Letters
to
Salthill

Nicole Wirth

Best Wishes,
Nicole Wirth

Washington, DC

Library of Congress Cataloging-in-Publication Data

Wirth, Nicole.

Letters to Salthill / Nicole Wirth. – 1st ed.

Summary: "A correspondence with an Irish teenager helps Marielle through the awkwardness of high school, and the drama of a family led by a violent alcoholic... until she visits her pen pal in Galway, and the real drama begins." –Provided by publisher

ISBN-13: 978-0692749074

[1. Family Drama—Fiction. 2. Coming of Age—Fiction. 3. Romance—Fiction. 4. Travel—Fiction.] I. Title.

The text of this book is set in 11-point Times New Roman

Printed in the United States of America

July 2016

First edition

For Isabella, my starry-eyed girl.

Acknowledgements

What follows is a fictionalized account inspired by real events, but I would be remiss if I didn't thank those who proved pivotal as the real story unfolded.

Thank you Colleen Dooley who signed me up for the pen pal club, and without whom there would be no Irish story. Thank you Erin Riley-Stroebel who listened patiently to my teenaged Irish obsession and who was there to pick up the pieces when I returned home. Thank you Laura Dobrowits; Amy Pofahl; Susan Russo; Karine Chevalier; Isabel Fernandez; Steve Greene; and Erin who convinced me this was a story worth telling.

Dr. John Neary played no small part in teaching me to write (though any grammatical mistakes are my fault, not his), and I'd like to thank him for it. He also gave me an A on a paper I wrote at St. Norbert College during my Freshman year which chronicled the hours before I was kicked out of my Irish pen pal's house. If I could find that paper, it would have made writing that chapter a great deal easier, but I still appreciate the A.

I would like to thank our friends/family in Dublin whose hysterical comments and turns of phrase are quoted far too liberally in my writing: Thomas (the elder), Thomas (the younger), Joan, Rachelle, and Aaron Campbell; David Rice; Caroline and Anton McGrath; Declan and Elaine Murphy; and many children of the aforementioned. Without their love and support, Ireland wouldn't feel at all like the second home it is today.

Last but not least, I would like to thank all of my friends and family who have generously volunteered to edit these words over the years, most notably: Susan Russo; Dr. Eleanor Hanold; Elizabeth Knox (www.elizabethknoxonline.com); Susan Ezell; Ed Cornely; Andy Rolle; Jackie Hall; Will Siss; my mother-in-law Betty Smith; and my amazing husband Brian.

Author's Note

American English spellings are utilized when a U.S. person is speaking or describing an object. Irish English spellings are utilized when an Irish person is speaking or describing an object. For example, "curb", "dialed", "license", "skeptical", "theater", and "utilize" when spoken by a U.S. person, become "kerb", "dialled", "licence", "sceptical", "theatre", and "utilise" when spoken by an Irish person.

… more than kisses, letters mingle souls.

—John Donne

Prologue

There was nothing distinctly Irish about the view from Salthill, save distant shadows of the Aran Islands. The laughter of teenagers on a rock jetty before her might very well have been that of classmates, but it was still early morning in the Midwest and everyone Marielle knew was likely still in bed.

Locals passed directly in front of her bench as they walked leisurely down the seaside promenade, but she didn't see them and she felt certain they didn't see her. It was all for the best. No one could help her now and they would likely shun her when they discovered what she had done.

Upon hearing she was traveling to Ireland, friends and family either cautioned her on the weather or on the war in the North, but neither had proven a factor. The breeze off the water felt nearly as warm as the sun overhead, and as it turned out, the war she fought had nothing at all to do with Northern Ireland.

Marielle scanned the coastline when she heard someone call his name, then implored herself to stop. She couldn't bear to search for a boy who wasn't there, who would never in fact come looking for her. His declarations of love seemed strange now, but not yet hollow.

Again, she pondered whether there was a way to go forward or a way to go back, but she was left without an answer. All she knew for certain was life would be easier with a boy from Freedom, but she wanted the boy imprisoned in Galway.

Chapter One

Most Violent Ways

—W.B. Yeats – *No Second Troy*

Summer 1985

It's hard to say whether the impatient bell or a door kicked off its hinges interrupted Marielle's version of slumber. She expected this disruption in sleep. She even expected an angry voice to yell "Bones!" as drunken footsteps tread heavily toward the room her older brothers shared. She could roll over and pretend it was a bad dream, but the screaming would surely wake her later, and her brothers probably deserved to be saved.

Marielle leapt from bed, quickly making her way to her parents' room through the adjoining closet. "Mom!" she whispered forcefully, then leaned farther into the bedroom. "Mom! Dad is choking John again!"

"Wh-what?" Maria asked, rolling toward the door.

"Dad is choking John!" Marielle repeated, barely masking impatience.

"Are you sure?" her mother asked, sitting up and pushing off her covers with one motion.

The only honest answer was "probably," but Marielle knew the situation warranted a more decisive response, so she said "yes" instead.

Maria jumped from bed, then ran through her bedroom door into the living room, and toward the rear of the house. Retreating through the closet, Marielle knew she'd find out soon enough if her words were a lie or prophecy, and either way she was in trouble.

Progress slowed as Marielle climbed over piles of clothes and backpacks in the room she shared with two sisters. After all, she didn't know for a *fact* that her father was choking John, and had her father broken from custom, Maria would be waiting in her sons' room demanding an explanation for her daughter's paranoid slander. Strangely, it was a comforting thought. Denial died quickly.

Sounds of yelling as objects or people hit other objects or people intruded upon the fantasy that Marielle was the worst-behaved member of the household. She bolted from her room.

She reached the dining room when Stephen yelled, "Dad!" and was nearly through it when her father growled, "You little punk!" Marielle was in the kitchen when a loud thump preceded a woman's screaming, and she ran into the adjoining hall where she found the source of the shrill protest.

What made John the usual target of their father's pre-dawn drunken rage is hard to say. He was the oldest of five children, and—although thin as the nickname "Bones" indicated—most able to survive a good choking, but Jack didn't generally analyze the pros and cons of whom to safely victimize after a dozen beers and the standard argument in Dusty's Bar. The boys' bedroom was closest to the back door, and John's bed wasn't elevated like Stephen's, which aided Jack in his decision-making process. If asked for a rationale, Marielle imagined her father would surely expound upon John's status as a "jag off" and might even reference the "cool" or "tough" thoughts he was sure his son had about himself. This would be his response during a normal attack, but tonight was by no means normal.

At approximately 8 o'clock on the previous evening, a mostly one-sided fight between Jack and his eldest son had taken place behind the boys' bedroom door. No one bothered to learn the details of the fight because their father's rage was more than common and far from rational. What wasn't common, however, was the sound of John yelling, "Stop being an ASSHOLE and start being a father!"

Maria and her four remaining children stared wide-eyed at one another in the living room, waiting for Jack to throttle John into the next time zone, which had recently moved east. But the quiet that followed resonated off the walls until Jack marched into the kitchen and yelled, "I'm going to Dusty's!"

Now, Marielle didn't expect alcohol drunk in a bar frequented by "stupid farmers," as her father described the local clientele, to improve his overall mood, but she was unprepared for the amount of rage he would unleash upon the family when returning to what the children loosely called "home."

Moments after yelling "Bones!" and stomping through the kitchen, Jack threw open John's bedroom door and began choking his 17-year-old son with vigor.

Jack's energy for the task at hand was surprising given his aversion to most activities which might divert his attention from the TV. He wasn't

4

necessarily a lazy man, just a choosy one. If he enjoyed his job, he put forth the extra effort, and tonight his job was felonious assault.

John was a moderately athletic boy, but no match for his father's 101st Airborne training, or his element of surprise. The sound of John choking and his violent thrashing terrified his 16-year-old brother enough to intervene. Stephen jumped off his bed and onto his father's back. In quick reply, Jack turned on Stephen, throwing him three feet into the wall behind him, and at that very moment, Maria unleashed a blood-curdling scream which paralyzed the chaos... for a moment.

What Stephen failed to accomplish through force, Maria's voice achieved efficiently. So irritated by the shrill interruption was Jack, that he determined a switching of victims was in order. Suddenly, John was in the clear, and Maria was on the run.

By now, Marielle and her two sisters stood assembled in the kitchen. It was the place where all family gatherings occurred. It was a big kitchen. It was here that the retreating Maria made a stand with her daughters behind the oak hand-me-down table and awaited her charging husband. They didn't wait long.

Despite his drunken state, Jack was a quick pursuer and reached the room seconds after Maria. Fists clenched nearly as tight as his jaw, he turned suddenly before reaching his wife. Changing his gait from a swift one to a purposeful lumber, he continued past the table toward the dining/living room and into his bedroom beyond.

A fluorescent under-cabinet light cast shadows across the room and onto the faces of those within it as John and Stephen ran into the kitchen. The light exaggerated their terrified expressions, but only slightly. The boys read their mother's expression and the absence of their father correctly. They stared at one another, silently asking if they should flee, or stand together, but there was no time for an answer as cursing and heavy boots approached. The boys joined their family behind the table, and Jack found them literally standing together when he returned with his loaded .357 Magnum.

Now, no one *knew* it was loaded, but it was the case seven years earlier when during a family meeting Jack pulled out the weapon and declared, "I'm gonna put this in a shoe box under my bed. If someone breaks in, I want one of you to grab it. It's not on a live round. Cock back the hammer and it will be." And with caution and a snicker he added, "But don't pick it up unless you intend to kill somebody."

Marielle and her younger sister Anna nodded assent as best they could, and left the gun alone each time their ball rolled under their parents' bed since, at the time, they had no one to kill. But clearly the same could not be said for their father on this particular night.

The kitchen erupted into hysteria when Jack cocked his weapon and leveled it at his wife. Cries of "Dad don't!", "Stop PLEASE!", and "NO!" came from every child with varying degrees of desperation and authority. Marielle ran around the table toward her father, pleading with him to put the gun down, but he ignored the request as if no words were spoken—as if no voice could be heard except the one inside his head, telling him to shoot his wife.

"I'm going to kill you, you stupid bitch!" Jack said as if he hadn't already made his intentions clear. He had made similar threats before with the same weapon, but tonight he seemed more angry, more sincere, or maybe just more drunk. In any event, everyone believed him.

Marielle saw horror turn to helplessness on her mother's face, and then acceptance. She could almost see where the bullet would rip through her mother's plum-colored satin nightgown, and imagine how she would fall against the counter. The decision had been made. There was nothing to do but wait.

Everyone's eyes welled-up with tears at the realization that their mother's life—and their own—was over. They waited agonizing seconds for the inevitable shot. They were terrorized by the shaking gun and its shadow on the kitchen cabinets, but it didn't fire.

"Well, go ahead!" Maria cried.

Jack narrowed his eyes and squeezed his grip more firmly on the gun, and for a moment, it didn't shake.

"*Please*, Daddy!" someone called out between sobs. "*Please* stop!"

This annoyed Marielle a great deal. Her father had already said he was going to kill his wife. Pleading just delayed the inevitable. She could no longer take the suspense or the feeling of helplessness. If her father was going to shoot her mother, she wanted him to shoot now and let it be over.

"Wait!" John yelled with a voice older than his own as he stepped in front of his mother, "You'll have to shoot me too!" he said, his chin held high like a soldier at reveille while his arms pushed backward to prevent his mother from moving to the side.

"No, John! Move out of the way!" Maria said with irritation. She attempted to move her son, but his stance was solid and he was stronger than she.

John's heroism seemed to confuse Jack. Were he a man of science, he would have taken the shot, realizing that firing now would accomplish his original goal of killing his first-born son, but he wasn't that man, so he dropped his aim to the table instead.

Stephen rushed to his father's side, imploring him to put the gun down, which he did with an air of defeat. Stephen swiftly grabbed the weapon, then stepped behind his father, studying the cabinets for a likely hiding place.

Maria—emboldened by her husband's disarmed status, and attempting to divert attention from Stephen—yelled, "You stupid drunken bastard!"

Now, Marielle didn't regard herself as a deep thinker, but she judged her mother's words as ill advised. Her father's surprisingly tan face turned red to his blond hairline before continuing the pursuit of his wife—this time around the kitchen table—as the children stepped back to watch the ridiculousness unfold.

After several circuits—and for reasons known only to Jack—his false teeth became an impediment to an effective chase. He popped out his upper plate with the inevitable trailing spit, and said, "Hold these," to John as he turned his son's hand to accept the dentures. The kids looked between their father's teeth and their brother's horrified expression and nearly laughed until Jack's behavior once again demanded attention.

No longer encumbered by his teeth, Jack failed to catch his wife just the same. Ever adaptable, he determined a change in tactics was in order. He flipped the kitchen table onto its side, sending 24 cupcakes into the air before leaping over it toward his wife. He grabbed the shoulder of her nightgown, but she twisted from his grasp and narrowly escaped.

After nearly 20 years of her husband's brutal and sometimes bizarre behavior, Maria still managed to look surprised. She ran to the interior kitchen door before Jack caught her firmly by her right arm, spinning her clockwise, and—despite the renewed screams of all present—throwing her sideways toward the picture window. Maria lost her footing just before her elbow and shoulder shattered the glass.

Chaotic screams halted as blood-colored glass fell to the floor along with Maria. If she or the window made a sound, Marielle didn't hear it. Her eyes turned to her father for direction or an explanation she knew would never come.

Jack ignored judging eyes and called his wife a moron before turning away in disgust. The sight of blood made him queasy and he had no plans to clean up this mess. He walked through the dining room into the darkened living room, pulled the small switch whose position he had memorized, then flipped the knob to channel six. Blue hues flooded the room and lighted the way to a well-worn, orange La-Z-Boy knock-off where Jack then sat.

The eldest girl, Jeanette, switched on the kitchen's overhead light and assessed the room as her older brothers helped their mother into the bathroom. Clean-up would take longer than usual, and without speaking, the girls moved together to right the table so recently wronged.

"Anna, you clean up the cupcakes while Marielle cleans up the glass," Jeanette ordered before walking to the back door to assess the damage.

Marielle sat back to consider her task. The largest shards of glass were easily removed, but smaller pieces proved more challenging as each movement of the hand broom embedded tiny shrapnel more deeply into the olive green kitchen carpet. It required vacuuming, she thought, but her father wouldn't like the noise.

As if on cue, Jack yelled, "Marielle, bring me a beer!"

She sighed audibly, but only loud enough for Anna to hear. *Gee, Dad, I'd love to fill your beverage request, but I'm cleaning bloody glass off the floor right now*, she said to herself as she walked to the refrigerator. She had mastered the art of sarcastic thought, but needed to wait many years to demonstrate this talent publicly.

She peered inside the refrigerator before sighing again. The proportion of food to alcohol would likely shift when John left, along with the pay checks he frequently converted into groceries. Soon, the refrigerator would return to storing mostly bottles and cans… if they had a refrigerator… if they had a house.

Contempt led the way to her father and his blaring television set.

"Do you have a problem?" Jack asked as he looked up at his daughter.

"N-no," Marielle muttered. Drunk or not, this man could not be underestimated.

"Then wipe that look off your face!" he spat.

Marielle twisted the cap off the beer bottle before handing it to her father. Time was when Marielle's bottle cap twisting proficiency was a source of great pride to Jack. He'd smile, chuckle even. While placing his arm around his daughter he'd proudly declare to visitors, "This one's built

8

like a brick shit house." And she was.

He used the term "this one" because he had difficulty recalling the correct child's name in a pinch. Marielle generally smiled without comment since the proper response to such a compliment eluded her. She couldn't pretend, however, that she didn't feel the smallest tinge of pride.

Now, she was nearly a teenager and her bare-hand bottle-cap-twisting evoked no response. Thank yous weren't customary, so she didn't wait for one. Instead, she returned to her task with more ammunition for sarcastic thought.

This is bullshit! she thought as she made the carpet suffer. *He kicks in the door; nearly kills John and Mom; throws Mom into a window; murders the cupcakes; and the problem tonight is* my *attitude!*

Rebellious thoughts led quickly to a realization. Her mission in life was to leave this house, and any house subsequently bought or rented by her parents, and get as far away from her father as soon as was legally possible.

She made a halfhearted effort to remove the remaining glass, and helped Anna render the frosting invisible before declaring a truce with the carpet. Kitchen duties complete, she walked with her sisters to the bathroom as their brothers wrapped Maria's arm with the last of the gauze.

Determining that their mother's care was well in hand, the three girls returned to the bedroom they shared.

The bedroom door skimmed the side of a wide, frameless mattress before hitting a thickly painted compressed-wood dresser. Jeanette pushed past her sisters to access her loft's ladder near the window, then turned on the radio when she reached the top. Marielle allowed Anna to crawl onto the mattress first before collapsing beside her.

***

Within a short time, the remainder of the household made their way to their respective rooms and turned off their lights—everyone except Jack. He sat alone in a TV-lit room that smelled of smoke and beer, his elbows resting on the threadbare arms of a half-reclined chair. He laced his hands over his flat stomach while his feet rested on the inside edge of the foot rest, and his knees splayed outward. His expression was intensely serious and mildly hostile. He would stew for awhile longer, but he wouldn't boil again tonight.

Almost everyone went to bed knowing the drama was over and that Jack would apologize tomorrow in a playful and sweet way. He might even wear the boys' boxing gloves while approaching Maria tentatively, hiding behind the gloves or ducking and weaving. She would stare at him angrily as she said he wasn't funny, but his antics would eventually cause the slightest grin to appear, and then the argument was over. Jack would grab his wife, pull her close, and rock her in a dance-like fashion. He'd whisper into her ear that he was sorry and that he loved her, and at that moment, he meant it.

***

Marielle listened as Anna's breathing became slow and steady, then lifted a blanket over her fetal form. She considered getting under the blanket herself, but she wasn't planning to sleep tonight. Even if the bedroom door absorbed enough TV noise to obscure the dialog, she couldn't relax. There were responsibilities to the family in the short term, and plans to make long term, and sleep wouldn't come if she had a job to do. Ever.

Writing lists made every situation clearer. Writing a list was really what she needed to do, but the flashlight was dead—the victim of reading *Encyclopedia Brown* books misdelivered to their house. So, she watched truck lights glide across the bedroom ceiling and repeated those things which required listing. If she repeated them ten times, she would remember them in the morning, she decided, but she didn't really believe that. It would be a relief to write them down now and not worry about forgetting. She could technically write in the dark, but she had no idea where her pen and notebook were hiding. For all she knew, they were under the dirty clothes on the floor.

A louder-than-usual diesel engine paused, engaging a lower gear as it made its way through the nearby curve. It sounded like a logging truck, but it was heading in the wrong direction. Logging trucks always traveled south, as did produce (mostly potatoes and corn), and desperate-looking cattle. At this time of night, pre-packaged food and oil trucks traveled north—probably not heating oil, but one never knew. Some people prepared their storm windows, firewood, and furnaces in the early summer. It was unusual and slightly paranoid, but Marielle appreciated a disciplined approach to seasonal preparedness. Those same people probably made lists.

Another vehicle passed the house. The lights on the ceiling told her it was a passenger car, or a small truck. At first, she thought it was a third-shift paper mill worker, but it traveled slower than the speed limit, and that

10

made Marielle wonder if the driver was drunk. Drunks drove too slowly or too fast, she determined long ago. They were also too happy, or too sad; too mean or too complimentary. Her father was too fast, too sad, and too mean, and she wished that just for once he would try too slow, too happy, and too complimentary. Then, he would just be pathetic and not so much terrifying.

The Richter house sat on a street cleverly named "Main" which represented one-tenth of all of the streets in the town of Kleiner. The house also sat near a ninety degree turn in the road, but not near enough to be hit by sleeping truck drivers or drunk motorists.

She wondered which truck was statistically most likely pick up a 12 ¾-year-old hitchhiker before disregarding the idea. They were probably only going as far as Rhinelander, and everyone knew hitchhikers were tortured and murdered.

Marielle turned over to borrow heat from her back.

Buses no longer traveled to Kleiner, and the train stopped in the '60s. As a slap in the face to anyone who might hope for its return, the railroad ties were ripped-up and replaced with snowmobile trails a few years ago. Marielle didn't own a snowmobile, but even if she did, its effectiveness during the summer would be seriously compromised, she decided, then chuckled.

The closest city of any real note was Green Bay and it was three hours south by car and much farther by bicycle. Her new ten-speed Huffy was faster than her old Blue Bell, but her feet barely reached the pedals with her legs fully extended, and until she hit a growth spurt, it just wasn't safe to ride.

The horrible reality was that she was in a town where she didn't belong, in a family that hated itself, and there was no hope of escaping either any time soon. If she wrote a list, she could determine exactly when that time would come, but she had already explored that disappointment. She implored herself to let it go while at the same time the list began running through her mind in a loop: *make friends overseas; get a scholarship to summer camp; babysit as much as possible; get a real job in two years; study abroad during high school; go to college anywhere or join the convent.*

She crawled under a blanket as she weighed the pros and cons of sleep. She had Sister School early in the morning, but with the back door kicked in and the house undefended, sleeping tonight wasn't an option.

Her dad would be comatose soon and it was up to her to raise the alarm if any ne'er-do-well wandered inside.

Some would say a break-in was unlikely in a town that rarely logged an unnatural death—barring suicides and stupidity—and where the neighbors left their houses unlocked even while away on vacation. But Marielle's house wasn't like her neighbors'. Bad things happened in her house. And if a ne'er-do-well wandered into *any* house, he would wander into hers.

Marielle heard the National Anthem before the station went off the air. She waited for her father to turn off the TV or turn the dial, but neither occurred.

She slipped out of bed, opening her door carefully. A light was now on and it took her eyes a moment to adjust. She plugged her ears in response to the TV static as she tip-toed past her father whose head cocked violently toward his left shoulder. His chair still rested in a semi-reclined position and the cigarette between his fingers had recently burned itself out. She studied her father as she slowly turned down the volume over several long seconds, having learned through much trial and error that turning off the TV abruptly would wake him.

After turning off the television, she walked to the back of the rust-colored, low-back couch to remove a pale-blue, cream, and tan plaid throw-blanket with fringe. Slowly, she placed it above her father's lap before dropping it. When he didn't move, she released her breath.

To her chagrin, the half-table/half-lamp between the recliner and the dark-paneled wall cast the offending glow. With the recliner blocking most of her access, it was the most difficult lamp in the room to reach. She would need to scoot between the recliner and the wall and pray she didn't lose her balance and fall into her dad's lap. Waking Jack from a passed-out state was like waking a bear from hibernation, and she would have taken odds on surviving the bear. She needed to do all of this without looking at the shadow on the ceiling. If she looked up, it was all over—her life, her dad's life, everything.

She willed her eyes not to move, but they never did what they were told, and a moment later she stood paralyzed under the three-pronged shadow the lightshade created. It resembled Jesus on the cross, and since Jesus was dead, and it hung over her father while he was sleeping, it was a sign that her dad would die soon as well. This wasn't the rule when people were awake, only when they were asleep. She didn't know why. It just

12

was.

She softly chanted the antidote, "Our Father Who art in Heaven...", as she reached for the light switch and turned it off.

Retreating required more concentration, which was good because it distracted her from the monsters that grabbed in the dark. She wouldn't stop her chant until the prayer was finished, and since the shadow cast three prongs, she said three Our Fathers.

As badly as her father behaved and as much as he scared her, she couldn't bear for anything bad to happen to him. If she got up every night to shut off the TV; cover him with a blanket; turn off the lights; and ensure his cigarette was out, maybe God would see that someone loved him and spare his life. It was worth a shot anyway.

Back in bed, Marielle could hear the clock radio on Jeanette's loft playing pop music from a station in Michigan. It was *Sunday Bloody Sunday* which never played on Sunday out of respect for conservative sensibilities. Coincidentally, or maybe out of protest, the DJ generally played it before dawn on Monday morning. Marielle liked the company the music provided, and she was a fan of this band in particular. As she looked up at her sister's loft, she imagined the scene the song painted and considered herself lucky to be in Kleiner and not there.

On many nights she imagined her soul floating out the window into God's giant palm where it was safe to lie down and sleep. But tonight she didn't have the luxury of sleep, comfort, or escape. She was stuck in her bed in Kleiner, Wisconsin, waiting for someone to push aside a broken door and terrorize their home—again.

Chapter Two

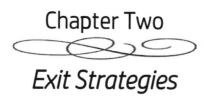

Exit Strategies

Marielle and Anna awakened before all but two members of their household. Their mother left a half-hour earlier for her bookkeeping job in Eagle River while their dad made his way to bed at some point during the early morning. He wouldn't awaken any time soon since he was still technically drunk, and he had no job for which to wake. Marielle realized she would have heard her mother leave the house and her father leave his chair if she had stayed awake as planned. With clenched teeth, she rebuked herself.

Marielle and Anna walked past the broken kitchen window, and through a plain interior door. Three steps down led to a landing where they stopped. Leaning toward the frame before them was the heavy wooden door so recently liberated from its hinges. Marielle released a guttural sigh while Anna crossed her arms, awaiting her sister's exit strategy. Marielle nodded in response. She was older. It was her job.

The top corners of the door rested upon the frame at an angle that created an inch-wide gap on top. Why Jeanette decided to tip the door against the molding from the outside when the door opened inward—and by rights should be tipped outward—mystified Marielle. Had Jeanette tipped it in the proper direction, Marielle could have pulled back the top of the door slowly and angled it to hit the closet to her right. Then, she and Anna might have jumped over the side to freedom. Marielle became agitated as she considered how easy that would have been before scolding herself for wasting time pondering a situation that wasn't.

She opened the hall closet, squinting in the dark to find anything that might assist her in her escape. There were musty hunting boots, and scarves, and mittens which had fallen onto the boots from the shelf above; large black snowmobile suits with one white and one turquoise stripe down the side; orange hunting jackets; wooden skis with cable bindings; more jackets; more scarves; more mittens; more boots; and Fala's leash which was just a long yellow nylon rope reattached to itself with electrical tape.

Marielle wondered where Fala had gone last night. She was a half-deaf, mostly-blind white cockapoo whose usual resting spot was in the boys' room. She could do little to protect herself when teenagers sailed through the air, but this wasn't an issue because she was never around when bad things happened. Fala had a sixth sense for violence. In fact, she probably hid in the basement shortly after John yelled "asshole" the night before.

Their German shepherd would have attacked their father last night, Marielle mused. Checkers had done it before... just before Jack chased him with a broom and gave him away to a farmer. As much as she loved Fala, Marielle preferred the justice a German shepherd could mete out, and right then and there she added "adopt a German shepherd" to her mental list.

Marielle abandoned the closet before studying the door again. "STUPID! STUPID! STUPID!" she said.

"We're going to be late," Anna protested.

Marielle turned to her sister with narrowing eyes. "No shit, Sherlock!" she said before quickly covering her mouth.

"Oh!" Anna pointed at her sister, "I'm telling Mom!"

"Go ahead, I don't care," Marielle replied, feeling quite the opposite.

She returned her focus to the task at hand, studying the window beside the door as she thought out loud. "The window is painted shut, and the upstairs windows might be too high to jump out of."

"I'm not jumping out of a window!" Anna snapped.

"You would if the house was on fire."

"*Ja*, well it's not."

"Go get me a match!" Marielle ordered before giving in to a chuckle.

"What about the front door?" Anna asked as if she was the only one to remember the house had two.

"Do you know where the dead bolt key is?" Marielle asked with condescension.

"No," her sister admitted.

"Then shut up! The only way out is to rotate the right side of the door outward and hope the left corner doesn't fall off the bottom, or get a ladder and climb out a basement window."

Before Anna could reply, Marielle placed one hand on the left edge of the door, then pushed the right side outward. The door rotated to the left easier than expected until it pinched Marielle's fingers, causing her to both curse and release the door in the same breath. The door teetered on an edge before falling onto the concrete sidewalk, making an impressive bang.

Marielle ran from the house, grabbing her sister's arm on her way to the alley. Once gaining the cover of their small garage, they released hands and walked quietly toward an abandoned lot.

Had last night's chaos surprised Marielle, she might have considered discussing it, but she said nothing. It was true that her father reserved his big performances for the holidays, but John's imminent departure for the Army probably qualified as a special occasion. With John, Stephen, and Jeanette all separated by one year, Marielle scheduled mayhem in her mental calendar for the next two Junes.

Today began the second—and last—week of Sister School, which usually caused Marielle no small measure of sadness and stress, but the Sisters' impending departure wasn't the reason for her angst. First, she came without the snack she had promised the class—these being the victims of the overturned kitchen table the night before; and second, she had engaged in an argument with Jimmy Hendrickson last Friday wherein she feared her insults went too far.

"My dad says your dad is a drunk," Jimmy announced, "and he got fired 'cause he couldn't handle the pressure."

"That's interesting," Marielle replied more calmly than she felt, "'cause I heard your dad's never seen a skirt he didn't lift."

Jimmy's face registered shock, presumably because Marielle said it, but also because he feared as much.

"And he's a porn freak, by the way," Marielle continued. "If you don't believe me, check the top shelf of your parents' closet in a box marked *National Geographic.*"

Unfortunately for Marielle, the last insult fell short of its mark since there are few things more impressive to Catholic boys than the discovery of unguarded porn.

No one asked the obvious question: how could Marielle possibly know where Jimmy's dad kept his girlie magazines? They lived in a small town after all, and everyone knew everything about everyone else. If asked, she would have lied anyway. Eavesdropping on Jeanette and Jimmy's older sister was less intriguing than the prospect that Marielle was either psychic or a spy. She liked being mysterious and she liked being feared, but deep down, she also felt guilty, and she didn't like that at all.

16

It's true Jimmy started it, but Marielle had a way of taking things too far. The penalty for rudeness wasn't death, after all, even if she sometimes wished otherwise.

Halfway across the vacant lot, Marielle contemplated whether her temper would be her ticket to hell. Just then, she heard a loud diesel truck lumbering down the street a block away. In an instant, she was off and running.

If she could make it to the sidewalk before the truck passed church, she would go to heaven, she decided. If she didn't, well, she didn't want to think about the end of that sentence. It was a risky bargain and she instantly regretted making it, but once begun, it was non-negotiable. If she stopped now, who was to say the devil would call off his part of the bet? In the end, stopping wasn't worth the risk of losing her soul if she had a chance to run for it.

Her short, chubby frame hid a quick runner and it seemed that her $7 running shoes wouldn't hinder her progress... until she reached shaded grass and the inevitable dew. The moisture combined with the plastic soles to create a slick running surface, causing each step to squeak and slip. Marielle grimaced. The idea that she would lose her soul because her parents were too poor to buy Nikes filled her with a sense of injustice and self-pity. She considered stopping, but couldn't. Social injustice or not, the bet was still on and the truck had just entered the intersection closest to church.

Anna yelled after her sister—not being privy to Marielle's deal for redemption. Marielle ignored the distraction and remained focused on the finish line as she began to pump her arms.

She was within ten feet of the sidewalk when the truck passed the rectory—five feet when the truck passed in front of the church stairs. She feared all was lost until the truck slowed as it spied the running child, which gave Marielle just enough time to place her left foot onto the sidewalk before the truck cleared the church hall which was still considered part of the church, she reasoned.

Marielle had beaten the devil. Her soul wouldn't be condemned to hell today.

As the truck driver passed the doubled-over girl, he looked at her with irritation and concern. *He's definitely from out of town*, she thought before reaching under her gray parachute pants to pull up the red and white tube socks whose elastic had given up just before her brother gave up on them.

There was little time to celebrate the reinstatement of Marielle's soul with her little sister closing in fast and complaining loudly. Marielle—too tired to issue a clever response and too clever to tell her sister the truth—instead responded with a very simple directive.

Marielle didn't bother to guide her sister across the street—not because she was irritated with her, but because the odds a vehicle would follow another so closely on this street, in this town was statistically improbable. Within a few short minutes, the girls passed through the small church parking lot, and inside the side door closest to the church hall's kitchen.

In general, Marielle tended to be exactly on time for most events. It had the benefit of injecting drama into everyday activities and made awkward small talk with her classmates less likely. Today, she arrived early enough to pass through the vinyl yellow and lime-colored, accordion-shaped room dividers just before they were closed, but late enough to avoid speaking to anyone. With a miracle and a well-planned entrance under her belt, it was shaping-up to be a good day.

Jimmy sat opposite Marielle in the square arrangement of folding tables so eye contact was usually unavoidable. Today, however, the waving of Shannon's arms commanded Marielle's attention instead.

"I," Shannon mouthed, pointing to her eye, "have the paper," she mouthed again while holding up a small piece of blue-bordered yellow paper.

"Huh?" Marielle responded.

"Pen," Shannon mouthed, holding up a pencil, "pal."

"Oh," Marielle mouthed in return. "Thank you."

The previous year—being granted admission into high school Spanish—Shannon recruited three seventh-graders to the Pen Pal Club for extra credit. Marielle didn't want to stand between Shannon and an A-, so she parted with the $3 administration fee and forgot the matter. That was until Saturday afternoon when Shannon informed her that everyone's pen pal information had arrived.

Sister Margaret busied herself examining the inappropriateness of the phrase "Oh, my God," but Marielle wasn't paying attention. She remembered asking for a boy pen pal because she generally liked boys better than girls—Shannon and Jimmy excluded. She also remembered asking for a pen pal from Ireland since she had already begun her descent into U2 mania, and Shannon said the band was definitely from Ireland, not

Israel as Marielle had previously thought.

Marielle expected her pen pal's name to sound like Sean O'Malley or Patrick O'Flanahan. *Was O'Flanahan a name?* she wondered as she stared at the paper in front of Shannon. O'Gill was definitely an Irish name, or so Disney said, but she hoped Darby wasn't... or at least not a popular first name among her age group. She didn't know why it mattered. It just did.

Within a few minutes, Marielle felt sure she would die if she couldn't determine whether her wishes were granted by the pen pal powers that be. She stared at Shannon to convey this fact psychically, but Shannon wasn't psychic. She also wasn't the type of girl to pass a note during Sister School, and Marielle wasn't the type of girl to ask. Actually, she was, but Shannon wouldn't be persuaded to break the rules which Marielle found both admirable and annoying.

"—and Marielle," asked Sister Margaret, "whom do *you* address in prayer most often?"

Marielle looked up at Sister with sudden attention. "Uhh, well, I, uh, pray to God, my Nona, Uncle Franz, and—"

"What about Jesus?" Sister interrupted with curiosity.

"Well, I, uhh, don't like praying to strangers," she admitted, pulling back the corners of her mouth in a pained apology.

Sister raised her eyebrows, paused for a moment, then called on another student.

It wasn't Marielle's best Sister School moment, but by the end of the day, it wouldn't be her worst. In a few minutes, the day's Mass would begin, and Mass was less of a spiritual experience than a test in self-control, and this test tormented Marielle in an unnatural way.

For reasons beyond her control or understanding, she lived in mortal fear of standing up and cursing or screaming, "Blasphemy!" during Mass. And because she was a student of either irony or masochism, she was especially tempted during General Intercessions, specifically during the moment of silence. Marielle knew such a dramatic interruption would make her a social outcast, but she felt a strong secondary force motivating her to be bad.

Holding the pew tightly with both hands prevented her legs from jumping up, but suppressing inappropriate language was always touch-and-go. While everyone else silently offered the intentions within their hearts, Marielle shook from the strain of holding her body down and clenching her jaw closed. She would try to think of something else, to stare at the missalette in the pocket in front of her or count the ceiling fan blades, but her ears rang with the inappropriate words she begged God not to say until the moment of silence was over and Father Joseph rescued her by continuing Mass.

Marielle had already defeated the devil today, and he would likely be anxious to get even, but she had more important matters on her mind. Today, her class was responsible for the Mass, and she was responsible for the Second Reading. The anticipation of that was torment enough.

She was sure nothing good could come of this. Sister held her in too high a regard by giving her a reading, and now it was too late to back out. Marielle's grandparents already sat in the back of church, waiting for their second-youngest grandchild to own the pulpit and wow the world with a few lines from the New Testament. Marielle hadn't seen their car outside, but she knew they were there. She also knew Grandma and Grandpa Richter had bored the extended family all weekend with news of her public speaking debut.

"She's a very good reader," Frieda Richter had told aunts, uncles and much older cousins. "And she has outstanding penmanship!"

Everyone smiled in a vaguely polite way, having no idea what penmanship had to do with reading.

"Everyone, line-up!" Sister Margaret said in a voice that sounded too urgent.

Marielle jumped up, quickly weaving her way to Shannon's side. Shannon anticipated Marielle's enthusiasm and already held the slip of tissue-thin paper in front of her.

Although excited to read the paper, Marielle couldn't help but notice the wider-than-normal grin on Shannon's face. She looked at her friend questioningly before looking down at the paper for the answer. It took only a moment for Marielle to understand Shannon's amusement, but it took much longer to pronounce the name on the slip of paper, and by that time Shannon was doubled-over in spasms of a silent laughter.

"Fergus MacManus?" Marielle asked with dismay.

Shannon attempted to straighten her body and say "yes" but her convulsing cheeks and restricted breathing made sound impossible. Instead, she nodded.

"OH – MY – GOD!" Marielle said, violating Sister's restriction on the phrase. "That's awful!"

"Hush now, children!" Sister called impatiently. She had a young face with freckles on and around her nose, and a lock of chestnut hair peeking-out from her mostly black habit. She was a kind soul, but where bad behavior met Mass, she displayed no patience.

The class quieted, then created a reasonably straight line by the door. Sister walked down the line handing-out neatly typed pieces of paper. She handed Billy the First Reading and Mary the Responsorial Psalm. She walked five more paces to give Marielle the Second Reading.

Marielle carefully fed her pen pal information into the pocket of her pants with her right hand while her trembling left hand held the reading. She attempted to read the paper several times before giving up. There was no way to practice when her hand wouldn't hold still.

The accordion dividers opened as children began streaming through the classroom.

The church loaded in ascending class order. So, even though Marielle's class sat closest to the hall and the connecting door, they waited while lines of younger children passed them before receiving the all clear. Anna had passed by at some point as well, but so distracted was Marielle that she forgot to trip her.

Marielle's class began moving forward as the pit in her stomach moved upward. She felt sure she would vomit or faint, but dutifully followed the line of the condemned and awaited her body's decision.

Frieda waved from the rear of the church as her granddaughter passed through the threshold of the adjoining side door. Johan raised his head and smiled proudly, but didn't wave. His silver hair was slicked back and his mustache was neatly groomed. He wore an expensive black pin-striped suit with a white silk shirt and a navy blue and white striped tie. Placed carefully on the pew beside him was a black fedora and on his feet were polished black, wing-tipped shoes. He didn't care that he stood out in a church of casual dressers, and he would never wear a Packers jacket with jeans if he did. He knew he was different from everyone else, and he enjoyed the fact that everyone else in church knew it too.

Frieda, on the other hand, resembled many of the women her age with her beige knit hat whose shade matched exactly her polyester perma-crease slacks and sweater vest. However, the quality of her hat and blouse as well as the presence of a broach on her left breast indicated an outsider to any discriminating local... and they were all discriminating.

The Richter family had lived in Kleiner for over 20 years, but they were newcomers by local standards. Marielle's dad would say, "Because it wasn't enough that you suffered. Generations before you had to suffer too." The reward for lineage was acceptance from the same people Jack went out of his way to shock and dismiss. Jack's father had his own way of shocking and dismissing the locals, and so he wore a pin-striped suit.

Marielle's class filled the first two pews on the left side of church, sitting directly across from the pulpit. The rectangular, stained-glass-shaded pendent lights were switched on owing to a lack of windows in the front of church, but the sanctuary was still under-lit. Having been built seven years earlier, the stout A-frame structure was larger than the one it replaced, but the modern dark-paneled walls, false ceiling, and absence of a choir loft made it inferior in Marielle's eyes.

Everyone rose as the organ began playing.

Marielle mouthed the opening hymn, but didn't sing. Her eyes were fixed firmly on the reading in front of her which she read in a loop without comprehending any of the words her mind recited.

They were halfway through the first chorus when Father Joseph walked past, flanked by two altar boys. Father mounted three steps before sitting dead center on a stone bench under a large wooden crucifix.

Billy Mueller rose from the pew and made his way to the pulpit to begin the First Reading. He looked confident, almost aggressive in his gait—like he just needed to get through this speech before he could apply to Harvard.

Marielle turned around to spot Billy's parents in the fifth row. It was reserved for students this morning, but they sat there anyway.

Everyone jumped, then cringed while Billy belted-out his reading. He was a close-microphone-talker and the microphone feed was especially loud.

His spit will be all over it, Marielle thought with contempt, which turned to panic when Billy stopped talking. His was a short reading. She shook her head. Lucky bastard.

Sister tapped Marielle's shoulder from the pew behind her. She stood without turning around, then stepped thoughtlessly on the toes of her classmates as she squeezed toward the middle aisle. She mechanically said "sorry" each time, but she wouldn't remember this later. She forgot to bow in front of the altar as she mounted the only step separating the congregation from the pulpit, but she reached the pulpit without falling which pleased her a great deal. She stepped upon the box available for short readers, placed her paper under the brass reading light, then began.

"The Second Reading," she paused, startled to hear such a loud version of her voice, "is a Letter from Paul to the Genitals." Marielle stopped as the church gasped audibly. She looked up at the dark congregation as the grades higher than fifth began to giggle. She knew she had said something very, very wrong, but she didn't know exactly what.

Frieda looked horrified while Johan's face simply showed concern. Sister was in the midst of covering an "Oh my!" with her hand while Father rocked forward on the stone bench to her left, ready to stand up for Jesus and save Mass.

"This is not good," she nearly said, but quickly summoned the courage to go on, being more efficient in a crisis than during peacetime. It took two sentences to leave behind the loudest laughter, but she finished the reading with no more gaffes. The lack of listeners helped.

Marielle returned to her pew with her head down, feeling officially shamed and cursed. After stepping on numerous toes, she sat once again beside Shannon who stared straight ahead with a confused look on her face. Marielle's eyes remained fixed on the pulpit until her grandmother crossed before her during communion. Minutes later, both grandparents slipped out the back of church like teenagers.

Departures immediately following communion had always infuriated Frieda. She spent many post-Mass brunches condemning them—along with people who arrived late; allowed their kids to wear jeans; didn't know their prayers or when to stand up, sit down, or kneel. Her grandmother's change in behavior was mind-shattering to Marielle. There was no explanation other than shame brought upon the family at the hands of her granddaughter.

Marielle sat alone, staring at a gold stripe on the altar cloth when Sister appeared beside her.

"It's time to go now. Did you bring the snack for today?"

"Um, no." Marielle dropped her head further. "I'm sorry, Sister. My cat got into the cupcakes last night."

It was clear that Sister knew she was lying, and doing so in God's house, but her face displayed disappointment rather than anger. "I'm sorry to hear that. Come now," she said with a smile and a motioning of her hand. "Everyone will be glad to hear they can go directly outside."

Marielle smiled gratefully as she stood, but made no move toward the aisle. "Sister, could I be a nun some day?" she asked.

Sister Margaret stopped walking to turn around. It was the last question she expected from a girl who said "genitals" in Mass and lied about cupcakes. "Well, of course you could," she replied.

"How soon?" she asked reflexively.

"Well," Sister looked up as if trying to remember, "some orders take girls at 18, but most require you to attend college first, so," Sister calculated, "I guess when you're 21."

Marielle nodded, then continued walking in silence. "Which one lets you in at 18?" she asked as they reached the aisle.

Sister stopped again, looking concernedly at the child beside her. "Marielle, why are you in such a hurry to join the convent?"

This was a much bigger question than Marielle's brain could process or truthfully answer so she said, "I don't know exactly. I just think it would be nice to play the guitar and pray whenever I wanted to."

Sister laughed as she placed her arm around the child.

When Marielle arrived home, she opened the top, middle drawer of her dresser, placing the thin slip of paper on top. She wouldn't write Fergus today, she decided. She would wait until there was something new or interesting to say.

Chapter Three

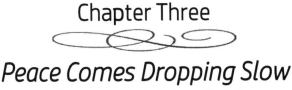

Peace Comes Dropping Slow
—W.B. Yeats – *The Lake Isle of Innisfree*

03/01/1988 Tuesday

Dear Fergus,

My name is Marielle Richter. I'm a 15-year-old American from Wisconsin. I got your address from the Pen Pal Club a few years ago, and I've written you several letters that I didn't send because they seemed really boring when I reread them. I'm sure this will seem boring too, but I'll send it anyway since there's a chance I'll be touring Europe this summer (including Ireland) with our city's drum and bugle corps.

I play the tenor saxophone in school and for competitions, but I play the trumpet during marching band and I'll play it during the tour. Do you play any instruments?

I'm 5'6" tall with blonde hair and blue eyes and my birthday is August 29th. I have two brothers: John is 20 and Stephen is 19. They are both in the Army. John is in South Korea and Stephen is in West Germany. I also have two sisters: Jeanette is 18 and Anna is 13. Jeanette goes to college 30 minutes away at UWGB (University of Wisconsin - Green Bay). Anna is in junior high and she's a typical bratty little sister.

I live in a city called Appleton, but we've only lived here about a year and a half. Before that, we lived in a town of 200 people called Kleiner which is 3 ½ hours north of here, near the border with Northern Michigan. There are a lot more people in Appleton (about 50,000) and the rest of our family is still back in Kleiner, so the move was a big adjustment for us, but I love it here now and wouldn't move back for the world! After all, we can walk to fast food restaurants (instead of driving 30 minutes to Eagle River) and there is a city bus that takes my sister and me to school and anywhere else we want to go... which is great because in Kleiner you have to drive everywhere.

St. Patrick's Day is coming up soon, so Happy St. Patrick's Day to you! I traditionally drink a Shamrock Shake every year to celebrate the occasion—since drinking Guinness is frowned-upon by my parents. ☺ I haven't gotten one yet (a shake not a beer), so I had better get to it.

Anyway, I hope this letter isn't boring when I reread it or I'll have to tear it up like I did all the others... but that won't bother you because you'll never know. Isn't that strange?

Sincerely,

Marielle

Marielle read the letter twice before smiling. She was proud of herself for determining Guinness was an Irish beer. It added just the right amount of sophistication.

She walked to the roll-top desk to find a crisp, white, business-sized envelope, then returned to the table to address it. Once the envelope was stuffed and sealed, she sat back, regarding the industrial whiteness of the paper with disapproval.

She returned to the desk to find two markers in a small basket, using them to create a border of red and blue around Fergus' address and to write a greeting on the back of the envelope. After examining it again, she nodded. The letter and the envelope weren't perfect, but she knew nothing ever would be. All in all it was a good effort, and more importantly, she was done.

She stretched her arms above her head and smiled at the ceiling. There were a few small cracks leading to the chandelier, but it was freshly painted and bright. The color was an unimaginative shade of rental white which matched the walls in every room in the house save two.

Marielle squinted through the doorway to determine if the paint in the kitchen was the same shade as her bedroom, but it was impossible to say. The light was different owing to the room's position on the opposite side of the house and on a different floor. If both rooms were the same shade, she was sure her bedroom was the original target of the pale yellow paint and the kitchen just got the left-overs. She didn't know why this mattered. It just did.

To the left of the kitchen doorway stood an eight track/turntable/sarcophagus-sized stereo which held multiple knick-knacks and doubled as a side-board during the holidays. Marielle's grandfather called it a "hi-fi," but she had no idea what that meant. It was just a radio to her, and only her father ever used it. She was willing to bet a dollar that a gold, semi-transparent Elvis album sat on the turn table right now, but she was too lazy to check.

Three 10" x 12" graduation pictures in matching dark wooden frames broke the monotony above the sarcopha-stereo. The backgrounds matched in all three pictures except around John's head where the color lightened to tan. This prevented John's hair and skin from blending into the background completely, but gave him an angelic look at odds with his age. Stephen's and Jeanette's light blond hair stood out against the background so they flanked their brother for symmetry.

Jeanette's long hair transformed to sunlight at the edges as it stood tall, wide, and curly, and just long enough to skim the shoulders of her cream-colored, V-necked, popcorn-stitched sweater.

In most ways, Marielle was the younger version of her sister (with less makeup and no perm). They had the same eyes, the same hair color, and the same skin when Jeanette washed her face. However, there was a difference between the two that makeup neither created nor covered.

To the world, Jeanette's smile was a half-attempt or possibly even a smirk, but to Marielle it was more than that. It was evidence that her sister knew she was popular and all the boys wanted her—and most did. Jeanette didn't need to work for this look. It had always come naturally to her. In fact, she probably didn't need to work for anything at all because right now there were men in the military and in at least two colleges who would work hard, study hard, and get a good job to win her love.

Marielle shook her head, appreciating how effectively boys thwarted female ambition. She decided long ago to never coast through school or skip a career, or trust another person with her physical or financial well-being. She would never plead with a bank for refinancing they wouldn't give, and she wouldn't sit helplessly at the dining room table while an eviction notice was taped to her front door. She wouldn't explain to her children how the new landlord wouldn't accept pets, or try to remain unaffected as they hugged throw pillows and cried. She would never grin and bear it because this was the life she had chosen, and changing paths now left the painful impression that she had wasted time in a life everyone said was short.

She sighed with disappointment at her sister's picture, wondering why Jeanette couldn't see what Marielle did. They shared the same genes.

They lived through the same experiences. They should have learned the same lessons. But Jeanette was walking blindly into a town called Pain with a grin on her face, and there was nothing Marielle—or anyone else—could do about it.

Marielle's eyes moved to her brothers' photographs. They wore gray sweaters over oxford shirts while their crossed arms rested on an invisible platform. Taken a year apart, it was essentially the same picture of the same sweater on the same set by the same photographer. John's face betrayed a smirk similar to his sister's, but it didn't say he was insanely attractive or wildly popular. It said he didn't care what people thought because in a few short months he would be gone and no bus or airplane or police car would ever bring him back.

Stephen's face appeared completely different from the others. It displayed a weak smile on white, freckled skin on a rounder than normal head. He also had a gap between his two front teeth that his closed mouth hid. Within a year, he would blossom into someone tall, tan, and muscular whose attention women wanted, but this didn't happen in time for his senior picture.

Marielle sighed again. Stephen never recovered from the blows he sustained as punishment for stuttering. She could still see him curled up against the wall, rolling to his right, pulling his knees against his stomach as Jack swiped his open hand at his son's head yelling, "Wha-wha-what?!"

Marielle closed her eyes as she shook away the memory. She felt grateful she didn't need to worry about Stephen anymore. In fact, she didn't need to worry about John either because now her brothers were safe and sound in the Army.

To the right of the pictures, a telephone rested inside a half-egg-shaped recessed stand. It rang only once or twice a night for Marielle, and every two nights for Anna. It rang on Sunday for Jack and once a month for Maria, usually the day after her brother drank his disability check. It delivered a weekly prank call, and on holidays it rang from South Korea or West Germany, but it mostly didn't ring at all. Marielle didn't check to see if the phone still worked the way Anna did. She knew that what was wrong had nothing to do with the telephone.

Marielle looked into the kitchen. Right now, there were two glasses resting on the counter/ledge below the 1920s-style maple cabinets. There were dishes stacked in the sink as well and it was Anna's turn to wash them.

A shiver went up Marielle's spine. She wasn't dreading anything. She was just cold. She exhaled into the air, but couldn't see her breath. She considered turning up the thermostat, but she was leaving for the post office soon and she couldn't risk forgetting to turn it back down before her parents returned from work.

She looked down at the only pair of name-brand jeans she owned and her pink polyester faux turtleneck sweater. *This should be enough clothing to feel warm indoors*, she thought with annoyance, then wondered if winters were changing or she was. It's true they seemed longer each year she got older, but maybe she was just more aware of them now. In any event, she was ready to be rid of snow that never canceled school and cheap clothes that never canceled cold.

When she was older, she would buy a down jacket, a down comforter, and live in a house with a fireplace and lots and lots of firewood. She would also ski in and out of her house with brand new Rossignol skis and poles. All she needed to do was implement her chairlift design, and find a place in Wisconsin with mountain-like hills.

Her teeth began to chatter. Leaving Wisconsin might be in order too, but she felt like a traitor for even considering it.

Wisconsin transplants and visitors who complained about the weather irritated her. She would call them wimps to her friends and family and they would agree, but she could be honest with herself right here, right now, shivering in a sweater and jeans on the first day of March and admit she was sick of being cold. And by association, she was sick of Wisconsin.

Marielle wouldn't be the first member of her family to pack up and leave her birthplace. In fact, since arriving in the United States, no Richter had ever died in the same state in which he was born. The culprit was usually joblessness, but Marielle suspected restlessness as well since it seemed strange to her that a person would leave the Wild West for any reason at all.

Grandpa Richter told her once that he could see Mount Hood from his bed through the cracks in the cabin walls. Marielle envisioned cattle ranches in the shadow of the mountains, overlooking turquoise streams and green meadows. She eagerly asked for more details about his upbringing, and by that she meant unrealistically romantic details. Fully prepared to smell the hickory smoke and imagine a friendly baby grizzly bear doubling as a pillow, she listened as her grandfather paused, took a deep breath and said, "I just remember being cold. All the time."

He squinted at the other side of the room like it was colder over there before looking back at his granddaughter. "We didn't have indoor plumbing so we couldn't take baths very often—well, people didn't think baths were good for you anyway." He laughed as a thought occurred to him. "I remember sitting in school and after about an hour or so my brother and sister and I would start thawing out, and oh man! That's when the smell would start," he laughed again, but it wasn't the kind of laugh one joined. "No one wanted to sit by us after that first hour, but we didn't care much. We thought school was great. Free heat, free books, and a place to read in peace."

Marielle attempted to hide her disappointment at this story. There were no cowboys, or mountains, or grizzly bears in it at all! She wondered why her grandfather's house wasn't peaceful, but she knew he would never say. Although disappointing, the story told her a great deal about her grandfather: why he married young to a girl whose family owned two houses in Chicago—both with indoor plumbing; why he worked himself into two heart attacks so he could buy expensive clothes, a new Packard every other year, and a TV before anyone else could afford one; and why he never owned jeans, second-hand clothes, or could be caught in his pajamas after six in the morning. Her grandfather was running from something too, Marielle thought before looking down again at her letter.

She knew she needed to cut musing short if she wanted to return from the post office and clean the living room before her parents arrived home, but urgency hadn't found her yet.

She looked left toward the double windows over the low-back orange couch which was exiled to the dining room shortly after the move. Sideways shafts of light told her it was still early afternoon. She looked toward the opposite wall to the clock on top of the desk to confirm this.

It had taken her last bit of courage to sit down well over an hour ago and commit thoughts to paper. And now that it was over, more than two years of guilt dropped off her shoulders like clothes off a prostitute. She was free—and cold—but she was mostly just free.

She basked in accomplishment a moment longer before a louder than usual television commercial intruded upon her thoughts, forcing her to turn around and address the watcher.

"Anna, you have kitchen duty today," she said as a directive.

"And?" the curly-haired brunette replied without energy, looking in the direction of the remote she held.

"Make sure you're done before Mom and Dad get home."

Anna rolled her eyes. The high-backed, navy velour couch absorbed her slumped frame and with it her ambition. Her posture suggested she wasn't wearing her brace, but Marielle lacked the will to police her. Anna would pay once their mother returned home, she decided.

Marielle glanced at the coffee table in front of her sister. On an average day, Anna would rest her feet on the table, but two empty cans of Meister Brau and an overflowing ash tray impeded her leisure. Cleaning the living room was Marielle's responsibility today, and it was probably time to start, but clearing the table added to her sister's comfort which only made her want to wait.

"Oh, Marielle, Mom said if the dishes aren't in the kitchen before I begin washing, *you* have to wash them," Anna said with a mischievous grin.

"Well, I was just about to clear them," Marielle lied, jumping up and walking to the coffee table. She collected the stale-smelling beer cans and ash tray, then turned her attention to the side table near Anna before stopping.

Their grandmother said Marielle had two speeds: daydream and sprint. The former usually caused the latter and a window usually caused the former. Across the street, their elderly landlord escorted the last customer of the day between 10-year-old used cars. He wore an old tweed jacket and dark brown polyester pants and he looked too old to be working so hard. She watched until customer and salesman became obscured by the turd brown porch pillar, then turned to the right.

The parking lot of St. Elizabeth's Hospital was still filled with the cars of patients and staff who would begin filing in and out in about an hour, but nothing was going on now. She wondered if the helicopter pad was empty. She thought it would be a good sign if it was, but she didn't know why. Maybe a person not being rushed to the hospital was good luck... unless the person needed the hospital and wasn't there. Now, she couldn't decide if an empty helipad would be lucky or not.

"What are you doing?" Anna asked impatiently.

"Nothing. Just looking," Marielle responded, wanting to sound more stern than her voice allowed, but her smile lingered a second too long.

"Well, you're in my way," Anna protested.

"What?!" Marielle looked behind her, "How's that? I'm on your left and the TV's on your right."

"You're still in my way," Anna responded with a self-satisfied smirk. She had just pushed Marielle's "illogic" button, and she was waiting for her sister's head to explode.

"If the TV were in the middle of the archway, I still wouldn't be in your way! If the TV were sitting on the opposite wall, I'd barely be in your way! And with the TV over *there*—" Marielle turned too quickly toward the inside corner, dislodging a beer can from between her forearm and chest, causing the can to fall silently onto the beige carpet.

Anna mouthed, "Good job," but Marielle ignored her.

"The only way I can be in your way is if I stand—" she moved to the other corner of the cocktail table, "here."

Anna craned her neck to see around her sister, a look of genuine irritation overtaking her amusement.

"So, am I in your way now?" Marielle asked with wild eyes.

"Move!" Anna ordered, still craning.

"So, I wasn't in your way after all, WAS I?" she leaned forward to better enunciate the last two words, a hateful German expression overtaking her face.

Anna narrowed her eyes at the TV and mumbled. She was the only child who resembled the Italian side of the family. It allowed for superior tanning genetics, but she couldn't combat the "German look," nor convincingly replicate it, requiring her to avoid eye contact when it was in use.

Marielle pulled back. "I'm sorry," she said, less wild-eyed, but not sorry at all, "I didn't hear that." She waited, pondering if she would beat defeat out of Anna or let it go. She finally decided that victory would require a noogie and no small amount of wrestling, and she wasn't in a noogie sort of mood.

Marielle retrieved the can she had dropped before walking into the kitchen—a room which was large enough to house a dishwasher, but didn't, and too small to hold a homemade plywood island with bar stools, but did. She dropped the cans into a paper grocery bag recently designated as "Recycling" by Marielle's black marker, then dumped the ashes into the bin before leaving. Without stopping, she closed the roll-top desk with a thud and continued to the living room where she pushed Anna's feet off the table before replacing the ash tray.

Anna's feet rebounded quickly, but Marielle pretended not to notice

32

while her eyes scanned the living room one last time for rogue dishes. Finding none, she made a mental note of the tasks which required completing once she returned from the post office. She needed to vacuum the ashes that had fallen onto the carpet while she was throwing her head around (or maybe when they fell from her father's cigarette last night), polish the furniture, and redistribute the blue, ruffled, circular pillows whose navy fabric and center button matched the furniture.

The tan linen drapes (also ruffled) were already pulled back to one side of all three living room windows, leaving enough drooping in the center to satisfy her mother, who had probably fixed them during lunch.

Looking at the curtains was one of two ways to see if her mother had come home for lunch. If Jack walked home alone, the blue plaid blanket would still be in a ball at the bottom of the couch. Marielle looked at the neatly folded blanket draped over the lonely chair in the corner. Her mother definitely walked home for lunch.

It struck her as funny that her mother folded every day what Marielle unfolded every night. Had her mother known it was Marielle and not her husband who disturbed the blanket, she might have been annoyed. Had Jack known it was his daughter who covered him every night and not his wife, he might have been hurt, but conversation was rare enough to make those chances unlikely until Marielle was gone. She paused as she stared at the blanket a little longer, silently telling it that staying wasn't an option even if it meant someone else picked it up to cover her father every night, and even if no one ever did.

Marielle turned her attention to the lonely chair for a moment. Since the recliner met the county dump, her father's default position was the couch—himself fully reclined. By rights, the chair/footstool combination should have replaced the recliner in paternal popularity, but its current position—too near the TV and outside arm's reach of any table—meant beer cans would either be placed on the window sill behind the chair, or precariously on the carpet.

Even Jack in his normal drunken state knew a can on the floor would eventually get kicked over. And everyone knew that the event would be announced with a hearty curse to God and a wake-up call to Maria who really should have known better than to place a chair so far from a table. Marielle shook her head, wondering if this was what her library book called "passive aggressive."

At the end of the day, it was just as well that her father preferred the couch. It was easier to cover him there and easier to reach the light on the end table beside him. His life was lonely enough without the help of the chair, Marielle decided. Still, she disliked finding him lying down, his right hand resting on his chest, his left hand dangling to the floor, and his mouth half open with lips collapsed into his tooth-free mouth. He appeared more dead than was tolerable at three in the morning, and Marielle fought the desire to flee each time she turned the corner of the dining room and saw him.

Escape would be easier if the door between the living room and the foyer was open rather than blocked by the lonely chair and foot stool. It was idiocy to block a perfectly good door because American Furniture had a sale on a four-piece living room set, especially when there was a sale on a two-piece set at the same time—the only drawback being a person didn't save as much money by buying only two pieces of furniture.

Jack laughed and shook his head when he heard this explanation. Elbows on his knees, he looked down at the floor, rubbed the back of his neck with his left hand and looked up at his wife using his eyebrows, another snicker, and a shake of his head to call her a moron. Translations would come later.

Maria pretended not see her husband's condescending expression. She didn't wish to waste precious sober time by picking a fight, and she didn't want to risk emotion by telling Jack the truth. Although sales were very important to Maria, having a place for all five children to sit was her real motivation. She knew her eldest three children were—for all intents and purposes—gone, and the remaining two would leave within five years. The chances of both boys earning leave at the same time was minimal, and the probability that Jeanette would choose to spend college vacations at home instead of with a boyfriend was less so.

Still, the children never had the luxury of sitting on furniture at the same time in the same room, and the irony was that now that they were gone, Maria could afford to provide it. With tears in her eyes, she told the sales attendant that she wanted all four matching pieces—hoping against logic that this goodwill gesture would somehow bring her children home.

Marielle moved the pillows to the corners of the couch and loveseat, save the one Anna held against her chest. She would fix the last pillow when she returned. She looked around one more time, then walked back to the dining room, spying the clock on top of the desk. With a curse, she grabbed her letter and green canvas backpack from the table before running into the hallway.

Turning right toward the front door, she tripped on Anna's shoes, but caught herself on a staircase finial before falling to the floor. "Damn it, Anna! Don't drop your crap in the middle of the hallway!" she yelled, noting Anna's coat had also fallen from its hook under a higher step. She thought about yelling again, but instead damned every living thing while kicking Anna's shoes to the side.

Marielle continued toward the front door, then made an abrupt U-turn with the assistance of the square block on top of the banister. She made another U-turn at the top of the stairs, thus avoiding her parents' room, then passed two open bedroom doors as she bounced to the end of the hall.

Marielle's bedroom faced east, but it was still bright in the afternoon owing not only to its color, but the two large windows overlooking the metal porch roof. This was the obvious emergency exit in case of fire or domestic disturbance, but the roof sagged between the joists and was hot enough to bake bread during the summer. All in all, it wasn't a place to go if one had alternatives.

The door in Jeanette's room accessed the same roof, but only Jeanette had ever used it. Her sister wasn't a seasoned assessor of risk, Marielle thought—a point made evident years ago when she made-out with her boyfriend in the middle of his front seat while he steered with one finger and one eye down a curvy county road traveling at 60 miles per hour. If Jeanette didn't appreciate the need to stay on her side of the car and wear a seat belt, she wouldn't notice the remnants of a railing around the edge of a roof, nor wonder why someone discouraged roof walking by removing the pretense of safety a railing might provide.

Marielle shook her head. Some people were blind.

She pushed aside the white sheer curtains which didn't discourage the sun by day or the street lights by night. She installed them over a year ago, and since then decided there were worse things than the sun waking you up every morning; getting changed with the lights off at night; and watching aircraft lights dance on the walls as helicopters descended toward St. Elizabeth's.

She chuckled as she remembered seeing a helicopter land for the first time. The noise and the vibration were enough for Jack to mute the television, kneel upon the couch, and exclaim, "Well, I'll be damned," as he peered through the window. Five gaping mouths soon joined him, breathing like dogs in July after running from their respective rooms.

Only watching Soviet paratroopers land outside their school could top the drama of that, Marielle thought, dropping the curtain as she turned toward her dresser.

Her room was small, but she didn't have much in the way of furniture to fill it. The head of her single bed stood immediately to the left upon entering the room, barely fitting between the door and the windows. The dresser—still painted blue and cream to match her old room—filled most of the opposite interior wall. To the left of the dresser were two clothing rods—one for the clothes of short people and another for giants or people on stilts. A large black scarf-like material with a white picture matching the *Joshua Tree* album cover hung from the giant's rod and was one of Marielle's most prized possessions—second only to the American flag hanging behind her door. To the left of the scarf, a cheap tennis racket hung horizontally from two hooks she fashioned from wire hanger pieces.

Marielle opened her jewelry box, causing a ballerina to pop-up and dance. She looked from the box to the old canopy bed with no canopy before deciding she needed grown-up things. She would get a job and save for bedroom furniture after returning from Europe. *If she returned from Europe*, she thought before immediately dismissing the idea.

It was true they had colleges and convents in Europe too, but Marielle wasn't sure she could undo all of her great-grandparents' work by returning to the place they started. If they were content to lie in graves an ocean away from their parents, she needed to give that place a chance to redeem itself from the sins of her father.

Marielle removed several notes from her jewelry box which were folded in a way to be self-closing, then grabbed the six one dollar bills they hid—her wages from babysitting her teacher's children the previous weekend. She stuffed the money into the outside pocket of her backpack, then glanced anxiously under the windows where an overturned green milk crate supported a miniature boom box and a digital clock. The latter read 20 minutes to three.

She bolted from the room and abused the stairs on her way down. She needed to mail her letter, and return by 3:30 to finish her chores. Had she planned ahead, she could have exited the bus at the library where she transferred anyway. There, she could have written her letter, walked the short distance to the post office, and caught the Number 10 bus home. If she accomplished all of this within an hour, her transfer would still be valid. However, she didn't remember to bring money to school and she didn't remember it was a half-day either.

She hastily pulled her coat from the hook under the stairs as she chastised herself for not being more organized. Clearly, she needed to write more lists.

Running through the dining room, Marielle called out, "I'll be back in a little bit."

"Where are you going?" Anna asked without looking up from the TV.

"Out," she responded, approaching the kitchen door.

Marielle ran down four narrow stairs curving 90 degrees to the right, then pulled open the exterior door which already hung open an inch or so. Normally, she would run back inside to confront her sister for wasting heat, but that effort seemed futile today. Both of them knew there was no heat in the house. To the stairs she yelled, "Were you born in a barn?" not because Anna would close the door next time or even hear her this time, but because yelling was her job as an older sister.

Marielle allowed the wooden screen door to creak to a close behind her. Her dark blue canvas shoes jumped over patches of ice along the narrow path leading to the side garage door which required a shoulder to open even though it was unlocked. The door gave way, but immediately bounced back, colliding with her face. Marielle grunted like a Viking before touching her mouth and regarding her finger with disdain. Although her lip pulsed, it had released an unsatisfying lack of blood.

She sucked in her stomach to slide between the side door and the snow blower, then shook her head at the large garage door which stood open.

Marielle grabbed her blue 10-speed bike and rode cautiously down the gravel driveway, avoiding areas of packed snow and ice every few feet. Much less snow had fallen this winter than normal and Marielle was grateful for it. Biking to the post office this early in the spring during nearly any other year would have been nearly impossible. She reached the bottom of the driveway with only two near wipe-outs before turning left onto the sidewalk.

Small, dirty ice banks stood against the curb, but the sidewalk was mostly clear owing to a strict city ordinance requiring property owners to clear public walks before noon the day following a storm. A narrow strip of cleared walk the length of the property line was technically legal, but rarely straight and such was the stigma of a messy sidewalk that half-hearted shoveling was the exception in Appleton and not the rule.

Marielle's bike gained speed as she coasted down Oneida Street to the bridge—which had a proper name, but no one used it. They called it the Oneida Street Bridge. It connected the north of Appleton to the south as it soared over a defunct paper mill, the Fox River, a biker bar and a hydroelectric plant. The bridge looked new and in good repair, but it was higher and more arched than it needed to be with a set of round steel rails which were lower than was wise for a bicyclist... or an NBA player. There were no NBA players in Appleton, but there were plenty of bikes, and Marielle easily imagined a gust of wind might cause her bike to collide with the wall, sending her over the railing to her death.

She considered walking her bike or joining the two lanes of 35 mph north-bound traffic on the other side of the street, but the 11-inch designated bike lane—or maybe it was just a line denoting the curb—wouldn't discourage anyone from running a bicyclist down from behind. Marielle trusted her ability to ride on a narrow, black-ice-covered sidewalk with a low railing more than anyone else's ability to drive safely beside her.

Her front tire jerked right to left, then back again with each push of the pedal and she twice talked herself out of walking the bike before the large, square spectrum atop Houdini Plaza came into view. The grade would soon be flat, and—more importantly—she would soon reach firm ground.

A few seconds later, the bike passed over a metal tooth-like expansion joint, reminding Marielle what a clever idea this was. Appleton was full of clever ideas. Another was the left-turn arrow at major intersections. It took a few honking motorists for her family to appreciate the arrow's intent, but now they turned left like pros. She made a mental note to wait for the arrow at the next intersection before entering the crosswalk.

Houdini Plaza was a tall building by Marielle's standards—six whole stories—and it spoke to the snob in her that she preferred to tell people she was from a city with tall buildings rather than the small farming town whose tallest building had barely three floors (if you counted the middle school basement—which everyone did).

Appleton wasn't a place people passed through or visited only during the summer or hunting season. It was a city where people stayed. They had the largest mall north of Milwaukee—bigger than Port Plaza in Green Bay even—and there were jobs which didn't involve lumber, farming, or county services at all. They had public transportation, multiple schools at every level, and even a mayor. And all of this gave Marielle social standing as well as bragging rights.

Marielle breathed a sigh of relief as her bike returned to land. Two stop lights and a minor bridge—not over water—were all that stood between her and the center of the city. She consulted her watch before standing up on her pedals.

She passed the *Metamorphosis* sculpture on her right without much notice. She didn't know what it meant and she didn't care. She categorized the precariously balanced cube opening to the sky with the exploding chain surrounding it as modern art—and to Marielle's mind, "modern" wasn't a compliment. It was art's equivalent of literary fiction, she thought, and she recognized neither the talent nor the point.

If she still lived in Kleiner, she would have reached the post office by now, it being only three short blocks from the house. In fact, she might even be there and back. Convenience, she determined, was something small town people didn't appreciate until it was gone.

Marielle locked her bike to the rack in front of the post office and checked her watch again. Her parents would return home in 35 minutes.

She stood in line as she studied each postal worker, attempting to predict the distribution of the line before her. She bet herself a cookie she would get the nice, red-haired lady in the middle, but this was less science than wishful thinking since the attitudes of the other two employees ranged from unpleasant to prison-work-release. It was the latter who called "Next" when Marielle reached the front of the line.

Mr. Work Release balanced precariously on his high stool, sighing instead of greeting as though he held the weight of the stool and not the other way around. He must have been concentrating on not falling, Marielle thought, because he neither smiled nor seemed surprised when she confirmed "Ireland" as her letter's destination. He simply flicked the letter onto a shiny digital scale near the glass, typed-in a few numbers, then requested forty-eight cents for a sticker he printed.

Marielle handed over a dollar before watching in horror as the bald man used an ugly white and pink sticker to vandalize the front of her letter. How he didn't see the large red and blue block letters on the back announcing "Hello from the USA!!!" as a sign that a colorful stamp might be appreciated, eluded her.

Mr. Work Release pushed Marielle her change before carelessly tossing her letter into a large trash-like canvas bin while asking for the next customer. She twitched in response to the implied order, but she didn't leave. She didn't want to anger the large man, but she needed to know why he took such an important letter and threw it away. If he didn't think she was old enough to send a letter to Ireland, why didn't he just say so?

A stern glance encouraged Marielle to move aside, and she exited the post office before stopping. She considered getting back into line, but worried she might get the same man again. Even if she spoke to a different postal worker, she feared Mr. Work Release might see her questioning his judgement and destroy her letter in retaliation.

Marielle cursed quietly as she returned to her bike. If Fergus didn't write back, she would always wonder if her letter was of no interest to him, or if it had never reached him at all. She could go home and write another letter, but if he received the first and didn't write back because he didn't want to, receiving a second letter would only make her look desperate and annoying.

Marielle rode her bike with her head down, determined to call Shelly when she returned home.

Shelly would never worry so much about sending a letter to a pen pal. She'd say that Marielle saw potential problems everywhere, and she was mostly right, but Marielle never made the first move toward friendship before, even with Shelly. Doing so would create the false impression that she needed people, and in her opinion she needed no one... until now.

Marielle didn't have time to stop inside the library to return the psychology book she only half understood, so she dropped it into the night drop box which sat in the middle of the parking lot... which looked remarkably like a Dumpster. At this moment, she realized the library drop box was a sign from God that just because something looked like a garbage can, it didn't mean it actually was. She smiled at her watch before riding toward the bridge.

***

That night, Marielle worked as a gas station attendant on a black and white version of the Andy Griffith Show. She wore gray overalls as she stood on a median between two old fashioned gas pumps with rounded corners. She stared past a two-lane road devoid of traffic to a field devoid of agriculture before an angry horn turned her attention to a 1957 black Packard pulling into the station in front of her. She plugged her ears against the sound that didn't abate, and as she bent down to look inside the passenger side window, the car exploded.

Marielle opened her eyes. She stared at the dark ceiling as she wondered if the noise was only her dream, then determined that only an actual sound could make her ears ring so persistently.

She sat up. The light through her curtains showed no sign of fire or flashing lights, and there were no sounds of yelling, horns, or sirens from the street. She turned to her right side, then pulled her door open only a crack, listening for any movement inside the house. Hearing nothing over several minutes—or maybe it was only seconds that felt like minutes—she determined the noise was only in her mind. Despite her ears and her best judgment, she lay back down... until she heard creaking on the stairs.

The house didn't needlessly creak often, but when it did, it creaked on the stairs. She attempted to recall the number of creaks she heard and how many steps that would equate to if the creaks were the product of a person and not a house settling. The first two steps never creaked and the next five didn't creak if one walked with one foot on each side... unless you took two stairs at a time which only her father did. So, a burglar was either on the fourth stair or her father was on the sixth which wouldn't do either of them any good unless they had enough patience to wait for everyone to go back to sleep—patience her father wasn't known to possess and a burglar with a gun didn't need.

Marielle relaxed, convincing herself that the sounds were just her imagination or the house settling, then wondered how many people were murdered in their beds believing the same thing.

Truth was, she had never heard of anyone breaking into a house in Appleton—with or without a weapon... while people were home, anyway—and the only person she had ever seen level a weapon against anyone was her father.

If her father's gun was the explosion that woke her up, Marielle knew her mother was dead because in crazy drunk man logic, he loved her best. She also knew that Anna was the next victim—being situated next door and being loved second best.

Marielle looked around the room frantically for a weapon she knew she wouldn't have the courage to use. Regardless, a cheap jewelry box, a lamp, and a pen were unlikely to stop a man with a 12-gauge shot gun, a .357 Magnum, or a hunting rifle whose caliber she couldn't quite remember. Her only hope was her tennis racket and the element of surprise... or maybe a sudden tornado or a visit from God. But as luck would have it, it wasn't tornado season, and God rarely stopped her father from shooting things... or maybe He did.

41

Marielle decided to stay in her bed and pray, *and die like a coward,* she added before deciding that the suspense was too much. She needed to go to her parents' room now and either meet her fate, or find everyone safe and sound.

She slowly pulled off her covers, slid off her bed, opened the door, and took one step into the hall. The window at the top of the stairs cast enough light to illuminate most of the hallway. She looked over the railing to study the shadows for a moment. Seeing nothing move, and deciding she had more patience than a non-Edgar Allen Poe murderer, she declared the stairs empty.

It was possible that her father killed her mother, then went out for a beer or lay down and took a nap, but Marielle doubted it. If Jack had killed tonight, he would either be up staring at Maria's body, sorrowfully telling her how much he loved her, or he would be busily looking for ammunition in one of his disorganized top dresser drawers—saddened only that he shot his wife before yelling at her for misplacing his stuff.

So, he was either sleeping beside a dead woman, missing, or the noise that woke her was simply a car back-firing, and that noise somehow made her ears ring.

Marielle pushed open the door of her parents' room, then stopped. She could now hear the soft snoring of her mother and see the outline of her father beside her.

She blinked hard as she returned the door to its three inch mark. She should have known her father was passed his killing phase. He hadn't threatened anyone with death since the move. Maybe he was shamed by the loss of their house in Kleiner or maybe he was happier in the city. Either way, things were better now and Marielle's dreams needed to follow suit.

Chapter Four

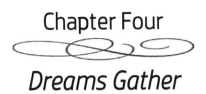

Dreams Gather
—W.B. Yeats – *The Valley of the Black Pig*

A week after mailing her letter, Marielle began running from the bus stop to the mailbox after school. It was a yellow, wooden box with a brown lid attached to the right side railing of the porch. The mailbox matched the house, and the paint on both was peeling. If the mailman arrived before lunch, her parents placed the mail on the dining room table. If the mailman arrived after lunch, the mail would still be in the box. Sixty percent of the time, the mailman arrived before lunch.

On April 4th, Marielle found only a small postcard in the mailbox which had fallen from a *Newsweek* magazine over a week ago. No one felt compelled to remove it. She didn't know why. They just wouldn't. She sighed as she flipped closed the lid, then easily caught up to Anna who had just pushed open the unlocked side door.

They walked silently upstairs to the kitchen where Anna stopped to drop her backpack on the island, thereby stopping the flow of traffic. Marielle squeezed through with force and without apology before walking quickly toward a pile of white envelopes on the dining room table.

They were all legal-sized, and all were type-written except one. It was addressed to Marielle in a handwritten style that made the number ones look sad, though the colorful postage and purple "Par Avion" did its best to cheer them up. No one in the house received colorful letters with foreign words on them. Even Stephen's and John's letters, routed through the Army mail system, looked no more foreign than letters she received from friends in Kleiner. She looked at the back of the envelope as she tore it open, noticing the words "Hello From Ireland!" written in large, garish, green letters. She smiled. Fergus had a sense of humor.

Marielle skipped to the dining room couch and threw herself down before eagerly removing the envelope's contents. Two 3" x 5" pictures dropped into her lap so Marielle studied those first. One photo displayed the back of a boy in white shorts, and a maroon and black long-sleeved shirt that matched his long socks. He clearly hit a ball with force using a small, hockey-esque stick. There was an arrow over the boy's head and the word "me" written in pen, but all that could be gleaned from the picture was that Fergus had brown hair, muscular legs, and good hand/eye coordination.

The next picture, taken with the entire team, showed Fergus' face only slightly better since he turned to the left as he looked down at the sticks his teammates crossed in front of him. The picture showed a lean, muscular frame and tan skin, but the angle and distance frustrated Marielle's desire to see his face clearly. He resembled five of ten athletic boys in school, she thought, except for the dark hair and skin.

Just the same, Marielle was sure Fergus was handsome and his horrible name was the curse of heredity. After all, she knew a kid at school whose dad's name was Adolph. He was named after his father, and he had the good sense to name his only son Karl, but clearly some people weren't so lucky.

Marielle set down the pictures and picked up the single sheet of lined notebook paper which was marked with blue ink and jagged handwriting as though the writer wanted to inflict pain upon the paper with every pen stroke. The margins, which featured pictures of odd looking faces with wild hair, missiles and planes, confirmed these violent thoughts. The paper smelled fresh. Not like Irish Spring soap, which was a disappointment, but more like it sat in a damp garden for a day or two before hanging on the line.

26-Mar-1988

Hi Marielle!

Thanks for your letter! Sorry I didn't write but I was really busy. I'm sending you some photos of my last hurling match. I hope you had a nice St. Patrick's Day. It was really good here even though it rained. I saw American parades on T.V. – they were really big (as usual!). I got a real surprise when I opened your letter — I had forgotten about joining the pen pal club!

About myself, I have brown hair and brown eyes and I'm 180cm tall. I'm 15 and my birthday is on the 13th of October. I have one sister, called Fiona, who is 17. In school she's in sixth year and I'm in fourth. I like hurling (similar to field hockey), cycling, swimming, windsurfing, and what you call soccer. Hurling is my favourite sport and it takes up a lot of time. My sister doesn't do much sport, but she's really good at music and she plays the piano, violin, guitar, and lots of little plastic thingies with holes in them (anything that makes noise!). I love listening to pop music and Sting is my favourite singer. Who do you like best? In school, the subjects I hate least are science and Irish.

I saw some pictures of Wisconsin on T.V. last night. It looks really nice. I also heard that Jesse Jackson will probably be the next president. I think he would be great! It would be great if you could come to Ireland in the summer! Please tell me if you are able to come as soon as you find out! I better finish my letter now because I have to go windsurfing and then get to Mass. Please write back soon and send me a photo!

See ya!

Love,
Dermot (I'm called by my middle name)

P.S. Please send me your birthday again because I (ahem) kind of lost the last part of your letter somewhere......

"Dermot!" she said to herself with relief. She had never heard the name before, but it was a whole lot better than Fergus. After all, "Fergus MacManus" seemed like the ending to a Roman joke. She didn't know any Roman jokes, but she had seen *History of the World, Part I*.

Marielle reread the letter with the name Dermot replacing Fergus in her mind, but stopped to curse at his mention of sports. She had forgotten to say she liked sports in her letter. It would have been a lie since she didn't like playing sports at all, but people who said they liked sports always sounded cooler than people who said they didn't. In fact, most people didn't admit they didn't like to play sports, she thought before wondering why.

She gave up on wonder to study the pictures again before rereading the letter and examining closely his doodling around the edges. He was left-handed, she determined, not only because of the way he held his stick, but by the crossing of his T's which trailed off to the left rather than the right. Marielle's father was a lefty too, but she decided to let Dermot slide since she was sure all lefties couldn't be violent alcoholics.

All in all, the letter was everything she had hoped. He sounded nice and fun and he even extended himself by writing "Love" before his name. People in Wisconsin would never do that in a first letter. It made her feel unexpectedly tingly which made her put off kitchen duty to run to her backpack for notepaper.

4 /4 /1988 Monday

Hi Dermot!

Thank you for writing back and sending pictures! It was great to hear from you!

It sounds like school, hurling, and water sports keep you very busy. I wish I could say the same (well, I'm not envious about the water sports part because I'm afraid of water, but the busy part would be great). I've taken extra classes both semesters this year to avoid boredom, but it hasn't worked so far.

I'm in the standard Biology, Geometry, English, German and History classes which are alright, but the classes I enjoy most are my three music classes: Wind Symphony (playing tenor saxophone [I made first chair this year]); Women's Choir, and a mixed guy's/girl's choir called "Easterners".

Symphony is my favorite music class even though my teacher is short and angry. He even wears tiny glasses at the end of his nose. (I think there's a law somewhere that says band directors have to have these.) When he smashes his baton on the music stand and yells your last name, he can seem pretty intimidating, but every once in awhile I make him laugh, and he doesn't seem so scary at all.

On the other hand, my choir teacher is tall and mean and barely tolerates me. I know this because he told me so at my last audition (that he barely tolerates me, not that he's mean). He says my "incessant talking irritates him greatly," which is, of course, an exaggeration because I only talk when I'm not singing! Friday, he was working with the sopranos (I'm an alto) and mid-way through my conversation with a tenor he yelled, "RICHTER!! (choir teachers only call you by your last name too) WHAT is the key in which we are singing today?" Everyone in the room was quiet except the tenor who murmured, "Oh sh$%." And I can't tell you *how I knew the note (since I was talking through his whole explanation), but I winged it and said, "Uhhh... D... Flat," and low and behold I was right!! Go figure! I think he might hate me more after that, but it's worth it because now I'm famous. By the end of the day, even my ex-boyfriend Guy (he's a senior [that's two years older]) knew about it... and he doesn't even take music classes! He's in architecture and engineering classes, but in any event he's an ass, but that's a subject for another letter.*

Just so you don't think I regularly try to irritate my teachers, I'll say that I know I'm supposed to be quiet when the teachers are working with individual groups and people, but I just can't control myself. There's really a lot to say and not a lot of time to do it (since I don't have a lunch hour this year) so I'm afraid my teachers and I are at an impasse.

Regarding popular music, I like at least one song from just about anyone who has ever recorded an album, but I generally don't listen to just one style or band. I'm actually wild about the song "Pink Cadillac" right now (I think Aretha Franklin sings that).

Anyway, I'd better go and write my friend Heidi now. (I met her at band camp last summer.) I received a postcard from her on Saturday with a picture of Garfield in Hell with the caption, "Wish you were here." It occurred to me while reading this that A) I should do a better job of writing Heidi, and B) There's a real lack of insulting cards at the pharmacy. They all say, "Hope you are feeling better", or "Happy Birthday, dear, sweet brother," but none of them say, "When we first broke up, I considered what I might have done to hurt the relationship, but now I've come to the conclusion that you're just an ass!" Now, that's a card I'd pay good money for! I'll have to ask Heidi where she got her postcard...

Anyway, take care!
Love,
Marielle

PS My birthday is August 29th.

PPS I've enclosed my latest school picture which was taken last September. I wanted to get retakes, but my grandmother forced me to keep these.

PPPS I live in a pretty conservative part of a pretty conservative state (Senator Joseph McCarthy was from Appleton [do you know him?]). We regularly insult people at school by calling them "red" which means they're communists... which makes people pretty mad. My grandfather is active in the Republican Party and he gets invited to all the Republican Presidential Inaugurations (although he never goes). My parents have never voted for anyone who wasn't Republican and we used to have a huge Ronald Reagan sign on our front lawn. So, I haven't heard that Jesse Jackson will be the next president, but that doesn't mean anything. I'm sure I wouldn't hear that news even if it were true... which I'm not saying it isn't. In any event, my grandfather is visiting this weekend so I'll ask him.

Marielle reread her letter the requisite number of times, paying particular attention to the last postscript. She was a little concerned that it sounded abrasive, but she had taken care to reciprocate with "love" in the closing even though she didn't feel it.

Overall, it was a much better letter than her first, even if she made herself sound more rebellious than she was. Truth be known, it mattered if her choir teacher liked her. It mattered a lot. But she was convinced he had big buttons that were easily pushed. She walked on egg shells at home. She refused to do so at school.

She also lied about not liking any particular band, but that couldn't be helped. If he knew the truth, he would think her U2 obsession was the only reason she wrote to him, and that would be hurtful and mostly untrue.

She regarded her school picture one more time before determining it was good enough to send. It had a bright blue background which brought out the blue of her eyes and contrasted nicely with her crisp white linen mock turtleneck blouse with three flat pleats down the middle. Her skin looked luminous and clear, almost porcelain, and her blonde hair's failure to achieve Christy Brinkley bangs was less apparent from the photographer's chosen angle. Her shoulders slouched forward slightly, giving the appearance of a low self-esteem which was the reason she wanted retakes, but all in all it was a good picture.

She placed the letter and picture inside a plain envelope, addressed it, and rested it upright against the ruby glass fruit dish which held coupons and change, but no fruit. The only thing left to do was call Shelly and tell her every single thing she read, wrote, and thought that day, then do the dishes before her parents got home. Marielle looked at the clock. Shelly would have to wait.

***

"Hello there!" Marielle's father said as he walked through the kitchen door.

"Oh, hello," replied Marielle, looking up from the dishwater, surprised to hear her father use his Friday voice on a Monday.

"Is your mom home yet?"

Marielle shook her head. "No, sir. Not yet."

"Well, I'm gonna grab myself a cold one and wait for her in the next room," he said, laughing as he patted her three times on the back.

Marielle turned her head to smile, then looked back at the dishes, hoping her father's good humor had nothing to do with the giggling she heard from her parents' room that morning. She shivered before bringing the silverware up for air.

She didn't know why her parents' intimate life disturbed her more than violence. One just felt more natural than the other. She would complain about this to Shelly because she was pretty sure girls were supposed to complain about their parents' sex life to their best friends, whereas fears of drowning dishes was something to keep to oneself.

She felt around the bottom of the sink for rogue silverware, remembering with shame the day the water drained, leaving suds and pieces of kidney bean on top of a drowned knife. She felt only a small glass under the water now, but everyone knew a glass could hold its breath longer than silverware.

"Well, it's good you don't really believe that because imagine what would happen to the dishes when you weren't around," Shelly said after Marielle confessed her fears, then retracted them when Shelly's eyebrows furrowed a second too long.

Marielle thought about Shelly's words before deciding she couldn't worry about the silverware when she wasn't around just like her brothers couldn't worry about their sisters when they weren't around either. Once Marielle left, she would be as unlikely to call the silverware as her siblings were to call her.

After drying and putting away the dishes, Marielle fetched her father another beer to pre-empt an imminent request, then ran up the stairs to call Shelly from the French phone at the top.

Shelly Schwartz was the first good friend Marielle made in Appleton.

She was three inches shorter than Marielle, but she had much bigger hair. It was dark blonde, and well-permed with bangs that were frozen into one long curl. Above the bangs, her hair flipped high and to the back. Shelly spent an hour and 15 minutes on makeup and hair each morning (twice as long as Marielle), but her efforts paid off in sheer volume.

Shelly's hair wasn't the only thing that was better than Marielle's. She had the latest clothes, real Penny Loafers (not the knock-offs Marielle wore), and a new Navy Pea Coat which she wore with various scarves of varying colors, depending upon her mood. Unlike most of the fashion-conscious girls at school, Shelly didn't display the Guess, Swatch, Outback Red, Tretorn or Benetton clothing tags on the inside of her locker like expensive trophies. Doing so would remove Shelly from Marielle's friend pool, which was small, but not shallow.

Shelly's parents were divorced and she lived with her mom in a duplex near Appleton East High School. Her house was clean, warm, and quiet with a faint smell of apple-cinnamon air freshener. She had never met Shelly's dad, and Shelly never talked about him, but Marielle had the sneaking suspicion she knew him almost as well as Shelly did.

Marielle's parents liked Shelly even though her mom was a teacher, and Shelly's mom liked Marielle even though her parents never attended college. It was in all ways a perfect friendship.

***

That night, Marielle lay in her dark room thinking about Dermot and Ireland, her head spinning with ideas of an imaginary future. It was entirely possible that Dermot was a jerk—as Shelly cautioned—but he made the effort to write back and that made him better than 98% of American boys. Besides, a jerk with an Irish accent probably didn't sound like a jerk at all, she reasoned, and Shelly agreed.

Marielle said her prayers while lying down. She felt badly for not kneeling on the floor, but her bed was too high to accommodate her elbows and the temperature was too cold to accommodate clear thought. In fact, she was probably just lazy, but she couldn't admit that without God finding out.

She settled deeper into her covers, trying to stop her teeth from chattering. Her bedding was two blankets lighter than usual, but after ten minutes, she began to rethink the optimism of removing two-fifths of her cold weather arsenal. She could get up, walk to the end of the hall and grab another blanket from the closet, but that seemed like a lot of work. If

50

she went to sleep quickly, maybe she wouldn't feel the cold. In any event, this was a good opportunity to test her mind over her body. She relaxed her eyes, cleared her mind, and drifted off to sleep.

Chapter Five

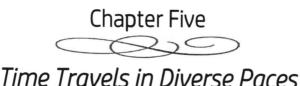

Time Travels in Diverse Paces
—William Shakespeare – *As You Like It*

"Hi, Blondie!" Johan Richter said as he hugged Marielle tightly. "How's my little *Fraulein*?"

Marielle returned the hug, smiling like her cheeks would explode. "Do you have it?" she asked, stepping backward to catch her breath.

"Of course," he replied, pulling a gold-colored, disc-shaped piece of candy from his right pocket while smiling more broadly than usual.

Marielle examined the candy before her smile vanished and her eyebrows furrowed. "But, this isn't soft like the last time," she said, knowing this wasn't the same candy at all, but looking up at her grandpa with confusion rather than betrayal simply out of respect.

Her grandfather laughed heartily, but didn't reply.

"What happened to the other one?" she asked, smiling with him, but feeling nothing approaching happy.

"I think I accidentally ate it," he explained, still laughing.

"Oh," she said, finally amused, "okay, then."

Marielle hugged her grandmother with two gentle pats on her back. She was taller than her grandmother now, but wouldn't call her *Shorty* like Jeanette did as she found the term disrespectful. Marielle also disliked the use of *Gran* or *Gram*, and thought the word *Gramps* should be illegal.

"Where's your coat?" Frieda asked her granddaughter.

"Ah, Grandma, aren't you tired of wearing a winter coat? It's so inconvenient," Marielle replied.

"Well, kid, there's nothing convenient about dead."

Marielle laughed. "That's true, but I have superior Richter genetics which makes me impervious to pneumonia."

Frieda rolled her eyes. "You sure are a Richter, kid," she said, shaking her head.

Marielle picked up her grandparents' small suitcase before walking carefully toward the front porch. "Watch your step," she cautioned.

"I see your father hasn't gotten around to clearing the path yet," Johan noted.

Marielle nodded. "*Ja*, Dad said he's tired of chopping ice this year. He said, 'God put it there, and God can take it away.' "

She walked through the front door, placing the bag at the bottom of the stairs, then held the door open as her grandparents crossed the threshold. The door wasn't in danger of closing on its own, but she noticed her mother held the door open for company and thought it more welcoming.

"Can I take your coats?" she asked.

"We can just put them on the hooks here," Frieda said, holding out her hand to receive her husband's coat.

Marielle normally carried the bags to Jeanette's room immediately, but this time she broke with tradition and followed her grandparents to the living room instead. It wasn't payback for the candy fraud, she told herself. She would move the suitcase later and get her grandparents settled in first... although the candy still annoyed her more than she was accustomed to being annoyed by her grandfather.

***

He had given it as a gift or maybe as a distraction almost two autumns ago, after the last of her family's belongings were packed into a single U-Haul truck and the back door of the house in Kleiner was closed for the last time. Marielle's parents and grandmother lingered near the back door, staring at the side yard while she and her grandfather removed themselves, pretending not to hear the conversation or be affected by the moment as Frieda bid her son and daughter-in-law goodbye for the last time as residents of the same town.

Marielle asked her grandfather to pet the horses for her, but her mind wasn't on horses, or the butterscotch candy in her hand. It was on the shiny black door behind her grandfather's shoulder. By rights, the door should have looked happy, knowing it would be kicked in no longer, but to her surprise it didn't. It looked sad and abandoned like the three-legged cat they dropped off at a farm the previous weekend.

Jack exchanged final hugs with his mother, but he didn't move from her. Hands in his pockets, he alternately looked down, then around at the backyard, his lips pulled back into a painful smile, and his body rocking back and forth as he felt things he didn't say.

Marielle and her grandfather looked over before sighing in unison. One needed to get into the car and get on with one's life and forget about the door, the cat, the house, and the life that would have been lived there.

Marielle gave her grandfather a hug strong enough to be received as final. She exchanged a stoic nod, then turned to walk to the small, red pickup truck in the alley. Anna—having given up on emotion before her sisters—already sat in the truck, taking her designated spot in the middle of the bench seat, her legs barely clearing the stick shift which could have been charged with assault each time it was placed into reverse. As a sign of positive things to come, however, reverse was unnecessary since the truck already pointed in the proper direction called "away."

Marielle watched her grandfather walk toward Jeanette who leaned against the U-Haul with arms crossed and an expression to match. Whether Jeanette was annoyed at her father's spectacle or leaving her boyfriend, her cat, and her popularity behind was hard to say, but riding with her father to Appleton was cause enough for annoyance.

It was true that the U-Haul cabin provided more space than the pickup, and Jack always traveled with licorice to spare, but his inevitable ranting at his wife's driving with no way to communicate his displeasure (aside from flashing his headlights and frantically switching his directional on and off) would make for an uncomfortable trip.

About 10 miles into the journey south, Jack began educating Jeanette on the proper usage of every curse word from B to S in the alphabet. It was a repeat lesson which ended with a "son of a bitch," an unhappy laugh, and a shaking of his head as he glanced at Jeanette for concurrence. It was incumbent upon Jeanette to make eye contact with her father and smile in uncomfortable agreement. Not smiling or making eye contact was considered disrespectful to her father. Smiling too much was disrespectful to her mother, and her father wouldn't stand for that either.

Thirty seconds after the first rant, Jack lit up a cigarette to calm down, then took two puffs before considering the air space of his passenger—or maybe himself—and rolled down his window a crack. Jeanette attempted to hold her breath, but experience showed that one risked serious light-headedness before giving up and gulping a mouthful of smoke. Jeanette could pray for more ventilation, but in Northern Wisconsin in November a vehicle traveling at 57 miles per hour with its window cracked one inch would somehow let in enough air to freeze a person's nose hairs without admitting enough air to breathe.

During the three hour—and mostly two lane—trip to Appleton, Marielle was tempted to eat the candy her grandfather gave her, but placed it into her right pocket instead while covertly spying the flashing lights in her side mirror. She would eat the candy and tell her mom about the lights eventually, just not yet.

A month after the U-Haul pulled into their new driveway, Johan and Frieda Richter visited for the first time. At the end of two short days, Johan shifted the Buick into reverse and smiled an unhappy "this is it" to people who were not yet sufficiently settled to welcome anyone's leaving. Before the car could move, Marielle ran up to her grandfather's open window and handed back the month-old candy.

Johan Richter was a man no one had ever seen cry (except during his dad's funeral; but that was during the Depression and most of those people were either in Chicago or dead). This occasion was no exception, but her grandfather's eyes looked suddenly more glassy at the realization that in a small way, the candy now represented the bond between his granddaughter and himself.

From then on, the same candy passed between them during each visit. Sometimes during a greeting and sometimes during a final goodbye, but it always exchanged hands, until now.

Marielle stifled sadness. *Did you think you could keep the same tradition for the rest of your life?* she chastised herself before her grandfather's voice returned her to the present.

"When do your mom and dad get home from work, young lady?" Johan asked amiably.

Marielle looked down at the VCR clock only she knew how to set. "Well, they should be home right now, actually, but I think Mom said the owner was coming to tour the nursing home and the administrator wanted everyone to stay until he was gone."

Her grandparents nodded.

"Can I get you something to drink?" she asked.

"No, no," her grandfather replied.

"Grandma?" Marielle asked.

"No, thank you," she responded in a high, discordant voice. "We stopped at Hardees before we left Green Bay."

After Marielle quizzed her grandfather in depth on his meetings for the state planning commission, the kitchen door drew everyone's attention to the back of the house.

"Well, hello there, Shorty," Jack said, walking briskly into the dining room to hug his mother.

Frieda abruptly stepped back. Placing her hands on her hips and pursing her lips she said, "I'll have you know I didn't shrink at all since my last doctor's appointment." Her tone attempted sincere affront, but a half-smile betrayed her.

"Ah, so you're still four-nothin', then?" Jack responded, laughing at his own joke. "Did they use a special midget scale for you?" he continued before his father's approach and handshake interrupted him.

"Hello there, sir," Jack said, shaking his father's hand firmly.

The two men were the same height and Jack's hand was by no means small, but it was dwarfed by his father's. This fact became obvious each time they said their hellos or goodbyes.

Jack attempted to turn a handshake into a hug once—when he was an adult and his mother was in the hospital—but his father reflexively pushed him into the waiting room wall and so the preference for a handshake was understood.

Jack told this story on the rare occasion when he was both drunk and reflective and usually with Elvis in the too-near background. On such nights, the children were expected to show empathy they didn't feel and keep their father company until he passed out. This ensured a reflective father didn't become a violent one, but it was a painful middle-of-the-night journey through hypocrisy just the same.

In his defense, Jack made a point to hug his sons when he wasn't choking them, and Marielle imagined John and Stephen would hug their sons and not choke them at all. Each generation was getting better and better, she thought.

"How was your trip?" Maria asked as she hugged her father-in-law.

"Fine," he said. "It's still cool enough that we didn't need to worry about the air conditioner."

"We haven't gotten that fixed since the belt broke and Gerry Brady helped us near Crandon last summer," Frieda explained.

"Well, you have a couple months before you'll need it anyway. So, how's everything up North?" Jack asked out of habit rather than curiosity. He sat down with his father in the living room while the women retreated to the dining room table.

The general rule was that women and girls sat around a table while men and boys sat in the living room or outside. Once the crowd grew to greater than ten or so people, the rule was strictly observed. When the crowd was less than ten, the custom was less clear, but Marielle had an "in" with someone in the living room, so she almost always sat near her grandfather to the narrow-eyed expressions of most women around the table.

"Good, good," Johan responded. "Once the ground thaws, we're putting in a new septic tank."

"That should be soon, eh?" Jack asked.

"Yeah, I'm not exactly sure. I always wait for the cemetery to start burying people before I start digging," he said with a chuckle.

"You know what they do around here, Dad?" Maria called from the dining room table. "They burn a tire on the plot. It burns slowly for a couple of days, and then they break ground with a back-hoe."

"You don't say?" he responded with interest. Maria was one of the few women who could interject into a man's conversation with Johan's approval and appreciation. "I'll have to mention that to Otto Ziegler when I get back. He was complaining the other day that they were running short on vault space."

"Is that the building that looks like a concrete garage?" Marielle asked, knowing it was, but surprised by the word "vault."

"Yeah," her grandfather replied. "We actually just voted to put a new garage door on it."

"And don't forget to tell Jack about the new lights," Frieda said proudly.

Jack rolled his eyes, shook his head, and laughed before looking around the room for sympathetic faces. He had heard about the new Main Street lights during every Sunday phone call for the last two months. Each time he hung up the telephone he said a variation of, "Why the hell would *anyone* be excited about a few lights on a crappy little street in a crappy little town?"

Everyone in the house was expected to laugh and they did, but Marielle thought her father had forgotten his small town perspective just the same. New lights would be a huge development!

"Right," Johan said, downplaying his enthusiasm in response to his son's head shaking. "We received a grant to install new lights on Main Street."

"The black old-fashioned kind you can add banners to," Frieda said, nodding her head in satisfaction as she was generally immune to her son's sarcasm.

"Oh, how nice," Maria said with sincerity.

Jack reached for the TV Guide on the cocktail table. "Well, let's see how I'll be spending my weekend," he said with happy defiance as he looked around the room wearing a childish grin.

Most smiled back in a mechanical way meant to hide the rude things they felt—with varying degrees of effectiveness. Johan smiled a death-stare at his son. He wasn't in the mood for a fight, but he wasn't pleased either. Jack knew his parents only watched TV after dark and only when the news or Vanna White were available. Pulling out the TV Guide during the day so early into the visit was an act of rebellion, but only the latest in a long string of rebellions.

Frieda turned her false smile to Maria who met it with a "what an idiot" look of her own.

"Gail and Mike are putting in new windows in their bedroom," Frieda said, eager to change the subject.

"Really?" Maria replied. "Aren't their windows brand new?"

Frieda nodded her head and pursed her lips like she was taking the old windows' side. "You bet. I asked Mike why they would do that when they only just built the house five years ago. He said Gail wanted the large crank-open kind they could leave open when it gets warm. I asked him what happens if a raccoon or a black bear comes along during the night."

Her grandmother's comments intrigued Marielle, not because black bear hadn't approached most houses since the '60s, or because her grandmother was expressing dissatisfaction with her cousin's wife, but because she said Gail's name first.

The male name preceding the female was always the custom unless Grandma thought the woman was uppity and not properly controlled by her husband. As recently as last month, the order had always been Mike and Gail. In fact, Joanne and Robby had been Robby and Joanne until just before the divorce. So, if Mike and Gail were now Gail and Mike it was for reasons more important than black bears and bedroom windows.

Marielle walked into the dining room to investigate as well as to escape the noise of the newly switched on television.

Johan would not be emasculated by sitting in the dining room—not to eat and not to socialize—so he stayed in the living room and read the *Post Crescent*, sighing loudly every few minutes.

"Did I tell you I finished my painting?" Frieda asked Maria.

"Oh, no, you didn't. Is this the one of the Alps?" Maria asked.

"You're painting the Alps?" Marielle interrupted with excitement.

"I am," Frieda replied, happy with her granddaughter's enthusiasm. "I found a picture of a place in Tyrol in my magazine and I decided to paint it."

"Ooh, can I see it?" Marielle asked eagerly.

"Sure. In fact, you can have it."

"Really?" Marielle asked, leaning forward.

"Marielle," Maria warned, then to her mother-in-law she said, "You should keep your paintings, Mom."

"Why?" Frieda asked, "God knows how long I'll be around and I want my kids and grandkids to have something to remember me by. You know Judy's living room is filled with paintings and knick-knacks I've made for her, and every time I see the kids, they're wearing the clothes I gave them. Gail—well, I don't know WHAT she does with the things I give her. They're never in the house and the kids never wear them."

Aha, Marielle thought. She was getting closer to the reason behind Grandma's name order reversal.

"Marielle, why don't you put on a pot of coffee and see what your father and grandfather would like to drink," her mother suggested.

Marielle's sighed. Her mother had a way of deflecting angry gossip. *Besides, it wouldn't take a rocket scientist to figure out what Dad wants to drink,* she thought. *Like today is the day he switches to milk?*

"Where's Anna?" Frieda asked Maria as Marielle stood up.

"Oh, she—" Maria began.

"She's assumed her pouty position," Marielle interjected.

"Marielle, go!" her mother scolded. Turning to her mother-in-law she said, "She is still having a hard time with the transition and having to wear the brace, so she spends a lot of time in her room."

That was a bullshit answer, Marielle thought as she dispatched with her beverage duties. So, she didn't want to move. It's been almost two years. *Get over it!* And she has to wear a back brace. It could be worse. A girl Marielle knew at East had rods installed in her back. They caught Anna's scoliosis early. By all accounts, she was lucky. Why her parents let her pout her way through life perplexed Marielle.

"Do you want me to go get her?" she asked after returning to the table.

Maria narrowed her eyes at her daughter. "Just tell her Grandma and Grandpa are here and ask her to come down and say hello."

She already knows Grandma and Grandpa are here, Marielle thought. *She'd be deaf not to hear them. She's just being difficult because she likes the other side of the family better—the side no one ever saw unless they needed bail money.* "Stupid WOP!" Marielle said as she ran up the stairs. She turned left, then threw open Anna's door. "Grandma and Grandpa are here. Go downstairs and say hi."

Anna lay on her right side facing the window, her dark, curly hair resting on her pillow. Marielle waited a minute, ignoring the desire to ask her little sister what was wrong. Anna stopped confiding in her a long time ago, and Marielle was tired of trying to resurrect a relationship that was dead. The final attempt came in the very same doorway the night Anna returned home wearing a back brace, and it ended quickly in a command to go away. Since then, Marielle suppressed any desire she had to show her sister either kindness or mercy.

"Did you hear me? Get – your – butt – up – and – say – hello – to – your – grandparents!" she demanded.

"Go away!" Anna responded with her left hand and a cup of whine in her voice.

Marielle turned away without closing the door. She walked to her own room to pull three gold medals and one silver from her top middle dresser drawer, all of which were cut in the shape of Wisconsin and attached to a pin held by small blue ribbons. She shut the drawer heavily before returning downstairs.

She made eye contact with her mother, raised and lowered her shoulders, then tip-toed to the loveseat. She couldn't interrupt her grandmother mid-rant to tell Maria of Anna's insubordination, and waiting for a pause in her grandmother's speech was time-prohibitive.

In a hushed tone, Marielle addressed her grandfather, "Grandpa, here are my medals from this year's Solo and Ensemble competition. I forgot to show you last time."

Johan set the paper down to regard the medals with interest a moment before Jack asked with narrowing eyes, "When did you get those?"

"Ah, in March, I think," Marielle said nervously.

Her father wouldn't yell at her in front of her grandfather without extreme cause, but there were few things he liked less than being reminded of the distance between himself and his children.

"Well, those are lovely, honey," Johan said, "What are they for?"

"This one is for my sax solo, and this one is for a sax quartet. That one is for singing a solo and the silver one is for a singing duet."

"You should show your grandmother," he said, and to the dining room he called, "Hey Frieda, take a look at Marielle's medals."

Jack gave his father a dirty look for disturbing his program at the same time Frieda turned toward the living room with a similar expression. She waited for Marielle to place the medals in front of her before dispatching the requisite compliments, then quickly continued with her story just before her husband interrupted again.

"Hey, Marielle, maybe you can play your saxophone for me later on," he suggested.

"Well, sure," Marielle responded in a tone lower than her grandfather's, looking around to see how many dirty looks were aimed in her direction.

"What's your sister doing?" Maria asked Marielle, then added, "Sorry, Mom," quickly to her mother-in-law before looking back at her daughter.

Frieda pretended not to be irritated, but it was the third interruption in five minutes and her nerves were beginning to fray.

"Uh, it looks like she's crying in bed again," Marielle replied.

Maria appeared concerned, but she was too polite to leave the table. "Okay, I'm sorry," she said to her mother-in-law. "So you say the bullet didn't actually hit the girl?"

"No, she had just pushed back her seat to take a nap. Had she been sitting upright though, Robby said she would have been killed. I asked Nancy, 'What's this world coming to?' "

"Who's this?" Marielle asked.

"Your cousin Robby's friend's daughter," her mother replied.

Rob didn't like to be called Robby and only his mother, aunts, and grandmother did so since he left the Navy.

"Someone shot at his daughter?" Marielle asked, knowing her grandmother didn't mind repeating salacious gossip.

"Uh-huh," Frieda nodded in a childlike way, forgetting complaints about her slipped discs. "He was driving from Iron Mountain to North Dickinson and a sniper shot at his car."

"Did they catch the guy?" Marielle asked, herself shocked and thrilled.

"No, not yet. Robby and his friend Darren are talking about camping along the highway and hunting down the shooter themselves." Frieda turned to Maria as she continued, "I told Nancy they need to let the police handle it, but she says he's all grown up now and he can make his own decisions."

"Maybe she's happy he's finally taking the initiative," Marielle said, amused with herself. She was alone. "Sorry," she said.

"So, what'll they do if they find him?" Maria asked with wide eyes.

"Shoot him, I suppose," Frieda said, looking down at the paper napkin she folded as if responding "cream and sugar" to how she liked her coffee.

"I imagine they could just say it was a hunting accident, eh?" Marielle suggested to her mother.

"Except it's not hunting season," Maria replied as though her displeasure with Marielle might stop her nephew from shooting a sniper. "Can you go get the Tollhouse Bars please?"

"Ooh, right," Marielle said. "You'll have one, right Grandma?"

"Well, my doctor says I should lay off the sugar, but I suppose one bar won't kill me," she replied, raising her shoulders while wearing a mischievous grin.

Marielle returned to the dining room, holding a plate of chocolate chip bars in the air as she mouthed "Do you want one?" to her grandfather.

After retrieving small plates from the kitchen, she delivered a bar to her grandfather, but ignored her father entirely.

Jack disliked sweets almost as much as he disliked being bothered and "being bothered" extended to people walking near or in front of his TV. So, when he looked up, narrowed his eyes, and held his breath, his daughter got the point. *These aren't the kind of bars you like,* Marielle silently replied before smiling at herself.

"Your Uncle Jim and Aunt Judy are on a vacation in Las Vegas this week," Frieda said when Marielle returned to the table.

"Oh, so who's taking care of the animals?" Marielle asked.

"Your cousin Robby," Frieda replied. She had a habit of adding "your cousin" in front of his name, as though the context wouldn't make his identity obvious. She turned toward Maria. "We're paying him $10 a day," she added in a matter-of-fact way.

"To feed the horses?" Maria asked with surprise.

"*Ja,*" Frieda said. "I asked Nancy if Robby would do it and she said that she thought he would if we paid him."

"That's crap!" Marielle said before quickly placing her hand over her mouth, exchanging a flash of anger for one of remorse. She watched her mother's shocked expression turn into an angry one before apologizing quietly.

"You're right, little lady. It *is* crap!" her grandfather said behind her. He had entered the dining room for another Tollhouse Bar, having almost finished the first. "You make the best Tollhouse Bars, Maria," he continued, holding up the remains of the bar with his left hand.

"Marielle actually helped me with those last night," she replied, having not fully recovered from her daughter's public use of the word "crap."

"Good job, Blondie," Johan said, squeezing her left shoulder with his right hand.

Marielle smiled up at her grandfather. "Ooh, Grandpa, next time you visit, we need to hunt for night-crawlers. Last summer, I found a spot in the back yard that's just full of them after it rains. It's probably too early for them to come out yet, eh?"

"Probably, but you can show me this weekend anyway," he replied.

"They say it's supposed to rain tomorrow," Maria added.

"Excellent," Johan remarked. "While you ladies are out at the mall, Jack and I can go to the junk shop. Then, we'll hunt for night-crawlers after dinner."

Jack looked up from the TV to give his father the hairy eyeball. "I punch a clock at work. I'm not going to punch it at home," he'd say. He punched other things at home.

Johan ignored his son, but everyone knew the look was there. Marielle smiled broadly at her grandfather. She knew of no one else who so consistently and remorselessly annoyed her father. "If people have big buttons, it's your responsibility to push them," he said once as he flashed an ageless smile. And he lived by those words.

***

It was unusual for the women, and the "little girls" (as Maria described Marielle and Anna) to shop at every local craft store and still return home before the men, but that was the case the next day.

Maria had already steamed the lobster tail for Johan and Jack, and was layering lasagna noodles for everyone else when her husband and father-in-law walked through the front door laughing, their hair and overcoats dripping rain.

"What happened to you two?" Frieda asked as they entered the dining room.

"We had to park a mile away from the junk store and walk," Jack replied, still slightly out of breath. "Everybody and their brother was out buying junk today."

"So, what did you get?" Maria called from the kitchen.

"I got a machine that crushes aluminum cans," Johan said, pulling a

63

brand new cream-colored, plastic, tubular-shaped gadget from a box labeled, "As Seen on TV."

He received "oohs" from all assembled, save his wife.

Johan wasn't the type to drink pop so the only beverage he might consume in can form was beer and his wife strictly rationed his consumption of beer... which is why it could be found in the basement behind the fire wood, inside the pockets of hunting jackets, boots, and pants, and between large workshop tools.

In Frieda's estimation, there would be no reason to buy a beverage crushing device for the meager amount of beer she saw her husband consume each month. So, he was either wasting money on a new device, or he was drinking more beer than he admitted, and either way, she was annoyed.

"What did you get, Dad?" Marielle asked to take the heat off her grandfather.

Johan smiled in a broad, mischievous way as Jack removed a question-mark-shaped scrub brush with a short wooden handle from a paper bag. Everyone's eyebrows furrowed, including Jack's who looked confused at the lack of enthusiasm.

"What's that?" his wife asked with a critical air.

"It's a coffee pot scrubber," Jack explained before looking at his father for support, but Johan stepped back, raising his hands in full-blown silent laughter.

"For cry-yi-yi," Frieda said, turning to her daughter-in-law to laugh in a way that made her eyes disappear.

"What?" Jack asked, genuinely confused.

When speech was again possible his mother continued, "You went through that huge warehouse and that's all you found?"

"It's perfect for cleaning coffee pots," he explained with more patience than usual. "You just feed it into the pot and it fits into the rounded sides."

"*Ja,* but your wife's coffee pot is square on the sides, not round. That's for restaurant coffee pots with small openings on top that you can't stick your hands into."

"Oh," he said before he chuckled. "Well, I'll be damned." He looked at the scrub brush one last time before throwing it onto the table and turning toward his father. "So, Dad, do you want a beer?"

***

The next morning, the women and girls left for church while the men

64

watched political talk shows and read the paper.

Maria and Anna were halfway across Oneida Street when Frieda teetered off the curb and leaned more heavily than usual on Marielle's elbow.

"Are you alright, Grandma?" Marielle asked, alarmed by her grandmother's rigid unsteadiness.

"*Ja,* sure," she replied. "I was just thinking."

Marielle didn't say anything. She determined long ago that people were more likely to give up information if one didn't ask too many questions. Instead, she stared at her grandmother while her grandmother stared straight ahead.

"My mother died 45 years ago today and it was on a Sunday too."

Marielle nodded, expecting a familiar story to follow.

"I know you guys think I'm short, but my mom was only four-foot-eight," she looked up at Marielle who was now looking straight ahead. "She had gray-blue eyes, just like yours. They looked especially gray when she got angry, which wasn't very often, but when she did, oh man!" Frieda paused for a moment. "Your eyes do the same thing, kid."

"Do they?" Marielle asked with a slight grin.

"Oh yeah. She would sometimes grab a broom and chase my father down the basement steps and he knew better than to come back up."

Frieda laughed as her granddaughter smiled.

"He would sometimes say, 'Pack your bags, Anna, we're going back to Austria.' He knew that made her crazy. My mom would say, 'Go ahead, Emmett! I'll pack your suitcase for you, but you're going back alone!' " Frieda paused for a moment to catch her breath. "My brother Franz was born over there, and my mother was pregnant with another child during the trip across, but she lost the baby on the ship, and a couple more after that. That's why there's ten years between my brother and me.

"When they first got here, my mother knew five languages and none of them English. She tried to order sauerkraut at a shop in Chicago, but the man couldn't understand a blessed word she was saying. She got so mad, she cursed in Hungarian and it sounded enough like 'sauerkraut' that the man gave her what she wanted."

Marielle heard these stories countless times, but today they sounded different. Grandma wasn't reciting history today. She was inside the story, and for the first time Marielle found her grandmother fascinating.

They caught up to her mother and sister who were waiting at the next corner. Maria feigned patience on her smiling face while Anna feigned nothing.

"Sorry, Maria," Frieda apologized.

"Don't worry, Mom, take your time," she said before she and Anna turned around to continue at their previous pace.

"When I was a kid, I didn't like sauerkraut *at all*," Frieda continued. "Well, I still don't like it. And one night my father told me I had to eat it. Yech!" she said from the back of her throat as she wrinkled up her nose. "Well, after I ate it I got sick right at the table, and my mom was so mad she yelled at my father, 'The next time you make her eat sauerkraut, you're going to clean up the mess yourself, *blödmann!*'" Frieda laughed a short hiccup, then paused as her eyes began to water.

Marielle turned to share laughter with her grandmother, startled to find a sadness overtaking her face. "It sounds like your mom was very spunky," Marielle offered weakly.

"Oh, she was," her grandmother replied mechanically, no longer a time traveler. "Well, until she got sick. She was doing the wash for a woman from church. When she carried a basket full of laundry from the warm cellar to the outside, her glasses fogged up—she had those small, round glasses with wire frames—and she hit the back of her head on a bolt on the door frame. After that, she started having headaches every day and when she went to the doctor, he said the blow gave her a brain tumor."

Marielle nodded her head unquestioningly.

"That was a rough time, I'll tell ya," Frieda continued as she began to travel again. "As she became sicker, she started wandering off. Nancy could sometimes find her, and sometimes I would go out with Jack. He was just two years old at the time. If we couldn't find her, we'd have to call the police."

"Didn't Grandpa and your father help too?" Marielle asked.

"You're kidding, right?" her grandmother asked aggressively. "Your grandfather was still playing drums so he was either at the club or asleep, and my father was out getting drunk half the time, feeling sorry for himself—well, when he wasn't working at the hospital across the street, that is."

Marielle's eyes darted toward St. Elizabeth's parking lot.

"He was the grounds keeper at Martha Washington hospital," Frieda explained to her granddaughter's silent question.

That's funny, thought Marielle. *What were the chances that they would both live across the street from a hospital?*

"I thought I would have a nervous breakdown," Frieda continued, shaking her head. "Mom was dying; I had a nine-year-old and a two-year-old running around the house; and every day I waited for a telegram from the War Department saying my little brother had been killed in Okinawa."

"That's horrible," Marielle said with glassy eyes, thinking of her own brothers.

"It was," Frieda agreed with decreased energy. "It really, really was."

She clicked her tongue against her upper dental plate as she returned to the present, noting her granddaughter's sympathetic face before pulsing her eyebrows to defuse it.

Marielle looked down as she stroked her grandmother's hand, noting the abundance of ugly, brown liver spots and tissue-paper-thin skin. She was startled when her grandmother next spoke and answered the question she subconsciously asked.

"I don't mind getting old," Frieda said. "Wrinkles and gray hair don't bother me. In fact, it's sometimes comforting to see another wrinkle and know the time is getting closer to the day when I see my parents again."

Marielle lowered her head as a tear formed in her eye. Frieda didn't see it, preoccupied as she was with correcting her posture, and fixing a pained grin on her face. Mass was clearly no place for unchecked emotion.

Frieda held her crystal rosary in her shaking hands as she moved her lips to the prayers in her mind. Every few minutes, she stopped, took a deep breath, pursed her lips, then continued. She had almost finished the first decade when the organ began.

Marielle looked around church and was pleased to note no impending infringement on her aisle space. The beginning of Mass went off without a hitch as well. She couldn't hear the First Reading on account of the short reader failing to adjust the microphone, but the second reader was taller and didn't stumble over the word "gentiles."

The priest delivered the Gospel in melancholy tones, and his Homily veered into a familiar place called "uninspiring." In fact, the thoughts of most parishioners wandered toward breakfast or the projects they'd complete that day before a highland terrier shot from the side door like a clown from a canon. He ran in front of the altar, then down the middle aisle toward the back of church. Suddenly, everyone was awake and most were laughing.

Sister Patricia abandoned the piano in the front of church to run after her dog, appearing both amused and embarrassed as she sprinted down the nave in her brown, plaid skirt and cream-colored blouse.

Marielle smiled at the dog and Sister before becoming distracted by the angry expression on Father Bernard's face. The dog obviously didn't fit into his Homily and mirth didn't fit into his Mass. Marielle's eyes narrowed toward Father as they turned more gray than blue, and right then and there she decided she wouldn't take any crap from a priest when she became a nun.

***

"I don't understand why a 30-year-old priest gets to tell a 50-year-old nun what to do," Marielle said to her grandmother when they returned to the dining room table.

"Well, those are the rules, kiddo, and you should get used to them if you're gonna be a nun."

She nodded sharply. "*Ja,* but I think I'm gonna push back on that one."

"Oh, you ARE a Richter!" her grandmother exclaimed. "You know, your father wanted to be a priest—"

Marielle had heard this story before, but she was never convinced of its veracity. She didn't think her grandmother was lying, per se. She was sure her father displayed a genuine interest, but the sentence she knew would follow proved in Marielle's mind that her dad had a sense of humor, or was afraid to tell his parents the truth.

"But he brought a date to the dinner for prospective priests. Can you imagine?" Frieda's eyes disappeared as she surrendered to laughter. "Do you remember that, Jack?" she barely asked the living room.

"Yeah, Ma," he replied, rolling his eyes in the direction of his father.

"Father Kramer patted him on the shoulder and said maybe he wasn't cut out for the priesthood after all."

Frieda allowed her amusement to peter out before addressing her granddaughter again. "If I were you, kid, I'd date for awhile. A life without a family isn't for everyone."

"*Ja,*" Marielle replied. *And a life* with *a family isn't for everyone either*, she thought.

Johan walked into the dining room to retrieve another Kaiser roll.

"Hey, Grandpa," Marielle said, "my Irish pen pal said he thought Jesse Jackson would be the next president. What do you think?"

An "oh, you've stepped in it" laugh came from her father in the living room while Johan stared at his granddaughter as if he no longer respected her intellect.

"What?" Marielle asked, pretending to be more perplexed than she was.

"Does your pen pal even *get* the news?" Johan asked. "There isn't a chance on God's green earth that the Democrats will win the election, and there isn't a chance in hell that Jackson will get the nomination anyway. I don't know what your friend's been drinking, but tell him he should stick with water."

Johan laughed as he walked his roll back to the living room.

Marielle smiled in an unhappy way before looking back at her grandmother and mother. She didn't appreciate her grandfather's condescension. He began his visit by losing her butterscotch and ended it by insulting her pen pal. She wondered if disappointment in her grandfather was a fluke, or the norm between them, now that she was a teenager.

"Well, we'd better get going," Johan said upon finishing his roll, prompting his son to rise to his feet and ignore the TV for the first time in two days.

"Well, it was great having you," both of Marielle's parents said—and one meant—as they escorted their guests to their car.

Johan nodded his head once, raising his right index finger in a modified wave before backing down the driveway.

After the car disappeared, Marielle and her parents returned to the house. Jack read his newspaper while Maria and Marielle cleared the dining room table.

"Damn it, Maria! He did it again!" Jack yelled.

"Did what?" his wife asked innocently.

"He screwed-up my newspaper!"

Marielle turned away to hide amusement. Her grandfather had a history of rearranging his son's newspaper, and he had a way of getting even with people who watched too much TV.

Chapter Six

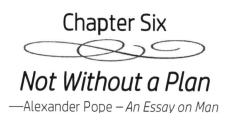

Not Without a Plan
—Alexander Pope – *An Essay on Man*

Dermot lied, and it was only his second letter. Marielle sat on her bed with her back against the wall wondering why, but the only explanation she could determine was that he didn't trust her. She read the letter one more time to confirm her assessment was fair.

22-Apr-1988

Hi Marielle!

Sorry I didn't write – I was in Dublin and I didn't have time to write. At the weekend I went to Trinity for a hurling match. My team did very well. We beat all the other teams in our section. Now, we're qualified to compete in the Irish Championship. I'll be very busy swotting (studying) for the next 3 weeks because of the 'inter' (it's really the Intermediate Certificate Examination, but that's what everyone calls it.) The grades I get in this exam will decide whether I do Pass or Honours in school next year.

Oh well! That's enough about school! I don't suppose you've ever heard of Sinéad O'Connor? I thought so! Well, she's a really good singer and she's going to have a concert here in Galway in July. I think I'll go to it – it should be really great.

There's a McDonald's take-away opening here in a few weeks – now I can ask for my Shamrock Shake!! Everyone I know thinks it will be great, but I think it'll probably be the same as Supermac's or any other take-away. My friend is getting a job there so I should be able to get lots and lots of free food! Yummee!

Did you get my last letter? I got my dad to mail it, but I had forgotten to write U.S.A. on it. My dad wasn't sure if you lived in Canada or the U.S.A. so he wrote both on the envelope!

Marielle stopped reading. Judging from the postmark on Dermot's first letter, mail required one week to cross the Atlantic. So, assuming Marielle and Dermot turned around a letter the day they received one, each could only hope to receive a letter every two weeks. So, Dermot wouldn't know Marielle didn't receive the letter his dad addressed to Canada until her response failed to arrive... today. So, why he wrote a letter a week after he claimed to have written the Canada letter, apologizing for not writing when he said he had, mystified her.

My sister is giving out to me again for having my walkman too loud. Sometimes she can be a real pain. She keeps telling me I'm too old to read comics. Imagine that! I'd die if I didn't read a comic every week.

You must be beginning to think I don't do much except go to school and compete in hurling matches. Well, I do. It's just that they're pretty important to me so I find it hard not to write about them. Anyhow, I met this really nice girl at Trinity but when I told her I was just 15 she laughed and walked off. Some people are really weird. My perverted friend said that she had a lovely ti...ti...t-shirt. Naturally, I told him that I was a good boy and didn't like his rude jokes (<—of course, that was a joke as well).

My friend Sean spent the entire day photographing everything with his new camera. When we got home, he found out there was no film in the camera!!

I don't think this is going to be one of those super-ultra-hyper-absolutely-unbelievably long letters. By the way, the new number 1 song is absolutely useless so I won't even tell you its name (which is just as bad). You are right! Pink Cadillac is a super song! My friend says that in the U.S. you say 'awesome.' Is that true?

I'm looking out my window now, and I can see my dog jumping through the neighbour's hedges. He's really bold—even for a dog. Today, I heard my neighbours are trying to sell their house and move. I hope it's nothing to do with me (or my dog)!

I might be going to Greece for my holidays this summer. I promise to send you a cool postcard if I do go anywhere (If I don't, I'll send you a horrible Irish one with ponies or horses looking over a stone wall). Most Irish postcards are 50 years old, but there are some really nice ones. Sorry about the horribly neat writing and no nice drawings – I'm just not in the mood, ya know? I better go! À bientôt!

Love.........Dermot

Marielle considered her next move while ignoring the voices on the ground floor that elevated in both pitch and volume. She could harass Dermot for an explanation, but there was no way to do this without openly suggesting he was a liar, and she would never do that... to a non-relative.

She imagined Dermot in an oatmeal-colored fisherman's turtleneck sweater, smiling through his window at a mischievous dog. Not having a clear image of his face made the task more difficult, but she placed herself outside in a misty rain several yards from the window to a vantage point consistent with his group photograph.

His small stone cottage held a warm fireplace in the main living room where Dermot sat. In fact, it looked much like the cottage in *Hansel and Gretel*, save the witch.

Dermot looked down as Marielle remembered his melancholy tone. And that was another thing! There was something clearly wrong with Dermot, but he wouldn't tell her.

As yelling continued downstairs, Marielle had no option but to assume he didn't trust her, and at the end of the day, she couldn't blame him. She had lied to him too. Well, it wasn't so much a lie as misplaced trust in her father, but either way she wasn't going to Ireland.

Earlier that evening, Marielle walked into the living room, holding another letter she received that day. She sat beside Jeanette—who was home from college to do laundry and sleep, one presumed—while she waited for her father to end his phone conversation.

Jack spoke on a cordless phone with a chunky block earpiece and an 18-inch metal antenna which matched the 2 ½ foot antenna on the base in the dining room. It was a new phone.

Marielle could tell by her father's manner that he spoke to a man he wanted to impress. She could tell by his word usage that the man was younger than himself. She guessed it was Robby.

"Do you want me to come up there and take him out for you?" Jack asked with bravado.

Marielle rolled her eyes. It was just like her father to offer to kill someone and not follow through.

"Do you have a problem?" Jack asked, holding his hand over the mouth piece as he stared at her.

"Uh, no, sir," she replied.

He narrowed his eyes slowly, then shook his head in a way that said he was happy to take care of his daughter's attitude problem, and on that she was sure he'd follow through.

Marielle left the living room to speak to her mother who busily washed the dishes Anna neglected.

"Hi, Mom," Marielle said, walking to the island to sit on the nearby stool. She placed the letter and pamphlet on top of the island, then waited a moment to collect her thoughts.

On matters of unreasonable dreams, her father was the soft target. The optimal time to approach him was 1 ½ beers and at least one cigarette into a weekday and well before the tipping point of 8 p.m. Close family knew about the tipping point, so they never called after that time. As little as John and Stephen knew about their host countries, they quickly determined what time equated to 8 p.m. in Appleton, Wisconsin.

Maria still wore the black pencil skirt, nylons and white blouse she wore into the office, reminding Marielle of how hard her mother worked, and adding guilt to her next words. "The payment deadline for the drum and bugle corps is this week."

Maria stopped washing a glass as she sighed. "How much do they need?" she asked, still looking down at the water.

Marielle shifted uncomfortably. She knew money was tight. The previous house reverting to the bank was her first big clue. Her father's reaction to her asking for $5 for the movies was the second. He apparently wasn't made of money and he wanted this impression to remain with his daughter. It did, but he had offered to pay for her trip to Europe all the same. Actually, it was more a halfhearted shrug during a commercial break in a *Barney Miller* rerun, but he could've just said no, and her mother could have disagreed instead of raising her eyebrows and giving her husband a disbelieving sideways glance.

"Well, the whole trip is $1,100 and we missed the 25% deadline, so this is the 50% deadline which is... uh... $550."

Maria rested soapy palms against the lip of the sink. She turned her head without moving her feet, then said with what little energy she had left, "Marielle, there is just no way we can do that right now."

Maria didn't wait to see her daughter's reaction before turning back to the dishes and she didn't explain that $550 equated to more than a month's rent. Marielle was mature enough to know this fact and to appreciate the unreasonableness of her request. The conversation was over.

Marielle looked down at the brochure and swallowed with difficulty. It wasn't an unexpected result, but it stung just the same. She rose quietly to leave the kitchen. She considered throwing the brochure into the garbage, but that would be viewed as a protest which would yield at least two weeks of restriction.

Marielle walked slowly to her room even though she wanted to get there quickly. She felt badly for herself, but worse, she felt stupid—stupid for asking if she could go, and stupid for expecting her parents to follow through on a promise. She knew better than to make plans based upon what her father said was possible. She had let hope cloud her judgment, and she promised herself this would never happen again.

"Hey, honey, we should drive to Orlando to stay with your Uncle Mike," Marielle heard her father say nearly every year for the past five. "We can visit with your family while the kids run around Disney."

Marielle shook her head. It had been a long time since this offer made her and Anna jump up and down. The fact that they had never traveled to Florida was bad enough. The fact that her father still promised to go was worse.

"This family is pathetic!" she said, kicking her backpack, and immediately regretting it. None of this was the backpack's fault.

***

Marielle stared at the opposite wall, but saw nothing, save the fuzzy mental image of Dermot's disappointment. Dermot didn't know her family so he'd be unfamiliar with broken promises. The worst part was that he would see her as she saw her parents—full of big ideas, but too lazy or too poor to follow through. Grandpa Richter said that all you have is your word, and now it was *her* word that was no good. There was no choice for her but to fix this. If she didn't, she was no better than her father and unworthy of her grandfather's name.

She picked up the turquoise notebook beside her and began to make a list. She had written "1) Babysitting 2) McDonalds" before an escalation of the yelling downstairs interrupted her train of thought.

Jeanette still sat in the living room with her father when Marielle walked past, but so consumed with self-pity was Marielle that she didn't question her sister's change in behavior or stay to determine its source.

Since moving to Appleton, the girls watched TV in their parents' room and left their father to himself and his new remote control. Most of the time, the bedroom contingent included only Anna, Marielle, and her mother, but if Jeanette was home from college, it included her as well. If Jeanette voluntarily spent time in the living room, it had more to do with making the news than watching it.

Marielle wondered if Jeanette was pregnant, then quickly discarded the idea. Although the *Cosmo* quiz Jeanette carelessly threw away said she was no virgin (and that her sex life was a 6 out of 10), Jeanette and Doug had broken up more than four months ago. If Jeanette approached her father first, it was because she thought he would be more sympathetic, and he would definitely *not* be more sympathetic if Jeanette was pregnant—although who might be the more violent parent was a toss-up. In any event, Jeanette probably knew that running half a state north to Canada was her safest option.

Marielle continued to wrack her brain. The only circumstances under which their father would show more sympathy were alcohol-related offenses or school trouble. A moment later, her father called her name.

Marielle ran from her room to join Anna at the top of the stairs. "Did Dad just call my name?" she asked, looking down at the dark hall below.

"No, I think he said 'aerial,' " Anna replied, her arms crossed.

Marielle narrowed her eyes. "Why would he say *aerial*?" she asked as she shook her head, but she stayed put just the same. She needed a more explicit directive to join this conversation.

Jack didn't see much use in going to college. As far as he was concerned, college was filled with draft-dodging war protesters, too busy doing drugs and having sex to serve their country, but not too busy to spit on the people who did. His opinion dated back to a very different time, but two decades were unlikely to change it.

Marielle could hear the pain in her mother's voice and knew why she was so animated. Maria, unlike her husband, had wanted to go to college, but she grew up during a time when getting married and having children was the only logical goal for a woman in a small mining town. Hastily marrying to escape an abusive home, only to land in another, was a gift her drunken mother and absentee father gave her. So, right now Maria was watching her eldest daughter throw away an opportunity she had always wanted, and giving up college was more difficult the second time.

"What did mom just say?" Anna asked.

Marielle smiled. "She accused Jeanette of sleeping through her classes. In Jeanette's defense though, going to class would be difficult when her clothes smell like beer and vomit all the time," Marielle said with a chuckle.

"Marielle!" Jack yelled again.

The upstairs hall cast enough light for Marielle to safely make her way down, but she clutched the wooden railing anyway as her hand studied the wide grooves on both sides. So hurried was she to run up and down these stairs on most days that she never noticed the softness of the varnish or the ease with which her fingernails penetrated it.

She turned toward the wall, noticing the sparseness of the decoration. True, it was a rental home, but how long did it take to hang pictures? Their old house displayed all five children's 5"x7" kindergarten photos above the stairs. Marielle wondered what happened to those. Dad would say he didn't want to fill a bunch of nail holes when they bought a house and moved out, but how likely was that? Besides, white toothpaste could easily camouflage small holes, making spackle unnecessary… or so said her grandfather.

Marielle studied the street lights through the lace curtains on the front door before using the banister to make a U-turn. The bathroom door would conclude her trip if she continued walking straight, and she couldn't say she wasn't tempted or didn't have a need, but the dining room door stood to the left, and she dutifully walked through it.

"You always said she was slower than molasses in January," Maria complained to Jack before Marielle stepped into the light cast by the living room lamps.

Aside from Maria's comment, conversation had not resumed since Marielle's name was last called.

Jack sat with his legs wide apart. His forearms rested on his knees as he held his beer with both hands. He smiled at his daughter's terrified expression before motioning with his eyes in the direction of his wife and shaking his head.

Marielle relaxed. This was obviously Maria's fight alone—and an angry mother, she could handle.

Chapter Seven

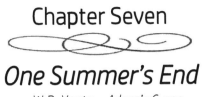

One Summer's End
—W.B. Yeats – *Adam's Curse*

5/27/1988 Friday

Dear Dermot,

How are you? I'm fine. Sorry it has taken me so long to write back. I was visiting my sister in college for a week and although I arrived home two weeks ago, I spent the first week catching up on homework and the second week catching up on gossip—I find both equally tiring.

You may wonder why my parents let me spend an entire week living in the dorms and leading the "wild college life," but I'm afraid the answer to that will disappoint you. See, my sister told my parents a few weeks ago that she was on academic probation and might be kicked out of school if she couldn't bring up her grades—especially algebra. My parents, being overly impressed with my study habits, suggested I attend classes with her. So, I went.

Figuring out why Jeanette was bad in math didn't turn out to be rocket science since, instead of taking notes, she and her friend Stacy couldn't stop teasing the guy who sat in front of them. They kept slowly slipping on and off their shoes and giggling which didn't make much sense until they told me he had a shoe fetish. I had a sheet full of notes before the Professor's wrapping-up got their attention, and by then it was obviously too late.

I tried explaining to my sister and her friend what they missed when we were back at the dorms, but that was a waste of time since my Grandpa Healy's monthly allowance check arrived in the mail, and Stacy and Jeanette were planning their alcohol purchases for the weekend... which included a half-keg of beer for a Hawaiian party... which was to be held at one of their friend's off-campus apartments... which was to include me.

The fact that we had a pretty severe cold snap (not unusual for Wisconsin) *didn't discourage anyone from dressing in Bermuda shorts, t-shirts, and lei. My sister suggested I not bring a coat into the party 'cause college parties are notorious for people stealing other people's coats, or coats getting lost or left behind when the police arrive and everyone scatters (since the drinking age is 21, and the fine for drinking is $300 per person...and judging from the crappy cars everyone drives and the amount of instant noodles everyone eats, I'm thinking no one has that kind of money).*

Anyway, I took my sister's advice and left my coat inside the car (wherein I suggested to the driver that "the closest distance between two points being a straight line doesn't apply when the road is curved." [I don't think he appreciated my opinion a whole lot.]) and I shivered the 100ft or so between the car and the apartment building...which was OK because somehow the temperature inside the party was 110° F (slight exaggeration) even though every window and patio door in the apartment was open (no exaggeration).

My sister was definitely the life of the party and it seemed that all the guys were competing for her attention...until they got drunk and tired of her ignoring them and decided to invade my personal space by drooling to me how I was "going to look just like Jeanette when I grew up" at the same time they were giving me eyes that said they weren't in the mood to wait.

You'd have thought it wouldn't have been wise for me to drink alcohol in this kind of environment (and usually I wouldn't), but some of my brother's friends were there (the ones that went to UWGB instead of going into the military), and I assumed they'd look out for me. So, I drank a couple of Fuzzy Navels (I'm not sure what's in them, but they tasted really good), and about three Kamikazes (I think that's vodka) before I thought that I had had enough...which was about five minutes before the cops arrived.

I'm not really sure who called the police, but I have a vague recollection of a neighbor knocking on the door and asking whoever opened it to turn down the music....which they did....for about five minutes. The only thing I remember about the police arriving is someone in the kitchen yelling "Police!" and my sister running from the dining room into the living room, grabbing my arm, and pulling me through the sliding glass doors.

Once we got outside, we ran as fast as we could to the railroad tracks behind the building. I turned around to see if anyone was chasing us just as my sister tackled me into the ditch alongside the tracks which happened to be filled with a couple of inches of water which I didn't really notice at the time because there was a search light beaming over our heads (it was attached to a police car in the parking lot) which was the reason Jeanette tackled me. My sister decided we should crawl along the ditch to get away which was when I finally noticed the water, and the inevitable mud, and the really low temperature, and I thought that college parties might not be so great after all.

We crawled for about 20 minutes before it was clear that no one was actually chasing us, and that's when my sister had the bright idea to run back to the apartment (completely undoing all our crawling), and look in the windows to see if the cops were gone. She dragged me along with her which was fine with me 'cause even if we got caught I'd've rather sat in a warm jail cell than slowly freeze to death in the mud next to those railroad tracks.

As it turned out, the cops were gone and there were only about five suddenly sober college kids inside the apartment. Luckily, one of them happened to be the guy who drove us to the party so we left right away. I don't actually remember driving back to the dorms, or getting cleaned up, or crawling into my sleeping bag on the floor since once I realized we were safe, I felt drunk again (I'm not really sure how the chemistry of that works), but my sister's roommate said we poured in at around 2:30am. And wouldn't you know that same roommate's overly-possessive out-of-state boyfriend called at 8:00am sharp the next morning (well, actually the same morning) and woke me up (bastard!), and he got angry at Darcy (the roommate) 'cause he said I answered the phone hung-over (which was true), and that meant she had had a wild party in her room the night before (which was obviously bullshit!), and he wanted to know if men were there, and if she got drunk, and what she was wearing at the party, etc, etc. I told my sister that I wasn't real sure why Darcy would date her stalker since she was pretty enough to date a guy without a future criminal record. Jeanette just laughed 'cause she thought I was joking.

ANYWAY, so that was two weeks ago and I think my eyes are still red, but it could just be the cold I got in that ditch... which is probably God's way of saying that a 15-year-old has no business going to an off-campus college party... which I'm not sure is unreasonable.

I hope you're not disillusioned with my behavior. I'm really the last person any of my friends would expect to get drunk and run from the cops. In fact, I have a long-standing tradition of preaching against excessive drinking... or drinking at all... so I guess this makes me a hypocrite... which I'm OK with....most of the time.

Anyway, regarding some of your questions: It's true that a lot of people use the word "awesome" here. In fact, most people overuse it. In fact, if you had been sitting in women's choir with me today (which would've been weird for you and the choir) you would've heard my irritating friend Joy say something like, "Sherry, tell Marielle about the <u>totally</u> hot guys playing for the Appleton Foxes [a minor league baseball team] this season. It's <u>SO AWESOME</u>! You should come to a game with us this summer. Wouldn't that be awesome? We always have SUCH an <u>AWESOME</u> time!"

It's also true that I haven't heard of Sinéad O'Connor, but her album is available through my record club so I ordered it. I'll let you know what I think when it gets here.

I'm afraid I didn't get your last letter (the one your dad mailed). Maybe it will arrive in 50 years and I'll be like one of those 80-year-old women on the news saying how grateful I am that it arrived at all. By the way, your next letter may not get here either if you keep adding my phone number to the address line (it's the number that begins with 414). ☺

I'm jealous that you'll be going to Greece this summer. My parents' idea of a vacation is driving 12 hours to Columbus, Ohio to see my mom's dad... which would be great if we were on our way to Greece... although I'm not sure driving to Greece is a good idea. ☺

I'm also jealous that you have a dog (stupid or not). Our dog died two years ago and we haven't gotten a new one yet. I'm beginning to lose hope we ever will since whenever I bring up the subject, my parents find something else to talk about.

Oh! My parents told me that my brother John isn't reenlisting in the Army so he'll be coming home from Korea in a few weeks. Yay!!

Anyway, I must go now. Congratulations on your match and good luck with your exams!

Love,

Marielle

PS If you don't mind me asking you a personal question, what religion are you? I'm Catholic.

PPS We only have a couple weeks left of school. When do you get out for the summer?

PPPS I was elected President of the Pep Club this week and my friend Shelly will be the VP. We should be able to rule the school next year....well, at least the school pep rallies.

PPPPS Is this the longest letter you've ever received?

Marielle looked down at the letter, swallowing guilt. Each paragraph was meant to relay the *real* news—that she wouldn't be visiting during the summer—but she lost her courage and began a new paragraph instead. By the time she reached the PSs, it was too late and the letter was too long. She could add another postscript, but bad news warranted a paragraph in the first third of a letter, not as an afterthought at the end. She could rewrite the letter, but aside from making it seem like she was cooler than she was, it was a darned good letter. She would mail it as-is and tell Dermot the news later, after she devised a plan.

She picked up her turquoise folder to review her list of potential jobs with the predicted hourly earnings for each. There was no way babysitting could pay for her trip. If a family was generous, she made $2 an hour, but that was unusual. A dollar-fifty was more common, especially if the woman took her home and paid her instead of the man. A check was also more likely to bounce if a woman wrote it. She wasn't sure why. Maybe men never wrote checks.

Shelly made $3.35 an hour at McDonald's and Jeanette made $3.81 at the nursing home. It was good money, but it wasn't good enough. Marielle heard of people making $10 an hour at the paper mill, but they already had their high school diplomas and they usually knew someone at the plant who got them the job. You couldn't just walk in and ask for a job like that.

Marielle did some more math before calling Shelly.

"Well, you could work with me, but unless my manager scheduled us together, you'd have to get your parents to drive you back and forth," Shelly cautioned.

Marielle thought about the Plymouth Reliant that was anything but, and the potential issues with asking her parents for transportation.

"Well, do you think he'd schedule us together?" she asked.

"He'd say he would, but he wouldn't. He's such a dumbass that he usually calls me on my days off to ask why I'm not at work."

Marielle briefly considered riding her bike, but memories of her trip to Kimberly the previous summer—cars and trucks roaring past on the county road with no sidewalk and barely a shoulder to provide safety—dissuaded her.

"How much do they pay at the theater?" she asked.

"At the mall?" Shelly asked.

"*Ja.*"

"I think they make less than minimum wage. They get away with it 'cause you can technically earn tips at the concession stand."

"That's BS!" Marielle protested. "No one tips at the movies!"

"I know," said Shelly. "That's why only the rich kids can afford to work there."

Marielle thought about Shelly's words for a moment. The movie staff appeared wealthy in tuxedos, plum-colored cummerbunds, and matching bow ties, but they probably weren't rich in a "going to Europe with the drum and bugle corps" way. Regardless, she decided she hated rich kids and Shelly agreed before they hung up.

Marielle retreated to her room and jumped onto her bed, dangling her feet off the side to avoid removing her shoes. She laced her hands behind her head while thinking about all the kids whose parents had enough money to send them to Europe. She allowed herself to indulge in jealousy for a moment before shaking it off. Wishing she was someone else wouldn't solve her problem. *They probably won't appreciate the trip anyway*, she thought with an air of superiority. She could still envy them, but she'd pity them at the same time.

She considered working at the nursing home next door, but four people from the same family working in the same place seemed both complicated and eccentric. Besides, none of the cool people in high school worked at the nursing home and she didn't want it to matter, but it did.

In any event, working at the nursing home wouldn't earn her $1,100 by June. It was mathematically impossible. Whatever job she chose, it would take at least six months, and that was far too late to join the tour.

She counted months on her fingers. Maybe she didn't need a tour to go to Europe at all. Maybe it would be cheaper to go on her own. A plane ticket alone should only cost $300, she reasoned, before deciding to confirm this.

She opened the Yellow Pages, found a travel agent near Valley Fair Mall, then held her finger below the number for a moment. It was unrealistic to assume her parents would allow her to go alone... unless she distracted them by asking to visit Stephen as well. A short stop in Ireland wouldn't seem so dangerous if West Germany was the intended destination. If she stayed three or four days in Ireland, she wouldn't technically be breaking her promise to Dermot since a visit was a visit whether she was with the band or not.

Marielle dialed the number. A moment later, a receptionist directed her to the international agent. *International Agent* sounded like a pretty cool title, thought Marielle. She expected the agent to have a certain air of superiority when she answered her extension—to ask what right a teenager had in taking up her valuable international time, even—but the lady sounded disarmingly normal and Marielle couldn't decide if this was refreshing or disappointing. She didn't reflect on this matter long, however, since the cost of the flight shocked Marielle into momentary silence before she asked the agent to repeat the number. It wasn't a mistake. To fly to Dublin for three days, then to Frankfurt for four during the off-season with a 21-day advance purchase cost $750 or—properly translated—over four months of work. There was no way around time, and first, disappointing Dermot.

10-Jun-1988

Marielle!

I got your letter yesterday. Thanks, it was really funny! Today was really great. It was 25 degrees, the sun was shining, and we got a day off school! My friend Sean came back to my house and we swapped letters - I read his pen pal's and he read your letter. His wasn't much good, but suddenly everybody's talking about my red-eyed pen pal who likes getting drunk in Bermuda shorts and being chased through ditches by policemen. You're famous! I couldn't believe that there was a $300 fine for having alcohol. Here in Ireland, the policemen would probably ask for a drink themselves! Police in Ireland don't carry guns either and most of them are fat or senile.

To answer your question, I'm Catholic. It's not really such a personal question and where I live nobody would mind being asked. In Northern Ireland, it's different - wear a T-shirt with an Irish or English flag on it and the other side just might decide to shoot you! Two days ago, two British soldiers were shot and yesterday 20 Kalashnikov machine-guns were found. Two hours ago a gunman was shot in the leg. You see, violence is pretty normal there and no one really takes much notice now.

The situation in 'The North' (that's what everyone calls it) is simple - The IRA (anti-British terrorists) are murderers and the British were stupid to colonise Ireland.

It now looks like Dukakis is going to be the next president. I hope you're not insulted, but I think he couldn't be much worse than Ronald Reagan. Anyway, I just saw a programme about the American Army. I can't blame your brother for not going back. Oh, sorry about writing your phone number on the letter, but once I had a German pen pal and I forgot to write her post code - the letter took two months to reach her.

Oh, in your perpetually long letter you said I might be disillusioned by your party. Well... I'm not. I don't drink, but I love parties (especially ones that last until 2:30 am).

Next Sunday, I'll be in yet another hurling match. When I get the film developed, I'll send you a proper photo of myself. For now, I'll just send you a photo of me and my sister in the Canary Islands (we went there at Christmas). Oh, I found Green Bay on my atlas. It's on the little thingy that sticks out of Lake Michigan (I hate geography. How did you guess?) Yesterday, the geography teacher wasn't in school so we all started setting fire to paper jets and throwing them at each other. It was great! We used to throw marbles until one boy got a tooth knocked out.

I won't say I hope the cold you got at the party is better, because if it isn't better by the time this letter reaches you, you'll probably be dead or something like that!? As my friend said today 'You know what? She probably thinks you're normal!' I was very insulted, but he was 6'2" so I just muttered something about his sense of humour being as warped as his face. Well, as you can see, I'm getting kind of tired and my letter is getting kind of long so I better stop.

Yours (almost) normally,

Dermot

PS Keep up your perpetually long and detailed letters. They're really great. I love them!

13-Jun 1988

Hi again!

I forgot to post this letter today so now I can write another sheet of boring letters! It was really warm and sunny again today so I got a chance to show off my new shades.

I went to the dentist (augh!) but I was really lucky. He did nothing to me - no teeth ripped out, no drilling for oil, etc. But he did take out this huge automatic toothbrush (kind of) just in case I got away without him doing something rotten to me. In Ireland, dentists cost an awful lot. I think one filling costs 60 pounds.

That's enough about dentists, even though I'm sure this is really thrilling you.

Before I forget, please please please please please please PLEASE... just to stop me tearing out my hair from suspense... tell me is your band going to come to Ireland? If you don't, I'll fly over to your house in my personal jet and drop my personal bodyguard (Iranian) through your roof!

I decided not to be modest and I cut out an article from a newspaper about me winning at Trinity (what a big head!). I got a new Prince album today. Like Michael Jackson, he's weird, but he can sing. My poor mutt of a friend keeps singing the same line "drive her to Tennessee, yeah, yeah." It's enough to drive you mad! He's the only person I know that's stupid enough to fail a blood test (I told him that).

Everyone brought water pistols into school today and we had great fun. Sometimes we act very immaturely, but it is fun! We made such a mess of the school, we had to get a half-day.

I need to post this letter now.

Love,
Dermot

A blind person could have seen Marielle beaming. Dermot had written back quickly, and he had complimentary things to say. It wasn't a high bar, but he was the first to fly over it.

Another amazing fact was that he didn't drink. What were the chances that an Irish pen pal wouldn't drink? It was hard to find Americans her age who didn't drink, and they didn't have a reputation for drinking... until college anyway. She wondered if drink was what kept John from coming home last night, and the night before that. That would be a lot of drink, she thought, but knew her brother's attentions laid elsewhere.

Marielle tried not to stare at the 35mm picture Dermot enclosed. Taken from the balcony above a hotel pool, it showed a frustrating lack of facial detail, but an alarming amount of non-facial detail. Dermot's shirtless body looked dark tan, almost bronze, against the sky-blue chaise lounge. He rested on his left elbow, facing the camera, but he wasn't looking up. Instead, he smiled down at his sister whose eyes cinched tightly against the sun, matching perfectly the grimace on her pink face. A love for the sun obviously skipped Fiona in favor of the second-born child. The tan genetic naturally followed suit, causing her legs to nearly blend into the white towel she rested upon. She wore a light blue bikini top, but shorts rather than swim suit bottoms. It was clear from Dermot's body language that he adored his sister and he was completely oblivious to her less than impressive physique.

For a moment Marielle's smile slipped, remembering her own brothers' tendency to beep if she or Jeanette stepped backward.

Marielle jumped from the dining room couch as her sisters entered the room, then hastily skipped in front of them to the hall doorway, letter and picture in hand.

"Watch it!" Anna yelled, emboldened by her proximity to Jeanette.

Marielle ran upstairs, then closed the door to her room. Strictly speaking, the use of the deadbolt locks on each bedroom door (remnants of the house's time as a boarding house) was forbidden, but it was potentially only a few minutes before her sisters realized she wanted privacy and did whatever they could to deny it.

If her sisters found Dermot's swimsuit picture, they would show it to their mother. If their mother saw it, she would disallow any further correspondence with Dermot, and—although Marielle couldn't blame her—she couldn't risk it.

Marielle threw the bolt, then turned to her dresser in search of a hiding place.

She remembered a story *Frau* told about an American exchange student who woke up her first morning in Germany to find the entire host family in the backyard sun-bathing together. Nude. Marielle stared at her dresser, wondering why the Germans in Wisconsin were so conservative while the Germans in Germany were so... naked. *Maybe our ancestors left because of all the nude sun-bathing*, Marielle thought, and was grateful Dermot at least wore a Speedo.

She studied the picture again. Although Dermot's coloring appeared more Italian than Irish, she could divine no more. The picture angle was so extreme that only the tops of Dermot's and his sister's head were clearly visible, leaving only a slight indication of a nose and cheek bones. Marielle sighed in frustration before looking away to avoid further study of Dermot's body.

It was hard to find anyone that dark in Wisconsin, she thought, after slipping the picture under some school papers she never had the heart to throw out. She closed the drawer, then opened it again to make sure the picture was still concealed. It was, but she felt momentary panic when she couldn't easily locate it.

A moment later, she sat on her bed, staring between the door and the dresser drawer. It was clear her sisters weren't en route, and it was debatable whether examining the picture was an immediate ticket to hell. She tip-toed to her drawer to retrieve the photograph, then placed it on her dresser top to assess it without the hindrance of a shaking hand. She studied the line and color of Dermot's body, surprised that it made her feel strange in new places. It felt like butterflies in her stomach... if they had been fast and warm... and if they had been lower. She immediately became disgusted with herself and hid the picture like a salesman hid a second family.

She unbolted the door slowly before walking downstairs as normally as possible, passing only Anna on the stairs.

The schedule on the refrigerator said Marielle was in charge of dishes today. Jeanette—no longer a college student—had bathroom duty, and Anna was lucky enough to pull living room/dining room duty.

Throwing their father's beer cans into the trash bag instead of recycling them was an easy way to tick Marielle off, so Anna would probably do it. A few cans wouldn't change the pay-out at the gas station near Fleet Farm, but Marielle couldn't bear to look at condemned cans, covered in trash when she knew she could save them. It would be easier for Marielle to pick up the cans from the cocktail table now, than to fish them out of the trash bin later, but that had the unfortunate side-effect of removing one task from Anna's already too short list. She stared into the living room and thought some more. If Anna was doing something other than lying on her bed, moping, Marielle would pick up the cans for her.

She returned upstairs to peer inside Anna's room. Anna would bring the cans into the kitchen herself today.

Jack arrived home as Marielle sprayed the sides of the sink, using enough water to obliterate the suds near the drain. "So, what are we watching tonight, kiddo?" he asked, smiling at her left cheek as he held her shoulders.

Her father's conviviality surprised Marielle. True, he was grateful to have company during his nightly TV marathons, but she expected her brother's MIA status to negatively impact his mood. Compartmentalizing hostility wasn't Jack's strength so she wondered if the rules didn't apply to boys, or at least to John, or to John since he was discharged from the Army.

"Hmm, I don't know. I haven't looked at the *TV Guide* yet," Marielle said as if she didn't have the schedule memorized, and as if she had any real say in the matter. She attempted to sound as upbeat as her father, but she failed. She was taking one for the team and no one knew it. Worse still, she was probably stuck watching *Newhart* while her sisters and mother watched a rerun of the only *MacGyver* episode she missed last season. And unless her sisters or mother were willing to put in their time with Jack, Marielle was stuck watching *M*A*S*H* reruns and NASCAR all summer.

"*Auch*," she said in the same guttural tones her grandmother employed when frustrated or annoyed.

Marielle thought to protest her sisters' lack of fair time, but she could see the face of each one saying, "Then don't do it." And no attempt to explain her father's feelings or point of view would dissuade them from their decision. She considered explaining the pattern of a hurt father turning into a violent one, but they likely didn't believe that either logic or predictability controlled their father's actions. They also wouldn't think their sister knew their father any better than they did, but Marielle heard him in the kitchen that night and they didn't.

It was over a month ago now. Jack held his wife by the shoulders in an attempt to gain her full attention, and to show her that he was as upset as she was about Jeanette's grades. He wasn't. Finally, he gave up on comfort and turned to self-pity. Embracing his wife, he said with a wry laugh, "Well, I should've known something was up when she decided to watch TV with me."

Marielle heard manipulation in her father's words, but she also heard sincerity. He knew he was being shunned, and he was sentient enough to feel badly about it. This made Marielle feel guilty, but it also annoyed her. It was easier to live with a monster than a violent man with complicated feelings. Now, while her sisters and mother watched TV, lounging on a king-sized bed in the middle of a dark room with a cool cross breeze, Marielle was stuck watching a too-loud TV aimed at a too-old audience in an unventilated dark room with a chain smoker.

On most nights, Marielle stared at the TV, wondering if she could turn on a light without risking offense before deciding she couldn't. Only her parents had light privileges, and unless her father left the room for a beer or noticed the lack of sunlight, there was nothing to be done but rub one's eyes and hope the strain wouldn't be permanent.

That night, Marielle's eye rubbing was interrupted by her father's musing.

"You know, you don't have to be faster than the bear, you just have to be faster than your friend," Jack said with a chuckle.

"What's that, Dad?" she asked, turning toward her father.

"That news report. You don't have to run faster than the bear, you just have to run faster than the people you're with." He laughed while looking sideways at his daughter, expecting a similar reaction.

"Ha," Marielle complied, but she didn't know what he was talking about until the evening news advertisement re-aired.

"Can you outrun a charging bear? Tune in at 10 for news on your side," the anchor announced.

Jack rested on the couch, crossing his ankles as his elbow supported his upper body. He stopped chewing the nail of his middle finger long enough to say, "Now, if they were *really* on your side, wouldn't they tell you that at *9* o'clock?" He laughed suddenly with an inhaled breath. "You know, I never watch that news anyway," he continued. "That lady has the face of a prize fighter!"

Jack's last remark caught Marielle off guard and she laughed in a way she normally wouldn't at a comment from an adult, much less a parent, much less her father. She attempted to pull back toward the end, but it was too late. Jack was staring at her with pride as they connected over sacrificing friends and ugly anchor women.

An hour later, Marielle unwrapped a mostly white cassette, placed it into her boom box, then examined its cover. She had never seen an Irish woman with a crew cut before, but she had to admit she knew very little about Irish women. The woman crossed her arms like a corpse, which slightly obscured the blue tank top she wore. Marielle wondered if the singer had forgotten to dress up for picture day and crossed her arms to hide her shirt. It had happened at school before—not to her, but she heard genuine angst in curse-filled sentences immediately following the question, "It's picture day?"

Admittedly, she never saw anyone wear a tank top to school, but they would have hidden it behind their arms, just like this woman, if they had.

The cover alone made Marielle skeptical she would like the music—and bedtime was hardly the time to try something new—but she promised Dermot she would listen to Sinéad O'Connor and she could hardly turn her back on another promise.

Two minor chords into the first song revealed that the singer didn't care much for subtle harmonies and was probably less interested in picture day than one might imagine. Marielle didn't say, "What the hell?" or pounce on the stop button, but she considered doing both. Instead, she turned down the volume before walking calmly to her bed.

The second song was an improvement on the first, but the third returned to what Odysseus must have heard in the Underworld. Marielle began laughing as she rolled to her left side. She would give it one more song and if Sinéad didn't have anything nice to say, she was done!

Marielle stopped laughing at the break. She sat up to listen, then jumped at the boom box without turning the light on first. Her action had less to do with the screeching tape than a noise downstairs, but lunging toward the boom box was just a matter of time.

"Who the hell do you think you are?!" Jack yelled. "You don't waltz in here after whoring around Green Bay all week!"

This was an exaggeration, thought Marielle. John was only whoring around Green Bay for *two* nights. Moral indignation was a new emotion for Jack, and Marielle didn't take it seriously. Maria did, however, and was on the stairs before she had time to tie her bathrobe.

"Let's relax for a minute," Maria said upon reaching the dining room.

"John, could you just call the next time you're going to be out all night? Your dad and I were worried about you."

"I wasn't worried!" Jack countered. "I knew what he was up to. That girl can't keep her legs closed!" Then, to his son he yelled, "If you knock her up, you're on your own!"

That was a stupid thing to say, thought Marielle. Aren't *all* guys on their own when they knock up a girl? Not as much *on their own* as the girl is, but one's father doesn't generally jump in and say, "Don't worry, son, I've got this one."

Marielle opened the door to confirm that her sisters were listening at the top of the stairs. She could see Jeanette's less-than-pleased expression, presumably as a result of her father calling her friend a whore, but as far as Marielle was concerned, Stacy deserved it. John also deserved whatever he got for violating the rules—not the rules about whoring around (because as far as she knew there 't any for boys), but the rules about engaging with and seeking approval from their father first.

Going out on the first night home instead of drinking, watching TV, and sharing Army stories was a shot across his father's bow. Spending the night with a girl without calling home first denied his father the opportunity to feel like a player in his son's life, and—more importantly—a member in the conspiracy against his wife.

One call containing the sentences, "Hey Dad, don't tell anyone, but I think I might get lucky with Stacy tonight. Can you cover for me with Mom?" would have made his father's week. The opportunity to yell, "Don't pretend you know anything about your son's life!" would have made his year.

Marielle shook her head. John knew the rules and either forgot them in the Army or woefully disregarded them now. There was no point in joining her sisters' hate fest at the top of the stairs. Taking her father's side against her brother wouldn't bring anyone together, and bringing the family together was John's job, not hers. Disappointment helped her close the door.

She lay down again and stared up at the ceiling, reviewing all of the things that should have been fixed by her brother's return. According to Marielle's plan, John should have confronted their father about his drinking in an understanding but forceful way. He should've sent Jeanette back to school with more self-esteem and ambition, and he should've adjusted Anna's attitude. Instead, John had fixed nothing.

While away, John had devolved into a kid his own age, and kids his age didn't fix problems, they created them, and more problems was something this house didn't need.

Marielle got up to hit the play button on her boom box. She turned up the volume, then lay back on her bed. She didn't cry because she couldn't and she couldn't hear John yell, "Fine! I'll be gone by the end of the week!"

6/26/1988 Sunday

Hi Dermot!

How are you? I'm fine. Thanks for your compliments on my writing, although I usually bore myself—it must be because I spend so much time with me and familiarity breeds contempt. ☺

Anyway, my cold is long gone and it's summer break. Yay! It's hard to imagine how I'll survive 2 ½ months of sleeping-in and basically doing nothing, but I will face the challenge bravely.

In reality though, it appears I will need to get a real job soon (instead of just babysitting) since one of the many things that occurred to me while running from the cops was that I should've taken driver's ed in school this past semester and if I don't take private lessons over the summer, I can't get my license in August when I turn 16.

Another barrier to sleeping in is of course my brother John who is now out of the Army and for whatever reason likes to wake me up at 5:30am to play Trivial Pursuit—I think he hates me (my parents say it's jet lag, but I'm sticking with hatred). Anyway, it's great to have him home again. I know South Korea isn't the most dangerous military assignment, but I did worry about him. Right now, he's thinking about either working for the CIA, or painting his 1972 Mustang yellow and driving it to L.A.—I'm trying to figure out how those things are related.

You may be right about the Dukakis thing, but in commercials I'm seeing he's taking quite a beating... but he would since they're paid for by the Republicans and I'm sure they don't want to say anything nice about him on their dime. Anyway, Minnesota, New York, Massachusetts, California, and DC always go Democratic (except in the last election when Reagan beat Mondale... and then I think only Washington, DC, and Minnesota went Democrat... but Mondale was from Minnesota, and DC isn't even a state!). Wisconsin is much more independent and whichever way Wisconsin goes is usually the way the election goes (or so says my grandpa... but he's probably giving Wisconsin more importance than is warranted because he's the state's unofficial chief booster [or so says my dad]). (I just determined that my sentences would be less complicated if I stopped listening to my family.)

Actually, the funny thing about my grandpa is that he's not even from Wisconsin. He's from Chicago. He only moved here after he retired, and all his kids and their families followed him. On the one hand, I think by rights I should be living in Chicago and enjoying "big city life." On the other hand, I'd hate to be a FIB (f*^#ing Illinois bastard) which is what some Wisconsinites (people from Wisconsin) call Illini (people from Illinois). It would take too long to explain why and I'm already rambling, so I'll save it for another letter.

Speaking of bastards, I've officially declared war on my ex-boyfriend, Guy. See, after Guy and I broke up (well, to be honest, he dumped me after two weeks to go back to his ex-girlfriend who's in college [she's a year older than him]), he kept meeting me at my locker and walking me to my classes and at first I was flattered, but eventually I realized he was only hanging around me so no one else would. So, I asked him if lifting his leg on my locker wouldn't be more effective, and although he's a self-proclaimed genius, he didn't get my point. Anyway, he wouldn't stop coming to my locker in a "this is my girlfriend" sort of way so I sprayed my perfume on his defenseless jacket (which was hanging in a locker to which I knew the combination) just before Loser Girl (his new/old girlfriend) picked him up from school one Friday. I figured once she smelled my perfume he'd A) be in trouble, and B) try to avoid hanging on me, so it was a win/win for me. (Did I tell you she smelled my perfume on him before they broke up?) Anyway, he didn't mention her reaction to smelling it again which was very disappointing, but he did stop coming to my locker, AND whenever Loser Girl sees me she grabs Guy and kisses him in a "he's mine, not yours" sort of way. So, I both know she smelled my perfume and understand where Guy gets his territory-marking tendencies.

Anyway, on Guy's last day of high school, Loser Girl was standing outside his architecture class (as usual for a Friday), and she muttered something when I walked by so I stopped, looked at her and said, "Jillian, I love your clothes. Do they come in small sizes too?" That wasn't very nice, but she could stand to drop a few pounds and whatever she said to me was probably not a compliment.

Anyway, the reason I'm declaring war is because last Thursday Guy asked me <u>twice</u> to call him after school and he seemed really concerned that I not forget. Well, I forgot, and around 8:30pm that night I saw Guy's car slow down in front of my house with a girl (I assume Loser Girl) in the passenger's seat flipping off my house. Then, this morning I got a prank phone call at 6am which I've gotten every Saturday since I started dating Guy. So, it occurred to me that the only reason Guy would ask me to call his house when his girlfriend was in town, or take her past my house, was to make her jealous at my expense, and him fanning the flames is why she's pranking me and flipping me off. To confirm my theory, I asked Guy's best friend Chad if Guy made any comments to him about my "still wanting him." He smiled in an "I know all about how crazy you are" sort of way and claimed he "didn't want to get involved" which he clearly already was. So, I assured him that Guy held no interest for me at all, but I could tell that our conversation made him think the opposite more strongly. SO, I haven't decided yet what I'll do to get even with Guy, but in the words of my favorite actress on Cheers (do you get this show?), "Revenge is a dish best served cold," so I have some time.

I'm surprised by what you say about the IRA. I'm not fond of their tendency to blow the kneecaps off of people, but from everything I read, the Protestants don't give Catholics much choice but to blow them up (i.e., keeping them from high paying jobs and marching through their neighborhood beating drums and taunting them). I read a few things about Ian Paisley that made me want to shoot him myself. Anyway, I probably don't know enough about the Protestant point of view to disagree with you so feel free to tell me what you think.

It sounds like you guys give the janitors at your school quite a headache. I assume your school is all boys? I say this because girls would never stand for flaming objects flying past their heads—assuming the girls there use as much hair spray as they do here, and dislike it catching fire as much as we do (myself included). Although, it's been awhile since my hair caught fire in school, and that was a Bunsen Burner gone bad (or so I told my 9th grade science teacher), but the truth was my lab partner and I unscrewed the burner shaft too far and the gas leaked out the bottom, and we were holding the flint near the top so the gas didn't ignite until the whole area was filled which caused a minor explosion that ruined my sweater, burned my bangs, and singed my lab partner's eyebrows. Did you know that burning hair smells like rotting flesh? Well, then and there I decided not to become a coroner, but I also decided that dying by explosion wouldn't be bad at all since it feels like a warm blanket launching itself at you.

Anyway, on a positive note, the guys at my school have abandoned squirt guns, paper airplanes, wetting toilet paper and throwing it on the ceiling, sucking on Skittles and pelting them at our legally blind Geometry teacher, and coating every pay phone receiver with Vaseline. On a not-so-positive note, they've begun throwing condoms on girls' desks, and betting on who can say the word "penis" loudest in class without getting into trouble. Once, a condom landed on my desk and my Geometry teacher thought it was a note someone passed to me so he asked me to read it to the class. I said, "I would, sir, but it's no longer in its wrapper." In any event, I didn't get into trouble because he was too embarrassed to yell.

It's funny how you say that 25 degrees is good weather. We have an exchange student from Venezuela who's freezing his butt off in 70 degree weather. The last week of school, everyone was wearing shorts and he stood up in the Commons, looked around, pulled his sweater together, and fearfully asked if anyone felt a draft (or so I heard)—as if a draft was equivalent to nuclear fallout. Oh, it just occurred to me that you're talking about 25 degrees Celsius. I consider it a matter of American pride not to know the Metric System, but I will look up that temperature on the Fahrenheit Scale anyway... as long as you don't tell anyone.

Well, this letter could rival The Odyssey in length and ramblings (although I did like that book a lot [we read it in 8th grade], but I would've preferred Odysseus not repeat his entire saga each time he met a new person, or maybe he could've just met fewer people. That Circe was a bitch. Am I rambling again?).

BYE!!!
Love,
Marielle

PS I've enclosed a few postcards I got for you on our class trip to Great America. The roller coasters were AWESOME, but the lines were awful.

PPS Thank you for sending your article and picture! I've never written to someone famous before!

PPPS Do you have any friends that would like to write to my friend Shelly? She decided that she'd like to have an Irish pen pal too. I'm not sure why. In fact, I tried to talk her out of it. ☺

PPPPS One more thing, my parents told me last week that I can't go to Europe with the drum and bugle corps this summer, but they generously offered to let me fly to Ireland for four days, and then fly to West Germany to see my brother for another four days. It's a real disappointment, but the tour was only supposed to spend three days in Ireland and this way I get an extra day. I hope you're not disappointed. Please don't hate me!

PPPPPS I stopped at the public library on the way home from school last Thursday and I had just enough time between bus transfers to look for Galway on the east side of the Irish map. I couldn't find it, but I'll search the west side next time I'm in the library.

She had just broken her own rule regarding PSs, but it couldn't be helped. The information was too sad to go into the body of the letter and she couldn't avoid telling Dermot the bad news much longer. She had hoped to tell him that she had a job and a plan, but she had submitted job applications at Dairy Queen, Pizza Hut and Burger King over a week ago and none had called back. She also hadn't spoken to her parents about her backup plan for getting to Ireland. So, that part of the letter was a lie, but no more of a lie than Dermot pretending to write and accidentally sending the letter to Canada.

Marielle thought about Guy for a moment as her eyes narrowed. She and her grandfather had just finished night crawler hunting in the back yard and were standing on the sidewalk beside the front porch when Guy's car slowed and Jillian's hand emerged from the window, middle finger first. Guy sped away, but it wasn't clear if he saw Marielle or not.

"Are those friends of yours, little lady?" Johan asked, looking after the car as it turned left onto Fremont Street.

"No, sir," Marielle said, assuring herself this wasn't a lie.

"Well, if they come by here again, I'll rip out their rib cages," he said with a smile that lacked humor.

In the days that followed, Guy didn't call to explain or apologize, but that didn't prove he hadn't seen Marielle since she now believed him to be a coward. Embarrassing her in front of her friends was one thing.

Embarrassing her in front of her grandfather was quite another. He was beyond the pale now, and if he thought she would become less angry with time, he was mistaken.

***

The next Monday, Marielle stood in front of a recent high school dropout and begrudgingly asked for an employment application. The girl didn't smile or frown. In fact, her face betrayed nothing except vacant eyes.

"Fill this out and give it to Sharon," she said. "She's sitting over there." The girl moved her head toward a woman sitting in a booth near the windows.

Sharon wore a skeletal-sized Hardees uniform and 1960s glasses whose edges gathered and pointed out to the sides. Her age was somewhere between 20 and 50, but Marielle couldn't wager one side of the scale over the other. In the past, she openly wondered how people couldn't know a woman's age from looking at her face, and now she knew.

Before Marielle reached the exit Sharon said, "You can fill it out here," pushing five pens toward the edge of the table without looking up from her documents.

Marielle sighed inaudibly as she walked toward the booth. She sat down across from the ageless stranger and began filling out the form in the one area of the table not occupied by paper.

"That's fine," Sharon said, putting her hand out to stop Marielle as she nearly wrote in the gray area marked, "INTERNAL USE ONLY." "So, have you held a job before?" Sharon asked.

"No, I haven't," Marielle said, smiling apologetically.

Sharon looked up for the first time, but didn't smile before her eyes returned to the form. "And you're 15 years old?"

"Almost 16. My birthday is at the end of August."

"You say you're willing to work nights?"

"Yes, ma'am. I need to start taking driver's ed soon during the day."

Sharon sighed. "The majority of our business takes place before 2 p.m., so nights don't help me much," she said to the form.

"Well, I only need 30 hours of classroom experience. Once that's done, I can schedule my behind-the-wheel training around my work schedule."

"Hmm. That might work," Sharon mused, making eye contact with Marielle, and allowing a slight upturn of her mouth as she gathered two pamphlets. "Here's a booklet on our menu and code of conduct. Tracy will give you a uniform to take home. If it doesn't fit, let us know before your first shift so we can find another one for you."

Marielle looked back toward the counter and the unhappy girl whose nametag read *Tracy*. A young, portly woman with a thick, blonde ponytail peeked around the corner from the drive-through window just before a mustachioed cook looked over the high counter. Marielle's interview was clearly the most interesting event in Hardees this morning.

Sharon moved a sheet of paper from the bottom of a small pile. "How about Wednesday at 9 a.m.?"

"Oh, okay," Marielle replied, wondering if she wasn't clear about her preference for evenings, but driver's ed hadn't started yet and she didn't want to challenge her new boss so soon.

"Very good," Sharon said, writing Marielle's name in pencil too dark to be completely erasable. "See you then," she said before returning to her papers.

Marielle rose quietly and left, but she was in tears before she reached the sidewalk. It's true that Sharon wasn't the friendliest person in the world, but she would have cried anyway. A suffocating sense of responsibility covered her like a heavy wet blanket. It was only June, and for all intents and purposes, her summer was over.

Chapter Eight

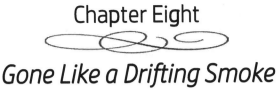

Gone Like a Drifting Smoke
—W.B. Yeats – *The Host of the Air*

"Wake up!" John said, the roughness of his shoulder-push camouflaging his discomfort at standing inside his sister's bedroom.

"What?" Marielle asked, rolling over as she squinted at the light in the middle of her ceiling.

"I want to talk to you. Get up and come downstairs. I made a pot of coffee," he said, then left before she could push back her covers.

Marielle grabbed her royal blue, fleece bathrobe before tip-toeing downstairs.

Two cups of steaming coffee sat on the table, and one looked blonder than the other so she assumed it was hers. She scanned the table for the Trivial Pursuit game as she sat down, but it was still inside its box beside the orange couch.

John rotated his coffee cup, covering his hand with the handle before looking at her in earnest like the old John used to do. "I want to talk to you about Dad," he said.

Marielle looked from the coffee cup handle to her brother without changing her furrowed eyebrows.

"How much is he drinking now?" John asked.

"Ten to twelve cans per night," Marielle responded like a navigator reciting the coordinates of her ship.

John's left eye squinted, "How do you know?"

"Because I recycle the cans now."

John nodded. "Has he been violent with Mom lately?"

Marielle shook her head. "Not so much since we moved."

"What about the guns?"

"Well," she chuckled, "you know how he likes to break-in new guns."

They both laughed until John resumed his mature face. "It seems like they're doing better financially, though," he said, glancing at the living room furniture.

At that moment, Marielle realized John was leaving and this

99

discussion had less to do with getting to core truth than with easing his mind. For a moment, she felt rebellious and determined to tell the truth—or an even worse version of the truth—but she knew that John had done his time. He had gone through enough.

"Well, as far as I know, they haven't been late on the rent and the truck is paid off now."

"Yeah. There seems to be more food in the fridge, too," John said.

Marielle nodded. "When are you leaving?" she asked, impatient to come to the point.

"Soon," he said, looking from his sister to the windows behind her. "Maybe tonight. I need to get the oil changed, and pick up some snacks for the trip."

Marielle nodded again, then took her first sip of coffee. "Holy Jesus! How much sugar did you put *in* this?" she asked.

"Two tablespoons. Isn't that how you take it?"

"No. Two *teaspoons* just like Dad."

"Oh," he laughed, "you can chuck it."

"No." She smiled. "It'll be like a science experiment. I'll see if I contract diabetes by the end of this cup."

***

At 6 p.m., with the sun still well above the horizon, the yellow Mustang sat packed and pointed down the driveway. Jack stood several feet behind the trunk, the top half of his fingers pushed inside his pockets like the pockets were fighting back. He began to rock back and forth as it seemed his son's preparations were at an end. Maria stood beside him on the gravel, forgetting the slippers on her feet. Jeanette stood between her mother and Anna with tears in her eyes, but Anna just looked angry.

Marielle held open her brother's door even though the angle of the driveway held the door open on its own. She waited for her brother to hug everyone else, then said sternly, "Remember, bridges and ramps freeze first," in an effort to cut short her own hug.

John laughed before looking back at his mother with concern.

"I wish I would've known you were leaving today," she said, breaking down. "I would have made a pot roast."

"There's no way for him to keep a pot roast in the car in the summer time," Jack said. "Jeesh." He widened his eyes while shaking his head and pointed his thumb toward his wife amiably.

John smiled unhappily before sitting in his car. Marielle closed his door with finality.

"Oh, wait!" Jack yelled. "Just a second." He held up his index finger while running into the house. A moment later, he passed a bag of red licorice through the driver's-side window, whispering something to John before the Mustang rolled down the driveway.

The plume of smoke dissipated with the help of a sudden breeze, but the canary yellow car could be heard long after everyone lost sight of it. They waited motionless until the sound blended into normal traffic.

Jack was the first person inside the house, and whether it was out of necessity or privacy, the women found the bathroom door closed when they returned to the foyer.

"I don't understand why John didn't wait to leave until the morning," Anna remarked to her mother.

"He wants to avoid the traffic around Madison," her mother replied, staring at the bottom step.

"Is there traffic around Madison?" Marielle asked.

Her mom raised her head, but no one answered. In fact, no one knew. They had never been to Madison.

"What did your father say to John before he left?" Maria asked Marielle.

"He said that eating the licorice would keep him awake," Marielle paused, "and that John always had a home here."

Jeanette scoffed before walking up the stairs with Anna in tow.

"*Dumme Esel,*" Maria said quietly, grabbing the hand rail to follow her daughters.

Marielle looked after her mother with a furrowed brow. There was something wrong with an Italian criticizing an Aryan in German.

***

"You okay, Dad?" Marielle asked as her father entered the living room.

"Yeah, yeah. Just ate something that's not sitting right," he explained, rubbing his flat stomach in a circular motion while walking to the couch.

"Ah," she responded. "How long do you suppose it will take for John to get to Los Angeles?"

"We figured it would take a little over 34 hours if he's lucky."

Marielle nodded. There was nothing more anyone could say on the matter without stumbling upon something real.

Looking to change the subject, Marielle mused, "Grandma Richter

101

said something strange last weekend."

"Oh, yeah?" Jack said to the TV. "What else is new?"

Marielle smiled at the air in front of her father's face. "She said something about Uncle Paul getting murdered in Michigan."

The word "something" was an understatement. What Frieda *really* said was "I know it's a terrible thing to say, but sometimes I really do wish it *had* been my dad and not Uncle Paul."

Jack sat back on the couch as he squinted at the wall above his daughter. "Now, I don't know much about that. I think they only lived in Michigan for a year or two before they pulled-up stakes and went back to Chicago."

Marielle nodded, hiding her disappointment. This wasn't new information.

"Let me think about that while I watch my program," he said, turning the channel.

Marielle's imagination ran wild as the familiar rerun exhausted the next hour.

"I think my grandpa brought over his youngest brother Paul from Austria after his parents died in World War I," Jack reflected in the direction of the television. "Grandpa Riess needed help running the farm, I suppose. Now, Paul either knocked up someone in town or got into debt with the wrong people. In any event, he turned up dead one morning in front of the barn."

"Did they ever find the killer?" Marielle asked.

"Well, now, *that* I don't know for sure. You'd have to ask your grandmother."

She looked at her father hopefully. "Wouldn't Grandpa know too?"

"Maybe, but he won't tell you." Jack smiled at his daughter in a menacing way as if he knew something shocking about Grandpa Richter she didn't.

Marielle had seen the look before and she didn't appreciate it. She knew everything she needed to know about her grandfather and nothing negative about him stayed in her head for long.

At the beginning of the next commercial break, Marielle asked, "Isn't it strange that the parents and not the son would die in World War I?"

Jack raised his eyebrows at his daughter, causing her to shrink back. He didn't like his memory questioned, and the topic was closed.

102

Chapter Nine

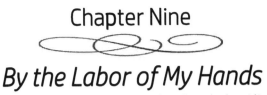

By the Labor of My Hands
—Henry David Thoreau – *Where I lived, and what I lived for*

Marielle awoke two hours before her first shift at Hardees and well before her family. For the first time, she tried on the polyester turd-brown pants and matching white, brown, and 70s-orange plaid shirt. Although a size too large, she felt grateful that the pants were not toddler-sized as they had been in her dream the night before. She applied her blush, eyeliner, and lip gloss, but there was no point in doing her hair since the round cap and brim would kill any poofy bangs she managed to create.

She tiptoed downstairs, and threw her hat on the loveseat before walking into the kitchen. The louder than normal squeaking of the cabinet door caused her to look up at the ceiling and wait. Hearing nothing, she retrieved a bowl, then proceeded to pour her cereal.

She didn't know why she hadn't told her father about her new job. Maybe there was no good time or maybe it was part of her quiet rebellion. Either way, her punishment would be swift and absolute if she coupled new information with her father's unwillingness to wake before his alarm clock.

In truth, she had many opportunities to tell her father the news, but she convinced herself his mood was too taxed by John staying, and then by his going. If she had followed her own advice, she would have asked her father what *he* thought about applying to Hardees before she applied, even if she suspected nothing would come of the visit. She silently chastised herself. There was no excuse for failing to do things the right way.

Marielle walked her bowl into the living room, placing it carefully onto the cocktail table. What happened next required two hands. She picked up the remote control, and with one thumb on the volume down arrow, she pushed the power button. She had under two seconds to bring the speakers down to a whisper before the previous night's volume awakened the house and the bear upstairs.

She turned the channel to CNN, attempting to read the anchor's lips when her crunching drowned-out his voice. The major news was either about the election or a prison break. In any event, there were criminals involved.

Marielle froze as she heard a groan from upstairs, then heavy footsteps, and a creak from her parents' bedroom door. She reached for the mute button when the footsteps reached the stairs, and as they approached the bottom, she held her breath. She should have set her cereal bowl down when she heard the first groan, but it was too late to do anything now except watch as milk threatened to jump from its container.

In all probability, Jack just needed to use the bathroom since only a camel could hold the amount of liquid he drank, but if he walked to the kitchen for a glass of water, she was screwed.

The anchor silently chatted away like nothing was wrong at all—as if he was so oblivious in his safe Atlanta studio that he might even un-mute himself. People who didn't understand the insanity of other families made her crazy!

Marielle stared at her hat across the room, then exhaled when the door closed to the bathroom. She allowed a dozen or so exaggerated breaths before the bathroom door opened again, and a moment later, the creaking of the stairs ushered-in normal breathing and a new appreciation for God.

Marielle studied the VCR clock. She could either leave by eight o'clock and kill an hour walking along the river, or sneak into her room and risk her father's work preparations trapping her upstairs. She walked into the kitchen as she considered this question further, then placed her bowl into the sink a second before picking it up again. No matter what her decision, she needed to wash and replace the bowl in the cabinet to remove it as evidence.

She turned toward the dining room as she dried her bowl, trying to remember if she left her room door open six inches wider than she did when she slept. She walked upstairs along the edge of the treads to minimize creaking. Two thirds of the way upstairs, she confirmed the door hung open at the proper angle, but her nerves were frayed enough to make walking along the chilly river seem a good alternative.

She passed the landlord's house, the country club condominiums, and the too-late-to-obscure-the-ugly-condominium hedges. Her watch told her it was 7:45 a.m. which placed her just outside the risk window of a passing car belonging to one of her parents' co-workers. If their shift started at 8, they would pass this spot at around 7:52, no earlier. No one wanted to arrive at the nursing home early, she decided, and this rule extended to both employees and residents.

Only two cars passed Marielle before she crossed the street and descended into the safety of Olde Oneida.

Since the main artery of traffic was rerouted to the soaring Skyline Bridge to her left, Olde Oneida looked and felt more like a ghost town from the Old West with abandoned buildings and unused parking lots surrounding them. Thin strips of land rested among three bridges: two over calm water and one over the angry dam-fed river.

Marielle walked along the dam-fed side of the island, eventually passing a small plaque commemorating Houdini, but she didn't stop to read it. Everyone knew this spot gave the escape artist the idea for his water illusions. If he had an idea for a happy family illusion, she might have stopped.

She turned right onto Lawe Street before climbing up one of the few hills in Appleton. Several blocks and a turn later, she walked into Hardees.

Two cashiers stood at the counter, each helping her own customer, as a blonde pony-tailed woman reached through the drive-through window.

Marielle consulted her watch. She had ten minutes to spare, so she waited patiently several feet from the counter until Tracy's customer walked away.

"This is your first day, right?" Tracy asked without any noticeable interest.

"Yes. I don't know who I'm supposed to talk to," Marielle replied as politely as she could.

"I'll get Sharon," Tracy said with fatigue.

The cashier, whose nametag read *Tara,* smiled broadly at Marielle when her own customer departed. "Do you go to East?" the girl asked.

"I do. You go to Xavier?" Marielle asked without considering the analysis behind her question. The girl wore diamond-studded earrings and shaded her eyelids like the Clinique lady at the mall. So, in Marielle's mind she had money, and kids who had money attended Xavier... even if they weren't Catholic.

"Not yet. I'm a transfer student," Tara replied a moment before Tracy returned to her register with Sharon in tow.

"Good morning," Sharon said in a nearly genial tone as she opened the cypher-locked door to the right of the counter. "Please follow me."

Marielle walked tentatively through the door, still not convinced she had the right.

"I'm going to get you started on the third register today," Sharon said, gesturing to her left. "Becky is our lead cashier so she'll train you when she isn't busy with the drive-through."

The pony-tailed, plump figure turned from the window briefly to wave at Marielle.

"This is the kitchen," Sharon said to the left just before turning right, "and here is the office." Sharon stopped outside a dark office where a broad-shouldered 30-something man sat on a small vinyl swivel chair behind a two-way mirror.

"This is our manager, Chris. This is Marielle," Sharon said to the office more than the man.

"Welcome to Hardees," Chris said as though he had said the same words a hundred times before and expected to say them hundreds more before retirement. His blond mustache matched perfectly his hair color, but there was nothing red to match his face.

Chris abandoned the chair which squeaked in protest, stood up six feet, and picked up the cash register drawer from his desk to hand it to Marielle. "You have $50 in small bills and coins to start, but let us know if you run low on any one thing. Your name tag is in the tray."

Marielle looked down and smiled at the newly etched black name tag with white lettering. So excited was she about the proper spelling of her name that she didn't notice her name tag was a different size and font than everyone else's.

"I'm gonna run to the bank," he said to Sharon. "I assume you have Becky training her?"

Sharon nodded, then made way for her boss. A moment later, she dropped an index card into the top of a buzzing square metal clock to the right of the office door. She placed the card at the top of a vertical-slotted rack before turning to Marielle to explain. "You've just punched in. Be sure to punch *out* before you go on break or leave, and *in* when you come back. Make sure you push it down hard or it won't mark the card."

Sharon turned toward the back of the building. "The refrigerator is back there," she said as the mustachioed cook walked out holding a box of frozen hamburger patties, smiling broadly when he spied Marielle, "and the dumpster is out the back door and behind the parking lot, but that's enough for now," she said briskly. "Take your tray up to the front and Becky will get you started."

As Marielle approached her register, Tracy cursed loudly.

"A bus?" Tara asked, but it wasn't really a question.

Becky looked back from the drive-through window after handing change and a receipt to her customer. "What's your name again?" she asked.

Marielle answered, though in a moderate state of shock.

"Marielle," Becky began, "push the button on the bottom right of the register. Now, place your tray inside and close it. I just want you to fill the drink orders for Tracy and Tara as they come in."

The Xavier student appeared mesmerized by the seemingly endless line of elderly people streaming from what looked to be the largest coach bus in North America.

"Tara," Becky said, interrupting the girl's concentration, "don't forget that the bus driver gets a free meal. Also, the Senior Citizen discount button is on the middle-left side, but don't push it until you total the order."

"Got it," said Tara, still staring at the human river.

Becky filled three baskets with frozen French fries and submerged them in the grease vat before pushing the timer buttons above them. "Marielle, come here quick," she said.

Marielle jogged to the French fry holding area.

"This is how you fill a regular fry," she instructed, placing a paper sleeve at the end of her shovel-ladle, and tipping it up toward the heat lamp until the sleeve dripped fries, "and this is how you fill a large." She did the same with a larger cardboard version of the sleeve. "Do you think you could put the remainder of these fries in sleeves—more regular than large—and place them on the rack until Tracy and Tara need you?"

"Sure," said Marielle, feeling as nervous as she did taking the Pre-SATs.

Three sleeves into her task, the side doors opened and stayed that way as two long lines formed in front of Tracy and Tara.

Ten sleeves later, Marielle ran to Tracy's register, read her drink order, guessed which were the medium cups, lids, and the proper amount of ice, then filled two cups with soda simultaneously. A few seconds later, the drinks were capped and sitting on the customer's tray. She did the same for Tara, then ran back to the grease vat alarm before using the same fry basket grease removal technique she had seen Becky employ.

"Nice!" said Becky as she rounded the fry corner. "Now, dump them here, salt them with this big shaker, stir them and bag them."

"Yes, ma'am," Marielle said happily.

"Ma'am?" asked Becky in a quarter laugh.

For the next 10 minutes, "Can I take your order please" morphed with grease vat alarms; beeping drive-through alerts; and "Thank you. Please come again."

"How old are you?" asked Becky as passengers turned upstream toward their bus, leaving calm in their wake.

"I'm 15 and three quarters," she replied.

Becky laughed. "Well, I just turned 21, so there's no need to call me ma'am."

"Okay... I'll try," she said, then after a pause she asked, "Are you in college?"

"I am. I'll be a senior at Stout."

"I was thinking of going to Stout," Marielle reflected.

"Oh, yeah? What for?"

"Hotel management. I may want to work on a cruise line."

Becky nodded. "Well, Stout would be the place for you, then."

"What's your major?" Tara asked Becky, turning away from her register.

"Psychology," Becky replied, looking past Tara to Tracy who leaned forward against the counter, staring out the windows that faced Oneida Street.

"Cool!" said Marielle. "I got a book from the library this spring that talked about obsessive compulsive disorder. I couldn't put it down!"

"Good one!" Becky said, a full two seconds before Marielle understood her own joke. "Did you read that for school?" she asked.

"No. To be honest, I'm really not sure what I want to be so I thought I should start reading up on the harder stuff like medicine and psychology to get a head start."

"So, you *don't* want to work on a cruise ship," Tracy said with irritation.

"Well, I do, but I'm really interested in everything. Actually, I'm not so much interested in medicine since I almost fainted during a biology video of open heart surgery."

"Eww," said Becky and Tara in unison.

"I know. My teacher got super mad at me because when I left class, I ran downstairs to the second floor to use the bathroom. Most of my classes are on the second floor and I was so freaked out by the video that I completely forgot that each floor has its own bathroom."

"Which high school is that?" asked the mustachioed cook who somehow stood beside the fry vat without anyone noticing.

Tracy jumped more than the others, but Marielle had the feeling it wasn't because she was startled.

"Uh... East," Marielle replied.

"We need to get back to work," Becky said, more to the boy than the rest.

"I'm Mark, by the way," the mustache said to Marielle before she could move away.

"I'm Marielle," she replied tentatively as Mark raised his eyebrows at her.

***

"I spoke to Becky and she said you did a great job today," Sharon noted as Marielle returned her cash tray.

"Thank you," she replied, smiling broadly. "It was fun."

Sharon studied Marielle to determine if she was employing sarcasm. Once satisfied, she looked back at the tray. "You'll probably want this," she said, pulling Marielle's name tag from the empty large bill slot.

"Oh, right," Marielle replied, looking nervously at a face which clearly began to question Becky's judgment.

***

Marielle glanced at her watch as she emerged from the over-air-conditioned building. It was only six hours ago that she entered Hardees for the first time as an employee, but she felt a decade more mature when she left.

"I'm home!" Marielle yelled to the stairs as the porch screen door slammed behind her. She walked down the hall, then stopped as she heard the call letters of her favorite radio station from the direction of the kitchen.

"I'm home now," she said to her sisters as they sun bathed beneath the kitchen window. "Did Dad ask where I was at lunch?"

Jeanette squinted upside down toward the window. "He didn't come home for lunch."

"Really?" asked Marielle, feeling sure she couldn't be that lucky. "I wonder why."

"How are we supposed to know?" Anna asked impatiently.

"Well, I was thinking you might try using your evil powers for good someday," Marielle replied before running upstairs to remove clothes which smelled like a grease vat.

After changing into cut-off jeans and her favorite mint polo shirt, Marielle retrieved a purple notebook from her top middle drawer. Turning to a blank page, she wrote, "June 29, 1988 – Hardees – 6 Hours." She smiled with satisfaction. She was now $20.10 closer to going to Ireland.

***

After the news signed off, Marielle looked at her father and said, "I got a job at Hardees today."

"You did? That's great, honey. When do you start?"

"Well, they asked me to work tomorrow," she replied, threading the needle between truth and lie.

"That's quick! Did you ask your mother?"

"Yes, sir. She didn't have a problem with it."

"How much are they paying?"

"Just minimum wage, but they will consider a 10 cent raise after a three month probationary period."

"Good, good," he said, inhaling through his cigarette.

During the next commercial he asked, "Is this just for spending money?"

"Well, I need to pay for driver's ed training, but after that I was thinking I'd like to save for a car or a motorcycle. Joy actually has a motor scooter that only cost her $800, so that's an idea too," she said, studying her father's face for the response she expected.

He puffed thoughtfully on his cigarette before squinting at the TV. "I'd prefer you save for a car," he said, turning his attention to his daughter. "I don't want you on the road without metal protecting you."

Marielle smiled at her father before looking back at the TV.

Ten minutes later, Jack regarded his daughter again and said, "Well, what about that trip you wanted to take with your band?"

"It's too late now. They're leaving next week." She paused for dramatic effect before continuing. "I was thinking of flying into Frankfurt to see Stephen on my own, then stopping to see my pen pal in Ireland on the way home, but I thought getting a car or a moped might be more practical," she lied.

"Well, now, let's think about that," her father said, exhaling smoke. "You can buy a car any time, but your brother won't be in West Germany forever."

Marielle nodded while suppressing a smile.

Her dad loved big ideas, and traveling to Europe was a much bigger idea than buying a car. It was also a much less realistic idea. So, the chances his daughter wouldn't follow through was likely in the forefront of his mind.

"I can write Stephen and ask if he'd be okay with me visiting," Marielle suggested.

"If he says no, let me know," Jack smirked in an "I'll change that" kind of way while rocking on his left elbow.

"Yes, sir," Marielle replied, finally unable to hide her smile.

***

"Marielle, if the phone rings, pick it up! I'm expecting an important phone call," Jeanette demanded before running into the bathroom.

She threw the door closed behind her, but it failed to latch, popping open about an inch. It seemed she had waited as long as she could for whomever was that important. Marielle imagined that person was Doug, but she hoped against hope that the latest drama had severed that relationship once and for all.

Fifteen seconds later, the phone rang. Marielle heard her sister curse just before she asked, "Can you get that?"

Marielle smiled. Her sister's tone was far more agreeable with her pants down and the door ajar.

"Hello?" Marielle asked the caller.

"Jeanette?" Doug replied.

She sighed. He had been burned by this question before, but Marielle was too disappointed to pretend she was her sister. "No, it's Marielle," she admitted.

"Oh," his tone changed from apologetic to aggressive. "Can you put your sister on the phone, please?"

"I'm afraid I can't do that. She's on the can right now, and from the sounds of it, she'll be there for awhile."

The phone was silent for a moment and Marielle felt no compunction to fill the void.

"Okay," he finally said. "Well, let her know I called."

"Of course," she said before pushing the off button and dropping the phone an inch above its cradle.

"Who was it?" asked Jeanette through the door as Marielle passed.

"It was Doug," she replied. "He's dead."

"WHAT?!" yelled Jeanette, as though she believed for a moment that one could call with this kind of news.

Marielle ran up the stairs, then locked her door. She would only be unsafe for the next half-hour. After that, her father would be home and there was no way Jeanette would bring up the incident, or Doug in general, to him.

Five minutes later, the bathroom door opened, and numbers beeped from a phone on its way up the stairs.

"Sorry about that," Jeanette said, trying too hard to sound aloof. "I was outside when you called."

Marielle chuckled. Strange that Jeanette thought her sister would protect her dignity... and she might have... but not for Doug.

***

"Hey, Dad," Marielle said genially. "How was work?"

"Oh, just peachy," he replied, placing his beer inside a new credit union cosy before continuing. "Same old shit, different day," he laughed unhappily.

Inspiring, thought Marielle with her normal amount of sarcasm. "Just so you know, Jeanette is mad at me," she said.

"Really? What did you do?"

Marielle flashed a mischievous grin. "I might have told her that Doug called to say he was dead."

It took a moment for her father's mind to disengage from the TV, but he laughed when it did. "Any particular reason?" he asked.

"Yeah, Jeanette found a cigarette butt with lipstick on it in Doug's car last weekend."

"Hmm," he said, eyes narrowing against his cigarette smoke. "Any idea whose lipstick?"

"No, he said it was his dad's, but I don't remember Mr. Miller wearing lipstick. Also, Janet Elroy said he's been seen running around Rhinelander with a married woman who happens to have two kids."

Jack's left eye squinted without the assistance of smoke. "Did you tell Jeanette that?"

"Yeah, but she just got a call from him a little while ago and he seems to have explained it all away." Marielle moved her left hand as though it was a piece of tissue on fire.

"I'll take care of it," Jack said, chewing his fingernail as he stared at the TV.

"Marielle, I want to see you upstairs NOW!" Maria demanded from the dining room doorway as Jeanette stood behind her left shoulder with arms crossed.

Marielle started, then looked toward her father.

"Wait a second," said Jack, his left arm motioning for Marielle to stay put. "What do you need Marielle for?"

Maria's expression changed from hardened to surprised, then back again. "She lied to her sister today," she explained.

"About what?" Jack asked aggressively, knowing neither she nor Jeanette could answer that question honestly without confiding in him.

"She told Jeanette that Doug was dead."

"Well, now, that's not the whole story is it? If you're gonna lie, then you need to get your big ass back upstairs and watch your program with your two daughters."

Marielle winced. There was definitely a downside to using her father as a human shield. Her mother stared at Marielle in a way that said her daughter was a traitor and she would pay later, while Jeanette's expression promised more violence.

"I don't know what you mean," Maria said innocently.

"I think you do. The only thing Marielle said was that Doug called to say he was dead. Maybe your IQ isn't much better than your daughter's, but it's impossible for a dead person to make a phone call—long distance or local," he added.

Marielle covered her mouth quickly to suppress laughter. Her father saw it and began laughing hard enough for his feet to leave the carpet while he held his stomach.

Maria and Jeanette looked at one other before turning away. As they passed the closed living room door, Jack managed to yell, "And don't think I don't know Doug is running around on Jeanette. We're gonna talk about that before she spends another minute up north!"

Jack gave in to laughter again, but amusement turned to brooding during the news. Moments after the anchor signed off, he said a curse to God before ascending the steps two at a time.

Marielle cursed as well, though to no one in particular, as her father threw open his bedroom door and began to yell. Marielle knew she had caused this problem, but she felt wary of the aftermath. There was nothing to be done but sit and wait for her father to return; get another beer; stew through four to six sitcoms; and hope the TV and her presence improved his mood. The futility of the plan became obvious, however, when one sitcom of stewing resulted in another trip upstairs and a fresh round of cursing and insults.

Marielle retired to her bedroom in defeat, and began playing her saxophone as loudly as possible. Practicing while her parents were home was strictly forbidden, but they wouldn't yell at her when they had each other.

Halfway through Sousa, Marielle thought about visiting her grandparents for a few weeks, but work and driver's ed killed that possibility for the summer. She blasted through the next stanza. This was her life now, and she needed to stop making trouble.

Jack abruptly ended his conversation with a "You stupid, fat bitch!" and a slammed door. His presence on the stairs indicated that practice was over and Marielle's presence was now required. Her father would likely recount his opinion of his wife until at least midnight, and strictly speaking she could leave him alone to do this, but that would risk an explosion well into the morning. He would wake up his wife with the overhead bedroom light, and his daughters with the yelling, and first day of driver's ed tomorrow or not, there was no sleep ahead for Marielle.

She rested her saxophone inside its case fully assembled before walking downstairs, knowing she might need it later, but the ringing of the telephone pulled her attention from sleep and family drama for a moment.

"May I speak to Marielle, please?" a polite teenaged voice asked.

"This is she speaking," Marielle replied as her father groaned while reaching for his beer.

"Oh," said the boy, seemingly startled. "This is Mark."

"Mark?" she asked, sharing a questioning look with her father.

"Yeah, from Hardees. Chris gave me your number."

It took a moment for Marielle to place the name Chris with the Hardees manager. "Oh, do I need to work tomorrow, because I asked off and I have driver's ed."

"Oh, no. Well, I don't know when you're supposed to work, but I was wondering if you wanted to go out with me tomorrow night?"

"Oh." Marielle stopped for a moment. She really didn't know if she did or not, but she was too surprised to reason it through and too polite to say *no* outright. "Just a second. Let me ask my father. Is this a movie or dinner?"

"Both."

"Just us or with a group?"

"Well, I thought just us."

"Oh, okay. Just a second."

Marielle covered the end of the phone, then waited for her father to look up. "There's a boy on the phone from Hardees. He wants to know if I'll go out with him to dinner and a movie tomorrow night. I don't care either way."

Jack nodded, seemingly amused by his daughter's attitude. "Okay, but you need to be home by ten o'clock."

"Alright," Marielle replied, both excited and disappointed at the same time. "I can go, but I need to be home before ten."

"Cool. I'll pick you up at 6:30."

"Alright, see you then," she said, then hung up the phone before wondering if Mark knew her address.

***

"There's a van in the driveway with 'Make Love Not War' spray painted on the side!" Anna yelled up the stairs she ascended.

"What?!" Marielle called over the railing.

"*Oh*, yeah," Anna replied, wearing a smile she hadn't used for awhile.

"Bloody!" Marielle said, returning to her room to grab her hair spray.

"What are you, British?" Anna asked with distaste.

"Has Mom or Dad seen it yet?" Marielle asked, removing the can top.

"No, but they're about to. He's walking toward the front porch with a blue Hawaiian shirt on," she said, looking out the window at the top of the stairs.

"You're joking!" Marielle said, more as a plea than an exclamation.

"*Ohhhh*, no I'm not."

"Shit, bloody hell, damn it!" Marielle managed to say before the sound of knocking caused her to freeze. She didn't know if she wanted to wait upstairs until the yelling stopped or run downstairs to tell Mark to leave first.

"Hi, my name is Mark, I'm here to take your daughter to dinner if she's still available," Marielle and Anna heard him say.

Marielle looked above her bedroom door waiting for a male or female voice to answer. Anna leaned against Marielle's door jam, smiling with arms crossed.

"Well, come in," Jack said politely.

Marielle closed her eyes as Anna laughed in two loud bursts.

"This is a nice home you have here, Mr. Richter."

"Well, thank you very much," he replied before calling for Marielle.

A "damn it" wafting downstairs prompted Jack to continue, "Let me run upstairs and get my daughter for you."

"Thanks so much," Mark responded with an air of politeness which bordered on mockery.

"Hey, what's the holdup?" Jack asked as he approached Marielle's room.

"I don't think she wants to go on her date anymore," Anna whispered.

Jack looked at his panicked middle daughter. "Well, you can't leave the poor kid hanging," he said.

Both girls looked at their father like he was a whole new person.

Marielle exhaled with defeat, then walked past her sister and father who were now laughing in the exact same way. She walked down the stairs knowing she was watched from above and below—all eyes smiling for different reasons.

Mark's wardrobe in no way resembled the last boy who picked her up for a date. Although both wore jeans, Guy's oxford shirt had been replaced with the bowling shirt of a middle-aged man. Guy's penny loafers were Mark's Doc Martins, and Guy's clean-shaven face and short blond hair were now Mark's long, dark mullet and mustache. Marielle knew about the mustache, but somehow Mark's hair didn't seem so rock musician-esque under his chef's cap.

Marielle managed a slight curvature of the mouth while saying hello, and nodding a let's go.

Walking toward the old brown cargo van bearing appalling paint, Marielle thought she would prefer to be just about anywhere right now than on a date with Mark from Kimberly.

"Tell me again how you got my phone number and address?" she asked as she rounded the front of the van.

"Chris and my mom are friends," Mark said in a way that suggested they were more than friends, or maybe that's what Marielle assumed because, as far as she knew, adults of opposite genders were never just friends.

"And this is your car?" she asked, spying the mattress in back while wondering why her dad allowed her to leave the house.

"My van, yeah. Do you like Rush?" he asked, pushing buttons on his after-market tape deck.

"I don't know Rush, but you should put on anything you like," she said, fighting the urge to cross her arms.

"You don't have your seat belt on," Marielle said after they successfully backed onto Oneida Street.

"Yeah, I don't like to wear them. I think I'd rather die in a car accident than become a vegetable."

Marielle turned toward the boy with disrespect. "Well, that presumes vegetative status is your only option with a seat belt."

Mark was quiet for a moment, and Marielle wondered if he needed to look up the word "presumes."

"You're the kind of girl who can buy a six pack and party all weekend, aren't you?" he asked.

"Oh, a six pack would last me a *lot* longer than a weekend," she said, crossing her arms.

They turned into the Hardees' parking lot.

"Where are we going?" Marielle asked anxiously.

"Oh, Chris said we could use his Cadillac if you preferred, and it sounds like you might prefer that."

"No, no, no. I'm good," she said, looking frantically at the restaurant windows for anyone who might see them together.

"Are you sure?" he asked in earnest as they drove around the back of the restaurant to the spot where the gold Cadillac always parked.

"I'm sure," she said, fighting the urge to get as far away from the mattress as possible.

"Okay. Have you seen *Big*, *Funny Farm*, or the latest Crocodile Dundee movie?" he asked as they approached the side exit of the parking lot.

"I haven't seen any of them."

"Well, which one you choose depends on whether we go to Valley Fair or the Fox River Mall for dinner."

"Which ones are at Valley Fair?" Marielle asked, wanting to stay within walking distance of home.

"*Big* is for sure."

"Well, *Big* it is, then."

"Okay. Do you want to eat at that Mexican place?" he asked, indicating a restaurant in the mall.

"That would be just awesome," she replied with sarcasm she didn't hide.

***

Marielle scanned the menu past the virgin daiquiris. Even though she wanted one, she had no intention of opening that line of questioning. The cheapest dinner was two tacos with rice and refried beans. She reached into her pocket to confirm it still held a $20 bill. Offering to pay would remove any doubt that they were on a serious date, she decided—if his shirt and hair hadn't done the work for her.

"What? Me?" Mark asked pointing to his chest as he looked over Marielle's right shoulder.

Marielle turned around, but saw no one. She turned back to Mark with a judging face, but he was already laughing.

"So, are you going to talk to me now?" he asked.

"Sure," she said, but sighed anyway. "So, why does Becky hate you?"

"Did she say she hated me?" he asked, sitting back in his chair.

"No, but she doesn't look at you when you come to the front so I just got that wild and crazy idea. Did you two date or did you dump her sister or something?"

He shook his head. "No. I don't date fat chicks."

"Nice," Marielle said with distaste, though she was more flattered for herself than offended on behalf of her friend.

"I told you that my mom is friends with Chris?" he asked.

She nodded.

"Well, he got me my job and he lets me choose my schedule and stuff and she's just jealous. She's also an uptight college chick and I have no plans to go to anything but technical school. In fact, I told her that she was wasting money on school since she's clearly going for an MRS degree. So, the long and short of it is that she's a bitch."

Marielle took a drink of Pepsi from her straw before she said, "Hmm. She's always nice to me."

"That's because she thinks you're like her, and you're a hard worker."

Marielle nodded. "You could be a hard worker too if you wanted to."

"True, but I don't see the point. I get paid the same amount of money whether I throw frozen hamburger patties at Paul or on the grill."

"Don't you want the satisfaction of doing a good job?" Marielle asked with some dismay.

"I get no satisfaction from that. Look, as far as I see it, we get paid minimum wage to do a job that should pay at least a dollar more per hour.

118

So, we're being taken advantage of and the managers know it. They make us punch out during slow periods and they give us a crappy 15% discount on food that we wouldn't even be eating if we didn't work there. They even fired the guy before me because he was eating a French fry in back without paying for it. It's bullshit!"

"So, why don't you tell Chris this?"

"Oh, he knows it, and he may be the manager, but he's not the worst of them. Sharon is a frickin' Nazi! I wish I could punch her in her ugly frickin' face! She doesn't even talk to me anymore 'cause she knows I hate her. I don't even try to hide it. The other day, I saw her spying on me through the two way mirror in the office. I just mouthed 'fuck off' at her. A little while later she came out and told me to clean the grill again. I told her I'd get right on that, but I didn't move. It cracks me up 'cause she can't do anything about it! She can't even go to the owner 'cause Chris is best friends with her. She's an old widow and Chris takes her to all of her doctors' appointments, and the grocery store. He also makes sure her lawn is mowed and her driveway gets plowed. Anyway, Sharon should quit and work at McDonald's except they wouldn't hire her because she's too frickin' hideous."

"I didn't know McDonald's was that selective," Marielle said with a smile.

"Probably not, but there's gotta be a reason she stays."

Marielle nodded. "I heard she's pregnant."

"No frickin' way!" Mark exclaimed, nearly leaping out of his chair. "She must've found the only blind guy in Appleton."

Marielle laughed.

"Okay, so let me ask you something," Mark said, leaning in and waiting.

"*Ja?*" Marielle asked impatiently.

"Do you like guys?"

Marielle's eyes squinted. "What do you mean by that?!"

"Paul says you don't really date anyone at East and you never seem that interested in going out."

She sighed. "Well, boys are kind of a distraction from my plans to get into a good college and move out. Also, my parents are pretty strict and it's easier to stay at home than to ask their permission to leave the house and explain everything I did when I got home."

"Not strict enough to keep you home when a guy with a van comes aknockin'," Mark said happily.

"Yeah, well, I have no idea what to say about that. I'm as surprised as anyone that my dad let me leave the house. If my mom was around, there's no way I'd be here."

"Where's your mom?" Mark asked with concern.

"I don't know. The store, probably."

His face relaxed. "Oh, I thought you were going to say your mom abandoned you at birth."

"No, I'm not that interesting," she said, sipping her drink.

"I'd be happy to have a boring family," Mark replied, looking past her as though he had seen a lot in 17 years.

"I heard you're a Golden Glove," Marielle said, eager to change the subject.

"I was," he replied, looking back at her. "I went to Colorado last year to compete, but I didn't win."

"Are you going this year?"

"No, we couldn't afford it, so I quit."

Marielle set down her drink. "But you have a job now. You can save your money for it," she said, more than asked, not sure how to question a person who would give up his dreams so easily.

"No. I can't get to work without a car and I have to work to pay for my van. It's a vicious cycle."

"Sorry about that," she said with genuine sympathy.

"Them's the breaks," Mark said in the exact same way Marielle had heard her father say the same words.

***

Marielle walked through the door fifteen minutes before ten.

"How was your date?" her father asked with a smirk on his face as she rounded the corner of the dining room.

"Fine," she said, plopping into the living room chair. "He didn't try to hold my hand during the movie, so that was great."

"That's my girl," Jack said, taking a drink of his beer. "What movie did you see?"

"*Big* with Tom Hanks. It's the one where he's a kid and he wakes up as an adult."

"Hmm," Jack said, looking toward the TV.

"Where's Mom?"

"Up in her room. Where else? She's pissed that I let you go out with that boy. Your sister told her about the van." He rolled his eyes. "I told her if anyone could handle themselves, it was you."

"Wow. Thanks, Dad." Marielle smiled at her father, then quickly turned toward the television.

"By the way, you had a phone call while you were out. I think it was Guy, but you should ask your sister. She took the call."

"Bah," said Marielle, throwing her head back.

"Something wrong?" asked Jack, removing the finger he chewed from his mouth with sudden annoyance.

The VCR clock reminded Marielle that it was past the 8 p.m. tipping point and reasonable Jack had expired.

"No, sir," she said before rising to kiss her father goodnight.

Chapter Ten

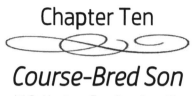

Course-Bred Son
—W.B. Yeats – *Ego Dominus Tuus*

"Do you know what this asswipe from West said when I was leaving driver's ed?" Marielle asked Shelly before the crackling of the handset prompted her to move closer to the phone's base. "He pulled out this stupid phrase that must be from 1910. It goes something like 'West is best, East is least, and Kimberly can't compete.' "

"Why bring Kimberly into it?" asked Shelly as though she was more interested in her nails drying.

"I have no idea. He must not like small towns. All I know is I want him dead. He's such a dumbass though that I'm pretty sure his driving will do it for me."

"Really?" Shelly asked, finally paying attention.

"I have no idea, but a girl can hope," Marielle remarked before giving in to an awkward silence.

"Look, I need to call Tim," Shelly finally said. "Can I call you back tomorrow?"

Marielle stuck out her tongue before she could stop herself. "I'm working in the morning, but I'll be home by four."

"Okay. Bye, then."

"Bye, then?" Marielle asked while placing the phone onto its charger. Whether or not the change in Shelly's personality was Tim's fault she didn't know. She only knew that Shelly became boring the moment she began dating him. Boys were a curse, she thought… which reminded her of Mark.

To say she had no physical attraction to him was an understatement, but this wasn't the entire reason he repelled her. His plan to live and die in Kimberly, and give up any dream that presented an obstacle was the real problem. Not only did she not respect him, but she feared his influence, since his were all of the bad choices she feared making.

Excuses prevented her from going out with him more than once a week, but she wasn't sure why she bothered except he kept his hands to himself, and breaking up with one's newly promoted supervisor seemed awkward at best.

***

"We got a letter from your brother today," Jack said, not aware of the scrutiny Marielle gave every letter which entered the house.

It had been over a month since she received a letter from Dermot which was at least 10 months in teenager time. There was no way around the conclusion that he was either disappointed or angry with her over her canceled trip. She didn't really blame him, but if he saw her bank account right now—over $140 even after she paid $64 for her driver's ed lessons—he would understand how serious she was about making good on her promise to visit. Each night, she prayed he would write while each day she wondered if she was past caring.

"What did Stephen have to say?" she asked.

"He said he's coming home on leave in August. You can read the letter yourself. It's in the fruit bowl," Jack said, nodding toward the dining room table.

8-Aug-1988

Hi Marielle,

Happy Birthday!!! I'm sorry I didn't write. I couldn't because I was in Irish college. It's just like a summer camp except that everyone speaks Irish. It's really great fun (Awwwwesome?). If you speak English, you get sent home, but that didn't happen to anyone. I made LOADS of friends (about three hundred). Yesterday, I wrote to two people who I got really friendly with there – Séamus (that's a boy) and Sinéad (that's a girl). Everybody stays with a family in the area (there were seven others staying in our house) and goes to school (not really "school" – it's great fun). Then there are discos at night. I got a beautiful girlfriend called Paula and all my friends (and enemies) were envying me. After a week, I found out that she was a snobby bitch so I left her... well, I didn't leave her. I told her I thought she was a snobby bitch and she left me. Anyhow, I made friends with loads of people who live in Galway but who I never met.

I hope you like your t-shirt. I don't think 'Ireland' t-shirts are great, but Americans seem to love them. I was going to send you a Porsche, but I couldn't find a big enough envelope. (Ha, Ha!)

I have so much to tell you, but if I don't send this package in the next five minutes it will get to you a day late and Ronnie will be firing cruise missiles at me. I'll try to find a pen pal for your friend. Most of my friends don't like writing and I wouldn't insult your friend with the creeps who have offered.

Wow! You must have had a brilliant time on the roller coasters! I'd be terrified!

Last night I read all your letters. We're almost "old friends" at this stage.

Well, I better run unless I'm going to swim across the Atlantic with your letter. I'm not that fit (yet!).

Did you see the race between Ben Johnson and Carl Lewis? It was brilliant, but I hope Johnson wins the Olympics. Well, I hope you get loads and loads of lovely presents.

I'm sorry you couldn't come to Ireland this summer. Maybe this fall, or this winter (at Christmas maybe)? I can wait until spring, but I'll likely die if I wait any longer.

Byeee!
Lots and Lots and Lots and Lots and Lots of Love,
Dermot

Marielle held the letter against her chest which was now covered by a new t-shirt across which the word "Ireland" was written in blue print over a green shamrock. She had seen people hold letters to their chests on TV, but she didn't know why before today. The smell of the t-shirt and the envelope along with the thinness of the paper spoke of a place both far away and perfect. It also spoke of women with smaller torsos or maybe just smaller breasts because the shirt was too tight to ever wear outside the house without earning a whole new reputation. In any event, it didn't matter because she would only wear the shirt to bed.

She had never received a present from a boy after telling him something disappointing. It didn't make sense. In fact, the implications to her theories—and previous certainties—about human nature were vast. Not only was he *not* angry with her for breaking her word, but the delay only seemed to make him more eager to see her. Dermot wasn't the kind of boy who gave up on his dreams or shrank from new experiences. She knew these people existed, but other than Grandpa Richter, she hadn't found them in the male form before.

She stared at the stamp and the postmark which read 08-08-88. It was a lucky number in China the news had said on the morning of the eighth, and it felt that way to Marielle until she remembered that it was now the 22nd and the package had taken fourteen days instead of the normal seven.

Marielle cursed as she sat forward. Dermot would expect a return letter to arrive soon... She added the days on her fingers... *today,* in fact. If it didn't arrive, he'd either think she was angry, or pretending to be angry, about his lapse in writing. Either way, she needed to find a way to tell him she wasn't the type of girl who became angry easily or played games. Too much was riding on this relationship to make Dermot wait another week.

Marielle thought to call Shelly, but listening to, "Oh, no... well... hmm... I'm sure it'll be fine," wasn't the reassurance she needed right now. She lay back on the orange couch, looking at a ceiling she didn't see before an idea emerged before her.

She jumped toward the roll top desk to grab a piece of paper and pencil, then sat at the dining room table. Cordless phone in hand, she took a deep breath before pressing zero.

"Hello. Can you tell me how I might find a phone number in Ireland, please?" she asked, employing the most adult version of her voice.

Hearing the answer, she hung up, then called 00. Thirty seconds after the initial "One moment, please," the American operator spoke to an Irish operator while asking Marielle for the specifics of the phone number needed.

"I don't have the father's first name, but the last name is MacManus and they live on Taylor's Hill Road in Galway."

Marielle wrote a seven digit number without knowing how one would call a number without an area code.

"Will that be all?" the Irish operator asked.

"Yes, thank you," replied the American operator, waiting for her Irish counterpart to disconnect before asking Marielle, "Do you know how to complete this call?"

"No, ma'am, I don't," she replied, out of breath for no good reason.

"Okay, so you need to dial 011 for an international number, then 353. That's the country code for Ireland. Then, add the number the Irish operator gave to you and you should be all set."

"Great! Thank you *so* much!" Marielle said, wondering if it was appropriate to send an operator a thank you note, but the line went dead before she could consider the matter further.

"Okay, okay, okay," she said to herself, pacing between the desk and table while biting her thumbnail. She had never crossed a foreign border in person or by phone. If there was a protocol for engaging in a live conversation with a foreign person, she was sure the operator or one of the exchange students would have mentioned it. This wasn't the kind of secret people kept... unlike the ending of a movie. After all, if you knew the daughter died at the end of *Terms of Endearment*, would you really watch it? Well, people watched *Romeo and Juliet* even though they knew both kids died, but Shakespeare was a genius. The only permission she probably needed was that of her parents, but they didn't get home for three hours, and that would probably make it too late to call... though she really had no idea what time it was in Ireland.

Marielle retrieved the phone and her paper before running up to her room and locking the door.

She pressed the numbers carefully, reading them aloud before punching them into the hand set. When she didn't hear the beeping of a number, she hung up, then started again. After the fourth attempt, all numbers beeped appropriately and a long silence ended with a very serious low-pitched double ring, then a pause, then another double ring.

"Hello?" said an Irish girl's voice through a tunnel.

"Hello. Is this Fiona?" Marielle asked excitedly.

"Yes?" replied the girl tentatively.

"Hi, my name is Marielle. I'm Dermot's pen pal from the U.S. Is he home by chance?" She said all three sentences without breathing, then covered the mouthpiece to catch her breath privately.

"Let me check," Fiona replied before calling her brother's name.

Marielle began to tremble when she heard a boy's voice approach the phone.

"Dermot here," he said in a silky soft brogue.

"Hi, Dermot. This is Marielle," she replied before breathing away from the phone again.

"Marielle?" he asked, making her name sound more French than anyone had ever done before.

"Yes. I hope I'm not disturbing you, but I just got your letter today and the t-shirt, and I wanted to thank you for both."

"W-Well, it's really nothing a'tall. It took me ages to write, but I was in Irish college and—"

126

"Please don't worry about that. I'll write you back today, but I noticed that you mailed the package on the eighth and I didn't get it until today and I didn't want you to think I was mad or dead when my letter didn't arrive when you expected it. *If* you expected it," she said anxiously, pulling back the corners of her mouth.

"Thank you. I'm glad you rang. I was looking for a letter from you to arrive shortly."

"Well, you should get it by next week, I promise! By the way, what time is it there? Am I calling you too late?"

"Not a'tall. It's... let's see... it's nearly half-six."

"Great. So, you're six hours ahead. I'll remember that. Okay. So, I have to go. I'm not sure how much this will cost and I didn't ask my parents' permission first."

"Ah-right. I hope they don't place you on restriction, now."

Marielle exhaled slowly as she felt Dermot's voice calm her. "I'm sure they will only make me pay for it."

"Well, it's lovely to hear your voice."

She smiled. "Yours too. I'm surprised it's so easy to understand you."

"Did you think I'd sound like a leprechaun?" he asked in mock offense.

"No." She paused. "Well, I thought maybe someone from Darby O'Gill and I guess half the cast were leprechauns, but I didn't think you'd sound that short."

Dermot laughed, then asked softly, "Did you really only ring to say thank you? You're not meaning to surprise me with a visit, now?"

Marielle released guilt with a sigh. "No, I wish I were."

Dermot inhaled into the phone. "Bad luck, that."

"Yes. For both of us. I hope my calling didn't get your hopes up, but I didn't want you to worry and—" Marielle stopped abruptly as someone began banging on her door.

"Ah-right. Well, I'm glad you did. What's that noise in the background, there?"

"Just a sec." Marielle put her hand over the receiver before she yelled, "Shut the hell up!" through clenched teeth. "Sorry about that," she said to Dermot. "You're lucky you don't have a little sister."

"I am. Or a choir instructor who can't tolerate me."

"You're right. I haven't seen him all summer, but he'll probably hate

127

me in the new school year. I've decided that I must remind him of a girl who wouldn't date him in high school."

Dermot chuckled. "Isn't that a bit big-headed of you?"

"Probably, but I'm okay with that," she replied, causing both to laugh before she wondered how much laughing would cost and said goodbye again.

Marielle held the phone against her ear even though the line was most assuredly dead. She had allowed Dermot to hang up first, but this was a mistake. It was much easier to leave than to be left. Either way, it was hard to leave the first real conversation she had ever had with a boy. She didn't know if it was his calm manner or his soft flowing accent, but she was pretty sure she wanted to hear Dermot's voice every day of her life and last thing before she died.

8/22/1988 Monday

Hi Dermot!

Thank you again for my t-shirt! I'm wearing it right now and it fits me perfectly! It was so nice of you to send it to me!! Thank you also for understanding about my visit. I promise I'm working very hard to make enough money to see you, but according to my calculations, the earliest I can get there is next spring. Is this alright? I should have mentioned this to you on the phone, but I didn't think of it until I hung up.

Please don't worry about not writing. This summer has been pretty hectic with working, taking driver's ed, dating, and my oldest brother at home before he left for California. (My other brother is coming home on leave from West Germany in a couple of weeks.)

Irish college does sound like a lot of fun (except for the speaking Irish part). Ooh, but a lady my parents work with is Irish (she's from a place called Gort) and she taught me one Irish phrase that's supposed to mean "kiss my ass" which would have been particularly useful to you in your breakup with Paula. By the way, did you break up in Irish or once you started fighting did you switch to English? If your Irish isn't very good, you might've been talking about something completely different and maybe you didn't break up at all. ☺ Anyway, I don't know how to spell this Irish phrase, but it sounds like "poag ma'hone." Do you know it? It's fun to say. In general, I find it's fun to swear or otherwise be insulting in another language. I also think it's the first thing foreign language teachers should teach because they know they have the whole class' attention and they can guarantee the class will be speaking the new language all day.

Back to the summer, though. Last month, I started dating a guy who works with me. He's technically my supervisor now, but he's only 17 which means I don't have to listen to him, or maybe I don't listen to him because I'm dating him, or maybe it's because I'm a model employee, or possibly I'm on the verge of being fired and I don't know it yet. Anyway, he's from a town called Kimberly, but you probably haven't heard of it. It's between Appleton and a town called Kaukauna which is a smelly town you probably haven't heard of either. I say it's smelly because the paper mill there periodically releases this rotten-egg-smelling vapor that could literally choke a horse. (I use the word "literally" loosely here because I've never seen a horse in Appleton... though the smell from Kaukauna may be the reason why.) In fact, whenever you smell rotten eggs in Appleton, people look at each other, say, "Kaukauna" and never blame each other. Anyway, he's a Golden Glove boxer which makes him a little grabby, BUT easily trained. EXAMPLE: He tried to persuade me to go parking after a movie the other night, and when I told him "no" he didn't whine like the average American guy.

Speaking of the average American guy, "Operation Revenge" is off to a good start. For Phase One, we (my friends Sherry, Joy, and I) carefully wrapped Guy's house 1 ½ times with good quality duct tape which of course made the house doors unopenable (if that's not a word, it should be). Then we bribed Sherry's brother to call Guy pretending to be a concerned neighbor and said that it looked like someone was breaking into his girlfriend's car in the driveway. I wish I could've seen Guy frantically trying to pry that screen door open, but I have a pretty vivid imagination. As far as I know, we got away with it 'cause the cops haven't come to my house yet. I wonder what the statute of limitations is on duct taping houses...

Phase II of Operation Revenge is a letter I'm writing "from Guy" to Loser Girl's mom. (Guy has this distinctive backward slanted handwriting and I'm pretty sure I can forge it.) In the letter, I'm going to say that "I'm a respectable man and I believe not only should a guy ask a woman's parents for her hand in marriage, but he should also ask for the parents' permission before he takes a girl to his bed." Then, I'm going to say that "I know the first time can be painful for a woman so I promise to 'take it easy on her.' " Finally, I'm going to say that Guy promises to ask for Loser Girl's hand in marriage before Christmas—just before his 19th birthday and not too young to commit, I'm thinking. The only thing I need to do is find someone who can mail the letter from Madison (that's where Guy is going to college in the fall), and wait 'til he leaves for school to send it off. Like I said before, the worst part about revenge is not being able to see the fallout, but asking questions and possibly getting caught is something I'm not willing to do... but I can't pretend I'm not tempted.

In any event, Guy keeps calling my house and leaving messages for me to call him back. At first, I thought he was calling about the duct tape, but my mom said he was really polite, so I assume not. Plus, he didn't rat me out to my parents which he'd do in a second if he knew anything. Anyway, ignoring him should make him crazy so I'll keep doing it! OH! I also heard some guy (I assume <u>the</u> Guy) came into Hardees looking for me on my night off and Mark (my current boyfriend) was working and none-too-pleased to see him. Anyway, Mark hasn't said anything to me about that incident yet so I guess he's not a big "leg-lifter."

I finished taking driver's ed a couple of weeks ago, so I'm all set to take my road test on my birthday. Yay! At first, I had a really cool teacher who would let me drive through Hardees' drive-through or he'd just go to sleep while I drove around town, but he left and we got an old guy who's fond of the "Blood Runs Red on the Highway" videos. I have to say, watching images of dead and dying teenagers is a real downer when all you want to do is learn how to apply your make-up and drive at the same time. I asked my teacher how to do this, but he had NO sense of humor. Something tells me he's trying to put the fear of God into us, but that's difficult when you're immortal. ☺

I'm glad you liked my roller coaster postcards. The large wooden one is called The American Eagle (which I guess the postcard says on the back). It's the largest wooden roller coaster in the world, which sounds pretty cool, but it occurred to me while the roller coaster car was clicking its way up the first "hill" that they must've stopped making roller coasters out of wood for a reason and maybe riding one wasn't the greatest idea ever.

I must get to bed now. Thank you again for my awesome shirt!

130

Lots of Love,
Marielle

Marielle tip-toed past the dining room table as her brother slept on the other side of the room. The orange couch wasn't short, but Stephen had easily grown three inches since Marielle saw him last and his legs extended over the end. If not comfortable, he was still soundly asleep after a marathon "get to know you again" conversation with their father the night before.

Stephen knew the rules at least as well as Marielle which meant she'd only be responsible for a blanket during his leave. On paper, "company and blanket" didn't seem like a lot of responsibility, but it felt a lot bigger than that, and she could tolerate any of her brother's antics as long as he kept their father company.

Marielle heard voices through the floor until just before 1 a.m., but they hadn't kept her up. She had other issues to ponder and her brother's return gave her time away from the TV to do so. The problem was that she had only saved a little over $200, it was already the end of August, and tickets to Ireland weren't getting any cheaper. She would need another job soon if she planned to buy a ticket in the spring.

"We flew over Ireland on the way to Chicago," Stephen said yesterday, like it was nothing at all.

"What did it look like?" Marielle asked eagerly.

Surprised by his sister's excitement, Stephen was quick to crush it. "It looked like Wisconsin... but a little less flat."

"Really?" Marielle asked, clearly deflated.

"Really. What do you want to go to a Third World country for anyhow?"

Marielle's eyes narrowed. "It's not a Third World country, Stephen!"

He smiled in a self-satisfied way. "Oh, it is. Their economy is like the size of Rhode Island's."

"Where did you hear that?" Marielle asked with full confidence that her brother had never read about the economy of Ireland.

"Everyone knows it."

"No, it's not."

Stephen looked up through fluttering eyelids as he calmly replied, "Yes, it is."

Jeanette laughed in the way she only did with her "Irish Twin" and partner in crime.

"She's obsessed with Ireland," Jeanette explained. "She listens to U2 constantly and she calls her pen pal every other day. What was your last phone bill, Marielle?"

She sighed in response.

"Where's your checkbook?" Jeanette asked, scanning the room.

"I don't know," Marielle replied, involuntarily glancing at a nearby dining room chair.

"It's on the back of that chair!" Anna announced.

Marielle lunged forward, but didn't reach her purse before her brother.

"Let me see here," Stephen said, paging through the checkbook ledger a foot above Marielle's head. "Twenty dollars to *Ireland of the Welcomes*. What the hell is that?" He shared a smile with Jeanette before both laughed.

Marielle didn't respond. She had stopped reaching for the ledger, preoccupied instead with crossing her arms and turning red.

"Ooh, is this it? Thirty-five dollars made out to Mom."

"She's not answering," Anna said, determined to state the obvious.

Stephen raised the checkbook to better make eye contact with Marielle. "How many times did you call Ireland?"

"Only twice," she replied.

In fact, she had called Ireland three times, but on one occasion she spoke to Dermot's father about the Senior Hurling Final since Dermot wasn't home. Speaking to Dermot's father didn't technically count, she decided... even if the phone company said it did.

"How long did you talk?"

"Only 30 minutes total. It's over a dollar a minute."

Stephen chuckled. "Holy crap! So, that's like 10 times more than what you earn in an hour... Wait...," he looked up for the answer, then began laughing with two of his sisters. "Math isn't my subject. Anyway, it's a shitload of money!"

"I don't call all the time," Marielle protested in a vain attempt to make the charge seem more reasonable.

"No, from the looks of it, you only call every pay day. That's pretty funny. So, it takes you two weeks to earn what you blow in a single phone call."

Marielle looked up at her brother's face with impatience. "That's an exaggeration."

"Okay. So, how much do you earn in two weeks?"

"It varies."

"Is it more than $150?" Stephen asked.

Marielle shook her head.

"Okay. So, assuming you earn $100 bucks in two weeks, you blew more than 30% of that in *two* phone calls."

Marielle's eyes helped the top of her brain calculate before she shrugged her shoulders in an "I don't care" manner while trying to ignore the horror of the truth.

"So, how are you gonna get over to Ireland if you can't stop talking to this guy on the phone?" Stephen barely finished his question before the irony of his words sent him into a new bout of laughter which only ceased with mock brotherly concern, and a hand upon Marielle's shoulder. "So, what's so great about this guy?" He turned to smile at Jeanette for a moment. "Are you gonna marry him?" He chuckled briefly before returning to his serious face. "Well, at least we don't have to worry about him getting you pregnant... unless those are some pretty dirty phone calls."

The room erupted in laughter too loud for anyone to hear Marielle's insults or notice her departure—without her purse or her checkbook.

From her room, Marielle could hear her brother read her driver's license.

"One hundred and eighteen pounds. I'm gonna call bullshit on that one. Well, maybe not."

Marielle looked in the mirror. It was possible she had gained weight during the summer. Her Hardees uniform was tighter around the hips for which she credited French fries and limited time to bounce a ball off a plywood board at a nearby tennis court. She began thinking of ways to return to her size seven jeans before the ringing phone demanded her attention.

"Hello?" she asked from the French phone at the top of the stairs.

"Marielle?" a boy asked in a voice remarkably like Guy's.

"Yeah," she replied, immediately wishing she had pretended to be Jeanette.

"Hey, it's Guy," he said as though the party could start now.

"Hey Guy, what's up?" Marielle replied as if she didn't hear the music.

"Well, I haven't talked to you in awhile and I'm about to leave for Madison and I was just wondering if you were free to get some dinner or lunch or something?"

Her eyes closed involuntarily for a moment. "Probably not. I have to go shopping for some new clothes and school supplies."

"When does school start?"

"Tuesday."

"Ha, well, that sucks for you. At least you won't be a sssssophomore anymore," he hissed as if resurrecting an old joke absolved him of his role in flipping off her house.

"Like I said, I'm pretty busy this week. My brother is home from the Army and I'm working a lot."

"Oh, okay," he said, then paused. The music stopped playing for him too. "Well, maybe I could stop by Hardees and—"

"Didn't you do that already?" Marielle asked with waning patience.

"What? No. What are you talking about?" he asked unconvincingly.

"Someone came into Hardees when I wasn't there and asked my boyfriend if I was working."

"No. That wasn't—"

"MARIELLE! Who are you talking to?!" Stephen demanded across the telephone line.

"Jesus, Stephen, get off the phone!" Marielle yelled down the stairs.

"What's your name and what intentions do you have with my sister? Are you the Irish guy? Why aren't you talking?" Stephen asked in rapid succession, not allowing anyone time to respond.

"I'm just a friend," Guy replied.

"That's good," said Stephen, "because I'm home from Germany and I'll beat your ass if you step out of line!"

"Oh my God," Marielle said to the hand that was heading toward her forehead. "Are you done, Stephen?'

"Sure. I'll hang up now," he replied, clicking the zero button on the cordless phone instead of "off." His sister's laughing preceded his own across the otherwise silent line.

"Why don't I just call you sometime this week and see if you're free?" Guy suggested.

Marielle agreed in order to expedite goodbyes, then dropped the handset in a manner for which the French phone was never designed.

"Ah, c'mon! We were just getting started!" Stephen yelled from below before running up the stairs at his father's angry pace. "So, who's this guy?" he asked, following her to her bedroom, but stopping at the doorway.

Marielle pretended to look through her backpack for something important. "No one," she replied.

"Her old boyfriend!" Anna yelled from below.

"What's his name?" Stephen asked over his shoulder.

"Guy," Anna responded.

Stephen chuckled through the word "What?" He turned toward his youngest sister. "The guy's name is Guy? What kind of rich asshole name is that?"

"A rich asshole," Marielle said, giving up on her backpack.

"Is he really rich? How much money does he have? Who broke up with who? Do you think you can make it work?" he asked, leaning against her door frame.

"*He* broke up with *her*," Jeanette clarified from the stairs.

Stephen nodded. "I see. Is that because you wouldn't put out? Because if it is, I'll kick his ass."

"You're just dying to kick somebody's ass, aren't you?" Jeanette noted with amusement.

He looked at her with arms crossed to better push up his larger than average biceps. "I am," he replied. "I really, really am. Do you know someone who needs it?"

"*I* know someone who needs it," Marielle said with feeling.

"Ooh, who?" Stephen asked like an anxious puppy.

Jeanette narrowed her eyes at her sister, but Marielle continued anyway, "Doug, for one."

"What? Why? What did he do?" Stephen looked back and forth between his sisters with concern

"Well—" Marielle began.

"Don't listen to her! She doesn't know what she's talking about!" Jeanette interrupted with too much emotion to sound credible.

"What is it?" Stephen asked Marielle, convinced now that whatever she was about to say was true.

"He's poking a married woman who's got two kids. Her name is Wendy."

"That's bullshit!" Jeanette exclaimed.

"That's not what people up north are saying," Marielle replied confidently.

Jeanette pointed her finger at her sister. "They don't know shit!"

"Really? Well there's only one orange bomber in Kleiner and the last time I checked it was the same car where *you* found lipstick on a cigarette butt in the ash tray."

"I'm gonna kill you!" Jeanette threatened as she attempted to push through the doorway her brother blocked with one arm.

"Hold on, hold on," Stephen said, suddenly calm. "What does Doug say about this?"

Jeanette stopped struggling against her brother. "He said he lent his car to his dad to bring his aunt to the store and his aunt was smoking."

"Oh, so his dad *is* talking to his sister now AND decided to use the orange bomber instead of the truck he always drives or his wife's brand new Toyota? Well, I guess a trip to the store isn't really a trip to the store unless you can worry about the car breaking down on County N."

"Shut up!" Jeanette said, using only half of her brain to speak, and the other half to consider the veracity her sister's words.

"Do you want me to talk to him?" Stephen asked without energy, like the last thing he wanted to do was get in the middle of a domestic dispute.

"What?! Five seconds ago you wanted to kill somebody!" Marielle protested. "I suppose different rules apply when the *guy* is your best friend!"

"What? We're not talking about Guy now." Stephen smiled. "What kind of person names their kid Guy, anyway?" he continued. "It's like naming your daughter 'Chick.' Hey, Guy, come here. Not *you* guy, *that* guy. Actually, bring that chick over here too."

Marielle crossed her arms again as she waited for her brother to stop. It was clear that no real conversation was going to happen with Stephen that day—or possibly *any* day—and she feared his was going to be a long leave.

Stephen still slept on the couch when the mail arrived the next day. Marielle sat at the nearby table, studying a grey-blue aerogramme displaying pictures of the four Irish Province shields on the back and the General Post Office in Dublin on the front. The paper looked too thin to hold an actual letter which explained the warning on the back which read "Enclosures not allowed." Beside the warning, Dermot had written, "No Enclosures! Absolutely Forbidden! Death sentence even! Don't risk it! He who encloses enclosures shall be infested with the fleas of a thousand camels, as decreed by Moses the Great!"

Marielle laughed. Dermot was bold enough to provoke a Postal Service he expected to deliver his letter. She thought about the bald postal worker from months before and wished she had been as bold... or maybe she didn't.

The postmark was smudged, but by now she could spell *Gaillimh*—the Irish word for Galway—in her sleep.

29-Aug- 1988

Marielle! Marielle! Marielle!

I saw this "Airmail letter" and it looked really cool so I took one. Sorry I didn't write much last time - I was in an awful hurry. I hope you're having a great birthday! Oh! By the way, I found (after much searching, threatening, battle, bloodshed, and murder) a pen pal for Shelly. His name is Ronan. He's 16. He's on my hurling team and we're in the same class. SIX other people wanted her too... but I think he's the most suitable. I won't bother with his address. He said he'd write first.

Today, I was in the cinema (Eddie Murphy, Coming to America) and three punks kind of attacked me. Well, my 20 year-old, 6'4" friend came along, and you can guess the rest.

I'm going back to school in one week. When do you go back? I'll be in 5th year, then 6th, and then I go to college. It's called U.C.G. (University College Galway).

Your last letter was great. I must have read it 50 times. After all those things you did to your boyfriend, you would have a special Irish name— Bad Bitch (in a Northern Ireland accent, it sounds even bitchier!) Now, I have loads of friends who are girls but no girlfriends - WEIRD!!?

Today, I went windsurfing. The wind was Force 7-8 (gale force) and I could hardly even stand up - never mind windsurf.

I've decided that when I go to college, I'm going to fly 'across the pond' (<—redneck Irish) to America in my summer holidays and arrive outside your house and start throwing stones at your window. THAT would give you a fright.

This letter's too short - the next one will be l o n g. Well, nothing exciting is happening in Ireland apart from the usual crap. The army found a few hundred IRA mortar bombs. The IRA killed 8 soldiers, a 2-year-old girl, etc., etc...

Wow! These American elections are boring. By the time they finish them, the candidates will be dead.

By the way, you never told me what your parents do—my mom is a French professor at U.C.G. and my dad is a Dean.

Marielle turned over the page.

Ah! More space to write on. Howya! Bejabbers do ya know 'tis three in the mornin'? I do be just in from the disco - dancing, ya know 'tis great craic!! ...Not really when your pen pal is in the U.S. Oh! When you write to me (which WILL be soon, won't it (threat!)) please tell me if it's true that 90% of teenage American girls diet - my friend told me that!

I went to an island called Inis Oirr for a few days. It's only got 50 inhabitants and it's tiny and nobody speaks English. That must sound like crap, but if your Irish is good it's really nice. There are two other islands beside Inis Oirr (in English - Western Island) and there's a castle on one of them called Dún Aengus.

Look, I better go. I'll ring you later... if I get the chance (I might be going away).

Bye! See you in a few years or when you send a video tape.

Lots of Love,
Dermot

"Why is the car in the back yard?" Maria demanded as she stormed through the kitchen and into the dining room.

Marielle jumped as she looked up from Dermot's letter, then realized the question wasn't directed toward her.

"Stephen wake up!"

Maria pushed her son's shoulder back and forth until she could see his eyeballs move to the front of his head. "Why is the car in the back yard?"

"Ah, we had some trouble with the cops last night," he said in a sleepy voice.

"What?!" Maria asked.

Marielle had heard Stephen ask their father if he and Jeanette could go out to the Skyline Club the night before. She had even heard her father reply, "You're an adult now. You don't have to ask me," like he really meant it. "Just let me know when to expect you back. Your mother worries," he said, rolling his eyes at how irrational women were.

Marielle rolled her eyes for a different reason, then wondered if women's reputation for emotional anger was at least in part due to men blaming their feelings on women.

"I said, we were hiding from the cops," Stephen said impatiently, his eyes remaining closed.

"Holy crap!" Marielle said under her breath.

"Stephen, wake up!" his mother demanded.

"I'm awake, Ma," he replied, moving his left elbow toward the ceiling while rubbing his eyes.

"Explain to me exactly what happened last night!"

"Some guy started a fight and I ended it," Stephen said, his arm falling back to his side.

"Where?"

"On the bridge."

The obvious question was why were they on the bridge when the Skyline and their house were on the same side of the river? The second question was why did they have the car if the Skyline was only two blocks away? But no one except their father would ask those kinds of questions.

"Talk to Dad. He knows all about it. He thought the best place for the car was behind the garage."

Stephen rolled toward the window, indicating the conversation was over.

Maria's shocked expression turned toward her daughter for an ally.

"That's insane," Marielle replied as she released the hand that smothered a smile.

Maria had three choices: she could either challenge her son; go back to work to challenge her husband; or press Jeanette for more information. Marielle knew the direction she was about to follow.

"What happened last night?!" Maria demanded as they entered Jeanette's room.

Marielle and Jeanette wore matching red and white candy-striped flannel nightgowns, but Marielle looked far more pious in hers.

Jeanette lifted her head an inch off the pillow before yawning a response. "This guy pushed past Stephen at the club and Stephen asked him if he had a problem. The guy said no, but ended up telling his friend who was almost as big as Stephen. The friend came over and said he heard Stephen had a problem and this was their hangout. He asked

Stephen if he went to Lawrence University and Stephen got CRAZY and started poking the guy in the chest as the guy started walking backward. He said he would kill his college punk ass with his bare hands and they could go outside if he had a problem with it. The guy walked away, but they must've followed us outside 'cause they pulled up next to us in the right lane while we were waiting to turn left. That's when the driver rolled down his window and said something we couldn't hear, then he flipped Stephen off and peeled out toward the bridge. Stephen turned right from the left lane and punched it. He passed the guy's Beretta, and turned sideways, blocking both lanes."

"Oh my God!" Marielle said, but only because she never thought their sedan could out accelerate a Beretta.

"What were *you* doing?" Maria asked.

"I was praying," Jeanette said with feeling while sitting up. "I was sure Stephen would either drive off the bridge or the other car was going to hit us on *my* side. So, Stephen starts pounding on the hood of this guy's car and there are four guys inside, but no one will get out, which I completely understand because Stephen was going ape shit! Anyway, the driver still had his window down and Stephen pulled him through it."

Maria exclaimed, but Marielle only shook her head. It was poetic justice for not wearing a seat belt.

"Stephen punched the guy so hard that he landed in the oncoming lane."

Maria placed her hand over her mouth, then released it to ask, "Were there cars coming?"

Jeanette shook her head. "No. Not on that side, but there were one or two cars stopped behind the Beretta. I think they were also from the club.

Anyway, one car behind us did a youie and I was sure they were going back to the club to call the cops so I told Stephen to leave the guy alone and come back to the car. He did and we did a youie too, then went up the driveway and tried to get into the garage, but there was too much crap inside so Dad said to hide the car in the back yard."

Maria looked to the side, seemingly in order to calculate the distance between the house and the garage.

"Didn't they see you come up the driveway?" Marielle asked.

"No," Jeanette replied. "We looked in the rear view mirror before we turned and we couldn't see them, so we assumed they couldn't see us either, but later on we saw a cop car drive slowly down Oneida Street. So, they must've thought we were close by."

"What did your father say about this?" Maria asked, clearly hoping for some anger or at least a dash of retribution.

"He said we'd talk about it in the morning. So, I went to bed, but I think Stephen stayed up and talked to him the rest of the night."

"Well, I need to go back to work now, but we'll discuss it when I get home," Maria promised, exchanging a look of disapproval with Marielle.

***

"Hey, Ma. What's up with you?" Stephen asked, arms crossed as he reclined on the loveseat. He smiled brightly at his mother while she ate dinner alone at the dining room table.

"She's not talking to us," Jack remarked from the couch, glancing coyly at his son over his left shoulder before addressing his wife. "Hey, Maria. What's for dinner?" he asked.

His wife's eyes shifted between the windows and her bowl without responding.

"Hey, Ma, any chance you could whip up some homemade lasagna?" Stephen asked.

"Ooh, or some *Bunya Calda?*" Jack laughed before leaning forward to drink his beer. "I'd hate to drink my dinner tonight, but she's giving me no other choice. Do you want a beer, son?"

"He's not legal!" Maria protested, finally turning toward the living room with the most irrelevant sentence she could manage.

Stephen scoffed in reply. "Ma, I've been drinking since middle school."

"What?!" she yelled more than asked.

"I'm just joking." He turned to his father before continuing. "It could've been elementary school. When did I start serving Mass?"

"You expect *me* to know that?" Jack asked.

Both laughed at the absurdity of the question. Church wasn't Jack's area.

"I raised you better than this!" Maria erupted. "The Army was supposed to teach you discipline, but you come back here acting like a hoodlum!"

Marielle sat in the lonely chair in front of the TV, wondering why her mother would challenge both her husband and her son if she wasn't possessed by either an angel or the devil. Then, she wondered how old a spirit needed to be to use the word "hoodlum."

"I like to think that I had discipline *before* I went into the service," Stephen replied. "The Army taught me the futility of that."

Good word, Marielle thought, looking up from the disappointing class schedule she received that afternoon.

"Do you want something to eat?" Maria asked Marielle as though the loudness of her thoughts had gotten her mother's attention.

Marielle looked nervously between her mother and both men. "I'm good for now, Mom, thanks."

"Do *you* want something to eat?" Maria finally asked the men.

"No, thanks. I'm not hungry anymore," Jack replied. "Maybe if you had asked me ten minutes ago..."

"I filled up on junk, but thanks," Stephen added. "Wanna Pop Tart, Dad? It takes away the hunger pangs."

"Only if they come in beer flavor."

"I'll run to the bar to check... or maybe the Skyline."

Maria narrowed her eyes, finished her red broth soup, then walked away from the table without clearing her bowl.

Marielle looked at the dish twice to confirm she had seen this correctly.

"Ahhhhh, c'mon. Where ya goin'?" Jack called playfully as his wife walked upstairs.

After the bedroom door closed, Stephen sighed with finality as he pushed himself up. "Marielle, what do you say we take a ride to Hardees?"

She nodded.

"Dad, would you like a roast beef sandwich?" Stephen asked.

"Sure. Let me give you some money."

Stephen raised his hand. "No, no, I got it. Can we take your truck? The car is still behind the garage."

A few minutes later, the Ranger sat beside the Hardees drive-through intercom.

"Well, I'm not sure if I would like fries with that. What did you say your name was?" Stephen asked the speaker using his seductive voice.

"Stop, Stephen!" Marielle demanded.

After a pause, the girl responded, "Tara."

"Well, Tara, do *you* recommend the fries?"

"Uh, yeah, sure."

"Did you make them yourself... in hot oil?"

"Nooo." She lingered too long on the vowel to sound mature to anyone but Stephen.

"What are they wearing right now? Are they naked with a sprinkling of salt?"

"Stephen! Leave her alone. She's *my* age!" Marielle said, slapping him on the arm.

"Sorry?" Tara asked.

"I said I think I'll pass on the fries. By the way, how old are you?"

"I'm 15," Tara answered without requisite caution.

Stephen looked up at the roof of the truck. "Oh, man," he said, cupping his hand on his mouth in the direction of his sister. "I thought she was older than that."

Marielle widened her eyes as far as they could naturally go while wondering if she could get out and walk home without making a scene. "You could've just asked me! I know everyone who works here," she said.

"Oh, right," he laughed.

"Will that be all?" the speaker asked.

"Ah, yes," Stephen said, adopting an air of professionalism. "That will be all, thank you."

Marielle continued to cast parental eyes at her brother.

"That was pretty bad, wasn't it?" he asked, still amused with himself. "I don't think I want to go up to that window now."

Marielle looked sideways at her brother. "You don't have a choice," she said, but she knew he was the kind of person who created choices.

Just then, Stephen shifted into first gear, then pointed the truck toward the parking lot.

"What are you doing, Stephen? You can't just leave!"

"Hold your horses," he replied, abruptly stopping and shifting into reverse before re-entering the drive-through lane, truck bed first.

"Are you kidding me? We can't go through backwards!" she said as the truck did just that.

"Who says? Besides, I shouldn't have to face Tara after asking all of those embarrassing questions," he reasoned.

"Stop! Really! I mean it!" Marielle said, holding the handle of a door she knew she wouldn't open.

"Oh, hi Marielle, what are you doing?" Tara asked after looking from the back to the front of the truck.

"Hi. I just made the mistake of getting into a vehicle with my brother. His name is Stephen. He just got out of prison."

"Really?" Tara asked with alarm.

"Yeah—"

"No!" Stephen interrupted.

"Don't listen to him. He's drunk," Marielle explained. "He always drives backwards and tries to pick up minors when he drinks too much. I'm just thankful you're not a little boy like—"

"Marielle! That's enough!" Stephen yelled, then leaned past his sister to make eye contact with Tara. "She's just joking. How much do we owe you?"

"Uh, seven dollars and fifty-three cents," Tara replied, confused by the sibling interaction.

"Here's ten," Stephen said, assuming a commanding "adult in the room" tone.

Marielle smarted. She had probably gone too far, but it was Stephen who made it a competition. If she had it to do all over again, she would've said he assaulted small farm animals rather than boys, but the latter just popped out. It was probably CNN's fault.

"Uh-oh. We should probably get something for Jeanette too," Stephen said after Tara closed the window.

"You wanna change your order now? After we've already paid? While we're sitting backwards in a drive-through? With a girl who thinks you're a drunken pedophile?" Marielle finally began to laugh, bringing her brother with her.

"Well, when you put it like that, she can probably eat Mom's soup."

"Yeah, I'll stash the wrappers in the garbage can in the garage before she gets home from work. As long as you and Dad don't say anything, we're home free."

Stephen looked at his sister in a whole new way. She had changed since he left for the Army, and it was clear he didn't hate all of the changes.

Chapter Eleven

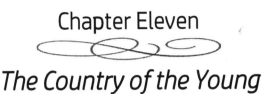

The Country of the Young

—W.B. Yeats – He thinks of his Past Greatness when a Part of the Constellations of Heaven

"This is crap, Shelly!" Marielle protested one last time before she'd let the subject rest.

"I know, but there's nothing we can do about it. We're on two different tracks. There's no way we'll have the same lunch hour our last two years."

Shelly was right and Marielle knew it. She was just in denial about the major force that would be the death knell of their friendship. Shelly was on a vocational track and Marielle was college prep. Whether it was by design or by accident, there was no way to sync the schedules of kids with marketing projects to those taking Advanced Algebra.

"Yeah, I know. It just sucks," Marielle said with defeat, reprimanding herself silently for not having scheduled classes through lunch like last year.

"Well, I'm sure you'll find someone to sit with," Shelly consoled.

Marielle stiffened. Was the reason for her irritation so transparent? She wanted to deny it, but she respected her friend too much. If she and Shelly were on two different tracks, it was important to leave the station on good terms.

"Thanks, Shelly. I guess I'll see you in the halls."

"And in Pep Club," Shelly comforted. "And I might even pass you in the Commons on my way out. What are you wearing tomorrow?"

"Just a polo shirt and jeans, although I was thinking of wearing a mock turtleneck sweater my sister said I could borrow. I'll have to see how warm it is. What are you wearing?"

"I haven't decided yet, but probably a new sweater and my Guess jeans."

"The light ones?"

"No, the acid washed ones. They're new."

Marielle rolled her eyes. *It must be hard to decide between* two *pairs*

145

of $50 jeans, she thought, then regretted. She was turning her rich wrath on her poor friend. It was probably time to end the call.

Shelly hadn't asked yet about Mark and it was just as well. He was dead to her, and the sooner people stopped asking about him, the sooner she could bury him.

The next day, Jeanette drove Marielle up Appleton East High School's semi-circular driveway. A large—and mostly windowless—three-story brick silo dominated the façade. It also held most of the academic classrooms and doubled as a tornado-proof nuclear fallout shelter. The main entrance rested outside the safety of the silo, within the two-story flat façade on the left.

Kids streamed through all school entrances, allowing traffic to move efficiently despite the line of teachers parking in their designated spots along the driveway.

"Thanks," Marielle said to her sister before closing the door and stepping backward onto the curb.

Jeanette pulled away as Marielle stared at a car which reversed from, then entered into the same parking spot three times without changing either its angle or its distance to surrounding cars. After identifying the driver, she walked slightly uphill to a line of eight glass doors.

A year after entering East for the first time as a student, the school still awed Marielle. The wooden counter within the glass-fronted office to her left extended at least 30 feet. Beyond it, the main hall curved to the right at an angle necessitated by its proximity to the silo. The angle allowed visitors to view the polished black granite Y-shaped staircase between the auditorium's main doors, while laying open the vastness of the Commons farther ahead.

This morning, the staircase gleamed only slightly brighter than the freshly buffed floors whose darkness was easily balanced by the walls and the soaring ceiling above. In fact, a student could easily make use of sunglasses if walking as far as the Commons whose exterior wall of windows illuminated the room in all four seasons and shined off the hallway's off-white and pastel tiled surface.

Marielle took pains to enter East through the main entrance every day to remind herself that kids mattered here—their safety, their education, their happiness, and their dignity were valued at Appleton East. She would never say it out loud, but she loved this place. She loved the tornado-proof silo, the principal, the staff, and most of the teachers. If it weren't for interacting with other teenagers, high school would have been perfect.

She walked up the right side of the granite stairs as the first bell rang. She had five minutes to make it to homeroom, but it was the same homeroom she had last year, and it would be the same homeroom next year. She was sure she could find homeroom blindfolded and shackled in less than five minutes. Next year, she might be able to make it backwards through an obstacle course and still have time to snarl at the girl sitting in front of her before the tardy bell rang.

Three hellos into the hallway, she began noticing pockets of fresh faces and felt an unexpected pang of sadness. There was no chance of running into Guy or any of his classmates this year. The Class of 1988 had been replaced by the Class of 1991—boys and girls who looked much younger than Marielle remembered her classmates looking a year ago. New seniors walked tall and proud near sophomores who looked up to them. Marielle rolled her eyes. The Class of 1989 was in charge this year, but they could never measure up to the class that went before them—with or without a senior named Guy.

***

"She did it again, Shelly! I'm going to kill her!" Marielle said to the back of Shelly's head.

Shelly smiled, turning away from her gray locker which rested inside the core of the silo. "Who's that?" she asked.

"Laurie Rich. I sat down in homeroom and she flipped her hair onto my desk and just let it lay there. I stabbed it with my pencil until Mr. King asked her to sit up properly. Then, just the tips of her hair invaded my air space, but I stabbed at them with my eyes."

"Why don't you ask Mr. King to move you?"

"We're in alphabetical order, just like last year. HOW is a person named Richter supposed to get away from a cheerleader named Rich in a Q to T homeroom with a teacher who loves alphabetical order?"

Shelly knew Marielle's rant would end soon so she just smiled as they walked around the second floor.

"I'm going to start calling it 'hell room' instead of homeroom!" Marielle announced as they stopped in front of Shelly's next class.

"Is your class this way?" Shelly asked, knowing it wasn't.

Marielle looked up, startled. "No, it isn't. I'll see you later!" she called, while running toward the silo's second floor exit.

147

Marielle made it through the classroom doorway as the second bell rang, and in any other class it would have been too late to pick a good seat, but this was the only stadium-style classroom in the school and at any given hour on any given day, only 20 of the 50 available seats would ever be filled.

"*Guten tag*, Marielle," the middle-aged, auburn-haired instructor said more as a greeting than a reprimand.

"*Guten tag, Frau*," Marielle said out of breath as she stepped up to the first row.

"*Sitzen Sie hier, bitte*," Frau said, more for practice than as a direction since she indicated the seat where Marielle had always sat in her class.

"*Guten tag*, Marielle," a boy seductively whispered from the second row as Marielle pulled out her chair, causing her to turn more from annoyance than curiosity. As she stared eye to eye with the speaker, she recalled seeing him once or twice at the mall.

In truth, she had seen thousands of people at the Fox River Mall, but it wasn't every day you saw a freckle-faced skater with a red Afro lusting after a sporting goods store mannequin. In his defense, boys did stupid things when surrounded by other boys, and in that outfit, the mannequin might've been asking for it.

Marielle narrowed her eyes at the boy, but didn't respond. There would be time—far too much time—for introductions.

"Hey," she whispered genially to the girl to her left while nudging her elbow.

The short blonde-haired girl smiled. "Hey, Marielle."

She had known Celia since her first year in Appleton, but they had rarely spoken before taking German together. Marielle was about to ask her a question before the thundering Frau continued.

"*Ich heiße Frau Schaefer und ich werde Ihre Deutschlehrerin...*"

Marielle sighed. It was too early in the morning for German.

After twenty minutes and a page full of halfhearted notes, she turned to the notebook page which concealed her schedule.

0745-0800 Homeroom
0800-0815 German
0815-0900 Creative Writing
0905-0950 Easterners
0955-1035 Wind Symphony

1040-1125 American History
1130-1215 Advanced Algebra
1220-1:05 Lunch – B Period
1:10-1:55 Chemistry
2:00-2:45 Women's Choir
2:50-3:35 Physical Education

She had six classes between now and lunch, and somehow it wasn't enough time to determine where to sit in the Commons... and not a lot of learning would take place until she did.

"Excuse me, *Frau*," the skater interrupted.

"Uh, yes?" Frau responded, turning away from the blackboard.

"You just said that the majority of Germans speak English."

"Yes?" Frau repeated, eager to get to the point.

The skater leaned back on his chair, wearing a smirk. "Can you tell me why we're wasting our time learning German if we can just speak English when we get there?"

Frau's face immediately turned red, or maybe it had always been red. "Mr. Fitzgerald, if you prefer to take another class, then by all means do."

"No, ma'am. I just thought it was an important point, but you can carry on now," he said, pushing his fingertips in Frau's direction.

Marielle smiled despite a strong urge to judge. If the enemy of learning was boredom, there would be plenty of learning in this class.

After Advanced Algebra, Marielle took care and abundant time in exchanging folders and notebooks inside her locker. She had decided to wait for people and groups to establish themselves in the Commons before arriving so she could choose where to sit instead of sitting first and risking the wrong people, or—worse—*no people* sitting beside her.

Of course, arriving late presented its own risks such as scanning the area for friendly faces longer than was dignified, but she had a plan for that as well. She would skim the tables carelessly as she passed them on the way to the school store. While inside the store, she would pretend to look at new logo items near the windows while really studying the seating arrangement of the Commons. Once she determined who sat where, she would make her move.

Tables, joined end to end, extended from the hallway to the windows like long bony fingers. Halfway down the hallway she noticed the "Closed" sign on the school store's door. She hesitated before continuing

149

forward. She would pretend to read the hours of operation, then turn around in mock disappointment. It wasn't a great plan, but it bought her time for a real one.

As she approached the store, a familiar voice called her name from halfway down the last table. Marielle shielded her eyes from the light long enough to see Sherry standing beside a seated Joy. She turned to walk toward Sherry a moment before the tardy bell caused her to jump.

"I didn't know you had B Period," Marielle said with too much relief to appear cool.

"I don't," Sherry replied. "I'm late. I just needed to borrow money from Joy."

"Ah," Marielle said, barely maintaining her smile as her head nodded.

Marielle genuinely liked Sherry, and she tolerated Joy because they were a package deal. Just the same, she had no plans to waste lunch period every day sitting beside a short, round girl who permed, highlighted, and curled her hair into a split-ended rebellion. She also couldn't imagine eating lunch to the dulcet tones of "OH MY GOD!" declared for information and events that didn't include car crashes or natural disasters.

Marielle continued to stand while scanning the Commons, using Sherry's proximity as a cool shield until she departed with a "see ya later."

"Well, aren't you going to sit down?" Joy asked through cracked makeup on a raised forehead. Sherry's departure had left a vacancy beside Joy that needed filling.

Marielle pretended to be oblivious, but deep down she knew her independence expired as soon as she saw Joy's face.

"Sorry, I thought Shelly said she had B Period, and I was trying to find her," Marielle lied, still scanning the distance for effect as she sat down.

"She's in A Period," a thin, pale boy with dark, curly hair said from across the table. "I saw her leaving when I walked into the Commons."

"Oh, hi, Tom," Marielle replied, relieved to see someone from band nearby even if he was an oboe and, therefore, unknowable.

Tom had the ability to blend into most crowds, but his proximity to Joy surprised Marielle. She turned to her left, finding the answer in other members of the Quiz Bowl Team eating their lunches. There was no reason to say hello to the team since they were distanced by their books, and too preoccupied to engage either Marielle or one another in conversation. Even the sandwiches they held near their lips seemed an uninvited distraction. With only one exception, they sat upright and against the table, and that exception was Tom. His chair sat away from the table, allowing him to rest the ankle of one leg on the knee of the other. He held a book, like the other members of his team, but his slouching allowed the book to rest on his stomach, giving one the impression that the book enhanced his life instead of separating him from it.

"You know my cousin, Joel, right?" Joy asked, indicating the boy across the table and technically beside Tom, though a missing chair stood between them.

The word "know" was a stretch. Marielle *knew* Joy had a cousin at East named Joel and that boy sat in the back row of her German class. She also *knew* Joy called Joel to get the duct tape they used to wrap Guy's house during the summer. Marielle told Joy she would pay Joel back, but Joy brushed away the thought. For whatever reason, he had massive quantities of duct tape he would never use. And that was all Marielle really *knew* about Joel.

"Hi," Marielle said tentatively, suddenly realizing that owing people you barely knew was only tolerable until you met them.

Joel raised his right hand an inch from the table where an empty candy bar wrapper sat, but he didn't respond. This wasn't unusual for boys with Doc Martins, studded belts, and Mohawks, Marielle thought, even though she suspected residual anger from the loss of his duct tape.

Although officially acquaintances for only 20 seconds, there were a lot of things Marielle didn't understand about Joel and the list was growing rapidly: why he was a collector of duct tape; why he sat with a cousin who had no problem taking his things; why he sat in the Commons at all, rather than standing at the smoking doors like everyone else who wore a similar outfit; and why he wore a rebellious haircut which sat idle to the side instead of defying gravity in its "natural" state?

"Are we having a Pep Club meeting tonight?" Joy asked Marielle with more excitement than the question merited.

"No. We'll have them every Thursday so we can decorate the gym in time for the games, but not so soon that people tear down the posters."

"Ah," said Joy, clearly not listening after the word "no." A good-looking boy who walked behind Tom and Joel had engaged her laser-like focus. She exchanged nudges with the girl to her right, and after an "I know, right?", a shiver, and an "oh my God," she turned back to Marielle. "Do we have a sponsor yet?" she asked.

"We" was a reach for Joy since she was the type of volunteer who only attended meetings and decorated for dances until Homecoming. Marielle wanted to ban people like her the year before, but the President at the time wisely argued that they needed seasonal workers to pull off the bigger events. Since then, people like Joy still made Marielle angry, but a lot less so than people who only showed up for the yearbook photo.

"No, but Mrs. Carpenter said we can use her room for our meetings until we find one."

"Cool," Joy replied before returning to her assessment of the boy who now stood outside the windows.

Marielle noticed the boy twirling his car keys around his finger before deciding she hated him—or maybe she just hated that he had his license and she didn't. It technically wasn't the boy's fault that the DMV didn't know how to schedule road tests, but she still regarded the careless twirling of keys as a call to arms.

"Is your gorgeous brother still home?" Joy asked Marielle suddenly as the boy walked away.

"No, he left last weekend," she replied with feigned patience.

"Ah, that sucks," Joy said, still studying the window.

"That depends on whether you like having your brother assault your boyfriend and drive backwards through your workplace."

"Yeah," Joy said, lost in a hormonal trance.

Marielle shook her head before opening the German notebook she forgot to leave in her locker and began writing a letter to Dermot. She didn't technically owe him one, but writing now served as a diversion from awkward conversation and the equally awkward pauses in the only type of discussion which might result from sitting with kids she either barely knew or barely liked.

She could technically move to another table, but not without provoking Joy's wrath, and although not the most clever adversary, Joy had a lot of time for wrath. More importantly, there was no table in the vast open space of the Commons that held kids with whom she felt more comfortable. Marielle's biggest mistake heretofore was preferring the company of vocational kids while aspiring to be college prep.

"You didn't bring lunch?" Joy asked Marielle, finally attentive to her own table.

"No, I forgot."

"Bummer. You want money for the vending machines?" she asked.

Marielle shook her head. "No, I'm good. Thanks."

Tom glanced at her before returning to his book.

"Do you have Chemistry with Farr or Schmidt?" Joy asked, spying Marielle's yellow notebook labeled in capital letters.

"Ah, Schmidt," she replied. "What about you?"

"We have Farr. I didn't understand a thing he said this morning. Did you, Tom?"

"I understood a few things," Tom replied to his book.

"Of course you did! You could probably *teach* that class," Joy mocked.

Tom raised, then lowered his right shoulder, but didn't look up.

Joel took a deep breath and glanced away before he spoke. "I can deal with the lectures just fine. It's the labs I dread." He shook his head with an angry intensity. "I just want to SIT in my seat, TAKE notes, and be left ALONE! I don't want to choose a partner, grab a bib, and start mixing things. If he STICKS with lectures, I'll be fine." Joel dropped his right hand before leaning back in his chair with finality.

Marielle took a moment to absorb the shock wave of emotion elicited by science labs, then composed herself enough to say, "Yeah, it's like going to church before Easter. Suddenly, zoning-out and staring at ceiling fans isn't good enough. You have to stand and kneel every three minutes while reading a script that makes you sound like an asshole."

Tom smiled at his book. He had thoughts he had no plans to share, and that was the way with oboes, but his unwillingness to make eye contact gave Marielle the opportunity to study him without detection.

Tom wore a white Polo shirt and raspberry-colored Levis just like a German exchange student, but they looked cooler on Tom—not because he didn't know that raspberry jeans weren't in style, but because he didn't care. Marielle couldn't see his shoes under the table, but she was pretty sure they were boat shoes. Half of the male boat-shoe-wearers at East didn't wear socks in an ode to Don Johnson, but Tom wasn't a Don-Johnson-worshipping kind of guy.

He sat on a canary yellow plastic chair which highlighted his outfit nicely. The pastel green and blue chairs of the same style didn't clash, per se, but they sat at the wrong end of the light spectrum for today's attire. Since Tom belonged to a rare breed of brainiac who obsessed over his appearance, Marielle wondered if he chose his chair based upon its color. Scanning the room, she found 27 other yellow chairs along their table, but only 21 across the remainder of the Commons.

"The store is open," Joel said, his head jerking to dislodge a large piece of blond Mohawk from his round-rimmed glasses.

It took a moment for Marielle to appreciate the comment was directed toward her since the desire to go was never genuine. Her eyes shifted toward Joel before she turned around to eye the store windows. "Oh, okay, thanks," she replied, but she made no move to stand.

Joel narrowed his eyebrows, then looked down at his drawing.

Marielle imagined having conversations with each group assembled at each table, but she knew she would find each of them equally uncomfortable. She knew enough about science to engage a brainiac, and enough about boys and nail polish to speak with the cheerleaders. She watched enough football and NASCAR to interest a jock, and she listened to enough new age music to have a remotely interesting discussion with a Goth. In fact, she was fragments of each of these tables, but she belonged to all and none of them. She would never belong to a winning Quiz Bowl Team or make a basket in an important game. She'd never tell off a teacher, then walk outside to smoke a cigarette while the principal was called and suspension papers were organized. She was part of the filler group of students who would be famous or infamous for nothing.

"So, tell me what you think about this," Joy said, uncertain whether to address Marielle or Joel. "I was riding my moped to work and a blue jay flew across the road in front of me. Then, on my way home, a blue jay flew in front of me again in the same spot. What do you think that means?" She glanced rapidly between Marielle and Joel.

"That a bird has a nest on the other side of the road," Joel replied dismissively while Marielle merely shrugged her shoulders.

"I think it's a sign from Knut," Joy proclaimed, like she just found evidence of alien life.

Marielle's eyebrows narrowed. "Why do you think that?"

"Because he had blue eyes and I saw a blue jay during his burial."

"He was Dutch!" Marielle protested.

"And you weren't at his burial," added Joel.

"No, but I saw a blue jay at about the same time *as* his burial."

"Are you sure?" Marielle asked. "I didn't know he was dead until a week after the funeral."

Joy's mouth opened seconds before she spoke. "You don't believe in signs?" she asked, as though she couldn't believe someone who went to

154

church wouldn't.

"No, I do," replied Marielle matter-of-factly, "but I'd think Knut would be more likely to give a sign to someone he actually knew."

"What do you mean?" asked Joy with exasperation. "He and I were friends!"

"You mean in middle school?" Marielle asked, willing to concede a relationship existed before she knew either of them.

"No. I went with him to see *The Last Emperor* last year."

"That was a school field trip!" Joel said impatiently. "You weren't happy about sitting next to him and you called him a weirdo."

"Wha—," Joy began to say, knowing she was caught, but a girl asking for money released her.

Marielle shook her head as she and Joel exchanged a smile. This afternoon, between bus transfers, she would check out a new book at the library—this one on mental disorders. She looked down at what was turning out to be a disappointing letter before Joel reading his Coke can distracted her.

"Why do you think they add caramel color to pop?" he asked.

"To make it more appealing, I imagine," she replied.

His eyebrows furrowed. "Why would brown sugar water be more appealing than clear sugar water?"

"Hmm. Good point. Maybe it's the color that gives it that zip."

He grinned slightly. "You know, I believe that. Yellow #3 makes me CRAZY!"

"Red #2 used to be lethal," Marielle said with enthusiasm.

"No, it didn't," Tom retorted, looking up from his book.

"That's why they stopped making red M&Ms in the '60s," said Marielle, losing confidence at the end of her sentence.

Tom shook his head. "The stoppage was brought about by hysteria."

"What *are* you, a teacher?" Joy scoffed, interrupting her own conversation to interrupt theirs.

Tom leveled his eyes at her. "No, I'm just someone who's read more books than you."

"Woe-hoe!" Marielle said, more to herself than anyone else. She had never seen a conflict develop so quickly between two sober people.

"Dis!" said Joel leaning forward, and ignoring his cousin's scowl.

The table remained quiet for a moment, awaiting a rebuttal from Joy that didn't materialize.

"Hey, will you conjugate 'facere' for me again?" Joel asked Tom admiringly. They apparently had a past about which Marielle knew nothing.

"Of course," said Tom with a coy smile.

"Facio, Facis, Facit—"

"Wait, wait, wait, stop!" Joel said, his face trembling with laughter while he held his stomach. A few seconds later, he said to the ceiling, "Fauk-it. I just love that one!"

Tom smiled broadly as he returned his attention to his book.

"What *is* that word?" Joy asked.

"Latin," Marielle replied, amused by the boys, but not laughing. She had heard far too many versions of the word "fuck" to associate it with fun or originality.

Joy sighed.

"I guess that's another book you haven't read," said Joel.

9 /6 /1988 Tuesday

Dear Dermot,

I'm so jealous! I've been back in school for a week and your first day was yesterday! AUGH! I hope your last week of vacation wasn't riddled with guilt for being a slacker while your friend "across the pond" was working her butt off in a fluorescent-lit hell (I can't decide if that would be work or school). In any event, it's a gross exaggeration, but you should still feel guilty... or did I tell you not to feel guilty? In any event, don't listen to me... about the first part... the not feeling guilty part... you're supposed to feel guilty. Am I making you crazy yet?

Speaking of crazy, I'm in Chemistry class right now and I have some time 'cause my teacher is rearranging her chalk (she's got Obsessive Compulsive Disorder [I diagnosed her myself after watching her park her car] and since I spread this rumor, everyone messes with the precise organization of her chalkboard tray when she's not in the room which gives us an extra 10 minutes to talk every time she comes in. You may be wondering why she doesn't yell at us, but then she'd have to admit she has a problem and I'm betting she's in denial. Also, sending someone to the principal's office for chalk rearranging would make her look like the crazy woman she is. So, she's stuck putting up with us. You may think we're mean, but we're really just trying to make her appreciate she's got a problem... and isn't that God's work?).

Anyway, I tried to write to you last week, but I was in a bad mood and I would have written to you last period (during lunch [yes, I have lunch this year!]) but everyone was complaining about their summer jobs and it was too funny to stop listening.

   I left Chemistry and I'm in Women's Choir now. Our teacher is droning on about musical theory and I'm pretending to take notes.

My friend Joel said he was promised a job as a cashier at a grocery store near school, but when he arrived for work they put him behind the meat counter. This was fine except there were two other guys working there and one was missing a hand while the other was missing a finger (no lie). He said the missing hand guy was named "Lucky" and he was too surprised to catch the other one's name. Anyway, he quit 30 seconds after they turned on the meat grinder and told him to try his "hand" at it. This put my "brother assaulting my supervisor" story to shame which was very disappointing (that my story didn't win, not that my brother assaulted my supervisor). Did I tell you this story yet? Hmmm.

Well, I think I told you I was dating someone from work and that he was a nice (atypical) American guy, right? Well, the only part about that last sentence that's true is that I work with him, and he's American.

I'm at home now, but I need to leave for work soon

I found out at the end of last week that he's been telling everyone at work that I'm having sex with him which is COMPLETELY untrue!! I was so upset when I heard this that I told my brother Stephen who was on leave from the Army. I didn't think Stephen was paying attention because he didn't look up at me or respond at all. He just put his shoes on and left the house (without the car), and he didn't return for about a half-hour. When he got back, he told me I didn't need to worry about Mark anymore. When I asked him why, he said, "Because I just pulled him over the counter at Hardees and threatened to kill him if he went near you or said anything about you again!" This got me thinking a few things:

1) *So much for Mark being a Golden Glove,*
2) *How am I going to work at Hardees again?, and*
3) *I need to rethink the circumstances under which I confide in Stephen*

in the future.

Don't get me wrong, I always knew my brother was dangerous, but only in a hollow-tipped Intercontinental Ballistic Missile sort of way. Now, I've re-categorized him as the "nuclear option"–only to be used in case of extreme bodily threat.

You may be thinking this kind of craziness runs in my family, but I actually canceled Phase II of "Operation Revenge." I realized that sending a letter to Guy's "in-laws" was technically "bearing false witness" and as sins go, breaking a commandment is a biggy, and Guy is definitely not worth losing my soul over.

Gotta run to work now

OK. I'm back. Quick, eh? ☺

The last time I talked to Guy, I asked him to stop calling my house and he sounded so hurt that I actually felt guilty for about 30 seconds, but then I got over it. Anyway, as long as he stops contacting me and lying about me, we'll call it even. Well, it's not really even, but I'm satisfied knowing I could reduce him to a slobbering mass of humanity at any time... which is not meant to sound arrogant, but might.

I need to go to bed now. I promise to finish this tomorrow at school.

Anyway, back to Mark, I was scheduled to work with him this past weekend and I was a little nervous about showing up, but no one said anything about my brother's little outburst (thank God!), and Mark didn't show up either which means he coincidentally got sick or proves my theory that he's a—

Marielle looked up at Tom. "How do you spell wuss?" she asked.

Tom placed his finger against a passage in his book before looking up. "Pardon?"

"Wuss. How do you spell it? One S or two?"

Tom considered the question for a moment, then said, "The proper masculine form would be one S."

"Wouldn't the usage make it neuter?" she asked, smiling.

"It ends in US. So, assuming it's of Latin origin, it's a second declension noun which would be masculine."

Marielle placed the pencil eraser against her mouth, then said, "Ah, interesting" in mock intellectual tones.

Tom smiled before returning to his reading.

Wus (a vulgar term the guys here use which is a combination of the words "wimp" and "pus..." well, another name for a cat. It's the cowardly equivalent of a double negative—which in this case doesn't make a positive).

So, I've tried to avoid talking about this because it makes me so angry, but to address the most important problem in recent history (no exaggeration!), I arrived at the DMV (Department of Motor Vehicles) with my mom on my birthday and they informed me that the appointment I thought I had made for that day was actually made for the day before and I couldn't take my driver's test until I made a new appointment. My mom was really irritated 'cause she had taken off of work to bring me there, and she saw this as a sign of my irresponsible nature. In my own defense though, I gotta think the DMV made a mistake! I mean, what are the chances I would tell them that my birthday was on the wrong day? After all, I'm pretty used to it being on the same date every year.

Anyway, the worst part is that I was fairly cocky when I left school for my test. When my Chemistry lab partner asked where I was going, I said, "To get my license," to which she responded in her usual condescending way, "You mean to take your test," and I replied, "No, I was right the first time." So, I looked like a real dumbass coming to school the next day without a license... which my snotty lab partner took as proof that I failed my test... and I couldn't convince her otherwise. Bitch.

Marielle spied her lab partner across the Commons. Michelle Morris hung out with the trendy girls who taped the tags from their trendy clothes inside their lockers.

Before Marielle returned to her letter, Tom caught her eye, staring at her as she stared at Michelle. Marielle quickly turned her expression into a pleasant one, but Tom had already seen the hate in her eyes, and he was about to say something when a girl walked up to him, asking if she could get his opinion on something.

Anyway, I'd better actually get some studying done now since I completely zoned-out in Chemistry class yesterday thinking about how much I want a new lab partner... and we have a Chemistry quiz today... I think... though given my luck, we had it yesterday and I was too angry to notice. That would be more happiness than my lab partner rightfully deserves... especially since God hates her. I actually told her that in response to her declaring that she was a vampire. She says there are over 10,000 vampires in the Great Lakes area alone. I thought she was trying to scare me so I looked at her and said, "God hates you. I talk to Him. He tells me these things." She said she was going to smite me, but I thought that was a privilege reserved for Christians and Jews. What are your thoughts?

Love,
Marielle

"Done," Marielle said to herself since no one else was listening.

Joy spoke to her neighbor while a girl named Tanya sat in Joel's chair, having moved that chair closer to Tom's than it had ever been before.

It took Marielle a minute to recall Joel saying something about the new computer lab which sat behind the long row of vending machines on the other side of the Commons.

In theory, Marielle understood that an empty chair could be occupied by anyone, but she didn't appreciate Tanya filling it when Joel could return at any moment. Tanya needed to go back to her friends at the window end of the table instead of mining for sympathy from a boy she would never date.

"He told me he was doing *me* the favor by dating me and then he said, 'You'll never date anyone as popular as me.' "

"What!?" Marielle exclaimed, her head snapping toward Tanya. "Ooh, sorry," she said, remembering this wasn't her conversation.

Tonya's alarm turned to irritation until she decided that another sympathetic ear couldn't hurt.

"Is that the phrase he used?" Tom asked.

Tonya said it was.

"What an arrogant bastard!" Marielle declared.

Tom turned toward her. "Do you think so? I think he's actually demonstrating humility."

Both girls looked at him as if he had just condoned incest.

"Well," Tom continued. "He used an objective pronoun where a subjective pronoun is required. So, clearly he doesn't mind looking stupid."

Marielle threw her head back to laugh while Tonya smiled in a hollow "you've just changed the focus away from me and I don't appreciate it" way.

After Tonya walked away, Marielle leaned across the table toward Tom. "You know, you're a nice guy so you might not know this, but girls like that are just fishing for guys to tell them how much better they deserve to be treated. Once she thinks she could date you whenever she wants, she'll go back to her table and ignore you again."

Tom leaned toward Marielle. "I'm not that nice," he said with a glint in his eye.

Marielle smiled brightly. "Well, good for you," she said, looking down the table to see how Tanya wore rejection at the hands of the Quiz Bowl Captain. When her attention returned to Tom, she found him staring through the glass of the school store with a blank expression on his face. "You know," Marielle said, "I think I know why America is wealthier than Europe."

Tom shifted his gaze toward her. "Why's that?" he asked mechanically.

"Well, isn't Europe inhabited by the descendants of the siblings of our ancestors?" She stopped to consider the matter for a moment. "*Ja*," she continued. "So, they are the ones that said, 'I'm right behind you,' to our great-grandparents as they headed off to the docks, but they were too lazy to get off the couch and go."

"Hmm," Tom said. "Using that logic, the laziest people on the planet would be living where human-kind originated, having never left the *original* couch."

"Exactly!" Marielle said excitedly. She barely paused to say hello to the returning Joel before she continued. "If they were too lazy to leave after watching U-Haul Camels pass them for thousands of years, there's really no hope. Note to self: never invest in the Middle East or North Africa."

"Maybe they just loved their couch," suggested Tom.

"Or maybe they were optimists," interjected Joel. "Maybe they thought, 'This isn't such a bad plague. I'm gonna ride this one out.'"

Tom laughed. "That's pretty optimistic."

Marielle nodded. "*Ja*. You can almost hear them say, 'The Huns have to get tired sooner or later.' "

"So, you're saying that Europe must be entirely populated with optimists and sloths, and either way, it's no good for their economy," Tom stated more than asked.

"Yes!" replied Marielle.

"That's brilliant," Tom declared.

Chapter Twelve

Eine Kleine Revenge

"If you're done with your application, I'll take it to Sandy when I go to work," Jeanette offered as she stood beside the dining room table in her brown smock, white pants, and hair net.

"Shouldn't I bring it in person?" Marielle asked, setting down her pen.

Jeanette shook her head. "It shouldn't matter. You've got the job anyway."

Marielle looked up at her sister with wide eyes. "Really?!"

"Yeah. They're about to fire the airhead because she never comes in on time, and sometimes she doesn't come in at all. She actually told me that her period made her forgetful. Can you believe that? The last time I complained about her to Sandy she said that if she could have another worker like me, she'd replace her. So, I told her you're the next best thing."

Marielle smiled at Jeanette, then quickly forced herself to stop. She wasn't sure how to respond to a compliment from her sister. "Can you mention to Sandy that I'm still working at Hardees from 5 a.m. to noon every weekend?"

"Sure," Jeanette replied, taking her sister's application, "but she won't have a problem with it. She needs you during week nights anyway."

"Awesome! Thanks."

"This way I can kick your ass if you're late," Jeanette explained. Complimenting her sister made her uncomfortable as well.

"Nice language, young lady," Johan remarked as he entered the dining room.

Jeanette cringed, but didn't apologize. She was old enough to swear even if she wasn't too old to blush.

"Did you have a nice nap, Grandpa?" Marielle asked, smiling at her grandfather like he had been gone longer than an hour.

He straightened his hair with his fingers. "Well, I'm not sure I slept, but it felt good to lie down."

"You still take a nap every day?" she asked as he made his way into the living room.

"Yeah. I probably don't need to. I suppose it's just a habit now."

Frieda peeked through the doorway of the kitchen. "Pa, I need you to run me to the store before Jack and Maria get home. I want to pick up something for supper."

"I'm sure there's no need, Grandma. Mom went shopping last night," Marielle reasoned, knowing full well her grandmother's main mission was to buy junk food.

"You've got a lot to learn about manners, kid," Frieda replied. "You don't stay four days in someone else's house without buying food."

After her grandparents returned from Piggly Wiggly, Marielle helped her grandmother place the microwave popcorn and Little Debbies above the refrigerator.

"Will you be able to reach them all the way up here?" she asked playfully.

"No, but I know where to find you," Frieda said with a wink.

Marielle breathed in as if to say something.

"What?" her grandmother asked.

Marielle stepped back from the refrigerator to better make eye contact. "I was just wondering about your Uncle Paul."

"What made you think of him?" Frieda asked with no obvious emotion.

"I don't know. I was just wondering if they ever caught the man who killed him."

Frieda's right eye squinted. "You assume it was a man."

"Wasn't it?"

She shook her head. "I always thought it was a woman of ill-repute. A widow who lived outside town."

Marielle's confused expression encouraged her grandmother to continue. "Well, my father liked this woman a lot." She paused to convey the true meaning of her sentence, then continued when she saw a lightbulb go off in Marielle's eyes, "and Uncle Paul was always very protective of my mother."

"But I thought Uncle Paul was your *father's* brother?"

"He was, but he and my father had a falling out over his behavior just before Uncle Paul died. I always thought the old witch shot my uncle to get him out of the way."

Marielle leaned against the counter. "Did she go to prison?"

"No, there was no evidence she did it. Back then we didn't have all these scientific tests you hear about on the news. I wish she *had* gone to prison though. She made our life hell and she ended up killing my father too in the end."

Alarm washed over Marielle's face as she wondered how a woman in Michigan could kill a man in Chicago decades after killing his younger brother and get away with both murders.

Frieda inhaled deeply before continuing. "She ended up moving to Chicago around the time my mom got sick. After my mom died, she and my dad got married and they lived in the apartment on the top floor of our house." Frieda's mouth stiffened at the memory. "You know, she took all of my mom's china and linen and gave it to her ugly nieces?"

Marielle shook her head. "How did she kill your father? I thought he died of a heart attack?"

"Let's sit down," Frieda suggested before leading her granddaughter to the dining room table. "Your Grandpa Riess wasn't feeling well and he wanted to stay home from work. That old—" she paused for a moment, deciding if the next word would start with a B, "*witch* told him to get up and go to work anyway. It was September, but it was an especially hot day and the grounds of Martha Washington Hospital took up nearly an entire city block. I saw him walking back and forth, mowing that lawn all day long. When he got home, he laid down on his bed and died."

Frieda shook her head with more anger than grief, then released her jaw. "Do you want a Nutty Bar?" she asked.

"No, thanks, Grandma. I'll have one for dessert though if that's okay?"

"Suit yourself. You can grab one for me though," she said, smiling cutely.

After retrieving the bar for her grandmother, Marielle asked, "Were you home when Uncle Paul died?"

"No, I was in boarding school. I had actually just gone back after my injury. Didn't I tell you about getting dragged by the horse?"

Marielle shook her head.

"Her name was Midnight. My dad told me not to let her go or I would get it, so I held on when she bolted out of the pasture. It was my father's fault. He always let her run from the pasture to the wagon on her own, and I never saw a horse as set in her ways as that one. Once she was hooked up to the wagon, she was fine. In fact, you barely needed to steer her at all. Some nights, I'd have to drive the buggy home because my father was passed out drunk beside me and no matter how hard I pulled her reins or whipped her, she always took the same route home."

"How old were you?"

"Maybe eight or nine," Frieda said, biting into her bar.

"Your parents let you drive when you were only eight or nine?!"

Frieda struggled to swallow quickly. "Well, driving a horse and buggy isn't the same as driving a car. If you had the right horse, there was almost no reason to hold the reins at all. I used to love seeing that horse pull up in front of my boarding school on a Friday, but when my mother dropped me off at the end of the weekend, I'd run upstairs and cry until I fogged up the window and I couldn't see her anymore."

Marielle studied her grandmother's eyes, certain they were glassier than a moment ago. "Wasn't there a school closer to your house?"

Frieda shook her head as she creased her napkin. "Not a Catholic one. Boy, was I happy when I was too hurt to go back to school that week... but I was happier still when we sold the farm and moved back to Chicago, that's for sure. After the murder, my mom put her foot down and demanded they move back, but the state built a highway through the property the next year and my father never let her forget it."

"Why?" Marielle asked.

"Because the highway would've given us more money than the people who bought the farm."

Marielle had never heard this rationale before. She assumed the government wouldn't pay top dollar if they could force you to sell your property anyway.

"Did your brothers go to school with you?" she asked.

"No, my younger brother was too young for school and my older brother had already graduated."

Marielle nodded. "How old was Uncle Paul when he died?"

"He was in his late 20s, but he looked much younger than that. I sometimes had a hard time telling him and my brother apart actually... except Uncle Paul's hair was darker, and he had a much better personality." She smiled until the kitchen door opened abruptly, gaining everyone's attention.

An out of breath Jeanette ran into the dining room, explaining that Sandy wanted Marielle to begin working immediately.

Marielle looked at her grandmother, unsure how she should respond.

"You'd better get going, kid," Frieda urged.

"But, what do I wear?" she asked her sister, wanting to work any night but this one.

"You can grab a pair of white work pants from my closet and Sandy will give you a smock when you get there."

Five minutes later, Marielle abused the stairs on the way down while pulling her hair into a ponytail.

"Bye, Grandpa," she said, kissing her grandfather's cheek as he rearranged the newspaper.

Johan moved the newspaper to the side. "Where are you off to, young lady?"

"I'm starting my new job at the nursing home."

"That's too bad. I brought some movies from the library I was hoping we'd watch."

"I should be home by eight if that's not too late?" she asked hopefully, backing into the dining room and touching her grandmother's shoulder on the way past.

"Bye, Marielle," Frieda said while reading an article about Princess Di's latest nanny troubles.

Marielle laughed at her grandmother's tabloid as she ran out the side door.

"Can you imagine finding out your nanny has AIDS?" Frieda had asked during her previous visit.

"Grandma, where did you read that?" Marielle replied while exchanging a knowing look with her grandfather.

Johan normally didn't allow for signs of disrespect toward his wife, except where her reading habits were concerned. "There's no reason to read unless it's non-fiction," he said a moment before Marielle agreed.

Frieda held up her tabloid. "It's a newspaper. Of course it's non-fiction."

Johan shook his head. "I disagree, and I'm not just talking about the newspaper."

"If you're not learning something, you're wasting your time," Marielle reasoned.

Frieda looked defiantly at her husband and granddaughter. "That's ridiculous! I learn things reading fiction all the time. For example, I learned that English women say their 'tights ladder' instead of their 'stockings run.' I wouldn't learn that reading Ronald Reagan's biography."

"One hopes," Marielle said with a mischievous grin. "But you could read a book about fashion industry terms in the U.S. verses those in the U.K.," she suggested.

"But I wouldn't!" Frieda argued. "Besides, stories are *supposed* to be fiction."

"How do you figure?" Johan asked while wearing a smirk.

"Because book categories are *fiction* and *non-fiction*. If stories were supposed to be true, the categories would be *fact* and *non-fact*."

Marielle raised her eyebrows. "That's actually a good point, Grandma."

"Well, you don't need to look so surprised, kid," Frieda remarked before smiling back at her newspaper.

***

"Four people from the same family working at the same place looks like a coup," Sandy said genially while handing Marielle her short-sleeved tan smock outside her office.

Marielle chuckled. "I suppose it is, but we promise not to invade the east wing tonight."

"Not before dinner is served, anyway," Jeanette added on her way to the walk-in refrigerator nearby.

"I'll hold you to that," Sandy said to Jeanette before returning her attention to Marielle. "I don't know if your sister had a chance to tell you your responsibilities, but you will set the tables in the dining room with linen table clothes and napkins. You'll get them from the laundry room when you come in first thing, but this has been done for you tonight. Then, you stand at the window over there." She nodded at the area to the left of the swinging door 10 yards directly in front of them. "You will help your sister make up plates for the nurse's aides who will serve the dining room. After that, the bed trays should start coming back and you can clear those, and wash the dishes."

Sandy's eyes moved to the dish room to the right side of the swinging door. "By that time, the residents should be done with their dinner in the dining room so you'll use that cart—" she pointed to the cart at the entrance to the dish room "—to clear and wash the tables. Wash the dining room dishes, put them away, wash the dish room, bring the dirty linens back to the laundry, and you're done."

"Got it," Marielle said, knowing she barely had part of it.

"Time to start," Jeanette called from the serving area.

"Good luck," Sandy offered before taking her leave.

***

"So, I'm the potato woman tonight or every night?" Marielle asked as she released an ice cream ladle of instant potatoes onto a thick white ceramic plate.

"Pretty much every night," Jeanette replied. "When you get better, I'll let you scoop the vegetable too."

"So, *you* always get the meat?"

"I do. When you work here long enough, you get meat privileges."

"Hmm," Marielle said, studying the tray of pulled pork. "Maybe you could establish a sort of bonus system where I can scoop the meat on one of three plates if I do a good job with the potato and the vegetable on the first 15 plates."

Jeanette smiled. "I'd hate for you to get a big head."

"So, where did you come from?" a nurse's aide asked Marielle over the serving counter. "I thought I was seeing your sister until I saw her standing next to you.

Marielle smiled in reply. She didn't consider it a real question and it was a comment she had heard too many times to find interesting.

10-Sep-1988

Dearest Marielle,

It's one in the morning, but it's still like Saturday night (MUCH better than Sunday morning) so I just thought I'd write. Sorry I didn't write earlier, but I thought you'd send a letter and I was waiting to get it first.

My sister is out at a disco now – everyone in her school who left this year and is going to college is out too. You see, after they do their Leaving Cert (the BIG one) they all go out for one night. First, they eat out in a restaurant; then they go to a disco; then (at around 3:00 a.m.) they go to someone's house and have a party. Fiona should be home in time for breakfast. She's got a boyfriend called Ryan. He's really nice (cool?).

Oh! I heard a BRILLIANT joke today. It's slightly perverted (VERY, VERY slightly by my standards) so avert your eyes unless you really want me to taint the purity of your (so far) perfect mind... Ha! I knew you'd read on. Well, ya see now, this boy was walking past his parents'

169

bedroom at around 12:00 a.m. and the door was open. He stopped and looked in for about 5 minutes and then he said – "and you had the cheek to slap me for sucking my thumb?!" Now, thou art perverted! (If you don't get that one, you've got a lot to learn. I'm a good teacher!)

Enough unclean humour! School is really shit! I'm back now and I've got loads of homework. I'm doing Maths, Irish, English, French, Physics, Chemistry, and Biology. I think I could get a scholarship into college, my science and Maths teachers said I could anyhow. All I have to do is swot for 2 years. (Aaagh!) If I do get a scholarship, I keep the fees (what you pay to go to college) for myself. That's £1,500! If I do, I promise I'll fly over to see you! I'll also get a new sailboard.

Next week, I'll start training for hurling again. I plan to stop next year so I'll train really hard this year!

Today, I lifted 200lbs with my weights. (I have my own at home.) I only have to use 100lb. weights for hurling. I'm probably boring you to death! Please don't die!

I wrote an obscene letter to my ex-girlfriend and bitch from the Irish College today. My friend told me she was really annoyed because somebody actually left her before she got the chance to leave them. She was such a bitch! And to think I actually fell in love with her (and for almost three days too). I was a stupid fool! However, I have learnt.

I can't wait for the Olympics! I love watching the gymnastics.

I was watching the news today and I saw pictures of the famine in Africa. I can't stand looking at the children starving to death, especially when I see money being spent on missiles and tanks – I'm not going to go on about it and I can't blame anyone but I'd love to help. That's why I was thinking of spending a year or more over there after I do my final exam. Well, we'll see...

Me again. It's now 1:40 a.m. I can't get asleep because I'm thinking about you. I just don't know what's wrong with me tonight. My friends were absolutely and totally and completely SHOCKED when I said that you were staying in my house when you visit. You'd think it was the same bed, not house! I think you'll be sleeping in my room (don't worry, I'll be downstairs sleeping on the cold, bare floorboards of our humble cottage. [You'll have the electric blanket, you lucky b....]). It's so cool! I mean,

170

when girls are coming from the U.S. just to see you, you must be really beautiful, right? (Only joking)

My friend's cousin is coming from Australia for 2 months – she's only 16 and she wants to live here! I have so much to tell you, I don't have enough room. I'll write again soon. Please write back! Ya know, for two people who've never actually seen each other, I think we're getting to know each other pretty well. I hope this letter gets to you really quickly. I promise to write when I get your next letter.

Yours,
The ever psychopathic, schizophrenic, and can't wait to see you,
Dermot

"Bah!" yelled Marielle silently. Dermot should have received her letter on the day he mailed his... or he *would* have received it if she had finished it on time. It had been a bad couple of weeks and it wasn't getting any better.

9/19/1988 Monday

Hi Dermot!

How are you? I'm fine. It seems you didn't get my last letter before you wrote yours. Sorry! I hope you've since received it and don't reply to it before I reply to you. It stinks having to wait two weeks between letters!!! Maybe I should call you and tell you to wait, but then I'd be tempted to tell you everything I'm going to write. AUGH!

I'm writing in Chemistry class and I just spent my lunch hour talking instead of eating. You'd never know I didn't start talking until I was five. My mom says I'm making up for it now. Anyway, today our lunch discussion revolved around names and initials which on the surface seems less interesting than who's dating who and which teachers are usually drunk by third period, but it was actually very amusing since one of my friends' initials are "TP" (which is what some people call toilet paper) and mine are "MER" which as you know, means "sea" in French which is pretty cool since I've decided that my grave marker will read "Lost at Sea" no matter how I die. I just think it sounds cool. The chances of me really being lost at sea are remote though... being deathly afraid of water and all. Oh! But the coolest thing about my initials is that my favorite

Bobby Darin (have you heard of him?) song was originally sung in French (by someone else) and was called "La Mer" (or so says my mom).

Actually, to tell the truth, my favorite Bobby Darin song is "Mack the Knife," but it doesn't fit my initials... though "Mac" is part of your name... so if I was one of those annoying people who looks for obscure signs to why life fits, I guess I'd be pretty happy right now. Actually, I'm not very happy right now, and it has nothing to do with Mack the Knife. The brochure I got from the pen pal club said "never write when you're in a bad mood," but they haven't had the week I've had so fuck them. Anyway, I'll complain in really small print so you can barely see it and it will be easily skipped. Plus, once it goes down on paper and travels across the Atlantic, I should feel much better—at least that's the hope. So here it goes:

1) My grandparents visited last weekend (they live three hours north of here), and I didn't get a chance to see them as much as usual because I started a second job (I'm working in the kitchen of a nursing home), and on their way home my grandma's heart stopped for some unknown reason and she blacked-out. My grandpa pulled-over at the nearest building which happened to be a restaurant which happened to have a member of the local rescue squad inside. They did CPR on her and rushed her to the hospital, and they were able to save her, but she's still in intensive care and they're not sure how long she'll be there or what her chances are for recovery. My grandpa sounds so sad on the phone that I can't help crying every time he calls. I heard my dad tell my mom that Grandpa wouldn't last long without Grandma and I can't stand the thought of losing them both. I know they will die someday, but that's not something I can handle right now... or any time soon. I also can't stand the guilt that I might've missed my last weekend with my grandma because I didn't ask for time off from work. Sometimes I think I am so distracted by my goals that I forget to make time for people around me... which brings me to #2.

2) Yesterday, I got a letter from my friend Heidi that basically said I stink as a friend and she was tired of waiting for letters from me that never arrived. She also said she had been in a pretty bad car accident over the summer (she flipped over her driver's ed car on the highway—an accident I coincidentally heard about from my driver's ed teacher, but disregarded because he didn't name names and I just thought it was one of his pre-driving scare tactics). Anyway, she said I was a pretty crappy friend to not be there for her. The last thing she wrote was that her mom is sick and they're not sure if it's cancer. I called her a little while ago and

172

her brother said she wasn't home, but I'm not sure she'd talk to me if she was.

3) Friday, I took my driving test (yes, this time I actually had an appointment) and I was SURE I would pass since my driver's ed teacher said I was his best student and he "knew I would have no trouble." I guess I wasn't as careful as I should have been because I went through an unmarked intersection without stopping and made a couple of turns that were too wide, and when the instructor asked me to parallel park, I paid too much attention to getting close to the curb and didn't notice the fire hydrant next to my parking space. It was pretty painful, but I was still shocked and horrified when he looked at me with pity and said, "Maybe next time." My mom told me it could happen to anyone, but the truth is it doesn't! No one in my family ever failed their driver's test and at school it's an honor reserved for the seriously stupid. Anyway, now I have to wait three weeks to take the test again and I will literally die if I don't pass. Literally.

4) Stupid Guy still won't leave me alone! He's written me three letters since he got to UWM which chronicle all the parties he's going to and all the alcohol he's consuming and only reminds me how little he knows me 'cause getting drunk and wandering around campus only qualifies him for the title of "party ass" in my book. His letters are also sprinkled with references to women he's staggering around campus with... which I guess I'm supposed to find either threatening or chivalrous. The level to which he irritates me cannot be overstated! Anyway, in keeping with the universal "three strikes and you're out" rule, I gave him a pass on the first two letters, but if he sends one more, he's done! I don't know what that means, but I know enough about me to know it'll be bad.

5) I had a date on Saturday with the spawn of Satan. He's actually the kid of a preacher, but I've determined they're the same thing. I assumed his dad's public ranting about "evil gay people" meant his son was conservative enough to wait for marriage before having sex, but that was clearly not his game plan—even on a first date. We were only at the movie about five minutes when he reached for my hand which I promptly moved to cross my arms. Incapable of taking a not-so-subtle hint, the weasel crossed his arms too and reached one hand under my crossed arm to grab my chest. I tried to elbow him away, but the worm had this suction cup hand that wasn't going anywhere. So, I leaned over and said that if he didn't move his hand, I was getting up and calling my dad. This did the trick.

The rest of the movie was uneventful so I didn't think I needed my parents to pick me up, but I was wrong. Instead of taking College Avenue out of the mall, he got on HWY 41 North which I assumed was an innocent navigational error so I chalked it up to his clueless nature... until he missed the Richmond Street exit (the exit due north of my house). I told him he could exit Ballard (the next exit), but that meant he had to back-track to my house. This was the point where he told me he wasn't taking me home yet. I was really annoyed (a 12 on a scale of 1 to 10), but it was clear he was unstable so I didn't make any whiny "my parents will be worried about me" excuses, or any insulting "you're a clueless prick" comments even though I was thinking both. I just told myself to calm down and think of a way to get control of that car.

I saw a story on the news once of a woman making her car crash into a light pole 'cause a guy had kidnapped her and was making her drive out of town. Although I was wearing my seat belt, I didn't have the nerve to grab the steering wheel and crash the car, and I also thought how credible a kid of a preacher looks in court verses just about anyone else. So, I said "Oh, okay," and then I told him I would be very grateful if he would teach me how to drive his parents' car (a stick shift) since I only knew how to drive automatics and sticks were cooler. (This was a complete lie since my grandpa taught me to drive his WWII-era Army Jeep when I was 13, but the beauty of a guy throwing himself at someone on the first date is that he doesn't know little facts like that.) He said, "maybe later" and proceeded to drive into a very dark Plamann Park.

Most parks here close after dark so there's usually a cop at the entrance waiting to pounce on you as soon as you come through the gate, but as unluck would have it there wasn't anyone there that night. I suggested that Hugh (aka Dickweed) park the car near the main road, but he drove into the park anyway. As soon as the main gate disappeared behind us, he stopped the car, pushed my seat back, and he was all over me. It happened so quickly I had no idea what was going on until he planted his face on top of mine. He was kissing me so hard I could barely breathe which I told him and added that it felt like I had a sea lamprey on my face. He didn't think this was funny at all and suggested we move to the back seat. I agreed, but I opened my door and bolted down the hill next to the parking lot instead.

I always thought I was a pretty fast runner, but Mr. Raging Hormone caught and tackled me pretty easily and with enough force to bring down a football player during a Homecoming game. At that moment, I thought that it was a good thing I had brothers and I could take a hit, but I also thought that I might be in trouble. Luckily for me, I laugh when I'm nervous so Hughsifer thought I was joking around or being one of those dramatic playing-hard-to-get chicks that I hate. Anyway, he pinned me to the ground and the only way out was to kiss the bastard

174

for about ten disgusting minutes... or maybe it was three but it felt like ten... actually, it felt like a thousand, but I finally reminded him that he promised to teach me how to drive a stick and the park was the perfect place for me to learn and we could always come back to kissing later. The whiny boy moaned and groaned all the way back to the car, but he let me get into the driver's seat and two minutes later, I was driving his parents' car onto Ballard Avenue... which is when Dickhead went BALLISTIC and said that I was a f..ing liar and I wasn't allowed to drive his parents' car on the street without a license and he would get into trouble if the cops stopped us, etc. etc. I kept telling him he needed to calm down until he finally did and soon after we were in my driveway.

I haven't ever seen Olympic sprinters run in person, but I'm pretty sure I broke a land speed record running into my house that night. My parents were surprised to see me home so early, but they didn't look concerned or upset at all. In fact, they seemed as calm as they'd've been had I spent an evening with our parish priest since for some reason a kid of a preacher (KOP) wearing a polo shirt and driving a Subaru seems inherently trust-worthy. I found it ironic that my mom trusted Dickweed and had nothing but contempt for Mark who showed up in his cargo van with the words "Make Love Not War" spray-painted on the side. Anyway, I chose not to disillusion her... mostly because my dad has guns and a temper, but also because I've sworn off dating for the rest of my life. I've decided that being a nun is a much better alternative than ever dealing with guys again. This sounds like I'm being hysterical, but I'm really quite serious.

6)   I was in German class on Friday when my friend Celia whispered, "Ich bin schwanger" to me. I had to look up the last word in my German dictionary since it's never come up in our usual vocabulary drills, but it apparently means "pregnant"...which she was/is. I showed her no end of sympathy since I assumed it was an accident, but she informed me that it wasn't which I just can't understand 'cause what kind of dumbass plans to get pregnant at 16?!! And it's not like she's from a broken home or anything. Her parents are married and they're a little weird (vegetarian ex-hippies), but they're doctors... who I imagine think their daughter is high on crack (an illegal drug)... which is the most likely explanation.

7)   My mom, sister, and I ate at the Burger King downtown last weekend and I normally don't carry a purse, but I wanted to pay for lunch so I grabbed it, and hung it on the back of my chair while we ate... then forgot it when we left. As soon as we got home, I realized I had left it and that my birth certificate was still inside (ever since I took my driver's test) and if anyone took it, it would be a

175

nightmare 'cause they could get a license under my name (well, assuming they drive better than I do) and pretend they were me, and waiting for a replacement birth certificate would postpone getting a passport, etc. etc. Anyway, I was too irrational to ask my sister for a ride back to Burger King, so I ran. When I got there, my purse was still hanging on the chair where I left it and everything was still inside, thank God! So, I guess this isn't as much a horrible occurrence as a *nearly* horrible occurrence, but it felt pretty horrible when I was running across the bridge.

8)   The same day, I decided to listen to my new INXS tape on my new walkman and halfway into the first song I got panicked thinking I hadn't seen a piece of butterscotch my grandpa and I pass back and forth every visit. So, I walked to the dining room, set the walkman on the table, checked my purse, and walked away without grabbing my walkman. Since my headphones were still on my head, the walkman skidded off the table and broke on the floor. Cheap piece of Japanese crap!

I should say something positive right now or you'll start dreading my letters. My dad always asks people if they'd "like some cheese with their *whine*" so maybe I should get some. ☺ Ooh, the bell just rang……

I'm happy to say that the bell saved me from saying anything positive. I'm at home now, but I have to work soon. Celia wasn't at school today so maybe her parents drowned her over the weekend. I'm not sure if my parents would kill me outright or kill the guy and shun me like an Amish kid. I don't even want to think about it though so I'll change the subject.

Frau passed back our tests and this freckle-faced kid with a huge head of curly red hair yelled, "I must've been smoking a crack pipe when I took this test!" Frau wasn't impressed. The other day, he grabbed my arm and said in a breathless voice, "May I lick... your... elbow?" By the time he got to "elbow" Frau was about to pass out. The whole class thinks he's a riot which is why they usually let him copy off their papers during tests... which I guess didn't work out for him this time.

Today, I determined that my Advanced Algebra teacher is a god. At first, I thought he was crazy 'cause he walks around school with mistletoe hanging from a string, attached to an up-side-down L-shaped wire, connected to a crown, attached to his head... and it's clearly nowhere near Christmas. But yesterday he joked that his method for grading test papers was to throw them down the stairwell and give the ones that landed on top

176

A's, and the ones that landed on the bottom F's. You could actually hear the self-proclaimed pre-Harvard kids in the front row gasp... which made everyone in the room with a sense of humor laugh... which didn't include the front row kids. Maybe you don't have many pseudo-intellectuals at your school, but they're pretty common here. Well, we have grits (lower caliber students) here too, but we have enough pseudo-intellectuals to categorize them into five distinct groups (which I've done). The group I'm talking about is a type IV pseudo-intellectual (PI). They usually belong to the Debate Team, make twirling a pencil between their fingers an Olympic sport (when they're not tapping the eraser against their teeth or holding the stem of their glasses between their lips), take only classes that guarantee them an A, and believe every word they say should be gilded which is why they speak s o s l o w l y a n d p r e c i s e l y. 'Cause what you lack in original thought can always be made up for in elocution. Anyway, I know this sounds judgmental, but I can't help myself. If I have to explain one more time to a "superior intellect" that I end sentences with prepositions not because I'm ignorant, but because I'm rebellious, I may scream! Add the characteristic, "Is too stupid to see the intelligence in other" to my list of PI IV characteristics.

I forgot to mention in my last letter that I was surprised that you already know what college you're going to (<—purposeful preposition-ending sentence). I've narrowed it down to about a dozen schools, but that list could expand or contract at any time. The front-runner this week is Syracuse in New York, although I'm not a big fan of orange. What is your favorite color? Mine is green. Anyway, they have a foreign exchange program with Trinity College which I assume is in a place called Trinity, Ireland?

I've actually been reading medical books since I was 12 (so I could get a leg-up on the competition) so if I start understanding what I've been reading, I may qualify for Johns Hopkins (the best medical school in the U.S.), but that's not going to happen unless medical books stop using so much Latin. ☺

I'm also surprised that people are so shocked that I would stay at your house. If it's not seen as appropriate, maybe I should get a hotel or something? It's really no trouble at all for me to do this. Also, maybe I should only stay a weekend and spend more time in Germany? I'd hate to upset your parents or put your good Catholic reputation into question. ☺

For no apparent reason, I've started writing down some of the more interesting vanity license plates around here. Most are people's nicknames or some version of their last name. They have to be six characters or less, but in Illinois they can be seven—lucky FIBs! Anyway, here are a few:

WE 1 IT– I think this plate encourages you to steal the car since it was only dumb luck that it's theirs to begin with.

FUQ2– This may only be a legend, but someone in my driver's ed class said a kid from Appleton West has this plate.

MY GRLZ– I assume a man bought this car for his girlfriend or wife, but the plate would never make sense if she were actually driving.

I 4 GV U– I imagine this car was also a gift from a man to a woman and the plate was wishful thinking on his part... or maybe the owners just assume they'll always be victims in a traffic accident... or maybe they want to guilt a cop into not giving them a speeding ticket. That one's difficult to pin down.

My grandpa made a wooden license plate for his forty-niner (1949 truck) that reads "Red Baron" but he's technically not supposed to be making his own license plates. The police don't really bother him about it though since he's friends with the sheriff and he rarely drives it off his ranch.

Now, I will regale you with the two jokes I can remember, although I'm sure I've heard at least a hundred that I can't remember:

Q: How did the Italians get to America?
A: The first hundred swam, and the rest walked over the dead fish.

My dad told my mom that one and she wasn't impressed... well, more impressed than when he calls her food "WOP slop" but less impressed than she'd be with an actual compliment.

Here's one my friend Will made up a few years ago:

Q: What was green and flew over London in the '40s?
A: The Snotzies.

Anyway, I should go before I force up the price of paper. By the way, I'm glad you're back in school, darling. 'Twould be a pity if I was the only one to suffer. ☺ Speaking of which, it's only September and there are already frost warnings here most nights. BAH!

Thank you for listening to my rantings. I advise you to burn this letter and save your sanity!

I love you very, very, very, very, very much!

Marielle

PS You asked about American girls and dieting a couple of letters back and I only eat about once per day, but that's not because I'm dieting. Between work, Pep Club activities, and socializing during lunch hour, eating generally suffers.

PPS I read that much of the world thinks we cheated by using a catameran instead of a regular boat in the America's Cup. I think they're just jealous that we always demonstrate such a high degree of intelligence in almost all technical matters. What do you think?

Marielle reread the letter at lunch, carelessly placing the read pages in front of her instead of tucking them inside her folder.

"You had a date with Hugh?" Joel asked, equal parts annoyed and interested.

"How did you read that upside down?" Marielle asked, looking down at the letter.

"Get this!" Joy said. "Marielle decided to be a nun. Can you believe it?"

Marielle sighed. "Don't you have a report to do?"

"*You* want to be a nun?" asked Joel. "That's the stupidest thing I ever heard."

"*Stupidest?*" Marielle asked, eyebrows raised.

"Yeah. You're the kind of girl who needs a guy. Just look at how much effort you put into writing to that *Kartoffelkopf.*"

Marielle's eyes fluttered. "Did you just demonstrate everything you learned during two years of German?"

"Yeah. *Frau*'s an idiot."

Marielle leaned forward. "No, you're a dumbass."

"Well, maybe you should pray for me," Joel retorted.

"I would, but I don't know who the patron saint for hopeless losers is!"

"You're a bitch," Joel said with less emotion Marielle expected.

"*Danke*," she replied, smiling as she organized her letter. When she was done, she opened a small notebook and began writing.

"What's that?" Joel asked with a head nod.

"I'm adding a 'Patron Saint for Hopeless Losers' card to my list of mean greeting cards. I think it's a winner. By the way, I heard you were so bad you got kicked out of home school. Is that true?" Marielle asked innocently, causing Tom to chuckle at his book.

Joel displayed a menacing glare before succumbing to laughter as well.

Joy glanced between her cousin and Marielle wearing an expressionless face. "Is it 100 bottles of beer on the wall or 1,000?"

"99," Marielle and Tom replied in unison.

"That doesn't make any sense. Why would you start with an uneven number?"

Joel rolled his eyes. "Why does it matter?"

"I don't know. Just does."

"Out of curiosity," said Marielle, "why do you ask?"

"Because I'm doing a report on folk songs."

Marielle shared a chuckle with the boys before addressing Joy. "Since when is *99 Bottles of Beer on the Wall* a folk song?"

"Since my folks sang it," she replied.

Joel shook his head impatiently. "That's not what it means, dumbass."

"Whatever," Joy responded with little concern. "It's what I'm writing about."

"So, you're going through the effort of writing about something you know is wrong?" Marielle asked with dismay.

"It's not wrong because you *say* it's wrong. It's just your opinion."

Marielle's eyes rapidly shifted from the ceiling to Joy. "Uh, no. It's just a fact! Getting athlete's foot doesn't make you an athlete, and your folks singing a song doesn't make it a folk song."

Joy shrugged her shoulders. "Well, I don't see why you'd sing a song that long anyway."

"To kill time," Marielle replied. "Like, say for example, you were on a school bus with a broken heater from Laona to Kleiner. It was dark so you couldn't read and you didn't bring your walkman 'cause you thought it would get stolen if you left it on the bus during your Solo and Ensemble competition, and you're pretty sure you're going to poke your eyes out if you see another single blue-white light next to another farmhouse in the

180

distance, or scream if the bus stops and opens the door for another railroad crossing where there's no train."

Joel waited a moment before he said, "That's very specific."

"Sometimes life is that way," Marielle replied.

Tom looked up from his book. "I spoke to Jillian's little brother the other day during band."

"Wait. Which one is he?" Marielle asked.

"The new bass clarinet."

Marielle displayed less interest than she felt, allowing an awkward pause to overtake the conversation.

"So, what did he say?" Joy asked impatiently.

"He said he would be very interested in seeing any letters Guy's been sending Marielle since Guy's convinced Jillian and her family that Marielle can't stop calling and writing him."

Marielle's mouth opened as her face rapidly became red. "That piece of crap!" she yelled, slamming her hand down on her notebook hard enough for two members of the Quiz Bowl Team to look down at the table, then at each other.

Joel and Joy regarded Marielle with the same shocked bemusement.

Tom seemed neither shocked nor upset. He concentrated on Marielle's face as if awaiting the response foretold to him.

"Tell him I'll bring two letters tomorrow. In both, Guy begs me to write him."

"That should go far toward clearing all of this up," Tom said, satisfied with the result.

***

Only the raising of Tom's head in a "hello" fashion signaled the arrival of Jillian's brother the following day. Marielle turned to her left, pencil still firmly connected to her notebook as Tom made the introductions. She awkwardly greeted the boy at the exact same time and with the exact same word he used.

The short, red-haired, oxford and khaki wearing sophomore sat between Marielle and her Quiz Bowl neighbor, looking across the table for help even though Tom's attention appeared dedicated to his book.

"Tom told me you had a question about Guy," Marielle said in an attempt to release tension.

The boy exhaled rapidly. "Yeah. He said Guy's been writing you even though you told him to stop."

181

"That's right." Marielle nodded curtly, opening her Trapper Keeper to find the letters she promised.

"Do you need these back?" he asked with a pained expression, as though any hope that Marielle was lying had been dashed by the small gray envelopes, backward slanted markings, and the expensive blue fountain pen that made them.

"No, you can keep them or burn them," Marielle replied, smiling in a failed attempt to lighten the mood.

"Thanks," he said as he stood up, his head an inch lower leaving than when he arrived.

"Why did he need a chair for that?" Joy scoffed.

"I have no idea," replied Marielle reflexively, too distracted by a downcast sophomore walking toward the granite staircase to pay attention to the words leaving Joy's mouth.

"I can't wait to hear what happens when Jillian reads those letters," Joel said, arms crossed and slouching as he shook his head. "He's gonna be in fer it."

"That's the hope," said Marielle, beginning to regret revenge's collateral damage.

"I expect they'll go to Jillian's parents first," Tom remarked, amused by his book, or something entirely different.

"Hey, did you hear that Hugh's car got keyed last night?" Joel asked, smiling like the information made his day.

His comment was enough to pull Marielle's attention from the hall. "Really?" she asked.

"Yeah, it was sad, actually. Someone wrote *Dick Sucker* on his driver's-side door."

"Why's that sad?" asked Joy.

"Because they spelled it wrong," Joel explained. "No one's gonna take you seriously if you can't spell 'dick' right."

"Maybe they misspelled it on purpose," Tom said to his book.

"How does *that* make sense?" asked Joy.

A lightbulb went off in Marielle's brain with enough force to move her head up. Tom saw the movement and knew she was looking at him, but he forced himself not to look back.

Chapter Thirteen

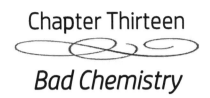

Bad Chemistry

"Your mother got a call from your school today," Jack said to his daughter during a commercial break. "Do you know what that's about?"

"No, sir," Marielle replied, losing confidence this was true even though nothing leapt to mind. She had spent homeroom planning the next pep rally with the principal and he hadn't mentioned anything non-rally related.

"Well, your mom should know more," Jack added, seemingly accepting his daughter's word.

***

"Your Chemistry teacher called today asking if there were any problems at home!" Maria said aggressively while standing in the dining room's archway.

It wasn't a question so Marielle didn't answer it, but the implication was clear. She had broken the family's code of silence.

"Why would she ask that?" Jack asked, accusing his wife and daughter at the same time.

"I have no idea," Marielle replied, adopting an expression of one innocently accused, though ideas of chalk rearranging leapt to mind.

"She said Marielle's grades have dropped since the start of the year and she seems upset and distracted," Maria explained.

"That's because I hate my lab partner and I can't stand Chemistry," Marielle protested, failing to mention it was the class immediately after lunch—a time when she generally finished her letters to Dermot.

"The lady asked for a meeting on Wednesday," Maria continued, annoyed with the inherent action item.

Marielle's eyes closed involuntarily.

"Well, we'll have to run over there during lunch, then," Jack replied, unhappy with the task as well, but doing his best to take it like a man.

***

"Where are you going?" Joy asked as Marielle stood and began loading books and school supplies onto her left arm.

"I have a meeting with my parents and Mrs. Schmidt."

Tom looked up with interest, but without speaking.

"Where's Joel?" Marielle asked.

"The computer lab," Joy responded. "He thinks he can make naked pictures of women using only ones and zeros. Why don't you leave your books here?"

"I don't know how long this will take," she said as she spied Hugh watching her from the vending machines.

Minutes later, Marielle stood behind the glass doors, watching her parents park their car in the teachers-only parking area.

"Hello, Marielle," a woman's voice said behind her.

Marielle looked over her shoulder. "Hi, Mrs. Schmidt. My parents are on their way in now."

"I see that. I'll wait for you in the small conference room," she said, withdrawing into the glass-enclosed administration area.

"Your father wants to finish his cigarette," Maria explained as she entered the school alone.

Marielle spied her father with concern as he stood with his back against the silo like he had all the time in the world to ponder Emmers Drive. "How long is that going to take?" she asked her mother.

Maria shook her head in disgust. "Who the hell knows?"

"Did you want to go inside?" Marielle asked hopefully. "My teacher is waiting in the conference room."

"No," Maria said with a sigh. "We'd better not."

Five minutes later, Marielle and her parents walked past the reception counter to the conference room whose windows looked onto the street.

"Sorry we're late," Jack said with a chuckle, expecting his wit and good looks to pass for promptness.

"Yeah, I saw you outside," said Mrs. Schmidt coolly, offering her hand without a smile or any obvious fear of Jack. "Please have a seat."

Jack's smile quickly turned into a warning sign.

Maria smiled broadly to counteract her husband's impending hostility while Marielle looked nervously between the adults before sitting down.

"So, what's she done?" Jack asked impatiently as though the target of his annoyance had suddenly turned to his daughter.

"She hasn't done anything," Mrs. Schmidt began somewhat defensively, "but I think it's important to inform parents when their child is on the wrong... what shall we say?... trajectory. Now, your daughter is bright and her homework is generally complete and on time, but I have concerns about her participation during class and in labs. Additionally, her quizzes thus far haven't indicated a complete grasp of the material. If she wishes, she can stay after school for tutoring."

"Which nights do you work after school?" Jack asked Marielle with simmering hostility.

"Every night except Thursday," she murmured.

"She has Pep Club on Thursdays," Maria interjected.

"Well, maybe she needs to drop that activity or one of her jobs!" Jack countered aggressively.

"That is none of my business," Mrs. Schmidt said efficiently while rising to her feet, "and you will have to work that out amongst yourselves. I must return to the Commons."

"Of course, thank you for your time," Maria said, half standing and only half smiling.

Jack followed Mrs. Schmidt's departure with his eyes, but said nothing. He never liked teachers—not as a student, and not as a school janitor—and Mrs. Schmidt was doing nothing to change his opinion.

Marielle returned to her table, sitting as though someone pulled the batteries from her back.

"How'd it go?" asked Joy.

"It looks like I'm quitting one of my jobs," Marielle muttered.

"That sucks!" Joy exclaimed.

"Yeah, I've only saved $400 so far." She looked up to groan at the ceiling.

"How much do you need?" asked Joel.

"Seven hundred and fifty dollars for my ticket and at least $100 for spending money."

Tom looked up from his book. "Can your parents help you?"

Marielle shook her head as she said "no," breathing in instead of out.

***

"Doug is visiting this weekend and I don't want any trouble from you," Jack warned Marielle, narrowing his eyes as his beer can hissed.

She thought to protest, but her father was right. Trouble between her and Doug was likely.

Marielle remained in the living room until the next commercial break, then walked upstairs to review her History notes. She had a sinking feeling while clearing the second cart of bed trays that something in

History was due, but she still felt shocked enough to curse when she read her notebook.

She consulted her clock radio, knowing before confirming that it was too late to go to the library. She opened the door to her parents' TV-lit room, then waited for her mother and sisters to notice. "Do you mind if I use the phone, Mom?"

"Isn't it a little late?" her mother asked, lifting her head to eye the digital clock on her dresser.

"Yeah, I didn't realize that I had a paper due tomorrow on the fall of the Roman Empire."

"I can tell you how the Roman Empire fell," Maria offered confidently.

Marielle listened to her mother's explanation, then delicately asked to use the phone anyway. Moments later, she consulted Tom over a crackling phone line.

"I don't imagine you have a book about this at your house," Tom mused.

"No. We only have exactly two books in the house: *The Bible* and *The Rise and Fall of the Third Reich.*"

Tom chuckled. "Your mom should know how it fell. Isn't she Italian?"

"She is. She said it fell because of orgies and gays in the military," Marielle explained, waiting a respectable time for Tom to stop laughing before he offered to consult his father.

"My dad said he could send a copy of his thesis with me tomorrow, but that would be too late for you. He said you might get by if you say that the Empire expanded to a level that was too large to defend. This meant that they were easily attacked by people like the Vandals and the Huns. In the end, they spent too much money on defense. There was some corruption and mismanagement too."

Marielle wrote feverishly as Tom recited statistics and sources from his father's paper.

"Do you need more?" Tom asked.

"No, that should be enough," she said before conveying her gratitude and goodbyes.

"Would a person who ravages be a ravager?" she asked Tom the following day during lunch.

Tom set his book on the table. "I thought that paper was due today."

186

Marielle blushed slightly. "Sorry, I thought today was Friday."

"What's the question?" asked Joel, having just arrived at the table.

"What do you call a person who ravages?" Marielle asked.

"An asshole!" Joel interjected, laughing.

Tom glanced at Joel while smiling. "I don't know. I've only ever heard *ravage* used as a verb."

"I wonder why that is?" Marielle asked, staring past Joel as two boys pushed one another playfully near the vending machines.

Tom sat back as he considered the question. "Maybe there's just never been enough work in ravaging or pillaging to give the doer a title."

Marielle nodded slowly. "*Ja,* I suppose it would happen in fits and starts and who would want something like that on their resume anyway?"

"It would suck to be pillaged," Joy not so much added as subtracted.

Marielle replied mechanically without turning toward her. "I guess it would depend on who was doing the pillaging."

"Yeah," Joel added, "a lazy pillager wouldn't be so bad."

"I agree," said Tom with a nod, "but no one wants to be pillaged by an overachieving pillager."

"Aha!" said Marielle. "Is *pillager* a word?"

Tom shrugged his shoulders a moment before Marielle threw down her pen.

That evening, Marielle entered the living room to find Doug drinking beer with her father. Doug looked up, but didn't smile, his grimace matching perfectly the expression on Marielle's face.

Doug appeared just as red-haired and freckle-faced as Marielle remembered, but the shape of his head seemed rounder. She scanned him quickly as she thought, *I see you wore your* good *Big Johnson t-shirt.*

"Where's Jeanette?" her father asked.

"I don't know. Tonight was my Pep Club night. I don't think she expected to see Doug here until tomorrow."

Marielle didn't want to make eye contact with Doug or say his name, but she had determined that one was better than the other.

"Is her shift over?" asked Doug.

Marielle sighed. Now she had to do both. "It would be if we were working together. Well, I have a paper due tomorrow. I'm going to head upstairs," she said, withdrawing through the dining room.

"She'll come around," said Jack. "And even if she doesn't, who cares? You're not dating that one anyway." He chuckled.

Marielle thought words she would never print all the way to the second floor. She opened her parents' bedroom door at the top of the stairs and collapsed on the bed beside her mother. Tonight she would watch *Dynasty* without feeling guilty about it.

The following night, Marielle beat an equally hasty retreat as her sister greeted Doug with too much enthusiasm to be tolerated. A few minutes later, Marielle's uniform lay on the floor of her bedroom and U2 was in the air.

"Marielle! Phone!" Anna called from the upstairs hallway.

"Just a second!" Marielle replied, slipping her nightgown over her head before making her way to the French phone.

"Are you coming to the dance tonight?" Shelly asked as Billy Idol yelled in the background.

"Oh, no. Sorry. I forgot to tell you that I had to work tonight."

Shelly paused. "But you're home now."

"Right, but I have to be up at 5 a.m. tomorrow."

"I thought you were quitting Hardees."

"I am, but I haven't yet."

Shelly breathed into the phone. "Okay, but you have to promise me you'll be at the next dance."

"Of course," Marielle replied. "It's Homecoming."

She returned to her room feeling guilty and a little depressed. Kids her age were yelling alternate lyrics to *Mony Mony* right now while jumping around like pogo sticks. She crawled into bed feeling older than her age, convinced she might feel better if she could only dream about Dermot.

***

"What the fuck are you doing up?" Jack thundered, seconds after opening the bathroom door to find a uniformed Marielle rounding the banister.

"I'm going to work," she said, voice shaking along with her hands.

Jack took two angry steps toward his daughter before she turned and darted up the stairs. She had nearly reached the top when he seized her ankle, pulling her a third of the way down the stairs. Marielle feverishly grasped at staircase finials, holding one long enough to see Doug sitting up on the orange couch, looking at her through the dining room doorway.

"What on earth is going on?!" Maria demanded from the second floor.

Jack stomped past his prostrate daughter. "Ask that stupid bitch what she is doing in her uniform at 4:30 a.m.!" Jack slurred as he pointed to the stairs.

"She's going to work," Maria answered, stepping backward as her husband continued forward.

"You're as stupid as she is," he said, his face painfully close to his wife's.

Marielle rose to her feet, still shaking as she held the railing tightly.

"We agreed on Wednesday that she was going to quit this job!" Jack roared.

"Well, she has to give two weeks' notice first. She can't just quit," Maria reasoned, losing her vehemence on the last word.

"Oh, because a bad reference from Hardees could ruin her career in the hamburger industry?!" Jack scoffed.

"No, because it's the right thing to do," Maria replied, ignoring her husband's sarcasm.

"Both of you can go to hell! I'm going to bed!" Jack declared, pushing past his wife, still unaware that he wore only a white t-shirt and matching briefs. The house vibrated as he slammed the bedroom door.

"Just go to work," Maria said impatiently, looking toward Marielle's bedroom as the only logical place to sleep.

Doug turned away from the door before Marielle walked through the dining room which was for the best. Worse than getting pulled down the stairs at 4:30 a.m. was getting pulled down the stairs in front of Doug.

***

"Did you give your notice today?" Maria asked anxiously as Marielle entered her mother's bedroom. There was no way Jack could hear them downstairs, but she lowered her voice anyway.

"I did," replied Marielle like a soldier confirming her orders.

"How did they take it?" asked Jeanette.

"Chris didn't look fazed at all. He just said, 'Okay. That's fine.'"

"Wow, that's cold," Jeanette reflected.

"Yeah, well, I'm sure he wasn't too pleased when Stephen kicked the crap out of one of his managers."

"I imagine," Jeanette replied, sending more concern than usual in her sister's direction. "Doug said he was about to get up and kick the crap out of Dad this morning," she continued as though she believed it.

Due to a mixture of both respect and fatigue, Marielle didn't say what she was thinking, but she realized at that moment that Jeanette was especially anxious for her sister to like her boyfriend, and that indicated a more permanent attitude toward Doug.

"Mom, can you wake me up in twenty minutes?" Marielle asked, still holding the doorknob. She had already changed from one uniform into another to maximize her sleeping time.

Her mother nodded.

"Thanks," Marielle said, closing the door behind her. She had interrupted a discussion between her mother and sister moments before, and that discussion was clearly not over. Her only hope was that this morning's events weren't used by Jeanette as an excuse to marry quickly or badly.

Marielle slept very little that night, distracted as she was by her own plight as well as that of her sister. A list after midnight, however, yielded an unexpectedly happy result, giving her the date she would earn enough money to buy her ticket to Ireland, as well as a subsequent date when she'd earn enough spending money to travel.

Though she could ill afford a call to Dermot, she felt certain she deserved to hear his voice. So, minutes before her pre-dawn shift began, Marielle sat with her back against the kitchen cabinets, listening impatiently to the familiar double-buzz of an Irish telephone while her eyes darted across a room lit only by the hood light above the stove.

"Hi Dermot! It's Marielle," she whispered suddenly.

"I assumed," he replied happily. "People with strange American accents don't often ring me."

"Hee, hee," Marielle said in mocking tones. "I'm calling for three reasons, but I have to be quick 'cause I have to work in... ah..." she stretched to see the oven clock, "four minutes, but wait, did you receive my very long letter yet?"

"I did, indeed. I was sorry to hear about your grandmother. Is she still in hospital?"

"No. She's doing better now. She and my grandfather may come to see us in a couple of weeks."

"Ah, that's grand," he said softly. "I'm planning to write you today so I refuse to tell you what I mean to say or you'll likely throw my letter into the bin when it arrives."

Marielle shivered unexpectedly. "That's not likely. It should be crossing your birthday present in the air. I mailed it yesterday. The nice lady at the post office said it should arrive in plenty of time."

"Ooh, wha'tis it?" Dermot asked with sudden excitement.

"I'm not going to tell you. I want it to be a surprise."

"I hate waiting. Give me just a wee hint," he said playfully.

Marielle refused which caused him to beg repeatedly and her to finally relent. "Alright, it commemorates a recent event."

"Is it a piece of the Iranian jetliner you shot down last summer?" he asked.

Marielle gasped. "No! You're mean! That was an accident!"

"I'm not cheap," Dermot countered.

"Sorry?"

"You said I was mean."

Marielle's eyebrows furrowed. "Mean doesn't mean cheap. It means rude."

"Like bold?" Dermot asked.

She shook her head. "No, bold means strong-willed."

He drew a sharp breath. "I presume you Americans think you can change the meaning of any word you like."

"Yes," she said, then paused, "but I'm not changing the meaning of anything. Bold and mean mean what they mean."

"Do they, now?" he asked with a thicker version of his accent.

Marielle smiled. "So, I need to tell you about the second thing."

Dermot groaned as if in pain. "Please don't tell me you've passed your driving test."

Her smile widened as she said she did.

"You lucky sod," he said with exasperation.

"Uhhh, it's not luck. It's skill. But my parents don't trust me enough to let me take the car anywhere yet so I had to balance your gift on my bike all the way to the post office." Her words picked up speed, lest Dermot ask her again what she mailed and she be tempted to admit it was an Olympic t-shirt. "Ooh, but there's one more thing I want to tell you— ask you, actually. How 'bout if I fly there for my spring break during the third week in April? I calculated that I should have enough money saved by then and I was going to go on my choir trip to New York, but why would I spend my break with a teacher who yells my last name like he's condemning people to the underworld when I could spend time with you instead?"

"Wow, I'm… flattered," Dermot said with an air of dismay.

"I didn't mean to say you're a close second to a married, middle-aged man who hates me. You definitely beat him… by most measures." She chuckled before she remembered the time. "Look, I have to run."

"Alright—" Dermot began sadly, the end of his sentence barely audible.

"What's that?" Marielle asked, hoping she heard correctly.

He cleared his throat before repeating, "I miss you."

Marielle paused for a moment, hoping to leave a tender moment alone just like Billy Joel suggested, but not sure she could manage it. "I miss you too," she confessed.

***

"So, he never responded about whether you should come in April?" Joel asked, a look of concern overtaking his face. "If I were you, I wouldn't keep calling this guy. He'll think you're a freak."

Two days had passed since Marielle's conversation with Dermot, but the glow hadn't faded yet. His last words and the sincerity behind them relentlessly lingered.

Joy sneered at her cousin before remarking, "This from the guy who waited outside a girl's school for two hours holding flowers."

Joel leaned toward her aggressively. "Yeah, well, I didn't know she had forensics practice that night."

"But she already told you she liked another guy."

"Yeah, well, that doesn't count."

"Why's that?" Marielle asked Joel, finally interested.

"Because that was during my stalking phase," he answered matter-of-factly.

"He's still *in* his stalking phase," Joy declared.

Marielle smiled as her eyes shifted between the cousins. "Why do you say that?"

"Because he goes down Northland Avenue to Badger when he could easily just stay on 41 for another exit."

This comment piqued Marielle's interest, not only because Joel held a flame for longer than a few weeks, but because Joy's observation was at least partial proof that she noticed more than boys' asses.

Joel's face contorted as a precursor to either lashing out or saying something painfully honest.

"Don't worry," Marielle said quickly. "You'll get over her soon."

"Right," countered Joy. "He hasn't gotten over Goose dying yet."

"That's not fair!" Joel exclaimed, barely modifying his pained expression. "I didn't see that coming! Here I thought the whole movie was going to be about winning Top Gun and they throw in emotional tragedy. I kept thinking, *how can this happen? It's a training mission and Maverick pushed eject.*"

"Pulled, actually," Tom said from behind his book.

"I know," Joel continued, "and the next thing you see is Maverick walking alone down the hallway." Joel paused, gathering himself for his final sentence. "And let me ask you, who could ever replace Goose?"

"No one," said Tom, shaking his head slowly with equally exaggerated sadness.

"So, this girl is your Goose?" Marielle asked.

Joel nodded.

"And you're Maverick?" she asked.

"Yeah," he said with abundant breath, "but I'd give anything to be the canopy."

5-Sep-1988

Hi Marielle, my perpetually paranoid psychedelic phosphorescent pretty perverted pondering paradoxical pen pal!

How are you? I'm fine (well, that's what you always write)! Thanks for ringing and for your letter!

I can't wait for you to get here in April! First of all, WHEN you come to Ireland you WILL stay at LEAST four days. That's minimum! In fact, you can stay for a month if you really want to! We Irish people are very welcoming (at least that's what Americans seem to think). Please don't insult my intelligence with any more of your pathetic jokes! Also, colour is spelled "colour" not "color." Why can't you Americans just accept that you're wrong!?

Now, I'll explain about the colleges to you. O.K. – Trinity College is in Dublin. There is nowhere in Ireland called "Trinity." Trinity is for semi-intelligent snobs. The Royal College of Surgeons is where you qualify to be a doctor. Then there are U.C.D, U.C.C., and U.C.G: University College Dublin, one in Cork, and one in Galway. They're for intelligent good-looking superior humans like you and me. Did you know that after the Japanese, the Irish are the best educated in the world? It's true. There's a really high standard here.

What do you think about the Olympics? You know, there's an Irish swimmer who broke the Irish swimming record in his first heat and didn't even qualify?! That's pathetic. I read that 30% less Americans are watching the Olympics than in '84. It's probably because the East Germans and Russians are beating you!!!! Gloat, Gloat. (Only joking).

I'm training to be a lifeguard. Did you know that there is no 50m pool in Ireland? Aaagh! And the sea would freeze your b...b...b*@!# off!

I'm very disappointed at what you said about American lads (no, I don't mean I'm disappointed because I'm homosexual, not that you'd think that). Well, you don't have to worry about being seduced by me in a car park. I don't have a car. Ha! Ha! Forgive me! I had heard American "guys" were like that, but I hear a lot of things which aren't really true! There's loads of lads like that in Ireland, but what's really weird is that there's just as many girls like that as well! (e.g. Paula: "Well, Dermot, nice and quiet isn't it? Nobody but the two of us...") That was the first night. I mean French kissing is great, but not when you're worried about being eaten! I suppose there are lots of girls like that where you are as well.

What's this about the America's Cup? I'd say you'll be beaten (as usual). You're not cheating with the catamaran (not "catameran"), but there's no need to be so f....ing big-headed about "high degree of intelligence." I have yet to meet an American who wasn't big-headed about the "U. S. of A." Don't forget, America was only discovered by accident! Hah! It's also pretty pathetic that you had to copy English instead of inventing "American." Enough of this! (No more rude comments)

Please, please, please don't become a nun because if you do, we won't be able to... but that never occurred to me because I'm Irish. What I mean is that black really isn't your colour (note correct spelling).

I get loads and loads and loads of homework. I had an English test and a French test yesterday. I got 96% and 98%. Isn't that just "awesome"? I don't study a lot, I'm just another modest genius. In three days, I will get my Inter Cert (BIG exam) results. I'll go out to a disco to celebrate (hopefully celebrate) with my friends, and my parents have given me permission to let all my half-drunk friends stay the night in my house. It'll be MAD!

I think it's absolutely sick! What? That you only eat once a day, of course. I eat a lot: breakfast, dinner, dinner, dinner, and dinner. Most of my friends have about ten main meals a day too. I train five days a week which means I'm a mere 11 ½ stone, but I do have one friend who diets—Ronan. He's about 12 stone, 5'9" and he's been dieting for the last 16 years or so. In fact, he's the only lad I know who has steak for breakfast!

I never heard of anyone who left their walkman on something and then walked away with the earphones on. I did it myself twice when I first got my walkman, but it didn't break. It's an Aiwa—just another Japanese product.

I'm sorry about your first driving test, but it's really annoying that you Americans get your driving licence at 16! I've been able to drive for years and I won't be able to get one for another year.

If you ever write that small again, I'll kill you! Luckily I have a good microscope.

NOW, MARIELLE! I have something to say (write, actually) to you. I know what crack is, thank you (we DO subscribe to Time magazine, you know). "Craic" (pronounced 'crack') here means fun. What's the difference? One kills you, I suppose. I'm glad you're so glad I'm back to school, darling (said in a bitchy fashion). I'm glad you're slowly freezing to death!!

I've just noticed how much easier I find it to write to you now. It takes about half the time and I can write more freely or something. Did you know that you use less than half the number of exclamation points in every page you write now? Weird! No, SERIOUSLY, what was I about to say? Oh yes, I can't wait to see you! I'm still trying to figure out where you'll sleep. You couldn't sleep outside with my dog! No. And you can't sleep in the kitchen, and my bedroom is tiny. I'll probably sleep downstairs, in fact! I'm beginning to think I wrote this in my last letter. Crap! I did, didn't I?

I will now tell you some FUNNY jokes which you seem to lack, darling!

Q: How do you stop a teacher from drowning?
A: Take your foot off his head.

Q: What do you call a Russian with three balls?
A: Whoojanickabolikov. ("Nick" means steal, you know.)

You know what??? My mother won't be here when you come because she's going on a free holiday to Cuba. Yeah, Cuba! That's grrrreat! I didn't think of it until now. She's not very strict, but dad is a walkover! Good thing you're not in the hands of a disreputable AMERICAN pervert! (I'm not American.)

You were really lucky to find your purse. I don't know about the U.S., but Ireland is so slow that you need to apply for a passport about 95 years in advance.

My God! I've just finished your letter. Do you really love me "very, very, very, very, very much"? Well, I suppose I know you better than I know most of my friends. Especially after the last letter you sent me. Oh yeah, tell Hugh Shit-m-head (or whatever!) that your pen pal will get the IRA after him unless he minds himself!

I had a great time yesterday. Me and a few friends went out on our mountain-bikes, found a nice big golf course and kind of wrecked it (as well as our mountain bikes). I'm still finding bits of grass and mud in my gears. I heard golf is a real snobby game in the U.S. It's not in Ireland, but lots of lads who play it are... saps? Nerds? Creeps?

I got a COOL Swatch for myself last week! Do you know what Swatches are? I'll show you in April if you don't. I also got two new albums— Tracy Chapman and the Cure—"Man Standing on a Beach" or something like that. Tracy Chapman has a pretty good voice. INXS is O.K. too! Did you ever hear "Hotel California" (I hope so!) (The Eagles)? It's awesome! (spiffing, old chappie/old bean/old man/my fellow, as the British would say!)

At last, I'm on the final page.

Augh! I've school tomorrow. Why? Why? Why? And if so, why me? Why me? Why me? I think I should retire.

Now for my revenge! This is going to be SMALL!

My friend's girlfriend dumped him! What would you do if your boyfriend met you at a disco and didn't even say "hi"? I hope you have a good magnifying glass. Ha! Ha! She slapped him on the face and almost broke his nose!

I won three pounds from my Maths teacher today 'cos I had a bet with him (again) that he couldn't work out a sum. Naturally, I, the genius, had it already worked out. Please don't show this to your friends. They'll think I'm a stingy bastard!

Your last letter was really brilliant. I wish I could write as well as you! Well, in fact I can in Irish...

Álainn Marielle, Tá mé ag scríobh i nGaeilge amháin chun cur as duit. Mar sin féin ní féidir liom a bheith in ann aon rud a rá go maith i scríbhinn. Is féidir liom a bheith ag rá go bhfuil tú saille nó ghránna, ach nach bhfuil tú. I mo thuairimse, tá mé iontach, grá mór duit, Marielle. Is é sin i bhfad níos éasca a rá i nGaeilge. Slon. Dermot

Ah, that's a load off my mind! And you'll never know, will you? Ha!

Don't ask me why I did that.

I think you're working too much. You look really tired and you sound exhausted. (I'm a genius at finding out about people from their handwriting.) I'd advise two aspirin, a facial massage, and a new pair of socks. Also, avoid plutonium cyanide and flying psychopaths.

I'm getting absolutely SICK of writing about nothing so I think I'll take up some space.

Well, I promise to teach you how to windsurf if you actually make it across yon far-stretching horizon (sorry, I've been doing Shakespearean sonnets). If zee wind is strong, sailing might be safer, but it's better fun for me watching you trying to stand up on the board.

I'm really glad you're coming to Ireland. Please mind yourself! I'm getting desperate now. I love you! I love your phone calls, your letters and your photographs, that is. I wish I lived in America (next door to you, in fact). I'm sure we'd get on really well 'cos you seem to have a lot of the same thoughts as me about things. I'm looking forward to seeing you. I'll probably sneak up behind you at the airport (I've grown a little since my last photograph so you won't recognize me at all) and I'll jab my finger into your neck and say, "Hi! Betcha' don't know who I am."

I love you!
Dermot

Marielle dropped the letter onto her dresser with no plans to write back quickly. The last two paragraphs made up for much of her annoyance, but Dermot had insulted Americans while declaring himself a genius three times. Worse still, he wore a Swatch like all of the snobs at school, and he had enough money for an Aiwa which cost at least $60. For the first time, she wondered if Dermot would sit at a completely different table in the Commons even if he *did* live next door.

Chapter Fourteen

What Instruments We Have
—W.H. Auden – *In Memory of W.B. Yeats*

Marielle collapsed onto the loveseat still wearing her church clothes. She placed her elbow on the armrest and tilted her head to meet her open hand.

"How was Mass?" her father asked, rocking on his left forearm from his normal reclined position.

"Fine," Marielle replied. "The lector mumbled into the microphone so it was hard to hear."

Jack chuckled through his nose. "Why didn't you just open the missalette?"

"I was too lazy," she said smiling.

He nodded knowingly. "My favorite part of Mass is always the 'thanks be to God.' When I served Mass as a kid, I thought everyone was saying 'thanks be to God' because Mass was over."

"That's probably how it started," Marielle mused, "and people tend to say that sentence the loudest."

Jack chuckled. "God, I used to hate holding that big, heavy Bible during the Gospel. That thing must have weighed 50 pounds and the priest always talked so damned slow. I always got the old ones who were retired and filling in for priests on vacation."

"How long were you a server?" Marielle asked.

"A good few years. I stopped before Grandpa Riess died, but Grandma asked me to serve his funeral Mass, so that would've been the last time, but I can't remember how old I was then."

"Grandma said her father's second wife wouldn't let him get buried next to her mother and *Tante* Mueller."

Jack took a puff of his cigarette before he shook his head. "No, she didn't. She put him clear across the cemetery from Grandma."

Marielle's face registered distaste. "I'm surprised Grandma never poisoned that lady's schnitzel."

Jack laughed through his nose, trailing smoke. "Boy, those two used to get into it. That woman was crazy. She once threw an open can of paint down the stairs at my mom."

"Jesus!" Marielle said, her mouth remaining open.

"Yeah. Your Grandma and Grandpa tried to evict her, but there was something in Grandpa Riess' will that gave her free rent until she died."

"How long was that?"

Jack shook his head slowly. "I don't know. She was still there when I moved out, but luckily she died just before they had to sell and move up north."

Marielle's eyebrows rose slightly. "That was lucky. I imagine she's burning in hell now."

"Probably," Jack said, biting the skin on the side of his right thumb. "She actually wasn't that bad though. She would hide me in her apartment when I skipped school and she'd buy me and my friends beer when we were only 13 years old."

"Whoa!" Marielle said, lifting her head from her hand.

Jack employed the coy smile of a bad teenager.

"That must've made Grandma crazy!"

"As far as I know, your grandmother never found out. The only time she caught me drinking was down the block at Shine's."

"Sunshine's?" Marielle asked, having heard the traumatic version of this story many times.

Jack nodded.

Marielle narrowed her eyes at the corner above the TV set. So, the same woman who killed Uncle Paul and Grandpa Riess had started her father on the path to alcoholism. If the woman wasn't already dead, Marielle would've been tempted to kill her.

***

Marielle dropped a stack of books and writing pads on the lunch table with a thud, causing everyone to look toward her.

"What's with all the books?" Joy asked with distaste.

"I've been avoiding my locker," Marielle muttered, sitting down.

"Why?" asked Tom with genuine interest.

"Because Richie Zoeller wants to ask me to Homecoming."

"How do you know *that*?" Joy asked, unconvinced.

"Because he told Shelly he was going to ask me when I wasn't here yesterday and he wanted to know where I was."

"And where were you?" Joy asked.

200

Marielle coughed halfheartedly into her fist. "I was sick."

"So, why can't you just tell him *no*?" Tom inquired. "I mean, I assume you don't want to date him if you're avoiding your locker."

Marielle blew an errant strand of hair from her left eye. "Oh, I don't know," she replied. "I like his older brother and it would be awkward to eventually date the older one if I turned down the younger one."

"How likely is that?" asked Joy with less sarcasm than usual.

"Not very," Marielle replied. "He doesn't actually know I exist."

"That's a good thing for you," Joy remarked. "I heard he practically *lives* at church and he helps his dad run Bible Study, and religious retreats, and crap like that."

"Isn't that expected when your dad's a deacon?" Tom asked.

"Ahhhhh, NO!" Joy erupted. "Richie doesn't do any of that! OH! And I heard that he's going to that Bible thumper college outside of Minneapolis. What's that called?"

"I have no idea," Marielle said, sorry she brought it up.

"You know. The one where all those girls go to get their M-R-S degrees?" Joy pressed.

Marielle looked up at the ceiling, willing her hair to reverse course and cover her eyes.

"Anyway, I heard he won't have sex before marriage and won't marry a girl who has!" Joy continued, like she had verifiable proof of psychosis.

"Well, that takes you out of the running, then," Marielle noted.

Joy responded with her nose first. "So, when's your next driving test?"

"As you know, I already passed. Why? Do you have any tips on how one can fail a second time?"

Joy's eyes narrowed. "Wow, that's red! I don't even know what to say to you!"

Marielle nodded. "Clearly."

"I'm getting something from the vending machine," Joy declared, standing. "Does anyone *besides* Marielle want anything?"

Both boys shook their heads.

Marielle smiled triumphantly before retrieving the letter she wrote the day before. It had been over three weeks since she received Dermot's last letter and nearly two weeks since she stopped feeling actively annoyed at his rude comments about Americans. In fact, the "intellectual inferiority" and "big-headed" comments still bothered her, but she no longer held his Swatch against him since she noticed some of her favorite people at school wore the same.

10/13/1988 Thursday

HAPPY BIRTHDAY! HAPPY BIRTHDAY! HAPPY BIRTHDAY! HAPPY BIRTHDAY! HAPPY BIRTHDAY! (I was going to write that 16 times, but thought it might annoy you... which is actually a good reason to do it given your rude comments about Americans.)

Sorry I woke you up this morning. I wanted to make sure I didn't miss you before you went to school and I had no idea you'd still be in bed at 7am. What time do you get up for school anyhow? If I were still in bed at 7, I would never get to school on time... since it starts at 7:45am. Can I go to your school instead?... It being superior to an American school and all. By the way, I agree with you that America's educational system is inferior to yours. You must be grateful for this though. Can you imagine how powerful we'd be if we were educated? Does this sound arrogant? I can't help myself... since I'm a big-headed American. I found it humorous that you called Americans "big-headed" in the same letter you complimented your amazing intellect three times. You must be studying irony in school. (OK, I'll stop now.)

Speaking of studying, I'm doing none of that today. I abdicated this responsibility and stayed home sick. I either have tuberculosis or the bubonic plague—I can't decide which. I've become so whiny and self-pitying that I'm irritating even myself. I'll try to get this letter into the mail box before the mailman comes... if I don't collapse from the effort (more self-pity). AUGH!

It's amazing that you can deduce from my handwriting that I'm tired. I deduce from yours that you're left-handed. I say this because every time you make a T you begin the horizontal line from the right and trail off to the left which is exactly the opposite of what I do... and I'm right-handed... which is clearly superior to your hand... because it's American, of course. Ha!

Congratulations on getting a 96 and 98 on your tests! I wish my last two tests went as well. Did I tell you that my parents are convinced work is interfering with my "studies" (as you say)? I'm working 30 hours/week now so when they heard that my Chemistry grades were slipping, they

FLIPPED! They said I had to quit one job and they met with my teacher. This makes them sound like concerned parents, but I think they just wanted to yell at me in public.

Marielle wrote the next section of her letter in a circular pattern which diminished to a single point.

Did I tell you that it's Homecoming in a couple of weeks? It's a huge event here where the alumni come back to our school and there's a pep rally during the day, a football game at night, and a dance afterward. Because I'm president of the Pep Club, I'm in charge of decorating the gym for the pep rally, and decorating the Commons for the dance (the Commons is HUGE, but we get a lot of people to help for that). On top of that, I have to perform in the marching band during halftime. Oh! And the worst part is that I have to make a speech during the pep rally. It's a nightmare! You have no idea how bad I am at public speaking (I'll explain sometime) and no one wants to hear what I have to say about "the meaning of Homecoming" anyway. Maybe I'll tell a lame joke or something. Can I borrow one of yours? ☺ Sorry, I'm REALLY going to stop insulting you this time... and I'm going to stop writing in a circle. You must be tired of walking around your table. A hint for next time (in case you reread this) is to rotate the letter instead of yourself. You should visit an inferior American school. They teach you that stuff here. O.K., that was technically another insult after I promised to stop, but I'm really, really going to stop this time. Please don't send the IRA after me (and that's not an insult if it's potentially true)...

She ended her circular print.

...especially since I may need you to send them to Hughsifer's house. (Thank you for the offer, by the way!)

I'm starting to feel better about failing my first driver's test since my friend Heather just failed for the THIRD time. The first time, she decided to drive a stick shift since she thought the instructor would be impressed (most people drive automatics here) and give her a break on her generally bad driving. She said everything was fine until the instructor asked her to turn around in someone's driveway. It was a short driveway so her car smashed easily into the garage door when her foot slipped off the clutch.

The second time, she had an instructor who was a stickler for stopping at yellow lights (I subscribe to the "speed-up at yellow light" school of thought). He yelled at her a couple of times which made her so nervous that she slammed on the brakes as soon as a light turned yellow. Unfortunately, she was already inside the intersection, but on the plus side, she was speeding so the car skidded right through and didn't cause an accident. The instructor, however, was NOT impressed.

The third time, Heather got the same instructor she had the first time which I think is a little unfair. He must've still been upset about filling out that accident report 'cause as soon as she turned too far on a left-hand turn and hit the median (picture an upside-down J in your head starting from the bottom), he told her to drive back to the DMV and refused to talk to her. She assumes she failed although he never bothered to say so.

Ooh! My favorite song just came on MTV!! It's Never Gonna Give You Up by Rick Astley. Not only do I love that song, but I think Rick Astley is totally hot in the video! Did I ever tell you that I saw Def Leppard in concert last summer in Green Bay? It was AWESOME! Did you see Sinéad O'Connor last summer after all? Regarding your question, of course I know the song Hotel California! It's a requirement for all Americans. People who don't know it are deported to Canada. That's a true story. ☺ I also know what Swatches are even though that's definitely NOT an American requirement.

I forgot to mention on the phone that I might actually have enough money to buy my ticket just before Christmas and I have everything I need to apply for my passport so I'll do that this week. My mom has to sign a waiver (since I'm under 18), but then I'm all set! I can't believe I'll be there in six months! I'm already making a list of things to pack. Let me know if there's anything you want me to bring so I can add it to the list. Also, tell me what I can bring for your sister and parents.

Oh! Thank you for offering to teach me how to windsurf! I really appreciate the thought, but I must warn you that me getting into the ocean at any time during my visit is not a good idea. I don't mean to be a spoil sport so if you say you can't respect me unless I try, then I will, but if I were to see anything under the water that used to be above it like a boat/car/log, I'd forget what little I know about swimming and drown in a hysterical fit. Really. It sounds like I'm exaggerating, but I'm not. I'm a horrible swimmer and a water phobe (hydrophobe?) and I'm both embarrassed and accepting of this. PLUS, I assume you have sharks, dolphins, and/or small fish there? Any of those would make the water unfit for me to swim in it. Really. Unless you want to test your lifeguarding skills on me, I need to stay on dry land.

In an effort to make up for any disappointment you may feel over my water aversion, I've started studying Irish history so we can talk about that while I'm there... sitting... on dry land. Last week, I stopped at the library between bus transfers and started reading about the Irish Potato Famine. I can't believe how many people starved to death and no one did anything to help! It's insane!! I could see why there might be some hard feelings toward the British since they were happy to hold your country as a possession, but not-so-interested in helping you when you needed them... well, not actually "you" since you weren't alive in 1848 (unless you're a vampire like my lab partner). Anyway, I only had time to read a few paragraphs before I ran out to catch my bus so maybe the British came through for you in the end. In any event, I promise to pay my library fine so I can check these books out and stop writing with incomplete historical information. Oh! In flipping through the book, I saw a picture of an "Irish need not apply" sign that met Irish immigrants when they arrived in the States. I have to say, I'm pretty embarrassed about that, and feel honor-bound to tell you that everyone here loves the Irish now so I hope there are no hard feelings.

Speaking of hard feelings, Guy called me out of the blue a few days ago to say he "misses me" and wants to "work things out." I think he was actually crying which shocked me all to hell 'cause I thought he was an evil robot AND I would've thought the letters I gave his girlfriend's brother would've placed me squarely on his list of enemies by now. I told him I didn't see how we were supposed to work anything out since A) He lives in Madison, B) I don't trust him, and C) He's banned from calling my house (by me, of course). He said he'd send me a letter explaining how he felt, but I told him that was a bad idea, and "rang off" as you say. If he sends me a letter, I swear to God I don't know what I'll do! He's definitely the rare breed of idiot that isn't happy unless he's dating a girl and has two waiting in the wings. Now, why would I want to be any girl in that equation? The only possible reason might be because I like his cologne, and he's not a horrible kisser. I know exactly what you mean about crappy *kissers. Mark was complete shit! He used to alternate between using his tongue to clean my gums and scraping it under the bottom of my top teeth which was neither a turn-on, nor sanitary. I've also kissed a few suction-cup kissers (aka sea lamprey) and the only thing you can do with them is pray for an end, and avoid resting your head against an unmovable object.*

You're right that there are a lot of American girls who are only after one thing. My friend Joy pursued multiple members of the Appleton Foxes baseball team and when she finally landed one (i.e. had sex with him), she called everyone in Women's Choir to tell them about it. I'm not entirely sure why that was necessary—the class is similarly confused—and I'm beginning to wonder why I began the last sentence with the words "my friend." Anyway, predictably the guy isn't returning her phone calls and she's somehow surprised which leads me back to the question of why are so many people having meaningless sex? If the act is more important than the person you're doing it with, maybe you shouldn't be doing it at all! Am I crazy, or is everyone else? I'm done preaching now. On the lighter side of meaningless sex, here are some good jokes for you (I've been asking around for "good jokes" since you insulted my last offering ☺):

Q: How does a blonde (not me) turn on the light after having sex?
A: She opens the car door.

Q: Why did the blonde have a black and blue belly button?
A: Because her boyfriend was blond too.

You may be wondering why I tell blonde jokes when I'm blonde myself, but everyone in Wisconsin is blond (well, not quite everyone. There are three brunettes ☺ so it's not necessarily directed at me.) One more:

Q: Why do Scottish men wear kilts?
A: Because a sheep can hear a zipper a mile away.

Incidentally, isn't your last name Scottish? I don't ask for any particular reason... just curious. Ha! (Now, that's not technically an insult since I made no direct connection between you and the sheep. If you made the connection, that's between you and your flock.)

AUGH! THERE'S NOTHING ON TV!!! I suppose watching MTV is better than making hydrogen which I'd be doing right now if I was in Chemistry. I guess I could watch another Olympic retrospective. Speaking of which, I also read that 30% FEWER Americans (you said

"30% less Americans" and one uses the word "fewer" when the subject can be counted... which clearly Americans do... they count quite a lot actually) watched the Olympics this year. The article didn't list a reason, but I think the time difference killed it for us. You had to get up at 4am to see anything live and everything else was taped with a commercial break every five minutes. By the time they showed 10 minutes of pole vaulting, you'd seen 15 commercials and nobody cared anymore. I would also say that Seoul has nothing on L.A. as an Olympic venue, but that would be arrogant—although true.

Don't worry about telling me what you said in Irish at the end of your last letter. I'll just ask your mom when I get there... although you said she'll be in Cuba, right? Hey, what's there to see in Cuba? I assume you don't have family there. My friend's mom used to vacation in Cuba when she was a little girl, but back then it was a tourist attraction. Now, it's just filled with communists and '58 Chevys, or so I've heard.

Sorry that your t-shirt and tape haven't made it there yet. I blame the terrorists... and the communists, of course.

Oh me Lord! It's almost time for the mailman. I need to wrap this up.

I CAN'T WAIT TO SEE YOU!! I become crazy when I think about it so I need to distract myself all the time... which is where jogging and work come in handy. School is usually too boring to be distracting... except when I'm rereading your letters or writing to you... but that certainly doesn't distract me from thinking about you!

On your recommendation, I'm putting-off the decision to join the convent... though I'm very tempted to get it all over with and sign up now. Celia says she has a guy friend who is very sweet and has a hard time finding a date because of it. She wants to set us up on a blind date since she's sure I'll fall madly in love with him. I'm skeptical, but my dad went to Catholic school and he always complains he was taught by the "Order of the Bitter Spinsters" and I'd hate to accidentally join that group so maybe I should give dating another shot.

I love you! I love you! I love you!
Marielle

PS You still haven't told me what your FAVORITE COLOR is. (Please note the original English spelling, not the post-Norman Conquest modification. [It's true. I looked it up.] I guess it's just harder for Americans to be conquered than Europeans—although you don't need to know much about history to know that. Ha! Oops, was that another insult? I can't say for sure because I'm undereducated. If only I went to school in Japan...)

PPS We won the America's Cup. You can apologize in your next letter.

PPPS I'm enclosing this year's school picture. I hate it, but feel free to compliment me anyway.

Marielle laughed. She felt much better about Dermot's anti-American comments now that they were even. How normal people got over anger without revenge, she couldn't imagine.

"Do you think you could've written 'I love you' one more time?" asked Joel, nodding toward Marielle's letter.

"Probably," Marielle replied, "but then it would've been insincere since I only love him three times, not four."

"How can you love someone you've never met?" derided Joy before glancing across the table for allies.

"I have no problem with this," Tom remarked. "It's the people I've met that I have trouble loving."

Marielle smiled broadly at Tom before he turned away. She had determined that he was a cello at heart, or maybe he *was* an oboe after all and she didn't know very much about oboes.

"Why are you looking at Tom like that?" asked Joel accusingly. "Do you have a crush on him or something?"

"What?! No!" Marielle said as Tom looked up with interest. "I was trying to determine if he was a cello."

"What does that mean?" Joy asked with narrowing eyes.

"Whenever I meet people, I equate them to a certain musical instrument. Tom is definitely a string and complicated enough to be a violin, but I thought he'd prefer to be in the background which would make him a cello. Violins get too many solos."

"Ah," Joel said, satisfied. "So, what am I?"

Marielle glanced toward the windows as she sighed. Freely stating what she thought about people didn't feel natural unless it was an insult. "You're hard to pin down and this could change. You're rebellious so my first inclination is to make you percussion, but percussion needs to work as a team, and you're too independent. You're also kind of macho so I threw out guitar in favor of a tuba."

"I play guitar," Joel said eagerly.

"You can play *any* instrument, but it doesn't mean it's who you are."

"But tuba?" he said with disappointment.

"Yeah, but you're minor chords and angry keys like the *Jaws* theme. I'm pretty sure that was played on a tuba."

"Oh, okay," Joel said, somewhat appeased.

"What am I?" Joy asked with childlike enthusiasm.

Marielle began to smile at the response she knew she'd throw away. "You're a flute," she said quickly.

"Really? Why?"

"Because a flute is what all girls choose when they don't know what to play."

"*You* don't know, or *I* don't know?" Joy asked.

"*You* don't know," Marielle said confidently.

"But some girls may be called to the flute," Tom argued.

Marielle nodded as she said, "Absolutely."

Joy looked around with abundant confusion. "What are you saying? Is the flute a bad instrument?"

Marielle shook her head. "There are no bad instruments, just bad musicians."

Chapter Fifteen

Kindred Spirits
—John Keats – *O Solitude!*

"They're here!" Marielle called to her sisters as the white Buick inched delicately up the driveway.

Marielle ran out the front door and opened the passenger's-side door before the car came to a complete stop. "Ooh, sorry! I was too anxious to wait," she said to her grandmother who looked slightly startled and noticeably more frail since her last visit. "How's my lovely grandmother?"

"Oh," Frieda said, voice cracking. "I think I'm not long for this world." She smiled as she willed herself to turn her body toward the door.

"Nonsense! You look great. Let me give you a hand," Marielle replied, expecting to only steady her grandmother's right arm as she stood.

"Just give me a second," Frieda said, out of breath after dangling her short legs over the driveway.

"Stay right there!" Marielle said to her grandmother, running to the other side of the car as her grandfather emerged from the driver's seat. "I don't want you to feel neglected," she said, giving her grandfather a bear hug he struggled to return. Somehow, her grandmother's illness had made him more frail as well. Marielle was too shocked to think of anything to say or do besides run back to her grandmother's side of the car.

"Are you ready, Grandma? I can give you a hand. I help people at the nursing home sometimes, and I'm getting pretty good at it now."

Marielle placed one leg between her grandmother's, bent down, then reached under her grandmother's arms, lacing her fingers behind Frieda's back. "Tell me when you're ready. I won't move until you say go," she said calmly.

Frieda wheezed once into her granddaughter's ear, then weakly said, "Go."

Marielle pulled straight back to clear her grandmother's head from the doorframe before pulling up, successfully moving Frieda to a standing position.

210

"See. Easy, peasy, Japaneasey," Marielle barely said as water welled inside her eyes. She hugged her grandmother, closing her eyes tightly as tears fell.

Johan cleared his throat. Still standing outside the driver's-side door, he steadied his palm against the roof of the car as he studied his granddaughter, tears of his own accumulating inside his eyes.

"What's *this* all about?" Jeanette asked, approaching the car and attempting to lighten the uncomfortably heavy mood. "You'd think she never saw Shorty before."

Johan smiled at Jeanette with gratitude.

"Sorry," Marielle said, wiping away her tears as she eyed her grandmother. "Let's get you inside."

***

"If you don't get your ass downstairs and say hello to your grandparents, I swear to God I'll kick the crap out of you!" Marielle threatened Anna, looking and feeling equally wild.

"Like you could," Anna said dismissively, smiling as Jeanette appeared behind Marielle.

"You heard Marielle. Get your ass downstairs," Jeanette ordered, startling both sisters.

Anna sighed dramatically as she scooted to the side of her bed, then stood up. "Get out of my way," she said, looking Marielle eye to eye.

Marielle thought to push Anna back onto her bed, pin her down, and yell at her until she gave up trying to push and kick back, but she knew this wasn't a silent maneuver, and her grandparents had experienced enough drama in their lives.

Jeanette walked Anna to the living room, supervising her less than warm hellos, while Marielle started a pot of coffee and organized a selection of sweets for the dining room table.

"You know, when I woke up in the hospital I thought I saw my mother standing at the end of the bed," Frieda confided in Marielle shortly after Jeanette left for work and Anna returned to her room. "She looked exactly the way I remembered her, sitting on the porch, watching the traffic the way she did before she got really sick and began to wander. I probably told you this, but sometimes the police would bring her home before I knew she was gone. She always looked so frightened and they told me she'd sometimes say, 'I didn't do it' when they approached her. I asked her once what it was she didn't do and she said, 'I didn't kill Paul. You

211

have to believe me, Frieda. I would never hurt Paul.' "

"Did people think she had?" Marielle asked, setting down her miniature cinnamon roll.

"I hadn't thought so. I was old enough to see that things were never the same between my parents after we moved back to Chicago, but I thought that was because my father lost money on the farm, and, well, because of the witch. Maybe the police assumed a wife would resent her brother-in-law living in her house." Frieda paused as she considered whether to confide in her granddaughter further. "But the real problem was her footprints. It snowed the night Paul died and the only footprints between the house and the barn were my mother's, but she was the one who found him dead so that stands to reason."

"Did he get shot before or after it snowed?" Marielle asked.

"Now, that I don't know," Frieda said regretfully before clicking her tongue against her upper denture plate.

"Do you remember seeing the witch on your farm when you were home from school that week?"

"No, I never did, but I stayed in my room most of that week. I always regretted that," she said with a shaking of her head. "It was the last week of Uncle Paul's life and I barely saw him."

"Because he was working?" Marielle asked innocently, well aware this wasn't Uncle Paul's only distraction.

"No," Frieda said hesitantly. "My Uncle Paul was very handsome and so naturally he was popular with the ladies. After dinner, he usually went into town—to one tavern in particular—where he would play cards, drink, and flirt with the owner's daughter."

"Did the owner mind very much?"

"Not the drinking or playing cards part," Frieda said with a twinkle in her eye. "But he began to run a pretty big debt with the bar and his card buddies. So, there was enough suspicion to go around when he died and they didn't bother my mother too much, but of course moving away helped too."

"But you said the witch killed him. What made you think that?" Marielle asked as she pushed a napkin closer for her grandmother to reach.

"It was something she said after my dad died. I was coming up the stairs to pick up the suit for his burial. The witch spoke *Low* German, but I understood her anyway. She was talking to her ugly spinster niece and she said that her only regret was in not arranging things more perfectly the night Uncle Paul died."

Marielle's face immediately registered shock. "Did you ask her what she meant by that?"

"I did and she flew into a rage." Frieda shook her head. "She was crazy. She said I was a spy and I should mind my own business or I would end up just like my uncle. From that moment on, I forbade the kids or your grandfather from going up to her apartment and I prayed every night for her to move or die and just leave us in peace."

"Did that work?" Marielle asked with a mischievous smile.

Frieda laughed as color returned to her cheeks. "Not right away," she said.

Marielle leaned in confidentially. "I was wondering, is there any way we can exhume your father and move him to the grave next to your mother?"

Frieda leaned slightly toward her granddaughter. "You know, I wondered that myself."

"What are you two lovely ladies plotting?" Johan asked as he approached the table for another cinnamon roll.

Marielle jumped. "Nothing at all, Grandpa. We just thought we might want to set some things straight."

"Does it require a shovel?" he asked without the smile Marielle expected.

"It may, but Grandma needs to regain some strength before we can try it. Any chance you might want to help?"

Johan held his plate, looking thoughtfully for a moment. "No. The past is better left that way."

Frieda said nothing, but made a face at her husband after he turned his back. "Are you working this weekend?" she asked her granddaughter.

"No. I don't work at Hardees anymore and I took the weekend off from the nursing home for your visit."

"That's wonderful, kid. Your grandfather and I agree you're working too hard. You need to go out with your friends and have fun. When I was your age, I hated spending time with the old people. I couldn't wait until my mom said I had done my time and I could run around with my friends."

"We had Homecoming a couple of weeks ago, but it was too exhausting to be fun. Wait," Marielle said suddenly as a thought occurred to her. "When you were young, hadn't the old folks lived through World War I and the Civil War? Didn't you want to sit down and pick their

213

brains about what that was like?"

"No," her grandmother said vehemently. "The old folks we knew were born in the Austro-Hungarian Empire. They weren't here during the Civil War. Most were here by the time World War I started, but no one liked to talk about it since people called us names in the streets."

"Well, didn't you want to know what that was like?" Marielle turned toward the living room for back up. "Grandpa, didn't you ask your parents what it was like to come over on the boat or to travel out west when it was really wild?"

He shook his head. "No, I never did. I think about that now and wonder why. I know they were in Butte and Billings, Montana and I was born in Oregon, of course. I remember living above my father's shop in Seattle, but we never really brought up those days when we lived in Chicago. I wish I could go back now and ask my parents, 'Okay, you started here, and then where did you go?' But you think about those things too late. Your grandmother's right. We never saw much use in the old people and their stories when we were young, and I regret that now."

"I don't regret it!" Frieda said defiantly. "I couldn't stand listening to them criticize us kids and say we were disrespectful, and we didn't know what real suffering was like. It was always the same old stories and they always ended the same sad way."

Marielle reflected for a moment on how the optimistic first-generation Americans felt alienated from the people who sacrificed everything to bring them here.

"Well, I'm not going out while you're here," Marielle said. "I'd rather hear your stories than spend time with kids who think getting drunk and acting stupid is fun."

"Well, that's where we had you guys beat," said Frieda, shaking her head. "We went to clubs and danced all night—not this silly stuff where you hold onto the back of a boy's neck and dance in a circle. Our generation *knew* how to dance."

"Ooh, did you know the Landler?" Marielle asked, having seen *The Sound of Music* the previous weekend.

"No, that was for old people," Frieda replied, scrunching up her nose in the same way Joy did.

"Every Austrian wedding our band played had to end with the Landler," Johan said, shaking his head from behind Jack's newspaper. "And all the old folks would get up and dance to it."

Marielle sat silently processing everything she just heard: The same kids who criticized the dancing and cynicism of old people, grew up to regard the generations that followed with cynicism. She wondered if she had stumbled upon a universal truth, or if this behavior was merely anomalous.

Marielle attempted to steer conversation toward Uncle Paul during the remainder of the week since several new questions had occurred to her. Unfortunately, no mention of the smell of fertilizer from farms off the highway or the move to Appleton elicited any movement toward Michigan.

"So, why are you so interested in the past, kid?" Frieda asked as though sensing Marielle's anxiety.

"Oh, she can't stop talking about history," Jeanette interjected from the orange couch while leaning into Doug as he read a thick, hardcover book. "What were you droning on about the other day?"

"Oliver Cromwell," Marielle muttered.

"Yeah, apparently he used little Irish kids as shields or something."

Marielle refused to pursue this topic to either educate her sister or defend herself. She was close to cracking a family mystery and she had no plans to move off course. "I don't know," she said, returning to her grandmother's question. "I suppose if history repeats itself, I'll be like a fortune teller."

"I suppose that's as good a reason as any," her grandmother agreed.

Johan eyed his granddaughter over the top of the newspaper, then shifted his gaze toward his wife. Marielle took this as the warning it was meant to convey. She could speak to her grandmother about the past as long as her grandmother found it more pleasant than upsetting.

"You said your stepmother spoke German," Marielle began.

"*Low* German," Frieda clarified.

"Right." Marielle smiled. "Was that common for people in and around your town in Michigan?"

"No, actually. The town was Dutch."

"Did your parents know anyone there from somewhere else?"

"From Chicago?" Frieda asked.

"From anywhere. Like, for example, was anyone else from Austria?"

Frieda shook her head. "No, I don't think so."

"Did your parents speak any English then?"

"My mom and dad did, but not Uncle Paul. My brother Franz always

215

went with him into town whenever he bought or sold anything for the farm so he could translate."

Marielle ignored the snide comments her sister and Doug shared. "Is that the only time Uncle Franz went into town, or did he go out with Uncle Paul when he went to the bar?"

"No. Franz didn't have any friends, and he was a homebody anyway. He sat next to the fire reading most nights."

"So, there's no chance someone meant to kill Uncle Franz, but killed Uncle Paul instead?"

Frieda shook her head.

"Wait," Marielle said abruptly. "How did Uncle Paul socialize when he didn't speak English?"

Frieda smiled. "Well, he knew enough to order a beer, but you don't need to speak much English to lay down cards, and make eyes at girls."

Doug snorted, while Jeanette laughed under her breath.

"Is it possible that other people knew the highway was going through your property, but they didn't tell your dad because they wanted to buy the property out from under him to make money?"

"Maybe, but my parents weren't planning to leave until Uncle Paul died."

"Exactly!" Marielle declared.

"I don't see what you're getting at," Frieda said.

"Maybe the person who bought the farm from you was the same person who killed Uncle Paul."

"No. I don't believe that. The bar owner—the one whose daughter ran around with Uncle Paul—bought the farm."

"Well, maybe he didn't like his daughter dating Uncle Paul and he hit two birds with one stone?" Marielle asked hopefully.

Frieda shook her head before giving her verdict. "No," she said decisively.

"Why?" Marielle asked, slightly deflated.

"Because," Frieda sighed, "the girl was engaged to Uncle Paul and she was *in the family way*. No one would touch her after Uncle Paul died. It was because of this and to settle my uncle's debts that my dad sold the farm to the bar owner for less than he bought it for... and a whole lot less than the highway would've paid."

Marielle smiled unhappily. "Well, I guess we can't *all* be *Poirot*."

That afternoon, Marielle rested on the orange couch, quietly reading the *Time* magazine she purchased from the gas station across the street. Knowing Dermot's family received and read the same magazine made her feel closer to him, although she became distracted easily and often needed to reread paragraphs.

"You know," said Johan quietly from the living room, "that sniper in North Dickinson was found dead in the woods last week."

"No shit?" replied Jack. "Did Robbie have anything to do with that?"

"I assume not, but I don't know for sure. It got me thinking about what we discussed before. In other words, what we would do if anyone ever harmed one of the girls."

"I remember," said Jack. "I'm not gonna be a hero."

"It's not about being a hero, Jack. It's about what makes sense. I'm 77 years old. If they lock me up, it won't be for long anyway."

"I know, Dad. I'll let you handle it," Jack said like he was accepting an order from a superior officer.

So, this is what men talk about when they don't know women are listening, thought Marielle as she slowly rested the magazine upon her chest. She would pretend to be asleep if either man got up and walked into the kitchen or bathroom. She had seen enough horror films to know it wasn't safe to overhear plans about murder, even if they were chivalrous plans.

***

"I didn't want to rain on your parade yesterday," Frieda said as Maria excused herself to make brunch.

Marielle laughed at her grandmother's usage of teenaged jargon. "You didn't, Grandma."

"I know you think I'm only saying this because I hated my stepmother, and I did, but you should've seen her face when I overheard her that day. I think she would've murdered *me* if she hadn't been so damn old and slow."

Marielle nodded agreeably. "I just wish she had been seen on your farm or Uncle Paul was shot with her rifle. Do you know what kind of gun shot him?"

"Well, I don't remember people doing those gun tests back then. What are they called?"

"Ballistics," Jack answered from the living room, rolling his eyes for his father's benefit before turning the channel to *Meet the Press*.

"Anyway," Frieda continued, "anyone who lived on a farm had a

217

gun."

Marielle's eyebrows furrowed. "And the gun that killed Uncle Paul wasn't found near him?"

Frieda said it wasn't.

Marielle leaned toward her grandmother. "Do you remember anything about what led up to the murder? Any arguments or strange occurrences?"

"Leave your grandmother alone!" Maria ordered from the kitchen.

"Oh, it's fine, Mar. I don't mind," Frieda replied before addressing her granddaughter again. "Other than getting pulled by a horse and my dad getting sick, I don't remember anything strange."

"Were your parents fighting about anything unusual or did anyone visit the farm who wasn't normally there?"

"No. Wait now. I remember my mother throwing away food the day Uncle Paul died. I saw her smashing jam jars in the sink. I suppose that was only natural after finding Uncle Paul the way she did."

Marielle's face brightened. "Ooh, is it possible your father was sick because he was poisoned?"

"No," Frieda said firmly. "My father had a cold. He had a terrible cough. It kept the family up half the night."

"They were up half the night, but no one heard a gunshot," Marielle stated more than asked, but her grandmother shook her head in response. "Okay, so the only reason your father didn't go into town was because he was sick?"

"Well, my father usually *said* he was going into town with Paul, but he almost never got past the widow's house—that's, of course, how Paul *knew*," Frieda tipped her head to the right to bring Marielle to the proper conclusion, then continued, "but his cold was probably the reason he didn't go to the widow's house that night. That's also why my mom was the first one up the next day to start chores."

Marielle's head shot up. "Did your mom do the outside chores?"

"No, the men did."

"Then, wouldn't your older brother be the first one to the barn if your father was sick and Uncle Paul was dead?"

The corners of Frieda's mouth rose slightly. "Now that I think about it, he should have been. Pa, do you remember why Franz didn't go out to the barn before my mother?"

Johan shifted the newspaper in his hands impatiently. "I thought I made it clear that I didn't want any part of this," he replied.

Marielle stiffened until her grandmother made another face at her husband.

"Anyway, I'll call my little brother. He was too young to remember any of this, but he might have heard something later," Frieda explained.

Marielle steadied herself through a wave of sadness. Uncle Franz would have been the best source for this information. He lived beside their house in Kleiner for nearly half of Marielle's life—until late one summer night. She could still see the ambulance lights from her bedroom window and hear her mother say it was Uncle Franz just before she heard her father run toward the back door.

Marielle had cried the loudest during the funeral until sideways glances told her to stop. She thought about all of the questions she asked Uncle Franz about his dog, his garden, and the weather, but she had squandered her chance to ask him the important questions—the ones which could have been the difference between solving a family mystery or leaving it in oblivion.

"When we prove that it was your stepmother who murdered your uncle, can we still bring her up on charges?" Marielle asked. "There's no statute of limitations on murder, right?"

Frieda shook her head. "No, but I don't think the state bothers when the murderer is dead. I'd just be happy to write *Murderer* on her headstone."

"I'll buy the spray paint!" Marielle offered.

***

After five days in Appleton, both Frieda and Johan looked far less frail than when they arrived.

"Are you sure you won't stay longer?" Jack asked with sincerity as he rose to stretch.

"No, you guys have to go back to work and we would just be in the way," Frieda said lightly. "Besides, the winter hay should be arriving tomorrow, and I don't want Bobby Kendrick thinking he can dump green stuff on us like he did the last time. We were lucky he didn't burn the barn down! Did I tell you about that?"

Johan grabbed his wife's shoulders as he stood behind her. "We should get past Green Bay before the game lets out," he urged.

"Aren't you going to miss the second half?" Marielle asked, attempting to keep one eye on the TV to see the result of an attempted field goal.

"Yeah, but we can listen to it on the radio," he explained.

"Okay," Marielle replied, approaching her grandfather, "but don't let Grandma get too upset if the Packers start to lose. We don't need a repeat of your last trip home." She smiled to diffuse the strength of her directive even though she was completely serious.

"I won't, Blondie," he replied warmly. "I'll pretend we've lost the station and change it to Paul Harvey."

"Good plan," she said, hugging him vigorously.

Marielle and Jack settled back into the furniture after Johan and Frieda departed, trying to determine what had occurred in the game since they walked away.

"Oh, c'mon!" Marielle yelled. "If that ref had one more eye, he'd be a Cyclops!"

She turned toward her father to share in her cleverness, but he was too busy chewing his nails to hear her. For a moment, she thought her father didn't approve of her rooting for the Packers, but no station was carrying the Bears game anyway. So even if she *did* like Chicago, there was no way to root for them.

Jack picked up the remote control in the middle of a play to turn down the volume.

Marielle cringed imperceptibly as she waited for her father to speak.

"Your grandfather and I talked and we want you to stop asking your grandmother questions about Uncle Paul," he said, narrowing his eyes at the play no one heard.

Marielle opened her mouth, but she didn't reply. There was no method to defy both her father and grandfather. This directive had the strength of ten brick walls.

"What if Grandma brings it up?" Marielle asked, grasping at straws.

"She won't." He glared at his daughter. "Your grandfather is telling her the same thing on the way home."

So, we go back to talking about who came in late to church and who doesn't know their prayers? Marielle thought, but had the wisdom not to say. Instead she nodded, then excused herself from the game to lie on her bed.

A half-hour into moping, she determined that there was only one way to feel better without Dermot. No matter what it cost, she was going to call him right now and sit on the phone as long as their conversation naturally lasted. She consulted the clock to ensure calling was still

220

possible, then ran to the kitchen as though she was still hungry. On the return trip, she nonchalantly grabbed the cordless phone before rushing it upstairs.

"Hello?" a calm Irish voice asked across a buzzing line.

"Ello, might I speak with Dermot please?" Marielle said in her best Cockney accent.

"Yes? Dermot here."

Marielle dropped the accent and blurted out, "Ha! It's me. Did my crappy accent throw you?"

"Whenever I hear a crappy accent, I think of you, but I must admit the accent was quite good."

"Well, it was supposed to be Irish, but I didn't quite manage it."

"In that case, it was complete shite! I thought you were going for an East-Ender."

"No. I think I watched *My Fair Lady* too many times."

"I despise that movie!" Dermot said with feeling. "I can't watch it without wanting Audrey Hepburn to go driving with Grace Kelly."

"Eww," Marielle said, covering her right eye while laughing.

"Sorry. So, have you terrorized your neighbours with your family car yet?"

Marielle shook her head. "Not yet. I've asked my mom tons of times if she needs me to run to the store for milk or eggs, but she just sends me to the gas station across the street instead. It's very disappointing."

"Bad luck, that. I meant to ask you, what sort of questions does one need answer to get a licence in America?"

"Well, the hard part is your road test. I passed my written test months ago, but on the day you get your license you have to take an eye exam and give them your birth certificate and they ask you your height and weight and—"

"What's your height?" Dermot interrupted.

"I'm 5'6". It's horrible! I'm the shortest person in the state!"

"That can't be true."

"It's not," Marielle said, straightening her back against her dresser, "but it feels true."

"Did I tell you I'm over six feet tall?" Dermot said playfully.

Marielle rolled her eyes. "You did and you're a mean bastard... *mean* as in *not nice*. I certainly wouldn't say being tall makes you stingy. Hey, what's that music?" Marielle asked, looking toward her boom box even though she knew it was off.

"The Police. Sorry, I'll turn it down," Dermot said with a strained voice as though reaching for the radio.

"No, no, it's fine. I just thought it was Rick Astley."

"You're joking! I despise Rick Astley *and* his blasted song."

"Really?" Marielle asked matter-of-factly. "We have something in common then 'cause I hate The Police."

"You're just saying that because I insulted your boyfriend," Dermot said dismissively.

"Maybe," Marielle conceded. "Actually, I usually change the station when The Police come on so I *might* be telling the truth. I can't say for sure though 'cause I'm blinded by your insult. Is everything alright? You sound odd." And by "odd" she meant aggressive.

"Do I? I had a bit of a lay-in this morning and I've felt dodgy all day."

"Did you just say that you slept in, and now you're feeling groggy?"

He chuckled. "Yes, I did."

"Excellent!" she said, looking up at her ceiling. "I can finally translate Irish. Did I tell you that Celia asked me if you speak English?"

"Really? What did you say?"

"I said *nearly*."

"Very bitchy!" he proclaimed while laughing.

Marielle heard her father curse downstairs, but attempted to ignore it. "I have to say, I sometimes wish you didn't speak English at all."

"Why's that?" Dermot asked softly.

She shivered. "Because you're pretty good at insulting me."

"Well, thank you, but you deserve some of the credit since you generally give me cause. Is this to do with the Olympics?"

"No, it's just a general observation. Did I tell you that my friend's brother rowed in the Olympics?... Actually, we're not so much friends as acquaintances. She *did* tell me I had perfect pitch in choir once so I certainly wouldn't say I dislike her, but I don't think a compliment makes us friends. Do you think compliments make us friends?"

"You and me?" he asked, using an especially soft brogue.

She smiled. "Sure."

"Hmm. I think a lot of things make us friends."

"What time is it there?" she asked quickly.

"It's ten past nine."

"Ah, so you're still six hours ahead of us, then."

"Did you think our continents drifted closer together and changed the number of time zones between us?" Dermot asked aggressively.

"No, dumbass," Marielle replied with equal aggression, "I wasn't sure if you fell back with us in the fall. It must be cool to be six hours ahead, though. You know what's going to happen in the U.S. six hours before we do."

"Uhhhh, that's not actually how it works, Marielle," Dermot chided.

"I know. I was joking," she replied, briefly considering Dermot for Pseudo-Intellectual Category III. "You really *do* think Americans are morons, don't you?"

"Even if I did, I would never say so... to you that is."

"Why's that?"

"Because you're mildly intelligent, and because you scare me."

"Excellent!" she proclaimed. "I'd prefer if you went fetal upon hearing my voice, but I'll settle for scared. So, I'm surprised you slept in and no one knocked-you-up for Mass this morning." She looked up at her bed as she laughed.

"No. I attended Mass last night. Why's that funny?"

"Because here getting knocked-up means getting pregnant. My teacher told me that for you it means to wake someone up. I think it's a riot."

"A ride?" Dermot asked, himself sounding scandalised.

"No, a riot, R-I-O-T. Why? What does a *ride* mean?"

"It's a crass way of saying you want to have sex with someone."

Marielle laughed. "Well, I guess that's one way to get knocked-up."

"The only way I'm aware of, actually," Dermot murmured.

"Ahem," Marielle cleared her throat, "not if you're Mary."

"Right, sorry, I forgot about her."

"I'm starting to question whether you actually *did* go to church last night," Marielle said in parental tones.

"Because I forgot Mary was a virgin?"

"Exactly."

"Well, I'm not certain I actually buy that story. After all, what was her alternative to saying an angel did it? Getting stoned to death?"

Marielle nearly hyperventilated at Dermot's brazen attempt to refute the purity of Jesus' mother.

"Are you alright, there?" Dermot asked.

"Oh, yeah. Sorry. I thought I heard my sister at the door. Aren't Irish people supposed to be more Catholic than just about anyone else on the planet?"

"Well, the Church runs nearly everything here, so they're a good target for ridicule."

Marielle thought to pursue this further, but she was tired of jousting. "Sorry about my last letter, by the way," she said, exhaling. "I was sick and in a bad mood. Have you gotten it yet?"

"No. It didn't arrive in yesterday's post anyway."

"Crap! I mailed it the day after your birthday, but I put it in my mailbox instead of going to the post office. I knew that was a bad idea!"

"You can post a letter from your house?" Dermot asked with surprise.

"*Ja,* as long as you have the proper postage. If not, they'll send it back... although my friend Heidi writes 'Free postage for the Blind' on her letters and she says they always go through without a problem."

Dermot chuckled. "You say 'yes' like a German."

"Do I?"

"Uh-huh. So, you're speaking to her again?" Dermot asked with surprise.

"Heidi? No, I just have a good memory. Do you know if Ronan got Shelly's letter yet? She'll be asking me tomorrow at school and I have plenty of other reasons to disappoint her."

Dermot laughed. "I don't know. I'll see him at practice tomorrow so I'll ask."

"Thanks. Ooh!" she said, suddenly excited, "did I tell you I finally found out how the Potato Famine ended?"

"You didn't, no. I'm told it didn't end well."

"My book said the same." Marielle paused for a moment as stress from mentioning school a moment ago distracted her. "I have to ask your opinion about something," she said with far less enthusiasm than the Potato Famine elicited. "This guy at school asked me to the Homecoming Dance a couple of weeks ago, and I told him I'd get back to him, but I never did. Well, he didn't mention it again either so I was hoping he forgot and I didn't need to address it, but—"

"He didn't forget," Dermot interrupted.

Marielle groaned. "So, should I apologize?"

"Yes."

"That's what my friend Joel said, but I told him I had my reasons for avoiding him."

"And what were those?" Dermot asked, like he believed she may actually have a good excuse.

"He's good-looking, Catholic, and nice so there's gotta be something wrong with him. Now, I generally don't think looks matter, but when they go with all the other things that would make my mom WAY too happy, then I'm suspicious."

"Would you rather a mean ugly Protestant?" Dermot asked.

"Well, I'm not sure I'd *rather*, but I'd be more comfortable with him."

"It sounds like you want to be the more powerful person in a relationship. I believe it means you lack self-confidence."

Marielle's mouth opened well before she spoke. "You say that like it's news to me!" she exclaimed.

Dermot erupted into laughter which eventually subsided into a gentle voice. "Well, I must change that whilst you're here. Did I tell you you'll definitely be staying in my room?"

"No," Marielle said with finality. "I won't. I'll sleep on the couch."

"No," Dermot said, matching her tone. "You'll take my room."

Marielle sighed. "I refuse, and I'm not familiar with the laws over there, but I'm pretty sure you can't make me."

"You're an infuriating American!" he declared with more amusement than exasperation.

"And you're a stubborn Irishman. Ooh! I have a good joke: How can you tell if a girl from West Virginia is a virgin?"

"That's a poor attempt at changing the subject," Dermot argued.

"Maybe, but it's a good joke. So?"

"Hmm, I don't know. If she's American, I imagine she's not a virgin a'tall."

"Funny boy. The answer is: She runs faster than her brother."

"Eww, yuck!" he said away from the receiver. "Is that sort of thing common?"

"Rumor has it only in rural West Virginia... and the West of Ireland."

"Did you ring for the sole purpose of insulting me?" Dermot asked, amused.

"Not entirely, but I think you're frustrated because you expect to win more easily. You actually may be able to win a verbal war with most of my classmates, but I'm from a big family where weakness is not tolerated and sarcasm is the preferred means of communication."

"Lucky me. Might you give me one of your friends' addresses then—

preferably an only child?"

Marielle rested her forearms on her knees as she pulled them closer to her chest. "I could, but I'm afraid you'd find her dull and unsatisfying now that you're used to me."

"That's an arrogant thing to say from a girl who lacks self-confidence."

"*Ja,* well, I'm a walking enigma." She shifted uncomfortably. "Did I use that word correctly?"

"Maybe," he replied, "I have a headache now so my brain isn't functioning properly."

"Sorry about that. Take a couple aspirin and call me back in an hour."

"I'm going to be in bed in an hour," he objected.

"I know. I was joking. Hey," she lowered her voice to a whisper, "what's this about Americans not being virgins? My friend Joy isn't, but plenty of us are."

"Really?" Dermot asked with enthusiasm. "That's not the American stereotype."

"I know. I saw *A Fish Called Wanda.* It's hardly fair. The Irish stereotype is of hard-working, hard-fighting, and hard-drinking people who pray a lot."

"We don't actually pray a lot," he admitted.

"I'm beginning to realize that, but you drink? Really?" she asked, beginning to deflate.

"No, I don't. You sound worried."

"I'm not worried, just surprised," she lied.

"You would be the first American to show surprise at an Irishman who liked the odd drink."

Marielle nodded. "Well, I had hoped you weren't like that."

"I'm not, but let's get back to your virginity," he said eagerly.

Marielle rolled her eyes. "I am... well, I'm a virgin by technicality given some of the dates I've had, but those weren't my fault. Speaking of dating, last weekend I had the worst lunch date of my life!"

"You had a date in the middle of the day?" he asked, showing no annoyance at being put off.

"I didn't know the guy so I didn't want to commit to anything longer than that. Good thing too 'cause it went so badly that I think all blind dates should be outlawed from now on!"

"Ooh, that sounds serious," Dermot said with interest.

"It is. I met the guy (Celia's friend) at the mall and, for starters, he looked like a short, pear-shaped troll."

Dermot laughed, then stopped. "Hey, I thought you said looks didn't matter?"

"I did, but I didn't mean by that much. The height and face aren't his fault, but the shape is just pure laziness... which brings me to his personality. If staring at a girl and raising your eyebrows every ten minutes is considered good conversation, then I would have no complaints. But it's just irritating, and praying for death was the only thing that got me through walking around the mall with him and his eyebrows."

"I hope he bought you lunch at least."

"No. I bought it myself. I didn't want him to think I owed him anything."

"Did he talk to you then?"

"He might've. I wasn't paying attention anymore. I decided that my salad was much better company. I have a date with *it* next Friday."

Dermot guffawed. "Jesus! That's brilliant!"

Marielle smiled at the curtains. "Thank you, thank you."

"Hey, you never told me what happened to that bloke. I think his name was Mark."

Marielle sighed. "Oh, he never really talked to me after my brother attacked him. He's such a coward! At least Stephen had the decency to declare war openly, and that was only because Mark declared war on me covertly."

"Why would he do that?" Dermot asked with amusement.

"Because I turned down his repeated sexual advances."

"*I'd* declare war on you if you turned down my sexual advances," Dermot said through a smile.

"No, you wouldn't," Marielle said with confidence. "You'd just pout until I changed my mind."

"You're right! How do you know me so well?"

"I'm psychotic—I mean, psychic." She laughed. "Actually, speaking of which, does being psychic include the power of willing things to happen?"

"I don't believe so, why?"

"Because during my date from hell, I sent out powerful psychic transmissions to my friends so they'd walk by with a life or death problem only I could solve, allowing me to escape. But no one walked by. So, either willing things to happen isn't a psychic power, or I'm not psychic at all."

"Did you think you *were* psychic?" Dermot asked concernedly.

"No, but I knew you'd ask me that question."

"You're mad!" Dermot declared.

"Well, I only mean about 30% of what I say."

"Then, why say anything a'tall?"

"Because I hate awkward pauses. I have six possible conversations in my head at any one time so I'm never at risk of hearing an awkward pause. Now, statistically speaking, I can't possibly have that many true statements rolling around in my brain, so I often have to say things that I don't mean. By the way, I think you're very smart."

"Thank you," Dermot said without appreciating her joke. "You know, you talk nearly as much as you write?"

"Should I stop now?" Marielle asked, surprised that she didn't feel offended.

"Not a'tall. I'm home alone, and you're the only person keeping me sane right now," he said, the final three words expending the last of his breath.

"Are things alright by you?" Marielle asked, using her own soft voice.

"Yes, well, they're fine. *I'm fine*, as you always say."

Marielle paused for a moment, wondering if she should press the issue before deciding to treat Dermot the way she wanted to be treated.

"Where are your parents?" she asked.

"They were in Dublin for the weekend. They've not arrived home yet."

"Isn't it a little freaky being home alone in an old country like Ireland?" Marielle asked, only half joking, and grateful it was still light outside.

"Well, I'm not alone with you and your letters to keep me company."

"Ooh, very smooth," Marielle said, smiling. "You know, now that I think about it, maybe my letter not getting there is *your* fault. Is your country on strike again or do they not deliver the mail when it rains?"

"If that were the case, the post would never arrive."

"Did I ever tell you that I love rain?" Marielle asked, looking up at her bedroom ceiling and sighing at the thought of it.

"You're daft," Dermot said dismissively.

"You already said that." She reached toward her radio for the beginning of the American music countdown.

"I did, but it bears repeating. So, what music do you like *besides* Rick Astley?" Dermot asked.

"Whoa!" she said, pulling her hand back. "It's like *you're* psychic. I was just reaching for my radio."

"Ooh, spooky. Do you like Tracy Chapman?"

"Her music is too depressing. If I wanted to commit suicide, I would play one of her songs."

"I think you don't like her because she's black and you're a racist," Dermot declared.

Marielle sat up, eyes fixed straight ahead. "Uhhh, either that or I just don't like her music and it wouldn't matter if she were white *or* black! So, by your rules I have to like a song if it happens to be sung by a black person? *Now*, who's the racist?"

"Relax, relax," Dermot said, comfortingly. "I was merely teasing you."

"Oh, sorry, you can't joke about racism with an Aryan. We're already on the defensive." She took a deep breath, then continued, "Did I tell you I quit my job at Hardees?"

"You didn't, actually. Is this because your brother attacked your supervisor?"

"No. Wait!" she said as two related stories collided in her brain. "Did I tell you my brother is leaving West Germany soon?"

"Oh, no! Really?" he asked, sounding more concerned than Marielle expected.

"*Ja*. Apparently, he was given the choice of either quitting the Army or getting kicked out. I don't know the whole story yet, but I think it had something to do with a German national."

"That sounds like an interesting story," Dermot remarked.

"It does. When I find out more, I'll tell you. Anyway, I quit Hardees because I'm beginning to suffer the effects of long-term sleep deprivation. Homecoming nearly killed me. I don't even remember what I said during my speech at the pep rally. More people are saying hi to me in the halls now, so it couldn't've been too bad. Actually, one of the chaperones said the Commons never looked nicer. We built a wall of streamers dividing the hall and we had a wooden footbridge connecting the two sides. Anyway, just thinking about it makes me tired." She sat back against the dresser. "The other day, I walked into the fridge at the nursing home and forgot why I was there. I nearly froze to death before I grabbed an open can of peaches and walked out."

"Well, at least you remembered why you were there."

"No, I didn't. I just didn't want to leave empty-handed. Ooh, before I forget! Is it true that the name *Erin* means Ireland? My friend Meghan says so."

"Is this part of the 70% you say, but don't mean?" Dermot asked with suspicion.

"No, it's a real question."

"No. It absolutely does NOT mean Ireland. Your friend is an imbecile," he said as though the matter was settled.

Marielle heard, but ignored his tone. "She'll be glad to hear it. You're right about golf, by the way."

"In what way?"

"You said you heard it's a snobby sport in the U.S. It is. A girl told me last year that I looked like I was on the school's golf team and I'm pretty sure that was an insult."

Dermot asked why.

"Because people on the golf team dress preppy—polo shirts, and sweaters tied around their necks, etcetera—and this chick wears only black clothes; dyes her hair black; wears black lipstick and nail polish; smokes slowly like a thought comes with each puff; and claims she's an atheistic nihilist. (She actually belongs to my Type V Pseudo-Intellectual category.) In any event, I read once that golf was a good walk ruined. I think Mark Twain said that. Do you golf?"

"No, but my dad's mad about it."

"Hmm. You'll have to ask him if he wouldn't prefer a good walk."

"Or if he wouldn't prefer to be a slow-smoking, atheistic nihilist," Dermot retorted.

"Exactly!" Marielle laughed, then rested her head against the dresser. "She's got some serious issues. I *love* when people assume a belief in an after-life and a generally perky demeanor mean you're simple."

"Aren't you?"

"Watch it! Hey, aren't nihilists automatically atheists?"

"I don't know for certain. I'll research it further and let you know," he said as if he meant to do just that.

"Thanks. I'd do it myself, but reading Nietzsche would flag me as a troubled student and I'd hate to get called into my school counselor's office. He already has his eye on me."

"Because you're mad?"

"No, he hasn't figured that out yet. It's because I bounce around school with a smile on my face all the time. I can tell he's trying to figure out if the smile is for real, or a front for inner turmoil. Of course, it's possible I'm paranoid and he's just considering how I might have applied my lip gloss better." Marielle looked away from the cobweb in the corner of her ceiling. "By the way, in answer to your question about music, I like INXS and the Ramones. Do you like either of them?"

"Do I need to choose only one?" he asked.

"No, you can choose both."

"Good. I choose both, then."

"Outstanding! I have one more thing to tell you and then I should probably let you go. Our school played a football game against Neenah at UWO, uh, University of Wisconsin at Oshkosh, and my dim-witted friend Joy didn't think to use the facilities before we left the stadium."

"Facilities?"

"Bathroom, toilet, whatever. Anyway, she yelled at our friend Sherry to stop the car at this bar near the highway and pleaded with us to walk inside with her. (She's one of those girls who has to pee in a pack.) Anyway, as soon as we opened the door of the bar, we could hear men hooting and hollering and we could see a naked woman dancing on the stage. Obviously, we stepped back, closed the door, and ran to the car. Well, stupid Joy was whining about how she was going to go to the bathroom in her pants if she didn't go right then and there so she conned us into going back inside and waiting for her by the bar. In any event, it was more awkward for Joy 'cause the bathroom was to the right of the stage so she had to walk past all the pig hunters (they don't hunt pigs, they just *are* pigs), but I was thinking that I should probably hang around with friends who are less stupid than Joy. What do you think?"

"I think you're glossing over the real question," Dermot replied.

"What's that?"

"Did you win the game?"

Marielle groaned as if in pain. "No, damn it! We lost. We were absolutely sure we'd win! I even made victory posters ahead of time to hang in the gym. I s'pose I could recycle them... or wait for our team to beat Neenah next year. Don't you hate Neenah?"

"Funny you should ask because I myself have hated Neenah from the

231

moment I laid eyes on it. It looks a bit dodgy with all those islands and inlets."

Marielle beamed. Dermot would have studied a map of the Fox Valley for a long time to know, much less remember, a minor detail of a neighboring city. No matter how aloof and aggressive he sounded, she was pretty sure he had it bad for her.

They exchanged a few more pleasantries before they hung up, but the conversation replayed happily in her mind for some time. She was under Dermot's skin now, and finally, they were even.

Chapter Sixteen

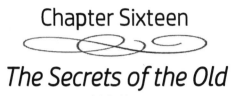

The Secrets of the Old
—W.B. Yeats

"Where is she?" Maria asked out of breath as she walked up the kitchen stairs.

"She's in the bathroom," Marielle replied, attempting to keep her eyes level without success.

"What did she say to you?" her mother asked, looking through the doorway into the dining room.

"You mean after she asked what I did to my face, or after she wondered out loud when I was going to lose my baby fat?"

Maria responded with a disapproving look.

"She said your father showed up at Uncle Ed's house and she made him decide which one of them would stay. He chose Grandpa."

Marielle followed her mother into the dining room, her arms firmly crossed. "Now, I'm no fan of your brother, but I'd say he made the right choice."

Maria turned toward Marielle with a sigh.

"I'm still not getting why Appleton, Wisconsin is a stopping point between Lower and Upper Michigan," Marielle whispered emphatically.

"She's afraid of the Mackinac Bridge so she goes around the lake."

"So, what kept her from stopping on the way down?" Marielle raised her hand quickly. "Not that I'm complaining."

The bathroom door opened, causing Maria to walk hurriedly toward it.

"Well, hello Mom!" she said, singing the last two words as she hugged the stylish woman of nearly the same height whose hair was still naturally black and whose skin was a deeper shade of olive.

"Hello there!" Lucia replied with a voice that sounded like wet gravel in a bag.

"Can I get you something to drink, Grandma?" Marielle asked, still trying to keep her eyeballs level.

"Get me a Schlitz," she demanded.

233

An hour later, Jack was sitting at the table with the only woman who could get him there or drink him under it.

"So, did you drive through Chicago this morning?" he asked genially.

"Yeah. The traffic was dreadful."

Jack nodded. "Yeah, if you don't make that turn in Indiana, you end up downtown."

"Well, now you tell me!" Lucia said with angry eyes over a beer can.

Marielle leaned closer to her mother near the stove. "How was Dad supposed to know she was in the area, much less on her way through Chicago? And how is it that she's afraid of a bridge, but not afraid of rush hour traffic through the south side of Chicago?"

Maria exhaled rapidly through her nose. "You're asking me to explain your grandmother to you?"

"Well, I'm still not getting why she had to leave your brother's house anyway. She had two kids with Grandpa Healy and *she* was the one who walked out on *him*."

"My parents are like fire and ice," Maria responded, turning off the oven.

"I think I know which one's ice," Marielle remarked.

Her mother narrowed her eyes. "Take this bread into the dining room for me."

"Get your grandmother another beer," Jack said to Marielle as she placed the bread on the dining room table.

She dutifully collected the empty cans before returning to the kitchen. "You know, your mother is already four cans into a six pack?" she said with abundant judgement.

"Do you have anything nice to say?" Maria asked with exasperation.

"*I* will when *she* does."

***

Marielle looked around the table at her sisters, parents, and grandmother. She couldn't remember the last time they all sat together for a meal, with or without their grandmother.

"*Salute balle tutte*," Lucia said, raising her beer.

"Mom!" Maria exclaimed, not appreciating the reference to testicles at the beginning of a meal.

Lucia smiled mischievously at her daughter before turning excitedly toward Jeanette. "So, how are things with Doug?" she asked as though the idea of Doug warmed her everywhere.

"Good," Jeanette responded, smiling with her chin an inch lower than normal.

"We think he's going to propose soon," Maria added excitedly.

"And why shouldn't he?" Lucia replied. "Jeanette is the prettiest girl around."

Anna and Marielle looked up from their plates at the same time.

"Now, you're going to look pretty when you grow into your face and get that horrible back brace off," Lucia said to Anna while squeezing the hand her granddaughter used to hold her knife. "After all, you look like a Sciarra," she declared as though that was all one needed for a successful modeling career. "John looks like your father's side of the family," Lucia remarked to Maria with disappointment after spying his picture from the corner of her eye.

"Yeah, he's the only one."

"Now, Stephen and Marielle are definitely Richters," Lucia said as if the last word made her stomach turn. Beaming at her eldest granddaughter she said, "Now, I don't know who Jeanette looks like."

"She's a Richter," Marielle said pointedly before she could stop herself.

"No," Lucia responded, losing her smile as she turned toward Marielle. "She's too good-looking to be a Richter."

Marielle turned to her father in an effort to gather the troops, but he had escaped the table without her notice. She turned toward her mother, noting how she nervously cut her manicotti, then looked back at her grandmother. "So, how is Uncle Ed?" she asked, not meaning to throw a dagger even though her subconscious obviously did.

"He's fine," Lucia said, narrowing her eyes like she didn't believe in a subconscious.

"How long were you there before Dad arrived?" Maria asked.

"Only three days."

"Did Ed know he was coming?"

Lucia shook her head.

That's what he said, Marielle thought, then looked up to see her grandmother reading the disrespect on her face.

"How are things with Joanna?" Maria asked.

Lucia waved away the question. "That woman doesn't know how to cook *or* keep a house. She asked me one night if I liked the lasagna she made and I told her it was shit."

"Mom!" Maria implored.

Lucia laughed as she looked around the table. "Well, it was! Do you want me to lie to her? The noodles were undercooked and the sauce came from a jar! She could've saved herself the effort and thawed out a TV dinner."

Maria grinned despite her best intentions. "So, what brought Dad to Michigan?"

"He said he and his brother got into the car in Ohio and just ended up there. He'll never change." Lucia looked down to remove a piece of lint from her black wool pants.

"So, Uncle Pat was with him?"

"No, Jim," Lucia clarified, still distracted by her pants.

"Well, it must have been nice to see Uncle Jim again," Maria hoped more than expected.

"No, he poured out of the passenger's seat with a tumbler of vodka in his hand. He told me I was still as thin and pretty as he remembered. I told him to go to hell. Then, I asked your brother if he planned to let them stay. He said he did so I got my things and left."

That seems like an awful lot of trouble for a temper tantrum, Marielle thought.

"So, tell me more about you and Doug!" Lucia said happily as she reached her hand out toward Jeanette's, her own sketchy history with love not preventing her from recommending it to others.

"Well, we went looking for rings last weekend and he wants to have a summer wedding," Jeanette replied with a coy smile.

Marielle continued to eat with difficulty even though their dinner definitely did not originate in a jar.

"Oh, how nice!" Lucia proclaimed through gravel.

Jeanette nodded. "His parents think the Eagle River Lodge would be nice for the reception."

"Why wouldn't you get married down here?" Marielle asked, looking up from her manicotti.

"Because all of our family and friends are still up north," Jeanette said coolly.

"You're gonna wait until he graduates, right?" Marielle stated more than asked.

"Probably," her sister responded.

Probably sounded to Marielle like a back-up plan in case Jeanette got pregnant, which meant they were having sex again, which meant reason wouldn't work with her sister anymore.

"Now, I told your mother this when she was your age." Lucia shook a long skinny finger toward Jeanette. "No matter what happens, you need to have the baby. We can forgive you getting pregnant, but we'll never forgive an abortion."

"What's this?" Jack asked aggressively, having just returned from the bathroom.

"Nothing, nothing," Maria consoled. "My mother is just giving Jeanette advice she'll never need."

"She'd better not!" Jack warned, settling into his chair and flashing his daughter a glare for good measure.

Lucia smiled knowingly at Jeanette who was doing her best to avoid making eye contact with both her grandmother and father. Clearly, neither bonding nor fighting over premarital sex was on her agenda tonight.

Marielle looked around the table, and—for the first time since her grandmother's arrival—she laughed.

Maria leaned toward her mother aggressively. "You know, Mom, not everyone is as crazy about sex as you are!"

"Well, you had five kids so you spent at least some of your time on your back!" Lucia retorted.

Gasps and mouth-covering mixed with a "Jesus Christ" as Jack turned his head toward the living room.

"I don't understand why everyone pretends to be so pure!" Lucia objected. "I had sex when I was young. I liked it and I was *good* at it!"

Maria put down her fork. "Really, Mom!"

"Fine, fine," Lucia said, shrugging her shoulders as she smiled cutely at Jeanette.

Lucia could be depended upon for three things during every visit: an insult, a discussion about sex, and revealing a deep, dark family secret. She had already delivered on two, and Marielle waited patiently for the third.

***

"Oh, it's not that bad," Marielle said while leaning against her mother's dresser.

Maria took off her blouse as she sighed.

"Well," Marielle consoled, "it's not as bad as last time when she declared you had a bastard brother you never met."

237

"No. Now she just made the rest of us bastards!" Maria declared, unzipping her skirt.

"Well, you have to appreciate how well she and Grandpa kept it a secret."

"And my sister for that matter. She apparently knew when she was in high school!"

"Well, it's not her father so why would she care if your parents were married or not? Besides, she has challenges figuring out the father of her own kids."

"Isn't that just ridiculous?" Maria said, near tears.

"Yeah, it's no wonder Grandma and Grandpa Richter can't stand her—your mom, I mean."

Maria shook her head as she sat on her bed. "Damn it!" she said, noticing the full slip she forgot to remove.

"Well, if you ask me, none of this is close to as bad as the way she treated *Nona*."

"That was terrible," Maria muttered.

"Yeah, you should tell her you plan to ridicule her, steal her car, and sell her things when she's too old and poor to resist. Can you imagine treating your mom so badly that her only wish on her birthday is to die? Your mother sucks!"

Maria shook her head at her daughter. "I don't approve of you talking that way."

Marielle nodded. "I know, but you'd give me some credit if you knew what I was thinking."

Maria began to laugh as she surrendered to temporary insanity.

***

Marielle paid little attention as Lucia's voice wafted from Jeanette's room into the hallway. She felt badly for Jeanette before remembering all the company she gave their father without her sister's sympathy or assistance. Jack had always said that payback was a bitch, and he was right. She was.

Chapter Seventeen

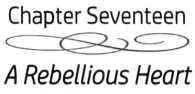

A Rebellious Heart
—The Bible – Jeremiah 23

"*You* get it!" Anna demanded from the kitchen as the phone rang a second time.

"Why should I get it?" Marielle asked, remote control poised to change the channel.

"Because it must be one of your stupid boyfriends. They keep hanging up on me."

Marielle answered the phone, out of breath from lunging on the fifth ring.

"Marielle?" a cracking voice whispered.

"Yes?"

"This is your grandmother. I don't have a lot of time. Your grandfather is outside feeding the dog. How is your German?"

"I'm getting an A, but I don't think I'll be hired by the U.N. anytime soon," she replied genially.

"Okay, well do the best you can and send me your questions in the mail."

"But Dad told me—"

"I know what he told you!" Frieda snapped. "Your grandfather told me the same thing, but that's a heck of a lot different than listening, kid."

Her grandmother instructed Marielle to alter her handwriting on both the letter and envelope, and address it from Sister Mary Margaret in Manitowoc.

Marielle ripped apart the desk looking for a pen and piece of blank scratch paper to write down the address. "Wait," she said suddenly. "Won't the postmark be obvious?"

"No," her grandmother replied with certainty. "Your grandfather doesn't look at letters that closely. Just use dark stamps that make the postmark hard to read."

"Okay. Are you sure about this?" Marielle asked with a mixture of excitement and caution.

"Don't you think I want to know how she did it?" Frieda replied hurriedly.

Marielle beamed at her grandmother's confidence, thinking it was probably the best compliment she had ever received. "Yes, ma'am," she replied.

"No, I think you have the wrong number," her grandmother said suddenly before the line went dead.

***

"I need your help with something," Marielle whispered, leaning across the lunch table as soon as Joy departed.

Joel glanced at Tom who busily indicated passages in his neighbor's book.

"I don't need Tom's help, I need yours," Marielle implored.

"Why?" Joel asked.

"Because you have experience with girls and you would know what it means when a guy writes a letter like this," Marielle said, revealing her latest letter from Dermot.

Joel sighed, but he eagerly accepted the letter just the same.

Monday the somethingth of October (I think),

Hi Marielle,

I won't say it's Dermot (I like to surprise you at the end of the letter). I only got your letter today (yeah, the 10/8/88 one)!! It took me all day to read it. Thanks for the BITCHY comments (e.g. "You can stop walking around the table now."). I'd actually give out to you now if I weren't madly in love with you. It's nice to know that you love me too. Seriously, I feel kind of weird loving someone I've never met.
This is going to be a super-long incredibly awesome, awesome letter. I know I have to write a big, long letter or you'll threaten to send Uncle Ronnie after me. Don't forget to write in ten years and tell me who got elected.

Joel chuckled.

Oh yeah... I'm really sorry to hear about your shitty taste in music. I s'pose it's not your fault (being an Am... ahem. Forget that Darrrrling!) I forgot to tell you I like The Cure, The Smiths, U2 (did you hear their new album yet?) and Sinéad O'Connor is pretty good too. Rick Astley SUCKS, as you Americans say. I didn't say I liked INXS and Bruce Springsteen cos' everyone does. Do you like U2?

It's really cool that your friend's brother rowed in the Olympics. I won't even mention the fact that East Germany and Russia beat them.

Joel's eyebrows furrowed.

Wow! You Americans get very insulted about your nationality. Everyone insults Ireland except the Americans so we just laugh it off. Here's an example:

This American came to Ireland. She met three farmers from Kerry. Being an American, she had brought a HUGE supply of condoms. Well, they all went to a 'pub' and got pissed, drunk (whatever!), and went back to the men's house (they were brothers). So, they all got into one big bed, BUT just as the first Kerryman was about to (guess!) she said, "No, you'll have to put on a condom." Then, they proceeded to (well, do you want a diagram?). The American went home the next day... three weeks later when the three rednecks were out on the farm milking the chickens, one said to the other "Bejaysus, Mickeen, ya know what? I don't care if that wan is going to get pregnant at all, at all. Whatever about if I don't take this thing off by tomorrow, I'll explode."

Joel shook his head.

Thanks for the t-shirt. You can only get ugly t-shirts in Ireland. My friends are begging me to find American pen pals who'll send them Olympic t-shirts. My sister is really jealous 'cos I got a COOL t-shirt from the U.S., a birthday card from my girlfriend who lives in Dublin (I'll explain later), and letters from everyone I was in Irish College with. I must spend ten pounds a week on stamps, notepaper, etc.

Oh yes! About my beautiful girlfriend. I met her in the Irish college and, well, nothing happened. We were "just good friends" and then we met again in Dublin and spent a few days together and, well...all we've been doing since then is writing love-letters to each other. (Sorry, my Biro just died...sniff... sniff!) She was supposed to come to my house for a few days. Now, she can't....

Look, Marielle, I'm really sorry to tell you this, but when you come to Ireland if you won't sleep upstairs, you can sleep outside with my bicycle and my dog (who has a strrraangeleey perverted liking for American girls—my dog that is, not my bike).

I showed your photo to my friends. Now, they ALL want American pen pals! My friend Sean said "I'll show Marielle all the IMPORTANT places in Galway!" (starting at certain parts of his body). Don't worry. I won't allow him near you!

I'm glad you're so interested in Irish history. You know more than me! I wouldn't mind the Famine—there were too many of us anyway. If you think what you read was bad, read about the Easter Uprising—then you get to the nasty bits. Sometimes I really hate the British. They're always talking about "wonderful, brilliant, super, perfect, GREAT BRITAIN." They'll shoot you for insulting their queen, and she IS a fat cow. Howwevverr, I must admit that any English people I ever met were really nice. I mean really wacko, super, tally-ho!

Ohhhh! I can't wait until April! I can't wait to see you! I thought you couldn't come when you said your brother wasn't in West Germany. My mother will be in Cuba which means I can shove my sister in somewhere and give you her room. Remind me to kill the rats and cockroaches...

You said you made hydrogen in science. I did that too LAST YEAR! I guess I'm just MUCH more advanced (Joke! Don't write in a circle again, please!) I dissected a worm last week. It's really cool, awesome, major (redneck—>ferocious). You have to pin back its skin like that <—| |—>. Did you know that a worm is both male AND female? That means they get twice as many babies when they have sex than we do when WE have sex (I mean "we" as in the human race [Actually, I don't really]). My friend made nitroglycerine again and almost blew himself up. He's really weird (example: he cut up the worm BEFORE he killed it).

Try my homework for tonight (this X 25): Establish the period of f(x): Sin 3x + Cos 4x.

Wow! I was shocked when you said you were a virgin.

Joel paused to eye Marielle before returning to the letter.

I didn't know there was such a thing as an American virgin! (Joke - nasty one too!) In your last letter, you really proved that you're different to the "American" I see on T.V. especially the bit about meaningless sex. I have sex regularly as part of my training. (Only joking, I'm a virgin too.) That's great. Now, when you come to my house, we can have meaningFUL sex!

"I assume this is what you wanted me to read?" Joel asked, holding his finger against the passage.

Marielle glanced nervously toward Joy as she sat down.

"I'll finish it," Joel continued.

And now, to my pen pal who writes almost as much as she talks... I'm going to write the last page of my letter in code. 1=A, 2=B, 3=C, etc... just to annoy you:

9 - 8,1,4 - 1 - 12,15,22,5,12,25 - 4,18,5,1,13 - 1,2,15,21,20 - 25,15,21 - 12,1,19,20 - 14,9,7,8,20. In it I - 23,1,19 - slowly - removing - 1,12,12 - 15,6 - 25,15,21,18 - 3,12,15,20,8,5,19! Then - 23,5 - began - 11,9,9,19,19,9,14,7 - (6,18,5,14,3,8 - style). Enough code. The rest is obvious - very obvious - very enjoyable!

"I'm not decoding this," Joel said impatiently. "What does it say?"

"It just says he had a dream about taking off my clothes and kissing me," Marielle murmured.

Joel sighed before finishing.

If you ever write a letter to me like the last one, I'll KILL YOU.

Are you still working 36 hours a day and living in the 'fridge'?! It's nice to know you do stupid things sometimes too. I brought home my Maths test with me when I was doing the Intercert exam. I still got a C 'cos it was only 15% in my paper. Well, thanks for congratulating me for getting six As! I s'pose you're intelligenter, superiorer or more gooder than me in some way? So dare! I don't mind. Do you think I mind you not mentioning it? Do I look like I'm making a big fuss about it? Go ahead. I don't care! I'm not bothered! Ca me fait rien!

I'm starving! Foooood!

Look! I'd better go!!!! I think I've written enough to keep even you happy! iF i hAveN'T - tOUgH luCk. i'M tRyINg tO dO sCRiBblY ilLiTeRaTE AmERicAn - Marielle- lIkE wRItiNG. iT's qUiTE eAsY - jUsT cLosE my eYEs aNd uSE my rIGht hAnd. (I <u>am</u> actually left-handed.)

I'm sorry this wasn't just one big love letter about how I can't wait to see you, touch you, run my fingers lovingly through your hair (the hair on your head you perverted American person!).

Voulez-vous (veux-tu) faire l'amour avec moi? J'espere.

Just in case you find out from someone else, that bit of Irish I sent you says, "I love you very, very much."
Well, for now, my ever-perfect pen pal,
i love you! (as Garfield would say)
I love you very, very, very, very, very much!!!!
I wish I could make my letters as interesting as yours.
Slan go foill! (see ya)
Lots of Love and Lust and Love and Lust,
Dermot

PS Ronan received Shelly's letter. I don't believe he wrote back yet.

PPS I hope your parents don't hang you for your telephone bill!

Joel set down the letter before issuing his judgement. "Number one, I'd say he's bi-polar."

"Why?" Marielle asked with concern.

"Well, he's either beckoning you to bed or insulting you. I'd say he's struggling between respecting you as a friend, and wanting to get into your pants."

Marielle smiled. "Are you saying he loves me?"

"Well, it's as close as any guy's gonna get."

"What are we talking about?" Joy asked, looking from Marielle to her cousin.

"Nothing," Marielle replied, sitting back.

"Aren't you bothered that he talks about his girlfriend, and asks you to have sex with him in the same letter?" Joel asked as if his respect for Marielle rested on her answer.

"Whoa!" exclaimed Joy.

Marielle puckered her lips in thought. "I'm not bothered by the

244

girlfriend. I talk to him about the boys I date all the time. I don't know why, but those things don't bother us. I was bothered about him bringing up sex before you confirmed that he respects and loves me though."

Joel stood up as though suddenly annoyed or preoccupied. "I'm gonna' get a Coke. Anyone want anything?"

Joy waited for her cousin to walk away, then leaned across the table toward Tom. "I heard Joel asked Cheryl Johnston to Winter Formal and she said no because—get this—her parents wouldn't approve. Who says that? God!" She rolled her eyes.

"Well, he does go out of his way to look scary," Tom noted.

"You're missing my point!" Joy said impatiently. "Who else do you know our age who brings up their parents when someone asks them out on a date?"

"Tonya's parents didn't let her go to Gwen's party because there was no parental supervision," Marielle remarked.

Joy sneered. "How did *they* know that?"

"She said she didn't expect her parents to ask, and when they did, she told them the truth."

"I could see that," Tom reflected as Joel returned with a Coke.

"What's up?" asked Joel, looking in Joy's direction while jerking his head up an inch or so.

"Well," Joy said, smiling at everyone else before continuing, "I heard someone, who will remain nameless, turned you down for Winter Formal."

Tom and Marielle opened their mouths, but neither spoke.

"What?" asked Joy defensively.

Joel turned his chair around to hold the back of it as he sat. "Well," he said, "you might've noticed that I'm a bit of a rebel and some parents don't approve of that."

"The most rebellious thing you've ever done is eat cereal out of a cup!" Joy said accusingly, laughing like she just shocked herself with hidden wit.

"You have no idea how much that pisses my mom off!" Joel retorted.

"Hey Joel," Tom interjected. "How did you like the college fair last night? Were you talking to UW Stout when I left?"

"I was, but I think I'll go to Fox Valley Tech instead. There's no way my parents will pay for college."

"Really?" Marielle asked. "I think I'm in the same boat. My parents said I could either go into the military or get a job to pay for it."

Joel nodded sympathetically. "My parents don't even want me going to college fairs. They said I'll get wrong ideas in my head. I once asked my mom what she thought about Houton and she said that was for smart kids, not me." He reflected on the word *bitch* as he said it.

"So, where did you tell them you were going last night?" Marielle inquired.

"I just told them I was going out. They didn't ask for any details until I got home. Then, I said I went parking with some chick."

Marielle regarded Joel with astonishment. "And they were okay with that?"

"Oh yeah," he replied matter-of-factly.

"But they're not okay with a college fair?"

"No," he said, shaking his head. He was about to continue when Joy interrupted.

"Well, I guess that's what happens when you get knocked-up in high school and you decide to keep the kid."

Tom and Marielle stared at one another, wondering what to say to a person who used information acquired in confidence as a weapon.

Marielle drew a deep breath as she turned to Joy. "Are you a bitch all of the time, or just during lunch?"

"What? It's true!"

"And what if I said—" Marielle stopped, afraid of what would come out of her mouth next. "Forget it."

"What? Can't think of anything?" Joy asked victoriously.

"Oh, I can think of plenty, but I'm not a callous bitch."

"That's not what Guy says," Joy replied with a grin.

"Alright," Marielle said, eyes narrowing. "You're an idiot and a tramp. No one wants to hear about your exploits with baseball players who are either too drunk to say no or have amazingly low standards. Additionally, we're tired of laughing at you behind your back when you get common words and phrases wrong. *Sloppy seconds* are not all things second-hand so stop apologizing for offering sloppy seconds when you lend someone your pen! Also, it's not *two of one, half-dozen of another*, it's *six*, and it's a *six*-pack of abs, not *twelve*."

Marielle's vision cleared sufficiently to notice the shocked faces of the boys just as the bell rang, but she picked up her books without apology and was still spitting venom as she walked up the main stairs.

"Hey, what's wrong?" Shelly asked near the entrance to the silo, moving to the center of the hall to remove herself from the flow of traffic.

"I may kill Joy Meyers," Marielle replied.

"Really?" Shelly asked as though she might be serious.

Marielle stared down the hall as the cloud of anger slowly cleared. "No, but I *really* don't like who I am when she provokes me."

"You should come over to my house tonight and we can plot revenge," Shelly offered amiably.

Marielle groaned. "I wish I could, but I'm working tonight."

"Tomorrow?"

"Working."

Shelly nodded once. "Well, I guess Joy's safe for now."

"Isn't that too bad?" Marielle said, finally smiling.

***

"So, you haven't told Dermot what a U2 freak you are," Joel reflected the following day. "Why's that exactly?"

Marielle glanced in the direction of Joy. Although speaking with her neighbor, Marielle suspected she was still listening. "Because I thought he'd think I was only writing him because I love U2."

Joel shook his head. "Guys don't think that way, and he loves himself too much to think you're writing him for any reason *other* than his amazing awesomeness."

Marielle looked over Joel's shoulder as she considered the truth of his comments. "I know it seems like that, but he's completely different on the phone."

Joel raised, then lowered his eyebrows. "Just tell him that if he hurts you or if he insults Americans again, I'll kick his ass."

Tom, Marielle, and Joy regarded Joel with surprise.

"Oh, and I checked with the manager at the record store. They don't expect another shipment of *Rattle and Hum* until just before Christmas," Joel continued as his can of Coke hissed open.

"Thanks," Marielle said as though her thoughts were far from *Rattle and Hum*.

11/4/1988 Friday

Dear Dermot,

Thank you for your letter! I'm writing this on a computer in our brand new computer lab. I can actually type faster than I can write and I need to make good time if I want to get this out by the end of my lunch period. Wow! This thing is much better than my friend's old Commodore!

Anyway, I hope you are well and enjoying your Monday. I'm always so very grateful to come back to school after two days of peace and relaxation! I find if you say that to your teachers while wearing a big blonde smile, they leave either confused or thinking you're an idiot. Either way, it's fun to mislead people.

We had a substitute Advanced Algebra teacher today named Mrs. Teets. That's right, Teets. The guys could barely contain themselves when she introduced herself, and they didn't do much better after that. To add to the problem, she's young and good-looking so you can imagine the things they whispered during class. Somehow she was completely oblivious to their talking and to the fact that their beginning each question with "Uh, Mrs. Teets..." was a joke. Part of me thinks she's gotta know her last name is a disaster (especially if you're teaching kids older than seven), but then why would she A) teach high school, B) take her husband's last name, and C) not crack a smile every time she said it? Either she's stupid, or she's the best actress I've ever seen. I spent most of the hour deciding which it was and laughing at the boys. In any event, not a lot of Algebra was learned. It was actually worse than the time a guy named "Mr. Heiny" substituted for our Biology class. Someone said his first name was Harry, but that's probably not true—unless his parents hated him. Anyway, every time he turned around to write something on the board, the class erupted in laughter. Now, I ask you, HOW AM I SUPPOSED TO GET INTO A GOOD COLLEGE WHEN I'M SO EASILY DISTRACTED???!!!

Speaking of distracted, I made a giant rookie mistake last week and if my parents find out they'll burn my driver's license in less time than it'll take them to agree on an appropriate punishment. See, my parents let me take the car to school on Friday for the first time ever, but they said I couldn't have ANYONE else in the car at ANY time for ANY reason. Of course, I disregarded this and offered to drive SIX of my friends home. Most of them were piled in the back seat yelling about what was on the radio while we were sitting at a stop sign. Anyway, they were so distracting that I convinced myself I was sitting at a stop light. So, when the three cars in front of me went into the intersection, so did I. Everyone screamed when they saw the cars on Calumet Street barreling toward us—one of which had another student in it who has taken to calling me "Crash" even though I missed all cars by several inches. In any event, I didn't get caught by my parents or the cops which is no small miracle.

My friend Joel got his license 11 months ago and he had to go to court this week on a reckless driving charge. He told the judge he was driving erratically because he was trying to get a girl inside the car to admit she liked him. The judge threw-out the charge, but told him that the next time he wants to impress a girl, he should do it on the dance floor. I crack-up every time I see him at lunch now. I also crack-up every time I see Hugh (aka "Hughsifer"). See, ever since I told people what happened on our "date," strange things have happened to Hugh's car. Did I tell you someone keyed the words "Dick Sucker" on the driver's-side door—twice? (The last time only days after he had the first scratches fixed.) Anyway, it stuck as a nickname and the more irritated he gets, the more people say it. You can actually track Hugh's position in school now by following shouts of "Hey D!"

DISCLAIMER: Although I find the keying of evil people's cars humorous, I neither encourage nor condone the destruction of private property whether the owner deserves it or not. I also have not taken part in said destruction even if I have a pretty good idea of who has.

SECONDARY DISCLAIMER: Playing "lookout" for car keyers is not technically taking part in property destruction—although I'm not sure this disclaimer would hold up in court.

TERTIARY (Are you impressed with my word usage?) DISCLAIMER: Just because I have a disclaimer for lookouts doesn't mean I'm implicating myself in that role. I wasn't a lookout... knowingly.

Anyway, I hope hearing about my near-miss, Joel's court case, and Hugh's car problems make you feel better about not having your license yet. I do think it's crazy that you can't drive until you're 18 though! Parents there must not trust their kids with the family car (with good reason based upon my driving so far). One question: how do you date without a car? Do you ride up to a girl's house on your bicycle to pick her up? Is it impolite to ring your bell from the sidewalk instead of walking to the door? As an aside, my dad would KILL a guy if he didn't get out of the car, come to the door, and introduce himself.

I know what you mean when you say you were "shocked" to hear I'm a virgin. I was equally shocked to hear you were sober. Actually, you didn't

249

SAY you were sober, but I could tell from the lack of slurring on the phone.

Before I forget, congratulations on your test results! I'm sorry I didn't mention it before, but I don't actually remember you telling me about them. But if by chance you did and I callously disregarded your accomplishment, I feel honor-bound to say how incredibly impressed I am. I categorically state that my failure to pay you the proper homage by no means represents my regard for you or your intelligence. In fact, I'm honored that the random pen pal computer gave me a correspondent with such a powerful mind. This sounds like sarcasm, but it mostly isn't. I would say "it isn't at all," but I can't—not because I don't think it, but because I'm a bitch. Ha! OK, it's not sarcasm "at all." My sincere congratulations to you!

One last thing and then I have to run: There's still no news about Guy's letters which is strange. Did I tell you I gave them to Jillian's little brother before Homecoming? I feel bad that Jillian will be hurt (I imagine her brother feels the same), but it's better she knows now what an ass Guy is instead of waiting 'til later. I'm also a firm believer in setting the record straight. In fact, my favorite quote by Kipling is, "Nothing is ever settled until it's settled right." (Don't tell my Creative Writing teacher though 'cause she and I aren't getting along right now and I'd hate for her to think I got anything out of her class. [That's a story for another letter]). Anyway, it felt strange to arm a nuclear weapon and not know when it will go off. (I guess that's how Reagan feels.) I have to admit that I'm a little afraid of what will happen even though I know I won't see Guy in person and if he calls me I'll just tell him to "bite off" as usual and hang up. Plus, I'm fairly confident I did the right thing, but I can't know that for sure and ruining someone's reputation (even with his own letter) is pretty big stuff. In any event, it's too late to worry about that now. I'm going to think about more pleasant things...

The bell is about to ring so I'd better finish this up and print it. I hope my failure to write to you hasn't made you think I don't care or think about you. Sometimes the thought of calling you and hearing your voice is the only thing that gets me out of bed in the morning. You are wonderful and sweet when you're not being an arrogant jackass, and every time I talk to you I feel happy the entire day—the entire week even. Feeling something so strong for someone I've never met surprises me a lot. I'm not sure what else to say except that I love you very, very much!!

Marielle

PS I don't mind sleeping outside with your dog or in the garage for that matter. Strangely enough, I usually don't have trouble sleeping anywhere, anytime, under any conditions... which comes down to my superior German genetics. ☺

Dear Dermot,

This is my second letter to you in the same day. I never thought I'd cram for correspondence, but here it is. I drove to the post office to mail the 2pm letter and a letter to my grandmother, but I forgot my purse so I just ripped open your envelope so I can add this letter since I promised to tell you about my fight with my Creative Writing teacher (actually, maybe I didn't promise, but I alluded to it and I'd hate to keep you waiting) so here it is:...

Wait! Actually, before I start, I want to say that I know it sounds like I'm always fighting with someone about something and clearly I must be at fault somewhere in at least one of these cases, but I honestly don't see it. My grandpa Richter has a trophy on his shelf that reads, "I'm never wrong. Once I thought I was wrong, but I was mistaken." I guess I got that gene from him. Seriously though, if you think I'm wrong I want you to say so. I respect your opinion enough to take what you say under advisement. OK, here it goes:

As a matter for the hateful and unfair column, I got a C- on my latest Creative Writing paper and I'm really pissed! The topic was "The Philosophy of Me" which I found both a gay idea and a transparent attempt by my teacher to collect juicy gossip for the teachers' lounge. I decided to duplicate part of my paper here so you can tell me how "A-worthy" it is... while still giving me your objective opinion. ☺

"I'm more often offensive than offended. While driving, I'm more likely to pass than be passed. I enjoy cursing, but think others who do so are both base and unsophisticated. I have an opinion about everything, but hate judgmental people and hypocrites. I'm not paranoid, but I'm sure my friends say I am behind my back. Sarcasm is my preferred means of communication. Do you wish I could write about myself forever?"

I go on for awhile like this and I don't mean to toot my own horn, but it's

251

damned funny... but clearly my teacher didn't agree. She said my paper "lacked courage and insight," but I'd say her assessment did since she clearly can't read between the lines. I mean, avoiding saying something meaningful about myself says something about me, doesn't it? And since when can a person's philosophy about herself be right or wrong? And what is "wrong" anyway? Bah! I think that woman needs a lot of alone time with her husband, if you know what I mean. Really, what other reason could she have for giving me a C-? I would yell at her, but she'd probably say it was my fault. Don't you hate people who avoid responsibility for their mistakes? Do you think I'll ever snap out of this state of sarcasm?

Anyway, this is what I get for taking Creative Writing instead of Wood Shop. I mean, how could creatively writing help me anyway? And my mom would've been really impressed if I'd made her a butcher block... although my brother made her one a few years back... but it's all scratched up and pretty much smells like onions all the time... even when it's clean... which I guess means it's never really clean at all. What do you think? I should suggest the next topic for a Creative Writing paper: "The Characteristics of a Clean Butcher Block." I'd like to see Mrs. Laughs-a-little say my paper on that "lacked courage and insight." Wench!!!!

I'll start reading about the Easter Uprising when I finish my book on Oliver Cromwell. Excuse my language, but he's a real prick! I imagine there's no question he's burning in hell right now—unless he thought what he was doing was right. Actually, I'm not sure how that works. I asked my mom once if seriously retarded people who kill people go to hell and she thought no because they didn't necessarily know what they were doing was wrong. Now, what if Cromwell or Hitler weren't so much evil as mentally unstable and they really thought killing the Irish or Jews was God's work? Would God punish them for being wrong or give them a pass 'cause their heart was in the right place? I don't think I'll ever know the answer to that, but if I make it to heaven and either Cromwell or Hitler are there, God and I will have issues—which is probably a good reason for God not to invite me to heaven in the first place.

On a Hitler-related note, we have a class of West German students and their teacher visiting our school right now. They don't seem terribly impressed with Wisconsin or the speed limit (they say driving here feels like moving in slow motion) and they've had enough of American boys asking if German women shave their legs. It's kind of embarrassing to sit in class day after day and hear the guys weave references to leg shaving and Nazis into every conversation. I'm waiting for the boys to get tired of either topic, but it's more likely the Germans will go home first. Can you see why I never date anyone my age? Two years older has always been the absolute minimum!!

By the way, congratulations on making hydrogen a year before us—even if you dissected a worm THREE years AFTER us. We advanced to dissecting fetal pigs last year. My pig's skull sprayed formaldehyde at me when I pierced it with a scalpel. It was REALLY gross. I think my lab partner must've read the lab instructions before we started (I never do) because she let me make the first incision. In any event, I guess we've determined that the Irish are more advanced in Chemistry and the Americans are more advanced in Biology—but, you must've known that just from looking at my picture. ☺

We were supposed to get our phone bill today, but it didn't arrive, damn it! God must be punishing me for provoking him on the Hitler thing because the phone bill always arrives by this time every month, and I'm pretty sure my share of the bill will hit an all-time high this month. Don't get me wrong, I'm not in a hurry to write my parents a check, but part of me is tired of worrying and just wants to get the yelling over with. AUGH!

Did I tell you my parents want to call your parents to make sure they're not ax murderers? Apparently, that's something you can determine over the phone now. I wonder if they'll make me pay for that call too! Shelly asked me if I want to go see Rattle and Hum tonight so maybe I should go before I'm grounded for being an irresponsible long-distance caller. Why, why, why do I have to talk so much? (You probably wonder the same thing.) ALTHOUGH... I might get out of punishment altogether if I win a $5,000 music scholarship I'm competing for. Did I tell you about this? Well, it'll have to wait for my next letter 'cause my hand is going numb from writing so much.

You asked me if I like U2 and the truth is I've been absolutely <u>mad</u> (as you say) about them since I was in Elementary School. They're the reason I chose a pen pal from Ireland on my form. So, I guess U2 is the reason you have to put up with me now. I didn't say this before because I imagined you were tired of people hearing you're Irish and bringing up U2. I've *been listening to The Joshua Tree album almost constantly since it was released and I've looked everywhere for Rattle and Hum, but it's sold out. A few months ago, I got my hands on a large, black, scarf-type thing that looks like the Joshua Tree album cover. It's hanging on my bedroom wall next to my tennis racket—which doesn't get used, but looks nice hanging on my wall.*

I have to finish this up now, but in case I didn't make it clear in my last letter, I've decided that I really like you a lot. I don't say this to a lot of people 'cause most people annoy the crap out of me. (I think I've given you plenty examples of this.) I can't wait to see you and hug you and kiss you. You are probably waiting to hear my response to the code in your letter so I'll write it now:

9-3,1,14'20-16,18,15,13,9,19,5-9-23,9,12,12-13,1,11,5-12,15,22,5-23,9,20,8-25,15,21-2,21,20-9-16,18,15,13,9,19,5-9,6-9-13,1,11,5-12,15,22,5-23,9,20,8-1,14,25,15,14,5-9,20-23,9,12,12-2,5-25,15,21.

Love,
Marielle

PS You haven't told me what I should buy your parents as a gift yet, damn it! I only have four months! ☺

PPS I know it's been out for awhile, but I still love the song "Wild West" by Escape Club. What sayeth ye?

"Marielle!" Jack thundered. "Get your ass downstairs NOW!"

Marielle closed her bedroom door behind her as Jeanette approached from the stairs.

"Two words," Jeanette said. "Phone. Bill."

Marielle closed her eyes for a moment, then returned to her room for her checkbook.

"Eighty-three dollars!" Jack held up the bill in front of her face. "Do you have eighty-three dollars to pay your part of the phone bill?!" he roared.

"I do," she replied coolly.

Jack studied her to see if she was employing sarcasm or not. "You do, hey? Well, write your mother the check right now and get your ass back to your room!"

"Well, that was less painful than it could've been," Jeanette remarked, holding her engagement ring hand over the cordless phone receiver.

"Yeah, I'm lucky I had the money," Marielle said with a sigh.

Until that afternoon, she was only one paycheck away from buying her ticket to Ireland.

Chapter Eighteen

Deep-Sworn Vow
—W.B. Yeats – *A Deep-Sworn Vow*

Joel walked to the table as though he wanted to kill the floor beneath his Doc Martins. Jaw clenched, he pulled his chair noisily toward himself.

"What's wrong with you?" Joy asked aggressively.

"Bess Truman got my blood boiling today," he replied.

"How'd she manage that?" Marielle asked, smiling as Tom lowered his book.

"Mr. Schmitz read us this letter Harry wrote after he surprised her by coming home for Christmas."

"What do you mean?" Marielle asked. "They didn't come home together?"

"Apparently not!" he said like he just discovered his kid cut class. "Apparently, she didn't like the whole First Lady gig and decided to stay home in Missouri instead."

"What a bitch," Marielle said with the last of her breath.

"Exactly! Your husband just won the Second freakin' World War and you can't get your lazy ass to Washington to keep him company?! And THEN when he surprises you by showing up at your door for Christmas, you treat him like crap. She's a useless freakin' cow!"

Tom bit his bottom lip to suppress laughter.

"Was she having an affair and he interrupted her exchanging gifts with her boyfriend?" Joy asked.

Joel shook his head. "I doubt it. She was fat and hideous."

"Hmm. It's too bad he didn't decide to spend Christmas with someone fat and hideous in DC," Marielle reflected. "It would've saved him the trip."

"Yeah, he went through a pretty bad snow storm to get there too," Joel said, his voice betraying only empathy now.

"Where did he meet her, I wonder?" asked Marielle. "I only ask because you may want to avoid that place in the future, lest you be sucked-in by a fat, hideous, Christmas-neglecting, venomous bitch wife."

Tom scanned the table, obviously amused by the reaction of his peers to history. "He met her in school when they were only five years old," he explained.

"From the same town, then," Marielle noted more than asked, but Tom answered "yes" anyway. "Well, that explains it," she said.

"What's that?" asked Joel.

"He wasn't her soul mate."

Joy's nose curled in a precursor to speech. "How do you know that?"

"Because they're from the same small town."

"And?" Joy sneered.

"And I'm from a small town and half of my brother's graduating class of 50-something kids married people from the same town. Now, what are the chances that 25 people just happened to be sitting in a desk, in a small school, in a small town, in a relatively small state, next to their one and only soul mate on the planet? It's statistically improbable."

Joy nodded slowly. "I agree. It's a little weird that people from Montana marry people from Montana."

Joel stared down his cousin. "Do you know this for a fact?"

Marielle leaned forward. "No, but people from Wisconsin tend to marry people from Wisconsin. So, we can assume the same is true across the country."

"So, you're saying the vast majority of people aren't married to their soul mates?" Joel asked, still skeptical.

"*I'm* suspicious of anyone who doesn't go to Milwaukee to find a spouse," declared Tom.

Marielle nodded her agreement. "How could they be soul mates unless everyone has, like 100,000 soul mates on the planet? And even then they're more likely to be in India or China than in Kleiner, Wisconsin sitting next to you in English class."

"Well, what if God put soul mates in the same geographic region on purpose?" Joel posited.

"So, we should only be suspicious of the people who marry outside their area?" Tom asked.

"Aren't we already?" Marielle suggested.

Everyone nodded.

Marielle smiled suddenly. "Well, if that's true, then people who move around a lot must really piss God off."

Everyone except Joel laughed. Instead, he declared he was going to the computer lab before walking away without pushing in his chair.

"Does Joel seem different to you?" Marielle asked Tom after Joy's attention became occupied by her neighbor. "He's been absent at least once a week this month and he's otherwise angry or tired."

Tom leaned forward. "I shouldn't be telling you this, but I know you can keep a secret. His father's been staying at the bar until closing time nearly every night since he lost his job. He got his third DUI, so now he wakes up Joel in the middle of the night and makes him pick him up from the bar to bring him home."

"Whoa," Marielle said, sitting back in her chair.

Tom nodded.

Marielle returned to her notebook with renewed respect for Joel. If there was anything dignified about alcoholism, it was the people behind the alcoholic who took care of the family, took care of the alcoholic, and did so without complaining.

That night, Marielle called Joel moments after locking herself inside her room. She asked only two questions before determining that only a confession by her would elicit a real conversation with him.

"You're not alone, ya know," she said.

"I know. I have my friends around me and they all love me," he said sarcastically.

"That's not what I mean," Marielle explained. "We moved here because we lost our house in Kleiner. My father was fired from his job for being an alcoholic. He also spent a good deal of money at the bar, and although my mom could cover the mortgage, no bank would give us a loan to pay-off the balloon payment."

Joel was quiet for a moment. "I'm sorry about that," he said.

"And I'm sorry about whatever is going on in your house."

Joel sighed before groaning loudly. "My mom is gone. She left a couple weeks ago," he said, then cleared his throat. "She didn't take me with her. She said she could only leave because she knew I'd be here to take care of the bastard when she was gone."

"Why is that your responsibility?" Marielle asked aggressively.

"Because she knows I'll feel guilty if anything happens to him."

"Even if he's the one killing himself?"

"I've thought about that. I think when you care about someone who's weaker than you are, you have to pick up the slack. When you don't and they get hurt, it's your fault."

"I disagree!" Marielle exclaimed. "Every night I make sure my dad is covered with a blanket and his cigarette is out, and I know I won't be able to do that when I go to college, but I'm still going. I can't sacrifice my life on the altar of his weakness."

"And what if he burns the house down while you're away and kills your family?"

"Then, that will be on his soul, not mine! I can't save him from himself and I can't save my mother if she refuses to leave him."

"What about your little sister?" Joel asked.

Marielle was quiet for a moment as tears filled her eyes. "Well, that's my only real problem."

"But you're still leaving?"

Marielle drew a slow, deep breath. "Well, there's no other way to provide her with a place to go if I don't leave. You need to think of it like that. By going to college, you can better provide for your family long term."

Joel scoffed. "Fat chance. I'm tanking in all my classes."

Marielle sat forward. "Talk to your guidance counselor and he'll talk to your teachers. You still have time to make this right before the end of the term. They'll let you make up papers and retake tests. I guarantee it and I can help you."

Joel laughed unhappily. "Why do you care?"

"If you're expecting me to say something nice to you, it won't happen!" Marielle shot back.

"Well, you obviously care about me or you wouldn't keep bothering me," he retorted.

She smiled. "So, now you have your answer and I didn't need to get all mushy"

"Okay, jackass," Joel began. "I'll talk to my counselor tomorrow."

"Thanks, dumbass. I appreciate it," Marielle replied before hanging up.

12-Nov-1988

Salut Marielle!

Thanks for your letter… thanks for your other letter. I love your typing— at least I can read it now. Sorry 'bout Guy, and the phone bill.

Did you like Rattle and Hum? I thought it was good.

I don't think you understand "pissed." It means drunk. You said, "I'm really pissed."... Well, maybe you were.

I don't understand what you mean about not dating without a car. Maybe we're unique in Ireland, but over here you have sex with your girlfriend, not a sunroof! Or maybe it's an American custom that you can only have sex in a car. I give up. I'm too confused! Pity you don't go out with guys younger than yourself. Did you know that (allowing for international time zones, the ozone, etc.) I'm actually five years, three months, six days, 19 hours, and 25 minutes OLDER than you!?

Oh yeah, my parents thought it was really funny that your parents are going to call. My mother said, "They probably think we don't even speak English." No, seriousssssleee, they're relieved. "Wow, you lucky thing Dermot, you've found an American with parents." Ouch! Nasty. You can kill me in April.

What does "bite off" mean? I hope (for my sake) it has nothing to do with oral sex.

I just had a really funny thought. If I answer the phone to your parents I'll say, "Bejaysus, how are ya? Mary, wud ya get da bloody cow outa tha kitchen? Well, Holy God!"

I think you're right about poor Ronnie. What do you think of "George Shrub"? Better than "Ducactus" anyway! Margaret Thatcher (a.k.a. "The Iron Maiden, Female Stalin, Terminator, etc.") is worse than Ronnie. I mean she has no excuse for being thick—she has a brain. The worst mistake she made yet was the Falklands. (Mistake? I call it murder.)

Last week was the reunion of the Remembrance Day bombing. (That was when people went to lay wreaths on the graves of dead soldiers and an IRA bomb went off beside them.) I was watching it on T.V. with a friend who used to live there and he started crying. I really pitied him. There was a tape of a man who was rescued after his daughter died beside him while they were trapped under rubble. To think something like that happens every week for a crappy little bit of a country. Oh well... you only get frustrated when you start thinking about it. Besides, you probably don't understand seeing as no one in this country does.

Oh yeah...you asked what my parents would like as presents. Anything like Ferraris, Piaget, Rolex watches, nuclear missiles, or other similar things will do. I asked them and they don't know. Imagine that. "Begorra, I s'pose an auld biteen o' turf for the hearth wouldn't go amiss, ha?" I want a present—your licence so I can shred it, burn it, digest it, etc. You can be such a BITCH sometimes (e.g. "I drove to the P.O."). I can make plenty of jokes about that: "At least I can fit in the door." From what I've seen of American tourists, I'll need a bigger house by April. ☺

Vous-avez (tu as) dit que je parle bien le français. Mais oui! J'y suis alle sept fois! Et je peux écrire aussi parce que je suis très intelligent. Et vous? Vous êtes intelligente aussi (pour une Américain!)

Thanks for the "bunch of beautiful" thing you wrote at the end of your letters. I need something to boost my already overgrown ego. You said I'm the reason you wake up. I'd sooner be there when you're getting into bed (or is it the back seat of a car I ask confusedly?). Don't get carried away, Dermot, you haven't even seen her yet! I have day dreams about you in certain parts of Biology class. The rest of the time, I just dream about you anyway. I think you're just "awesome." I dream about what you REALLY look like (you only sent me photos with your clothes on). I feel you deeply - NO! - I meant that I feel deeply for you. Hee! Hee! Hee!<— In case you're wondering, that's my "it's 4a.m., she's asleep, and I'm having a good time" laugh. Sick. Gross! My friend says that. No! Stop! Seriously! I'd love to just touch you now, or hold you because I think we know each other so well and it's annoying that we live so far away from each other. I'll probably be a complete child to you if you're used to guys two years older than you. Never mind, I have nothing against child molesters.

Oh yes! Brilliant joke: A man is thrown into a prison cell with another bloke.

"Hi, I'm in for murder. What did you do?"

"I'm a dog molester."

"Sick, how low can you go?"

"Jack Russell, actually." <—Breed of small dogs.

Gross! <—Typical U.S. saying.

Sorry about that! It was really GREAT to get two letters from you in one day. I told my friend Sean and he said I was a lucky bastard. Now, his pen pal writes every six months.

I love you. I dream about you. I love to write to you. I can't wait 'til

April—sooner than you think! Thanks for being you. I really wish you were here now!

Do chara dhil.

Au revoir! Je t'aime! (Grosses Bisous!)

Slan go foill!

Auf(whatever)sehen!

Dermot the perpetually infatuated one!

Marielle read the letter only three times before deciding—phone bill or no phone bill—she would die if she didn't hear Dermot's voice soon. So, she ran to her room to set her alarm for four in the morning on the off chance she might forget.

***

"I looked up nihilism the other day," Dermot said over a phone line that echoed. "Now *my* librarian is looking at me suspiciously."

"I guess librarians everywhere are nosy," Marielle noted. "Did you come to any conclusions?"

"Wait. I feel badly lying to you, just there. It was actually my religion teacher who answered the question for me. He said that nihilists are atheists, but not all atheists are nihilists."

"What's the difference?" Marielle asked, looking up at the kitchen window as a gust of wind rattled the pane in its channel.

"Ah, bloody. I knew you'd ask that. Moments after he told me, I forgot. Wait, now. Atheists don't believe in God or an afterlife, of course, but I think he said nihilists believe there's no meaning in life as well. Basically, there is no meaning in anything a'tall."

"That seems very dark," Marielle reflected. "I see now their need for black fingernail polish and lipstick."

"Exactly," Dermot agreed. "Your nihilist friends would *never* be taken seriously if they attended lectures wearing a t-shirt with a smiley face on it."

Marielle guffawed, then paused to take a deep breath. "You know, Dermot MacManus, you amaze me. You take your word seriously enough to follow through, and you're the only guy who consistently makes me laugh. *Why* do you live in Ireland?" she asked with frustration.

"I've wondered the same about yourself, living in America that is. You're really the only person I can talk to about loads of things. The only person I trust, really. And you're the only girl who doesn't bore me to

262

tears."

Marielle smiled brightly as she said, "I promise not to let another boy come near me until I see you. Well, I might kiss him—on the lips that is—and hold his hand, but that's it which isn't saying much because I find the boys here so irritating and they don't know how to kiss at all."

Dermot was quiet for a moment. "What do you mean, Marielle?" he muttered.

"Well, they're either trying to impress me with their clothes or their cars or—"

"That's not what I'm meaning to ask you," he interrupted.

"What are you asking me?" Marielle asked, biting the right side of her bottom lip.

Dermot moaned. "Please don't make me say it."

"You're the guy. It's your job to say it," she replied with as much determination as remorse.

"Just a sec," he said, setting down the receiver. A moment later, he returned. "Are you saying you'll allow me to make love to you, like?"

Marielle stared at the light above the oven. "I think I am," she replied.

"My God!" he declared.

She sat forward. "I'm sorry. Is that bad?"

"Not a'tall. I just need a moment," he said breathlessly.

She smiled mischievously. "To do what?"

"Not that!... yet," he said, then chuckled.

Marielle looked down as her cheeks became warm. "Should we talk about other things now to give you a minute?" she asked, then continued when he didn't respond. "I've been looking into transportation from the airport to Galway, and I was thinking I should take the train."

"No, we'll give you a lift from the airport," Dermot said, still short of breath.

"I don't want to put you guys out."

"There's no train from Shannon to Galway, Marielle. So, it's best you accept my offer."

She looked up as the window rattled again. "I think you're lying in a rare attempt at being polite, but I won't let you give me a ride."

"Hold it now! A ride and a lift are two separate things, and you just promised me you would!"

Marielle laughed. "Oh, right. I promise to never ask anyone else to give me a ride, then."

"Please don't. That's my job," Dermot said, then stopped to collect himself again. "I'm not misleading you about the train though. There isn't one."

"I thought Limerick was the second largest city in Ireland," Marielle said accusingly.

"'Tis."

"And Shannon is near Limerick?"

"'Tis, but trust me there's no train. Don't ask me why. I wouldn't make this up. If you were flying into Dublin, you could take the train, but you're not so you either accept my offer, or you can rent a donkey and cart from the local sheep farmer."

Marielle squinted at the oven door. "Hmmm... I do like sheep. We had a couple of brothers in my home town that always smelled like their farm animals... and I do miss that smell. Although, I don't think they had sheep. Maybe they did before one got a restraining order, actually. Anyway, this is too big a decision to make over the phone. I'll need to get back to you."

"So, transportation is a bigger decision to you than intercourse?" Dermot asked, using a more emphatic version of his voice.

"No," Marielle replied. "I made that decision when I received your last letter."

"Read it to me quickly! I want to make certain I send one exactly like it next time I write to you."

Marielle laughed. "I wish I could, but it's nearly time for me to go to work. I just have one request before I go though."

"Anything!" Dermot said vehemently.

Marielle sat back. "Wow! Boys are very compliant when you promise them sex."

"This isn't a new rule, Marielle."

"Well, my request is that this conversation not change anything between us. I'd feel awful if you stopped talking to me about who you're dating and I don't plan to stop telling you about the crappy boys I date. You're really the only person I can talk to about these things."

Dermot breathed into the phone before he spoke. "I promise. This changes nothing a'tall."

Marielle hung up the phone, then walked into the predawn darkness. It occurred to her that her first three hours of work would go towards paying for her phone call, but it was worth it. She would think of

Dermot's voice while she served food. She'd remember his words while clearing and washing tables. She'd hear his laugh while washing and stacking dishes, and she'd think of how much he wanted her while cleaning the dish room and cart. In fact, thoughts of Dermot would interject themselves throughout her shift, creating a disorder of thought she found both pleasing and irritating in its inability to be managed.

11/20/1988 Sunday

Dear Dermot,

Thanks so much for your letter and for speculating on my size. There are plenty of examples of fat Americans in Wisconsin, but I'm fairly certain I'm not one of them... at least I didn't used to be. Wait a second while I throw up my lunch. ☺

Thank you also for saying I'm "smart for an American" in French. Americans are generally not accustomed to hearing compliments in French... or so I'm told. Most people here are still pissed that the French didn't let us use their air space to bomb Libya so they're not interested in hearing what the French have to say at all.

By the way, in the U.S. "pissed" means angry. Don't feel bad about being wrong. You were probably drunk when you wrote that. ☺ *Did I tell you that if a person has a hangover, we say he has the "Irish Flu"? AND, if siblings are nine months apart, we call them "Irish Twins"? I don't imagine you say the same. Do you call a police van a "Paddy Wagon"? Speaking of which, it's funny that you seem so against war. The Irish have a reputation here for fighting everything from their boss to an empty beer can—once provoked of course (by the beer can, not their boss. They hit their boss for no reason at all!). The Irish also have a reputation for being stubborn (I think we covered that earlier). My mom is half Irish and I swear the woman can hold a grudge for nine years! <—That's actually not an exaggeration, by the way. She once didn't speak to her mother for nine years. I can't remember if that was the time Grandma paid a bar patron (she used to own a bar [I guess you say "pub"]) to beat up my dad, or the time she lied to my mom and told her that some random bar guy was her father. You'd never know that my mom comes from white trash though. She was raised by a very conservative, God-fearing, church-going Italian grandmother everyone called Nona, and my mom and Nona shunned my*

265

grandmother most of her life... which brings me back to the stubborn part. ☺

Last night, I couldn't sleep. So, I was lying in bed thinking of a way to solve the whole Northern Ireland problem—after I thought about you, of course. You'll never believe it, but I actually figured out a solution—at least it seemed like a solution at 3am. I thought I should write it down, but I was too lazy to get up, turn on the light, and find a notebook and pen. I also convinced myself I'd remember this morning, but I didn't. Sorry about that!

Speaking of dying though—wait, actually, I was talking about Northern Ireland, wasn't I? Anyway, dying and Northern Ireland are connected in my mind. So, our lunch discussion today was about preferred ways to die. Everyone agreed that dying like Elvis did would suck since—although he didn't technically die on the toilet—everyone thinks he did. My friend Tom was teased for saying he'd like to die while thwarting an assassination attempt on the Pope. I defended him by saying that dying while saving someone else was the best way anyone could die, but we sit with a bunch of Lutherans who're blinded by any reference to the Pope. To be honest though, I think dying during a gun battle after storming an SS officer's mountain chalet would be right up my alley... as long as I took a few SS officers with me, of course. Most everyone else said dying in your sleep would be best, but I disagree. I want to see death coming and not "wake up" wondering why my room looks like a cloud and who's playing that harp?

Anyway, I'll never die the way I want because there's a serious lack of SS officers hiding out in the Alps these days. I hear most of them ended up in Argentina, but I can't figure out why that is. I know Germans emigrated there in the '20s and '30s (they apparently got on the wrong boat), but I can't see why being German would make you sympathetic to the Nazis. My grandpa said we were called "Huns" in Chicago during WWI, but once WWII rolled around everyone was just considered American... unless you were of Japanese descent... which was too bad. Am I rambling? The thing is that most people in the U.S. feel closer to the British than to the country of their ancestry. I talked to my grandpa about this and he agreed it was true. I wonder if it's because of the language or our political/legal history. Hmm. Anyway, I know I'm rambling now because I've moved from dying to political history—which wouldn't seem unreasonable if you knew my old civics teacher.

As an aside, I have to disagree with you about the Falkland Islands War. I think several hundred sheep are definitely worth dying for ("A preposition is nothing to end a sentence with."—Sir Winston Churchill [You know, he was half American? ... That would be the smart, industrious half]). Anyway, I think sheep are just the cutest things.

Also during lunch, our gym teacher, Mr. O'Sullivan (he's Russian ☺), came over to talk to us and Joy was such a complete suck-up saying things like she was "waiting until Mr. O'Sullivan taught archery so she could take it" that once he left I asked her if she needed to have her nose surgically removed from his ass... which was unfortunate since he had doubled-back to say something else and heard my comment. (I guess I won't be taking swimming with him next semester.)

Did I tell you we can't graduate unless we take swimming? It's complete bullshit! I'd understand if we lived on an island like you, but you've gotta go out of your way to find water here. I suppose Lake Winnebago is a few miles from here, but that's only 15' deep for God's sake!... though no one is 15' tall so you'd still need to know how to swim, but 15' of water doesn't seem that dangerous somehow.

The Fox River is the closest body of water to us (do you say "body of water" if it's a river?), and with the dams and undertow, knowing how to swim doesn't help you much. The river is posted everywhere with "don't jump in or you're fucked" signs (well, they phrase it differently), but all they'd really have to do is make the "Houdini almost drowned here" plaque bigger. (Did I tell you Houdini was from Appleton?) Anyway, if a world-renown escape artist barely escaped that river, I want no part of it!

I just reread what I've written so far and it mostly sounds like I'm drunk, but I promise I'm not. My aunt who's a nurse told me that drinking before 18 damages your liver more than drinking <u>after</u> 18 so I'm staying away from alcohol until college. Most of my friends think that's lame, but it's not their liver! Anyway, the reason I think I'm rambling is because your last letter and our conversation made me more than a little crazy and I'm a little nervous about addressing it. You may not know it, but saying and hearing compliments or anything serious or sincere at all makes me nervous. Whenever I get a compliment I usually say "shut up" or my favorite "shut up or I'll punch you!" This sounds mean, but most people *only compliment me because they know I don't like it. In any event, I know that's not why you complimented me so thank you. If you were here right now, I promise I'd take you to see Houdini's plaque. (It's where a lot of kids go parking.)*

I really, really like you which I think is sometimes harder to say than "I love you" which I do... a lot. I think sometimes I'm just passing time until I can be with you. I don't mind that you're one month and ten days younger than me and I don't care what you look like. I just want to hear your voice for longer than 30 minutes at a time and see the places you see every day. Being near you would be a dream to me. When things get bad here, I think, "wouldn't it be great to run away together?", but then I tell myself I'm going crazy and "whatever you do, don't tell him you think that way" which I've clearly just done. BAH!!

I love you!
Marielle

PS Don't let this (and previous letters) make you think you have to end every letter with "I love you." I know you have a girlfriend now and it may seem uncomfortable for you.

PPS "Bite Off" means "go to Hell." I'm pretty sure most people do <u>not</u> engage in "biting off" during oral sex, but this certainly isn't my area of expertise so you'd have to ask Joy.

PPPS I had a dream about you the other night. I wish I could say it was similar to your dream, but in it you actually drowned and I couldn't swim fast enough to save you. Isn't that bizarre? I'm sure it doesn't mean anything, but stay away from the water anyway. I know living on an island makes this difficult, but please try!!!

PPPPS By asking how you date without a car, I only meant how do you get to the movies without a car. It had nothing to do with sex. Pervert. Going to the movies is generally considered a date thing to do... so is sex... but not for me.

PPPPPS I'm done PSing now.

Marielle sat inside the doorframe of her parents' room looking through the lace curtains of the hall window as she waited for Shelly's mom to retrieve her daughter.

"Hey, Mar!" Shelly said cheerfully.

"Hey there! What are you doing?"

"I'm cleaning my room. Saturday is sheet changing day."

Marielle furrowed her eyebrows. "Really? We're never that organized."

"Well, that's what happens when your mom is a teacher."

"*Ja,* I can see the good and bad of that. I had the worst dream last night and I need you to tell me what it means."

"That's not the kind of psychology class I'm taking. It's more like the psychology of marketing. You know, what works in an ad and what doesn't."

"Oh," said Marielle, attempting to sound less disappointed than she felt.

"Why, what did you dream about last night?" Shelly asked.

"Well, I dreamt that I was taking the city bus to Chicago to see U2 in concert and Bono was sitting next to me, but I couldn't see his face because he was serenading the girl across the aisle and the bus was approaching a crash scene, but it wasn't slowing down. I saw a guy in the middle of the road going through his trunk and it looked more like bedding from a house or apartment than stuff you'd keep in a car. We were in the left lane passing the guy and I was about to yell 'slow down' when all of a sudden the Budweiser dog was in the street and the bus didn't even try to stop before it ran right over him—"

"*Her,*" Shelly corrected. "The Budweiser dog is a girl."

"Okay, but in my dream it was a boy and I saw him run away with one of his rear legs in the air and I yelled 'Stop!' and the bus driver did and I said I had to go look for the dog and help it and no one else was willing to go so I said, 'Fine! Pick me up on the way back from the concert.' But as soon as I got off the bus and it pulled away, I saw the dog running with a pack of two or three dogs with no problem at all, and I realized I was in a dangerous part of Philadelphia—"

"Philadelphia?" Shelly asked.

"I know, it doesn't make sense, but I ran after the bus and had to run through a group of criminals who were counting money from a cash register they stole, and the bus finally stopped when I waved my white hat, and I got back on, but Bono stole my seat. Can you believe that?! I'm still so mad, I haven't listened to U2 all day!" Marielle paused, waiting for Shelly's analysis.

"Well, I think it's clear that you're still mad at your parents for not letting you go to Chicago to see U2."

"*Ja,* maybe," Marielle said, unsatisfied.

"What did you think it was about?" Shelly asked.

"I thought maybe the dog was my dad and I couldn't save him and trying to save him put me in danger and meant I'd miss the bus or any opportunity to be with Dermot who was represented by Bono."

"Hmm," Shelly said, then quickly continued, "I'd say it has more to do with the concert."

2-Dec-1988

Hi Marielle, my absolutely cool America pen pal!

Your letters are (slowly but surely) getting more big-headed and funny.

That was a bad joke about you liking the Falkland Islands War - it "sucked". (Yippee! I'm a qualified American. Just add 160 pounds, $1,000,000, and a camera).

Oh yes... indeed... about my girlfriend. I'm in a BAD situation. I've got Sinéad in Dublin and Katie in Galway. If I get caught by either one, I'm dead/fucked/finished—you get the idea. I'll blame it all on you, too— they're only practice so I'll be fit for my seven day/night obstacle course/endurance test with my advanced, mature (16+6(time-zone)=22 years) American pen pal. Aaagh. Guess who's going to kill me in April?

Bet you're wondering who Katie is. Just a female. Thanks for dreaming about me. I dream about you, but you wouldn't like me to go into detail (unless you're a perv).

My sister is a bitch!! Every time Katie phones me she (Fiona) says "Oh, hi Pauline, I mean Sinéad, or Marielle. Whatever." So Katie gets really angry and threatens to kill me.

Guess what? Guess what? You better pray my dad doesn't answer the phone when your parents ring. I told him about the "language barrier" so he's going to pretend he speaks no English! I can just imagine it. "Marielle, I won't let you stay with savage barbarian primitives!" <— (your mother) Don't worry. He was only joking.

I know "Bite off" doesn't refer to oral sex—it's just a painful thought.

Ouch. Even thinking about it induces phenomenal hormonal imbalances.

I didn't mean to imply <u>you</u> were a fat American. Just because you seem to DRIVE everywhere... do you A) live in a big car, or do you B) enjoy gloating?

What do you mean "I don't have to write 'I love you' at the end of my letters"? I do. Why shouldn't I?

I hope this reaches you soon. I might as well tell you that another girl rang me last night and we met the next day and guess what happened? Another girlfriend. Yippee. Her name is Róisín. If one finds out about the other(s) I'm dead... But, that's life. I better go now 'cos I've Irish love poetry to learn. I promise I'll be thinking about you. Thanks for phoning me. Happy Christmas. Enjoy yourself. Don't drink too much. I LOVE YOU.

See you in April, when you're <u>not</u> getting a train from the airport!

Dermot

Part II, Chapter 168, Book 3

Hi, it's me again. I had to write more. I had to tell you your name in upper-class English: Mariella, that's wot it is. Anyone with a name like that could qualify as a true snob.

I've just done my poetry. There's hundreds of words that describe you just perfectly. No, they're not insults you poor paranoid person.

Please tell all your family that I wish them a happy Christmas. My friend (Sean) keeps telling me to force you to bring friends because... well, that's pretty obvious.

Now, I REALLY have to go. I have to go swimming with Róisín who has the most incredibly beautiful body (which is why I like swimming with her). Sorry - I know - I'm boring you again. That's a common fault among Irish males.

Bye.........

Lots of Love,

Dermot

P.S. There IS no train from Shannon to Galway!

She opened the envelope to reinsert the letter when she made the discovery of another slip of paper.

I couldn't sleep, so I wrote down this poem for you:
I'm not alive, I'm just a dream.
When you wake, I'll not be seen.
But when you think of me alone,
You'll know I am your very own.
There are some words you know are true.
These words are, I Love You!

***

"Oh, he DEFINITELY wants to get into your pants!" Joel exclaimed.

Marielle turned around angrily. "Stop reading over my shoulder, dumbass!"

Joel laughed as he rounded the table. When he sat down he laced his hands together in front of him in a thoughtful pose. "I'm just trying to help you out. Way to kill the messenger. By the way, do they sell condoms in Ireland?"

Marielle narrowed her eyes in a failed attempt at appearing stern. "I have no idea. Why do you ask?"

"Because from the sound of that poem, you're going to need them. Well, at least one—extra small, I imagine."

"Very nice!" Tom exclaimed before mouthing "sorry" to Marielle.

"No, seriously," Joel continued. "You don't want to come home pregnant with a leprechaun baby. How would you explain that to your folks?"

Marielle leaned forward. "Number one, you don't need to worry about me getting pregnant. Number two, there wouldn't be time to explain that the baby was a leprechaun 'cause my father would shoot me before I had time to explain."

Joy cleared her throat. "You could always lie and say you were raped."

Marielle nodded slowly. "Good idea. I'll tell them Joel did it."

"Uh, didn't you say your dad has lots of guns?" Joel asked concernedly.

"*Ja,* but lucky for you he's not a good shot when he's drunk."

"What about when he's sober?" Tom inquired.

Marielle turned to Tom. "I don't know. I've never seen him shoot a gun sober."

Joel laughed, then suddenly adopted a serious expression. "Back to my original point. I bet they only sell condoms sanctioned by the Church in Ireland."

"There's no such thing as condoms sanctioned by the Church, dumbass."

"I know. Ooh, I just thought of a good idea for a new brand of condoms. What do you think about *Papal Condoms?*"

Marielle chuckled. "I think the Pope wouldn't like you borrowing his name for a brand of prophylactics."

"Big word, but *yes* he would."

"How's that?" Tom asked through laughter.

"Because my condoms would dissolve in water."

Marielle guffawed. "You'd make a killing at all the Pro-Life rallies."

"Nice pun, but I'm gonna get that idea trademarked and make a million dollars off the rights. Where's my notebook?" he asked, looking under the table.

"Your notebook of brilliant ideas?" Joy scoffed.

"YES!"

"It's probably in your locker," Marielle replied. "Do me a favor and write that one under *showering daily.*"

"I will, and just above *avoiding Marielle's sexual advances.*"

Marielle smiled. "If only I weren't promised to someone else."

"AHA, you admit it!" Joel declared.

"No, I was only joking," Marielle replied with too much feeling to be believed.

"Liar!" Joel declared.

Marielle began to blush before she asked, "So, if I *were* to buy condoms, where could I get them where I wouldn't be recognized by anyone who knows either me or my parents?"

Joel reflected on the question before he said, "Nowhere, but I'll buy them for you for $20."

Marielle consulted her right eye. "I don't think Dermot would like me bringing condoms another guy bought."

"WRONG!" Joel said in an outdoor voice. "He won't give a shit as long as he gets into your pants. If a girl flew across the Atlantic just to see me and she brought condoms with her, I wouldn't care if she got them from her pimp. I'd be too busy jumping her bones."

"You're a vulgarian," Marielle said dismissively.

"And you're an idiot if you think Irish guys are any different than Americans! Do you want me to buy you condoms or not?!"

Marielle shook her head. "No, thanks. I won't need them."

12/9/1988 Friday

Dear Dermot,

How are you? I'm fine. I have some important news for you. I did some more research on transportation between Shannon and Galway and guess what? There's no train! I knew you'd be <u>completely</u> shocked so I thought I'd tell you right away. Bus Éireann goes to Galway though so I'll take that. I'm studying Irish road maps right now. This seems kind of boring, but I like mapping out possible routes between two cool sounding places. (Obviously, Galway is always one of those places.) Aren't I a party animal? It looks like Carnagh East is the geographic center of Ireland, and I'm a real fan of a place called Skibbereen which I've decided to call Skedaddle.

I'm babysitting right now. I only mention this because I might have to jump up if the baby cries and I don't want you to wonder where I've gone. ☺

Thank God it's Friday! I had to see the school counselor today (not because I'm mental or because I got caught reading Nietzsche [though I told him you were investigating nihilism and he's planning to call your parents ☺]) but because he wanted to discuss what he described as my "overloaded class schedule" for next semester. I told him I appreciated his concern, but keeping busy distracted me from the horror of being under the thumb of my parents and, "oh, by the way, your picture is crooked" which is when he decided that I should A) talk to him about my relationship with my parents and B) get tested for OCD (Obsessive Compulsive Disorder). I told him I didn't want to be rude, but I didn't feel like talking about my parents and as regards the OCD, I could write him a 10-point paper on why I'm not. He chuckled 'cause he got my joke, but then he just looked concerned. Anyway, I promised to consider talking to him because he's a great guy and I don't want to disappoint him, but I'm not sure I'll have the time with my crazy class schedule. Ha!

Anyway, I think my friend Lisa might need counseling services more than I do 'cause she blurted-out today that she'd like to find the person responsible for assigning her to her homeroom and light him on fire. This was surprising, not because her homeroom doesn't suck, but because she's a pacifist. Anyway, I thought her comment was funny and related it to the mother of the kids I'm babysitting which was a mistake 'cause she looked really alarmed and asked if Lisa was serious. I said that I was sure she wasn't and if she was it wasn't in a body-engulfing-Vietnam-era-monk kinda way, but rather a cigarette-burning kind of way. She seemed confused so I added, "You know, the way people burn their foster kids?"

Apparently, this is <u>not</u> the thing to say to the mother of the kids you're babysitting 'cause she didn't laugh AT ALL! I was sure I disturbed her enough to make her come home early, but no luck. Maybe she found her sense of humor while she was out.

I still work at the nursing home, but I had to go back to babysitting to make up for the pay I lost when I left Hardees which screws up my already dysfunctional social life. Last week, I babysat for this pervert hockey player kid whose friends are my age and he's only 12. So, he calls me into his room after I told him to go to bed and I don't have proof, but his right hand was under his blankets and it looked to me like he was having a one man party. (By the way, you're the only guy I know who admits to doing this. All the guys at my lunch table say 99% of all guys do it... except them). I told him I wouldn't tell his parents this time, but from now on it's "hands above the covers" when I walk into the room.

Anyway, it was kind of awkward later on when Justin's mom asked how her son behaved for me. I tried to stay cool, but I'm a horrible liar and I'm pretty sure she knows he acted up... although, she probably didn't guess he treats his body like a petting zoo when she's not around. The mom is pregnant with another kid so we'll find out in a few years if being a pervert is genetic. In any event, I escaped that house as quick as I could and drove home.

I hate to harp on the driving stuff, but I have to say that the greatest thing about driving is not making awkward small talk with parents when they drive you home at the end of the night. You also don't need to time any conversation to end as soon as they pull into your driveway. I used to babysit for my Biology teacher's kids and I swear she drilled me about what we did, where we went, and what we ate from the time we left her house until the minute we arrived at mine. Her science tests were never that hard... and if they were, I was never that nervous.

Anyway, I'm just dreaming about going home now 'cause it's 2:30am and the parents aren't back yet. All that's on their whole three TV channels is some white-bearded preacher man gushing about his ugly Tennessee Walker horses. If they don't come home soon, I may go crazy!

Did I tell you I almost walked into the back of a hearse last week? It was about 9:30pm when I punched out and headed out the back door of the nursing home. The light above the door was out and my head was in the clouds and two steps after opening the door I bumped into the back of an open hearse. I FREAKED OUT and shrieked in a really undignified way. Thank God no one was there to hear me... or if they were, they didn't say anything... although my running like the wind didn't give them much of a chance. Anyway, I'm much more careful leaving the building now.

I've just reread your last letter and I have to say, you're very brave to date so many girls. I couldn't handle the drama of dating multiple guys. In fact, I'm happily dating no one right now which might seem unrealistic (the happily part, I mean), but guys are such an enormous pain in the ass! Besides, writing and calling you takes up most of my free time now and listening to some vapid snob tell me how he's wanted to date me since the first time he saw me across the Commons "with my hair sparkling in the sunlight" might cause me to vomit on his new boat shoes.

Do you think I'm too young to be so bitter? If you're wondering, this is probably in the category of the 70% of things I say and don't mean... or maybe I <u>do</u> mean it and saying I don't is part of the 70%... or maybe I <u>don't</u> mean it and saying it, then saying I mean it is part of the 70%. Are you crazy yet? WHEN ARE THEY COMING HOME?! Don't get me wrong, I love messing with your brain, but I have to work at 6:30am tomorrow and even if I was asleep right now I'd have less than 3 ½ hours before I had to get up. BASTARDS!!

Did I tell you that one of the residents at the nursing home told me he loves me only second in the world to his deceased wife? His name is Lars and he's from Denmark. He wears this cute, bright green cardigan and holds my hand every time I come into the room to talk to him... which I do

276

during most of my breaks. Sometimes he asks me to write a letter to his nephew for him, and he helps me by addressing letters to my grandmother (long story), but most of the time he just talks about Denmark and holds my hand.

The residents aren't all as coherent as Lars. One guy wears his white underwear on the outside of his dark blue dress pants every day (which looks great as he pushes his walker down the hall). If you ask him how he's doing, he'll either say, "Good, I just had a BM" or "Not good, young lady. I haven't had my BM." My dad says there's no good way to respond to this except to say, "Good, good," in the first case, and "I'm sorry to hear that," in the second.

There's also a really mean guy in our nursing home that everyone calls "The Judge" who used to be best friends with Senator Joseph McCarthy and every time I deliver his bed tray he goes OFF about how Senator McCarthy got the shaft. Sometimes he uses the word "railroaded," but it's always the same message. I hope when I'm in the last years of my life, I'm not sitting in a nursing home scaring off teenagers with rants about ex U.S. Senators. If I am, and we're still friends, you have my permission to kill me. Actually, you also have my permission to kill me if I wear my underwear outside my pants, and/or judge the value of a day by whether or not I've had a successful bathroom break.

I'm home now, and it's 4am so there's no point in going to sleep since I'd be up in two hours anyway. The cheap parents came home as soon as I finished writing the last paragraph. I call them "cheap" because they paid me $10 for nine hours of babysitting. I was tempted to say, "Couldn't you just buy me a sandwich?" At least I wouldn't need to hide that from the IRS... although the IRS probably doesn't care about my $10 anyway, but who knows. Getting paid in sandwich form would be one less thing to worry about.

OK, I'm officially rambling under the influence of sleep deprivation so I'm going to stop now. I'm also going to stop writing "I can't wait to see you!" because it makes me too crazy to think about. Actually, I can't control myself, I CAN'T WAIT TO SEE YOU!!

Lots and lots and lots of love,
Marielle

"So, how many Hmong chicks are going to commit suicide this year, I wonder?" Joel asked coldly. "We should start a pool."

Marielle looked up from her German workbook. "That's horrible, and you don't know that she committed suicide."

"Uhhh, yes I do. She just turned 16 and everyone knows they get sold off when they're 16."

"They're not sold off, they're married," Marielle argued.

Tom raised his head with purpose. "Their parents arrange the marriage, get money for the transaction, and she becomes the slave of the mother-in-law afterward. How is that different from slavery?" he asked.

Joy seized on the one point she understood to proclaim, "Arranged marriage? That's nuts. I'd be pissed if I had an arranged prom!" She erupted in a round of cackling which ended in a snort.

Marielle smiled as she shook her head.

"What's up with you?" Joel asked suspiciously.

Marielle's smile expanded. "Nothing," she replied.

"Bullshit," Joel said. "Tom?"

Tom nodded. "Something's definitely up."

"What? What is it?" Joy asked, wondering why Marielle was more interesting than her joke.

"Tell us. Now!" Joel demanded as he slapped his hand against the table.

"Fine!" Marielle replied, still smiling. "I have enough money to buy my ticket to Ireland. The travel agent is holding it for me so I can pick it up after school."

"No shit," Joel said with the last of his breath.

"No shit," Marielle replied.

"Why wouldn't you tell us?" he asked confusedly.

"It's too exciting to think about. I have to force myself to forget about it or I won't get through the day. Plus, part of me thinks I'll jinx myself if I talk about it before the ticket is actually in my hand."

"How much does it cost?" Joy asked.

"Seven-hundred and eighty-five dollars," Marielle answered.

"That's insane!" Joy exclaimed. "That's almost as much as my motor scooter."

"I'd rather see Dermot than ride a motor scooter," Marielle argued.

Joel stared at her for a moment before saying, "You mean you'd rather ride Dermot than a motor scooter."

"Alright," Marielle agreed, feeling nothing could faze her now.

"You're nuts!" Joel proclaimed unhappily. "There's no way this guy is going to live up to your idea of him! I have a definite feeling this is going to end badly."

"I'd rather see him for seven days and have it end badly than to never see him at all," Marielle said, still impenetrable.

"But you don't even know what he looks like!" Joy protested.

Marielle glanced at Joy. "I kind of do, but I honestly don't care."

Joel exhaled as his head turned sharply toward the windows.

"What!" Marielle demanded. "Why does this upset you so much?"

He turned back. "You'll be halfway around the world when he breaks your heart and none of us will be there to help you. You're just running away for the same reason I feel like running away, but I have the sense to stay put and wait until the bastard dies!"

Tears formed in Marielle's eyes as she stared at Joel. "But I can't wait that long," she said softly.

Joel stood up as his chair flew backward, scraping the floor loudly and gaining the attention of those nearby. Some students looked from Joel to Marielle, and some spoke in whispers about what her emotion meant, but only Tom read her perfectly. Escaping to Ireland was her plan, but abandoning people who needed her had never been part of her exit strategy.

Chapter Nineteen

A Chattering Wise and Sweet
—W.B. Yeats – *The Cap and Bells*

"Guess what?! Guess what?! Guess what?!" Marielle sang quietly into the phone receiver, praying her boom box disguised her voice and her father didn't notice the absence of the cordless phone downstairs.

"Hmm, did you tape some poor sod's house shut?" Dermot asked, yawning.

"No," she whispered vehemently.

"What time is it there?" he asked.

"Uhhh, 1am. So, guess again."

"Isn't it a bit early to guess?"

"Sure, if you lack the stamina to put together coherent thought, but if you're American, it's never too early."

"Alright," he said, as though shaking the cobwebs. "Did you get pissed, smash your car, and run from the police?"

"No. You're completely off base," Marielle said with more frustration than she felt.

"Did you quit school and join a traveling orchestra?"

"No. You're never going to guess so you should just surrender."

"Okay," Dermot relented, "but I want it noted that I only surrender to you."

Marielle smiled brightly. "So noted. Soooooo, I bought my ticket," she sang, and danced where she sat.

"Your airline ticket?"

She stopped dancing. "No, my ticket to ride."

"Hmm, I heard she don't care," he retorted.

"Ha! I heard the same. No, I bought my ticket to Shannon, you dumbass!"

"That's fantastic! I hope it wasn't terribly dear."

Marielle paused for a moment as she thought she heard someone on the stairs. "You don't want to know. It's better that we concentrate on the fact that I have it. It's in my hands right now, though it's too dark to read it, but I stared at it enough to know it's peach and green with all kinds of carbon paper attached to it. It doesn't look all that impressive, but it's supposed to get me there."

"At which point we will collect you at the airport," Dermot interjected.

A mischievous smile appeared on Marielle's face. "I was thinking about taking the bus."

"I refuse to fight with you on this matter," Dermot said with calm authority.

"Ooh, that sounds like a challenge," she replied in what she would later consider her sexy voice.

"You're the type of girl who likes a good row, aren't you?"

Marielle gazed from the corner of her eye. "That depends. What's a row?"

Dermot chuckled before he said, "An argument."

She reached up to her dresser to deposit her ticket. "Is that a serious question? Have you read ANY of my letters?"

"Alright then, I will annoy you by refusing to engage you in debate."

Marielle leaned back against the wall as she accused Dermot of sucking.

"Thank you," he replied. "Please give me your details now."

She smiled at Dermot's presumption of authority. "I arrive in Shannon the morning of Tuesday, April 18th, and I fly home Friday—"

"I don't want to think on you leaving. I only want to hear about your arrival," he said with unexpected tenderness.

Marielle quietly cleared her throat. "Alright. I arrive in Shannon at 11:30 a.m. on April 18th."

"That's brilliant!" Dermot said, as if sitting back into a comfortable chair. "I know it's a fair bit away, but I have a MILLION places to show you so bring along your runners or trainers or whatever you call them."

"We call them tennis shoes or sneakers."

"Even if you don't play tennis?" he asked.

"Yeah. It makes no sense. I won't ask where you're taking me since I know you won't tell me which will only cause me to harass you and since you refuse to engage me in debate, there would end our conversation."

"Right, so."

Marielle leaned forward. "Unless you want to tell me now, that is."

"No, I'll let you know when it's all sorted. I have a few minutes before I must prepare for school. So, why don't you tell me now what a homeroom is and why Lisa hates hers."

Marielle smiled as she studied the street light pouring through her curtains onto the bottom half of her bed. "Oh, good, you got my letter. A homeroom is the first room you go to in the morning. They generally just make announcements there. They assign you to your room alphabetically so it's nobody's fault Lisa's in hers. Well, I guess you could make the case that it's her dad's fault, but he couldn't know he was condemning his daughter to hell by giving her his last name. I, myself, will always have to sit behind Amy Rich and put up with her flicking her long blonde hair onto my desk like she's in a shampoo commercial. It's really enough to make anyone set someone on fire."

"So, Lisa has an Amy Rich in her class?"

"No, she doesn't. It's worse than that. It's a long story. Are you sure you want to hear it?"

"You're not usually opposed to telling long stories," Dermot reflected.

"Well, this one is sad and I'm morally opposed to telling sad stories first thing in the morning. Actually, it's first thing in the morning there. It's still night here so I get to crawl back into bed after I hang up with you. That must suck for you knowing I'm cuddled up in a warm bed hours after you have to get up for school. I imagine it's especially bad in the winter."

"I hadn't thought on that before, but it's torture now that I think of it. Thanks for bringing it up."

Marielle laughed quietly. "You're very welcome."

"So, you tell your story, and if I feel myself getting desperate I'll let you know."

"Okay, well, Lisa's last name is Ziegler which means she shares a homeroom with all the Xiongs, Yangs, and Vangs, etc.—basically, the entire Hmong community. Do you know who the Hmongs are?"

"Not a'tall."

"Well, they helped us during the Vietnam War and had to be evacuated when we left, and most of them came to Wisconsin. Anyway, there have been a lot of deaths among girls in the Hmong community and they usually announce these deaths during homeroom which causes most of Lisa's class to both erupt into fits of crying and get pushed into mandatory grief counseling. Since Lisa is the only non-Hmong in her homeroom, the administration can't discriminate against her by assuming she doesn't know the dead girls, so they send her to group counseling along with everyone else.

282

"So, nearly once a month she sits in a room with sobbing classmates who break into a language she can't understand every time they get really upset, and all she can do is hope the counselor doesn't ask her how all this affects her 'cause the only honest answer is that it doesn't... except that the counseling session just rolled into first period and she's missing English class, and to get into that class she'll need a pass from the counselor which makes her English teacher wonder why she's pretending to be upset to get out of his class."

"That's madness!" Dermot declared. "Why are so many girls dying?"

"Well, I don't really know, but everyone says they're sold into marriage at 16 and the girls are committing suicide to escape it."

"That sounds very Shakespearean."

"If I knew anything about Shakespeare, I'd agree with you," Marielle said, standing to watch a helicopter land at the hospital.

"You haven't read *Romeo and Juliet*?" Dermot asked with surprise.

"Yes, and the *Merchant of Venice*, and *Midsummer's Night Dream*, etc, etc. I was only feeding your intellectual superiority complex."

"Marielle," Dermot said in a teacher's voice. "Do you really think that's necessary?"

She dropped the curtain. "You make a good point. Hey, did you receive a package from me yet?"

"No, should I expect one?"

"No. I'm just wondering if packages I *don't* send arrive at your house."

"I'm ignoring your sarcasm and you'll feel especially guilty when you hear I sent you a gorgeous, brilliant Christmas gift yesterday."

"I don't suppose you'll tell me what it is?" she asked, sitting on the floor again.

"I won't, but I'll give you a hint. It looks a bit like a shield."

"Awesome! Does it come with a sword?"

"No, but you can buy one when you arrive. I love saying that, but I won't believe it until I see you at the airport." Dermot cleared his throat suddenly. "I'm after gettin' terrible looks from my mother so I'd best be off now."

For the next week, Marielle ran from the bus stop to the mailbox with more urgency than normal and was disappointed each day when it contained neither a package nor a letter. She was determined not to call Dermot until his gift arrived since her impending trip required a more disciplined fiscal approach, but restraint became more difficult with each package-less day until two days before Christmas.

Hi Marielle!

I got the HUGE parcel you sent me today and... guess what?... I opened it. I never even read the back telling me to wait. Thanks a lot. My friends think the blanket is a bit "suggestive." Yes, Marielle, they think you're one of "those" Americans, but I'm the only one who knows for sure.

I hope you like the REAL, GENUINE, Galway necklace I sent to you. Sorry it's so late. I had to get it specially made, you know? Don't worry, I'm only joking.

I had a laugh when I opened the package to find your reprimand. How did you know I would open it before Christmas? I think you're telepathic or something... And that day you told me to not go near water, I couldn't because there was a storm so I had to do a 10 mile run instead. (I hate running. I'd prefer to drown really.) Anyway, my friends found a dead woman in the river two days later. So it seems you dreamed of her instead of me. I'll try not to be jealous.

Anyway, thanks for the blanket!

Bye. Lots of Love. I can't wait to see you!

I love you very, very much.

Dermot

P.S. Hope you have a Happy Christmas.

Marielle continued to smile as she set down the letter. Knowing the contents of her present made waiting for its arrival much easier to manage. All the same, she wouldn't call Dermot until the necklace arrived to prevent disappointment and stress when the obvious question was asked. However, seconds after receiving it, she planned to call Dermot and tell him it was the most beautiful piece of jewelry she had ever seen even if it was hideous and made her skin turn green.

On December 30th a small, tattered box arrived from Ireland. Marielle struggled to rip it open since it was mostly comprised of tape, but finally uncovered a silver disc-shaped pendant embossed with several interwoven ropes attached to a 12" silver chain. She regarded it for many minutes before fully appreciating its beauty, then happily placed it around her neck.

She read the note folded inside the box which was one of apology from the U.S. Postal Service, explaining the box was damaged en route. *So, the box was mangled and delayed in transport,* Marielle thought. None of that mattered as she rubbed the black and silver Celtic knot between her fingers and felt the cool metal chain on the back of her neck. She decided to wear the necklace until she arrived in Ireland, then dialed Dermot's phone number which she now knew by heart.

"Hello, Mrs. MacManus. This is Marielle Richter, Dermot's pen pal from the U.S. I'm calling to thank Dermot for the lovely necklace that arrived today."

"Dermot isn't home at present," Mrs. MacManus replied efficiently.

"Do you know when I might catch him?" she asked.

"I don't."

"Oh," Marielle paused. "Would you mind telling him I called to thank him—"

"I shall. Thank you for ringing," she said in a voice that didn't sound thankful at all.

Marielle reflected on the conversation for a few minutes after she set down the receiver. It was clear Mrs. MacManus had other things on her mind and she hoped they had nothing to do with Marielle.

1/1/1989 Sunday

Dear Dermot,

Happy New Year!! I wanted to be the first person to write you and wish you a Happy New Year so I'm writing a couple minutes after midnight. Of course, now that I think about it, it's already 6am by you so I'm probably not the first person to wish you Happy New Year at all.

Don't ask me why I'm not at some wild party 'cause it has to do with babysitting a pervert kid whose parents pay well. (I checked to make sure he was asleep before I started writing 'cause I don't want him to sneak up behind me and grab an unprotected part of my body. You may think I'm being paranoid, but I'm not. This kid should really be put down! [Note to self: don't leave this letter at the house when I go home.])

Just tonight, he told me that he got to "third base" with a 15-year-old girl.

The whole time he was raising his eyebrows at me like he was willing to demonstrate. Now, why is it that annoying guys always raise their eyebrows at me? From now on, the raising of eyebrows will cause me to run from a guy as quickly as possible!

Did your mom tell you that my beautiful, lovely, wonderful, sweet necklace arrived on Friday? I put it on as soon as it arrived and I don't plan to take it off until I see you... or maybe never. I really, really love it! Thanks so much for sending it to me!! All my friends will be jealous when I show it off at school next Monday.

Did I tell you I bought my parents a rowing machine and an exercise bike for Christmas? I'm pretty sure they're not happy about it 'cause when they opened their gifts my mom said, "Oh... look, honey," to my dad who replied, "Oh, great," in the tone of voice he only uses when something isn't great at all. Right now, the machines are in the laundry room 'cause doesn't everyone hang out in the laundry room to work out? Actually, to be fair, there aren't a lot of other places to put them.

Both of my brothers are home right now. Well, they're probably out drinking and getting into fights to be honest. John drove home from California on Christmas Eve and Stephen arrived the same day at the airport. I think Stephen plans to go back to California with John in a few days, but I honestly don't know. I'm just praying they leave before they get arrested.

Ooh, I have a good joke for you. It might ruin it if I tell you the 12-year-old I'm babysitting told it to me, so I won't. ☺ Two guys from Southern Illinois are watching a dog lick himself and one says to the other (in a deep southern drawl), "I wish I could do thayit (that)." And the other responds, "He'd bot (bite) you!"

I just remembered that I promised to tell you why some people from Wisconsin call people from Illinois "FIB"s. Well, I'll do that when I see you. I don't want this letter getting held up in Chicago. ☺

I'm happy to say that Appleton is back in order after the two or so inches of snow shut down all operations. Being from Northern Wisconsin (more north than Appleton), I have to say it's embarrassing to share a zip code with people who run around screaming with their hands in the air when a few snowflakes fall. Good thing the terrorists don't know how to manufacture snow!

I'm home now. As God's punishment for complaining about Appletonians, I slid on ice on the way home while taking a corner too fast and skidded up on a curb, thereby smashing an innocent trash can. Unfortunately for me—and the trash can owner—it was metal which made a horrible noise and an even worse mess. Being the responsible citizen I am, I jumped out and picked up the can, but then the house lights went on, and I got scared and ran off before picking up the trash. So, guess who's going to confession next Saturday? Hopefully, my penance won't be telling my parents I skidded off the road and smashed a trash can with their car 'cause I'd have to renegotiate that one with the priest (are penances negotiable?)... or disregard the penance altogether which is a sin in itself, I imagine. Then, I'd have to go to confession for disregarding my penance and hope my penance wasn't to tell my parents I skidded of the road and smashed an innocent trash can with their car. (Do you feel like you've already read this? It's actually the Hotel California of paragraphs.) Anyway, the whole penance thing might be a moot point since the car is probably scratched or dented and I'll have to come clean with my parents on my own. It didn't look damaged when I got out, but it's dark outside and the street lights are this horrible yellowy-orange color that don't let your eyes focus on anything very well. Now, I know what you're thinking: It's New Year's Eve, I murdered a trash can with my parents' car, and I can't focus my eyes well enough to see if the car is damaged. Well, you're wrong!... I think... unless I'm so drunk I don't remember getting drunk. Does that ever happen?

Speaking of drunks, my Uncle Ed (my mom's brother) is visiting from Southern Michigan. He's a prison guard down there and my dad always says he's living on the wrong side of the bars. My mom is pretty embarrassed to be related to him (I'll explain in a minute) and my grandpa Richter makes fun of him pretty often—which is well-deserved—but the nice thing about Grandpa is he doesn't tell Ed he's a drunk, manipulative, thieving, cheating bastard to his face. My grandpa Healy (Ed and Mom's dad) on the other hand, doesn't work under the same constraints. See, Grandpa was in Pearl Harbor, and fought with Patton's Third Army in France. He was also among the first troops to liberate concentration camps in Germany. So, he has no use for anyone who would lie about serving in the military when he didn't... which brings us back to Ed... who claims he was in Vietnam when he wasn't. He also claims he served in Berlin and fathered a child in Helsinki—who is now a super model whose name he can never quite remember—but in reality he never even made it out of boot camp. He was discharged for "forgetting" to tell the Army that he had a knee injury from a motorcycle accident in high school.

So, all of that would be fun enough on its own, but Uncle Ed happens to be visiting at the same time as Grandpa Healy and every time Ed starts talking about his time in Delta Force, Grandpa goes into a five minute tirade about what a "useless piece of shit" he is and if he repeats his "bullshit stories" to the wrong people (i.e. people who actually served in Vietnam) he'll get his clock cleaned, etc, etc. Now, Grandpa is from Tennessee (Copper Hill to be exact. Have you heard of it? ☺) and he NEVER swears around us so you can tell he's really bothered by the son God gave him.

I have to admit, I'm enjoying this visit a lot. It makes me SICK to hear Grandma Lucia gush about what a wonderful person her son is and how all three of his failed marriages were the woman's fault, and how all of his other failings are Grandpa's fault. I'm pretty sure Grandma would still be breastfeeding Uncle Ed if it were possible. Now, that's disgusting, but it made my mom laugh once—just before she yelled at me for being disrespectful.

Anyway, I'm probably scaring you now and you might stop writing to me if I tell you how crazy my family is. Have I mentioned yet that my uncle tells me each and every time he visits that he's giving me everything he owns when he dies? I guess that's one way to get my grandma's stuff back. HA!

Okay, I need some sleep now. I'll write more in the morning. Sweet dreams!

So, it's the morning and I got a good look at the car before anyone else got up and it's not scratched at all. I keep thinking, "How the hell did that happen?" but I can only assume that I'm one of God's favorite children. Speaking of which, I think I just heard my Grandpa raise his voice at Uncle Ed. I'll be right back............

False alarm. Grandpa was just talking to my mom, but he stopped as soon as I walked into the dining room, so I left right away in the hopes he'd start gossiping again... which he hasn't done, or it's too soft for me to hear from upstairs. All I caught was him saying something about a bar, a woman named Marcy, and a bridge, but I couldn't piece it together. Don't you hate when people are discrete?

Marielle stopped writing as her sisters were called downstairs. A few minutes later, people walked into the house and people walked outside. She heard her father curse and she heard the car start, then back down the driveway.

Marielle returned to her letter.

Well, you've probably spent more time with my family than anyone rightfully should.

I can't WAIT to see you!!! I can't believe we're now in the year where we'll finally meet face to face.

HAPPY NEW YEAR!!!!!

Love,
Marielle

PS Did I ever tell you that my Grandpa Healy is Irish and his family is from Donegal? They were Protestants though so I apologize for that. ☺

PPS I realize I haven't sent you a picture in awhile so I'm sending an extra copy of my passport photo. It was sitting on my dresser and needed a good home so if you don't like it, you can just throw it out... or toss it onto your dresser. I'm just happy knowing it got a transatlantic trip before it died. ☺

PPPS Thank you for your lovely poem! I wrote you a poem in response, but decided that it was no good in comparison to yours. It didn't help that I read Sonnets from the Portuguese in school. You know, "How do I love thee? Let me count the ways..."? That one is really good... but obviously not as good as yours. ☺

Marielle looked down at her poem one more time before she ripped it into pieces:

The sky is dark. The moon shows no light.

My heart it runs rampant all through the night.
The sun which was bright so long before,
Has gone to bed and locked its great door.
You will see it again as the dawn rushes through,
Just as I shall await the great day I see you.

"Drivel," she said, standing beside her wastepaper basket for a moment before the quiet downstairs demanded her attention. There was no talking, no yelling, no laughter, and no TV.

Chapter Twenty

Wound in Mind's Pondering
—W.B. Yeats – *All Souls' Night*

Marielle awoke well before her alarm on the first day of the new semester, ensuring she had time to walk to school in her brand new Nikes with a light blue swish. Although planning to save her shoes until her trip, she decided the unveiling of her necklace was a special event, and vowed to return the shoes to storage that night.

To her delight, someone noticed Marielle's necklace in Women's Choir before she was forced to volunteer its provenance, though volunteerism was required every other hour, including lunch.

"It's just awesome," Joel said sarcastically. "Did you guys hear about the dumbass who drove into the Fox River on New Year's?"

"That was my uncle," Marielle said matter-of-factly, immediately receiving everyone's attention.

"Funny," Joel said smiling.

"I'm completely serious. A thirty-nine-year-old man from Lower Michigan, 1987 two-tone Ford Bronco."

"Seriously?" Joy asked, her mouth remaining open much longer than it took to ask the question.

"Seriously," Marielle confirmed.

"Whoa," Joel said, sitting back. "I'm sorry."

"You shouldn't be. He was a piece of shit," Marielle said before looking around at multiple gaping mouths. "Are you not allowed to say that?" she asked.

"I think you're not supposed to speak poorly of the dead," Tom reflected.

"Because all dead people were wonderful in life or because they can't defend themselves?" she asked.

Tom's eyebrows went up as he studied Marielle. "I have no idea, actually."

"Really?" Marielle asked with surprise. "I thought you analyzed everything before reaching a conclusion?"

"Well, I guess you found an exception," he said, seemingly surprised with himself.

"Hmm, anyway, he was a compulsive liar. I told my mother I wouldn't believe he was dead until I saw the body."

"And did you?" asked Joy.

"There was a wake, but he looked pretty waxy and unrealistic. I decided that I'd probably need to cut him open to know for sure."

"That's disgusting!" Joy exclaimed before looking at the boys for support.

Marielle pulsed her eyebrows with disinterest.

"Was this your mom's brother or your dad's?" Joel asked.

"Mom's."

Tom continued to stare at Marielle with concern. "Tell me you didn't share your feelings with your mom during the funeral."

"No. I shared them before and after. I told her he saved the country a lot of money in future incarceration charges. I also made the joke that if he were really dead, I should be able to feel it—spiritually that is." She chuckled before scanning her classmates' faces again. "What?!" she asked with frustration. "I refuse to feel something I don't, and I refuse to hide what I *do* feel! This is the same guy who pushed down my grandmother and broke her arm. He also pushed my mom when she got in the way of him going after my grandmother."

"You can't hold him accountable for what he did growing up," Tom decided.

"This was two years ago!" Marielle argued. "He was in a drunken rage. He also abandoned two kids, and cheated on three wives, and there was an investigation into his potential role in selling drugs in the prison where he worked. Do I need to continue?" She paused briefly. "The last time we visited him, he showed me a Picasso painting and told me he was the original painter. He also showed me a ruby-red vase and told me it was the oldest piece of glass on the planet. He said it was found in Egypt by Napoleon's troops." She lifted her hand. "I swear to God! Because if you're an invading army, the wisdom of carrying glass on horseback seems like a no brainer."

"You're making this up," Joel said, beginning to laugh.

She smiled unhappily. "I wish I was. Would you like me to go on?"

"Please," said Tom sharing an amused glance with Joel.

"Okay. He was trying to get disability from the Army last year by claiming he broke his back while painting the roof of an outhouse during basic training. That's right. Apparently one paints the roofs of outhouses. And apparently there are outhouses in camps with running water. And apparently it was *friendly fire* that hit him, causing him to fall down. Guys on the firing range were apparently terrible shots, but not with a regular weapon, but a grenade launcher. And apparently he didn't go to the doctor because he decided to be a man and suck it up which is why the V.A. was so confused when he made a claim decades later. Can you imagine that? How many men don't need to see the doctor after breaking their back?"

Tom's and Joel's faces succumbed to laughter, but Marielle went on with a dead-serious expression on her face.

"So, this past weekend he told us the V.A. settled with him for $350,000, but he didn't want any of his ex-wives to get the money, so he wrote a check for the entire amount to the Republican Party. He actually went to the trouble of typing this letter with President Reagan's signature on it thanking him for his donation. I actually saw it. It was a ridiculous Xeroxed copy of the Presidential shield and a pathetic forgery of Reagan's signature. He even spelled *gratitude* wrong. Are we done now? I'm holding a number of stories in reserve."

"No, no. You're good," Joel finally said, looking up at the ceiling for breath. "I'm so glad we sit together. Just promise me you won't forget any of these stories. I may need to call you for a pick-me-up someday."

Marielle nodded. "No problem. Just remind me to tell you about the geologist and the secret meteor hit next time."

"Oh, geez," Tom said, glancing at Joel.

"No. We're done now," Marielle declared. "I need to eat. I was only trying to prove a point, but you can tell me again how awesome my Irish necklace is," she said, holding out the pendant.

A chorus of halfhearted "oh yeah"s and "it's great"s could be heard a second before Marielle rolled her eyes. She pushed back her seat, then walked several yards toward the vending machines before she heard the boys laughing again.

Marielle held her necklace pendant with her left hand during most of the day, looking up at the clock as much as possible to determine the time in Ireland and to speculate on what Dermot might be doing at that moment. She copied her assignments happily when she managed to pay attention, not minding the impending requirements, and not minding her scheduled work that evening. She didn't even mind the bitter cold as she ran from the front door of school to the waiting car.

Marielle reached for her seat belt without saying a word to her sister since her recent rants about Grandma Lucia and Uncle Ed were less than well received. Equally unappreciated was Marielle's request for Doug to take his arm off Jeanette after the funeral, and her question regarding whether Doug had somewhere else to go instead of constantly stalking her sister.

"Guess what?" Jeanette said with an unpleasantly happy expression on her face.

"Is it good news?" Marielle asked with caution.

"Yeah, kind of," her sister said, still smiling.

"Hmm. Doug drove into the Fox River too?" she asked.

Jeanette sighed. "That comment would annoy me if I didn't know your trip to Ireland was canceled."

"Very funny," Marielle said dismissively as her sister turned left onto Emmers Drive.

"Oh, I'm serious," Jeanette replied. "Your little friend's mom called this morning after you left for school."

Marielle smirked at the street. "Well, I'm sorry I missed her."

"And Dad's pissed 'cause she was so rude," Jeanette continued.

Marielle's head turned quickly toward her sister. If Mrs. MacManus had called, there was no doubt in Marielle's mind that she would have been rude.

Jeanette noted her sister's quizzical expression before continuing. "The woman didn't introduce herself, or say hello, or anything. She just blurted out, 'I hope your daughter can get her money back for her ticket.' Just like that."

Marielle's eyes closed involuntarily for a moment.

"The phone woke Dad up. So, of course he was hung over, and he didn't know who the hell she was or what she was talking about."

"Oh, no," Marielle said, covering her mouth and dreading what her father might say when awakened by a foreign person he thought rude.

"Uh-huh," Jeanette replied, nodding her head.

"Why?" Marielle thought out loud.

"Apparently, they're going on vacation that week. Wait! I'm sorry. They're going on *holiday*." Jeanette said the last word with a fake British accent.

"And they waited until *now* to tell me?" Marielle asked with too much sadness to sound indignant.

"Yeah, it sounds like a bullshit story to everyone. Dad said 'what do you expect from a dingbat teacher?' "

"What did mom say?"

"She said she can't believe they almost let you go."

"So, that's it? I can't go now? I can't even go some other time?" Marielle asked desperately.

"Well, actually Dad asked Mrs. Mac-what's-her-name if you could go some other time and she said you'd have to work that out with Dermot." Jeanette drew-out the first syllable of the last word to better mock it as a name.

Marielle unexpectedly felt appreciation toward her father for working on her behalf. She then reflected on how cold the "work it out with Dermot" comment sounded. It was definitely a brush-off and she took it as such.

"That's all?" Marielle muttered.

Jeanette nodded.

"This really happened? On your soul?" she asked, even though she already knew the answer.

"You think I'm making this up? My imagination isn't this good. You can ask Doug if you want. I called him as soon as I found out. He thought it was funny that you worked so hard for nothing."

"Doug is a prick," Marielle said coolly.

"I'll tell Mom you said so."

"Go ahead," Marielle replied, and to herself she thought, *I have nothing to lose now anyway.*

Despite her apparent delight at her sister's misfortune, Jeanette took sympathy on Marielle that night, even offering to work her shift.

After crying in bed for several hours, Marielle decided that skipping work had been a mistake since there was nothing to distract her from her desperate situation. But upon further reflection, she changed her mind, remembering how rote tasks were only made bearable by talking and thinking about Dermot. She also couldn't face the possibility of someone asking about Ireland or noticing her eyes, and asking the obvious questions. Tonight, she wanted to lie in bed alone and cry.

To Marielle's surprise, her parents didn't demand she leave her room to eat or listen to the story of how rude Mrs. MacManus had been. They didn't ask why their daughter was in bed early; why the lights were off in her room; and why the radio was on louder than usual, and for this, Marielle was grateful.

It would have been a perfect night of unbridled wallowing had Anna followed her parents' example and left her sister in peace, but sometime between eight and nine o'clock Anna yelled for Marielle from the bottom of the stairs.

Marielle cursed to God as she rolled from her bed, lowering the volume on her boom box before walking down the hall. She lifted the receiver on the French phone, and yelled "Got it!" to the stairs before greeting the caller.

She heard the downstairs extension click off before her receiver responded, "Hey, it's Guy."

"Oh," she said, not knowing if she would end the sentence with "shit" or "hey," but either way her tone was tempered by several hours of crying, and a fear of doing the same over the phone.

"What's up?" was Guy's usual response even if he had something important to say, and tonight was no exception.

Comforted by what had usually been a sympathetic ear, Marielle lowered her guard, nearly saying "It's been such a bad day" before words became tears, and tears became sobs, and sobs became punctuated by the undignified gasping for air Marielle called hiccup-sobbing.

The line became silent for a moment or two and then Guy's harsh voice proclaimed, "I can't understand a thing you're saying!"

"I was supposed to go to Ireland and now I can't and..." more sobbing.

"Look," Guy said as if shaking off an annoying child, "I'm calling to ask why you gave my letters to Jillian."

This was enough to pull Marielle from her humiliating grief spiral, but she needed to stall for a moment to engage her brain. "What?" she asked.

"Why did you give Jillian the letters I wrote to you?!" he repeated with force.

"I… didn't," she responded truthfully, in the very technical sense.

"Then, how did she get her hands on letters I wrote to you?" Guy asked indignantly.

Marielle's brain was now alert. Attempting to restore its owner's dignity—as well as anyone who began the conversation with hiccup-sobbing could—she replied, "I gave them to someone who knows her."

"Why would you do that?!" he demanded.

"Because I was frustrated that you continued to write and call me when I told you to leave me alone!" she declared, finally on her game.

"Well, you don't need to worry about me writing or calling you anymore," Guy said in a lower voice than the one nature gave him. "You're not worth my time."

Marielle searched for a reply before deciding that Guy wasn't worth the effort. "Go fuck yourself," she finally said. And with that, the line went dead.

Marielle smiled only a fraction of the amount she would have done had she not humiliated herself at the beginning of the call. She walked the short distance to her room and turned on the light, squinting at the light the three yellow lightbulbs in the ceiling cast. The mirror beside her dresser caught her eye as she walked toward the boom box, so she stopped to regard herself for a moment. Her hair was clearly on strike, her eyes were red and overworked, and what little makeup she wore had worn off onto her pillowcase. "You look like hell," she said with satisfaction. At least her body knew how unhappy she was.

Had anything but catastrophe occurred that day, she would have reflected with delight over Guy's predicament. She would wonder how Jillian broke the news to him and the expression on his face when she produced his letters.

Marielle steadied herself against her dresser as the afternoon's events rushed passed her on all sides. She began feeling guilty over her public declarations against her dead uncle, and she wondered if her canceled trip was God's punishment.

She turned to her boom box, trying to find the mental bookmark she made before getting up to answer the phone. "Sobbing while listening to the radio" was an easy enough place to find. She turned up her radio, then lay down to continue where she left off.

Marielle heard her sisters and mother walk upstairs at varying times before closing their doors on the day. She heard her mother say something to her father when he entered their bedroom, but she didn't listen. She didn't listen to the top ten requested songs of the day either until the end of the countdown.

"And the number one requested song in the Fox Valley tonight is U2's *Angel of Harlem*," the DJ said as the familiar guitar riff began. The song inspired a new round of crying and contributed to the feeling that someone or something was mocking her tonight.

For a moment, Marielle feared she was throwing aside logic and discipline for drama and martyrdom. She saw and appreciated the signs of both and worried this was the beginning of a dark descent. She lay there attempting to employ logic before deciding she didn't care to act rationally. She knew this moment mattered. This pain mattered. And she was going to wallow in self-pity forever—well, at least for awhile—no matter what anyone (including herself) thought about it!

Rather than punishment for her harsh words about her uncle, Marielle wondered whether the trip cancellation might actually be God's retaliation for her decision to have sex. She looked up at her ceiling with her hands laced together saying three Our Fathers and three Hail Marys before brokering a deal with God. If she could just go to Ireland, she wouldn't have sex with Dermot or do anything inappropriate at all. She would be good. She promised this if He would just let her go! "PLEASE!" was the last thing she said before signing off.

She grabbed her pendant with her right hand, rubbing the disc like a worry stone.

A moment later, she felt angry again. She didn't ask a lot from God, she decided. She didn't ask Him for parents who didn't fight or a nice house, or even a house they actually owned. She didn't ask for a father who attended her recitals, halftime routines, parades, or even remained sober. She didn't ask Him to give her the money to go to Ireland or make her jobs easy. She would work hard on her own and earn her own money. In return, she just wanted to make plans and not have God cancel them because she was planning to have sex with a boy she loved! After all, wasn't this *her* decision to make?

She turned her head away from God before deciding she'd gone too far. She would go to the bottom of His favored list and stay there for awhile. She thought a curse to no one in particular before settling into a cry that sleep overtook.

Marielle woke up hard the next day. Getting out of bed, showering, dressing, and sitting through her classes required a level of effort heretofore unknown to her. She had floated through life so freely before yesterday that she had forgotten how hard the ground felt when it met her feet.

Again, Marielle found herself in bed before dinner, but unlike the previous night, sorrow and fatigue made way for deep thought. She looked up at the ceiling as she analyzed the potential reasons behind Mrs.

MacManus' phone call and her recent rudeness.

If Mrs. MacManus found one of Marielle's letters, and thought it inappropriate, surely she would have told her father about it. If she found one of Dermot's letters before he mailed it, or overheard Dermot with one of his friends, there was no way she would have left open the possibility of rescheduling.

Just then, Marielle remembered a line in Dermot's last letter that annoyed her. Was it possible that Mrs. MacManus assumed the University of Wisconsin blanket she sent was as suggestive as Dermot had? Marielle sighed. How could anyone equate a blanket with sex? Blankets were cozy and kept you warm. They were the opposite of sex. This was probably not the reason... unless it added to an unsettled feeling Mrs. MacManus had about Marielle.

Maybe Marielle seemed pushy and overly eager to communicate with Dermot and maybe that offended his mother's conservative views regarding female behavior. Maria always said that only desperate girls called boys, but that was if a girl wanted to date a boy. Marielle had no intentions of dating Dermot when she first called. Distance made that notion a ridiculous one. Surely, anyone could see it was camaraderie she sought and she was merely curious about Dermot's culture—how he talked, what he ate, and how he lived. How could curiosity seem desperate?

Wait! What if Dermot's family was poor and couldn't bear to have a foreign guest see this, especially one they might assume was wealthy by virtue of their country's overall income and the fact that Marielle bought a transatlantic ticket? Hmm. That was a possibility. She would put that idea into the "reasonable" column while continuing to search for others.

Marielle also added as reasonable the possibility that Mrs. MacManus forbade girls from staying at the house. After all, Dermot's plans to host his Dublin girlfriend were canceled as well. Marielle made a mental note to fish out the letter where Dermot mentioned this fact.

It was also possible that Dermot's family didn't like Americans. Surely, Dermot had made enough anti-American comments to make that a possibility. It also explained Mrs. MacManus' rude phone manner with both Marielle *and* her father. *But it's not like we ever invaded them or stole their land!* she thought. That didn't make any sense.

Marielle returned to the most logical explanation with displeasure. Mrs. MacManus had read a letter she was never meant to read or heard a conversation she was never meant to hear, and whatever she intercepted was really, really bad.

She thought hard to remember any inappropriate remarks she made to Dermot. She had written jokes, and statements of love, but nothing explicit or indecent. She couldn't think of any examples, anyway. It would assuredly be worse if Mrs. MacManus saw one of Dermot's letters before he sent it, or a copy of a letter he had already sent—if he was the type to make copies of his own letters. Marielle felt shamed when she imagined Mrs. MacManus reading some of the things Dermot wrote to her. Any woman would wonder why a boy thought he could talk to a girl in that manner if she was respectable. His lack of decency would be seen as Marielle's fault which wasn't entirely fair... until quite recently.

Marielle cursed as she realized that her New Year's Day letter had not yet arrived in Ireland. If Mrs. MacManus' motivation to cancel was an inappropriate letter, Marielle's latest letter would most assuredly be scrutinized by adult eyes. This began another round of brain wracking to determine if anything she wrote could be considered inappropriate. She was disrespectful about her uncle, but not inappropriate. Just the same, she questioned the wisdom of honestly describing her family in a letter that would be read aloud by Dermot's parents.

The word "why" ran through her brain in a loop. She now knew the dream of meeting Dermot was over, and she would eventually abandon this dream the way it had abandoned her. She would stop crying, get up, and determine how to live every day without Dermot, but this wasn't that day.

Self-induced mental torture continued for fifteen days until a letter from Ireland finally arrived.

11-Jan-1989

Hi Marielle!

Thanks for your letter. I'm really sorry you can't come to Galway because I was looking forward to it as much as you were.

I have to go to Wales for a hurling event and my parents decided they'd make it a holiday and come along for a week. The reason I didn't know was because our trainer thought we wouldn't have a chance of winning and I didn't find out until last week. Even then I only knew that we had entered a match and I only found out we'd qualified for a final in Wales two days after the match.

Marielle reread this paragraph three times, but the last two sentences still didn't make sense.

Do you get holidays in October? I do and it would be O.K. for you to come then—

Again she stopped. The periods between "O" and "K" made it sound like he was tentative or hedging. Was he tentative because he didn't know if she was amenable to a trip anymore, or because it really wasn't okay for her to visit at all?

(presuming that you've forgiven me – for all I know you could have burnt this letter without even reading it).

I'm really, really sorry. If I didn't go to this match I'd be letting down my coach and the rest of the team. I hope you can come in October.

Your stories about your uncle were brilliant! I reread that bit loads of times.

Were your parents not insulted when they saw the rowing machine and exercise bike? It looks like you were trying to give them a hint. Oh well... as long as you don't stick a picture of an elephant on the fridge....

I can't wait for you to show me around Ireland. I haven't seen most of it anyway. For some strange reason I can't write as much as you. I suppose you (being a girl, and an American ["Yankee"]) just write more, and talk more... So, as my more agricultural friends say, "how's life?"

She stopped again. The excessive talking comment was an attempt to reengage her in an old debate. The paragraph seemed awkward and somewhat desperate and she began to feel badly for Dermot.

I promise to send you a photo if I find one where I look nearly as good as you. I don't believe those photos are really yours. I think you just go through all your magazines and cut out the best looking photos.

Marielle rolled her eyes.

301

Oh great. I just remembered you can come over anytime in September or October. I'm still depressed that you can't come yet. I hope you're not too angry. Please don't stop writing to me because (this sounds kind of stupid, but I really mean it) I've really gotten to know you and I've kind of fallen in love with you since you first wrote. Actually, leave out the "kind of" back there. From what I thought Americans were, you must be the most un-American person I know (except for the way you GLOAT, (try to) drive and mis-speel every-things.)

This last paragraph confused Marielle a lot. Why would Dermot propose she come again or apologize so profusely if she wasn't really welcome? Mentioning his assumptions about Americans made her think she was right about his family not liking them. Additionally, her not visiting and her being American were in the same paragraph, so they were obviously linked in his mind.

It's not really my fault the situation arose but I apologise and I expect you to be really angry and send me hate mail and letter-bombs for a few months.

I reread all your letters last night. Ha! A "virgin by technicality" – what's that? Don't tell me the poor guy wasn't able. Please explain with the aid of a colour video. <—Don't worry, that was a joke. I'm still just a poor, simple, Catholic boy.

I'd really love to go to your house for summer and that pisses me off 'cos I won't be able to until I go to college. I'm doing super brilliant in my tests, even if I'm not a musical genius like you. There's a load of anti-American jokes going around our school, but I won't insult you because you're perturbed enough already.

My friend Sean saw your photo yesterday. He advised me to leave the hurling club in disgrace, kill my family, and invite you to come and live over here. I might try that, but not yet.

Please write soon. Please write. I'll promise to be really nice and I'll remain in love with you for the rest of my life if you forgive me and write.

I better go.
Aaaagh! (That's another attempted but failed suicide!)

Sorry!
Please wait until September/October and then you can personally kick my teeth in.
Bye,
Lots of Love,
Dermot

P.S. I love you!

It would be a lie to say Marielle read this letter 10 times because it was more like 15. The fact that it took Dermot a week to write after his mother's call annoyed her. Could embarrassment or sadness have accounted for that much avoidance? If he had really wanted her to come at a later date, wouldn't he have written right away before anger and sadness settled in as permanent companions?

Marielle considered giving Dermot a pass because he was a guy and guys weren't known for being proactive. Her mother frequently complained that her father avoided her when she was angry. He thought she would get over it on her own, but that never worked. In fact, her mother only became angrier. Her father's unwillingness to address her mother's anger could only be accounted for by stupidity or cowardice, and Marielle could handle Dermot being one of those things, but not the other.

***

"What are you doing tonight?" Joy asked Marielle.

"I have plans to wallow," she replied, flashing a halfhearted smile.

"So, is that a letter from your pen pal?" Joel asked gently, looking between Marielle and the pages she held.

She looked up at him blankly.

"Wait." Joel glanced at Tom. "Would he be a *pen foe* or a *penemy?*"

Marielle looked back down at Dermot's letter.

"I personally like pen foe," Tom decided.

Joel sat back, smiling at Tom. "That's good, isn't it? I have a couple ideas for *Saturday Night Live* commercials I'll run by you later. Can you just write to NBC or do you need to know someone who works for the show?"

"I think you have to know someone. Why? What's your idea?" Tom asked eagerly.

"Well, I was at church last weekend—"

Marielle looked up.

"I go to services sometimes!" Joel protested before addressing Tom again. "So, I'm sitting in church," he turned suddenly to regard Marielle as she returned to her letter without reading it, "and the reverend was so damned boring."

"Why's that so unusual?" Joy asked, turning toward Joel for the first time, and surprising everyone with her ability to listen to two conversations at once. Joy turned back to her alternate storyteller. "Wait, wait. So, how do you know this guy?"

Marielle sighed. It was a better question than the last since Joy needed to hear every last detail of the girl's first sexual experience, and no detail was too small, so to speak. Marielle knew a lot about this boy by the time she finished her peanut butter and jelly sandwich. In glancing at Joy's friend, she also knew that the boy was either half blind or completely desperate.

"So," Joel continued, "the weird thing is that it was a visiting reverend who was only like 25 and when we met him afterwards—"

"Donuts?" Marielle asked.

"Yeah," Joel said, surprised she joined the conversation. "He was really animated and funny. So, I got to thinking that maybe the problem isn't that reverends and priests are inherently boring, but that the sound system most churches buy changes their voices into a monotone rumble of boring shit."

"Hmm," Tom said. "So, maybe priests everywhere are yelling and joking and trying to connect with their congregants, but the Catholic Church sound system is suppressing it."

"Exactly!" Joel said excitedly. "Well, the Lutherans must buy the same systems."

"That *would* make for a good *SNL* skit," Tom agreed. "You could have a guy making a Martin Luther King *I Have a Dream*-type speech behind the pulpit, but out of the speakers you would hear the teacher from *Ferris Bueller's Day Off*."

"Yes!" Joel said, slapping his right hand on the table.

"That's good," Tom declared, chuckling for a moment, but the smile abandoned his face when he turned to Marielle. She had ignored the slap and her own hands shook under the weight of her letter. "So, what are you going to do?" he asked.

"I have no idea," she replied with vacant eyes.

"Let us see that," Joel said, holding out his hand.

Marielle handed over the letter, then looked at the hall as a boy pushed another into an unsuspecting girl. When she looked back, Tom was waiting for Joel to turn the page. A few minutes later, Tom looked up at Marielle without saying a word.

Joel handed back the letter as he asked, "Do you believe him?"

"No," she replied. "Well, about what?"

"About why the trip was canceled."

"No," Marielle repeated. "I think his mother doesn't like me."

"Does that matter?" Tom asked.

Marielle expelled a deep breath while considering the question. "It does if she can intercept any letter I write or phone call I make."

"But that doesn't mean he doesn't care about you," Tom argued.

"True," Marielle said without changing the expression on her face. "The problem is—" She leaned forward. "—I can't continue to write him if I think he's a liar. So, if I write back I need to give him the benefit of the doubt and never question him again, and I'm not ready to do that. Not yet."

Joel squinted slightly. "Is the truth really so important?"

Marielle nodded slowly.

"Well, he sounds pretty desperate for word from you," Tom noted as though the call to action was clear.

Marielle's eyes suddenly looked more steel-gray than blue. "Here's the thing. I'm already in too deep. I almost have no choice but to pretend I believe him, and I really, really resent that."

Joel groaned before he spoke. "If that's true, you need to just consider the cancellation an inconvenient change of plans. Can you get your money back for the ticket?"

"Yeah. As long as it's 21 days out, they refund the entire ticket price. My money is already in my bank account."

Tom's eyebrows furrowed. "How long have you had this letter?"

"Two days," she replied.

Joel and Tom exchanged a look that Marielle didn't see before quiet overcame the boys' need for answers.

Joel studied the school store windows for several minutes before he said, "Here's the thing, Marielle, kids like you and I don't have a lot of things going for us. How are you gonna get through the next year if you don't have Ireland to look forward to?"

"I don't think I will," she replied, then smiled weakly in an attempt to dispel the alarm on Tom's face. "Sorry. I'll get over this. I just need some time."

"I think you need to forgive him," Joel said suddenly.

"You do?" Marielle asked, as if she trusted his opinion above all others.

He nodded once, confirming he did before standing up and walking away, mumbling something about the computer lab.

Marielle glanced at her notebook as a curse escaped her mouth. She looked up at Tom while groaning. "I need to think of a really good short play by tomorrow for Creative Writing," she explained.

Tom placed a bag full of peanuts on the table, then nodded toward it in a silent offer to share. Marielle shook her head before Tom's gaze moved above her as though deep in thought. He cracked a peanut shell, emptying the contents into his left hand as Joel returned. "No binary porn?" he asked his friend.

Joel grinned slightly. "No, it's beginning to bore me, but I got some ones and zeros to look like a woman's who-ha the other day. Wanna see?"

Tom raised his peanut hand. "No, no, I'm good."

Joel looked down at Tom's bag. "That's a big sack of nuts you have there, Tom."

Tom smiled. "Why, thanks for noticing."

"Are they salty?" Joel asked.

"Always. Would you like to try my nuts?"

"Oh, would I!" Joel said with enthusiasm.

Joy turned to display her rolling eyes. "You guys are gay," she declared.

"In the happy sense?" asked Tom.

And right then, Marielle had the idea for her play.

1/22/1989 Sunday

Dear Dermot,

Thank you for your letter. There's no reason for you to worry about canceling. I understand how important a game like this is and I can easily reschedule for another time. In any event, things have taken a turn for the worse since we last spoke so I'd hate to cross you in case you have ancient Druid powers which could ruin my life. Now, that seems dramatic so I'll just start by telling you that only my brother John and my Richter grandparents are actively speaking to me since my uncle died and I refused to pretend this wasn't a good thing (yes, the uncle I made fun of in my last letter).

Just a warning: You may want to take Prozac before continuing. I'm obviously not sure yet how this letter will turn out, but I don't have a great feeling about it.

So, my list of enemies now includes my History teacher. Actually, he's just a substitute for the real teacher, but he still took offense when I proclaimed, "Come on!" at one of his insanely annoying lectures. See, he asks questions like "And WHAT is the color a stop light changes to after yellow?" as though it's profound. The questions are really beneath anyone to reply to, and instead of asking more challenging questions, he just looks around the room assuming we're too stupid to know the answer. After my wholly inappropriate proclamation, he asked if I had a problem. I told him I thought I spoke for the entire class when I said that contrary to popular opinion, there are such things as stupid questions, and he kept asking them. So, he sent me to the principal's office, but the principal loves me and actually laughed when I told him that this particular teacher is starving my brain of all available oxygen. If you have a non-violent answer to my History teacher problem, I'm open to suggestions. Right now, violence is the only solution I see.

So, the war with my Creative Writing teacher goes on. (<—I'm leaving that preposition at the end of the sentence just to piss her off.) Can you believe I have a "C" in that class? So, I wrote a play using old English words that used to be innocuous, but are now considered vulgar (like in Ivanhoe how they say "He ejaculated" but they mean "He exclaimed"). Anyway, the play is two pages long, but here's a snippet:

> *Two boys sat in the restaurant engaging in playful intercourse. It was a gay scene repeated all across the city.*
> *"What shall we eat?" one ejaculated.*
> *The other, startled, said nothing at first. He was busy removing a spot from his tie.*

Now, I know that sounds gross, but if you consider that intercourse is just discussion, and gay means happy, and ejaculate is to exclaim, I see no issues with it at all... but my teacher didn't agree because she's either not well educated or she's doesn't believe I am.

So, I was sent to see the principal again... but he didn't even look up when I walked into his office. He just handed me the paper over his desk and said, "Try to stay in the 20ᵗʰ Century, Miss Richter." I told him I would and thanked him because he knows I have every respect for him, and I really do. However, two trips to his office apparently triggers a mandatory counseling session.

I think I told you that I'm pretty good at putting off the counselor, but he seemed more determined this time so I threw him a bone and told him about my uncle driving into dam-fed water (near Houdini's plaque actually), as well as not going to Ireland, and instead of just giving me credit for time served, I now have to waste half of my lunch hour twice a week talking about my feelings which I really really hate... with anyone except you that is.

Oh, so I forgot to mention how a letch of a boy caused me to nearly get myself killed at a basketball game on Friday night.

So, it's too bad you don't live here for a number of reasons, but the most important one is that you could lend me your letterman's jacket and I wouldn't need to worry about random annoying guys asking me out. This sounds arrogant, but it's mostly true. I honestly can't deal with boys who think talking to them means you want them or think they have the right to stare at you across the Commons, then wink when you can't avoid looking at them anymore... and, if you look away you're a tease, not someone who just wants to be left alone. Sometimes I wish I went to an all girls' school except that most of my good friends are boys since girls are generally bitches.

Anyway, this guy (we'll call him Dick) asks me to go to JD's (a restaurant near school) nearly every day on the way to the Commons. I'm not sure how he times his locker routine so perfectly with mine since we are in completely different parts of the silo, but he does. (Did I explain the silo to you?) So, every day I tell him I either didn't bring money or I have a PB&J sandwich with my name on it and every day he says I don't need money or a wasted PB&J isn't a big loss. So, finally I got tired of this routine and decided if I just go to lunch with him once and insist on bringing my annoying friend Joy along, he'll leave me alone.

So, we went to JD's and I paid for myself and Joy, and we had the most boring conversation you can imagine—though to be honest, I really wasn't trying. The next day, he didn't meet me in the hall at all so I thought I was in the clear until I got to the Commons and two people told me he told their Chemistry class that we were dating. I nearly had a coronary! I forgot most of my English for most of the day, and tried to track him down to tell him what a clueless prick he was, but it's like he disappeared into the center of the silo—which is where an annoying red-haired boy in German class says we keep a nuclear missile. This was a week ago Friday, and I stopped actively looking for him on Monday because following a guy around isn't a good way to prove you're not dating him.

ANYWAY, this Friday I forced myself to get out of the house to play in the pep band since a giant tenor saxophone generally discourages people from talking to you... everyone except Dick, that is.

So, I see him talking to his friends and laughing and he keeps looking over at me and I do a pretty good job of ignoring him all the way through the third quarter. Let me just say at this point that we were playing Appleton West who we hate even more than Neenah, and I'm not just saying that because they live on the other side of town. Every time our pom-pom squad performs, their entire side of the gym opens a newspaper as if they can't be bothered to watch. AND they keep yelling, "JUST SAY NO!" to one of our players when he has the ball because he had an unfortunate experience with marijuana and the police recently. Now, I'm not saying the guy doesn't smoke pot like it's his job—and I admit I ridicule him myself—but that's none of Appleton West's business!

Anyway, I wasn't in a good mood to begin with and Dick's behavior in addition to Appleton West's, and the fact that we were only up by four points the entire game didn't help. Additionally, in the middle of the fourth quarter, Dick decides to abandon his friends and sit next to my saxophone... which doesn't like him any better than I do. I tried to ignore him by watching the game, but he kept talking. I told him we weren't dating and there was no chance of that ever happening and he got really quiet. So I felt bad for a second and I looked at him, but the ball caught my eye as someone lobbed it from way behind the three point line and it just swished into the net in front of me. So, I jumped up and yelled, but that was a bad move because it was West's basket, not ours. So, it was just me cheering on my side of the gym while both sides of the gym and my band director looked confused. So, now I need to find a new school. Does yours take girls? AUGH!!!!

I think that's all the angst I can fit into one letter. I honestly suggest you burn this one. At least promise me you won't show it to Sean or any of your other friends.

Love,
Marielle

"That's genius!" Joel said as he handed Marielle's play back to her.

She smiled a thanks. "I got called into Schneider's office for that."

"What did he say?" Joel asked, his eyes wide and alert.

"He just asked me to stay in the 20th Century."

"I love that man!" he declared.

Marielle agreed. "I pretended to be downcast when I returned to class so I didn't get him into trouble with the drunk, but it was hard with her looking so smug and powerful up there in front of class."

Joel nodded. "I can imagine. So, did you talk to Dermot yet?"

"No, well, I sent him a passive aggressive letter."

"What does that mean?" Joy asked reproachfully.

"It means I attacked him and he didn't see it coming."

Chapter Twenty-One

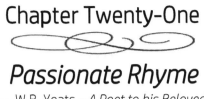

Passionate Rhyme
—W.B. Yeats – *A Poet to his Beloved*

"What's that?" asked Tom, eyeing the poem in front of Marielle.

"A peace offering for my Creative Writing teacher," she explained, nearly rolling her eyes.

"This should be good," he said, motioning for her to pass the paper over the table.

Writhing in reality, humult complete;
Twisting in history, surely repeat;
Fire breathes hot as dew catches cold;
Youth seeks lust as death catches old.

Tom puzzled over the sentences longer than it took to read them. "Did you write it?" he asked as Joel sauntered up to the table.

"Of course," she replied, somewhat offended.

He puckered his lips. "You made up *humult.*"

"Poetic license."

"Humiliation?"

Marielle nodded.

"Since when?" Joel countered.

Marielle regarded him with a serious expression before telling him to shut up.

Tom's eyebrows narrowed as he passed back the poem. "Not much of a peace offering, if you ask me."

"Why's that?" Marielle asked with concern.

"Because the last sentence is a threat."

"Which part?"

"The part where you say, 'I'll be having sex when you're dead.'"

"I didn't mean to say that!" she exclaimed, looking down at the paper.

"Oh, but you did," Joel remarked.

***

"Are you working tonight?" Shelly asked through a crackling telephone line.

Marielle shook her head as she sat on the top step. "I'm not, actually. I've decided to cut my hours since I already have enough money for my ticket."

"I thought you were going to New York with the choir?"

Marielle heard her dad curse downstairs in a way that didn't require her attention. "I haven't decided yet."

"Oh, well, I'm wondering if you want to go out with Tim and me to the movies tonight."

"What did you do?" Maria said to Jack in the living room.

"Isn't that a date night thing, Shel?" Marielle asked her friend.

"I think I burned a hole in the couch cushion," Jack admitted with more remorse than usual.

"Not really," Shelly replied. "He's actually starting to annoy me and I want you to tell me if I should break up with him."

Marielle drew a deep breath at the same time her mother did. "Does he know I'm invited?" she asked a second before her father said, "What's the problem? Now you can buy another set of furniture we don't need."

"No," said Shelly. "Not yet. I'll tell him if you say yes."

"It's not like your bony ass isn't sitting on this furniture more than the rest of us combined!" Maria argued.

"Are you driving?" Marielle asked Shelly.

"No, Tim is."

"Do we really want to discuss the size of our asses?" Jack asked. "Because I'm pretty sure your ass is doing a hell of a lot more damage than mine!"

"So, I can sit in the back seat while you two make out up front?" Marielle asked with irritation.

"Eww. No," Shelly replied. "I haven't made out with him for weeks."

"You're an asshole!" Maria yelled from the hallway below.

"Wow. And you need my opinion before you break up with him?" Marielle asked, sounding more like Joe Pesci than herself.

"And you're a fat ass!" Jack yelled from the living room.

"Please!" Shelly begged. "We haven't gone to the movies together in *such* a long time. You can even pick out the movie."

Marielle moved over to allow her mother to walk past on her way up the stairs. She wanted to see *The Three Fugitives* anyway, she thought.

"Okay," she said, causing Shelly to squeal happily in a way she hadn't done since the summer of *Top Gun*.

***

Marielle sat on one side of Shelly as Tim sat on the other, wondering why she was there. It hadn't taken Tim long to grab Shelly's hand like it was an unpleasant responsibility and play with it mechanically like it was a pocket knife. Each and every attractive girl standing up or moving down the theater's aisle received Tim's attention while Shelly's eyes remained fixed on the movie screen.

"What did you think, Mar?" Shelly asked as the lights came up.

"I liked it a lot," she replied, following Tim's line of sight to the breasts of a girl one row forward.

"Yeah, the little girl is darling," Shelly said before grinning at Tim. "Wanna go to Burger King?" she asked.

"Sure," Tim replied with a sigh, releasing Shelly's hand to stretch. "Gary is working right now. He'll give us free food."

"I thought he was rich," Shelly said.

"He is, but his parents want him to know the value of a dollar," Tim replied dismissively.

"That's commendable," Marielle remarked.

"I'm so glad you approve," Tim said sarcastically.

Marielle got into the third-wheel seat of Tim's Jeep, praying the stop at Burger King would be a quick one as they passed the exit for Northland Avenue. "Which Burger King are we going to?" she asked.

"The one in Kaukauna," Shelly replied.

"Isn't it a waste of Tim's gas to go all the way to Kaukauna, then back to Appleton to drop us off?" Marielle asked, not worried about Tim's gas so much as her proximity to home.

"He doesn't mind," Shelly said, turning toward Tim without a seat belt to restrict her movement.

***

"Does your car have heat?" Marielle asked Tim as they entered Burger King.

"It does. Didn't it make it to the back seat?"

"No, but I'm sure it's lost through your soft top."

"Yeah, well, Shelly and I make our own heat back there, don't we Shel?" Tim said, grabbing Shelly's waist like she was poised to fall off a cliff.

313

Marielle rolled her eyes, then froze as an attractive blond-haired boy behind the counter smiled at her.

"Gary!" Tim called as he approached the boy. "When's your shift over?"

Gary looked up at the clock. "Soon. What can I get for you guys?"

"I thought only girls were cashiers," Tim remarked, smiling.

"I'm running the register and the grill 'cause we're short-staffed. If you have a problem with it, I can spit on your hamburger before I push it through to the front."

"I'll definitely not order what he's ordering," Marielle said, causing only Gary to smile.

"Bye, Gary!" two girls said seductively as they walked through the cashier area to the adjoining door in their street clothes.

"Bye," he said, with half the attention they gave him before turning back to Marielle. "Wait," he said, putting his index finger up to address the girls again. "Jill, what time do you need me to cover for you?"

"Noon to seven. I wrote it on the schedule."

"Okay," he said, nodding them away. "What can I get for you fine people?" he asked, forcing himself to look at Tim and Shelly.

"I'll pay for mine separately," Marielle said, stepping back.

"No, you won't. It's free," Gary said, flashing a smile as his eyes locked onto Marielle's.

She glanced away.

"Don't worry. The manager isn't here and he loves me anyway," Gary explained. "I'm the only one who actually shows up for my shifts regularly."

Marielle nodded, then waited for Shelly and Tim to order before she did.

Gary gave them their drinks on a tray, then addressed the person at the drive-through window as they walked away. "Did Carrie come in yet?" he asked.

"She did," the girl replied. "I think she's getting changed now."

"Okay. I'll make up this order and punch out for the night, but I'll sit in the restaurant for a little bit in case you need me."

The girl nodded before placing her elbows on the stainless-steel counter, and staring out the customer-less window.

Marielle sat in a booth facing the counter, watching Gary as he worked until he unexpectedly glanced at her.

"Here you go," Gary said to Tim as he placed the tray in the middle of the table. "I'll sit with you guys after I punch out and get changed."

"Sounds good," Shelly said enthusiastically before lowering her head slightly. Judging from the reproachful look Tim gave Shelly, this wasn't her comment to make.

"What?" Tim asked Marielle after Gary walked away.

"Nothing," she said, relaxing her eyes. "I was just thinking of something irritating."

"Of course you were," Tim said, squeaking his straw against the cup lid with his teeth before drinking.

Marielle turned to Shelly. "Dave Allen asked me the other day if you were dating anyone."

Shelly looked nervously from Tim to Marielle. "What did you say?"

"I said I wasn't sure," she replied before biting the head off a French fry.

"Do I know this Dave Allen?" Tim asked unpleasantly.

"You would if you were a starter," Marielle replied. "Oh, and if Freedom was large enough to be in the same conference as East," she added.

Tim narrowed his eyes at Marielle as Shelly said, "Tim's a starter this year."

"Really?" Marielle replied, unimpressed. "Congratulations."

"What sports are you starting in this year?" Tim asked Marielle, grinning as he squeaked his straw again.

"She's too busy working," Shelly explained. "She earned enough money to fly to Ireland."

"You're going to Ireland?" he asked.

Marielle nodded. "In the fall."

"Well, since our mascot is The Irish, I'll give you a pass."

Marielle sneered at him as she ate another French fry.

"I like McDonald's French fries better than Burger King's," Shelly declared.

"I like Burger King's better," Tim said in a way that made Marielle wonder if he was just being contrarian.

"Hey!" Gary said happily as he approached the table wearing jeans and a *Joshua Tree* Tour shirt.

Marielle gasped.

"What?" Shelly asked, turning toward Gary before she gasped as well.

"Did you see the concert in Chicago?" Marielle asked Gary with wide eyes.

"I did. My parents took me," he said, smiling at the effect he was having on her.

"Oh my God!" Shelly proclaimed to Marielle.

"What?" Tim asked with irritation.

"Marielle wouldn't shut up about going. She nearly ran away when her parents wouldn't let her go on the bus to Chicago alone."

"I wish I'd have known," Gary said. "We could've given you a ride."

Marielle let out a short burst of laughter. "Sorry," she said, "I just thought of something else."

"Well, you *are* blonde," Tim said as an explanation.

"Hey!" Gary objected.

"Sorry, but blonde jokes only apply to women," Tim clarified.

"Since when is that a rule?" Marielle asked.

"It's always been a rule. Look it up."

"Where, dumbass? In *The New England Journal of Medicine*?" she asked, causing Gary to laugh.

Marielle scooted over to make room for Gary to sit. "That was the first leg, right?"

"It was," he said, smiling brightly as he sat beside her. "What's your favorite song on the album?" he asked, turning toward her as if no one else sat at the table.

She glanced away briefly. "It's a song no one really notices."

"Tell me," he said eagerly.

"*Running to Stand Still*," she answered.

"No way!" he proclaimed, glancing at Tim.

"Why? Do you hate it?" she asked.

"No. It's my favorite song too. Nobody else I know likes that song as much as I do."

"Seriously?!" Marielle asked with more enthusiasm than she had displayed since buying her ticket to Ireland.

Gary nodded as his eyes matched the wonder in Marielle's.

"Oh my God!" Tim said in a high voice as he waved his hands.

"You're a dick," Gary said with a grin while Marielle regarded Tim with contempt.

"He's just angry that I never found him this interesting."

"Why would I care what you think?" Tim replied aggressively.

316

"Because you're dating my best friend... for now."

"Well, Gary is my best friend and it looks like you're trying to date *him*."

Marielle leveled startlingly gray eyes at Tim. "I'm doing no such thing."

"Gary?" Tim asked.

He shook his head. "I have no idea, but I'd like to have her number," he said confidently.

Marielle cleared her throat, feeling her cheeks turn red as she turned to Shelly.

"I'll give you her number," Shelly offered happily.

"No," he said, still staring at Marielle. "I need it from her."

"Do you have a pen and paper?" Marielle asked.

"No, but I can run to the back to get some."

"So, what the hell?!" Tim exclaimed as Gary left.

"What? It's not just me," Marielle protested.

"Well, you batted those gray eyes at him and he's suddenly helpless."

"They're blue and that's not my fault," she said, ignoring the heat accumulating on her cheeks.

"Yeah, but now I'm stuck with you."

Marielle lost her smile. "Funny. That's what I was just thinking about you."

***

"Why don't you drive, Gary?" Tim suggested as they approached the Jeep. "Shelly and I will ride in back."

Gary caught the keys Tim threw, then smiled at Marielle.

"You drive a stick?" she asked as she held the door for Shelly to climb into the back seat.

"I do. Do you?"

"I do," she replied, sitting in the passenger's seat.

"Where are we going?" Gary asked the rear view mirror.

"Marielle needs to go home," Shelly said. "She's not allowed out past midnight."

"Really?" Gary asked Marielle with surprise.

"Yeah. My parents think all trouble is found after midnight."

"I'm not sure they're wrong," Gary said, smiling. "Will you tell me the way to your house?"

"Sure. I don't know where we are now, but if you get on 41 West, I can direct you from there."

"So, what are you doing Friday night?" Gary asked Marielle as he shifted into third gear.

"We have a basketball game Friday night," Tim called from the back seat seconds before Shelly giggled at whatever he was doing.

"You play on the basketball team?" Marielle asked.

Gary nodded.

"What position?"

"Point guard."

"My dad played that position on the Chicago All Star team in high school."

"Really? That's impressive," he said, adjusting his rear view mirror away from the back seat.

"It is, but he lost a big game once and he never got over it."

Gary nodded sympathetically. "I've seen that happen to guys before. I never really understood it—no offense to your dad."

Marielle shook her head. "I never understood it either. Even if you're the one who misses the winning shot, if you made 20 points in the game, why does the last shot matter? The team wouldn't have been one basket away from winning without you."

"Exactly," he said. Lights from a car illuminated his eyes before he turned toward her. "I'd really like to see you again," he said, then shifted into third gear as they ascended the ramp onto Highway 41.

"That would be nice," she replied, smiling as she looked down at his hand. "Why don't you call me with your schedule and I'll try to get time off from work."

"Or you could call me with your schedule and *I'll* try to get time off," he offered.

"I don't have your number," she said, briefly raising her shoulders.

"Okay. I'll call you tomorrow."

Marielle nodded, then looked back at the road. "Have you always lived in Freedom?" she asked.

"I have and so have my parents, and my grandparents… and my great-grandparents."

"Ah, so you're one of *those* families," she said, turning toward him with mischief.

"What families?"

"The families everyone knows, and the families that belong. Towns the size of Freedom don't appreciate newcomers, and by that I mean people who moved there since the '50s."

Gary laughed. "That's true, but I don't pay much attention to that. I don't see myself staying there after graduation anyway."

"Where will you go?"

"U.W. probably."

"I've thought of that myself, but Madison would be quite a culture shock. I hear there are freshman classes with hundreds of kids in them."

"Yeah, but the anonymity would be nice. I can't raise the blinds in my room without the neighbors commenting on my new wallpaper."

Marielle's head fell back as she laughed.

"That's a true story. I swear," he said, raising his shifting hand.

"Yes, well, then Madison would be great. I guarantee you there are two or three kids there who look exactly like us."

Gary exhaled audibly. "I seriously doubt there's anyone there who looks like you."

Marielle smiled at the highway. "I presume you mean that as a compliment."

"I do," he said softly, staring at her cheek.

***

"Oh my God!" Shelly said when Marielle picked up the phone the next morning.

Marielle beamed, waiting anxiously for Shelly to say more.

"As soon as we dropped you off, Gary put his head against the seat rest and said, 'I'm going to marry her.' "

"What?" Marielle asked with less enthusiasm than Shelly expected.

"He did. Can you believe it?"

"No," Marielle replied flatly.

"What's wrong? I thought you liked him."

"Oh, I do. Very much. But I hardly know him."

"Well, you hardly know Dermot and you're ready to marry *him*," Shelly objected.

"I wouldn't say that at all. I've never met him, but I feel we know each other as well as two people can."

"Oh come ON, Mar! What are the chances you'll ever meet Dermot? Gary is a real guy who's already madly in love with you."

Marielle looked at the non-existent pictures above the stairs. "You're right," she said with resignation. She needed to be more realistic. Gary's

319

t-shirt, favorite song, and school's mascot were a sign from God that it was time to do just that.

"Has he called you yet?" Shelly asked, sounding excited again. "He said he was going to try to sleep until the first possible minute he could call you."

"Well, it's only 8:30, Shel," Marielle replied. "Don't people generally wait until later to call on a Sunday? I mean, if they're *not* best friends."

"I suppose. You need to call me though as soon as you get off the phone with him."

Marielle agreed, then set down the phone. She couldn't pretend she wasn't flattered, but Gary's enthusiasm scared her and the entire situation didn't seem fair to Dermot. Geography was an unfair advantage.

***

"Marielle! Phone!" Anna yelled from the first floor.

"Got it," she replied to the stairs before greeting the caller.

"Hi, beautiful," Gary said brightly, immediately taking Marielle's breath away. "Do you mind me calling you that?" he asked.

"No, I've been called much worse," she replied happily.

Gary laughed. "I can't wait until next weekend to see you. Is there any chance I could spend time with you today?"

Marielle sat down on the top step, feeling the heat from her cheek with her right hand. "Well, I have Mass at 10:30, but I should be home by noon at the latest. We could go to the mall or out to lunch, but isn't Freedom pretty far away?" she asked, realizing she knew more about Irish geography than that of Wisconsin.

"No. I'm only 20 minutes from your house. I already asked my parents for the car. I can be there by noon."

"Wait," she said. "Let me ask my parents first just to make sure they're okay with it."

Marielle ran downstairs, finding both parents watching *Sunday Morning*. They looked up at her without annoyance even though it wasn't a commercial.

"Do you mind if I go to the mall later with a boy I met last night? He's a friend of Shelly's boyfriend."

Jack raised his eyebrows at his wife. "It's fine by me if it's okay with you."

"It's fine with me," Maria said, surprised by her daughter's enthusiasm for anything unrelated to Ireland.

"Great," Marielle said before running upstairs. "Sorry about that," she said to Gary. "I can go."

"Awesome. I'll pick you up at noon, then."

Marielle quickly called Shelly before running to her closet to find her favorite green ribbed turtleneck, jeans, and black penny loafers.

***

Marielle watched Gary's Lincoln Town Car pull up the driveway from the upstairs window before running to Jeanette's room. "Can you answer the door? A boy is here to pick me up and I'm really nervous."

"Really?" Jeanette asked in disbelief.

"Hurry! Please!" Marielle implored, looking behind her as if the front door was upstairs.

"Okay," she replied, walking past Marielle as Gary began to knock.

Marielle held the upstairs railing as the front door opened, her eyebrows furrowing as she heard Gary gasp.

"You look just like Marielle," he declared.

"I'm her older sister," Jeanette replied pleasantly.

"Hi, I'm Gary. I told Marielle there was no one as pretty as she is, but I didn't realize she had a twin."

Marielle didn't know if she wanted to smile or roll her eyes, so she did both.

"Wow! Welcome to the family," Jeanette proclaimed. "Marielle, your future husband is here," she called playfully.

"Hello there," Jack said as he approached Gary. "I'm Marielle's father."

"Hello, sir. It's nice to meet you."

"You have a very firm handshake," Jack noted approvingly.

"Well, my dad says you have to say hello like you mean it."

"He sounds like a good man," Jack replied, and Gary agreed.

Marielle's mother exited her bedroom, regarding her daughter with a questioning face. Marielle shook her head in reply.

"Well, hello," Maria said as she descended the stairs. "Is that your Town Car in the driveway?"

"It is. Yes, ma'am. Well, it belongs to my parents, actually."

"Well, it's lovely. I'm Marielle's mother, Maria."

"Hello, Mrs. Richter, it's a pleasure to meet you. I'm Gary."

Marielle took a deep breath before approaching the top of the stairs.

"There she is!" Jeanette exclaimed, widening her eyes at her sister as if this was a historic day.

Marielle looked down at Gary who wore an oatmeal-colored turtleneck sweater under a full-length charcoal gray coat. The sweater resembled one she had seen on the cover of an Irish magazine and the coat looked like a cashmere blend.

"Wow," Gary said as Marielle descended the stairs in her polyester-knit sweater and less-than-name-brand jeans.

"Why don't you take *my* coat," Jeanette whispered, pulling her more expensive coat off the hook.

"Thanks," Marielle replied, putting on the coat as she pretended not to notice Gary's appraisal of her. "Well, I imagine we'll be home in a couple of hours," she said to her family as she fixed her collar.

"Three at the latest," Gary added.

"Take your time," Jack said amiably. "We'll be home all day."

Marielle looked at her father with new eyes. Apparently, one only required an expensive car and a firm handshake to run off with his daughter.

"Well, you made quite an impression on my family," Marielle said to Gary as the front door closed behind them.

"I hope so," he replied, glancing at her. "I'd hate to marry you against their wishes."

Marielle's head snapped toward him, her face not relaxing until he smiled.

"I can't get over how much you look like your sister," he said, staring at her again.

"Yes, and she never lets me forget it," Marielle replied, finally smiling at the boy who stood as tall as her brothers.

"Let me get that for you," Gary said, opening the passenger's-side door, then waiting to close it behind Marielle.

"Oh, Jesus," she thought as she looked up at three smiling faces in the upstairs window.

"I have something for you," Gary said from the driver's seat before he reached past Marielle's legs to remove a tape from the glove compartment. "Shelly said you couldn't find *Rattle and Hum*, so I made you a copy."

Marielle's mouth opened as she looked down at the tape. "That's incredibly thoughtful," she murmured. "May I listen to it now?"

"Sure, but I put my tape in the player so it doesn't chew yours up."

She addressed him without words until a "thank you" escaped her lips.

Gary smiled lovingly before backing the car onto Oneida Street. "I know we discussed the mall, but there's a new restaurant I'd like to bring you to on College Avenue. My mom thought you'd like it."

Marielle turned toward Gary with surprise, still holding the tape. "Your mom knows about me?"

"Everybody knows about you. Well, everyone except my brother. He's in Spain right now and he only calls once a week. But I told my parents about you as soon as I got home last night."

"Why?" Marielle asked with a mixture of interest and fear.

"Because I think you're the one," he replied, smiling at the road before turning toward her.

"The one for what?" she asked.

Gary laughed, assuming she was joking.

"Don't your parents think we're too young to make plans like that?" she asked. "Aren't you 16?"

"Seventeen, but my parents met when they were our age and my grandparents were married at 17. They understand how this can happen at a young age."

"But you don't know anything about me," she said, closing her eyes for a moment. "I'm extremely irritating."

"I knew enough when I saw you walk into Burger King, rolling your eyes at Tim. It was really love at first sight. I've never experienced anything like it and I promise I've never said this to anyone before."

Marielle blushed as she looked out her window. "I'm not good at expressing myself, but I appreciate everything you've said."

He pulled the car over just before the intersection with College Avenue, then grabbed her hand. "I know this seems abrupt, and Shelly says you're very independent and you want to go to college and see the world and I respect that. If it wasn't love at first sight for you, I can live with that."

"I don't know what it was," she said, looking down at the hand that held hers. "It was something special, and I definitely feel a connection with you, but I can't say more than that."

Gary nodded, then looked longingly into Marielle's eyes.

"You may kiss me now," she replied to his silent request.

He smiled broadly, removing his seat belt to slide closer to her. He tilted his head to the left just before his lips touched hers. She opened her mouth a moment before his tongue attacked hers like it was on the front lines of a war.

What the hell? Marielle thought, but waited for a moment until it was polite to break free.

"Wow," he said, pulling away, eyes still closed in a manner Marielle found dramatic.

***

"You know, Madison has married housing for its students," Gary said, leaning across a table secluded from others by strategically placed palm bushes.

Marielle leaned forward slightly. "How about if you tell me your last name, and I'll tell you if I can marry you?"

"Pardon?" he asked.

"I have to go higher in the alphabet. I'm tired of being at the end."

Gary moved back slightly. "An R isn't so bad, is it?"

"It probably isn't, but I'm an overachiever. What's your last name?"

"Van den Plas," he said slowly, his face turning pale.

"Hmm," she said, looking down to her menu again, fighting the urge to say, "It looks like it won't work out, then."

"You don't really plan to choose a husband based on the alphabet, do you?" he asked with concern.

"Well, you may be able to change my mind, but it'll be an uphill battle."

"I'm okay with that," he said, allowing his gaze to linger on her before turning to his menu.

"So, you and Tim are friends, but I get the sense that he's an ass," Marielle said as she stabbed her Caesar salad.

Gary chuckled. "He is, but he's a good wing man."

Marielle looked up quickly.

"What I mean is that when we went out together *before* I met you, he and I used to make a good team," Gary added nervously.

Marielle nodded at her salad.

"You were only joking when you said a last name mattered, right?" he asked.

"I was," she lied.

Gary took a deep breath. "You had me frightened for a minute."

***

"Who the hell announces they want to marry someone they've only known for a half-hour?" Marielle asked her sister before collapsing onto

Jeanette's bed.

"I think it's very romantic," her mother remarked, standing near the closet door.

"I'm only 16, Mom!" Marielle protested.

"I met your father when I was 15."

"Exactly!" she exclaimed, then apologized. Marielle glanced at her sister where she stood by the dresser, not bothering to mention Jeanette and Doug began dating at 16 as well. "I'm sorry. I love you people, but I don't want to be part of this club," she continued, then winced. "Sorry. I don't mean that I think I'm better than you. I'm just saying that boys irritate me too much to consider starting marriage early. I'm going to put it off as long as possible. Plus, it was our first date and he's practically picking out kids' names, and he kisses like an epileptic, by the way—no offense to epileptics."

"How do you know how he kisses?" Maria asked sternly as Jeanette chuckled.

"Because minutes after leaving the driveway, he proclaimed his love for me and I said he could kiss me, but it was a test and he failed. Have you ever seen a giraffe's tongue on one of those *National Geographic* shows?" she asked her sister.

"Marielle! You kissed him with your tongue!" Maria objected.

"I did, yeah," she replied matter-of-factly before she and Jeanette laughed.

"I told you that only whores open-mouth kiss!"

Marielle looked at Jeanette. "Well, I guess we're all whores, then."

"Marielle!"

"You can be as exasperated as you like, Mom. It's not sex," she said dismissively, still lying on the bed.

"Well, it leads directly *to* sex!"

"How do you figure that?" Marielle asked, propping herself up on her elbow to better make eye contact with her mother. "I've open-mouth kissed, let's see," she looked up to the ceiling, "like five guys and I've never had sex. How about you, Jeanette?" Marielle asked with a mischievous grin.

Jeanette narrowed her eyes at her sister.

"That's a good question, Jeanette," Maria said, causing her daughters to hold their breath. "How many boys have you open-mouth kissed?"

Jeanette exhaled as Marielle lay back on the bed, laughing with abandon.

***

"No!" Joel exclaimed.

"I swear to God it's true!" Marielle replied.

"So, that's his letterman's jacket you're wearing?" he asked, looking at the green wool jacket with slightly darker green leather sleeves and a large white "F" attached to the left breast.

Marielle nodded.

"But you've only known him for two hours."

"Maybe three and a half, actually. He pulled it out of the trunk when he dropped me off at home. He asked me to wear it to school so other boys would know I was taken. He also wants me in Freedom for his basketball game on Friday and he wants me to wear his football jersey. He gave me that too."

"But why are you wearing his jacket here?" Tom asked.

Marielle looked at the leather sleeves. "Well, it's warm enough."

"Yeah, but boys will think you're actually taken," Joel argued.

"I'm good with that," she replied. "And I guess I *am* technically dating him."

"Why?" Joel asked with exasperation.

Marielle began to laugh. "I have no idea."

"Yes, you do," Tom said confidently.

"Well, I look at him and he's cute, and he's responsible, and hard working. He's close to his family and he's obviously athletic—"

"That matters to you, doesn't it?" Joel asked before sighing.

"I don't want it to, but yes, it does."

"Go on," Tom prompted.

"He's also charming and my family loves him already and dating him is a good chance to reconnect with Shelly and he's far enough away that I don't have to see him all that often."

"Are you going to have sex with him?" Joy asked.

Marielle's face contorted as she said, "Eww. No! He knows I'm waiting for marriage."

"But you're not!" Joel corrected. "You're waiting for an Irishman."

"Right. Well, marriage or an Irishman, whichever comes first, so to speak."

Marielle and the boys laughed, leaving Joy behind.

"Tell me you were lying about the last name thing," Joy said.

"I wasn't," Marielle replied. "I only told him I was because he seemed so bothered by it."

"So, you wouldn't marry Richie Zoeller?" she asked, naming one of the most popular boys in their class.

"I wouldn't."

Joy scrunched up her nose. "Why not?"

"Because I'm tired of waiting longer than everyone else to be seated, to get an award, or to be assigned a homeroom," Marielle explained. "I'm holding out for an Abel."

"You aim too high," Joel declared. "What about a Parker?"

"That only gets me two letters higher!"

"Yeah, but you may waste away your youth waiting for an Abel, eventually settling for a Zoeller just before your eggs fall to pieces when you could've married a Parker early on."

"True," she agreed, "but I'm okay with waiting. I'm thinking of my kids as much as myself. I don't want them waiting an extra half-hour to graduate from high school."

"It doesn't really matter, does it?" asked Tom. "Everyone has to wait 'til the end of graduation to leave anyhow."

"Yeah, but everyone stops paying attention after the N's. The S's wear them down and they're thinking downright belligerent thoughts about Y's. Nobody ever hears a Z graduate. It even takes the parents by surprise. Did you know that a lower alphabet student is half as likely to be fog-horned during graduation as a higher alphabet student?"

"I didn't, actually," Tom admitted.

"That's because I just made it up. But you believed me, didn't you? Marrying anything lower than an M is unacceptable!"

"Now, you're settling for an M?" asked Joel.

"Well, you wore me down."

"Hmm, and who do we know whose last name starts with an M?" he asked.

Chapter Twenty-Two

Promises to Keep

—Robert Frost – *Stopping by Woods on a Snowy Evening*

1/30/1998

Dearest Marielle the wonderful – forgiving – altruistic – brilliantly beautiful person,

Thanks for writing (and not sending a time-bomb)! I just put your passport photo on the wall beside my bed—it looks really good there.

I took your advice about simplifying my love life which is especially important since... wait for it... my hurling club has qualified for the All Ireland Junior Club Hurling Finals in three weeks! It's never happened before in the history of St. Clement's College Hurling Club! Our coach and the school are mad with excitement!

How are you? I'm glad you can come over in September/October. It means we both get to miss school.

I know I should be enormously happy right now, but I'm kind of depressed lately and I don't know why. I suppose I'm just going through one of those "teenage stages." I keep wondering what I'm doing studying and training six days a week, and the final means more training and more pressure for the entire team. I suppose I'll get out of it, but it's great to have you to write because I wouldn't really tell anyone else. I hope I'm not boring you here. Sorry!

My friend Sean got a girlfriend (I think it's his first). She's really nice. In fact, they suit each other perfectly. So, I have now got NO girlfriend except for Sinéad who I haven't seen in ages.

Do you like my super psychedelic purple envelope? Neither do I.

Dear Marielle, will you marry me?

I'm looking at your photo again. You know, you're really pretty!? You must get loads of guys following you, etc... I know just what you mean about being called a "tease" if you only want to be friends with some lad. Most of my friends think girls want to be their girlfriend if they even talk to them... and I thought Ireland was really different to America.

I see poor Colonel North is on trial. I suppose what he did was kind of stupid. ("Dumb? Red? Raw? Preposterously insolent?")

You know what? I wish you lived in Ireland because you think the same way as me about loads of things so we'd probably really like each other. Or maybe my dog would have bitten you and you'd hate me so it's great that you live on the other side of the world.

It's really considerate of you to visit me. As everyone I know probably says, "Imagine flying to Ireland just to see HIM!" When you come to Ireland, you can show me around and I'll teach you how to spell.

Now, for a big, long, love letter bit... wait for it... get ready... make sure no one's reading... lock the door... turn on the shredder... Ready?... Are you sure?... OK

I really, really, really, really love you and I love writing to you and reading your letters. I can't wait to meet you. I think you're the most beautiful person I've ever seen, but that doesn't matter 'cos you're so nice I'd love you even if you weren't attractive at all. I'm not very good at expressing myself, but I think I'd probably commit suicide if you stopped writing – or worse – if you stopped phoning me or (equally bad) if you died. Oops! You know what I mean.

Please think of me next time you're kissing one of your hundreds of boyfriends—even if it's in the back of a car while you're thinking I can't drive.

I love you! I love you more as each stamp finds its lonely way across our vast ocean of separation (How romantic!)

I have to go.
Please write soon.
Please.
Pretty please.
With Sugar.
Lots of Love,
Dermot

Marielle set down the letter with a sigh. It was impossible to stay angry with Dermot for long, she decided unhappily before looking down at her notebook.

"What's today's assignment?" Tom asked, following Marielle's line of sight.

She stared at Tom with the concentration of a Final Jeopardy contestant. "Finish this sentence: Persistence is... "

"Persistence is the companion of a keen mind," Tom replied.

Marielle nodded. "That's good, but it's not what I wrote."

"What did you write?" he asked, smiling.

"Persistence is... also known as stalking."

Tom laughed at the ceiling, then said, "I thought you and Mrs. Perkins made peace."

Marielle's face became indignant. "I tried, but she picked another fight with me!"

"About your poem?"

"Can you believe it?!"

He glanced at her notebook. "Did she perceive your threat on the last line?"

"No. Well, maybe, but she accused me of plagiarizing it!"

"From whom?"

"She said she didn't know. She just had a *feeling*," Marielle said, wiggling her fingers to make the sentence sound more ridiculous.

Joel looked up from his book, glancing at Tom with a half-smile before asking Marielle, "What did you say to her?"

"I asked her if that was a *glass* of Jack feeling, or a *bottle* of Jack feeling."

Tom and Joel laughed as Joy looked up from her bag of chips. "What did Schneider do? You *were* sent to the office, I assume?"

Marielle nodded. "He asked if I could limit my creativity to writing and not smart-assed comments. I said I would if it made his life easier, but I wanted him to know that it would be difficult for me. He said he had no doubt it would be, and he would consider it a personal favor."

"What did you say to that?" Joel asked.

She raised her right shoulder briefly. "What could I say except 'Yes, sir'?"

Joel shook his head as he chuckled. "You're lucky he didn't rat you out to your parents or you wouldn't be seeing Freedom guy for awhile." His smile widened as a thought occurred to him. "That's funny. Do you think kids in Freedom get grounded?"

Marielle's face became more serious. "They don't, actually. It's a city ordinance, but they're thinking of building a state prison there in furtherance of irony."

"You're lying!" Joy proclaimed. Four months at the same lunch table had not been long enough for her to understand Marielle's sense of humor.

Marielle turned from Joy to the boys. "Wouldn't it be funny to be incarcerated in Freedom?"

Tom agreed. "I imagine the inmates would be too embarrassed to write their return address."

"Hey, where's the letterman's jacket?" Joel asked, equating the jacket with prison.

Marielle moaned as she sat back. "It's in my locker. It didn't want to come out today. It was tired after Friday's basketball game, but it'll be out later. Gary's picking me up from school since he only has a half-day today."

Tom's face brightened before he asked, "So, how was the game?"

"You mean, how was my unveiling as Gary's future wife?" Marielle asked before blowing an errant strand of hair from her face. "Awkward. He's like a god there and I barely know him, but everyone assumes I know him at least as well as he purportedly knows me.

Shelly had to work so Gary sat me next to one of his teachers who went on and on about how great Gary is and how special I must be for him to care about me so much and how he couldn't stop talking about me, blah, blah, blah, blah, blah. I just kept looking at the guy wondering when he was going to say, 'But I told him you really shouldn't think about getting serious until college,' but he never did. I swear those small town people start pairing up in grade school!"

"Oh, come on!" Joy said impatiently. "You've been *dying* to have a boyfriend and now you're pretending you can't be bothered."

Marielle turned to Joy with no perceivable emotion. "I believe you're confusing you with me."

Joy glanced at the boys. "So, you're not loving the fact that this guy thinks the sun rises and sets on your ass?"

"I do, and he's right of course, but it's the long pauses when he's expecting me to reciprocate that I hate, and the way he kisses." She

331

shivered unpleasantly. "Thank God my parents let me drive their car on Friday so I didn't have to go parking with him on the way home."

"The shit box?" Joel asked.

"Yeah. My dad loves his truck too much to let me use it. Can you tell a guy his tongue shouldn't be used as a weapon without offending him?"

Tom shook his head.

"I made the mistake of correcting a girl's technique once," Joel said with regret.

"Did she flip?" Marielle asked.

"Like a Suzuki Samurai," Joel replied, causing her to guffaw.

"The tramp from West?" Joy asked.

Joel nodded.

Joy grinned in an unpleasant way. "She broke up with you, didn't she?"

Joel leaned forward to better make his point. "No. I canned her like tuna."

"That's lucky," Marielle said, wiping laughter from her eyes. "Now you don't need to buy her a Valentine's Day gift. By the way, what's a good gift for a guy you barely know who wants to marry you?" she asked, scanning her classmates' faces.

"Cuff links," Tom replied after a moment of looking into space.

"Good one," Joel agreed. "It's a long term gift since he won't be wearing them before your kids are born. Until then, he can store them in his hope chest." Joel threw back his head to laugh at his own joke.

"You amuse you, don't you?" Marielle asked, laughing again.

"Absolutely," Joel replied. "I can't wait 'til Spring Break to spend a whole week with me."

"A whole week of you doing your make-up homework, that is," Marielle said with the voice of her mother. "Did you get your Geography homework done?"

"Noooo," he said with mild rebellion. "I was going to do it during class today, but the substitute teacher was so hot, I explored myself instead."

"I imagine that was a short trip," she remarked.

Joel's eyes nearly twinkled. "No. A long one with Old Faithful at the end."

"Eww!" Marielle protested.

Joel smiled. "It's your fault! You provoked me."

"Well, I didn't expect you to take it to the land of the sick and inappropriate!"

"Sure ya did."

Marielle shook her head, then shared a smile with Tom. Joel was getting back to his old self.

"I'm surprised Gary didn't buy you your Valentine's gift already," Tom said as an afterthought, ready to leave it that way until Marielle blushed. "Did he already give you your Valentine's gift?" he pressed.

"What did he give you?" Joy asked.

Marielle groaned at the ceiling.

"What?!" Joel asked, genuinely interested.

Marielle closed her eyes for a moment, then sat up and reached under the neckline of her shirt.

"What are you doing?" Joy said reproachfully.

Marielle didn't reply. Instead, she exposed a bronze-colored chain and a pendant of a heart cut in half. She turned toward the hall with a mixture of amusement and shame.

"Eww!" Joel exclaimed. "It's one of those broken hearts that matches another half."

Tom chuckled as Marielle dropped her necklace and turned back toward them. "He's wearing the other half. He said every couple should have one."

"Well, I think it's sweet," Joy decided.

Joel scooted his chair closer to the table. "What did you say when he gave it to you?"

Marielle bit her lip for a moment. "I said I appreciated the thought."

"Well, *that* was bitchy!" Joy declared.

"Not as bitchy as what I was thinking!" Marielle protested, making eye contact with Joy for the first time.

"What were you thinking?" Joel asked happily.

"I was thinking, 'Please for the love of GOD, promise me we don't have a song!' "

Joel threw his head back and laughed hard enough to bring Marielle with him, and once she started, she couldn't stop. Her eyes began to water again as she wrapped her stomach with her forearms in a failed attempt to stop spasms.

***

"Hi gorgeous," Gary said as Marielle closed the passenger's-side door of his parents' Lincoln.

"Hi there," she replied, having forgotten since Friday how handsome Gary was.

He glanced toward the school. "May I kiss you here, or will you be teased?"

"Oh, I'll be teased, but you can kiss me anyway," she said, assuming their proximity to authority would make the kiss more brief than usual.

Gary approached Marielle slowly before his lips locked onto hers like a magnet, but a student yelling for another near the car window allowed the kiss to die a mercifully quick death.

Gary laughed through his nose at the disruption before resuming his seat and turning the key. "Where should I take you?" he asked.

Marielle drew a deep breath. "Where would you like to take me?"

"How about my house?" he asked, placing his car into gear. "My folks won't be home for at least three hours."

Marielle's eyebrows furrowed. "I'm not sure that's a good idea."

He lifted one hand from the steering wheel as he neared the end of the semi-circular drive. "I will be on my best behavior. I respect what you've said about waiting."

"Okay, but would your parents want me in their house when they're not at home?" she asked over the sound of the blinker.

Gary shook his head before briefly checking for traffic. "They won't mind. They know we're waiting."

"Whoa, whoa, whoa!" Marielle said as the car turned. "How does this come up in normal conversation?"

Gary glanced at her innocently. "My parents just ask and I answer them. They thought it was very respectable of you. In fact, my dad said how great it was for me not to have to think about you with other guys since I'd be your only... well, you know."

"But they don't expect the same restraint from you?" she asked.

Gary expelled air from his nose as though the question was a ridiculous one. "No. Well, they know I'm not a virgin anymore."

Marielle briefly scanned the crosswalk as they stopped abruptly at an intersection. "And they're okay with that?"

"Sure. My dad is actually the one who buys my condoms."

Marielle sat staring at Gary with her mouth open until she accumulated enough air to speak. "You're joking!" she exclaimed.

"I'm not," he replied, seemingly startled by the look of shock on her face.

She sat in silence, tossing around ideas in her brain before she asked, "Were your parents hippies?"

"Kind of. They conceived my brother at a Bob Dylan concert."

Marielle nodded at the road. "Do me a favor and never mention that story to my parents. They were part of the anti-hippie movement."

Gary glanced at her. "Was that a movement?"

"It was in my house."

"That's good to know," he replied, smiling as if it was a laughing matter.

"So, how did they decide on a name like Gary instead of Moonbeam?" she asked, finally matching Gary's smile.

"I'm named after one of their best friends."

"Lucky break," Marielle reflected, turning to the side window as her smile slowly disappeared.

"Are you alright?" he asked.

"Yes. I'm just wondering when you lost your virginity?" she asked, turning toward Gary in time to see the stress on his face.

He sighed. "Do I have to answer that question?"

"You do," she replied without remorse.

"Does this really matter?"

"It does if you expect me to trust you."

He ran his fingers through his hair before he spoke. "I was 15. She was the cousin of a friend of mine. She stayed with them for the summer. It was nothing really. I remember just wanting to do it and get it over with."

"That's beautiful," Marielle said, disarming Gary with her smile. "Was he your friend *after* the summer?"

Gary checked his rear view mirror as a car tailgated him. "Not really. Things were weird between us after that. Do you know this guy?" he asked as the car behind him flashed its lights.

Marielle turned around. "It looks like a kid from my German class."

"Is he crazy? He's almost in my trunk."

She chuckled as she admitted he was a bit crazy. "But you live in a small town," she said, getting back to the loss of Gary's virginity. "How did you get away from your friend?"

"I didn't. We just say hi in the halls or wave from our cars now and that's it."

335

"Right," Marielle nodded. "So, is she the only girl you've slept with?"

Gary groaned. "Is this really important to you?" he asked with frustration.

"Absolutely."

"No," he replied as if that might be the end of the questioning.

"How many others?" she asked, deciding she liked this game.

"Is this guy for real?!" Gary exclaimed as the loud, rusty Chevy Nova inched beside their car at a light, nearly hitting the side mirror.

Marielle rolled down her window in response to the red-headed kid leaning out of his.

"Hey," the boy said, moving his head up slightly with the word. "Do you want to get some cheese curds?"

"What?!" Gary protested as Marielle laughed.

"That sounds great, but I'm here with my boyfriend right now and he doesn't like cheese curds."

"WHAT IS HE, A COMMUNIST?!" the boy yelled.

Marielle tried to speak, but she was laughing too hard. The light turned green seconds later and Gary hit the gas in a way the old Chevy couldn't.

"Hey!" she protested mildly. "I don't think we were done talking."

"Seriously?" Gary asked, glancing at her face for the truth.

"No," she said happily. "Okay, so who else have you slept with?"

Gary squinted. "Do you want to know their names?"

"No, just your stats."

"A few girls in Kaukauna and one from Little Chute."

"Girls you work with?"

"A few."

"Like Jill?"

Gary snapped his head toward her. "Did Tim tell you that?"

Marielle thought to lie and say he had, but she wanted him to know how smart she was more than she wanted to ruin Tim's reputation. "No. I just figured it out when she said goodbye to you like you were on the dessert menu."

Gary finally laughed.

"Is that a yes, then?" Marielle asked.

"If you're forcing me to admit it. Yeah, that's a yes."

Marielle turned away from Gary as his stock plummeted on her market.

"Are you angry?" he asked with sincere angst.

Marielle shook her head slightly. "Why should I be?"

"Because I'll be your first, but you won't be mine."

She cleared her throat. "No," she said. "So, everyone at school says once you start having sex, you can't really stop. How do you plan to manage this?"

Gary's posture stiffened ever so slightly. "I haven't figured that out yet," he said.

"I think you have," she replied. "Surely, you've spoken to your parents about it. What do they suggest?"

"I'd rather not tell you."

"Well, that's not really an option," she said, convinced she already knew the answer.

"My dad said I should stay faithful as long as I can, then sleep with other girls until you're ready to have sex."

Marielle studied Gary's face as he blinked heavily. "So, sleep around while you're dating me," she summarized.

"Yes, but there was no way I was going to do that."

"Does your mom know about this plan?"

"I don't know. She thought it was a little strange in this day and age that you'd wait, but she probably wouldn't agree with my dad."

"Hmm," Marielle said, somewhat irritated at being regarded as strange. "You know, I believe in fair play in all things. If you kiss another girl, I'll kiss another boy. If you touch another girl, I'll touch another boy, etcetera."

"Wouldn't you be too hurt to go to another boy?" Gary asked with genuine confusion.

Marielle puckered her lips thoughtfully before indicating she wouldn't.

"Even though you're waiting for marriage?"

"Well, I'm not sure what I'd do if you took it all the way to having sex with someone else, but I'm leaving it open as a possibility. You should just know what you're dealing with before you do it."

"I wasn't planning to do it, Marielle!" he said with exasperation.

"Alright. Is this the same plan Tim has? To sleep around until Shelly is ready to have sex with him?"

"I don't know what Tim thinks," Gary said haltingly.

"I think you do," she replied with an unfriendly grin.

"Well, I'd rather not say."

"That's okay. When you said he was your wing man, I figured it out for myself."

"But wing man means *he* helped *me* get girls," Gary explained.

"I know what it means, but Tim isn't a selfless kind of guy."

Gary drew a deep breath before asking again if Marielle was angry, taking her at her word when she said she wasn't.

"But I don't understand why you and Tim date virgins if sex is so important to you. Why can't you just date the girls who give you what you want instead?"

"We don't want to date those girls," he said as if the hypocrisy was understandable.

"Well, Shelly and I don't want to date guys whose only interest in girls is sex—whether that's us or girls we don't know."

Gary nodded, then looked away as if his thoughts went with him. A moment later, he said, "I hope you don't think that's who I am. I mean, it sounds like me, but I promise that's not who I want to be."

Marielle sighed before nodding.

Fifteen minutes later, they pulled into the driveway of a slate-blue saltbox house on a freshly paved road.

"This looks new," Marielle said, exiting the car as she spied the lines in the sod and saplings planted near the curb.

"We moved in last fall. We used to live in my great-grandparents' big old house in town, but my parents got tired of fixing it up."

Marielle's eyebrows narrowed, thinking she would much rather live in a big old house with old trees and sidewalks than a new house in the middle of a corn field with no way to get anywhere without a car.

Gary opened the front door without using a key, revealing a curved staircase in the center, sitting rooms on either side, and a kitchen straight ahead. The sitting rooms held new furniture which appeared transported directly from the display room of a store.

"It's lovely," Marielle lied, preferring a less Garanimals approach to decorating.

"Are you hungry? I can make you a sandwich," he offered, unzipping his parka, then waiting for Marielle to hand him his letterman's jacket.

"No, I'm fine," she said.

"You're one of those girls who's too polite to say when you really want something, aren't you?" he asked as he hung both coats in the hall closet. "How 'bout this? I'll make two sandwiches and throw away the second

338

one if you don't eat it?"

"Okay," she replied happily, following Gary to the butcher block island. "So, why did you have a half-day today?"

"Teacher's conferences," he explained, pulling the bread from a container on the counter specifically designated to house it.

"Can I help you?" she asked.

"No. Well, you can hand me the plates behind you," he said, motioning toward the cabinet nearest her, "or you can just stand there and look beautiful," Gary continued.

"Is that sarcasm?" Marielle asked sharply.

Gary looked up with alarm on his face. "No. Isn't it okay that I say you're beautiful?"

"Sure, but I know how to make a sandwich. I also know how to put together one or two sentences and speak about current events with some clarity. For example, I know all about the plan by the Soviet Union to cut their troops by 10%."

Gary shook his head as he chuckled. "I don't know what my dad will make of you." He walked to the refrigerator for turkey, cheese, and mayonnaise.

"Why's that?" Marielle asked, placing the plates on the butcher block before retreating to the counter.

Gary held turkey above Marielle's bread. "Two slices or one?"

"One, please."

"Well, my dad thinks women can be good-looking or smart, but never both."

Marielle crossed her arms. "And which did you tell him I was?"

He looked up as he added only one slice of cheese to her sandwich, waiting for her to nod. "Well, good-looking because it's the most obvious."

"And what's your mother?"

"She's smart," he said, adding mayonnaise.

Marielle shook her head as a wry laugh escaped her lips. "Nice. So, let me get this straight: your father is okay with you marrying someone based strictly upon her looks and cheating on her until she's ready to *put out*, as they say?"

Gary cut her sandwich diagonally. "Well, that makes him sound shallow."

Marielle stared hard at Gary without speaking.

He exhaled audibly. "This isn't going the way I planned," he said with defeat.

"How did you think it would go?" she asked.

Gary abandoned the butcher block in favor of Marielle, then tilted his head to the side as he leaned down to kiss her.

"Wait," she said before his lips touched hers. "Something you should know is that I have asthma and I can't breathe well through my nose. If you expect to kiss me without sending me to the hospital, you need to be a little less aggressive with your tongue."

He looked from one of her eyes to the other. "Why didn't you tell me this before?" he asked.

"Because I didn't want to hurt your feelings or sound weak."

Gary kissed her again, this time using his tongue sparingly. Marielle fell back against the counter.

"Are you alright?" he asked, smiling as his lips remained near hers.

"I don't know. Do that again," she said, smiling back.

Gary repeated the kiss, making parts of Marielle's body rethink the whole marriage concept.

"We should stop now," she said breathlessly.

"What if I can't?" he asked, reaching down to touch her breast lightly through her polo shirt.

"We don't have a choice," she replied, stopping his hand, then looking down to avoid his eyes.

"Touch me and I'll leave you alone," he said, resting his forehead against hers.

"Touch you where?" she asked nervously.

"Marielle," he whined.

"How will that be helpful?" she protested weakly.

"I can't stop thinking about your hands on me. I just want you to touch me so I have something to think about when you're not here," he murmured.

Marielle closed her eyes involuntarily. "I'm afraid I can't do that."

"Why not?"

She looked up at him again. "I promised Dermot I wouldn't."

"Who's Dermot?" Gary asked with narrowing eyes.

Marielle turned away. "A friend of mine. Can we eat now?"

"I thought you weren't hungry?"

"I'm suddenly very hungry."

"Okay," he said, placing his forehead against the cabinet for a moment. He turned to look her in the eye. "You may kill me, ya know?"

"Oh, I think you'll survive," she decided.

"You know, sandwiches are named after the Earl of Sandwich," Marielle remarked after swallowing her final bite. "He had a gambling problem and he didn't want to take time to eat. So his staff put his food between two pieces of bread."

"Really?" Gary asked, moving his eyes from Marielle's breasts to her face.

She studied him to see if his interest in her comment was sincere, smiling when she confirmed it was.

"Let me show you around the house," Gary suggested, offering Marielle his hand.

He quickly showed her the living room, rec room, dining room, half-bath, and unfinished basement before leading her upstairs. He stopped only briefly at the doorway of his parents' master bedroom/bathroom, his brother's room, the guest room, and finally his own en suite.

"Are you tired?" he asked with a smile, moving his head toward the bed as he closed his bedroom door behind them.

"Is this your way of asking me to lie on the bed with you?" she asked.

"Please," he said.

"But we're not having sex," she warned.

"I'm not asking you to have sex with me, Marielle," he said with irritation.

Marielle shook her head. "Open your door and I'll lie on your bed."

"But no one's here," he protested.

"Then, there's no reason to close the door," she reasoned.

Gary opened the door, then waited for Marielle to lie on his double bed.

"This is very comfortable," she said, looking up at the ceiling with a nervous smile.

Gary climbed on the bed beside her, then grabbed her hip to turn her body toward him before inching his pelvis closer. He repeated compliments on her beauty before kissing her more strongly than he had in the kitchen.

"Give me a second," she said, turning her head away to breathe.

"I'm sorry. I forgot about your asthma." He kissed her cheek, then immediately reengaged her lips when she turned her head toward him again.

Marielle's legs moved involuntarily as Gary's tongue showed restraint. He squeezed her hip before his hand moved to the button of her jeans. She stopped his progress, but he unbuttoned his own jeans instead, exposing his penis. Marielle looked down at him with wonder a second before a woman's voice called Gary's name from the front door below.

Gary sighed as Marielle froze. "I'm up here with Marielle," he called back.

"Why did you say that?" she asked, scooting back to create distance between them. "She'll think we're having sex."

"Then she definitely won't come up," he replied, pulsing his eyebrows.

Marielle leaned back to better see Gary's face. "Were your parents home when you had sex with other girls?" she asked.

"Sometimes. I told you I have no secrets from my parents."

"Is this typical for kids in Freedom?" she asked, wondering if the name had anything to do with the attitude.

Gary smiled. "No. My parents are very unusual."

"Good. I thought I accidentally landed in the teenaged version of *The Stepford Wives*."

"Would you touch me?" he asked, rubbing her arm.

"No," she said, giggling uncomfortably as she glanced down.

"What did you s—" his mother said, peering into the room from halfway up the stairs. She gasped before making a hasty retreat.

Marielle covered her mouth. "Oh my God," she muttered, sitting up as Gary began to laugh.

He glanced over his shoulder. "I guess she didn't hear me," he said, smiling at Marielle's red face. "It's really nothing. She won't think anything about it."

"Even if that's true, I'd rather not have your mother see me for the first time while I'm lying on the bed with your penis exposed." She put her head into her hands as she quietly groaned.

"She couldn't see that from where she stood."

Marielle removed her hands, revealing her face's new shade. "Just the same, I think it's time for me to go home."

Minutes later, she stood in the kitchen in front of Mrs. Van den Plas.

"Mom, this is Marielle. Marielle, this is mom," Gary said proudly.

"It's wonderful to meet you," Mrs. Van den Plas said, foregoing a handshake to hug Marielle instead. "My son talks of little else but you, and you're just as pretty as he described. Are you Dutch?"

"No, I'm German."

"Oh," the woman said with no perceivable disappointment. "Gary told me you're as crazy about U2 as he is. It's too bad we didn't know you when we took him to the concert."

"I think most teenagers would die to have parents like you," Marielle remarked, not strictly referencing the concert.

"You're very sweet. Will you be staying for dinner?"

"No, ma'am. I need to get home. I have a ton of homework to do."

"Gary said you're very serious about your studies. I hope that rubs off on him." She smiled at her son, then gave Marielle another hug before they left.

2/12/1989 Sunday

Dear Dermot,

Congratulations on the Hurling Final! You must write me right away to tell me how you do. I'm sending you powerfully good thoughts and strength from across the Atlantic!

To answer your question, yes, I will marry you, but you have to wait eight years and you can't tell my boyfriend Gary because he asked me the same question and I put him off—forever, not just for eight years. I would marry you now, but it will take a year and a half to finish high school and four years to finish college and I'd like to have my Master's Degree before we get married. (I figure I can get my Doctorate afterward. Most people seem to manage that, I think.) Eight years will also give me time to date a string of losers so my family will forget you're not American, or German, or Gary and just be happy you're stable.

Regarding losers, I'm going to rename Guy "Lazarus" because he continues to be a clueless prick. About a month ago, he called to ask why I gave Jillian his letters and I said it was because he wouldn't leave me alone and I wanted him to stop contacting me. The conversation ended badly (with an "f" off on my side and a hang up on his) so I'm not sure where the confusion is, but I got a letter this week from him that said:

"I would appreciate it if you stopped writing me! I'm not sure if I can trust your motives! I feel as though you are trying to interfere with the relationship I have with Jillian. I don't feel as though a friendship exists

343

between us; if it ever did! So, to put it plain and simple, I don't want you to call or write me again!"

Uhhhh, am I in a parallel universe? The only thing I can think of is that this was great theater for Jillian's benefit as she sat next to him... Wait a second.....

Marielle jumped up to retrieve the envelope from the trash.

"Bastard!" she said before going back to her letter.

He's such an idiot! The postmark is from the city nearest Jillian's college, not his, so she clearly didn't trust him to mail it. Smart girl. Although he must've convinced her to stay with him and that his letters were somehow taken out of context (because "Why aren't you writing to me? Please write to me! I miss you!" can be so misleading sometimes), and that the problem is me for giving up the letters, not him for writing them. I take back my smart comment. She's an idiot. If a fake letter is ever enough for me to forgive a lying piece of crap, please have the IRA kill me. Does the IRA carry out hits in the US? Please check.

So, enough about Dickhead.

My grandparents are visiting for a whole week which is great, but all my grandma wants to talk about is my boyfriend which is unfortunate because I have a thousand questions to ask her about her dead uncle and my German isn't what it should be. Did I tell you I was trying to solve his 60-year-old murder? I've read enough Agatha Christie to believe I can do it and my dad always says that what I lack in knowledge, I make up for in enthusiasm. Anyway, we both think it was the tramp down the road, but I won't get to the truth of the matter if Grandma won't stop talking about Gary.

Regarding Gary, I've been dating him for a couple of weeks now and I either think he's great or I want to get as far away from him as possible. Are teenaged relationships supposed to be like that? He can't stop calling me "beautiful" which was nice at first, but then it made me wonder if he thinks I'm here strictly for his amusement.

Tell me truthfully, is it more important for a teenaged boy that a girl be smart or good-looking? For girls, it's all about looks at first, but the guy gets cuter or uglier depending upon his personality. You are, and always will be, good-looking even if you never send me a picture where I can actually see your face.

So, things got a little intense with Gary the other day when he drove me to his house after school, but I promise I'm still a virgin which is good for his health as well as mine because otherwise I would've killed him when Shelly told me that he shared our encounter with the entire basketball team. Apparently, he said he was sure he'd have sex with me by the summer. He doesn't know I know he said this yet. I'm waiting until we're alone to spring it on him.

Gary isn't a virgin—not by a long shot—so I'm not sure I want his pelvis that close to mine anyway. Is it unusual that I regard people as diseased if they've slept with a lot of people? (And by that I mean one person. Ha!)

My grandma just said to me, "Your Aunt Candice is cold. She's Norwegian ya know?" She's all excited that Gary is Dutch. Strange how we have a hierarchy here in Wisconsin... or maybe just in my family. If I were to rate the preference of my grandparents for boys I should marry, it would be: 1) German/Austrian; 2) Swiss; 3) Dutch; 4) Danish; 5) Swedish; 6) Norwegian; 7) Finnish; 8) Polish; and 9) the rest of Europe, but like I said, they love my mom even though she's in the number nine category so they'll accept you... eventually, without a problem.

So, I don't know where my mind has been lately, but I've made a rash of seriously blonde mistakes. If you promise not to share them with the basketball—I mean hurling—team, I'll tell you:

1) I gassed up my parents' car on the way to Shelly's house the other night and there was a cute guy working inside the glass gas station booth and I was sure he was looking at me while I walked back to my car (I'm arrogant that way) which made me nervous and I missed the car door handle when I reached for it (it was dark) and car doors here get stiff with the extremely cold weather so you generally have to pull up on the handle really hard. So, missing the handle pushed me completely off balance, along with the ice underneath my feet, and I slid nearly halfway under the car. I didn't even look up at the booth when I crawled out. I just got inside the car and left, vowing never to go back there again. HOWEVER, I was so frazzled I forgot that the shit box (I mean our car) kills whenever we turn left with the blinker on (not when we turn right, and not when we turn left <u>without</u> the blinker on. Don't ask me why.), and the car killed on Calumet Street very near where I earned my nickname of "Crash". Well, *cars stopped before they hit me, but it took me far too many seconds to remember I needed to put the car into neutral or park before trying to restart the engine and people were honking at me and I looked up at the guy in the booth and he was laughing (at me, not with me... I know because I wasn't laughing at all). AUGH!*

2) I was daydreaming in the nursing home break room the other day (my friend, Lars, was asleep when I went to his room to visit) and I suddenly noticed I was staring at this nurse's aide's face and she was winking at me. She did it once or twice and I thought she was joking around so I winked back at her, but then she got really annoyed and she wouldn't look at me anymore. So, later I was dishing out supper and I asked the cook why the lady got so mad at me when I winked at her and she said, 'Oh, she has a problem with her eye.' I have no idea what I'm supposed to do now except wait for the cook to gossip about it and the lady to understand that I wasn't making fun of her at all.

3) I was talking to the French exchange student the other day and I've been looking up words and phrases in French in an effort to better converse with her. Well, she went skiing in the Alps with her family over Christmas Break and I meant to say, "I envy you," because it's mostly flat around here which is crap for skiing, but I didn't know there were two ways to say "I envy you" in French. The first is "Je t'envie" and that's what I meant to say, but what I said was "J'ai envie de toi" which apparently means "I want to have sex with you" which I don't, obviously. Anyway, it took several awkward minutes to get that cleared up and now she can't pass me in the halls without laughing... and I can't say "Bonjour" without breaking into a cold sweat. By the way, thanks for warning me about how complicated French is!

On a positive note, I got my scores for the SATs and ACTs (tests you need to take to get into college) and I scored in the 80th percentile on the first, and 89th on the second. So, my blonde issues don't seem to be impacting my education... yet. Anyway, I've started receiving letters and big envelopes from universities across the country. Can you believe some colleges charge $14,000 a year for tuition?

I'm sorry about things on your side of the ocean. I get depressed myself sometimes and I don't know why. I used to think it was because my future husband was sad and I was feeling his pain. That seems cheesy now, and

I'm not sure what I think except small things when packaged together seem overwhelming sometimes, and it sounds like you are dealing with a lot of <u>big</u> things packaged together. I wish I was there to help you, even if I could only hold your hand and go for a walk and talk about nothing at all or plot revenge against anyone who bothers you. I'm very good at revenge as you know. I've even considered getting business cards that say, "Revenge is my business."

I'd better wrap this up now and spend some time with my grandparents. I've been meaning to ask you this for months, but I keep forgetting. Why is your address "Seaview Galway"? I can't find Seaview anywhere on the map.

Happy Valentine's Day!

I miss you!
Love,
Marielle

PS GOOD LUCK IN THE FINAL!

PPS I have to decide within the next week if I go to New York with our choir over Spring Break. If I do, I'll have to keep working crazy hours to make enough money for my ticket to Ireland in the fall. If I don't, I'll be able to spend more time with my boyfriend. Hmm... Both seem like bad alternatives. ☺

Marielle pushed aside guilt in a manner that had become disturbingly easy. Speaking as though she was still on track to visit Dermot was in all ways misleading. In fact, Maria wouldn't consider any conversation that included her daughter flying to Ireland. She may have very well used the phrase "over my dead body," but it was equally likely Marielle dreamed that since her mother's opposition was frequently in the forefront of her mind. Suffice it to say, there would be no trip to Ireland without divine intervention.

Chapter Twenty-Three

Fathomless Wisdom Come

—W.B. Yeats – *Her Dream*

Frieda looked conspiratorially to her left even though no one in the restaurant displayed the slightest interest in her conversation. "Did you understand my letters?" she asked her granddaughter.

Marielle leaned forward to match her grandmother's posture. "I think so, but I didn't understand the connection to Iwo Jima."

"My mother wrote to my younger brother when he was fighting in Iwo Jima saying she feared for her life after she ran into the witch at St. Benedict's in Chicago. My brother thought she was just paranoid because of her illness, but he saved the letter and he read it to me over the phone a couple of weeks ago. She told him that she thought my accident with Midnight had been intentional, and that Franz and my father had taken ill in Michigan when they ate jam the witch had made for the family. The strange thing about that is my father didn't like sweets and I don't ever remember him eating jam."

"So, if the witch were trying to kill everyone but your father, she would have poisoned something sweet, and your father must have suspected something was wrong with the jam to taste it," Marielle said, ignoring the idea that eating enough poison to get sick, but not enough to die was also a pretty good alibi.

"Exactly," Frieda replied.

"But Uncle Paul must not have eaten it."

"No. I guess he didn't like sweets either or maybe the jam wasn't in the house long enough."

"Or he stayed out of the house as much as possible because he and your father were fighting," Marielle reasoned.

Frieda shrugged her shoulders.

"Okay, but there's something really strange about this," Marielle said before stopping to tell the waitress their food tasted just fine.

"What's that?" Frieda asked.

"If your mother didn't think the incident with Midnight was an accident, she must have thought your father tried to kill you."

"She did, but I'm not sure I agree with my mom on that. My father said later he told me *not* to hold Midnight or I would be hurt, but what I heard him say was not to let go of Midnight or *he* would hurt *me*."

"Did he say it in German?" Marielle asked.

Frieda nodded.

"Is there a chance you just misunderstood?"

"It's possible. Even though I learned German before English, I had been living at the boarding school for months and we only spoke English there. Every time I came home, I had trouble switching back to German for a day or two."

"Were you hurt on your first day home?"

Frieda shook her head. "No, my second."

"So, his explanation might have merit," Marielle decided, the alternative being far too difficult to accept. "You said a few months ago you wished it *had* been your father who died. Did you think he had been the real target?"

Frieda inhaled slowly as she turned briefly toward the front door. "Oh, I don't know. Well, my father had been spending a lot less time away from the house after my accident and it occurred to me that maybe he and the witch were on the outs. So, I thought maybe the witch might've shot Uncle Paul when she meant to shoot my father instead."

"But Uncle Paul didn't look like your father."

"No, he didn't. He looked like my brother."

"Is there any chance your brother was the intended target and it was just a case of mistaken identity?" Marielle asked, though she couldn't imagine anyone wanting to hurt Uncle Franz, no matter what her grandma said about him.

"I don't see how. Franz rarely left the farm."

Marielle paused for a moment to collect her thoughts. "You said Uncle Paul had a female friend in town. Is it possible his activities with her or his gambling caused someone to want him dead, OR that the murder was a ploy to get you to sell your farm before the highway came through?"

"I've thought of both of those possibilities, but I'm telling you it had to be the witch. She confessed to it when she didn't think I was listening."

Marielle nodded again. She still couldn't get past the problem that Uncle Paul had been found dead in front of their barn and the only footprints leading to him came from the house.

"Thank you," Marielle said to the waitress as she collected their plates, waiting for her to walk away before she continued. "You said your father and Uncle Paul had a fight. Is it possible the witch used your dad to kill him?"

Frieda shook her head. "The only time I ever saw my father cry was at Uncle Paul's funeral."

"Not at your mom's?" Marielle asked with surprise.

"Nope," Frieda said with a clenched jaw and narrowing eyes.

"So, your mom said—"

"Wait a second," Frieda interrupted. "When is your friend supposed to be at the house?"

Marielle eyed her watch. "Soon, but he can wait."

Frieda raised her eyebrows. "Trouble in paradise?" she asked.

"I've never been to paradise," Marielle replied before a song she hated began to run through her brain. "You'll have to tell me what you think of him when you see him. It's possible I'm just not being very nice."

A slight grin appeared on Frieda's face just before she asked the wrong waitress for the check.

Marielle took a final drink of her lemonade. "Okay, so you said you went to the bar with your father sometimes. Did you ever see the witch in town or did she have any friends there who might have helped her?"

"She never had any friends that I know of—in Michigan or Chicago— just her ugly nieces. I never saw the witch in town either, but I only went out with my father when I was home from school. I think my mom wanted me to keep an eye on him."

"How did your father meet the witch, I wonder?"

"She sold us Midnight. She said it was her favorite horse, but she didn't have a lot of money after her husband died and she knew she'd get more money for him than one of her draft horses."

Marielle nodded once. "What made your mom suspect there was an affair?"

"It was Midnight, actually. On the way back from town, the horse stopped right in front of the witch's house, and it took some doing for my mom to get the horse to move again, but the whole time my mom said the witch was watching her from her front parlor window, laughing at her. God, I hated her big old spooky house with the car port in front that was half falling down. It looked just like a house in one of those scary movies. I wouldn't be surprised if she didn't kill other people too—even her first

350

husband."

Shivers went up and down Marielle's spine as her grandmother continued.

"My mom and dad had a terrible fight about the witch the night Uncle Paul died. Mom asked why Midnight had stopped in front of the witch's house, but my dad said it had been the witch's horse and it was a creature of habit."

"It's too bad they stopped burning witches before the '20s," Marielle reflected, causing Frieda to laugh in a way that made her eyes disappear for a moment.

"So, what do you make of your mom's letter?" Marielle asked, holding her grandmother's elbow as they walked to the car.

"I think she was genuinely scared."

"Because she knew the witch was guilty or because she thought the witch and your father were in cahoots?"

"Both. She had had brain surgery the year before and she was much worse after that. The surgery was only experimental and she had been warned it might make her worse, but my father forced her to have it. We didn't know at the time that the witch was already in Chicago and that my father was seeing her again."

Marielle shook her head until a question occurred to her. "Your mom never told you she saw the witch?" she asked with surprise, knowing her grandmother was in her late 20s at the time.

Frieda pursed her lips as her eyes becoming glassy with regret. "She did, actually, but I told her she was imagining things."

***

"So, what were you ladies up to?" Johan asked genially as Frieda and Marielle appeared in the dining room doorway.

"Marielle drove me to the mall and Perkins. Is her beau here?" Frieda asked, looking around the dining room in a valiant attempt to avoid follow-up questions.

"He's in the bathroom. He just got here," Jack answered from the couch.

Marielle studied her grandfather to see if a verdict had been reached on Gary, but he smiled brightly without giving away his thoughts.

"So, how long have you been friends with this boy?" Johan asked Marielle.

"A couple of weeks, but I don't see him much. He lives in Freedom."

"I'm not sure I know—" Johan began to say.

"It's very close to here," Gary interrupted as he entered the room.

Marielle studied her grandfather's face. She was sure she had never heard anyone interrupt him before.

"Hi there," Marielle said to Gary with an air of reserve, trying not to react to the image of him in his Levis and green and blue striped polo shirt. She abruptly looked back at her grandfather. "Is mom here?" she asked.

"She's at the bridal store with your sister," Jack replied.

"Maybe you should've gone with them," Gary suggested, raising his eyebrows with meaning.

Marielle shot her grandmother a look, but Frieda didn't see it. Having slipped a disc years before, her opportunities to jerk her head were limited and she had already moved toward the hall to hang up her hat and coat. Marielle shifted her gaze to her grandfather as he turned toward the living room. The only face Marielle could read was her father's, which said Gary was either amusing or presumptuous.

"Can I get anyone something to drink?" she asked.

"I'm fine," Gary said, smiling at her with eyes that looked a lighter shade of blue than she remembered.

"I'll get you a Coke," she replied, smiling at him briefly before looking at the other men.

"Just some coffee, little lady," Johan said.

"I'll have the same," Frieda called from the hallway.

Marielle didn't wait for her father to reply. She already knew what he wanted to drink.

Moments later, Gary sat with the men in the living room while Marielle spoke to her grandmother at the dining room table. Marielle used her mother's usual seat which allowed a full view of everyone in the other room.

"I see he learns quickly," Frieda said, gesturing with her thumb toward Gary.

"Yeah." Marielle exhaled. "But he doesn't seem to know that he's not allowed to talk in there."

Frieda chuckled. "So, have you always lived in Freedom, Gary?" she called before smiling mischievously at her granddaughter.

Gary knew enough to stand up and approach the dining room table before replying, if not enough to sit down. "We have," he replied, holding the back of the chair directly across from Marielle.

"They're like a founding family," Marielle remarked, opening her eyes wider with meaning. "I'm surprised the town isn't named Van den Plas. I looked in their phone book the other day and there were about 15 entries with Gary's last name."

Gary attempted to lock eyes with Marielle before he addressed her grandmother. "Marielle says you're from Chicago."

"We are. Well, my husband was born out west, but I was born in Chicago. Our home up north was just our cottage until my husband had a heart attack."

"Oh, really?" Gary asked with interest. "My parents just bought a cottage last fall."

Marielle looked at him with questioning eyes. She opened her mouth, but her father spoke before she could, breaking his own "talking between rooms" rule.

"Where abouts?" Jack asked.

Gary smiled as he turned around. "Not far from Freedom. They didn't want to be stuck in traffic on Friday and Sunday afternoons."

"That makes sense," Frieda decided. "Back in the '60s, we'd have to take a two lane highway all the way from Chicago to Kleiner. It would take us well over six hours to get there, and in a storm or with no air conditioning it was brutal, I can tell ya."

"I didn't know you had a cottage," Marielle finally said to Gary, slightly hurt that he hadn't mentioned it before.

"Yeah, my parents bought it the day after the election. They were so upset when Dukakis lost that they decided to treat themselves."

Marielle snapped her head in her grandmother's direction before both women turned toward the living room.

"What's wrong?" Gary asked Marielle as she watched the men exchange a look, and a shaking of their heads.

"We're a Republican family," she explained, omitting the other half of the problem—whimsically purchasing a cottage spoke of too much money to make Gary's family likable.

"Don't speak for me," Frieda argued.

"Sorry. Grandma won't say who she votes for. We suspect she's a Democrat."

"So, I have one friend at the table," Gary surmised, finally taking the chair before him.

"Do you hunt from your cottage," Jack asked, throwing Gary a bone.

"No, it's on a lake and it's close to other cottages. It's only good for power boating and water skiing really."

Jack laughed through his nose as he noticed the displeasure on his father's face.

"Do you get a whole week off school for hunting season?" Marielle asked Gary. "We always did in Kleiner."

"We do, but my mom usually wants me to take her Christmas shopping that week. We go down to Brookfield Mall."

"Near Milwaukee," Marielle explained to her grandmother.

"I know where Brookfield is, kid," Frieda replied. "But why would you do that? Isn't the Fox River Mall just as good?"

"No. The clothes are better in Milwaukee," Gary explained.

Johan cleared his throat. "You mean people would rather say they bought their clothes in Milwaukee than Appleton. They're the same shops, and chains buy in bulk so they're most likely the same clothes. You're just wasting time and gas buying something in Milwaukee you could've easily found in Appleton." He set down his coffee before he sat back on the couch.

Marielle looked from her grandfather to her father a second before Jack raised his shoulders. The verdict was in and there was nothing anyone could do about it.

"Did you know that Gary is the starting point guard on Freedom's basketball team?" Marielle asked the house at large.

"Ah, Jack used to play that position. He was on the All Star Team," Frieda said proudly as Jack rolled his eyes. "When they lost their game, he refused to get out of bed or go to school for three days. Do you remember that, Jack?" she asked as she turned toward the living room.

"How could I forget? You bring it up every other visit," he said, sharing a wry smile with his father. "You seem to forget that we won nearly every game up until that point."

"Oh, I didn't forget," his mother replied. "I just remember the last one the best. I think that's human nature."

"Do you still play?" Gary asked Marielle's father.

"No," Jack said as a warning before picking up his beer.

"Gary was thinking you might want to come to one of the Freedom games. They are smoking all the other teams in their division this year," Marielle said before abruptly turning away from her father's displeasure at being put on the spot.

"Do you think you'll go to state?" Frieda asked Gary.

"I hope so, but I hurt my ankle a couple games ago and the coach is worried. He made me sit in the whirlpool for 45 minutes the other day. That, in addition to my heart murmur, and ingrown toenail mean it may be a short season."

A laugh escaped Frieda's lips before she closed them.

"Can I get you more coffee?" Marielle asked her grandmother.

"Sure," she said, though her cup was mostly full.

"So, why did you suggest Marielle go to the bridal store earlier?" Frieda asked Gary as her granddaughter stood helplessly in the kitchen.

"Oh, to help her sister out, and prom is coming up soon. Don't girls usually find their dresses in the bridal stores?" Gary asked nervously.

"Did you ask Marielle to the prom?" Frieda asked.

"No, well, since we're dating, I just assumed she'd go with me."

"I'd schedule that with her well in advance," Jack said coolly. "She has plans to run off to New York and Ireland and God knows where else. And when she's not planning a trip, she's working next door or babysitting."

Marielle returned to the dining room with a full cup of coffee and a red face.

"Are you interested in going to the prom with me?" Gary asked as she set down the coffee in front of her grandmother.

"When is it?" she replied, well aware of the number of eyes upon her.

"At the end of April or the beginning of May. I'll need to find out and let you know."

"Well, as my dad said, I have a school trip to New York at the end of April." She looked quizzically at her father who hadn't given her permission to go to New York yet.

"When are you going to Ireland again?" Jack asked as if they had given her permission to make those plans as well.

"I don't think you and Mom decided I could go," she replied haltingly.

"Why wouldn't we let you go?" he asked, smiling menacingly at the back of Gary's head.

"I thought Mom wasn't happy with Mrs. MacManus' phone call."

"*I* was the one on the phone with the woman! What does it have to do with your mother?"

"I don't know. I just thought—"

"If you decide on a new date with your pen pal, I'm sure I can convince your mother it's fine," Jack said, ignoring the confusion on everyone's faces.

"Marielle said your parents took you to a concert in Chicago," Frieda said abruptly. "Do they like modern music?"

"Some, but they're crazy about the Beatles, especially the *Abbey Road* album. You know, the one where Paul is walking barefoot? It started the rumor that he was dead." He chuckled. "I never understood that. How can a dead body walk or move at all?"

Marielle's head shot up as Gary continued to talk.

"Apparently, if you play another one of their albums backward, it says, 'Paul is dead' or 'turn me on, I'm dead' or something like that."

Marielle stared at her grandmother trying to speak to her telepathically, and though her grandmother concentrated equally hard on Marielle, it wasn't working.

"Wait," Marielle said suddenly, then apologized to Gary before looking back at her grandmother. "Do you mind helping me with just a few phrases in German, Grandma?" She looked at Gary. "I promise it won't take long."

"Sure. I'll watch TV," he said, standing up while gathering a deep breath.

Marielle retrieved a purple notebook and a German dictionary from her room.

"Where Uncle Paul found?" she wrote in broken German.

Marielle looked up her grandmother's response, *"Vor dem Stall,"* in the dictionary to ensure it meant "In front of the barn."

"Were open the barn doors?" she wrote, again in German.

"Nein."

"Was he walking out, or in, or past the barn?" Marielle asked.

"Auch nicht," Frieda said, then wrote, "He was still in the carriage," in English, realizing the men wouldn't read the notebook, whatever the language.

"With which horse?"

"Midnight."

"How many routes into town were there?" Marielle asked, picking up speed.

"Two, but the horse preferred the route past the witch's house."

"Did your uncle make it into town that night?"

"Yes. He was shot after he returned home."

Marielle put her hand over her mouth as her eyes sparkled. "I have it!" she said, then scribbled as fast as she legibly could.

The widow shot Uncle Paul when the horse stopped at her house. The shot scared the horse and it ran back to your farm with Uncle Paul still in the carriage.

Frieda puzzled over the words for many seconds before her jaw dropped, either because the solution overwhelmed her or her granddaughter's handwriting did.

"*Mein Gott!*" Frieda exclaimed. "*Das ist es! Du bist sehr klug mein kind!*"

"I know what that means," Jack said proudly. "You got it right and you are apparently very clever," he said to Marielle. "See, I didn't forget all of my German, Ma." He stood up to retrieve a beer, then stopped in the archway, studying his mother's face. His knowledge of German hardly seemed like a reason to cry.

***

"Doug!" Jack exclaimed as Jeanette's fiancé walked through the kitchen.

"Since when is he allowed to walk into the house without knocking?" Marielle asked Maria as Gary held her hand at the table.

"Be nice," Frieda chided.

"*Ich bin sehr nett,*" Marielle replied.

"No, you're not," Anna commented from the orange couch.

"Hi everyone!" Doug said genially from the kitchen doorway. "Where's Jeanette?"

"She had a date," Marielle replied. "A big, hunky guy. He looked like George Michael, but with less facial hair."

Gary squeezed her hand.

Maria admonished her daughter, then spoke to Doug. "Don't listen to her, love. She's running some errands. She'll be back by dinner time."

"Oh, okay," he said with disappointment.

"How was your trip?" Johan asked.

"Fine until Pembine, then my muffler fell on one of those hills. I pulled over and secured it with a metal coat hanger, but it started scraping again a few miles ago."

"I can help you with that," Gary offered, rising to stand.

"Oh... thanks," Doug replied, not knowing how to address the speaker.

"Aren't you going to introduce Doug to your boyfriend?" Maria asked her daughter.

Marielle withheld sneering long enough to say, "Doug, this is my boyfriend, Gary. Gary, Doug. There we go."

Gary walked over to Doug to shake his hand before both took their leave.

"Any chance you can give me a hand with the brakes on the Jeep when the weather warms up?" Johan asked his son.

Marielle turned around to see the annoyance on her father's face.

"What about Robbie?" Jack asked.

"He won't do anything unless I pay him three times what I'd pay a garage."

Jack nodded as he bit his fingernail.

"I'll help you, Grandpa," Marielle offered.

"Have you replaced brake rotors before?" he asked with skepticism.

"No, but I can check out a book at the library."

"She can do it," Jack said. "She and I replaced the head pipe on the truck last year. Well, *she* replaced it. I told her what to do and came in to watch the end of the race. By the time they threw a caution flag, she was nearly done."

Marielle smiled at her father. "Well, Dad put Liquid Wrench on the bolts first. They were pretty rusty."

"Your friend can come too," Frieda suggested.

"Do you think that's a good idea?" Marielle asked.

"And how," Frieda replied, chuckling mischievously.

***

"Are you going to Minnesota?" Jeanette asked as she handed Marielle a large envelope from a university in Minneapolis.

"No. Ever since I took the SATs, I get at least one advertisement from a college every week."

Jeanette nodded before an idea occurred to her. "Why don't you guys come to the movies with us tonight?"

"Grandma and Grandpa are here," Marielle said as if the need to stay home was obvious.

"They won't care. Doug really likes Gary."

"Well, that's just awesome," Marielle replied, making no effort to hide her sarcasm.

"If you want to spend time with me after the wedding, you'll need to

358

get along with Doug," Jeanette said with raised eyebrows.

"Fine," Marielle acquiesced. "What stupid movie does your stupid fiancé want to watch?"

Jeanette smiled. "I'll find out. By the way, Doug told me to tell you not to screw this one up."

The right side of Marielle's nose twitched. "Well, tell him I said to do the opposite with you."

That night, Marielle sat beside her sister in a theater while Gary sat on her opposite side. She tried to remember the last time she had gone to the movies with Jeanette before determining she never had.

Gary placed his arm around her early into the movie, but she didn't feel confined for several minutes. In fact, she leaned into him at one point, grateful he had the ability to bring her closer to the people she loved.

Jeanette turned toward Marielle at least twice to share laughter before Marielle decided dating Gary wasn't so bad and she had probably been too hard on him. True, he was no Dermot, but as Shelly and Joel rightfully pointed out, chances were that Dermot himself didn't match her idea of him, and either way, she'd likely never meet him. It wasn't giving up on a dream as much as it was being realistic, and realistic wasn't so bad if you didn't live through it alone.

She turned to kiss Gary's lips briefly before looking back at the screen. He pulled her closer as he whispered "I love you" into her ear. Marielle closed her eyes in disgust. Gary had a way of ruining everything!

21-Feb-1989

Dear Marielle,

I won't leave you in suspense. I know you're dying to find out how our team did in the All-Ireland Final this past weekend, so I'll tell you straight away... So, how are you? Well done in your tests. You might even "scrape" your way into an Irish college yet... Of course, the standard here is so much higher. O.K. I better stop before you kill me.

The match was far too close, but in the end, we won by two points. If you're jumping up and down and going completely mental, then you look much the same as our teachers and headmaster. I feared for their sanity in fact and that of our parents. We arrived back at school today to pure madness with an assembly and speeches and photographs and let me say

359

there was very little learning done, but the best part was seeing my father near the end. I believe had tears in his eyes.

I have to say, I was never so nervous in my life, and your letter arrived just in time to cheer me. I almost died laughing when I read it! You really are confused, aren't you? You've been writing the wrong address for the last year as well. It's "Seaview" (name of house) then (and only THEN!) Taylor's Hill Road. Our house has a number too, but it's got three digits in it so it might be a bit too confusing for you.

I think you should go to U.C.G. and save yourself $7,000 a year. We have special courses to teach English to Americans.

I think I'll stop being nasty for awhile. I was reading Time magazine and it says 8,092 people were shot in 1985 in the U.S. That must be almost as good as Northern Ireland.

It's raining again and I have to go hurling. It's not fair! I hate it!

Look dearest darling, I think you should go with your class to New York— not because I want to keep you away from your new boyfriend (although that is a pleasant side-effect). I'll be missing our class trip to Amsterdam when we're in Wales, and I'm sure it would be loads more fun to be in Amsterdam than losing a big match in Great Britain.

I MUST GO.
Byeeee!
I love you!
Dermot

"Marielle said you told her she could go to Ireland!" Maria said aggressively from the dining room archway.

"I did. Do you have a problem with it?" Jack asked, more as a challenge than a question.

"I thought we agreed there was something fishy about that family and she shouldn't go!"

"Well, I changed my mind," he said, staring at his wife in a way that matched her intensity.

Maria swatted her right hand in her husband's direction before returning to the kitchen.

"Well, that went over well," Jack said playfully to Marielle before turning up the TV in an effort to drown-out the clanking pots and pans.

Chapter Twenty-Four

Picturesque Liar
—Mark Twain – *Private History of a Campaign that Failed*

"Are we rooming together or what?" asked Joy on the way to the Commons.

"Sure," Marielle replied as if the answer didn't impact her one way or the other.

"Cool. It's four people to a room so I asked Sherry and Meghan too."

Marielle stared ahead to kids leaving the gym area with wet heads. "Whatever you think."

"You don't care?" Joy objected.

Marielle finally looked at her friend. "I was supposed to be in Ireland that week. I don't care about much else."

"Are you going to be a downer during the whole week?" Joy asked as they approached their usual table.

"No. Just part of it," she said, managing a weak smile.

Joy sat down with an "ow" and a rubbing of her lower back.

"What's wrong?" Marielle asked, regretting the question as soon as it left her mouth.

"I think I broke my caucus," Joy replied.

"What?" Tom asked, laughing through the word.

"You know! My tail bone."

"Oh, coccyx," Tom said.

Joy scoffed. "Yeah, you didn't *actually* think it was a tail bone did you?"

"It *is* a tail bone, dumbass," Joel said.

"Next, you'll say the Golden Gate Bridge isn't golden," Joy replied.

The other teenagers reserved laughter until they confirmed that Joy did in fact believe the Golden Gate Bridge was painted gold. Marielle allowed Joel to educate his cousin while she pulled out her notebook.

"Dermot?" Tom asked.

Marielle nodded.

"I thought you stopped writing to him."

362

She furrowed her eyebrows suddenly. "No, why would I?"

"You haven't brought in his letters in a while and I haven't seen you write any."

"Oh, I sent him a congratulations card that wasn't very interesting, and he's been kind of weird with me since I started dating Gary, or maybe I've been weird with him since my trip was canceled. Anyway, I haven't had the energy to do more than 50% of the entertaining so my letters haven't really been worth your time."

"Are you planning to do more than 50% of the entertaining today?" he asked.

She nodded. "I'm going to give it my best effort."

"Okay. Carry on, then."

4/14/1989 Friday

Dear Dermot,

How are you? I'm fine. Actually, my day today has been most enjoyable since my nemesis (an exaggeration, but it's a better story this way) locker neighbor left our school a few minutes ago. (He's moving to Texas). I tried to sound all touched and empathetic when he walked over to me and said he didn't want to go and how sorry he was about his juvenile fit a couple months ago (he expressed it differently) that caused me to wish he'd been on a Pan Am flight a few months ago (Did I tell you about this? [the fit, not the Pan Am flight... I'm pretty sure you already know all about the Pan Am flight]). According to everyone who witnessed my reaction, I wasn't very convincing in my sympathy... which could be in part because I stepped back and offered my hand when he moved to hug me. I was never a wizard at diplomacy as you know, but as I get older I realize that I don't have as much patience for pretending I like someone when I don't.

I'm leaving for New York tomorrow which is pretty exciting, but I haven't packed yet, which is incredibly poor planning. It's the first time I'll be on a plane and if we don't crash I'll send you a postcard each day and try to call you with the roll of quarters I'm bringing with me... I wonder if it's cheaper to call Ireland from New York since it's at least a third closer... I guess we'll find out.

I have to babysit tonight which is <u>more</u> poor planning. I wasn't even thinking when the mom called me to ask if I could babysit on the 14th.

"What are you doing tonight?" Joy asked.

Marielle looked up from her notebook.

"Jesus!" Joel said to Marielle as Joy leaned away from her. "If looks could kill!"

"Sorry," Marielle said, her face relaxing. "What did you ask?"

"What are you doing tonight?" Joy repeated.

"Babysitting for the drunks."

"Do you like babysitting?" Joel asked.

"I love it," Marielle replied without feeling.

"It must be boring as hell," he reflected while admiring the Bolivian exchange student as she walked into the school store.

"It's torture if the kids aren't interesting," Marielle replied. "You have to distract yourself from looking at the clock, and study them like a lab experiment instead. I like to use those times to make random assessments about human nature. In summary, I've decided that anything you need to know about kids, you can learn in Halloween horror films: their singing is spooky as hell and they frequently act like the devil."

"That seems harsh," Joy remarked.

Marielle nodded curtly. "Maybe, but I have a powerful brain. You're not hampered by such things."

"What are you saying?" she asked.

"Exactly," Marielle replied before sharing a smile with Joel. "I have some rules for babysitting which I plan to add to the letter I'm writing. You can read it when I'm done."

She looked down at her notebook again.

It's worse than you can imagine since the kids have no imagination. For example, they've both dressed up as pirates for Halloween two years in a row. Their parents don't have any imagination either. They've sat on bar stools while I've taken their kids trick or treating both years.

I have some rules to help get through the times that try my soul, and here they are:

1. I'm not your tissue.

2. Your nose is not a buffet.

3. Bad things happen three seconds after "Watch this!"

I sometimes daydream while I'm there and the kids could be telling me their hand fell off and unless they're screaming and jumping in place, I won't hear them. I wonder if I should charge half as much per hour for that... Anyway, I've been daydreaming less since I solved the murder of my great Uncle Paul a few weeks ago. Actually, I'm not sure I solved it, but my grandma thinks I did and that's all that matters. In case I forgot to mention it and you're in suspense, it was the tramp my grandfather was cheating with, which I admit sounds a little convenient, but as I said, it makes my grandma happy.

I have to go to Gary's prom when I get back from New York. My parents said I could stay out all night for that, but I haven't told Gary. He won't shut up about sex and getting married... when he's not complaining about his aches and pains. Can you imagine what he'll be like when he's 70 (regarding the aches and pains, not the sex and marriage part)? My grandma told me during her last visit that he complains like an old lady and I have to agree with her on that. She'll have plenty of time to gather more ammunition against him when we visit their ranch in a couple weeks. BAH!! I don't know why I agreed to bring Gary to my grandparents' house. Doesn't that seem a little too serious? The worst part of it is that he'll tell all of his teachers and buddies what a bonding experience it was and how much closer we are to making a lifelong commitment. Auch! That just makes my stomach turn. Tell me truly, do I have a right to be disturbed or am I just a bitch?

I think New York will be fun, but I have to admit I'm nervous about being that far from Wisconsin for five days. I mean, what happens if my grandparents get sick and I can't get back here in time to see them? I don't know why this never occurs to me when I think of going to Ireland. Maybe I don't really want to go to New York at all. Sometimes I feel helpless and completely overwhelmed worrying about my grandparents. Every day, I see people their age dying at the nursing home, and I don't know if I could handle losing them. I'm probably just being stupid. I should stop now before you think I'm crazy.

As part of my self-imposed Irish literacy project, I've read a biography about William Butler Yeats and I'm reading his poems now. I have to say that if "Leda and the Swan" was read in more high school classrooms...

"Joel," Marielle said, briefly distracting him from the Bolivian on her return trip to her table.

"What?" he asked, maintaining his eye contact with the exchange student.

"Read this poem. It's perverted," Marielle said, pushing her open book toward him.

"What do you think she sees in him?" Joel asked Tom with a contorted expression as an acne-faced boy kissed the Bolivian.

Tom looked up from his notebook. "Citizenship," he replied, then craned his neck to see the poem Marielle placed before Joel.

...you'd have 100% attendance rates in English class. Wowee! Have you read it? I think it qualifies as soft porn... and it was right there in the library! I kept guarding my book every time the librarian walked by. I heard there are some pretty risqué parts of the Bible too, but finding them seems like too much trouble.

I just finished the book "Johnny Got his Gun" for English and I have to say, although it's pretty dark and depressing, the guy's thought patterns mirror my own in a really disturbing way.

Before I forget to brag, you should know that I won a First in my sax solo and a Star First in my sax quartet and quintet. For a Star First, you compete at State. So, I'll be doing that too when I get back from NYC.

Ooh, I also need to ask you what day I should fly in to Shannon and when I should fly out? I should be able to buy the ticket by the end of May if I don't spend too much money in New York. (Do you think I've mentioned New York City enough times in this letter?)
I miss you!
Good luck in Wales!
All My Love,
Marielle

PS We have only two more months until Summer Break! When do you get out?

Marielle stood at a pay phone in Penn Station as Joy and Sherry gossiped several yards away. She waited for the deep double-ring of an Irish phone after inserting eight dollars in quarters, and holding her free ear closed in an attempt to hear better.

"Hello?" she heard Fiona ask.

"Hi, Fiona, this is Marielle. Is Dermot there?"

"He's having a bit of a lie-in. Just a moment, I'll fetch him for you."

"Just a sec," Marielle said as she waited for the end of a loud-speaker announcement. "Sorry. Please don't disturb him on my account."

"Not a'tall. He'll be wanting to share his news with you."

"Ooh, did they win?" Marielle asked enthusiastically.

"I'll let him tell you that himself," Fiona replied before calling for her brother.

"Hello?" Dermot asked, his tone holding more of a question than usual.

"Hi," Marielle said as her eyebrows narrowed.

"How are you?" he asked concernedly, causing Marielle to begin searching her brain for a reason why.

"So, don't leave me in suspense. How did you do in Wales?" she asked with enthusiasm a moment before the date on the train arrivals board caught her eye. She hadn't noticed it when she walked to the phone, but there it was: April 18th—the day her plane was scheduled to arrive in Shannon. Her heart stopped or skipped a beat, or maybe just the earth stopped, but she felt it. Dermot wasn't supposed to be home yet.

"—three points," was what she heard before her attention returned to the conversation.

"I'm sorry," she said. "Did you say you won?"

"Only by a goal," he repeated with obvious pride.

"Yes, well, that counts. Congratulations," she said in a nearly normal voice.

"Thank you. I was just thinking about you. Have you gone to New York yet?"

"I'm here now. In Manhattan, actually. I would have called from our hotel next door, but one phone was being used, and the other was out of order. Anyway," she said, feeling her façade slipping, "I'm sorry to rush, but my friends are waiting and I need to send off your daily postcard."

They exchanged goodbyes before Marielle hung up the phone with more force than she had ever done with Dermot. From this day onward, there was a lie between them, and they both knew it.

Chapter Twenty-Five

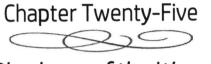

Shadows of the Wood
—W.B. Yeats – *Who Goes With Fergus?*

"Is this all you're taking?" Gary asked as Marielle handed him her gray duffel bag.

"Yeah. It's not the prom. We're going into the woods."

"What if there's a cold snap?" he asked with concern.

She chuckled. "How long have you lived here? This place is one giant cold snap. This flannel shirt and my winter jacket will never come off me so there's no reason to pack them."

"Oh," he said with disappointment. "I thought we might go out to dinner at a fancy place one night."

Marielle drew a deep breath. "You didn't get enough of that prom night?"

Gary smiled. "I didn't."

"Alright. If it's important to you, I'll go back upstairs and get something nice."

"No. It's fine," he said, placing her duffel bag into the trunk.

"What should we listen to on the way up north?" he asked with a twinkle in his eye.

Marielle returned Gary's smile as she opened the passenger's-side door. "I was thinking we could start with U2, then listen to a little more U2 before ending with U2."

Gary laughed. "Exactly what I was thinking!"

***

Marielle turned toward Gary as she ejected the third spent tape. "What?" she asked as she noticed his furrowed eyebrows.

"I was just thinking about what you said about your pen pal."

Marielle held her breath for a moment. "What did I say about my pen pal?"

"You said you promised him you wouldn't do anything physical with me."

"Right, well, I promised him I wouldn't do anything physical with anyone."

"Why would he ask you to promise him that?" Gary asked the highway before glancing at her.

"He didn't ask me to promise. I promised of my own free will, but that was before we started dating," she said quickly, hoping to bury the subject.

"But—"

"Do you have *The Unforgettable Fire*?" Marielle interrupted, looking at the box of tapes on the bench seat between them.

"It should be in the glove compartment unless my mom moved it."

Marielle rummaged through the glove compartment for a moment before Gary nervously said, "Forget it! It's not there."

Marielle looked from the glove compartment to Gary. "Okay," she said, too fatigued to get to the bottom of why he didn't want her exploring.

"So, how far is it to your grandparents' house?" he asked, staring at the seemingly endless vista of pine trees along the hilly, two lane road.

"You go past all civilized life, then it's another half-hour," she replied, chuckling.

Gary smiled. "You're funny for a girl."

Marielle's head snapped toward him. "Yeah. Imagine how funny I'd be if I had a penis. Now, is it having a penis that makes you funny or does having it make other people *think* you're funny? I've never understood that, but then I have a small female brain."

He turned toward her, his face asking the question before he did. "Are you joking?"

A blank expression overtook her face. "No. All my brain power is taken up with being beautiful. Are we driving?" she asked, looking around.

"Marielle," Gary chided.

Marielle began to laugh before she yelled. "Ooh, turn here!"

***

"Hello there, Blondie!" Johan said, standing on the cabin side of the large, circular driveway as his granddaughter leaned out the passenger side window.

Marielle barely waited for the car to stop before she opened the door and ran to him for their usual hug. She placed a butterscotch candy into her grandfather's hand before moving to her grandmother. "Where are the horses?" she asked, not seeing evidence of them in the pasture along the long drive or on the other side of the barn.

369

"They're in the meadow in back. You won't see them until dinner time."

"It's good to see you again," Frieda said to Gary with a pat on the back.

"Can I help you with your bags?" Johan asked after he shook Gary's hand.

"Oh, no. Marielle packed like a guy," Gary replied. "I think I can manage both bags." He walked to the back of the car with Johan behind him.

"You didn't bring your rifle?" Johan asked Marielle as he looked into the gun-free trunk.

Marielle pulled back the corners of her mouth. "I'm sorry. I didn't know I needed it."

"I thought we'd do some target shooting and you shouldn't walk into the woods this time of year without a gun."

"Oh, right," she said, chastising herself for forgetting.

Gary looked at her concernedly as he closed the trunk.

"Bears," she explained.

Gary approached her, not having lost the anxiety on his face. "You have a rifle?"

"No." She shook her head decisively. "It's a shotgun."

They walked in silence over the wooden footbridge toward the black log cabin with white stucco chimney and stone inlay.

"I love your house," Gary said, looking up at the two-story structure with dormer windows.

"Yeah, it would have been cheaper just to tear it down and rebuild it," Frieda said as she used her shoulder to open the door, "but we decided to fix it up instead. I hope you don't mind sleeping on the couch."

"Not at all. It's huge," Gary said, spying the large sofa inside the fireplace-lit room.

"We made that, Pa and I did."

"You did?" he asked in disbelief, walking over to the 6"x6" wood lacquer armrests.

"Yep. Pa made the wood frame and I sewed the cushions by hand. It took weeks for the blisters on my fingers to heal." Frieda turned toward her granddaughter. "Show Gary upstairs so he can drop your bag, then come into the kitchen for a drink."

Marielle led Gary up stairs which protested each step.

"Whose trophies are these?" Gary asked, stopping to look at bronze men holding guns on a handmade wooden shelf in the hall.

"My grandfather's. He won a bunch of skeet shooting competitions in Chicago in the '40s and '50s."

"So, you shoot," he said more than asked.

She shook her head as she regarded her grandfather's trophies. "I don't, no, not like Grandpa."

"But you *do* shoot."

Marielle looked at Gary's concerned face. "Only in the way everyone does."

"I've never shot a gun in my life!" he confessed.

Marielle opened her mouth for a moment without speaking. "Do me a favor and keep that information to yourself. Otherwise, Grandpa will declare this a shooting weekend."

"Really? Why?"

"No reason, other than he likes to screw with people," she said, smiling.

***

Johan smiled proudly as his granddaughter entered the small kitchen. It held the gray, roughly-hewn wooden cabinets, wine rack, and back door he had made decades before.

"So, I thought we'd walk back to camp to see if we can shore-up that porch," Johan said. "We should have time to do some fishing too, but I need your help with an outlet upstairs."

"What about the brakes on the Jeep?" Marielle asked.

"Oh, I had Robbie fix those last fall," Johan said with a mischievous grin.

Marielle smiled. "What's wrong with the outlet upstairs?"

"Oh, I wired it years ago with whatever I had on hand and it burned up the other night."

"Auch, the smell," Frieda protested. "I thought he was burning the house down." She turned a displeased face toward her husband who smiled through it.

"When you say you wired it with whatever you had on hand, what do you mean by that exactly?" Marielle asked, having heard stories about her grandfather's shoddy wiring nearly every time she held the flashlight for her father.

"Oh, you know, an old extension cord wire," he replied, still smiling like a bold child.

Marielle covered a gasp with her hand.

Gary looked from Marielle to Johan. "Is that bad?" he asked.

"You betcha'," Frieda replied.

***

Marielle knelt beside the blackened outlet cover in her grandfather's bedroom. "Is the fuse out?" she asked cautiously.

"I think so," Johan replied, then smiled at his granddaughter's displeased face.

"Okay. I'm trusting you now," she said, unscrewing the face plate before reaching for the outlet and its wiring. "AH!" she yelled.

Johan's mouth dropped.

"Only joking," she said.

Gary looked at Frieda concernedly from the other side of the bed, causing Frieda to shrug her shoulders in reply.

"Should you really be doing that?" Gary asked as Marielle unscrewed the wires from the side of the outlet receptacle.

"Probably not, but my parents have a good life insurance policy on me," she said, winking at her grandfather. "Do you have 12/2 wire for this?"

"No. Fourteen-two," Johan replied.

Marielle sighed. "I'd feel better with 12/2."

"Well, it's better than the extension cord," he argued.

Marielle opened her mouth, then closed it, trying not to shake her head. "Well, I suggest we attach the new wire to the old with electrical tape, then pull it through the wall so you don't need fish tape."

"Good idea," Johan agreed. "Did you hear that, Frieda? I told you Marielle would know what to do."

"Yeah, Pa, I heard you," she said without interest before turning toward Gary. "Why don't we go downstairs and look at Marielle's baby pictures?"

"Do I have baby pictures?" she asked without humor.

"I get the feeling your friend doesn't approve of you rewiring outlets," Johan said after Gary and Frieda walked downstairs.

Marielle smiled. "I think his family hires out for this sort of thing."

Johan replied by releasing an unpleasant grunt.

A half-hour later, Marielle ran down the stairs with a rifle in her hand.

"Which one is that?" Frieda asked from the table as Marielle made her way around the couch and into the open dining room.

"The Ruger," she replied before looking at Gary. "It's only a .22," she said in an effort to allay his concern. Marielle turned as her grandfather reached the landing overlooking both the living and dining rooms. "Is it true the Weatherby reverses the blood stream of a deer and kills it with a heart attack?" she asked.

Johan didn't respond until he reached his granddaughter. "Who told you that?"

"Dad."

"Well, it's possible. Shall we walk back to camp?" he asked, prompting Gary to stand. "You'll want to change those shoes, young man," Johan cautioned, eyeing Gary's new boat shoes.

"I didn't bring anything else," he said weakly.

"Well, I have some old boots for you," Johan offered before handing Marielle his gun.

Johan retrieved hunting boots from the basement which were two sizes too large for Gary's feet.

"That gun weighs a ton," Marielle said to her grandfather as she handed it back.

"It's a handmade stock," he explained.

"Oh, right," she said before asking Gary to hold her gun while she put on her coat.

Gary's eyes moved up and down the weapon as though it might go off without warning.

"When's the last time we went shooting together, *Fraulein*?" Johan asked as they alighted the cabin.

"Two summers ago, actually. I was thinking about that on the way up. I worked all last summer."

"Well, I'm glad you're not doing that anymore," he said, feeling the extra bullets he dropped inside his flannel trouser pockets. "Your grandmother and I were worried about you. You're only young once, you know."

Marielle smiled. "That's what people say, but youth seems to last a lifetime."

Johan laughed. "Well, being old lasts even longer."

"Did you make this?" Gary asked, looking up at a varnished wooden sign that read, "Frieda's Waterfowl Sanctuary."

"I did," Johan replied. "It's not official, but it's a better name than *the swamp.*"

"Where's the swamp?" Gary asked as though alligators might live inside.

"It's down the hill on the other side of these reeds," Marielle replied. "We'll walk through it on the way to camp."

"Really?" Gary asked.

Marielle smiled through a nod before glancing at her grandfather. "Will we be shooting snakes on the way?"

"Nah, I'd rather save my bullets," he decided.

"What if we see a water moccasin?" Gary asked uneasily.

"Shall I answer?" Marielle asked her grandfather, then continued when he nodded. "There are no water moccasins in Wisconsin. What you're thinking of are actually northern water snakes." She glanced at her grandfather. "Have you convinced Dad of this yet?"

"No, your father is a hard-headed man. He still thinks rain storms follow rivers."

"And that all jokes originate in prison," Marielle added before noticing Gary scanning the swamp as they walked through the slightly elevated muddy road. "You shouldn't see anything terribly poisonous," she consoled.

"That's right," added Johan. "Maybe a pine snake, but they'd only make you sick."

"The pit vipers are only in the south of the state, right Grandpa?"

Johan nodded. "Probably," he said, smiling as Gary's eyes widened.

Dead leaves crunched beneath their feet as the road gained distance from the swamp.

"It's so dark in here," Gary remarked, looking up at the tall trees.

"You should repeat that up ahead when the road splits," Marielle said before turning a smile toward her grandfather.

"Why?" Gary asked.

"Two roads diverged in a yellow wood," Johan quoted.

"And sorry I could not travel both," Marielle added. "Do you remember the rest?"

Johan shook his head with disappointment.

"I don't either. I seem to only remember the first and last lines of any poem."

"Which poem?" Gary asked.

"*The Road Not Taken,*" Marielle replied.

"I took the road less traveled and it's made all the difference?" Gary asked.

"Something like that," Johan said, still looking down the road.

"What does that have to do with dark woods?" Gary asked.

"Oh, well, I confused two of Robert Frost's poems," Marielle explained with embarrassment. "I do it all the time. Grandpa doesn't even bother to correct me anymore. I was thinking of the line 'the woods are lovely dark and deep.' "

"Oh," Gary replied vacantly.

"Stay here while I check on my blind," Johan said before he climbed a small hill toward an old hemlock tree.

Marielle smiled after her grandfather, then turned toward Gary, surprised to find a serious look on his face. "What's wrong?" she asked.

"I think I'm in an episode of the *Twilight Zone*," he said.

Marielle's eyebrows furrowed. "Why?"

"You're wiring outlets on live circuits—"

"It wasn't live. Grandpa was only joking."

"Can't he wire his own outlets?"

"Sure, but he doesn't want to so he pretends he doesn't know how. He does the same thing when his car needs gas or his tire is flat."

Gary shook his head. "I'm walking in the woods with two people carrying guns behind me, and I'm wearing boots big enough for Sasquatch."

"True, but you didn't pack properly and our safeties are on," she explained.

"That's not the point," Gary rebutted. "Were you really going to shoot snakes just for the fun of it?"

"No. Well, you seemed happy enough for me to shoot if we saw a water moccasin," she argued, then continued when Gary didn't reply. "Anyway, I shoot near them, but I miss on purpose. My dad does the same thing. He makes Grandpa really angry because a herd of deer could run right past their blind and my dad just waves and keeps smoking his cigarette. It took me five deer seasons to figure out he wasn't really trying. He's never actually killed anything that I'm aware of."

"What about your grandpa?" Gary asked, his eyes on the hill.

"Oh, yeah, he kills stuff all the time. He's actually the one who's sup—" Marielle stopped abruptly.

Gary turned from the deer blind to Marielle. "Supposed to what?" he

asked.

"Pardon?" Marielle asked innocently while turning red.

"What's he supposed to do?" Gary asked impatiently.

Marielle cleared her throat. "Kill anyone who hurts one of us girls, but I think that means hurt in a criminal sense, not someone who hurts our feelings."

"Are you sure?" Gary asked, looking back at the hill as Johan began to descend it.

"Pretty sure," she said, smiling.

Chapter Twenty-Six

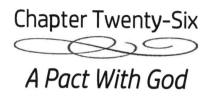

A Pact With God

29-May-1989

Hi Marielle!

Thanks for your hundreds of postcards, your letter and your phone call. You sounded different on the phone - maybe you're losing your American accent or something. This letter is probably going to be very late because there's a postal strike on in Dublin and they already have a build-up of over a million letters.

Sorry for not writing to you for so long. First, I was doing my summer exams (don't ask how I did in them, please...) and before that I was busy beating conceited little bastards in Wales. I am now on the first ever non-British hurling team in history to be a British champion. I know that doesn't really make sense. We only won the match by a goal and two points, or five points if you want to be accurate.

I must have had the best time of my life in Wales! There's an old tradition in St. Clement's Hurling Club that whenever we go anywhere we take all the posters and signs back with us. On the last night, I was on top of a 20-foot pole trying to take a flag off (at 3 a.m.) and a guard walked past with an Alsatian. I don't know how, but he didn't see me.

It was really embarrassing when we arrived in Wales because we're all around 16 or 17 years old and we were entered in the "under 19" category. (There were actually two lads on the team who were mistaken for primary school players.) No one thought we'd win when they saw how much bigger the teams from Wales were. Most of the other teams were really nice, but one was so snobby I couldn't believe it. One of them said, "Oh look, the Irish have come over for a jolly good beating!" because I was standing in front of him. I said nothing. Actions speak louder than words...

The British are really weird people. No matter what you do they say

"Cheers" but the way they say it sounds like "Chairrrs" or something.

The boat journey was great (from Ireland to Wales, I mean). I'm sure you'd enjoy being stuck on a car ferry with a force 7 wind. We were going to go by plane but the dates didn't fit.

So... how are you today, my supremely sexy, sweet, psychedelic, surreally sympathetic (I better stop before I start using a dictionary) pen pal. Did you ever notice the way my lines go up and down? Well, I can't help it. I'm looking at your passport photo - I have it stuck on the wall beside my bed so every morning I wake up and say... Aaggh! And jump out of bed (<— Only joking. I humbly beg your forgiveness on behalf of this insulting mind of mine!) Oh, what a beautiful pen pal I have... Now, if only that was her and not her photograph, but I'll be patient and wait until September. Imagine if you had arrived as planned. You'd be gone now and we'd have nothing to look forward to, unless we ran away and got married, which could be great fun. I was examining my schedule and it would be brilliant if you could travel here before school begins this fall which should be September 7th.

Poor me is really sick – I was awake 'til 4 a.m. with a bad cough and have to go training at 9:30 a.m.

Did you hear about the American scientist who says he's discovered fusion power in a "test-tube," or is everyone in your family normal (with no mad-scientists)? Anyway, if this comes true, we'll never need oil or coal or gas again. I hope I'm not boring you to death.

My sister's started driving. SHE is a health hazard (i.e. "if you don't like the way I drive, keep off the sidewalk"). "Sidewalk?" I'm turning into an American.

I met my ex-girlfriend yesterday. Her name is Ashley and she's from Australia. She's probably one of the few ex-girlfriends I've ever grown to actually like. One problem though (which she made me promise not to tell anyone, so feel lucky) - she used to giggle at the wrong time - and I mean the WRONG time. She dumped me, in case you're wondering. I'm going to get the book "Johnny Got His Gun" if I can. I'd like to know more about your "thought patterns"!!

I know just what you mean about feeling helpless and your grandparents getting old and everything getting too much for you. The only reason I do is because two of my grandparents are dead (I never met them) and my other grandparents are very old. I felt almost the exact same way when my granddad was in hospital but he got better. If you think about what he said it might help, then again it might not, but he thinks that anything would be better than having to spend an eternity on this planet. He also said if you're going to spend your whole life worrying about you or your friends dying, you're making a mess of your life while you ARE alive. Everything makes more sense when he says it than when I do, but one thing I'm really glad about is that I'm the one you decided to tell, even if there isn't much I can do. When you think of it, not many of your friends (well, my friends anyhow) are the kind of friends you tell things like that and I'm glad you trust me. Of course, I don't think you're just being stupid. At the moment, however, my greatest worry is that you have a licence and I don't.

I'm on summer holidays now and you're not. I was going to go to the beach, but it started raining. Irish weather changes every hour or so. I still haven't got used to it.

I think that's all my news and I'd love to bore you by telling you the details of the match in graphic detail but I don't like being a bore. The one thing I will say is that victory is even sweeter when it's mixed with revenge.

I better go.

Sorry for not writing.

I NOW have to go training. Do you know they only gave us one day off for winning in Wales? Slave drivers!!

I love you and I can't wait to get your next letter.

See ya!
Lots of Love,
Dermot

The French phone rang three times before Marielle made it from her room to the top of the stairs.

"Hey," Gary said with apprehension.

"Hey, what's up?" Marielle asked, wondering why a person who called another would sound so tentative.

379

"What are you doing?" he asked.

"Not much, I'm just binging on *Kokomo*," she said before chuckling.

"Huh?" Gary asked.

"I'm listening to the Beach Boys song over and over again. Actually, I got tired of getting up to rewind it so I taped it three times in a row. All you have to do is listen to the *Top Ten at Ten* for three nights."

"Oh. That's a good idea," he said before surrendering to an awkward pause.

"Is something wrong?" Marielle asked.

He cleared his throat. "Have you heard from Shelly lately?"

"No. Is she okay?"

Gary sighed. "She and I had a big fight last night and she threatened to tell you something."

Marielle leaned against her parents' doorway. "No. She hasn't called. What's this about?"

Gary hemmed and hawed before beginning a long description of a party at his house, and the inevitable drinking, and a girl from Kaukauna who attended.

"Oh, alright," Marielle said, looking out the window as Jeanette backed down the driveway. She tried to remember if Jeanette said she was going to Green Bay to see her friends or Marquette to see Doug before realizing another awkward pause had overtaken the line. "Is there anything else?" she asked as Jeanette's car pulled into the gas station across the street.

If Jeanette only stood at the pump for a few minutes, Marielle could assume she was going to Green Bay. Jeanette looked into her wallet as though wanting to spend all available funds on gas. Marielle sighed. Her sister was probably on her way to Marquette.

"... and when I woke up there were only two in my drawer," Gary said.

"Sorry. Two what?" Marielle asked.

"Condoms," he said.

"Are you telling me you had sex with the girl from Kaukauna?" she asked in disbelief.

"I didn't think so, but she says we did and I honestly can't remember."

"I don't understand how this could happen," Marielle said, her voice cracking involuntarily.

"I'm sorry. I was really drunk and she's a slut and she came on to me—"

"I think I'm done talking to you," Marielle said, hearing Gary call her name as she hung up the phone.

"Are you alright, Shel?" Marielle asked moments later.

"Did you hear from Gary?" Shelly asked delicately.

"Yeah. Dickweed just confessed."

"Good," Shelly said, releasing all of her breath. "I threatened to tell you, but I was hoping he would tell you first."

"How did you find out?"

"I had a fight with Tim when his ex-girlfriend called his house and left a message. He said 'Well, at least I'm not sleeping around like Gary.' "

"So, it wasn't just the one girl?" Marielle asked.

"Is that what Gary said?"

Marielle nodded before she remembered to say "yeah."

"I don't think it's just one girl, Mar, but I don't think Tim's a saint either. I'm thinking of breaking up with him."

"Ooh!" Marielle said with sudden energy. "That's a great idea! I'll break up with Gary and—"

"You didn't break up with him already?" Shelly asked.

"No. The conversation didn't get that far. I told him I was done talking to him and I hung up."

"But you're going to break up with him!" Shelly demanded more than asked.

"I'm torn. It's hard to get even with a guy if you're not dating him. Either way, I probably don't have to see him again. You and I can just spend the summer watching movies and tanning. Well, you can tan. I'll sit in the shade and drink Mountain Dew."

"You mean when you're not working," Shelly said with fatigue.

"True, BUT I can try to schedule my days off for the same as yours and we can have more time together."

"Okay. Good. Well, I feel better now," Shelly said unconvincingly.

"What are you doing now?"

"I'm going running. I'll think everything through on the bridge."

"What do you mean by that?!" Shelly asked with alarm.

Marielle laughed. "Sorry, I meant I'll think about it while I'm running over the bridge. I would never commit suicide over a boy, Shel, least of all Gary."

"Good," Shelly replied. "Well, have a good jog, then."

"Thanks," Marielle replied before drawing a deep breath. "And thanks for looking out for me."

"It's my job," Shelly said with kindness.

Marielle put on her old jogging shorts and t-shirt which fit better since her New York pictures shocked her into exercise. After stretching out, she took two puffs of her inhaler, then ran downstairs with her walkman as if her workout had already begun.

"I don't know why you're still running," Anna said as Marielle let the front screen door slam behind her. "It's not helping!"

After a week of running and pondering, Marielle finally accepted a phone call from Gary.

"Are you alright?" he asked with feeling.

"I'm fine. You?" she replied coldly.

"I've been miserable," he complained. "I don't know what to do with myself to feel better."

"Oh, I know what you can do with yourself," Marielle replied without humor.

"I don't blame you for being angry and I know what you said about fairness across the board, but please tell me you haven't gotten even with me yet."

Marielle smiled. "I haven't yet, but I haven't gone to Ireland yet either."

"What does that mean?" Gary asked desperately.

"I think we both know what that means."

"Do you have your ticket?"

"I do."

"Please forgive me, Marielle. I've been talking to my friends and my parents and they agree that you have every right to be angry with me."

"Excellent. I was waiting to hear their verdict before deciding how I

382

should feel. That said, I honestly don't see your father or Tim having any problem with your behavior."

"Tim hasn't been the same since Shelly broke up with him and my father has never seen me so upset. He's very worried about me."

Marielle suppressed the "poor baby" response which rattled around in her brain. Instead she said, "Well, you should go out with your wing man and help him drown his sorrows."

"Oh, Marielle. I've never heard you so cold before."

"You probably weren't listening."

"Can't you just scream and cry, or break up with me like most girls would?"

"No. If you were Catholic, you'd understand that an indefinite Purgatory is better punishment."

"What if I don't want to stay in Purgatory?" he said with sudden rebellion.

"That's your right as a Protestant."

"But then you'll never forgive me," he said, losing defiance as quickly as he found it.

"Probably not," she agreed.

"Can I just please come to your house and explain myself? Please."

"You should know that I've already told my family why I'm not accepting your phone calls. I'm not sure you'd find your visit a very comfortable one."

"Is your grandfather there?" Gary asked with sudden concern.

Marielle's hand covered laughter before she managed to say he was not.

"But you told your parents?" he asked as if *he* was the one betrayed.

"Yeah, I like to share everything with them," she said mockingly. "Though it's not like I announced it to my school or declared that I'd bed you by summer."

Gary was quiet for a moment before he said, "Just let me make this right, Marielle."

"How does one do that?" she asked, wondering why any high school relationship would be worth this much trouble. "Is there a way for you to un-screw her?"

"I still want to marry you," Gary declared, causing Marielle's mouth to drop and her stomach to turn.

"Look, I just realized I have to work this afternoon. Our little reunion will have to wait," she said, not waiting for a response before she hung up.

6/19/1989 Monday

DERMOT!!!!!

WHY DO BOYS SUCK?!! Make them go away!!

Sorry. That's not how I wanted to start this letter. Let me rewind...

How are you? I'm fine, thanks. I'm INSANELY excited that I'll be there in only two months!!

I'm sorry it has taken me awhile to return your lovely letter. It didn't arrive until a week ago and I've had boy troubles that started with Prom and didn't end after two nasty phone calls and a boyfriend I won't allow inside my house (and that's not just a euphemism). I'll tell you about it when I get there since Gary doesn't deserve any more of my paper or time, but the most important matter at hand is that I have my ticket in front of me and I thought I'd give you the details in writing. I also received my senior class pictures and I thought I'd send you one of each pose so you recognize me at the airport.

Let me also reiterate how proud I am that you and your team did so well in Wales. I would've been proud even if you lost, but I know losing would've bothered you and it would've bothered me that it bothered you. Am I making any sense? I should probably wait to write until I'm less angry... and can actually see straight.

This week, I marched in my last Flag Day Parade. You wouldn't think I'd get attached to marching in stifling heat, wearing a dark blue skirt, red wool crested coat, and white beret, but as we were coming down the main part of College Avenue with my little sister marching ten rows ahead of me—and me being a usual Nazi about the straightness of our line—it hit me that my parents and grandparents wouldn't be standing on the sidewalk to see both of us march next year, just Anna, and next year's first chair player might not keep the line of saxophones so straight, and maybe growing up and moving away isn't the best thing ever.

Anyway, that's enough of that.

I fear I've been a little reserved since the beginning of the year, and then after I started dating Gary I didn't feel like it was appropriate for me to tell you how much I care about you, but I feel no loyalty to him now and after rereading most of your letters, I have to say that you're a thousand times more interesting and smart and considerate than any guy here. Gary is a jackass and I wonder why that doesn't bother me more, but the truth is that I can't stop thinking about how much I want to spend time with you... which would be fine if I could stop thinking about what I'd like to do with you... which would be fine if I could catch my breath. So, in the end, I can't even spare enough time or mental energy to break up with Gary properly which is too bad for him because he still thinks he can win me back. To be honest though, he never really had me.

Thank you for all of your kind words and your grandfather's wisdom. He's right of course and I will remember what he said the next time I feel down.

Thank you also for mentioning that you were on summer break and I wasn't. Consider the rain there proof of my telekinetic ability to get even... so that gives you some sense of what I'm doing to Gary right now. ☺

I miss you terribly and can't wait to see you!

I love you!
Marielle

26-Jun-1989

Hi Marielle!

My parents went to Paris on Sunday and got back on Thursday. I had a wild 4 days. On Wednesday night, I went out to a disco, then a party, and got back at 7 a.m. and didn't bother going to bed. That was the best party of my life. I had a match the following Saturday. I almost fell asleep halfway through. Naturally, we lost! We came second to... guess... Shannon Hurling Club. We have a match next Saturday and we should win that, but it is going to be the hardest (and probably the last) match of my life. My parents think I need to spend more time on my studies, but my coach and team aren't pleased at all.

One of my friends went to live in Australia on Thursday (that's whose party was on Wednesday) and she was really sad going. She kept a pretty happy face until she was getting a taxi home and I was just saying goodbye and I said, "I'll miss you" and she broke down and started crying and I hate that. Being sad is the worst thing in the world. Ever since she's left, I've heard nothing but that song "Bang on the Ear" and I hear the line about someone going to Australia! Aagghh!

Fiona went to France for 3 months to work as an au pair (did I tell you that already?). We will see her in July/August when we visit France for a month. The pay is hardly anything, but she loves France so... she went. Besides, there's very little work in Galway. I wrote to her today. Do you know how small a place Ireland is? I'll tell you. When Fiona got to the airport, she met a bloke (Mike) from my class who she knows 'cos she went to Irish College with him and they were both going to Paris on the same flight.

Also, when my parents went to Paris, they met TWO of my teachers... who they know, of course.

There does be fearsome celebratin' goin' on in Paris, at all, at all! Y'see 'tis the 200th anniversary of the big CHOP (the French Revolution).

Someone tried to stab my ex-girlfriend's boyfriend. The guy who tried to stab him was also my friend so I heard great stories about it. In the end, my ex-girlfriend (the 5'11" Australian one) flattened the guy with the knife. Now, my friends know why I used to arrive scratched and bruised at training.

Did I ever tell you about my friend who smashed the beer glass on his head? Well, his mom found out she has cancer and Sean's very upset. It's up to me to keep an eye on him now - he'll probably do something really stupid. Speaking of strange friends, I can't wait until September. (Hee! Hee!)

What do you think of R.E.M., or do you even know their music? I was surprised with Jason Donovan. His last song made it into the "almost-listen-to-able" class. He's improving... I'll have to go get that Greenpeace album. It's a great organization and the music isn't bad.

I'd better go 'cos I don't really have any more news and I don't want to bore you.

ONE THING: I was telling my friend "Marielle is a real sadist. She loves teasing about having a car."

HE SAID: "Tell her that's NOT the kind of <u>drive</u> you like in a woman."

See you!

I LOVE YOU,
Dermot

"Who are you calling?" Anna asked from the top of the stairs as Marielle walked toward her carrying the cordless phone.

"Your boyfriend. Oops. I forgot you don't have one," Marielle replied.

"Neither do you," Anna declared victoriously.

Marielle continued walking. "*Au contraire.* I have like a hundred."

"Then why hasn't Gary called in a week?"

"Because he's too busy writing me cheesy letters. He can't stay away from me. I'm addictive, really," Marielle said as she closed, then locked her bedroom door.

***

"Can you believe I'm going to be there in 11 days?" she asked Dermot without saying hello or announcing herself first.

Dermot exhaled. "I know. It's fanTAStic!" he replied. "I can almost imagine you walking down the stairs in front of me. I honestly don't know how I'll manage it. My friends already think I'm going mad and smiling far too often."

"Same here. I'm alienating everyone, and my parents keep doing a double-take at me. You'd think happiness would be a good thing, but I get the distinct impression it disturbs them."

"I feel exactly the same. Just a sec," Dermot walked away from the phone for a minute. "Oh good, the car's gone. She must be out at the grocery."

"Who knew parents didn't like it when their kids were happy?" Marielle reflected.

"I think they worry over what teenagers might *do* when they're happy," Dermot suggested.

"Right, well, we should probably talk about that," Marielle said, feeling she couldn't put off the conversation any longer.

"Why? What's the matter?" Dermot asked softly as though his brogue

387

could solve any problem.

Marielle leaned forward as she whispered, "Well, when the trip was canceled in January, I made a pact with God that we wouldn't have sex if I could just make it to Ireland to see you."

"Oh, Jaysus, Marielle!" Dermot said with the last of his breath.

"Do you not want me to visit if we can't have sex?" she asked, prepared to be offended.

"Not a'tall, but I was just very much looking forward to... well... being each other's first experience."

"I know," Marielle moaned. "It's horrible. But I really think I wouldn't be able to visit if I hadn't made that pact."

Dermot breathed into the phone before he spoke. "I understand. I'll do my best to behave myself, but I promise you it won't be easy. You can't imagine the things your passport photo has seen from the wall beside my bed."

Marielle laughed. "If you had ever given me a decent picture of yourself, yours might have seen similar activity."

"I doubt that very much!" he protested.

"You shouldn't. I promise you it's true."

"I didn't think girls did that," he said with surprise.

"Well, consider your education beginning, then."

"Oh, wow. Really?" he asked excitedly. "What if you did your thing while I did my thing—in the same room, like? Would that go against your pact?"

Marielle thought for a moment. "No, I think that would be a loophole."

"Would kissing each other also be a loophole?" he asked.

"Yes, kissing is just fine," she decided.

"Marielle, I don't mean on the lips," Dermot clarified.

Marielle's eyes closed hard. When they opened, she scanned the room for her inhaler just in case. "I don't know how to do any of that," she replied as though ignorance would end discussion of the matter.

"Well, we can learn together," he said eagerly.

She drew a deep breath as areas of her body tingled. "You're making me crazy," she confessed.

"Tell me that's a good thing," he pleaded in the sexiest possible version of his voice.

"If I could think straight, I promise I'd say yes."

"Good," Dermot said decisively. "I don't want to be alone in my madness. May I ask you something you may find cheeky?"

She laughed through her nose. "Cheekier than what you've already asked?"

Dermot chuckled. "Good point. See, I know what you're saying about not having sex and I absolutely respect that, but if we use a loophole and you don't have anything with you, there's no way to get anything here and—"

"Stop," she said kindly. "Are you asking me to bring condoms?"

"Oh, God, yes," he said with relief.

"Does one use that sort of thing while kissing one another?" she asked.

"I haven't a clue."

"Okay, so I might be able to meet you halfway. My friend Joel bought me a box of six on my last day of school just in case I had a wild summer."

"*Did* you have a wild summer?" Dermot asked with too much concern to appear merely curious.

"Not wild enough to open the box. I did accidentally tell Gary just before summer break that I loved him while we were making out, but I retracted it immediately and he got pissed—angry that is. He also told me he wanted to make love to me and I started laughing at him, then told him that wasn't the proper phrase for what he wanted to do. The fighting got worse from there. Anyway, that's where it ended and that was as wild as my summer got."

Dermot released a large amount of breath.

"Are you jealous?" Marielle asked with surprise. "I thought we decided not to get jealous."

"I promise I tried to avoid it," he said with some embarrassment.

"Fine, then. I'll bring the box," she declared.

"Thank you, love," he murmured, causing her eyes to shut involuntarily.

"Marielle! Come downstairs!" Maria called from the foyer.

"Jesus!" Marielle declared. "That's my mom. I need to go."

"Alright," Dermot said. "The next time I speak with you, it will be face to face."

"Oh, God. I definitely need to get some alone time very soon," she joked.

"Where do you think I'm going right now?" he admitted.

Marielle laughed before her name was called a second time with less patience.

"I'll be right there!" she yelled toward her door.

"Sorry, love," she said to Dermot before hanging up the phone.

A moment later, she peeked over the railing, noting the frustration on her mother's face as she looked up. Whatever her parents had to say, it was important enough to waste the last 20 minutes of their lunch break.

Marielle ran downstairs, finding her parents together in the living room. She looked from her mother on the loveseat to her father on the couch, noticing more intensity from one than the other. She sat in the lonely chair which had recently moved to the area under the archway.

Jack leaned forward toward the cocktail table, holding his water glass with two hands as his knees supported his forearms. "Your mother and I have decided we don't want you going to Ireland," he declared.

Marielle gasped before looking from one parent to the other.

Maria spoke before her daughter could. "Your father and I think there's something funny going on over there and we don't feel comfortable with you traveling on your own."

"I don't understand," Marielle replied as pain mixed with confusion. "I skipped dances and parties and worked two jobs. It's less than two weeks away and I can't get my money back for the ticket anymore." She closed her eyes as tears immediately fell.

Pain registered on Jack's face as he turned toward the front windows. "Your daughter has a point," he said to his wife before grinding his back teeth.

Marielle opened her eyes in time to see the look of betrayal her mother shot at her father.

"If you didn't want her to go, you should've said so when she could still get her money back for her ticket," Jack elaborated.

"I told you in January I didn't want her to go and you agreed with me! YOU'RE the one who changed your mind so don't put this on me! You said you'd raise the boys and I'd raise the girls. So, you need to stay out of my way!"

Jack's face reddened as it picked up steam. "Who the fuck do you think you are?!" he thundered, slamming his glass on the table. "You're just angry because she didn't hide her feelings about your piece of shit brother! Don't deny it! The other two girls are so far up your family's ass it's disgusting! You didn't even ask Marielle to go to the police station with you."

"I didn't ask her because I knew she'd be no help. Just like you!" Maria yelled.

"No, that's not it. You knew we wouldn't go along with your perfect brother routine. The world is a better place now that he's dead, but it's hard to get sympathy when you admit that, and you just *love* everyone at work sending you sympathy cards and looking at you with pity, don't you? We're not built like you or your family. You think your weakness is charming, but the rest of the world just finds it pathetic!" he roared.

Marielle's eyes raced between her parents. She knew she was on her father's side, but she was beginning to wonder why.

"So, you're just going to let her go?" Maria asked in disbelief.

"Yes," Jack replied. "Marielle, you can go," he said as though the matter was settled... and Marielle had every confidence it was as she returned to her room.

21-Aug-1989

Hi Marielle!

I was going to wait for your letter before I wrote, but I'm writing this now to make certain it reaches you before you leave. My parents will both be at work on September 1st so (as I can't drive!) we won't be able to give you a lift home. I hope that's O.K. As you know, there are buses that go to Galway (no trains!) and if you ring (call?), I'll be able to meet you in Eyre Square because I won't be doing anything. My mother said she'd love to put on wellies and a straw hat and meet you at the airport with a horse

391

and cart and speak Irish, but I told her you would probably get a heart attack or something.

I went out last night (everyone goes out the day the exam results come out) and I didn't get up until 1 p.m. That's life in Ireland for ya!

My friend was really depressed 'cos he didn't get enough points (I'll explain when you arrive) to do medicine. He'll probably repeat with me next year (I used to be a year behind him).

There was a BIG article today about planes falling apart and pilots going asleep and other things like that. I hope you make it! ☺

Another man was shot and died in Ulster, but we won't be visiting there when you arrive. He's the 20th in 20 years to die (I think) from plastic bullets. I heard the IRA gets loads of money from America—you can tell me about it when you arrive…

I met two Americans from Texas on the boat from France to Ireland. One of them is eternally grateful because I found her gold bracelet on deck! I was disgusted at them—imagine they didn't even (stupid pen!) know 'Marielle Richter' from Wisconsin. I knew IMMEDIATELY they weren't Americans at all, at all!
That's all the news for now,
SEE You SOON
Lots of Love…
Dermot

Marielle hid the letter after only two readings, worried that her father might jump ship if he knew she needed to make her own way from Shannon to Galway.

She lay on her bed, listening to U2 as she considered her dilemma. Dermot again pointed to his mother as the source of their woes when he mentioned her in the same paragraph as the decision not to pick Marielle up from the airport.

She closed her eyes to the ceiling. There was no way the library would provide information on bus routes to and from Shannon Airport. This was something she needed to manage alone upon her arrival. However, her more immediate problem today was finding a decent suitcase, having searched for, then cast aside the soiled, red, hard case her mother received as a high school graduation present.

***

On the morning of August 30th, the phone rang twice before Jeanette answered it.

"Sure, she's right here," Jeanette said with widening eyes. "It's him!" she said, handing the phone to Marielle excitedly.

Marielle looked at her sister's face, hoping *him* didn't mean Gary. "Hello?" she asked tentatively,

"Hello, there," Dermot said as though easing into a soft pillow.

"Well, hello," she said brightly. "Do your parents know you're calling insanely long distance?"

Dermot laughed. "They do, actually. My father asked me to ring to tell you we'll be collecting you in Shannon Airport on Friday."

"Are you sure?" she asked gratefully.

"Quite, but I must be off. Friday cannot get here fast enough, I can tell you," he said before Marielle agreed and the line went dead.

Chapter Twenty-Seven

To an Isle in the Water

—W.B. Yeats – *To an Isle in the Water*

The last morning in August felt cooler than usual, but probably appropriate for the time of year. Marielle never noticed which morning was the last to feel like summer. That was probably a week ago now and each morning since seemed exponentially darker and colder. It was the type of morning teenagers wanted to be sick in bed, and 2% would convince their parents they were. A year ago, Marielle counted herself among the unlucky 98%—and maybe a month from now she would again—but this morning, she had showered, dressed, and tucked two more items into her suitcase well before dawn.

Marielle turned 17 the day before, but cake and a new bathrobe weren't the highlight of her week. That highlight was yet to come and would begin the second the doors closed on her plane at O'Hare since that was the moment parents on either side of the Atlantic could no longer cancel her trip.

Marielle sat on her bed, wracking her brain for anything she may have forgotten. Presents were safely packed inside the navy blue collapsible suitcase, and her bathrobe took up nearly three quarters of her gray canvas duffel bag. It was important for her mother that she bring her new bathrobe, and Marielle assumed this was meant as a talisman against Dermot seeing her not-so-sexy candy-striped, flannel nightgown.

Marielle scowled at her suitcases which were still an embarrassment, but they were new which made them appear less third-rate. Her outfit looked overly conservative in the full length mirror, but she needed to dispel Mrs. MacManus' fears as soon as she arrived. A black blouse, buttoned to the top and sealed with a broach, a green plaid drop-waist skirt with black nylons, and short-healed, black patent leather shoes would do the trick, she reasoned.

Although she packed size-seven jeans, wearing a skirt meant she didn't need to worry about the width of her thighs when she sat down in the car.

Marielle scanned her room, considering whether she would return to it the same person, or return at all. Accidents happened. There was no reason to think she might be immune to tragedy, but this seemed less likely than the possibility of running away with Dermot to get married, assuming one could marry in Ireland before turning 18.

She opened her passport to look at the twin of the photo Dermot treasured. She wore her favorite polo shirt and a wry smile, but there was nothing exceptional about it.

She walked to her dresser, deciding if she would bring extra copies of her senior pictures for anyone she might meet. There was no question the pictures were well taken. Her peach polo-esque sweater lit up her complexion of the same color and her hair nearly glowed in the back-lit, brown-hued background of the close-up photo, but the pose of her looking out the window from a distance nearly sparkled. It had been the photographer's suggestion to think of her boyfriend during this shot, and so she thought of Dermot.

Marielle grabbed one copy of each pose in case Dermot's were lost in transit, then left the remainder on her dresser for the friends and family she left behind.

She sat back on her bed to stare again at her luggage, then closed her eyes as a particular W.B. Yeats poem replayed in her mind.

I will rise and go now, and go to Innisfree... but an Irish song broke into her thoughts after the line's first reciting. She had listened to the song in a loop last week when it arrived from her record company, committing the lyrics to memory after only a half-hour.

So fill to me the parting glass,
And drink a health whate'er befalls;
Then gently rise and softly call,
Good night and joy be to you all.

***

"Are you sure you still want to go?" Jack asked as the road turned in front of Houdini Plaza. "It's not too late to change your mind ya know," he continued nervously, looking at his wife who turned to him hopefully.

"I promise I'll be fine, Dad. I won't change my mind," Marielle replied, hiding her fear well.

Jack shook his head toward his wife before Maria looked out the window again.

***

"Use the calling card to call us as soon as you arrive," Maria implored after hugging her daughter one last time.

"I promise, Mom. I'll call as soon as I get there, but don't worry. The plane ride should be easier than the bus."

"Don't talk to anyone in Milwaukee, do you understand?" Jack implored. "Just sit in the main terminal until they call the bus for O'Hare."

Marielle nodded dutifully. "I will, Dad."

She hugged her sister briefly as Jeanette told her to be safe, then watched the remnants of her family walk to the car. She waved one more time as her parents and Jeanette drove away, thinking back to Anna's goodbye earlier that morning. Anna used the same words Jeanette did, but her expression of loss surprised Marielle and she wondered what it meant.

***

Marielle sighed as the bus stopped far too long at a bank in the middle of Oshkosh. Exiting the highway and driving across town hardly seemed worthwhile when it yielded only two new passengers.

She looked out the window at the bridge on Main Street, vowing not to turn on her walkman until Fond du Lac. Although she carried two sets of spare batteries, stress over running out of power before O'Hare plagued her.

For several months, Marielle dreamed of her plane taking off at the precise moment *Where the Streets Have No Name* turned from a guitar riff into a full-fledged song. By her calculations, this occurred exactly one minute and eight seconds after the song began. If she began the song as the engines revved, she was pretty sure the wheels would leave the ground a minute later, but unfortunately she hadn't thought to test this theory on her way to New York. Anyway, the exercise was a moot one if her batteries were dead.

Marielle's head bounced against the bus window more often than it rested against it, but the discomfort provided a welcome distraction from going crazy. In 24 hours, she would arrive in Ireland, and this thought terrified her, but not more than changing buses in Milwaukee, and navigating O'Hare and Heathrow Airports did. She realized too late that she should have studied a map of the bus terminal as well as both airports, and she lamented the feeling that no list could prepare her for traveling to Ireland.

***

Marielle missed her Nikes on her walk from the bus to Milwaukee terminal, and she missed her shotgun as she sat in the dingy main seating

396

area. A homeless man felt each and every coin return of the nearby vending machines before kneeling to reach coins that rolled underneath. An elderly lady in a pink sweater held her pocketbook more closely as teenagers walked on either side of her. Two kids ran across the floor as a young mother employed the "f" word in an incomplete sentence to call them back. Not many people looked at Marielle or her suitcase, but she felt conspicuous and scrutinized just the same. She carried a library book by James Joyce, but she didn't want the distraction of reading when it seemed her life depended on remaining alert.

She looked up at the clock with regularity, wondering why her bus to Chicago hadn't boarded yet even though the schedule promised it would leave in less than 15 minutes. She got up to stand in line at the information counter before the boarding call was made and she moved to the ninth dimly-lit garage parking space where a bus displayed the words "Chicago O'Hare" above the windshield.

With trepidation, she abandoned her suitcase and duffel bag inside the open luggage compartment under the bus before sitting directly above the area to ensure no one walked away with her baggage.

She breathed a sigh of relief as the baggage compartment closed, but she didn't contemplate sleep until the bus merged onto I-94 South. However, no sooner had her eyes closed than she opened them again, afraid she might sleep through the O'Hare bus stop.

She looked out the window at the bleak highway and concrete walls until waysides became oases and signs included the name of Chicago-O'Hare.

Marielle moved to the front of the bus to ask the driver what she should expect in terms of a stop at O'Hare Airport. The man smiled at the road before asking on which airline she was traveling.

"British Air," she replied, thinking the name much more exotic than any domestic carrier.

"Well, young lady, your stop is the first one at the airport. I promise you won't miss it," he said comfortingly.

Marielle looked down at her watch as the bus drove through its second toll. It was 10:30 p.m. in Ireland.

Although technically rush hour, the traffic moved easily, only stopping briefly before the airport exit and again as the bus neared the enormous semi-circular glass and concrete airport structure.

"The next stop is yours, young lady," the bus driver said before announcing the stop to the remainder of the bus.

Marielle thanked the driver with enthusiasm before checking her purse again for her passport, tickets, and British pounds, careful to zip the purse closed before engaging the magnetic button. She scanned the seat and floor area to ensure nothing had fallen during her brief inspection, but she decided she needed to check her purse again just in case something fell and she couldn't see it.

After retrieving her bags and bidding her driver farewell, she turned to automatic doors that nearly remained open with the volume of businessmen and foreigners walking through them.

"I'm sorry, Miss. You can't check into this flight for another hour and a half," the ticket agent said after Marielle reached the front of the line. Marielle grimaced as she prepared to walk away.

"I'm only joking. Let me see your passport, please."

Marielle smiled broadly as she handed over her passport and placed her flimsy suitcase on the scale.

"Is this your first trip overseas?" the agent asked.

"Yes, ma'am. Can you tell?"

"I'm afraid so," the woman said, smiling over Marielle's passport. She efficiently detached the Chicago to London ticket from the packet, placing it on the outside of a paper sleeve before stapling the baggage claim to the inside of the sleeve along with the remainder of her tickets. The suitcase disappeared down the conveyor belt as the attendant said something about her bag and Heathrow Customs, then declared everything was in order and she could proceed to security.

Seconds after leaving the counter, Marielle looked back, realizing that in her excitement to leave, she hadn't really listened to the agent. Now, she didn't remember if the woman told her to pick up her suitcase in London or let it make its own way through Customs to Ireland. She stared at the counter, but the agent was busy with another customer and would be busy for some time given the line in front of her. Marielle turned away, but she chastised herself all the way to gate B17, and until another agent opened the boarding gate desk.

"Sorry to bother you about this," Marielle said, "but I'm wondering if you can tell me if I need to wait for my luggage in Heathrow before I go through Customs?"

"May I see your luggage claim?" the woman asked efficiently.

Marielle had no idea what the woman meant, but handed her the entire sleeve of tickets for good measure.

The woman opened the sleeve. "The baggage claim says your bags are checked through to Shannon," the woman replied.

Marielle thanked the woman before sitting down again near the window which looked eye to eye with her airplane whose cockpit appeared as a tumorous growth behind and above its nose.

She watched dusk turn into night as the airport staff attached and removed large hoses from the airplane and delivered sealed cabinets through elevated truck beds.

Baggage carts drove to and from the cargo hold with the speed and animation of circus cars, and Marielle noticed both the cart manufacturer and that of the nursing home's dishwasher were one and the same.

She looked at her watch. On just about any other night, she would be clearing the dining room right now. It seemed strange to think that someone else stood in her place, likely bored with her job and bored with life, while at the same time only a few hours south, Marielle's life was just beginning.

The flight crew greeted the gate agent as they walked through the door to the jetway. Moments later, cockpit lights switched on, illuminating the pilots.

Marielle's right hand began to shake as she debated whether she still had time to use the airport bathroom. She looked at her watch. It was nearly 2 a.m. in Ireland. Dermot was either asleep or lying in bed thinking of her. She closed her eyes for a moment to send him love as the sound system announced Flight 296 would board shortly.

Marielle stood for several minutes before her row was called, thinking the entire time that she might have easily managed the bathroom break she hadn't risked taking. Hands still shaking, she surrendered her ticket as requested, half expecting an error on the ticket, or the last-minute arrival of her parents to halt her progress. She looked around nervously as the airline worker examined her ticket, tore off two-thirds of it, and invited her to have a pleasant flight.

Marielle smiled at every airline worker and passenger with whom she made eye contact from the jetway to row 28 where a thin woman with well-coiffed, snow-white hair already sat nearest the aisle.

"I'm sorry. I'm in 28A," Marielle explained to the woman.

The lady sighed before standing, then again as Marielle remarked about how nice the airline was to already provide a blanket and pillow in her seat.

"Do you travel often?" Marielle asked as she secured her seat belt.

The woman raised her eyebrows before releasing a long breath. "I've traveled around the world," she said to the seat back in front of her.

"Do you have a favorite country or place?"

"Antarctica," the woman said, as if the word comprised a complete sentence.

"Really?" Marielle asked with excitement.

The lady said "yes" as she turned toward Marielle, but looked away again as she continued, "I'm glad I saw it so late or it would've ruined every other continent for me."

Marielle gasped as two men of Middle Eastern descent passed their row speaking in a very foreign tongue.

The woman finally grinned. "Is there something wrong?" she asked.

"No, nothing," Marielle said, beginning to look around for security. "Are people from the Middle East allowed on our planes?" she finally asked the woman confidentially.

"Why wouldn't they be? Have you never seen someone from the Middle East before?" the woman asked.

"Well, I had a boyfriend from Pakistan once, but he didn't talk like that and he dressed just like us."

"So, the only Middle Eastern people you've seen were on TV?"

"Yes, that's right. The news, actually. They were holding our embassy staff hostage, burning our flags, or wanted for questioning in either a hijacking or a bombing," Marielle said without humor. "Plus, after we accidentally blew that Iranian jetliner out of the sky last July, I gotta believe they're not happy with us."

The lady narrowed her eyes at Marielle. "You know, there's a whole population of Middle Eastern people who speak differently and dress differently and have no interest in blowing up our planes."

"Are you sure?" Marielle asked in earnest, finally causing the woman to laugh.

So preoccupied with the Middle Eastern passengers was Marielle that she didn't hear the cabin door close on flight 296. She forced herself to listen intently as the safety features of the cabin were described, following along using the card she found in the seat pocket in front of her.

She retrieved her walkman seconds after the airplane taxied over a highway, then pressed play as it turned onto the well-lit runway. She turned up the song as the engines revved, and held the cassette player tightly as sudden speed pushed Marielle against her seat. The front wheel left the ground a minute and five seconds into her song. The back wheels departed at a minute and eight!

"YES!" Marielle exclaimed, gaining the attention of several people near her before her too loud apology gained attention from the rest.

Marielle smiled at the lights and buttons above her as she listened to the *Joshua Tree* album in nearly complete peace.

An hour later, she exchanged her walkman for her James Joyce book, determined to increase her knowledge of Irish literature—if only by a few pages—before landing in London.

The white-haired lady looked at Marielle's book before turning away in disgust.

Marielle fell asleep on page ten and well before dinner, and didn't awake until the cabin crew began serving breakfast.

"Oh, no!" she said, looking out the window at what looked to be dense, snowy hills hundreds of feet below.

Her neighbor once again regarded her with annoyance.

"I think we're over Antarctica?" Marielle explained, certain the plane had taken a wrong turn.

The lady displayed shock at Marielle's ignorance before explaining those were only clouds.

"But they're so far down," she argued.

"Because we are so far up," the lady replied before turning away.

Marielle continued to look out her window, wondering if the woman could be trusted. She looked at her watch. It was 3 a.m. in Appleton and 9 a.m. in Ireland.

Before breakfast dishes were cleared, the captain confirmed they flew over Ireland, and Marielle breathed easier. It seemed strange that she would fly over the country only to return to it, but at the end of the day it was her own fault. She had the choice to change planes in JFK or Heathrow, but she chose the latter, not only because London sounded more exotic, but so her parents couldn't easily pull her home if they changed their minds.

"Where are you headed?" the white-haired lady asked Marielle, suddenly concerned or interested in her neighbor.

"I'm going to Ireland. I only have an hour and twenty minutes to change planes at Heathrow so I'm grateful I don't need to wait for my suitcase before I go through Customs."

"Are you sure?" the lady asked with skepticism.

Marielle began to worry anew. "That's what the lady at the gate said."

"I think she's wrong. You usually have to wait for your bag to go through Customs. Let's ask the stewardess," she said, pushing her own call button.

The elderly lady posed her question to the stewardess who asked to see Marielle's claim ticket before walking to the back of the plane with the entire ticket sleeve.

After several minutes, the stewardess returned. "So, I just asked a more experienced member of our crew and she said normally it would be checked through, but seeing as you're transferring to a different airline, you'll need to collect your bag before exiting Customs."

Marielle thanked the stewardess and accepted her tickets before thanking her neighbor.

"You don't have much time," the lady cautioned.

Marielle nodded before she began chewing her thumbnail. The lady looked back at Marielle twice before the plane landed as though either worried on her behalf or in awe at her ability to remain quiet.

The doors on flight 296 opened into Dermot's time zone, but Marielle didn't celebrate this fact or the opening of the cabin door in a foreign airport. She also didn't change the time on her watch since she forgot the time as soon as the stewardess made the announcement. Additionally, she felt too nervous to do the math. All she knew was that her Aer Lingus flight to Shannon left at 11:45 a.m.

Marielle stood at the baggage carousel until a nearby clock read 10:45, but no flimsy, blue, nylon bag arrived. She joined a long line at the information counter while keeping one eye on the carousel. By 11:00, she stood in front of the attendant. "Can you tell me if I need to continue to wait for my bags? My flight leaves in 45 minutes."

"You were never meant to wait on your bags, miss," the 20-something man replied. "They're checked through to Shannon."

Marielle cursed, apologized, and thanked the man before running from the carousel area. As she sped through a hall with men in white and dark blue uniforms, she asked where Customs could be found.

A blond man smiled. "You're running though it now, miss."

"Oh! Should I stop?" she asked.

"Not a'tall," he replied, chuckling.

She saw Terminal 4 signs, but knew her flight departed Terminal 1. She asked a woman at an information counter how to find Terminal 1 before questioning the answer. How could any airport be large enough to require a bus between terminals? She ran through the automatic doors to the street anyway since she was sure the information counter lady was watching. There, she asked a porter how one reached Terminal 1 and was told the same answer the information lady had given her.

"Take this bus here," the man said as a bus stopped.

"Thank you so much!" she said as she jumped onto the bus, still suspecting a hoax or a misunderstanding. She looked out the window as an Aer Lingus flight took off behind the airport. It was 11:15 a.m.

Marielle ran into the departures level of Terminal 1. Directly in front of her read a sign for International Flights; Gates 14-30; Gates 36-46; and the Eurolounge. To her left were multiple Aer Lingus check-in and baggage acceptance desks. She looked up at a monitor which displayed a gate not listed on the International Flight sign. She cursed again, then stood in line to ask a check-in clerk.

It was 11:30 a.m. when she reached the front of the line and the ticket agent searched for flight 834 in her computer.

"Is it still here?" Marielle asked anxiously.

"I'tis," the woman replied, nodding at her screen.

"Thank God!" Marielle exclaimed.

"But they've closed the cabin door," she added, looking up from her screen to Marielle.

Marielle's eyes closed as she held the counter for support. Tears began to collect in the corner of her eyes as a lump formed in her throat. "Can I get on the next one?" she barely asked.

"You'll need to fly stand-by."

"There's no other option?" she pleaded.

"You arrived with plenty of time to make this flight," the attendant scolded.

"Yes, but the—" was all Marielle could say without the lump stopping her.

The woman looked up at Marielle through the top of her eyelids.

"You are number 12 on the stand-by list, but I'll tell you now that it doesn't look good. This is a Bank Holiday weekend and all of our flights are oversold."

Marielle nodded. "Okay. Thank you," she said before walking to the one place she knew she could cry in peace.

She closed the nearly full-length door of the bathroom stall, placing her forehead against it. She glanced down at her watch before dissolving into tears. It was 11:45 a.m.

By 11:50, she told herself enough was enough. Falling to pieces wouldn't deliver her to Ireland any sooner. *Besides*, she thought, *pieces are harder to ship.* She grinned briefly at her joke before leaving the stall to wash her face in the bathroom sink. After brushing her teeth, fixing her hair, and reapplying her makeup, she left the bathroom with a more determined attitude.

She examined the black pay phone near the edge of the terminal before walking into a nearby shop to purchase a magazine, candy bar, and very foreign looking gum.

Outside the shop, Marielle paid more attention to the departures board than to her purse as she stuffed the receipt and 10 coins inside. The purse tilted wildly on its strap axis until it overturned, depositing her wallet, tickets, coins and a pack of American gum onto the floor. She looked down with foggy eyes as a man in a suit crouched down to offer assistance. After handing Marielle her items, he departed with a smile and a "cheers" just like Dermot said the British would.

She placed three coins onto a stainless steel tray before skimming the directions beside the black phone and lifting the heavy receiver. After decoding the leading numbers to dial Dermot's phone, Marielle heard a double-buzz and a "hello."

"Hello, Mrs. MacManus! This is Marielle. Have Dermot and Mr. MacManus left for the airport already?"

"Yes, they have. Is there a problem?" she asked in a disarmingly kind voice.

Marielle shut her eyes as she said, "I'm afraid so. There was a delay in Customs and I've missed my flight."

"Oh, dear. Is there a chance of you catching another?"

"I'm on stand-by for the 12:30 flight, but the ticket agent said the flights are all oversold."

"Oh, dear," Mrs. MacManus repeated.

"I'm so sorry," Marielle said quietly, near tears again.

"Not a'tall. I'll inform my husband and Dermot if they ring, but it would be best for you to ask the Aer Lingus staff to send a message to them at Shannon Airport as well."

"Right. I'll do that now," Marielle said, watching her money count down to 10 pence before adding another crown.

"I'll ring my travel agent friends to see if anything might be done on our end," Mrs. MacManus offered.

"Thank you. I'm told everything is complicated because it's a Bank Holiday weekend," Marielle added, deciding a lot of people must work in London banks for their vacation to impact the airlines.

"Ah-right. Well, phone when you know if you'll be on the half-twelve flight, then."

"Yes, ma'am," Marielle said, and added another "sorry" and a "thank you" before hanging up.

Marielle approached another ticket agent to request a message be sent to a Mr. MacManus at Shannon Airport notifying him of her missed flight.

"Certainly," the attendant said before asking the woman beside her how to send such a message.

Five minutes later, the message was sent, and Marielle made her way to a seat near a jolly, middle-aged woman who spoke to her young, bearded son. "I strongly suggest you buy them," she said.

"I don't fancy spending seven pounds on a pair of socks, Mum," he replied.

Marielle quickly did the math before siding with the son. There was no reason a person needed $12 socks.

"Well, I'm a bit tired of darning your socks, to be honest. You're old enough to buy your own," she said as amiably as one could.

The man rolled his eyes.

"You're on stand by for which flight?" the woman asked her son.

"Noon," he replied.

"To Shannon?" Marielle asked before she could stop herself.

The man looked past his mother with a grin on his face. "No, Amsterdam," he replied.

"Sorry," she said before sitting back.

"Did you miss your flight as well, dear?" the woman asked.

"I did. I'm waiting on the 12:30 flight to Shannon, but it doesn't look good."

"It's a Bank Holiday, see," the lady explained.

"I heard that, but how many people work for the banks here?" Marielle asked, causing mother and son to laugh.

"Sorry, dear. A Bank Holiday is a holiday for everyone."

"Why's that?" Marielle asked with abundant curiosity.

"I don't know, now," the lady replied as though she hadn't considered the question before. "My son missed his flight even though we left home with four hours to spare. The traffic in London is a scandal!"

"How frustrating," Marielle said, having a hard time imagining a four hour traffic jam anywhere.

"'Tis at that. Is this your first trip to London?"

"It is. It's my first time out of the country, actually. I'm terrified my parents will find out I've missed my plane and call the police to put me on the first flight back to Chicago."

"Is that where you're from, then?" the woman asked as her son regarded Marielle again.

"No, I'm from Wisconsin. It's three and a half hours north of Chicago."

"I'm not sure I know it," the woman said with a degree of remorse.

"I'm sure most people don't."

The woman chuckled before handing her son a 20-pound note with the directive to purchase two pair of socks from the shop.

Marielle's eyes widened. She was sure one could buy a package of five socks for the price the shop charged for one, but she kept the matter to herself. There was little chance the lady and her son would drive to Shopko in Menasha any time soon.

"So, do you have family in Ireland?" the lady asked.

"No, just a good friend. We're pen pals in fact, and I'm going over to meet him." Marielle felt heat rise on her face.

"Oh, how lovely," the lady replied. "What's *his* name," she asked with a twinkle in her eye.

"Dermot," Marielle said before glancing away.

"Well, mind yourself whilst you're there," the woman warned. "There's nothing as fierce as an Irish mother."

Marielle started. "Oh, well, I was worried about that, actually, but she was very kind when I called to tell her I missed my plane."

The woman chuckled. "I'm quite certain she's more than happy you missed your plane."

"I'm on the flight," the son said suddenly, holding a bag from the sock store in his hand. "I'd best be off."

Marielle said her goodbyes to both woman and son before approaching the stand-by desk.

"I'm not on the flight," Marielle said as a British Pound clicked away. "The next flight to Shannon is at 3 o'clock."

"Well, there's nothing to be done for it, then," Mrs. MacManus replied with ample breath. "Though, my travel agent friend suggested you might ask if they'll allow you to sit in a stewardess' seat."

Marielle felt a sudden shot of hope. "Okay. I will try that. Thank you and my apologies again. I will call you back as soon as I ask them."

"Are you or a member of your family employed by Aer Lingus?" the airline worker asked efficiently.

"No," Marielle admitted.

"Then, I'm afraid not."

Marielle called Mrs. MacManus again, and again she apologized.

"Not a'tall. Eamon and Dermot drove to Limerick to make a day of it. They haven't spent time, just the two of them, in ages."

Marielle felt less guilty as she set down the receiver, but she found another opportunity to apologize at 2:30 when she didn't make the 3:00 flight to Shannon either. Minutes later, she sat near several 20-something Irish men and women in the same predicament.

"Are you traveling to Dublin?" one of the men asked Marielle.

"No, Shannon," she replied.

"Well, you're in worse shape than us, then. There are far fewer flights to Shannon."

"I wonder if I could just switch to Dublin?" she pondered before a thin, dark-haired woman in a Guess shirt and jeans suggested she was traveling to Shannon as well. "Would it be wise to change to another airport?" Marielle asked.

"Not a'tall," the woman said. "We'll get a flight before these gobshites."

Marielle laughed. "If I don't make the 5 o'clock, I might just take a train to the coast and sail across."

The woman narrowed her left eye as though it was the most stupid idea she had ever heard.

"Are you from Galway?" Marielle asked.

"Not a'tall," the woman replied. "I'm from Limerick."

"Stab city," one of the men said.

She narrowed both eyes at him.

"Do you know anyone from Galway?" Marielle asked excitedly.

The woman sighed. "Well, that's a big question now, isn't it?"

Marielle sat back wondering why this woman wasn't wearing black lipstick. In any event, she was done talking to her.

***

Upon hearing she didn't make the 5:30 flight to Shannon, Marielle asked if there was anything to Dublin or Cork.

The attendant looked down at her screen. "Wait," she said hopefully. "We can actually get you onto the 5:40 flight to Cork," she said, looking up at Marielle for a split-second decision.

"Absolutely," Marielle replied.

"Alright, then," the woman said before a printer came to life.

"Really?" Marielle asked with thinly veiled enthusiasm.

The lady nodded with fatigue. This clearly hadn't been her day either.

"Oh, I love you!" Marielle declared.

The woman suddenly smiled. "Thanks a million. I needed that."

"Have a lovely day!" Marielle exclaimed while departing with her tickets.

"I'm on the 5:40 flight to Cork," she conveyed to Mrs. MacManus. "It leaves in 20 minutes so I need to run, but I will figure something out when I get there. I certainly don't expect anyone to pick me up."

"We have relation in Cork," Mrs. MacManus replied more coldly than earlier. "Let me see what can be arranged."

"Thank you so much!" Marielle said. "One quick thing though. I know Ireland uses pounds as well. Will my British money work there?"

Mrs. MacManus sighed audibly. "No. It won't. You'll need to change it when you arrive."

"Okay. I'll do that. Thank you again," she said before hanging up and running toward a sign that said "Domestic/Republic of Ireland Flights" rather than "International Flights."

Marielle sat happily in a center seat on a warm plane beside a long-haired 20-something-year-old man who had planned to go to Dublin and was angry for the inconvenience.

"I honestly don't care what airport we land in as long as it's in Ireland," Marielle said happily. "I'd gladly make my way from Belfast right now."

"You're mad," he replied, more annoyed than amused.

"Yeah, well, we fund the IRA so I thought I'd be safe as long as I go through the right sections."

The man gathered breath. "Your family supports the IRA?"

408

"No, people in the U.S. do. I'm using the collective *we*."

"Ah-right," he said, relaxing. "My band recently wrote an anti-IRA song."

Marielle looked at him with surprise. "Well, you're very brave."

"Not when you live in London."

She leaned toward him conspiratorially. "Well, I promise not to tell anyone in Cork just in case there's IRA among them."

The man smiled. "That would be much appreciated. So, you really have no idea what you'll do when we land?"

Marielle smiled broadly. "Not a clue."

"Well, fair play to you," he said, shaking his head before resting it on his seat.

Chapter Twenty-Eight

The Deep Heart's Core
—W.B. Yeats – *The Lake Isle of Innisfree*

The carousel in Cork was a fraction of the size it had been in Heathrow. In fact, it appeared even smaller than the one at Outagamie County Airport.

Marielle waited until the conveyor belt stopped before walking to the lost luggage counter to make a claim. As she moved to depart the baggage area with a red slip in hand, one of three elderly women sitting behind a long folding table requested she stop and allow the searching of her purse.

The elderly lady removed Marielle's passport, tickets, walkman, and wallet as Marielle waited with five or so passengers whose baggage, or that of a loved one, was searched as well. The woman pulled six condoms from a pocket in Marielle's wallet which should have concealed them better. The lady quickly replaced the prophylactics with a huff, but not before two men evaluated Marielle, then smiled at one another.

Marielle cringed as she retrieved her things from the woman's shaking hands while avoiding her judging eyes.

Seconds after escaping Customs through a metal door, a short middle-aged woman in a dark blue dress asked Marielle to take a survey. "Can you tell me how much you paid for your ticket from London to Cork? Was it between 50 and 80 pounds, 80 and 100 pounds, or over 100 pounds?"

"I'm sorry. I was supposed to go to Shannon. I was rerouted here and that was part of a larger ticket from Chicago."

"Oh," the lady said with disappointment just as an announcement was made for a Marielle Richter to pick up the white phone.

After scanning the walls in vain, Marielle walked to the information desk to ask where a white phone could be found. The 30-something-year-old lady motioned to her right, leading Marielle to a ringing phone around the corner. She lifted the receiver quickly, but found no one on the line. After replacing the receiver, the phone rang again.

"Hello?" Marielle said anxiously.

"Hello? Marielle?" an Irish woman's voice asked across a gravelly line.

"This is she."

"This is Margaret MacManus. Eamon and Dermot are on their way to collect you. They'll arrive shortly, and they have your luggage in hand."

Marielle leaned against the wall. "Oh, wow. That's wonderful. Thank you so much!"

"Not a'tall. We'll see you around ten, then," she said before ringing off.

Marielle glanced at the doors to Customs, knowing they were locked without testing them, and knowing she wouldn't return to retract her lost baggage claim as long as witnesses to her condom possession still stood around a table.

She scanned the faces of people in the near empty airport on the off chance Dermot was among them before remembering she only had a vague sense of his appearance. In any event, there were no six-foot-tall, teenaged boys among the waiting crowd.

She moved to a nearby chair, but sat only a moment before determining that sitting was both impossible and a waste of time if she could fix her hair and makeup before Dermot's arrival.

Marielle studied the bathroom mirror with surprise. Although her blush and lip gloss appeared faint, her face looked refreshed and happy. She also marveled at her Christie Brinkley bangs as they curved up and backward without a flaw or a break. Maximum-Super-Ultra-Hold hair spray had much to recommend itself, she decided. She reapplied her peach lip gloss before frowning at her too formal attire.

At O'Hare, a skirt, blouse, and broach only made her look Mormon. In London, it made her appear snobby. In Cork, well, she gathered from the waiting room that there was just no place for a person who dressed so formally outside of church. She rifled through her duffel bag to find her jeans and Nikes, locating a pair of Levis and one sock before feeling she had run out of time. In weighing the risk of Dermot walking into the airport while she was in the bathroom against the desire to change her clothes, the clothes lost.

Marielle zipped her bag, exited the restroom, and scanned the airport again before the setting sun drew her through sliding glass doors into the amber-tinted glass foyer beyond.

Sliding doors on either side separated the foyer from the footpath, and

Marielle made a mental note to use both sides of her peripheral vision to watch for Dermot and his father.

She scanned the parking lot, but was immediately distracted by a car driving under its own power on what she considered the wrong side of the road. After a brief moment, she reminded herself that the driver was on the proper side of the car and the proper side of the road for this particular country.

She turned her attention to the flagpole in the center of the roundabout immediately before her as a man tipped the pole onto its side. She crossed her arms and narrowed her eyebrows as she wondered if the man was fixing the pulley or retrieving the flag. The man reached for a hook just as Marielle heard the swish of sliding doors to her left and felt the space fill completely with the energy of another.

Marielle felt eyes upon her and knew without looking that they were Dermot's, which was fortuitous since she couldn't move her head. She blinked heavily, aware her inaction might be interpreted as gamesmanship, but it couldn't be helped. She wasn't above playing games, but her paralysis had nothing to do with a game and everything to do with fear. She was afraid to see the face of the boy she loved; afraid to be disappointed; afraid to be swept away; and afraid to meet the reality of too much time spent dreaming. As the boy, it was Dermot's job to be strong, Marielle decided, so she waited to be addressed or approached.

A familiar and gentle voice called Marielle's name as a question, and she summoned the nerve to turn only her head. There, two men stood frozen as if they waited many minutes in the same spot. A 60ish man wearing a tweed coat and matching hat stood in front of a teenaged boy several inches taller than himself. The boy rocked forward as though he wished to move past his father, but was precluded by propriety and the order in which they entered the space. If not for his Mediterranean complexion and short, curly, dark brown hair, Dermot might have easily passed for an American in his Levis and new running shoes whose swish matched the dark blue windbreaker he wore over a steel blue t-shirt.

Marielle stared too long into Dermot's golden brown eyes which reflected the sun and magnified his adoring smile. Instantly she realized that no human being had ever looked at her quite the same way before. Without thinking, she turned her entire body toward him, then shifted her gaze back to his father who smiled brightly in return.

She saw no resemblance between father and son. Mr. MacManus' pale, lined and dignified face reminded her of a stereotypical country lord or maybe a poet. She could even imagine him returning to his manor and shaking his head as he proclaimed there was trouble upon the moors. All he needed was a walking stick, she decided.

By the time her mind returned to the present, an awkwardness rested in the distance between them. It was the physical equivalent of a conversational pause and Marielle regretted the standoff her daydreaming caused. She would move now, or in a moment when feeling returned to her legs.

She had no idea why she felt so timid. Although she had never seen Dermot's face, she knew him well. In fact, he felt more familiar to her than anyone she had met before, and in spite of her nerves and in spite of her body's insubordination, Dermot's arrival in the foyer made this very public and strange place feel like home.

Marielle drew a deep breath to summon strength before abandoning her duffel bag. She stood on her tiptoes to deliver the hug of a clergyman, avoiding Dermot's disappointed eyes as she pulled away. She then turned to his father, looking him in the eye as she shook his hand. "I'm so sorry I kept you waiting," she said, her smile competing with her blue eyes for his attention.

"Not a'tall, young lady," Mr. MacManus replied, holding her hand with both of his. "Welcome to Ireland. We're relieved you've arrived safely. Let us grab your bag." He motioned for Dermot to retrieve the duffel bag before walking toward the doors with Marielle.

"I must thank you," Marielle began. "Mrs. MacManus said you picked up my suitcase in Shannon. How did you know it was mine?"

Dermot easily caught up to Marielle and his father to say, "Dad just waited until all the others had been collected, then assumed the last was yours. I'm only joking," he continued in response to the concern on Marielle's face. "The luggage tag from the airline displayed your name."

"Dermot, the boot should be open," his father said as they approached a newish silver Toyota.

Inside the trunk, Marielle's nylon suitcase looked more cheap and tacky than it did in the U.S., wrapped as it was by an embarrassingly bright fluorescent green strap with black lettering declaring it was added at Heathrow to secure the bag in transit.

Dermot placed the gray canvas duffel bag on top of the suitcase and closed the hatchback. He attempted to make eye contact with Marielle, but she effectively turned away, concealing her embarrassment. For all the money she earned and planning she had done, she still managed to bring a plastic purse, a boring duffel bag, and a tacky suitcase while arriving in Ireland shockingly late and overdressed. *Great first impression!* she chided herself.

"Why don't you sit in the back with Dermot," Mr. MacManus suggested as he approached the Irish version of the driver's-side door.

Dermot shared the surprise he found on Marielle's face, but climbed into the car behind the driver's seat without questioning his father. Marielle walked to the passenger's-side door, surprised to find Dermot had slid to that slide. She laughed as she ran around the back of the car to the driver's side, opening the rear door just as Dermot returned to that side. Before Marielle could close the door, Dermot lifted his hand as he said, "Wait!" then slid quickly to the passenger's side of the car, patting his recently vacated seat as his laughter became a smile.

Marielle turned from him as color rose on her cheeks, but her peripheral vision told her Dermot was staring at her. She secured her seat belt despite shaking hands, then looked at Mr. MacManus through the rear view mirror as he used the same to happily study his son's face. Seconds later, the car backed from its parking space at twice the speed Marielle's driving instructor would have endorsed.

"You've had quite a day now, haven't you, young lady?" Mr. MacManus remarked through the mirror while shifting into first gear.

She leaned forward, "Yes, sir. I feel terrible that you both spent your day driving around the country waiting for me."

"Not a'tall. Dermot and I rarely get the opportunity to spend time together, just the two of us. So, what exactly transpired at Heathrow?"

"Well, the stewardess on the flight from Chicago to London told me I needed to wait for my bags before going through Customs," she began, then related the events up to and until she asked for a message to be sent to Shannon.

"They sent it," Dermot interrupted, "but they made the announcement to a MRS. MacManus." He chuckled.

"Did they really?" Marielle asked with a smile that fear overtook.

"Would they not put you on the next flight since it was *their* affiliate's stewardess who made the error?" Mr. MacManus asked.

Marielle didn't know how to respond to this question without admitting that she hadn't told Aer Lingus of the error, having nearly broken down at the counter. "No, sir," she replied with less indignation than a moment ago. "They said I had plenty of time to make the connection and it was my fault I missed the flight. I asked them if there were any flights to anywhere in Ireland, even to Belfast—"

"Well, now, I'm afraid we wouldn't have been able to collect you from Belfast," replied Mr. MacManus with a serious face to match his tone.

Dermot nodded, and to Marielle he said, "It would be very dangerous to have a car reg from the Republic whilst inside the North."

Marielle glanced at Dermot. "The IRA wouldn't bother you, would they?"

"No, but the Orangemen might and you wouldn't risk it, like."

"I find a lot of people in the U.S. confuse Northern Ireland with the rest of the country," Marielle said with an air of superiority. "I told my parents' boss I would be perfectly safe in the south and she said it looked close enough to the North on a map."

Mr. MacManus drew a deep breath through his nose. "I suppose that's true, but we rarely see violence in the south now, I have to say. All the same, there seems little hope the Troubles will be over any time soon."

Marielle leaned forward again. "My dad said he doesn't understand why people in the North don't just move. He said when the south side of Chicago became dangerous, people moved out and they could do the same in Ireland."

It didn't take a great deal of silence for Marielle to appreciate she had said something terribly wrong. She sat back in her seat, determined not to allow her father's opinions on foreign policy issues to surface again. To Dermot she said, "You know, on the way to Chicago I saw a license plate with the letters T-Q-U-I-L-A on it. I thought that was a good way to give the police probable cause to stop you for drunk driving."

"Dad, did you know Americans can buy number plates with whatever they like on them?" Dermot asked.

Mr. MacManus nodded appreciatively.

"Well, not *anything* we like," Marielle countered. "You can't curse, for example, and it costs more than a regular plate."

"How much more?" Dermot asked, appraising her with a slight grin.

"About fifty dollars, I think."

Jealousy shook Dermot's head. "A while back, a license plate with the word 'VIP 1' was auctioned off for nearly 300,000 quid, I believe."

"That's nuts!" Marielle replied. "I don't know why you'd want a personalized plate anyway. If you were a kid, it would be too easy for your parents to track you down, and if you were a criminal, it would be too easy for witnesses to remember your license plate as you left the scene of a crime."

A smile overcame Dermot's face. "In both cases, that presumes you'd be doing something wrong, doesn't it?"

Marielle smiled back, then quickly turned again. "I suppose it does," she agreed. "Did I tell you that I asked a physics teacher about the car crash conundrum we discussed a few months ago? You know if two cars were the same size, weight and structure, and one was going 30mph while another was going 60 when they hit head on?"

"Right," Dermot said with a single nod. "And which car would sustain more damage?"

"Surprisingly, they'd have the same amount of damage, but the 30mph car would be pushed backwards a certain distance. I can't remember how far, now. My teacher said the force would be incredible and if you had the choice of hitting another car or a brick wall, you should choose the brick wall instead."

"It would be nice to have a choice in an accident," Dermot reflected.

"True," Marielle agreed. "If I had a choice, I'd choose NOT to be hit by a drunk driver. They always survive and the people they hit always die."

"Unless they hit a lorry or a tree," Dermot reasoned.

"*Ja,* but in a car a drunk driver always beats a sober one. I was thinking the other night that I'd like to buy an old WWII missile and attach it to the top of my car. That way, if a drunk driver kills me in an accident, I'd take him with me."

Dermot nodded thoughtfully. "But what if his family is in the car as well?"

Marielle turned toward him with an air of contempt. "Why are you ruining my fun? When someone's contemplating revenge she doesn't want to worry about those who may be hurt in the crossfire."

"Sorry," Dermot said as his eyes penetrated her.

Marielle turned away. "Do you know what the penalty is for the second drunk driving offense in El Salvador?" she asked.

"No, what?"

"Nothing. Because the penalty for the first offense is death."

"Is that true?" Dermot asked with a healthy degree of scepticism.

Marielle chuckled as she glanced back at him. "I don't know, actually. A kid at school said so once and it makes for a good story."

"Dermot tells me you have your driver's licence, Marielle," Mr. MacManus said through the rear view mirror.

"Yes, sir, I do. We get it when we're 16," she replied, casting a playful sideways glance toward Dermot.

"Do you have it on you?" Dermot asked. "I fancy destroying it, if I might."

"Sure," she said, looking for her license while taking pains to keep the condoms hidden. "You'll have a hard time ripping it though. It's laminated."

"This is quite small," Dermot noted, holding it up to the last of the day's light. "But it's not a terrible photo a'tall. I showed your latest photographs to Sean and he said what a pity you weren't here for the Rose of Tralee competition."

Marielle took a sudden breath as her eyebrows furrowed.

"What?" Dermot asked, looking up from the licence.

"Doesn't the Rose of Tralee have a reputation for being a tart?" she whispered.

He smiled. "Well, yes, but that's not how he meant it."

"Oh, sorry," she said. "What do your licenses look like... I mean, *if* you had a license?" Marielle asked, smiling mischievously while returning her card to her wallet.

"I refuse to answer that question on account of your rudeness!" Dermot declared.

"I'm sorry," she said, looking at him as he moved his gaze to the front of the car.

"You're not a'tall!" he protested.

She smiled at his cheek. "You're right, but I'm sorry I'm not sorry."

"I suppose that will have to do," he said, smiling as he reached for her hand.

Marielle looked quickly toward the front seat, then relaxed once she confirmed Mr. MacManus was unaware of his son's movement. "You have soft hands," she whispered.

"Yes, well, I'm not working two jobs like some people I know," he replied, staring at the side of Marielle's face as he squeezed her hand.

"I'm only working one job now. Although I suppose babysitting could count as the second." She squeezed back.

Dermot squeezed her hand harder which Marielle answered in kind.

If Dermot hadn't meant to engage Marielle in a game of Mercy, he was up for the challenge once presented. He tried valiantly to counter her escalating pressure, but a year of loading stacks of plates sideways into a dishwashing rack made Marielle a worthy opponent.

"Mercy!" he called out.

Marielle's eyes widened unnaturally in an attempt to quiet him. "No way!" she whispered. "You're just being nice."

"I'm not a'tall. I'm quite serious," he replied in an outdoor voice. "You almost crushed my hand." Dermot looked at his father. "Dad, she has the strongest hands of any girl I've ever met!"

Marielle watched Mr. MacManus nod once while his eyes smiled at his son.

"Okay, let's try again, and don't let me win this time," she said as her eyes narrowed slightly.

"Alright," he replied, "but I'm absolutely serious. Your hands are immensely strong."

"That's because I have superior German genetics. You should see a picture of my brother Stephen. He looks like Dolph Lundgren now."

"I'd rather not, thank you," Dermot said curtly

"Actually, he used to look like Boris Becker. People on the street in West Germany would ask him for his autograph all the time. He got tired of explaining he wasn't Boris, so he just started signing autographs."

"As Boris or as himself?" Dermot asked.

"As Boris. You'd think his inability to say anything in German unrelated to ordering beer would tip people off, but apparently not."

"Well, everyone in Germany speaks English anyway," Dermot remarked.

"That's what our German teacher said, and she got mad when someone asked why we were wasting time learning German, then."

"That lazy attitude must be why your test scores are so low," Dermot reflected a second before he smiled.

Marielle squeezed his hand until he cried "Mercy."

"By the way, those results are skewed," she said firmly. "Wisconsin, Minnesota, and Iowa always rank highest in the nation and would rank much higher internationally if not averaged together with underperforming states."

Mr. MacManus nodded as though accepting her explanation.

"Marielle, are there many illegal drugs in American schools?"

She replied without considering the question fully. "*Ja.* Actually, a boy sold marijuana out of his locker in Middle School, or so everyone said. I don't think it's generally a problem for a kid to get drugs in school. You just have to have the right upbringing to avoid them," she explained, then realized that in elevating herself, she just insulted her classmates, her school, and her country. She sat quietly for a moment, feeling like a traitor.

"I love how you say 'yes' like a German," Dermot remarked with amusement.

"Pardon?" she asked.

"You said '*ja*' instead of 'yeah' again."

"Oh right. It comes and goes, but no one ever notices it in Wisconsin."

"Marielle," Mr. MacManus began, "were both of your brothers in the Army?"

"*Ja,*" she said, then stopped for a second to smile at Dermot. "Yes, I mean. They were, but they're both out now. I guess you would call them Army veterans."

"Would you use the term 'veteran' to describe them?" Mr. MacManus asked.

Marielle squinted.

"For us, the word *veteran* refers to a person of retirement age," Mr. MacManus explained. "We wouldn't use it to describe a young ex-military person."

"Really?" Marielle asked, leaning forward. "For us, it means anyone who was previously in the military no matter what their age."

"Is your oldest brother still planning on working for the CIA?" Dermot asked.

"No, John is in California now. The CIA contacted him over six months after he applied and he was annoyed by the delay."

"I saw a documentary on the agency, and there is apparently a very high standard to qualify for a job there," Dermot remarked.

"Then you know more than me," she replied.

"More than *I*," Dermot corrected.

Marielle squeezed Dermot's hand, forgetting his eagerness to compete. Dermot squeezed back and they were playing Mercy again.

"Now, see, this is where Fiona would cry 'Mercy,' " Dermot remarked before a look of intensity overcame his face.

Marielle squeezed as hard as she could, determined to win or die trying.

"Ow! Mercy!" Dermot declared.

"Yes!" Marielle whisper-yelled, raising both arms in a half-field-goal pose.

"Wait, now, that's my right hand," Dermot said with sudden relief.

"And it's *my* left," Marielle argued.

"Ah-right," he replied, his disappointed eyes giving way to a smile.

"Do you want to play again?" she asked hopefully.

"Not a'tall!" Dermot said, pretending to brood.

"I'll let you win this time," she said leaning toward him.

"No. I'm officially retired. You've broken my spirit, and my hand… nearly."

Marielle sat back, looking at Dermot as he stared straight ahead. *A boy from Wisconsin would never admit to a girl beating him,* she thought. The last time she played Mercy with Gary, he allowed his hand to go limp rather than admitting defeat.

She drew a concerned breath. She knew she liked Dermot, but she was beginning to feel a great deal more for him than she liked.

"It's getting warm in here," Dermot said, removing his windcheater. "Hey, let me see your forearm," he requested, looking at Marielle's blouse-covered arms.

"Why?" she asked with suspicion.

"Please?" he asked, employing kind eyes and raised eyebrows.

Marielle unconsciously raised her own eyebrows before rolling up her left sleeve.

"Aha!" Dermot declared, holding his forearm against hers in the twilight. "My tan is darker than yours."

"It is. You win," she said matter-of-factly. "I actually stopped laying out in 5th grade. I read that it causes skin cancer."

Dermot looked at her as though she declared cannibalism a good source of protein. "Having skin cancer and a tan would be much better than the alternative," he argued.

"You mean living long and looking healthy?" she asked.

"No, looking white and pasty."

"You only say that because you don't see the sun that often. The sun is pretty common for us even when it's cold out. We get a tan skiing or doing everyday activities. See, you're not that much darker than me and I'm not even trying."

"Than *I*," Dermot said, correcting her grammar again, and causing Marielle to laugh.

"Marielle, how warm would it be in Wisconsin right now?" Mr. MacManus asked.

She felt startled at the reminder that Dermot's father could hear everything they said, compelling her once again to answer before seriously considering the truth. "About 95 degrees," she said, immediately realizing she was at least 15 degrees off. Good faith required her to correct herself, but she didn't wish to sound indecisive, and Mr. MacManus probably didn't know what 95 degrees Fahrenheit meant anyway, she reasoned. Just then, she noticed the speedometer displayed miles per hour rather than kilometers. *Maybe he knew what 95 degrees Fahrenheit meant after all.*

"I see the line separating opposing traffic is white and the line along the curb is yellow," she said in an effort to change the subject. "That's the opposite from home. It would be really confusing to drive a stick shift car using the opposite hand; on the opposite side of the road; on the opposite side of the car; when the lines mean the opposite of what they mean back home."

"Yeah, Americans are causing accidents here on a regular basis," Dermot said. "Dad, didn't Matthew Broderick kill an entire family a couple years back?"

"A woman and her daughter. In Enniskillen," he clarified.

An unfortunate name for a town, Marielle thought, wondering who would drive in a place with the word "kill" in it.

"I would never drive here," Marielle declared. "I'd be too afraid *I'd* kill an entire family. Did you have a hard time driving in France, Mr. MacManus?"

"Not a'tall," he replied. "We're accustomed to switching back and forth at this stage."

"We'd tell Dad if it was safe to change lanes though," Dermot noted.

"A fair few people looked at me twice on occasion when they didn't see anyone on the driver's side of the car now, I have to say," Mr. MacManus shared, chuckling quietly at the memory.

"I did the same thing in front of the airport," Marielle admitted, staring through Dermot's window. "I notice that the yellow line along the curb is sometimes zigzagged and sometimes straight. And when it's straight, it's sometimes a single line and sometimes doubled. What does that mean?" she asked.

"Well, a single yellow line beside the kerb means you can't park a'tall," Dermot explained.

"And the double yellow line?"

"You can't park a'tall, a'tall." He smiled.

"But there's a car—" Marielle pointed.

Dermot laughed. "Right, people park there anyway."

Yellow lines and Irish rebellion against them fascinated Marielle and she wondered why Dermot had never told her about them before. She was sure at this moment that he couldn't possibly say anything she wouldn't find noteworthy. "I approve of your country's rebellious nature," she declared.

"If you want to hear rebellion, you should read what people are saying about the new fishing licences. Hey, Dad?"

"Oh, stop!" Mr. MacManus said more as an exclamation than a command. "Do you see there the Blarney Stone, Marielle?"

She looked up, expecting to see the actual stone, but it was just a brown sign indicating one turned soon to reach Blarney Castle.

"One is said to get the gift of gab by kissing it. Have you ever heard of it, Marielle?" Mr. MacManus asked.

"Yes, sir. I read about it, actually. Didn't Queen Elizabeth I try to gain possession of the castle from someone named McCarthy and either he or the man she sent to negotiate responded to her with very flattering letters, but avoided giving her the land so she yelled, 'Blarney, Blarney. I cannot believe what he says!' or something like that?"

"I believe so," Mr. MacManus said, regarding her with new eyes.

"You know more about Irish history than I do," Dermot noted.

Marielle smiled as she appreciated Dermot's sentiment while doubting his sincerity. "I was expecting to see more thatched cottages," she said as a question to Mr. MacManus, but his son answered instead.

"The fire insurance is very expensive."

"Actually, you can't get insurance on them a'tall," Mr. MacManus interjected.

"That's too bad," said Marielle. "I always thought having a thatched cottage on a cliff overlooking the sea was the place I'd like to live and die."

Dermot squeezed Marielle's hand, but it wasn't a challenge. She smiled at him before looking out his window again.

Well-lit gas stations appeared every few miles with familiar names like "Shell" and "Texaco" along with unfamiliar names such as "Esso" and "Jet"—the latter painted a deep shade of purple. Marielle was sure gas stations never made it into movies about Ireland so she felt privileged to see the country behind its curtain.

At one point, she was certain she witnessed a scene from *The Quiet Man* as an elderly man wearing a fisherman's sweater and a tweed hat rode a bicycle along the side of the road. On second thought, the vision was probably a side-effect of fatigue, she decided before resting her head against the back of her seat.

"Please don't go to sleep," Dermot pleaded in a startlingly soft brogue.

Marielle lifted her head. "I'll try," she said, smiling. "But I haven't slept in," she counted in her head, then gave up, "31 hours, I think. Would you like a stick of gum?" she asked, reaching into her purse. "I bought a pack of English gum in Heathrow and I brought my favorite lime-green gum from America. You choose," she said, holding out both packs.

Dermot chose the American gum.

"Good choice," she said, grabbing the same for herself. "So, is it true that Galway City is the capital of one of the four provinces which is—" Her right eye squinted as Dermot waited expectantly and his father smiled. "—Connaught," she said.

"Well done!" Mr. MacManus replied.

"And Galway means foreigner," she continued.

"Right. There is a wall around Galway City," Mr. MacManus began, looking for Marielle to finish.

"*Ja,* and there were 14 tribes inside," she said tentatively.

"Families, actually, but well done again," he said happily.

Dermot looked between his father and Marielle, amused by the game they were playing.

"Right, right, and one was named Lynch," Marielle added. "The word lynching actually comes from a man being hanged from Lynch's Castle, right?"

"It does," Mr. MacManus said with enthusiasm.

"It's a bank now," Dermot noted.

"And another family is named Browne," Marielle continued, ignoring Dermot's comment.

Mr. MacManus nodded.

"And another was O'Brien?" she asked her right eye.

"Ah-no," Mr. MacManus said as if the game was over. "Actually, there was a saying that no Micks or O's were permitted inside the walls of Galway City."

"Bah, that sounds right now that you say it. I'm an abject failure," she said, only half in jest.

"Not a'tall," Dermot and his father nearly said in unison.

"You know, they're finding new bits of the wall nearly every day now," Dermot remarked.

"Do you never find it interesting that old things are always under so much dirt?" Marielle asked.

"What do you mean?" he asked. "You mean, below dirt rather than above the surface?"

"*Ja.* If no matter is ever created or destroyed, where does all this dirt come from? Is dirt just magnetically pulled toward old stuff? And would rotten leaves, trees, and dust account for all that dirt?"

"Well, in volcanic regions—" Dermot began.

"Okay, volcanic regions notwithstanding," Marielle interrupted. "I understand why Pompeii is buried, but I don't understand why a place like Galway would be."

"Hmm, good question," Dermot agreed. "Maybe that's just what happens when you stop sweeping."

Marielle guffawed. "That should be a warning to all messy people!"

Dermot's smile changed suddenly as he studied Marielle, causing her to stop laughing as her heart began to race. Dermot's eyes shifted toward his father's seat before he sighed.

The car slowed as it entered a small village, and they passed a car struggling to parallel park in front of a gas-lit pub.

"You know," Dermot said. "I invented a car that would parallel park with all four wheels turning?"

"They actually have those now," Marielle noted.

"Yeah, but in my car, the wheels would turn a full 90 degrees. So, one could pull up beside a spot and slide right into it."

"Ooh, that would be much easier," Marielle remarked. "I would've loved that car during my driving test. You know, I invented liposuction before plastic surgeons did? But with my invention you could hook up your thigh to the household vacuum."

"Eww, disgusting!" Dermot declared.

424

Marielle nodded. "I know. More so if it's your job to clean the vacuum."

Dermot laughed before moving his fingers lightly between hers. "You know, my friends will tease you mercilessly about your accent."

"Why's that?" his father interjected.

Dermot looked up quickly. "Well, Sean said American accents sound like silverware landing on ceramic tile."

"I rather like American accents," Mr. MacManus declared.

"Really?!" Dermot asked as though he had never heard anything positive about Americans in his life.

"I do."

Dermot eyed Marielle. "Well, at least yours isn't as bad as that girl's from Texas."

"On the ferry to France?" she asked.

"Back from France, actually. It was desperate. I couldn't understand a thing she said to me."

Marielle smiled. "My mom's dad has a southern accent. My dad always says it sounds like he has cow dung in his mouth. He actually puts it more rudely than that, but he never says it to Grandpa's face since Grandpa killed a few men in World War II. I actually saw my dad remove his arm from my mom when Grandpa told that story. It was really funny because he said, 'Don't let anyone tell you it doesn't bother you the first five times you kill a man with a dagger.' "

Dermot put his head back to laugh as Marielle grabbed the door handle to stabilize herself around a corner.

"By the way, I ask for no particular reason, but what is the speed limit here?" she asked Dermot quietly.

"Fifty-five, I think," he replied.

"Even on these roads?" she asked with surprise.

Dermot lowered his chin slightly. "What do you mean?"

"Well, I don't mean any offense at all, but they're so narrow, and there are so many blind corners, and potholes, and walls that look like they're ready to fall into the road."

Dermot chuckled. "You sound like our French friends. You should see the nice letter they left us about the very same thing."

"French friends?" Marielle asked.

"The people we switched houses with this summer. They left a note telling us everything they hated about Ireland."

"It's funny you say that because leaving a letter that rude is something Americans associate with the French."

"Yes, but you just said the very same thing," Dermot argued.

"True, but I didn't want you to take offense, and your *friends* probably didn't care whether you took offense or not."

"In defence of the French," Dermot began, "they have wonderful roads don't they, Dad? How are the roads in the U.S.?"

"County roads are always terrible, but the interstates are usually pretty good, except during the summer when they're always under construction. My dad says there are two seasons in Wisconsin—winter and construction. Last year, our economics class studied the impact of highways on local economies and you'd be amazed at how much road construction increases wealth. Specifically, we studied the positive economic impact of a new highway built between Milwaukee and Green Bay."

"And what was the impact?" Dermot asked with interest.

"Well, time-wise it reduced the trip by 30 minutes."

"And in terms of increased wealth?"

"Scientifically speaking," Marielle cupped her hand toward Dermot as she whispered, "it was a shitload."

Dermot guffawed.

"What was that, Marielle?" Mr. MacManus asked.

"She said—OW!" Dermot said as Marielle squeezed his hand.

"I said it was approximately $3.6 million dollars per year, sir. Did I tell you they served me liquor on the airplane? They asked if I wanted a liqueur, and I asked what that was and they picked up a Bailey's Irish Cream and I thought, "Oh, liquor.""

"It's not actually the same thing, Marielle," Mr. MacManus corrected.

Her eyebrows furrowed. "Really? I always thought saying liquor and liqueur was redundant, or is that synonymous?"

"What do you mean by redundant?" Mr. MacManus asked.

"That would be like saying George Washington's white horse was pale," Marielle explained. "The horse is obviously pale because it's white so the description is redundant."

"Ah," Mr. MacManus said with interest. "For us, something is redundant if it is no longer useful. So, for example, a horse and cart are redundant if you own a car."

"Really?! That's very interesting," Marielle replied. "It's almost a completely different language."

426

"Listen to this," Mr. MacManus said, reaching forward to turn up the radio. "It's your first taste of traditional Irish music."

Dermot rolled his eyes as a fiddler began to play.

"Would you call this Trad?" asked Marielle, leaning forward again.

"Exactly," Mr. MacManus said happily. "I have to say I'm impressed by your grasp of Irish history and culture."

Marielle said thank you as she looked away.

"What he's saying to you is that he thought, based upon your national test scores, that all Americans were eejits," Dermot said with a smile until his father looked at him through the mirror with his eyebrows furrowed.

"So, Dermot tells me you hold two jobs, you're musically inclined, and you study Irish culture in your spare time," Mr. MacManus said as if schooling his son on how to treat a guest.

"Well, I can't take credit for the musical thing since it's genetic," Marielle replied. "My grandfather was a professional drummer. He actually played for Al Capone in his hotel in Chicago for New Year's one year. But regarding everything else, I find there's an amazing amount of time available if you don't watch TV or sleep."

Mr. MacManus nodded with satisfaction.

"I actually checked out a James Joyce book at the library before I left Appleton so I could understand Irish literature better. So far, I've only read William Butler Yeats. But I'm only on page 10 now, so I won't be able to discuss Joyce intelligently for a few days."

"Which book is that, Marielle?" Mr. MacManus asked.

"Let me think for a second. I keep calling it the *Odyssey* but it's definitely not the title, but it's related somehow, and it's one word and it starts with a vowel."

"*Ulysses?*" asked Mr. MacManus, studying Marielle through the rear view mirror.

"That's it!" she exclaimed.

Dermot looked at the roof of the car as he and his father surrendered to laughter.

"What's wrong?" she asked, her eyes moving from one Irishman to the other.

"If you keep reading you'll discover soon enough," Mr. MacManus explained.

"Is it a bad book?" she asked with concern.

"It depends upon your definition of *bad*," Dermot replied. "It was banned here until, when would you say, Dad?"

"It's probably still banned," Mr. MacManus joked.

Marielle put her right hand over her mouth.

Dermot smiled. "It's okay, we shan't turn you in."

"Well, let's not be hasty, Dermot," his father said. "I'm not sure we can support the introduction of such filth into our society."

"But I thought James Joyce was a celebrated Irish author?" Marielle asked with dismay.

"He was," Mr. MacManus replied. "Just not here, during his lifetime. *Ulysses* in particular is sexually provocative and Joyce writes with thinly veiled references to people in Dublin. Anyone reading at the time might have easily understood to whom his writing referred."

"But I thought this was considered one of his best books and there's a festival in Dublin each year that follows the path the main character takes in the book," she said, still disheartened. "That's what my librarian told me. She never said a thing about it being banned. I was actually planning to check out *Portrait of An Artist* instead because it was thinner."

Dermot chuckled. "Well, maybe your librarian has a sense of humour."

"Or maybe she hates me!" Marielle said, feeling betrayed. "Is there a place in your house where I can hide the book during my stay, like a safe or a secret room?"

"Best of luck to you on that," Mr. MacManus replied. "The *Gardai* have dogs that are trained to sniff out that particular book."

Mr. MacManus and Dermot began a new round of laughter which Marielle eventually joined.

***

"I hope you don't mind, Marielle, but I'd like us to stop at one of my favourite pubs for a celebratory drink," Mr. MacManus proposed, slowing in front of a well-lit, one story, yellow stucco building several yards in front of a castle.

"Durty Nelly's?" Dermot asked.

"Naturally," his father replied, turning into the gravel car park.

As they walked toward the entrance, Mr. MacManus pointed at the sign above the entryway. "That's the Irish word for welcome."

"How do you pronounce it?" Marielle asked.

"Fall-cha," Mr. MacManus replied, then smiled at Marielle as she repeated *fáilte* twice. "Now, keep this stop secret you both," Mr.

428

MacManus urged as he opened the door, looking at his son in earnest. "Your mother wouldn't be impressed."

"On my honor," Marielle replied, raising her right hand. "So, why do they call it *durty*?"

"Because they didn't clean the glasses," Mr. MacManus answered as all three became awash in warm yellow light. "People placed their used glasses on the fireplace mantel or bar and someone else would pick them up to use them."

"But we have every assurance they wash them now," Dermot said, smiling.

"What would you like to drink?" Mr. MacManus asked Marielle enthusiastically as they stopped near a black fireplace mantel. "Anything a'tall."

Marielle smiled. "I honestly would just like a Coke if that's alright?"

"I'll have the same, Dad," Dermot said, turning to Marielle until he noticed his father still studied him for the truth. Dermot nodded a confirmation to his father before turning back to Marielle with a growing smile. "You're not looking at my spot are you?" he asked, reaching up to the tiniest blemish on his left cheek.

"No," she replied, pimples being the very last thing on her mind. "I didn't even see that before you pointed it out."

"Don't you hate when you go to sleep with perfectly clear skin and you wake up the next day with a giant spot on your cheek?"

"I wouldn't call that a giant spot," Marielle argued, "and, I haven't been to sleep in awhile, but I know what you mean."

Dermot inhaled slowly as he looked from one of her eyes to the other. "I can't believe you're really here. May I touch you to confirm you're real?"

"It depends on *where* you plan to touch me," Marielle replied, smiling mischievously.

Dermot's eyes expanded for a fraction of a second. "You must have a thousand boyfriends back home."

"No. Only one, and he annoys the crap out of me. Did I tell you about the case of the missing condom?" she asked as American tourists began singing Irish folk songs at the bar in the adjoining room.

"Not a'tall," Dermot said, prepared to be amused.

"So, Gary calls me one morning saying he's only telling me this story because he's sure I'll find out anyway, and he proceeds to say that this slutty girl from Kaukauna (he actually called her that) was at his house the night before with a bunch of other people—he was having a party—and everyone was too drunk to go home and this girl slept on his bed. So, I say, 'oh, alright' because I honestly couldn't give a crap who sleeps on his bed, but he's breathing funny and acting weird like he wants me to pursue this train of thought. So, I play along and ask if there's anything else he wants to tell me and he seems relieved actually and says really dramatically, 'I had three condoms in my top drawer when I went to bed, and only two were there when I woke up.' So, I'm thinking maybe someone at the party took one, but I finally ask him if he slept with the girl, and he said he doesn't remember doing it, but *she* says they did, and he wouldn't believe her except the condom is missing."

"You're joking!" Dermot exclaimed.

"I wish I was. So, I'm a little shocked that he slept with a girl he calls a slut and I'm a little shocked that he told me all about it. I'm also shocked that I don't give a crap, but it occurs to me that the only reason he told me is because I won't sleep with him and he must think this story will make me jealous enough to change my mind. So, that part I find amusing and I think I might laugh, and my voice cracks, and he thinks I'm crying and he actually sounds happy because I guess my role is to be crushed so he can call his friends to tell them how jealous and upset I am. I guess drama is how we determine how much we love each other."

"Do you love him?" Dermot asked, concernedly.

"Well, I don't want him dying in a fiery car crash, but, no, I don't love him. We were making out once in the back seat of his car and in the heat of the moment I accidentally told him I loved him, but I retracted it immediately. Wait. I think I told you that already."

"Perhaps. What did he say?" Dermot asked with enthusiasm.

"Again, he got really dramatic like he'd watched too many soap operas and said, 'Someday I'll deserve your love,' " Marielle said in a mockingly breathless voice.

"And you couldn't stop laughing," Dermot said proudly.

Marielle looked at him lovingly before she said, "God, you know me so well! I have to say, he's so emotional, I almost feel like a lesbian for dating him. He got out of the car and started walking along the road and he had the keys so I had to go after him and pretend I cared about his feelings or anything besides getting home safely. I also had to stop myself from asking if he was on his period."

They both laughed as Mr. MacManus arrived, handing each of them a small glass of lukewarm Coke.

Marielle thanked Mr. MacManus, took a drink, then raised the glass to examine the bottom.

Dermot did the same as his father laughed.

"Well, I can't tell you what it means that you'd use your hard-earned money to journey to our part of the world, Marielle," Mr. MacManus said, his posture relaxed and his expression appreciative.

"Thank you," she replied with an enormous grin. "I can't tell you what it means to visit your part of the world."

Mr. MacManus smiled at his son as Dermot beamed at Marielle, and in that one instant, everything in the world was perfect.

***

"Now, up the road here is where you were meant to land, Marielle," Mr. MacManus said as they drove along a dark road.

"I'm so sorry about that," she said as her breath escaped her.

"Not a'tall," Mr. MacManus replied.

"Is it true that Charles Lindbergh scouted out this area personally as an employee for Pan Am?" Marielle asked suddenly.

"I hadn't heard that, actually," Dermot replied.

"Nor have I," his father admitted.

"It was in a biography I read about him. He was tasked to find a good place for an international airport. He was only supposed to stay here for three days, but fog kept him for ten. That was of course before the war derailed the project." She took a sharp breath. "Wait. Isn't it the 50th anniversary of World War II soon?"

"T'tis," Mr. MacManus said happily. "Today is the 50th anniversary of the invasion of Poland and Sunday will be the anniversary of the official start of the war. Specifically, when France and Great Britain declared war on Germany."

"So, tell us more about your grandfather," Dermot urged. "Is the soldier the same as the musician?"

"No. The musician is my Grandpa Richter from Chicago. Grandpa Healy is the soldier from Tennessee. Grandpa Richter was too old to be a soldier when the war broke out so he managed a munitions plant instead. Grandpa Healy was on watch in Pearl Harbor the night before the attack. He swears there was something fishy there, but he has a lot of conspiracy theories and he doesn't trust the government at all. He was also in Patton's

431

Third Army later on in the war and liberated a concentration camp near Neuss, Germany."

"What's his idea about Pearl Harbor, Marielle?" Mr. MacManus asked.

Dermot smiled proudly at his father's interest.

"Well, he said they were manning guns 24 hours a day until three days before the attack, so he thought being called off high alert was fishy. He also says his watch position the night before the attack was high above the harbor where he could see everything between Diamond Head and another landmark I can't recall. Anyway, he was in the Army, but the Navy was in charge of a net that blocked the harbor and they were under orders not to move the net for any reason, but at some point during the night, my grandfather saw the net raised or retracted—I forget the word he used. He said he woke up a major who was sleeping on a cot next to him to complain. The major called down to the Navy to demand an explanation and got placed on permanent hold. The last my grandfather saw of the major, he was hopping out to his Jeep as he pulled on his long boots. I guess they still wore WWI uniforms up until that point. The next day, they were attacked. There's more to that story, but that's the *Cliffs Notes* version."

"I'd like to speak to you on that again before you leave, Marielle," Mr. MacManus said as his eyes squinted in thought.

"Absolutely," she replied. "He has some bizarre stories about the Pentagon removing his entry in the log book and asking him to change his story twice on an official report as well."

"Do you really wish you could die skiing through the Alps, killing SS Officers?" Dermot asked Marielle as if he had read that particular letter yesterday.

"No, well, that was a hypothetical situation," she explained.

"You mean if there were still Nazis?" Dermot asked.

"No, I mean if I were mortal," she replied, causing everyone in the car to laugh.

"You're great *craic*, Marielle," Dermot said, squeezing her hand. "Ooh, I considered your question about whether the Nazis or people equally evil might merit heaven if they didn't realise what they were doing was wrong."

"Really?" she asked, wondering if any boy besides Dermot had ever deeply considered anything she had ever said before.

"Yes, and I came up with an experiment."

"Ooh! Tell me!" she said excitedly.

"Well, you would only need to ask them to describe a nightmare they've had. If the nightmare was about a little girl picking lilies as she pranced around a field, then they don't subscribe to our moral code and they would probably be exempted from hell. However, if their nightmare was about being alone after Armageddon or their father being chased down the street by a man wielding a knife, then they know the difference between right and wrong and they should definitely be sent to hell."

"That's brilliant!" Marielle said with wide eyes. "So, we just need access to a few homicidal maniacs to run the experiment."

"Yes, well, that's the difficult part."

"You wouldn't say that if you knew my family," Marielle murmured, causing Dermot to laugh.

"So, what do you think of our Irish radio?" Mr. MacManus asked.

"I like it a great deal," Marielle replied.

"Ah, she's lying!" Dermot declared.

"I swear I'm not! I actually love the song *The Parting Glass.*"

He looked at her with abundant scepticism. "Really? So, you listen to Irish music on the radio in America?"

"No, on tape. We don't play Trad on the radio at home."

Dermot smiled at her word usage.

"I listen to Polka on some nights on some stations which I find fun for about seven minutes, but I mostly listen to pop music out of Green Bay... unless I'm babysitting, that is."

Dermot furrowed his eyebrows. "What type of music would you listen to babysitting?" he asked.

"Well, if I tell you, you'll think I'm a terrible babysitter, but I promise the kids I babysit for usually like me."

"Especially the hockey player," Dermot noted, raising his eyebrows for a moment.

She nodded. "Right, well he likes me far *too* much."

"Okay, we promise not to judge if you come clean," Dermot announced.

"Alright. So, in Appleton we have a radio station we call Wapple. Its call letters are WAPL, which I'm proud to say a radio station in New York unsuccessfully tried to steal. Anyway, they're a really good classic rock station, but they should really just be known as the Led Zeppelin station because every time I turn it on, Led Zeppelin is playing which is actually fortuitous for me because I babysit this really colicky baby. In fact, the parents resorted to going out at least twice a week just to get away from her—"

"Which is good for business," Dermot commented.

"True," Marielle replied, "but after you feed and burp the baby, and change the diaper, and give her gas medicine, and rock her, and sing to her, and she still screams, you begin to think you're going mad. Well, one night, I put the baby to bed, and in a fit of crazy I turned on WAPL downstairs as the baby cried upstairs. Well, the *Immigrant Song* was playing (of course) and it immediately drowned out the baby's cries which was weird because it wasn't a great stereo system and it wasn't on at ear-bursting decibels. So, I turned down the volume and for a second the baby was quiet, but then she started crying again. So, I turned it back up and I walked upstairs to confirm the baby wasn't crying, but she immediately started crying again when the song was over."

"That's madness!" Dermot proclaimed.

"I know, but I swear it's true. So, the next time I babysat, I turned on WAPL and she was less colicky overall, but completely quiet again when the *Immigrant Song* came on. So, I ran out and bought a Led Zeppelin tape and dubbed that song six times in a row. And—"

"Don't tell me she didn't cry a'tall," Dermot interrupted.

"Well, she cried until the entire feeding, bathing, and bedtime routine was over, so I gave up and turned off the music. But as soon as I laid her down and the nighttime crying began, I tried again. I actually turned on my boom box in her room and she stopped crying like she had an off switch. She actually went to sleep only two or three *Immigrant Songs* into the tape."

"Not a'tall!" Dermot said in disbelief.

Marielle lifted the hand that wasn't holding Dermot's. "I swear on my soul. A screaming baby wants to hear a screaming rock band—not too loudly though. I found you could turn the radio down quite a bit as long as she can hear the yelling clearly."

"Are you not worried you'll be scarring the poor child for life?" Dermot asked.

"My mom asked me the same thing, but I told her I was respecting the baby's right to choose her own music, and I swear the Disney tapes did no good."

"Do the parents know about this?" Mr. MacManus asked.

"Yes, sir, they do. I told them nearly right away. I even gave them the tape which they say they use every night. On the down side though, I only babysit for them once every couple of weeks now which is too bad because they paid well."

Mr. MacManus cleared his throat. "Now, I share my son's concern regarding scarring the child, but I have to say I'm impressed by your scientific method."

"Thank you, sir," Marielle said proudly, and to Dermot she said, "So, how goes your job hunt?"

"Em, did I say I was searching for a job?" he asked with considerable embarrassment.

"You did," she replied confidently.

"Well, the proper job hasn't exactly presented itself to me yet."

"And how would a job do that for you?" she pressed, causing Mr. MacManus to chuckle.

"It would need to fit into my study and training schedule, of course."

"True, but you just went through a summer of no studying, and didn't you quit hurling for the year?"

"Yes, well, we were in France for part of the summer and, em," he looked at her pleadingly as though asking to be let off the hook, but she allowed him to struggle while wearing an amused expression. "Well, I like to go out as well," he continued.

His father sighed loudly. "His girlfriend keeps him well occupied."

Dermot turned to his father with alarm before looking back at Marielle with concern, but she merely smiled in return.

"Really?" she said, feigning surprise. "I thought you and Ashley broke up?"

"Well, we did, but we got back together a while back and she's extremely jealous of my time."

"She's extremely jealous of everything!" his father declared.

Marielle smiled more broadly.

Dermot looked straight ahead as he said, "Dad doesn't appreciate her spirit."

"That's a diplomatic way of putting it," his father remarked.

Marielle's eyes shifted from one MacManus to the other. "Ooh, it sounds like there's a story here," she said excitedly.

"I'll tell you later," Dermot promised.

Marielle narrowed her eyebrows suddenly. "Wait. A jealous girl wouldn't like another girl visiting you."

Mr. MacManus laughed.

Marielle's gaze shifted to the front seat, then back again. "Ah, so you've had some drama lately. Shall I guess what happened?"

The darkness obscured Dermot, but Marielle knew he was blushing, and his father had a hard time concentrating on the road with the outline of his son's face as competition.

"Go ahead," Dermot said in defeat.

"Alright, so you probably should've told her I was visiting when you got back together, but you didn't want to ruin the euphoria of the moment by addressing reality. Additionally, all guys put off bad news as long as possible either in case circumstances change or to minimize the yelling. So, I assume you didn't tell her until this week, possibly yesterday."

Dermot placed his head against the seat as his groan turned into a chuckle.

"Okay, so you probably told her over the phone because you didn't want to face her wrath in person."

"Not a'tall," he replied, turning his head toward her.

"Ooh, alright. Sorry. I misjudged you. Well, you did it in front of an audience then so she couldn't flip out easily. I assume your mother or father were nearby?"

Mr. MacManus nodded.

"Okay, so based upon your father's previous comments, I assume his presence didn't stop her from going ballistic. I also assume she said things which might appear disrespectful or undignified."

"Spot-on, Marielle!" Mr. MacManus exclaimed.

"So, how late were you up fighting last night?" she asked.

"Jaysus, it must've been half-twelve, right Dad?

"I can't say. I went to bed after securing the knives."

Marielle laughed before breathing in suddenly. "Will I be safe, then?" she asked, only half in jest.

"I promise to protect you from her," Dermot said in earnest.

"So, are you still technically dating, then?"

"I think so. She said we'd discuss it when you left."

Marielle smiled confidently. "I bet you five pounds you discuss it *before* I leave."

Dermot shook his head slightly. "I don't have five quid, and I'm not certain I'd take that bet if I did."

"I'll lend you the quid, if that means money," Marielle replied.

Dermot laughed. "It does."

"I'll cover Dermot's bet, though I fear he'll lose," his father said as he down-shifted into a turn.

"Thanks, Dad," Dermot replied with no perceivable appreciation.

"You should really get a job," Marielle suggested. "If you don't want to see someone you're dating, it makes for a good excuse. If you *do* want to see them, you can usually switch shifts."

"So, do you have a boyfriend as well, Marielle?" Mr. MacManus asked.

Her mouth contorted unpleasantly before she said she did. Technically.

"But she doesn't like him," Dermot added.

Marielle nodded. "That's true too."

"Then why do you date him?" Mr. MacManus asked.

"It's for his letterman's jacket," she replied as if that's all she needed to say, but the silence told her she was wrong. "Well, I honestly don't want to date anyone at all until I go to college, and even then I have a pretty strict three year plan so I probably don't need the distraction."

Mr. MacManus chuckled.

"But not dating isn't an option with American guys because if they know you're available, they won't leave you alone. That sounds arrogant, but I promise it's just annoying. I actually had two guys pull into my driveway and demand I come outside to talk to them or they wouldn't leave. Then, a guy started calling me after each jazz band concert telling me I looked like a flower (he actually used that word) on stage and he wouldn't tell me who he was because he said he knew I would never date him, and at first I felt badly for him, but after the third concert, I began to agree with him."

"So, was Gary one of your stalkers?" Dermot asked.

"Not until I stopped talking to him, but he's hampered by living several towns away and me working so much. Even if I was talking to him though, I'd only see him a weekend every month anyway. He demands I wear his football jersey and letterman's jacket so the guys leave me alone which is just fine by me."

"However, Gary isn't the faithful sort," Dermot said to his father.

Marielle started for a moment, then silently agreed with Dermot. "No, he's not, but I honestly don't care as long as *I* can keep his jersey and jacket, and *he* keeps his hands to himself."

"So, what did you say to him when he said he had... em... dated the girl from—"

"Kaukauna," Marielle finished.

"Isn't that the town that smells?" Dermot asked.

"Good memory!" Marielle said excitedly. "Well, my voice cracked at the end of our conversation because of the strain not laughing had placed on it."

"And?"

"And I said I was done talking to him. That was well over a month ago and I haven't given him my verdict yet."

Dermot laughed. "But you knew you wouldn't break up with him because you still need his jacket."

"True, but he doesn't know that," Marielle said with vehemence. "I can't have him thinking he can walk all over me."

"I'm quite certain he thinks nothing of the kind, Marielle," Mr. MacManus said smiling. "So, what does Gary think of you visiting Ireland?"

"He didn't have a choice, of course, and he didn't ask me to stay or anything. He wrote me a few annoying, sappy letters about how he didn't know how much he cared about me until he messed everything up and no one else matters, blah, blah, blah, blah, blah."

"Did you answer his letters?" Dermot asked.

"No, but I know he called my sister to ask if I read them and she told him I had. Traitor."

"So, the cheating happened over a month ago, and you still haven't given him an answer? You like torturing lads, don't you?"

"Absolutely!" Marielle proclaimed. "He's a Protestant, but I decided to put him into Purgatory anyway."

"Can you do that?" Dermot asked, looking at his father for the amusement he expected to find.

Marielle shrugged her shoulders. "I wasn't sure myself, but it seems to be working."

Dermot smiled as he drew a deep breath. "So, how did you know it was Ashley I was dating?"

"Well, you started talking about her again in your letters and addressing me differently."

438

"How?" he asked, turning toward her with interest.

"It's to do with the way you begin your letters. If you say 'hi' with or without my name, you're always dating someone. If you use just my name with an exclamation point or 'dear' or 'dearest', you're not."

"I can't believe that's true!" Dermot replied, but his voice betrayed concern.

"Oh, it is. I noticed last fall."

"Why do you believe Dermot does this?" Mr. MacManus asked, displaying more interest than amusement.

Marielle released Dermot's hand to grab the back of Mr. MacManus' seat. "Well, if I can be so bold, I think people are more stand-offish to the opposite sex when they're dating and more exuberant when they're available. I think it's an evolutionary thing."

"Do you do the same?" Dermot asked, grabbing her hand again as she sat back.

"No. I make a point *not* to do the same thing. I'd hate to give myself away like that."

"That's fascinating," Mr. MacManus remarked.

"Thank you and I promise it's true. I would've brought Dermot's letters as proof if I'd known this topic would come up."

Dermot squeezed Marielle's hand before picking it up to kiss it. "We're nearly in Galway now," he said happily. "Dad, was it last year that that lorry became wedged under the bridge?"

"Maybe it was two years ago now," his father replied. To Marielle he said, "The lorry was too high to clear the bridge and caused a terrible crash. It took several days to free the vehicle."

"Do you know how they managed it?" she asked.

"I believe they shaved a couple inches off the top," he replied.

"If it was only a couple of inches, why didn't they just let the air out of the tires?" she asked.

"I'm quite certain they considered that," Dermot remarked.

"I'm not so sure they did," Mr. MacManus said pensively.

Chapter Twenty-Nine

Mingled Seas

—W.B. Yeats – *At Algeciras-A Meditation Upon Death*

Streets became narrower as stone walls, house façades, and eventually rows of shops jockeyed for space.

"I know you said the population of Galway is the same as Appleton, but it looks like a much larger city," Marielle said, looking out the window at the narrow sidewalks teeming with pedestrians.

"Have you told Marielle about our musicians?" Mr. MacManus asked as they passed a long-haired, middle-aged man leaning against a building while strumming a guitar.

"I hadn't, no. We're very near now," Dermot said excitedly as they crossed a bridge and the view to the left gave way to darkness Marielle assumed was the sea. "What does your house look like, Marielle? Did you bring a photo?"

"No, I didn't. It's a yellow cube and it's pretty boring," she said, and to herself she added, *and pretty small and not even ours.*

"Ours is *very* scary," Dermot replied. "There's ivy growing on the front so you can barely see through the windows in places."

His father's head twitched suddenly as though surprised or wounded by his son's comment.

As they made their way down the street, Marielle noticed townhouses fronted by either gated yards or parking pads to her left. She looked down the long line of homes, prepared to turn into one of those properties rather than the large houses across the street whose near park-like front yards and long driveways were protected by stone walls and large metal gates. The car slowed for a passing car, then turned right through one such gate.

For a moment, Marielle wondered if they hadn't turned into a double-gabled apartment complex, but only the first floor was illuminated on the two-story stone structure. A salmon-coloured foyer cast a warm glow onto the yard as the front door in the middle of the house opened.

Marielle's mouth remained agape as the car stopped and a Brittany spaniel ran toward the car, barking.

440

"You may want to sit here for a moment, Marielle," Dermot cautioned, but in her excitement, she didn't hear him. She opened her door and nearly closed it before the brown and white dog pinned her against the car.

"Gryphon!" Mr. MacManus yelled before Dermot could run to Marielle's aid.

"He's fine, sir. I love dogs," she said, scratching Gryphon's head and neck vigorously as his paws kneaded her stomach.

"Are you alright there?" Dermot asked happily. "He's not terribly clean or well mannered."

"He's lovely," Marielle said as Gryphon licked her hands with vigour.

"Will you look at that?" Mr. MacManus declared, unsure if Gryphon's or Marielle's reaction was more noteworthy.

"Are you coming inside or not?" a petite woman with short blonde hair and small, wire-framed glasses asked from the front door.

"Sorry," Marielle called genially to Mrs. MacManus before saying the same to Gryphon.

Dermot flashed a look of annoyance at the front door before joining his father at the boot, nervously watching Marielle as she approached the house alone.

"Well, finally you've arrived," Mrs. MacManus declared.

"Yes, thank God," Marielle said, opening her arms to hug Dermot's mother.

"Oh, my," Mrs. MacManus replied, looking past Marielle to her son as though a handshake would have suited her just fine.

Marielle felt Mrs. MacManus' reserve and pulled back.

"You need to call your parents straight away," the woman said as her son walked through the door.

Marielle looked around the expansive foyer which opened to rooms on three sides, with an L-shaped staircase at its center. The stairs began to the left of the middle door, then turned to the right at a landing whose front provided hooks for several jackets. Doors to the left and straight ahead stood closed, while the door to the right remained open at a 45 degree angle, displaying a bleached wood table and matching chairs.

"I thought you'd never arrive," Mrs. MacManus said as a question to Dermot which he pretended not to hear as he placed Marielle's suitcase near the stairs.

"Where did you go off to?" Mrs. MacManus asked her husband as he walked through the door she still guarded.

441

"We stopped at Durty Nelly's," he admitted, looking to her eyes for judgment.

She exhaled sharply through her nose before asking if anyone wanted a cup of tea.

"I'd say we could all use a cup of tea," her husband replied.

"May I help you with that?" Marielle asked Mrs. MacManus, causing father and son to exchange a grin.

"Not a'tall," she dismissed, "but let me show you the kitchen. Are you hungry a'tall?"

"No, ma'am. I'm not."

"When did you last eat?" Mrs. MacManus asked, walking between a small fireplace and the dining room table.

"I ate a candy bar in Heathrow," she replied, glancing at Dermot behind her as she entered the large, cabinet-lined kitchen.

"When was that?" Mrs. MacManus asked, grabbing the handle of the 1950s-sized refrigerator to the left of the doorway.

"Just after I realized I missed my plane. I guess that was around noon."

"You really must eat something else," Mrs. MacManus demanded, reaching inside a refrigerator containing no beer.

"I promise to ask for food if I'm hungry, but I swear I'm not. In fact, I have no idea why that would be, but it's true."

Mrs. MacManus looked away from the refrigerator with displeasure, then sighed as her son smiled shamelessly at Marielle.

Marielle spied an electric tea pot for the first time. "Are you sure I can't help you with the tea?" she asked.

"Not a'tall," Mrs. MacManus replied, turning toward the sink which was flanked by a dishwasher and built-in ovens. Above the sink, a window reflected Mrs. MacManus' unhappy expression, but above her head, a shelf held a red and white clock with a familiar logo.

"KitKat!" Marielle exclaimed, immediately feeling more at home even though she'd never seen a KitKat clock before.

Mrs. MacManus scoffed. "I thought you'd like that. Dermot, show Marielle the bathroom and the laundry."

Dermot sighed. Standing awkwardly in the middle of the room, he seemed in need of an occupation, but this was clearly not the job he had in mind.

Marielle raised her eyebrows impishly at Dermot, then followed him as the terracotta floor narrowed to the right of the ovens.

"This is the secondary toilet," he said, indicating a door, but not opening it or turning on the light. "The primary toilet is upstairs. Here is the laundry." He pointed toward a dark void across the hall from the bathroom.

"And that's the door to the outside?" Marielle asked, looking straight ahead. "Wow, quick tour," she said with mischief.

***

Dermot smiled across the dining room table while his father beamed from Marielle's right and Mrs. MacManus scowled from her left.

"Well, you've accomplished quite a feat in making your way to Ireland, I'll give you that," Mrs. MacManus said with slighter eyes than the ones God gave her.

"I appreciate you saying that," Marielle replied, "but I realized that flying to Ireland was no more complicated than taking the bus to Chicago, just on a much larger scale."

Mrs. MacManus expelled breath. Looking away from Marielle with disgust, she said, "Of course. She's chewing gum."

Marielle looked at Dermot as his eyes furrowed in his mother's direction.

"I'm sorry," Marielle replied nervously. "Do you mind if I dispose of it?" she asked, turning from Mrs. MacManus to the kitchen.

"Not a'tall," Mrs. MacManus replied, still looking away.

Marielle threw her gum into the trash can before asking if she could wash her hands.

"Please do," Mrs. MacManus replied with her back to the kitchen.

Marielle chastised herself as she washed her hands. She had noticed Dermot no longer chewed gum during the tour of the bathroom and laundry room, but she hadn't fully appreciated the importance of this. From now on, she needed to study Dermot's cues more carefully.

"Marielle, try one of Dermot's favourite biscuits," his father suggested, pushing a blue package of granola cookies towards her as she returned to her chair.

"Thank you," she replied, smiling as she reached for a cookie until she noticed the affronted look on Mrs. MacManus' face. Saying *no* to her offer of food while saying *yes* to her husband's was clearly a problem.

"Marielle, what would a typical kitchen look like in America?" Mr. MacManus asked, happily interrupting her thoughts.

"It would look very much the same," she replied, looking briefly toward the U-shaped configuration of bleached wood cabinets and the red ceramic backsplash. "It would have the same appliances you have, and it would be laid out very similarly," she continued.

Mr. MacManus displayed a look of surprise, causing Marielle to wonder if he knew her family couldn't afford a dishwasher or built-in ovens.

"You haven't phoned your parents yet," Mrs. MacManus said as Marielle swallowed the last of her biscuit.

"Oh, right," Marielle replied, pretending she'd forgotten. "I have a calling card so it won't be charged to you. Let me grab it from my purse."

Marielle stood up, trying to ignore Dermot's happy appraisal of her.

"Let me see that," Mrs. MacManus offered near the base of the stairs after Marielle studied the back of the plastic card for many seconds.

Mrs. MacManus read the same directions to no avail. In defeat, she called an operator, then hung up the phone. "They'll ring us back when they make the connection," she explained.

"Really?" Marielle asked reflexively, not having heard of anything like it before.

Marielle smiled brightly when her eyes met Dermot's, and he returned the smile until his mother intercepted it.

Mrs. MacManus turned towards Marielle with nothing resembling a smile. "After you ring off, you should have a nice bath," she suggested. "Shortly after I spoke with you in Cork, I ran a bath so I might finally relax."

"I'm very sorry for monopolizing everyone's day," Marielle said, looking around the table with regret until the intensity in Dermot's eyes distracted her. "I hope I didn't ruin anyone's plans."

"We had no plans a'tall," Mr. MacManus said comfortingly.

"Speak for yourself!" his wife objected. "I missed my friend's art exhibit tonight."

Dermot and his father turned displeased expressions at Mrs. MacManus while Marielle apologized again.

"Not a'tall," Mrs. MacManus said unconvincingly, looking down at her teacup for a moment. "So, why don't you tell us what happened to your connection in Heathrow?"

Marielle repeated her story and was nearly finished when the loud double-buzz of the phone caused her to jump. "Is that the phone?" she asked, still alarmed.

Dermot laughed.

"I'tis," his mother replied. "You should answer it. It's likely the operator."

After several hellos, a pause, and a command from the operator to "go-ahead," Marielle finally heard her mother's voice.

"Marielle? Is that you?" Maria asked as though her daughter had been gone for much longer than a day.

"It is. I'm safe in Galway now. Sorry I scared you guys."

"Well, we're just happy you're finally there. The airlines wouldn't tell us anything."

"Well, we were in the same boat, then," she replied, chuckling.

"Just a second. Your father wants to speak with you."

Ah, crap, Marielle thought, quickly calculating Appleton time in her head.

"So, you finally made it, kid," Jack said, equal parts relieved and proud.

"Yes, sir, I did. There was a misunderstanding about baggage and Customs."

"Well, let's hope there's no misunderstanding on the way home."

"I promise there won't be. I have a four hour layover on the way back so I could actually get arrested in Customs and still make my connection."

Jack laughed. "Alrighty, then. Thank the MacManuses for us."

"I definitely will. Love you. Bye," she said before setting down the receiver.

Although murmuring could be heard in the dining room throughout her conversation, it stopped abruptly after she hung up, giving Marielle the sense she had been overheard.

She returned to her seat wearing a smile. "My parents asked me to thank you for them."

"We're happy to have you," Mr. MacManus said kindly.

His wife drew a deep breath. "You should really complain to British Air upon your return. We had a dreadful experience on the ferry to France and I wrote a note of complaint. When we returned home, there was a letter of apology waiting for us."

Marielle shifted uncomfortably in her chair. "I really don't like to complain. I'm just happy to be here."

Mrs. MacManus sighed. "Well, it's *their* job to ensure their staff is well acquainted with connection procedures."

Marielle nodded slowly. "True, but I switched airlines and it's really my own fault for not studying the layout of the airport before I left Appleton. I also should have asked the baggage desk about my bags as soon as I arrived at Heathrow. There's really no excuse for me."

Two of the three MacManuses smiled.

"Well, sometimes if you complain they send refunds or discounts as well," Mrs. MacManus explained before noting the determined look in Marielle's eyes.

"Did you use your calling card to place your phone calls at Heathrow?" Dermot asked.

"No, I used pound coins," she replied.

"Was it terribly dear?"

"Well, I would put the coin into the phone and as soon as the connection was made it would immediately start ticking down from 100. It was probably a penny—do you say penny?"

"Pence," Mr. MacManus replied.

"Thank you. A pence a second. Maybe a little quicker. But if you hung up before the end of your pound, it didn't always give you back the remaining money. I was deeply annoyed by that."

"So, you exchanged money in Heathrow?" Dermot asked.

"No, in Appleton. My bank had to order it ahead of time. I asked them for Irish punts, but they said Ireland used British pounds. I hadn't brought my book with me from the library which proved otherwise so I just bought the British money instead."

Dermot took a sip of his tea. "Maybe they meant Northern Ireland."

"Maybe," Marielle replied as Mrs. MacManus protested through her nose again.

"Why don't we get Marielle's bags to her room," Mr. MacManus suggested to his son.

Marielle looked up at the men as they stood to leave, uneasy with the prospect of being left alone with Mrs. MacManus.

"So, you're finally in Ireland," Mrs. MacManus said, grinning unhappily at her mug.

Marielle became distracted by cream and red toile dinnerware displayed in the hutch behind Mrs. MacManus' chair.

"I love your china," she remarked.

Mrs. MacManus twitched as if tempted to look over her shoulder.

"It's wedding china. It belonged to my mother-in-law. We never met."

"Well, she had lovely taste. I've always liked the red toile better than the blue."

"I prefer the black," Mrs. MacManus said, leaning back in her chair.

Marielle looked from the cabinet to Mrs. MacManus. "Did you meet your father-in-law?"

"No," she said, amused with the girl for a moment. "He died well before my mother-in-law."

"Oh, I'm sorry about that."

Mrs. MacManus raised one shoulder briefly, then glanced at the window behind Dermot's empty chair. "You know, my friends worried when I didn't attend the art exhibit tonight. I was in the midst of fielding your phone calls as well as my husband's when they rang to ask why I hadn't arrived."

Marielle looked at Mrs. MacManus with purpose, determined to convey her sincerity. "I'm very sorry about that. I know it's my fault and I will change money on Monday to pay you for your gas. I know that doesn't help with your missed appointment, but I hope you can accept my apology."

Mrs. MacManus cleared her throat as the men returned.

"Marielle mentioned something interesting on the way home," Mr. MacManus said to his wife as he and Dermot resumed their seats. "She read that Charles Lindbergh was involved in determining the location for Shannon Airport."

"I believe I've heard that before," his wife said with faint interest.

"It's brilliant to think an American had a hand in making Shannon Airport, isn't it?!" Dermot exclaimed.

Mrs. MacManus turned her head sharply towards her son, causing the joy to leave his face.

"Why don't you show Marielle to her room and get her settled," Dermot's father suggested as he stared down his wife.

Dermot stood up, temporarily breaking his mother's hold over him.

"You should take your bath as well," Mrs. MacManus added, looking again at the window behind Dermot's chair.

Marielle nodded as she stood up. She followed Dermot from the room, turning back only briefly to revisit the intensity of the stare Mr. MacManus attempted to communicate to his wife.

Dermot grabbed Marielle's hand, kissing it gently as they reached the landing. He guided her past the open door on the left as they reached the top of the stairs before turning 180 degrees to the right. The narrow hallway led to an open space dominated by a table at least twice the size of the one in the dining room below. Stacks of books were barely visible by light which escaped the foyer below, and Marielle barely saw Dermot's hand reach down to retrieve a small box from the table.

"What's this?" she asked.

"It's your birthday gift," he replied, scarcely allowing her room to properly view the black, leaf-shaped earrings.

"They're lovely. Thank you," she said, reflexively grabbing her Irish necklace through her blouse.

"May I kiss you?" he asked, looking down at her with more longing than she had ever seen in a boy's eyes.

"Tell me if this is a dream first," she said as the dim light cast shadows across Dermot's face.

"It is and it isn't," he replied, closing his eyes as his lips approached hers.

"My God," she said, shivering as their lips barely touched.

He opened his eyes, smiling at her for a moment before approaching her again. His tongue parted her lips as she braced for aggressive play, then relaxed when he gently probed her mouth instead. Warm electricity flooded her lower body in a way that made coherent thought difficult. She reached up with her left hand, stroking the back of Dermot's neck as he reached down to cradle her head.

A chair scraped against the floor below, abruptly stopping the kiss, but Dermot and Marielle remained together, their lips inches apart, transfixed by the feeling that they were two halves of the same spirit.

"My God," she repeated. "I swear to you that is the best kiss I have ever had. Really. You could teach a college-level course in it."

Dermot laughed. "Ah, you're having me on."

"I swear on my soul I'm not!" she protested.

He smiled as he kissed her forehead. "I can't begin to tell you how lovely it is to have you on my side of the Atlantic."

"When I regain my ability to speak properly, I'll tell you how lovely it is for me to be here," she replied.

He smiled into her eyes before remembering his task. "Let me show you to your room," he said, returning to the door at the top of the stairs. He flicked on a switch from a raised electrical box behind the door, illuminating a single bed against the far wall, a dresser to their left, and a small wardrobe between the door and a window. The room's cream and green, fern-patterned wallpaper reminded Marielle of a Laura Ashley design while the deep walnut floorboards looked as though they belonged to a Nantucket beach house.

"You have Fee's room," Dermot announced

"It's lovely. Ooh," she said suddenly, spying her suitcase and duffel bag on the floor near the bed. "I need to take out my gifts for your parents before I forget."

"There's no need for gifts a'tall," Dermot said, but Marielle ignored him as she busily opened her duffel bag. She found the Cubs hat and the mug filled with potpourri easily enough, but she searched in vain for the book she brought for Dermot.

"This will take me five seconds," she said, running downstairs with Dermot following close behind.

Marielle presented the gifts to the MacManuses while Dermot stood in the doorway.

"Oh, I do like the smell of this," Mrs. MacManus said as she removed the mostly cinnamon potpourri from the coffee mug.

Dermot's laughter at his father turned everyone's attention to the end of the table.

"You look ridiculous!" Mrs. MacManus declared, barely smiling at the visage of her husband in a Chicago Cubs' cap.

Marielle smiled broadly. "That's from my dad, actually. That was his team when he was a kid. We bought it in Chicago a few weeks ago."

"Thank your father for me," Mr. MacManus replied, nodding his head once in Marielle's direction as he pushed down the hat's bill. "I think I'll wear it golfing tomorrow morning."

"You will indeed," Mrs. MacManus said dismissively.

"I will," he countered, causing his wife to shake her head.

"I need to find your present now," Marielle said to Dermot, expecting him to retreat so she could follow.

"Is it the book you were reading in school?" he asked eagerly while maintaining his position.

"It is."

"What's that, Marielle?" his father asked.

"It's called *Johnny Got His Gun*. It's about a man who's critically injured during World War I. He's a paraplegic and he can't speak or see, but his mind works perfectly. He's basically trapped inside his own body."

"That sounds a bit dark," Dermot's mother replied.

"It is, but I think it's very well written. Oh," Marielle said with concern. "Do you not want Dermot reading books like that?"

"Not a'tall," she replied as Dermot studied his mother. "Well, why don't you take your bath now," she suggested with less patience.

"Right," Marielle agreed before she and Dermot took their leave once again.

"You may go up first," Dermot said at the bottom of the stairs.

Marielle smiled shyly. "Any particular reason?" she whispered.

Dermot returned the smile. "None a'tall."

When Marielle reached the top of the stairs, she turned left suddenly into her room, catching Dermot staring at her backside.

"You went the wrong way," he said, grabbing her hand to pull her into the hall. "I'll give you a tour, but the bathroom is this way."

"Right, but I need my pajamas."

"And knickers," he added mischievously.

"No. Americans stopped wearing knickers in the '20s," Marielle said before Dermot lost his breath. "Ooh, a Benetton bear!" she exclaimed, noticing the stuffed animal on the bookshelves behind him.

"Now, that was a cruel lie," he said, pulling her hips closer to his.

"I would never lie to you," she replied.

Dermot looked up at the ceiling while taking a deep breath. "You're making me daft," he declared.

"Then we're even."

He grabbed her hand forcefully. "We'll begin our tour with my bedroom," he joked, causing Marielle to guffaw before covering her mouth.

They rounded the opening in the floor the stairs required before stopping in front of a closed door. "Mum's room," he said. "You'll be sharing a wall with her so you mustn't dream about me too loudly."

"That's easier said than done," Marielle remarked.

Dermot blinked hard before walking towards the table and pointing across the hall. "Dad's room."

Marielle narrowed her eyebrows wondering why a married couple under 70 years old wouldn't share a room.

Dermot walked beyond the table. "Bathroom," he said, turning on the light of a large room with mauve tile which held only a sink, a shower, and a tub. Although copious amounts of space might have easily held a toilet, it was missing.

"You could land a plane in here," Marielle said, scanning the room.

Dermot smiled as he led her down a short hallway to the left. "Toilet," he announced, revealing a closet-sized room. He continued to the end of the corridor. "My room," he declared happily as he turned on the light and a moment before he raised his eyebrows for a fraction of a second.

Marielle smiled. "Do you do that because I told you only annoying boys raise their eyebrows at me?"

"Yes," he said before doing it again.

Marielle laughed before peeking inside Dermot's room which was the smallest of the rooms she had seen thus far. A single bed rested against the exterior wall, taking up the vast majority of the space while a bookcase stood at the foot of the bed. A dresser sat to the right of the entrance on top of which folded clothes were neatly stacked, owing to the lack of both a closet and an armoire. A small stove and chimney obscured the bed's headboard, sitting as it did between the bed and door.

"Lovely," Marielle declared before Dermot's expression caused her to back up nervously. "Let me try to find that book I brought for you," she said, jogging toward her room.

After nearly tearing apart her suitcase and duffel bag, she found the *New Kids on the Block* poster meant for Fiona.

"Is this for me?" Dermot asked, sitting on her bed with his hands braced behind him to better lean backward.

"Sure," Marielle replied.

"Is it or isn't it?"

"I brought it for your sister, but since she's not here, there's no reason it can't be yours... though I'm pretty sure you're not a fan of this particular band."

"I try always to maintain an open mind," he said, reaching for the poster which was rolled into a plastic sleeve.

"Aha!" she declared, locating the small paperback book.

"Lovely," Dermot said, reaching down to accept the book. He took a moment to regard the cover which displayed a helmet resting on one finger of a peace sign. "I'll start reading this immediately."

Marielle turned toward him abruptly, happily surprised at his eagerness, but fearing he might not like the book. "There's no hurry," she said.

"What's that?" Dermot asked, eyeing her suitcase.

"Ooh, my yearbook," she replied, retrieving the dark blue, hardbound book.

"May I see it?" he asked, his hand extended.

Marielle complied, then replaced her clothes inside her cases. Moments later, she sat beside Dermot while he continued to stare at the first page.

"That's an aerial shot of our school," she explained. "Those are the baseball, football and track fields, and six tennis courts, of course. That structure is the gymnasium and that's the outline of the indoor pool."

"Go away with you," Dermot said breathlessly.

"Are you saying you don't have a pool at your school?" she asked, knowing full well he didn't.

"You're a cheeky monkey," he said, causing her to laugh. "What's that round structure?"

"Ah, that's the silo. It's our tornado-proof, nuclear fallout shelter."

"And missile silo," Dermot added.

"Yes. According to a burn-out in my German class. He says the presence of the missile is why the janitors get paid so much."

"To keep quiet, like?"

Marielle nodded.

"Are they well paid?"

"I have no idea," she replied happily as Dermot turned the page. "These are the seniors. Next spring, my picture will be in this section. Oh, did you get my senior pictures?"

Dermot smiled with mischief. "I did indeed."

Marielle studied his profile. "What does that mean?"

"Let's just say I liked your photos a great deal."

She looked down at the yearbook as she began to blush.

"Where are you?" he asked, scanning the page where the R's were featured.

"I'm in the juniors' section." Marielle turned several pages. "Here's my picture, which I believe I sent you last year, and here's a candid picture of my friend and I at a football game." She pointed to a large photograph in the middle of the page before turning it. "This picture shows the back of my football jersey. See, *Richter*? We were cleaning up the grounds the day after we TP'd the school."

Dermot observed the trees dripping with toilet paper. "Did you really vandalise your own school?"

"Sure, but they made us clean it up."

Dermot's eyes widened.

"Oh, and back here there are pictures of me in the Women's Choir, Easterners, Wind Symphony, and Pep Club."

"Jaysus!" Dermot exclaimed, a second before the door opened swiftly.

Mrs. MacManus looked at both teenagers as shock overcame her face.

"Hey, Mum. Look at this," Dermot said, only briefly looking up from the yearbook. "They printed an entire class in colour. Didn't you say that was quite dear?"

She collected herself enough to walk over to the yearbook, but not enough to avoid sighing as she looked down at the photographs. "They all look so American," she said with distaste.

"But didn't you say printing in colour was expensive?" Dermot pressed.

"I'tis," she replied, stepping back as she pointed towards him. "You, go to bed." She turned her finger towards Marielle. "You, bath."

"Yes, ma'am," Marielle replied while Dermot nodded, and a moment before Dermot's father entered the room holding a map.

"Let me show you how far you travelled today, Marielle," he said genially.

Marielle jumped up to stand beside his shoulder.

"I'm tryin' to get them off to bed!" Mrs. MacManus protested.

"Sure, love. In a minute," he replied without making eye contact. "So, look down there, Marielle. Do you see Cork City?"

"I do."

"And we're all the way up here." He pointed with a free finger to Galway.

"That's over halfway up the country!" she declared. "That's incredible. In the U.S. three and a half hours only gets you from Chicago to Appleton."

"Yes, well, we're a much smaller country, see."

"Ooh, Skibbereen!" Marielle said happily, looking down at County Cork.

"Does that hold some significance for you?" Mr. MacManus asked as Dermot laughed.

"She saw it on the map when she was searching for Galway and remembered it as Skedaddle," Dermot explained.

Mr. MacManus chuckled before deciding he shouldn't keep them any longer from their tasks.

"Thank you again for driving all that way to pick me up," Marielle said, looking at the man with genuine appreciation. "I really love being here."

Mr. MacManus glanced away shyly. "It's nothing a'tall," he said before departing.

Dermot smiled at his father's wake before turning to Marielle. "Let me fetch you that towel."

***

Marielle filled only a fifth of the tub and quickly found the water level inadequate to combat the cold of the room once she sat inside. She washed rapidly before sitting back to waste time. Everything she had done since arriving was negatively regarded by Mrs. MacManus, and she assumed a quick bath would be as well. She told herself to relax, at the same time she found relaxation impossible. She sat naked in a large room only two doors down from Dermot, but more distracting was the thought of Mrs. MacManus sitting naked in the same tub hours before. She told herself she held nothing against Mrs. MacManus or her tub, but baths in general seemed far too intimate and far less sanitary than showers.

Marielle stood up, allowing the water to drip from her body while looking across the room at the mirror above the sink. She had always felt chubby—and maybe she had always been—but she didn't appear chubby in the mirror right now. She placed one foot outside the tub, expecting to hit the floor three inches before she did. Her foot fell hard on the wet tiles, causing her to lose her balance before sliding into the shower in the corner of the room like a baseball player slides into home base. The sound of her exclamation was only eclipsed by a strip of aluminium which fell from the edge of the shower's glass enclosure before crashing to the floor.

Marielle released her hands from her ears, then looked quickly at the door. She jumped up to wrap the towel around herself, continuing to study the door carefully as she replaced the aluminium, rinsed out the tub, and brushed her teeth. Confirming a search party was not en route, she dressed in both her nightgown and bathrobe before opening the door slowly to peer outside.

Dermot's bedroom door immediately swung open at the end of the hall to her right. "Are you alright there?" he asked, lying in a dark room.

Marielle cringed. "I'm afraid I just broke your shower. I slipped on

454

my way out of the tub—"

"No, that was me. It came loose when I stepped out from the shower this morning."

"Oh, thank God!" she said, placing her hand against her chest. "If you have some clear caulk, we can fix it without a problem."

"Pardon?" he asked with a mischievous grin.

"You know very well," she said, smiling.

"I don't, but it sounds interesting." His smile suddenly slipped into a sigh. "I'll be gone in the morning. I have lifeguard training at nine o'clock in Salthill."

"Can I go with you?" she asked eagerly.

"Absolutely," he replied with tempered enthusiasm. "But wouldn't you prefer to have a bit of a lie-in instead?"

"Not at all," she replied in earnest.

He looked at her with questioning eyes.

"Really," she continued. "Do you mind waking me up? I only need a half-hour to get ready."

"You're certain now?"

"I am." She raised her right hand as if taking the Girl Scout oath. "I swear."

His smile returned. "Alright, then. I'll wake you at 8:15."

"Wonderful. Sweet dreams," she said with a little wave.

"Sweet dreams," he replied happily before reluctantly closing his door.

Marielle heard muffled voices as she looked down at the still illuminated foyer, but she had no intention of going down despite guilt over not saying goodnight properly.

Following Dermot's lead, she closed her bedroom door even though it was considered rude to do so in Appleton. She extinguished the light, but stood motionless for a moment before flipping the switch on again. After analyzing the distance between herself and the bed and determining a proper launching point, she turned the light off again. She walked two steps before jumping safely onto the bed without interference from monsters or murderers beneath it.

After placing her bathrobe at the end of the bed, she organized the fluffy comforter under her chin, then prayed with as much appreciation as one could fit between laced fingers. Dermot was lying only a few yards away and at long last they breathed the same air. By the end of her prayers, only her nose felt cold.

That night, Marielle dreamt she and Dermot sat alone on the deck of a catamaran, having recently won the America's Cup. He smiled as he appraised the boat, finally conceding it was the better design. Marielle smiled back, knowing no telephone or screaming parents could find them on the ocean. They looked at each other lovingly while discussing in which direction to point the bow, eventually deciding south. Dermot stared at her mouth, causing her to close it. He asked if they should begin their journey, but she asked for ten more minutes of precious sleep.

Chapter Thirty

Sails for Flight
—W.B. Yeats – *The Cloak, the Boat, and the Shoes*

Marielle opened her eyes abruptly before squinting at the digital clock on Fiona's dresser. It read 9:10 a.m. She dropped her head onto her pillow with disgust, knowing she had missed Dermot. If she dressed quickly, she might be able to find his class, she reasoned, though she had only a vague sense of where to find the sea.

She grabbed a pair of jeans, and a white t-shirt from her bag before placing her mostly white Appleton East football jersey over her head. She felt liberated having left Gary's jersey behind. If there was one thing she admired about Appleton East, it was the preference for girls to wear jerseys bearing their own families' name rather than that of their boyfriend's. If not in an effort to mislead people, Marielle saw no reason to ever wear a boy's jersey at all. Well, she would gladly wear Dermot's jersey, she decided as she pulled the top of her hair back into a barrette.

Marielle ran downstairs to find the dining room door mostly open. "Good morning," she said brightly as Mrs. MacManus drank her tea and Mr. MacManus read the *Irish Times*.

"Good morning, young lady. We were sure we wouldn't see you until noon," Mr. MacManus remarked happily.

"Well, I think the airport wore me out yesterday. I went right to sleep and slept like the dead. The bed is so comfortable and the blanket is incredible. We can't get comforters that thick in the U.S. without costing an arm and a leg."

"Really?" Mrs. MacManus asked, finally showing interest in something Marielle had to say. "How much do you think they would cost?"

"I'd be surprised if you could find them for less than $100," she said, realizing she had no idea what she was talking about, distracted as she was by Dermot's chair which sat squished between the table and the wall. "How did you guys sleep?" Marielle asked, amusing Mr. MacManus while offending his wife with the word "guys."

"Brilliantly," Mrs. MacManus replied. "Though my husband was up with the sun golfing."

"Ooh, how did you do?" she asked as she sat down.

"Well enough," he said coyly.

"He was soundly beaten by Sean's mother," his wife remarked.

"She's quite good," Mr. MacManus defended. "I was hoping to beat her by virtue of my new ball cap, but I'm afraid it didn't work."

"Did you wear the hat after all?" Marielle asked in disbelief.

"I did indeed," he said. "I was the envy of everyone on the links."

Marielle didn't bother to turn toward Mrs. MacManus, certain she could accurately guess her reaction, and preferring to smile at Mr. MacManus instead.

"Are you hungry, then?" Mrs. MacManus asked.

"I'm not at all," Marielle replied with surprise.

"Well, you must eat anyway. I'll make you an egg and some rashers."

"I hate to be a bother," Marielle protested, not having any idea what a rasher was.

Mrs. MacManus stood without reply before declining the help Marielle offered.

"Is there anything interesting in the paper today?" Marielle asked when Mr. MacManus finally looked up.

"It appears your Mr. Bush isn't pleased with Panama a'tall. He's cut ties and funding, in fact. The jobless rate is up in Ireland and a builder is in hot water over some funny business. There's meant to be a baby rescued, but I haven't read that article yet. Do you read the paper?"

"Sometimes. We get the local paper and I have to read *USA Today* in one of my classes, but I generally just watch CNN. I guess that's like your BBC."

"Not quite," Mr. MacManus said without clarifying. "So, does it feel strange to be on the east side of the Atlantic?"

"It does!" she replied. "Although, I've never seen the west side. I've never seen any body of water larger than the Great Lakes, actually."

"So, you've never swam in salt water?" he asked, pushing his paper to the side.

"I barely swim at all," she replied as Mrs. MacManus entered the dining room carrying Marielle's plate. "Thank you so much," Marielle said, relieved to find a smaller, more manageable portion of fried eggs and bacon than she would find at home.

"Would your parents not force you to take swimming lessons?" Mr. MacManus asked.

"No. I don't think they care. We have to go out of our way to find water in Appleton whereas it seems you need to go out of your way to avoid it here. Driving is much more important than swimming for us. However, our school has a pool and we need to take swimming before they'll let us graduate."

"Dermot raved about your school's pool," Mrs. MacManus said with fatigue.

Marielle turned toward her. "I showed him the pictures in our yearbook. He was almost as impressed with our principal letting us toilet paper the school for Homecoming."

"What do you mean by that?" she asked with an edge to her voice.

"Oh, they let us wrap trees and basically anything that stands still with toilet paper. The grounds are dripping in white when we're done. They make us leave homeroom to clean it up the next day though."

"That's disgraceful!" Mrs. MacManus declared.

Marielle twitched.

"To waste precious resources for a bit of fun is ridiculous!"

Mr. MacManus stood before excusing himself from the table. He tapped Marielle's shoulder as he passed behind her chair, causing his wife's eyes to grow more narrow.

"But I thought toilet paper was biodegradable," Marielle remarked.

"'T'is, but you don't see a problem with wasting it after it's been processed and packaged for another use?"

"I actually hadn't thought of it before," Marielle said, cutting the fat from her bacon.

"Well, it's important for you to think about it and for your teachers and headmaster to force you to think about it!"

"So, the university kids don't play pranks at UCG?" Marielle asked with curiosity.

"Not like that," she replied, turning away.

Marielle nodded once before looking down at her fried egg, surprised that Mrs. MacManus' rebuke didn't bother her more.

"So, how do you have time for such things when you're working two jobs?" Mrs. MacManus asked with less aggression.

Marielle looked up with a coy smile. "I think kids always have time for trouble."

"Do you only work for travel money, then?"

"No, I have to pay for my own expenses like school matriculation fees; school trips; driver's ed; my senior pictures; spending money, etcetera."

"Very good," she said before looking down at her lap to straighten her napkin. It was clear that Dermot's mother had come to a decision about Marielle, but it was impossible to say whether that decision hurt or favoured her.

"You need to eat," Mrs. MacManus urged, eyeing the plate Marielle barely touched. "We can walk down to meet Dermot's class when you've finished."

Marielle immediately brightened, making quick work of the food she never wanted.

"Don't be surprised if someone attempts to buy your shirt from you," Mrs. MacManus said as she buttoned her dark blue, quilted, knee-length jacket.

"Would they really be so bold?" Marielle asked, not wearing a coat.

"Do you think that bold?" Mrs. MacManus asked as she transferred her hair to the outside of her collar.

"Bold as in brave, not bold as in rude," Marielle clarified with a smile.

Mrs. MacManus nodded as they exited the house. "Please pull that door shut. My husband has a habit of leaving the door open when he takes his naps. The other day, I came home for lunch and he had left the door wide open!"

"Ajar?" Marielle asked as she looked back toward the shiny red door.

"No, unlocked."

Marielle nodded as they passed the car in the driveway. "Mr. MacManus would be happy in Appleton, then. We do that all the time."

Mrs. MacManus looked from the ground to the side of Marielle's face. "Even with no one home?"

"Absolutely. We only have a couple of keys for the house and we all come and go at different times of the day."

"That's not the stereotype for America," Mrs. MacManus said as they neared the iron gates which were held open by two large rocks.

"I think most of what you hear about America must be New York City and maybe the coasts in general. The Midwest is much safer and more conservative. I was shocked when our class visited New York in the spring."

Mrs. MacManus nodded her head, but she didn't reply until they turned south onto Salthill Road. "We read about the drug problem in America. Is this a problem in the Midwest as well?" Mrs. MacManus asked.

Marielle took a deep breath, determined to give the question more consideration than she had with Mr. MacManus. "I don't think we have an issue with anything besides marijuana in our town and even that is pretty limited. None of my close friends smoke marijuana, but everyone knows who does. Strangely enough, it's a worse problem with the rich kids. I suppose that's similar to drug use among famous people like Adam Clayton, for example," Marielle said, attempting to suppress a smile.

"Adam Clayton wasn't arrested for drug use," Mrs. MacManus said defiantly.

Marielle's eyebrows narrowed. If there was one subject she knew, it was U2. "Are you sure?" she asked. "My understanding is the Irish police caught him in possession of marijuana last month."

"Not a'tall," Mrs. MacManus said defiantly, though Marielle was sure she saw her twitch. "The offense was alcohol related. The judge made an example of him since he's a role model to children."

"Ah," Marielle said, nodding slowly. She was now convinced that no positive information about America, and no negative information about Ireland, could make the journey into Mrs. MacManus' head.

They walked past large properties on their right and a theatre on their left before the road turned and houses became town homes which eventually became businesses. Marielle stared at a large, modern-looking white church, set back from the road half a block until she bumped into Mrs. MacManus. "Excuse me," she said. "The gravitational pull of the earth must be different here. I'm having the worst time walking straight."

Mrs. MacManus didn't reply.

A short distance later, the road intersected with a rocky coast. They crossed the street near a public parking area before turning right onto a wide promenade.

Kids hopped from boulder to boulder as the dark sea sprayed between the rocks at intervals. Across the water, hills appeared charcoal-grey against a melancholy sky.

Marielle inhaled the cool sea air as Mrs. MacManus finally turned towards her. "Would it not have been wiser for you to spend your money backpacking through Europe rather than visiting us?"

Marielle glanced at Mrs. MacManus to judge her intensity. "There's no way my parents would allow me to wander around Europe. Even wandering around Heathrow pushed the limits of their patience," she said, smiling even though the question burned.

"Well, Fiona is working in France now as an au pair and she sees a good many classmates as they travel across Europe."

"Does she like her job?" Marielle asked in an effort to change the subject.

"She does," Mrs. MacManus replied, drawing a long breath. "She works for an unmarried couple and their two children." She shot a sidelong glance at Marielle.

"Really?" Marielle asked, having rarely heard of unmarried people raising children together.

"Well, there's no need for them to marry, I suppose," Mrs. MacManus said with European sophistication.

"But what about the children?" Marielle asked before glancing at Mrs. MacManus, wondering if the conversation was a test of her moral code. "That would never happen in Wisconsin," she declared.

"Why on earth not?" Mrs. MacManus asked.

"The stigma would be too much for the children. I'm not allowed to babysit for the children of divorced couples, much less unmarried ones."

"That seems rather closed-minded," Mrs. MacManus said, grinning at Marielle's animated response.

"Yes, well, it rarely comes up since there are so few of them," Marielle replied, still waiting for Mrs. MacManus to agree with her.

A collection of teenagers appeared farther along the beach near a large concrete pier with a diving tower at the end. As she neared, Marielle spied a CPR dummy lying on the ground before she saw Dermot beaming at her above it.

An attractive middle-aged man was among the spectators and the first to greet Mrs. MacManus and Marielle. Many minutes later, the man introduced his short, dark-haired daughter, Gráinne, who recently stood unusually close to Dermot. The girl shook Marielle's hand, but neither her smile nor her handshake felt like a greeting.

Marielle narrowed her eyes slightly until Dermot appeared behind Gráinne, his head standing at least six inches above hers. His smile and his vivid, golden brown eyes immediately stole Marielle's attention. Gráinne's father stopped talking to Mrs. MacManus as the intensity of the gaze shared by Dermot and Marielle distracted him. Gráinne said something no one heard before excusing herself to return to class.

"Should you not return to class yourself, Dermot?" his mother asked.

He glanced at his mother before reluctantly backing away.

A near trip caused Marielle and Dermot to laugh, and Mrs. MacManus to shake her head before he finally turned to jog back to the front of the CPR line.

Moments later, Marielle realized that Dermot hadn't actually said a word.

"Can I give you both a lift back to the house?" Gráinne's father asked as rain began to fall.

Marielle stared at Dermot, not wanting to leave him and not wanting to stay dry if he was left in the rain.

"That would be lovely, thank you," Mrs. MacManus said for both of them.

"So, when did you arrive, Marielle?" the man asked through the rear view mirror as she secured her safety belt.

"Yesterday," Marielle replied, feeling as though her stomach was attached to a cord Dermot pulled.

"What do you think of Galway so far?"

"I like it very much!" she replied with enthusiasm. "The colorful stucco buildings and the promenade are lovely. It must feel so liberating to have access to the ocean, knowing you could get into a boat and go anywhere in the world you want, anytime you like."

The man's eyebrows rose suddenly as if this was the first time he had considered the matter. "It's like anything, I suppose. You take it for granted after a time."

Marielle shook her head imperceptibly. "I've lived landlocked my entire life. I don't think there's any way I could take this for granted. Have you lived here since you were born?"

"I have, yeah. I guess I could never leave my parents," he replied, assuming Marielle asked why he hadn't left, rather than when he had arrived.

"You're a good son," Mrs. MacManus said with feeling as the man nodded appreciatively.

At that moment, Marielle realized there was a split between the Irish who stayed and the Irish who departed and that difference had much less to do with geography than she expected.

After returning to the house and saying their goodbyes to Gráinne's father, Mrs. MacManus suggested they walk to the city centre. Marielle agreed, though she feared they wouldn't return before Dermot did, and she knew this wasn't a question she could ask.

They crossed a busy intersection in silence before walking along a road that ended at another. After turning left, passing a park, and crossing the River Corrib, Marielle joined the congestion she remembered from the previous evening.

As they fought their way up Shop Street, Mrs. MacManus raised one arm in frustration towards a sign farther ahead. "Do you see that?! I don't know why they allowed a McDonald's to be built here. It ruins the entire look of the street!" she said, as though her protestations might still make a difference.

Marielle regarded the building's stone façade and old fashioned sign which matched the style of others on the street, wondering if Mrs. MacManus' annoyance had more to do with McDonald's being an American company than an eyesore.

Dermot's mother and Marielle walked again in silence until they arrived at a farmers' market which spilled onto the street with crates of fresh produce, and people browsing more than buying. As if to counteract the effect of McDonald's, Mrs. MacManus insisted Marielle have her picture taken in front of a pile of carrots which stood four feet tall and at least double that width.

After oohing and aahing as much as a Wisconsin girl could manage at a farmers' market, they walked to the modest home of Nora Barnacle.

"People said Nora was simple and uneducated, but she was James Joyce's inspiration for much of his writing," Mrs. MacManus argued.

Marielle bit her bottom lip, wondering if *Ulysses* was among those inspirations.

"Have you read any of Joyce's work?" Mrs. MacManus asked.

"I began to read one of his books, but I didn't finish it before I arrived. I've read a good many of William Butler Yeats' poems though."

"Very good," she replied, as though that was good enough. "We'll visit Yeats' Tower tomorrow while the country is enthralled with the hurling final."

Marielle gasped.

"Is something wrong?" Mrs. MacManus asked.

"No. Sorry. I didn't realize the final was tomorrow, but Thoor Ballylee would be lovely."

Mrs. MacManus narrowed her eyebrows before pressing onward towards the Church of St. Nicholas which had somehow earned the designation of Collegiate.

"It's very strict looking," Marielle said as they approached a dark stone building surrounded by a wrought iron fence. A large square clock tower stood above the centre, topped by a steeply-pitched green roof.

"It's said that Columbus stopped here briefly to pray before sailing to the New World," Mrs. MacManus remarked, staring at the façade.

Marielle glanced at Mrs. MacManus before asking: "Do you believe that?"

"No. It seems a bit out of the way."

Marielle chuckled. "It's also Anglican. What are the chances Columbus would seek out the only Protestant church in Galway to pray when he's Catholic?"

Mrs. MacManus regarded Marielle with pity. "There were no Protestants during Columbus' time. The Reformation hadn't occurred yet."

"Oh, right," Marielle said, beginning to blush.

Mrs. MacManus purchased a leaflet for ten pence before handing it to a grateful Marielle.

"It's amazing to think this church was built by 1330," she said as she studied the first diagram. "I'm used to new buildings and new sidewalks. Even just walking here I thought how strange it looked to see young people walking on such old streets. Do you ever think of the hundreds of years of footsteps under your feet?" Marielle asked.

Mrs. MacManus studied her before nodding her head, allowing herself the slightest grin.

Marielle walked her pamphlet through a set of peaked arches which gave onto the main nave, then sat down to read. When she finished, she found Mrs. MacManus in an isolated side chapel.

"So, did the Mayor of Galway really hang his son and did Cromwell's army really stable their horses inside here?" she asked with wonder.

"He did, and they were. You can see the hoof marks over there," Mrs. MacManus said, pointing to the opposite side of the nave. "And the mayor's son's tomb is farther along the right wing."

"Do you mind if I take a look?" Marielle asked in a near pleading tone. "I promise I'll be quick."

"Not a'tall," Mrs. MacManus replied quizzically.

Several minutes later, Marielle returned to Mrs. MacManus, wearing a huge smile. "The gentleman over there told me the tomb used to be outside the church, but a renovation brought it inside. The exciting part is that I knew the word lynching came from Galway, but I didn't realize it was Mayor Lynch who hung his own son from the castle after he murdered someone. Can you imagine hanging your own son?"

Mrs. MacManus shook her head.

"He also said Cromwell's army was responsible for some of the headless statues here. I wonder why they would deface a Protestant church when he was Protestant. The church was Anglican back then, right?" she asked, then continued without waiting for a reply. "Aside from being a jerk, Cromwell seems rather simple-minded as well."

Marielle studied the arches supporting the ceiling before turning back to Mrs. MacManus. "Thank you for bringing me here," she said excitedly. "I've never sat in a building that was over 600 years old before. In fact, I'd be surprised if I've sat in a building that was over 100 years old before." She looked at Mrs. MacManus in earnest. "Really. I can't think of an example. It says here that the rectory is on Taylor's Hill Road. Do you know Reverend Forrest?"

"Only in passing," Mrs. MacManus replied, still recovering from the flood of interest Marielle threw in her direction. "We should head back now. Dermot will wonder where we've gone off to."

"Oh, right," Marielle said happily. "Do you think he'd want to go to the library with me to look up Columbus' exact route to America?"

Mrs. MacManus nodded slowly. "I'm sure if anyone could convince him to research the matter further, it's you."

"Excellent," Marielle replied, allowing a smile to overtake her face as conversation ended.

As they walked over the River Corrib, a young woman stopped Mrs. MacManus to ask about an assignment. Owing to the narrowness of the footpath, Marielle stepped backward, then suddenly lost her balance, stepping for a moment into the roadway as a car raced by from a direction she didn't expect. She stepped up quickly before grabbing the rail of the bridge, deciding she needed to be much more careful in the future.

"That girl isn't the full shilling!" Mrs. MacManus declared as they continued their walk.

Marielle looked back nervously to ensure the woman was outside ear shot.

"We made plans to have an end-of-year party at a pub near Eyre

Square last semester and she had the CHEEK to suggest the place was too dirty. And you should see the pub her father owns in Salthill. It's a bloody kip!"

Marielle didn't know the proper response for this statement, so she smiled as she nodded her head.

"I don't know why she bothers taking my class! She understands very little and she and her friends have plans to be stewardesses. Can you imagine? They think it very glamorous, but I told them they're no better than waitresses in the air."

Marielle grimaced slightly. "Maybe it's the travel they find glamorous. If you can't afford to travel otherwise, it might seem like the only way out."

Mrs. MacManus sighed without responding.

As they passed Father Burke Park, two boys of similar height and frame turned the corner farther ahead—one strawberry blond with a fair complexion, and the other the exact opposite. The darker boy immediately attracted Marielle's attention before she realized it was Dermot. A smile overtook his face when he saw her and a smile overtook hers, becoming brighter when she realized he had come looking for her. As the distance between them diminished, Marielle finally noticed Sean's smile, which was nearly as broad as Dermot's, likely owing to something Dermot said.

"Sean, this is Marielle," Dermot said proudly.

Sean shook Marielle's hand as he appraised her wordlessly. "Em, well, I'm afraid I must be getting back to me mam," he said, backing up as everyone studied him. "She's certain another boarder will be knocking at our door before long and I'm meant to help with the bed clothes." And with that, Sean ran down the street in the opposite direction.

"Boarder indeed!" Mrs. MacManus said, passing Dermot as the footpath narrowed and turned.

"Well, his mum does run a B&B," Dermot explained before turning back to smile at Marielle.

"I know very well she runs a B&B, Dermot!" his mother snapped without turning to make eye contact. "My point is he should be well able to say hello properly."

Dermot seized Marielle's hand covertly. She smiled nervously as he turned to regard her. She felt her breathing become more shallow as he rubbed her pinkie. She pulled her hand away as her chest began to ache.

"So, where did you run off to?" Dermot asked Marielle in a soft voice, but his mother answered instead and didn't stop speaking until they reached the front door.

"Seaview," Marielle said happily as she pointed to the brass plate secured to a large stone on the house's façade.

"Oh, right," Dermot replied. "Mum, why is the house named Seaview?"

"I believe one could see the sea from here at one stage," she said, walking through the door without turning around.

"So you explored the market, did you?" Dermot asked Marielle as they entered the foyer.

She nodded, feeling one night wasn't enough time to steel herself against his accent or his eyes.

"It's madness. There's really no point in attempting to drive on Shop Street a'tall on a Saturday," Dermot continued as they walked towards the dining room.

"It's awfully warm out. Do you mind if I change into shorts?" Marielle asked Mrs. MacManus as Dermot turned to her with concern.

Minutes later, Marielle entered the dining room as Dermot and his mother approached the door.

"Those are just like Dermot's," Mrs. MacManus said, looking down at Marielle's jeans which were cut-off two inches above the knee and rolled twice.

Mrs. MacManus reached behind the dining room door to grab a picture from the bookcase. "Look at this photo. Dermot is wearing the same shorts. He nearly collapsed after hiking to the top of the Puy de Dôme in France." She regarded her son with an amused dismay. "A boy who won the British and All-Ireland hurling championships and he couldn't keep up with his father or me whilst hiking up a mountain."

"Well, those are completely different muscles," Dermot said before giving in to a grin.

Marielle looked down at the picture of Dermot lying back on a rock, his legs bent to allow his feet to touch the ground while his arms were held out to the sides as though in the middle of saying a Mass.

"Ah, and here's another of him about to hang glide from the top after he caught his breath." She handed Marielle a close-up of Dermot's smile with a colourful sail dominating the background.

"Is that safe?" Marielle asked with concern.

"Perfectly," Mrs. MacManus replied, taking the picture from Marielle before returning to the kitchen as she continued speaking. "You should've heard Sean in that very room the day Dermot received your latest photos. Dermot couldn't get a word in edge-wise. When I think he's the same boy who treated you so rudely in the street just now." Mrs. MacManus shook her head in disgust. "You should have just *heard* the things he was saying!" She looked through the doorway at Marielle as if expecting her to ask what those things were, then looked away when Marielle did nothing but smile.

Dermot and Marielle exchanged an amused look.

"Well, we had never seen anyone pose for a photo before," Dermot explained as his eyes remained on Marielle.

"Really?" Marielle asked, beginning to feel culture shock. "Everyone in the U.S. poses when they get their senior pictures taken."

Dermot nodded. "Did anyone ask to buy your shirt from you?" he asked, appraising either the shirt or what lay beneath it.

"No. Your mom suggested they might. Is this common?"

"Sure. Well, with any type of clothing people haven't seen before."

Her eyebrows furrowed. "But it has my name on the back."

"I doubt that would make a difference," he said, pulsing his eyebrows. "What time did you wake up?"

Marielle shivered before she said, "Nine-ten."

Dermot tilted his head back to laugh. "Ten past nine you mean?"

She shook her head. "No, I said it right. By the way, I thought you were going to wake me up," she said, trying not to betray how disappointed she felt.

Dermot shook his head as he narrowed his eyebrows, then tilted his head towards the kitchen. "Mum, would you mind if I take Marielle for a bit of a walk?"

"I don't mind, but fetch a tape from my dresser first. I must create a duplicate for my class on Monday."

"Ah-right," he replied, then looked away from Marielle with difficulty before running from the room.

"Marielle, there's a leaflet on Thoor Ballylee in the drawer of the hutch. You should read it," Mrs. MacManus said more as an order than a request.

Marielle opened the leftmost drawer of the dining room hutch, finding the leaflet without difficulty. She paged through it as Dermot returned.

"Why don't you read out loud, Marielle?" Mrs. MacManus suggested.

"It's been ages since we've visited."

Marielle looked up at Dermot as they shared a grin, and likely, a similar thought. A reading test was apparently part of the vetting process.

Marielle read without difficulty until the word *Celts*.

"You pronounced that wrong," Mrs. MacManus called from the kitchen. "It's Celts with a hard C."

"But what about the Boston Celtics?" Marielle asked, staring at Dermot as they awaited the verdict.

"They have it wrong," Mrs. MacManus replied.

The teenagers smiled before Marielle continued reading, only skipping those words which appeared unpronounceable while declaring them Gaelic.

"It's not Gaelic," Mrs. MacManus said with impatience. "It's Irish. Anyway, that's enough," she said as though disappointed by Marielle's literacy. "Is Dermot back?"

"He's right here," Marielle replied, smiling as she continued to stare at him.

"I can't find what you're looking for, Mum," he finally said.

Mrs. MacManus sighed while approaching the doorway. "I swear he can look directly at something and not see it," she complained to Marielle. "I'll go up a moment later and it's exactly where I described it."

"Do you want me to look?" Marielle asked before shooting Dermot a mischievous grin.

"Please," Mrs. MacManus replied gratefully. "It should be the only cassette tape on my dresser."

Dermot regarded his mother with concern either because she questioned his ability to search, or because she was putting Marielle to work.

Marielle ran up the stairs like she was in a race and rounded the banister before turning right into Mrs. MacManus' large room which was papered in rose and cream. It was an especially nice colour scheme against walnut furniture which seemed less dark owing to copious amounts of light streaming through sheer curtains on both sides of the dresser.

Marielle made an effort to filter her vision to cassette tapes only, hopeful nothing private would enter her line of sight. Within seconds, she held a dark grey cassette tape. She returned to the dining room victoriously, holding it up for Dermot's disappointed appraisal.

"Thank you, Marielle," Mrs. MacManus said with genuine

appreciation as she grabbed the tape and ignored the playful looks the teenagers exchanged. "Bloody!" she proclaimed seconds after placing the tape into slot one of the boom box which rested on a bookshelf behind the dining room door.

Dermot and Marielle turned toward her as she spun around.

"My blank cassettes aren't large enough to accept the information on this tape."

"Are they 60s?" Marielle asked.

Mrs. MacManus nodded.

"I have a 90 upstairs. It has songs I taped from the radio, but you should be able to tape over them without a problem. I'll be right back," she said before disappearing again.

Dermot intercepted the tape as soon as Marielle returned to the room. "We have nothing like this," he said, studying the mostly clear cassette with yellow wheels, and geometric shapes painted in blue and fuchsia. "Ah, you didn't remove the tab," he added with disappointment.

"What tab?" Marielle asked.

"The one that allows us to overwrite your information," he said, pointing to the side of the tape.

"So you can use it, then. That's good, right?" she asked, wondering why his face registered regret.

His mother clearly wondered the same as she waited beside the stereo for her son to hand over the tape.

Dermot looked at his mother concernedly. "Do you really think we should take Marielle's tape from her?" he asked.

Mrs. MacManus sighed while Marielle hurriedly spoke, "It's nothing, Dermot. It's just the top ten songs from a radio station in Green Bay and maybe some Led Zeppelin for emergency purposes," she said, attempting to make him smile. It worked, but only until he turned to his mother again.

"What's the problem, Dermot?" Mrs. MacManus asked with irritation. "Marielle has no issue with it. I scarcely see why you should."

Dermot closed his eyes as he handed over the tape, ignoring his mother's lingering appraisal. "Shall we go?" he asked Marielle in defeat.

"Sure," she replied, attempting to unfurrow her eyebrows.

"What was that about?" she asked kindly as Dermot closed the front door.

He sighed before he spoke. "I don't know. I couldn't bear to have her destroy your tape. I thought if I could listen to it whilst you're gone, it would feel less like we're apart."

Marielle stopped walking. "That's an incredibly nice thing to say, but I just got here. There's no reason to imagine me gone yet." She looked at him consolingly as they continued to walk.

Dermot nodded at the gravel, placing his fingers into his pockets as wind gusted in a single puff.

"Ah," Marielle exclaimed as she covered her left eye. "There's something in my eye. I need to run in for a second."

Minutes later, she returned to Dermot, halting his progress as he paced at the bottom of the driveway, and immediately turning his look of yearning into a smile.

"Sorry," she said as she reached him.

"Hello, Dermot!" a woman called from her garden across the street as she evaluated the blonde girl whose hand Dermot eagerly held.

"Hello, Mrs. Murphy," Dermot said, a thousand times more happily than his expression suggested before Marielle joined him.

Farther along the street, Dermot said, "She's the woman who fed Gryphon over the summer. It was very good of her. We didn't expect it a'tall, like."

Marielle drew a sharp breath. "Then who was supposed to feed him?"

"No one. My parents thought him well able to care for himself."

"Really?" Marielle asked with alarm.

"Certainly. Dogs here come and go as they please. I have no idea where he is now, for example. For all we know, he has another family laying claim to him as well."

Marielle finally smiled before looking down at their hands. "Aren't you worried Ashley or one of her friends will see us?"

"I honestly don't care," he replied with feeling, "unless you're concerned you might be at the centre of a bit of drama."

"Not at all," she replied happily. "Drama and I are good friends... though it seems to follow me more than I pursue it. If she starts yelling, I'll just pretend I don't speak any English. Does she know German?"

Dermot laughed. "Not a'tall. You know, my dad thinks we're mad for dating people we don't fancy."

Marielle nodded thoughtfully. "Yes, well, you can hardly explain that we're using them for company until you and I get married."

He shook his head slowly. "No. I class that as a much more awkward conversation."

Dermot shared a smile with Marielle before staring at the footpath with concern. "Do you think of me when you're with other lads?"

Marielle exhaled slowly while squinting slightly. "Not usually the first time I kiss them, but by the second week—when they start to bore or annoy me—I do. What about you?"

"The same," he replied with a short nod. "I suppose you can feel wonderful things for just about anyone you find attractive, or who's keen on you anyway."

"Yeah, but there are so many things that make an otherwise attractive person ugly," Marielle noted. "Though, you generally don't find that out until the second week."

"I doubt *any* of the lads find you ugly," Dermot said, glancing at her as he squeezed her hand.

She glanced back. "You say that, but I'm quite sure Gary would disagree with you, especially after prom night."

Dermot halted the swinging of their hands. "What happened on prom night?" he murmured.

"Well, Gary took me to his cabin by a lake. It was after midnight and no one else was there, but somehow all of the candles were lit. I think his parents were in on it which I find more than a little disturbing. Anyway, he shows me the view of the lake while he's hugging me from behind, and then asks me if I'm tired. When I say I am, he leads me into the bedroom where the bed is freshly made and turned down."

Dermot stopped walking, turning towards Marielle as if prepared for disappointment.

"So, I look at the bed and I say, 'I'm *not* having sex with you, Gary,' and he gets really irritated and says, 'I didn't ask you to have sex with me!' and I said, 'No, but your cabin did.' "

Marielle laughed with Dermot as they began to walk again. "So, I'm pretty sure Gary didn't find me attractive at all that night, especially when he could've spent it with any number of girls who were stupid enough to fall for his transparent romantic overtures."

"So, nothing happened, then?" Dermot asked, still using his soft voice.

"Well, we made out for awhile on the bed before we fell asleep, but that's all that happened. He's a horrible kisser, by the way. I didn't realize how bad until last night."

Dermot smiled proudly.

"It's gonna be harder to go back to kissing him when I return to

Wisconsin. I keep thinking it might be time to trade up, but I'd hate to abuse someone I respected."

"That presumes boys only want to date you with the aim of eventually marrying," Dermot remarked. "That thought doesn't occur to most lads."

Marielle raised her eyebrows briefly. "Maybe in other areas of the country or world, but Gary's already telling his family, and even one of his teachers, that I'm *the one*. I guess when I trade up I'll have to say, 'Look, I'm happy to date you, but I have no intention of marrying you, EVER, and it's good if you never bring up either marriage OR sex. Not once. Don't even ask me why those topics are off limits.' "

"That seems a bit off-putting," Dermot said happily.

"Yeah, but there's probably no way around it. I just need to date boys who deserve to be mistreated. Thank God there are so many of them."

Dermot squeezed Marielle's hand as both smiled.

"So, does Ashley deserve to be mistreated?" she asked.

"I'm wondering that myself. She cheated on her ex-boyfriend with me, but I'm cheating with you right now... well, I'm *always* cheating with you in a way. So, I guess the answer is no, but I don't see this as mistreating her. My relationship with you is completely different. With her, I'm just a teenager. With you, I'm looking to a life beyond university."

Marielle nodded. "I agree. It's completely different. I guess the only reason I abuse Gary is because he's such a typical male jackass. Only *his* jokes are funny. Only *his* friends are interesting. He wouldn't bother with girls at all if his hand could give him the satisfaction he required."

Dermot chuckled. "Speaking from experience, I don't see him casting you aside any time soon, then."

Marielle studied him briefly. "Speaking from experience with me or with your hand?"

"Both," he replied.

As they neared the sea, Marielle looked at Dermot in earnest. "Do you miss hurling?" she asked.

He held air in his cheeks for a moment before letting it go. "I do, yeah, but we thought I should concentrate on my studies during 6th year."

"Who's *we*?" Marielle asked.

"My parents and I."

She glanced at him again. "Both parents or just your mom?"

"I guess just my mum, but she didn't walk over me, like. It was my decision as well. In fact, it was good of her to take the blame with my coach and teammates."

Marielle nodded even as her eyebrows furrowed. "As someone who's no good at just about every sport, it's hard to imagine walking away from something when you're at the top of your game, so to speak."

Dermot closed his eyes abruptly.

"I'm sorry," she said immediately. "Did I upset you?"

He opened his eyes again, displaying nothing but pain. "You don't understand the cost of it, Marielle! I was constantly exhausted and my parents, well, my mother was terrified my grades would slip and it might jeopardise university. The pressure was immense!" He stared hard at the sea behind her. "I was sitting on the sea wall, the one near the pier, and two lads from my team were chatting beneath me. They didn't see me, like. One of them said 'Dermot is a bit of an ass, isn't he? He takes hurling far too seriously.' I didn't know what to say to that, so I yelled, 'I'd hope if my friends had something to say, they'd say it to my face!' but in truth they were right. I have no earthly idea how to engage in anything without taking it seriously. I was driven mad when any of them made a mistake on the pitch, let alone when *I* made a mistake. I would obsess over it for ages!"

"I understand," Marielle said, rubbing Dermot's hand as she looked up at him. "I'm that way about music and school, and even work. I know it shouldn't matter if a sax rests half a beat instead of a quarter—most of the audience won't notice—but I go insane if anyone screws up while we're performing. At work I'm just as bad. If the tablecloths are crooked or if the plates aren't stacked neatly, I fix them. I can't stand that my name might be associated with anything that isn't perfect. I know playing sax in a jazz concert or working in a nursing home kitchen are a far cry from being a hurling god, but it's the same concept. I guess if it's worth doing, it's worth doing better than anyone else on the planet does it," she said, smiling sympathetically.

"Exactly!" Dermot exclaimed. "Thank you for understanding."

"Well, my only concern is that later you don't regret giving it up."

He squeezed her hand appreciatively. "I imagine I'll miss it when they lose an important game and I think I might've made the winning goal, or worse, if they have a perfect season and everyone realises they never needed me a'tall."

"I very much doubt the latter will happen," Marielle said comfortingly before turning to walk again. "I can't imagine how anyone would think they don't need you. So, is Sean still hurling?"

"He is. He gives me no end of grief over it as well." Dermot paused as they waited to cross to the sea side of the road. "About earlier. I hope you weren't offended by his behaviour."

"Not at all," Marielle replied genially. "I thought it was funny. Though I don't usually scare boys away so quickly."

Dermot chuckled as he hurried her across the intersection. "Well, he knew you were lovely from your photographs, but I think he imagined you wouldn't look as beautiful in person."

Marielle stopped walking. "You need to insult me quickly," she said, her cheeks turning red.

"Pardon?"

"That's too nice of a compliment. If you don't insult me, I'll feel uncomfortable. Seriously," she said with urgency.

Dermot grabbed both of her hands while looking down at her blushing face. "You don't wake a'tall easily," he said.

Marielle laughed. "So you tried to wake me up?"

"I didn't, no. I watched you sleep for a time, but I couldn't bear to wake you."

"Oh, no!" she said, turning away as she placed her hand against her forehead.

"What, love?" he asked, equal parts amused and concerned.

"I can't breathe well through my nose so I sleep with my mouth open. It's horrible and undignified."

Dermot tried not to laugh as he said, "I swear to you, you looked lovely. It was all I could do not to kiss you."

She looked up at him with caution. "No open mouth?"

He shook his head as he confirmed, "No open mouth."

"Okay, then," she said, relaxing. "So, why didn't you wake me?"

"I thought you'd be cross with me."

Marielle's eyebrows narrowed. "But I *told* you to wake me up. I promise I'm not bi-polar."

He grabbed her hand again. "I know, but I hated to disturb your sleep."

"Wait. Go back. Do girls ask you to do something, then yell at you when you do it?"

He nodded as he said, "Sometimes."

"That's insane!" Marielle protested. "Why do you put up with that?"

"I thought that was the way with girls."

"No offense to whomever you have in mind, but that's only the case with crazy girls! Promise me you won't date crazy girls anymore. They're scary and unpredictable, and I need you in one piece when we get married."

Dermot nodded happily before a colourful sail on the bay caught his eye. "I love to sit here and watch the sailing yachts," he said, hugging Marielle from behind after she turned toward the bay.

Marielle smiled at the boats gliding across the water. "After we're married, can we buy one and sail to the Mediterranean or just circumnavigate Ireland?" she asked.

"Those yachts are quite dear, and you're afraid of water," Dermot said too near Marielle's ear to avoid causing tingling sensations down her spine.

"We'll promise not to sink it, then," she murmured.

Dermot chuckled. "Alright. What do you say we go to the Docks and you can show me what you have in mind? No catamarans though." He looked at her with a mischievous grin, not seeing her gasp as someone called his name from a passing car.

"Do you know them?" Marielle asked.

Dermot turned towards the car as it sped in the direction of the pier. "Probably," he said.

Marielle stared at a lighthouse at the end of a long jetty farther along the coast as Dermot squeezed her hand. "What's wrong, love?" he asked. "You're suddenly so quiet."

She glanced at him. "I'm afraid you won't believe me if I tell you."

"I swear to you, I will," he said, staring at her profile.

She took a deep breath. "Okay, have we ever talked about getting a sailboat or a catamaran before?"

He shook his head. "No, I don't believe we've discussed it."

"Are you sure?" she asked with urgency.

Dermot smiled. "I'm quite sure."

She glanced at him nervously before she said, "I had a dream last night that we were alone on the America's Cup catamaran deciding where to sail and it felt like we were married and no one else could find us or get to us. It was just you and me and we were free."

"Really?" he asked with more joy than wonder. "Well, the idea did occur to me a few weeks back, but I'm quite certain I never mentioned it. I'm taking you to the place where I first considered it. So, if it resembles your dream a'tall we should call a priest."

"To get married or to have me exorcised?" Marielle asked.

"Both," he said, smiling. "Well, one before the other. Wait. You must've seen the Docks on your way to the city centre with my mum."

"I was concentrating too hard on keeping up with your mother—verbally not physically—I saw some boats from the corner of my eye as I stepped off the curb and nearly got hit by a car though."

Dermot tugged on Marielle's hand as he looked at her with concern. "Did you really?"

She shook her head. "It just shocked me when the car came by so fast from the opposite direction I expected. I wasn't in any real danger."

"Would I sound like your father if I asked you to please look both ways before stepping off the kerb in future?"

"Not a'tall," she said, mimicking his accent.

"That's quite good," he said happily. "What else can you say?"

She took a deep breath. "I'll tell ya somethin' now, Aidan, and not a word of it's a lie."

"That's grand!" Dermot declared. "Where did you hear that?"

"Just a block or so ago. Two men were talking near a parked car. You must've zoned-out on that one."

"I did indeed. I was terrified you were cross with me."

"Because I was quiet?"

Dermot nodded.

"Please don't think that way. I can hardly imagine a scenario where I would be angry with you."

Dermot laughed. "That can't be true."

She smiled. "Actually, it's not. I *can* imagine it, but it would take a lot more effort than you've given it so far."

They walked along the street-side of a waterfront park before turning left where the River Corrib meets Galway Bay. A few feet farther along, Marielle spied a sign bearing the Claddagh symbol.

"I noticed your mother wears a Claddagh ring," she said.

Dermot nodded at the sign. "Everyone here does."

"Will we?"

He turned towards her. "If you wouldn't mind?"

"I wouldn't mind," she said decisively as she noticed the boats tied up

478

against the sea wall. "Are these the boats you wanted to show me?"

"No, the boats I'm considering are farther along, inside the locks."

"It must be amazing to live in a harbor town," she reflected, scanning the river and the colourful town homes on the opposite side. "I used to sit in my room thinking how trapped I was with nothing but vast open fields around me. You must feel the opposite with the ocean at your doorstep."

"I do," he said decisively. "I can't imagine ever living far from the sea."

"I don't see myself ever asking you to," she replied.

They walked until they stood across the street from a church and in front of lock-enclosed inlet which sheltered a dozen or so boats, resting side by side in four rows.

"We won't get a motorboat, will we?" Marielle asked with concern, leaning against the black iron railing as the largest boat caught her attention.

"Not a'tall. A sailing yacht is a bit more work, but I prefer the limitless potential of wind power. We should have a motor in case the wind dies though."

"Okay. I prefer a wheel to that hand thingy," she said, pointing toward a nearby boat.

"Tiller," Dermot said with amusement.

"Right. And it has to be big enough for a bathroom and a couple of bedrooms."

Dermot smiled at Marielle's lack of nautical terminology.

"Which one do you like best?" she asked, scanning the water.

"Why don't you tell me which *you* like best?" he asked, glancing at her before returning to his appraisal of the boats.

"Alright," she agreed. "This will be like a personality test. We'll know we're meant to sail around the world together—or at least around Ireland—if we choose the same boat, but you can't change your answer once I've given mine."

"I promise, I shan't," he replied, smiling at her.

"Okay," she said, looking back at the water as she began studying hull designs, main sail covers, and furling jibs without knowing what they were called. She finally settled on a 40 foot yacht with a tapered stern, low transom, and dark blue Bimini. "*Honora*," she said.

"You're joking?!" he replied.

"I'm not. Why? Is that a bad boat?"

"No, she's gorgeous!"

"What's your choice, then?"

He pointed at a cream-coloured boat with a maroon sail cover. "I initially chose *Honora* as well, but she's a bit long and the *Zephyr* might be easier for one person to sail."

"Why do you need to sail it alone?" Marielle asked with some dismay. "I'm going to be onboard."

Dermot smiled as he glanced at her. "But you don't sail."

"But you'll teach me."

He turned towards her. "You won't listen."

"I absolutely will! I admit that I'm not obedient on land, but I swear I'll listen to any command you give me on the water." She looked at him with intensity. "I swear on my soul."

"*Any* command?" he asked, a mischievous smile overtaking his face.

She smiled back. "Any."

"Well, we'll need to buy this yacht soon, then," he replied as the air became considerably warmer.

"Not before we agree on a name," she decided.

"Ah-right," Dermot replied. "Okay, so what to name our sailing yacht?"

Marielle looked back at the water. "Would you call it a yacht? It's just a boat."

"These are most definitely yachts," he said, studying them again with the tip of his left index finger touching his lips.

"We could name it after Gryphon," Marielle suggested.

Dermot shook his head twice. "No, it must be a girl's name for good luck."

"The *Zephyr* isn't."

"True, but I didn't name it, and I'm a traditionalist. No redheads aboard either."

Marielle laughed. "Is that a rule?"

Dermot nodded, still studying *Honora*. "It used to be."

"Poor Sean," she said with empathy.

Dermot laughed as Marielle finally broke his concentration. "I'll tell him you said that! He'll have no trouble giving out to you, then."

Marielle's mouth opened seconds before she spoke. "What's wrong with red hair? I thought all Irish people aspired to have red hair and freckles?"

"Not a'tall! We generally pity children and parents when a red-haired child is born."

"That's nuts! I've always wanted red hair."

"Well, we've already established that you're mad," Dermot replied, then reflexively said "ow" before she elbowed him.

Marielle raised her eyebrows briefly. "Well, I've established that you can't be captain of our boat if you can't even come up with a name."

"I'm thinking," he said, picking up her hand to kiss it. "What if we give it your name?" he asked suddenly.

She smiled as color rose on her cheeks. "I knew you were going to say that. I couldn't sail on a boat named after me without feeling overwhelmed by arrogance."

He nodded once. "Alright. It's settled. We'll name it after our daughter, then".

Pain washed over Marielle's face.

"Are you alright?" Dermot asked, bending his knees to better look into her eyes.

She nodded. "I am. You just keep throwing beautiful thoughts at me. I don't think I can take it."

"Well, you must try to manage it because I plan to spend my life throwing beautiful thoughts at you."

Marielle held the railing as she closed her eyes.

"Marielle," Dermot said softly.

"I just need a minute," she murmured, turning away briefly to wipe her eyes. She cleared her throat before she spoke again, staring at the boats instead of Dermot. "It's overwhelming to be near you. I was sure I had elevated you in my mind and you couldn't possibly be as handsome, and smart, and sweet as I imagined. But the truth is you're so much more than I expected. It feels wonderful to be wrong, but at the same time, you're beginning to terrify me."

"Why?" he asked, smiling as he gently turned her chin toward him.

"Because no other guy will ever live up to you and if you change your mind about us, I'm not sure I could ever be happy with anyone else."

Dermot pulled Marielle to him. "I won't change my mind about us," he said before kissing her in a way that made her forget about fear or anyone walking, driving, or sailing nearby.

Chapter Thirty-One

A Pitch of Passion Wrought

—W.B. Yeats — *All Souls' Night*

"Are you really taking me to McDonald's?" Marielle asked as Dermot held open the restaurant's door.

"Do you not like McDonald's?" he asked with concern.

"Oh, I do, but your mom was ready to throw a Molotov cocktail through the front window earlier."

He pressed the side of his index finger against his lips briefly. "We won't tell her, then."

"Well, how are you getting on, Dermot?" the cashier asked from a 15-year-old body using a 40-year-old's voice.

"I'm grand, Kevin. How are things yourself?"

"I'm in the middle of my second shift because Gerry never bothered turning up. He's a right eejit, that one."

Dermot laughed. "Kev, this is my good friend Marielle. She's visiting from America."

Kevin nodded towards Marielle before looking at Dermot again. "And you took her here to eat? Are you daft, man?"

Dermot regarded his friend with amusement. "Does your manager know how you talk about this fine establishment?"

"He knows himself. He never eats here. I never eat here either. My mother would give out murder."

"Is there something wrong with the food here?" Marielle asked, leaning toward Kevin confidentially.

"Not a'tall," he replied, "but we're nearly putting Supermac's out of business."

"Would you like Dermot and I to go to Supermac's instead?" she asked kindly.

"I suppose it'll be fine if you order drinks and chips," Kevin offered.

"Very good," she said. "Then, we'll go to Supermac's for a burger."

"There's a lot of guilt in this McDonald's," Marielle remarked as she and Dermot walked away from the counter.

Dermot chose a large, semi-circular, yellow booth with a clear view of the front door. He scooted beside Marielle before placing her right leg over his left and resting his left hand on her thigh.

Marielle analyzed the fry from which she had taken a bite. "Although dripping with guilt, Irish-Catholic McDonald's French fries are much better than Protestant-American McDonald's French fries," she noted.

"Are they really?" Dermot asked with interest.

"I have no idea. It could just be that I've never eaten a French fry with your hand on my thigh before."

Dermot nudged Marielle as Kevin rounded the table, employing a broom and dust pan. Dermot shook his head as Kevin walked away. "You know, they only pay a little over three quid an hour here? It's a scandal."

Marielle considered the matter for a moment. "That's actually better than what I get paid if you take into account the exchange rate."

"Really?" he asked with surprise.

She nodded as she picked up another French fry.

"So, you earned enough to journey here on such little pay?" Dermot asked as guilt moved from the French fry to the expression on his face.

Marielle opened her eyes wider for a fraction of a second to diffuse Dermot's angst before indicating she did.

"Your parents didn't help you a'tall, like?" he asked.

Marielle considered lying to remove Dermot's guilt before deciding on the truth.

"That's amazing, Marielle! You're a wonder," Dermot remarked.

"Well, I couldn't wait to kiss you and pick out a sailing yacht," she explained. "Plus, you wouldn't send me a decent picture of yourself. So, you left me with no other choice."

Dermot squeezed her thigh as he looked at her in earnest. "I'm immensely flattered that you worked so hard to visit me."

She smiled back as she picked up her drink. "And I'm flattered that you wanted me to come—I mean, to visit," she said, beginning to laugh.

"You *are* a pervert," he declared, smiling broadly.

She pulsed her eyebrows. "Lucky you."

"That's what I was thinking," he replied happily.

They had nearly finished their French fries when Dermot looked up with alarm at a middle-aged woman reaching for the front door handle. Marielle reflexively moved her leg and scooted farther from him. Seconds later, the woman made eye contact with Dermot before turning to Marielle.

"Hello, Dermot," the woman said coolly, narrowing her eyes at the discomfort on Dermot's face.

"Hello, Mrs. Brennan," Dermot replied in his adult voice.

The woman crossed her arms. "So, I heard you and my daughter had a bit of a row the night before last."

"I'm afraid so," he said, unconsciously leaning away from Marielle.

Mrs. Brennan turned to assess Marielle. "So, you're the American, then?"

"I am," Marielle replied as though national honor required her to say it clearly.

"Well, sure, you're in McDonald's after all," Mrs. Brennan said dismissively.

Marielle nodded. "That's right. I had to check in. It's like our embassy," she replied, then smiled.

Dermot bit his bottom lip.

Mrs. Brennan narrowed her eyes at Marielle without effect before returning her scrutiny to Dermot. "You'll want to ring Ashley sooner than later."

"Yes, Mrs. Brennan," he said dutifully.

"Right, so. Enjoy your—" She looked down at the single empty carton of fries, "day."

"Jaysus!" Dermot said to the ceiling after Mrs. Brennan walked to the back of the restaurant.

"She's fierce," Marielle added, looking after her.

He released a long breath before he looked over his shoulder. "She's usually very kind, actually."

Marielle nodded. "Just the same, I think we should get out of here."

"Right, so," he replied, exiting the booth.

They walked briskly toward the river, then onto Father Griffin Avenue before a voice yelled Dermot's name from behind.

"Feck!" he exclaimed as he turned around.

"Where the feck have you been?" Sean asked before saying "hi" to Marielle for the first time.

Dermot relaxed. "We're after running into Mrs. Brennan."

Sean smiled. "Bad luck, that."

"The worst!" Dermot agreed. "We saw no one on the Prom or the Docks or Eyre Square. I thought we were home free, like."

"Well, me mam wants to know if you're keen to fish on Lough Corrib.

She's willing to give us a lift an' all."

"That would be grand if Marielle is up to it," Dermot said, turning towards her.

"Absolutely," she replied, preferring as much distance as possible from Dermot's mother and Mrs. Brennan.

Sean nodded. "Donal's keen to go as well. It'll be a bit close"

"Marielle can always sit on my lap if we require more space," Dermot said, flashing her a smile.

***

Marielle asked Dermot in vain if he needed help organizing his fishing gear or snacks such as miniature cans of Coke and pretzels.

"Me mam is here," Sean called as he returned through the front door.

"Do you have bait, like?" Dermot asked when they intersected in the dining room.

"Nah, I thought we'd coax the fish onto the hook using only our amazing good looks," Sean replied.

Marielle laughed. "I'll go introduce myself to your mom," she said, walking past the boys.

"Well, you must be Marielle," a short, round, golden-haired lady said warmly as Marielle alighted from the front door.

"I am," Marielle replied with equal warmth as she extended her hand. "And you must be the woman who beat Mr. MacManus at golf this morning."

Mrs. Campbell laughed heartily as Dermot walked outside. "Well, he's quite good now, but I believe he thought the baseball cap would do all of the work for him. My God!" she said suddenly, looking down at Marielle's legs before looking back at Dermot. "Did you see the muscles on her?"

"I run a lot," she explained, praying her legs looked more lean than muscular.

"I see that. You must come closer so your ambition rubs off on me," she said, pulling Marielle in for a hug as her son joined Dermot outside.

Marielle hugged the woman happily before she said, "So, Dermot said you run a B&B."

"I do, indeed, and it's been quite the summer, I can tell you. We've had so many visitors to Galway and it's been so warm that will you believe the Guinness has gone off?"

"How?" Marielle asked, not having heard of beer going bad before.

"It's too fresh," Sean explained. "People are drinking it too fast."

"Well, there you have it. Who knew beer had to age like wine?" his mother said, turning towards Dermot as he held the door for his mother. "Have you changed your mind about allowing your lad to hurl yet?" she asked Mrs. MacManus before winking at Marielle.

Mrs. MacManus noticed the gesture, and although she ignored the question, she stared at Marielle as though she had influenced its asking.

Mrs. Campbell addressed Marielle again. "You know, Dermot is the best hurler any of us have seen in the flesh, like!"

"Thanks, Ma," Sean said, leaning down to pet Gryphon as the dog returned from his adventures beyond the front gates.

"Well, you know you're nearly as good," she said to Dermot's amusement before turning to Marielle. "Dermot played Full Forward which is quite difficult. You need tall players in that position, like Dermot, but they need to pass accurately as well, and the team is counting on them to score the majority of the goals. Dermot played it brilliantly! In fact, the paper said he was among the most promising young hurlers in Ireland."

Mrs. Campbell looked back at Mrs. MacManus who now sat against the front of the house with her feet resting on Gryphon's back. "Would you not reconsider allowing Dermot to play his last year?"

Marielle watched Dermot close his eyes.

"Not a'tall," Mrs. MacManus replied, smiling impassively.

"Well, it's a shame, that," Mrs. Campbell said before asking Sean and Dermot if they were ready to go.

"Why don't you take the front seat, Marielle?" Mrs. Campbell suggested to the apparent displeasure of her son. "Ah, give over, Sean!" she exclaimed. "Surely, sitting in the back seat for once won't kill you."

"Will she be driving as well?" Sean asked as Marielle stood on the wrong side of the car.

Marielle looked through the window at the steering wheel, then laughed as she ran to the passenger side.

"So, you're sitting in what would normally be your driver's seat," Mrs. Campbell said as they made their way down Taylor's Hill Road. "Does it feel strange, like?"

"It feels strange not to see a steering wheel in front of me, but I spend a lot of time in this seat now. I started driving when I was 15 and I've had my license to drive by myself for the last year."

486

"Ah, fer feck sake!" Sean declared from the back seat. "So, it's true, then?" he asked Dermot.

"I'tis," Dermot said with exasperation. "I've seen the licence an' all."

"I have it with me in fact," Marielle said, pulling the card from her back pocket to hand to Sean.

He looked up from the small, laminated card. "I see you're an organ donor which is important if your driving isn't brilliant."

Marielle glanced at Sean. "Oh, I can drive just fine."

"Indeed," Dermot objected. "She's blindly driven into an intersection, nearly causing an enormous crash, and she skidded onto a footpath murdering some poor sod's rubbish can."

Marielle gasped as she looked at the back seat, finding Dermot wearing a child's grin. "You can't use my own confessions against me!" she objected.

Dermot shrugged his shoulders. "I'm not a priest, like."

Her eyes narrowed. "I'm not either. Shall I mention some of your confessions, then?"

Dermot's mouth opened well before he spoke. "You wouldn't dare!"

"Oh, I dare," she replied before turning to Sean.

Dermot leaned forward anxiously. "Wait now! I wasn't daring you to tell us."

"*I* dare you to tell us," Sean said eagerly.

Marielle stared at Dermot as if transmitting telepathically the facts she might convey.

"Tell me!" Sean urged.

"Don't!" Dermot implored, still smiling anxiously, but using his golden brown eyes to soften her.

Marielle nodded. "Do you admit I could do a good deal of damage, then?" she asked.

"I do, absolutely," he said, using his hands to speak in a way she associated with Italians.

She tried not to smile. "And you won't use any more confessions against me?"

"Not in public," he replied.

Her eyes narrowed again. "Hmm, that's not quite good enough. So, I was thinking of the time you were in Irish College—"

"Stop!" he pleaded. "Okay, I categorically state I will never use another confession against you in public or private. I swear it on Sean's life."

Everyone in the car laughed except Sean.

"Swear it on your own feckin' life!" he protested.

Marielle glanced nervously between Sean and his mother. "You use that potty mouth with your mother in the car?" she asked.

"What potty mouth? I said feck, not—"

"Sean!" Mrs. Campbell interrupted.

Marielle's eyebrows furrowed. "That's not just the F word said with an Irish accent?" she asked.

"Not a'tall," Sean replied.

Dermot chuckled. "You should hear Sean curse with his Dublin accent. It's great *craic*."

"You must be mistaken, Dermot," Mrs. Campbell interjected, using her mirror to make eye contact with Dermot. "Sean never curses. You must be thinking of another lad out on the pitch."

Dermot glanced at Sean. "I believe you're right, Mrs. Campbell."

Marielle smiled. "Sean, don't take this the wrong way, but you have the smile of a serial killer right now."

"He does, indeed," Dermot noted, studying his friend a moment before Mrs. Campbell pulled the car to the side of the road.

"Sorry, dears," she said. "Mrs. Harper flagged us down. I imagine she saw Marielle and she'd like to meet her."

The boys sighed.

Marielle watched a car make a U-turn behind them, then park on the shoulder in front of Mrs. Campbell's car.

"How-ya?" Mrs. Campbell asked a tall, dark-haired woman of similar age.

Mrs. Harper and a young girl approached, greeting Mrs. Campbell while watching Marielle exit the car.

"My goodness! I thought she was Fiona," Mrs. Harper declared.

"Not a'tall," Mrs. Campbell said. "This is Dermot's friend Marielle visiting from America."

Marielle held out her hand as Mrs. Harper looked between her and Dermot.

"Nice to meet you," the woman said to Marielle, then to Dermot she asked, "Where's Ashley?"

"At home, I suppose," he replied, still smiling with his fingers carelessly pushed into his pockets.

Mrs. Harper's left eye narrowed as she studied Marielle for a reaction. Finding none, she asked Mrs. Campbell where they were off to and had they any plans for the hurling final.

"Blast!" Dermot said to Sean after returning to the car. "I forgot the match was tomorrow."

Marielle turned to the back seat. "I would love to watch it with you, but your mom said we're going to Thoor Ballylee instead. There's no reason I can't go with her alone while you stay at home and watch the game."

"Not a'tall," Dermot replied convincingly. "We can listen on the radio and there's no hope Antrim will beat Tipperary anyway. Sure there isn't, Sean?"

"Not a notion," his friend agreed.

"So, do you have a boyfriend back home, Marielle?" Mrs. Campbell asked.

Dermot chuckled as Sean studied him.

"Strictly speaking, I do," she replied.

"Now, that's a very interesting answer," Mrs. Campbell commented as they pulled into the driveway of a modest ranch home. "We'll need to discuss this further upon collecting Donal."

Everyone exited the car to greet a boy shorter than Sean and Dermot, but much stockier. His hair was a chestnut brown and his lip showed signs of the slightest moustache.

"Well, hello there," he said seductively to Marielle as he turned a handshake into a hug.

"That's quite enough," Dermot declared as he stepped forward.

"Ah, you have your own girlfriend, Dermot. It was kind of you to bring Marielle to Ireland for the rest of us."

Marielle looked around. "Rest of you? I can only disappoint one boyfriend at a time," she replied.

"You're great *craic*, aren't you? Let me give you another hug," Donal said, drawing her close again.

"Jaysus, Donal! Haven't you a girlfriend of your own?" Sean protested.

"Not a'tall. She died last night. Tragic story, that," he replied, causing Marielle to laugh.

"Alright, boys. The fish are waiting on you," Mrs. Campbell declared as she opened the driver's-side door.

"Does someone else want shotgun?" Marielle asked.

"Shotgun?" at least two boys asked.

"The front seat," she clarified.

"Dermot can," Donal replied, raising his eyebrows at Marielle.

"Not a'tall," Sean interjected on Dermot's behalf. "Donal can have shotgun, as the mad Americans say."

Dermot nodded appreciatively at Sean before holding the back door for Marielle.

"Who has my license?" she asked from the middle seat.

"Oh, I've confiscated it," Sean replied, looking down at the white, red, green, and blue laminated card. "It boggles the mind that they allow you to drive at our age in America," Sean reflected before handing it back to Marielle.

"Mightn't I see that?" Donal asked, holding out his hand to receive the licence.

"So, why do you call the passenger's seat shotgun?" Sean asked.

"It's from the Wild West," Marielle explained. "The person sitting next to the driver always held a shotgun."

"And do you now, like?" Donal asked.

"Rarely," she said, smiling. "There are very strict rules for shotgun. So, if you want to incorporate it into your everyday life, I'll need to write them down for you. Of course, you can always develop your own rules."

"What are some of the rules?" Dermot asked eagerly.

"Well, the first rule is you can't call shotgun over an adult. Shotgun only applies to people of similar ages and you shouldn't call it over the girlfriend or boyfriend of the driver, but rude people still do."

"But how does it work, like?" Sean asked impatiently. "You run to the car first or call out the word?"

"Oh, sorry. You have to say the word *shotgun* before anyone else. The first person to call it, gets it, but you can't call it until you're outside on the way to the car. So, for example, you can't get out of the car and call it for the next trip, but you can call it away from someone even if the person is sitting in the shotgun position if they didn't explicitly call it. So, for example, we could call it away from Donal at the next stop sign and then we'd need to engage in a limited Chinese Fire Drill."

"What's that?" Dermot asked with amusement.

"It's just where people jump out of the car and switch spots."

"Shotgun," Donal said with a smile. "So, must everyone be on the way to the car or just one person?" he asked.

"That's an excellent question. In fact, we debated this very point at school last spring. It's sufficient for one person to run outside to call it, but going back inside the building nullifies the call, and it doesn't count unless the driver hears you. If you want to call it and sit on the porch for two hours to wait for everyone else, that would be fine. It's your life. But if the driver didn't hear it and you're daydreaming when everyone else comes out of the building, someone can call shotgun away from you and you would have wasted your time waiting outside."

"What if the driver pretends not to hear your call?" Sean asked.

"Then civility goes out the window," Marielle replied. "This all hinges on the driver being completely objective, and it's also the inspiration for the *not calling shotgun over the girlfriend of the driver* rule."

Dermot pursed his lips before he spoke, "What if you're outside at a hurling match, for instance, and you call shotgun at the beginning of the match?"

"We haven't addressed that particular scenario in Wisconsin," Marielle admitted. "I guess you would have to vote on that one."

Sean and Donal spoke at the same time indicating opposite points of view.

"You might establish a time restriction of sorts," Mrs. Campbell suggested.

"Good idea," Dermot replied. "You can't call shotgun until you're within thirty minutes of any journey."

Marielle nodded. "That sounds reasonable. I'll bring that one back to Wisconsin with me."

"Is your family originally from Ireland?" Mrs. Campbell asked Marielle through the rear view mirror.

"One-fourth of my family is. I suppose all visiting Americans say they're Irish," she said reservedly.

"They do, but I love to hear it," Mrs. Campbell encouraged.

"Oh," Marielle said with surprise. "My Irish great-grandfather's name was James Healy. He was Protestant."

"Are you Protestant?" Donal asked.

"No, the Austrian and Italian sides of my family won the religion tug of war in America."

Dermot leaned forward to address Donal. "I told Marielle she's a bit of a mutt."

"I wouldn't describe her as that a'tall," he replied, winking at Marielle in a way she was sure was only meant to annoy Dermot.

Sean shared an annoyed glance with Dermot.

"So, from where in Ireland does your family hail?" Mrs. Campbell asked.

"Donegal," Marielle replied, pronouncing the word donna-gull, and causing everyone except Mrs. Campbell to mock the pronunciation.

"We pronounce it Doe-nay-gaul," Mrs. Campbell explained.

"Doe-nay-gaul," Marielle repeated as Dermot squeezed her hand.

"That's right," Mrs. Campbell replied with satisfaction.

Marielle squeezed back, but called "Mercy" before another game could commence.

"Not a'tall," Dermot protested.

"Marielle," Sean began, "why do Americans spell night N-I-T-E?"

She exhaled as she said, "We don't."

"Are you certain?" he asked.

"As of two days ago we didn't, but things change quickly in America. For example, banana clips are no longer the rage."

"I have no idea what your woman's sayin'," Sean said to Dermot.

Marielle smiled. "I see that you guys spell tire T-Y-R-E and check with a Q-U-E."

Dermot nodded, then pointed at a road sign. "Would you read that sign to us, Marielle?"

"The English?" she teased.

"No, you cheeky girl. The Irish above it."

"Alright. I would pronounce that 'bother cul de lock,' " she replied to everyone's amusement.

"And that?" Donal asked.

"Bother an choir elle. How would you pronounce it?" she asked, receiving three different versions in reply.

"Dermot's pronunciation is the correct one," Mrs. Campbell decided. "Did you hear your mother before we left, Dermot? She'd like you to practice your Irish whilst you're fishing."

"I did, yeah," Dermot replied, sighing softly.

"And who are you meant to practice with, like?" Sean asked. "My Irish score on the Inter was desperate."

"I scored an A," Donal bragged.

"Well, it's settled, then," Marielle decided. "Donal and Dermot will speak Irish while Sean and I speak English, but I'm open to learning some Irish as well."

"I'll teach you everything you need to know about Irish," Sean offered.

"She already knows how to say 'kiss my ass,' " Dermot remarked before apologising to Mrs. Campbell.

Marielle turned toward Sean. "I work with a lady from Gort," she explained.

Sean grinned in a self-satisfied way. "It's good we've sent missionaries abroad to spread proper Irish."

"So, now, Marielle," Mrs. Campbell interjected. "I'm interested in hearing about your boyfriend."

Dermot smiled at Marielle before she began.

"I date a boy from a town near mine. He's pretty full of himself owing to his football skills and his general popularity with the ladies. He also has certain expectations of a girlfriend, which I guess meets the stereotype of American teenagers. In any event, I'm a disappointment to his expectations, but he keeps doing things to try to make me fall in love with him which just annoys me." Marielle looked at Dermot. "Did I tell you he changed his football number to 29 in honor of my birthday?" She rolled her eyes.

"That's massive!" Dermot replied.

"And ridiculous. I never asked him to change it, and how am I supposed to break up with him before the end of football season now? I'm locked in. Thank God it's his senior year."

"But you said you weren't planning to break up with him a'tall," Dermot argued before Sean turned towards his friend, wearing a confused expression.

She exhaled. "No, but I'd at least feel like I have the option."

"Wait, now," Sean said. "You don't need to date anyone a'tall, you know. It's not a requirement, like."

"It is in Wisconsin," Dermot replied.

"Would you not date someone you liked, then?" Donal asked.

"Feeling anything for a bloke is a risk to her aggressive three year plan for university," Dermot explained.

Marielle squeezed Dermot's hand as she looked lovingly toward him. "You're a very good spokesman," she remarked.

Donal glanced down at Dermot's and Marielle's hands. "So, how is

Ashley coping with Marielle's arrival?" he asked.

"As you might expect," Dermot replied.

Donal looked at Marielle. "You can stay at my house if there's trouble."

Dermot narrowed his eyes at his friend. "She'll not be needing alternate arrangements. I'll cast Ashley aside if she makes trouble."

"Really?!" Sean asked, leaning forward to better see Dermot's face.

"Really," Dermot replied decisively.

Marielle looked from one boy to the other, flagging the topic for later discussion.

"Let's get back to Marielle," Dermot said happily. "She's done some terrible things to her boyfriends."

"No one wants to hear this," she said defiantly.

"Oh, I think we do," Sean rebutted.

Marielle began to blush. "I'm sure each of you has done something terrible while dating. Why don't we discuss that instead?"

"We will if you start," Donal offered.

"Do you promise?" she asked, looking around the car.

The boys nodded.

"Okay. So, Gary plays basketball as well as football and I was at his game one night in February, and Freedom—that's his town—was just killing this other town... I think it was Winneconne," she said to the corner of her right eye. "Anyway, they were leading by like 28 points, and Gary made at least half of those baskets, so they pulled him out of the game and put in their second string."

"Wait," Sean said with amusement. "What's the name of the town they were playing?"

"Winneconne. It's near Oshkosh. It means 'land of skull and bones' in some Native American language... which is interesting because it's near Lake Butte des Morts."

"Mounds of dead," Dermot translated.

"Yes!" Marielle replied. "I pronounced it with a French accent just so you'd get that, but I thought it meant lake of the dead, but your French is better than mine."

"There must be a link between Winne-whatever and Butte des Morts," Dermot mused.

"Do you not find it a little strange that you can say three words in French better than one Native American word?" Marielle asked, having never met any American with a similar strength or impediment.

Dermot shook his head as he said, "Not a'tall."

"Anyway," she continued. "Yes, there's a link, but I can't remember my 9th grade history class as well as I should. I believe the French killed the Fox Indians there. We live in the Fox Valley." Marielle suddenly chuckled. "I was just thinking how funny it is that a place named Freedom was killing a place that's already dead." She shook her head. "Anyway, by halftime, Freedom was still winning by twenty or thirty points so Shelly and I decided to go to this diner and get some hot chocolate. Well, when we got back to the gym at the beginning of the fourth quarter *Winneconne* was leading and I didn't see Gary anywhere—not on the court and not on the bench. So, I just sat there until the game was over, and I ran up to Shelly's boyfriend—he plays on the same team—and asked him where Gary went. He was pretty irritated with me and said they had to take him away in an ambulance during the third quarter because he hurt his knee. I guess they put him back in the game when they started losing their lead and a guy from Winneconne fouled him pretty hard." Marielle looked at the corner of her eye again. "It might have actually been a technical, now that I think about it. Anyway, Tim, Shelly's boyfriend, said Gary asked for me as they carried him off the court and they looked for me, but obviously I wasn't there, so one of the cheerleaders went with him instead. There was a dance afterward, so I just went to that and he showed up before it was over, but he couldn't dance, of course."

Marielle looked around the car, trying to gauge the level of amusement or offense. Sean smiled while Dermot chuckled at the window with the back of his left index finger pressed against his lips. Donal looked at Marielle as though he had never heard of a girl acting so coldly before.

"That's terrible," Dermot declared happily.

"So, you call yourself a good girlfriend, do you?" Sean asked.

"Not once!" Marielle objected, causing Sean to join Dermot in laughter.

"Did he talk to you again, like?" Donal asked.

"He did after I apologized, but he kept bringing it up and throwing digs in about the cheerleader being ever so worried and kind. So, eventually I said, 'Look, we're just dating. I'm not your mom and I'm not your wife. In the future, if you need to go to the hospital, you should just go without me... or take one of your cheerleaders.' "

"That's horrible!" Sean said, still amused.

"He's a hypochondriac," Dermot explained.

"Exactly," Marielle replied. "I promise I wouldn't be this horrible if I really liked or respected him as a human being. Okay, someone else's turn. Why don't we find out how Donal's girlfriend died last night? Did you kill her?"

Donal shook his head. "Not a'tall. In fact, she may still be alive. I haven't checked."

"That's not much of a story," Marielle said with disappointment.

"It's not, but you remind me of something I did to a previous girlfriend."

Marielle raised her eyebrows impatiently, waiting for him to continue.

"Maureen!" Dermot announced.

"Yeah," Donal confirmed.

"Oh, I love this story," Sean remarked, resting his head against his seat.

"I was dating this girl named Maureen. She attends an all-girls school in Galway and she studies like mad and we were training hard for hurling this past spring—sure, Dermot will tell you—and there was a long span of time, maybe three months, when I didn't see her. Well, next of all, she turns up at our match and I didn't recognise her a'tall because she had gotten so fat."

"In just three months?" Marielle asked.

Dermot nodded as his eyes opened wider.

"So, she waits for me after the match and asks if I'll take her out on Friday and I said sure because I couldn't think what else to say, but I began to rethink the relationship during the week."

Marielle noted the smiles on everyone's faces, including Mrs. Campbell's.

"So, I rang your man and Sean and asked them what I should do."

"Don't pin this on us!" Sean objected.

"I'm not pinnin' it on you, now. It was my decision at the end of the day—"

"And your idea from the start, if I remember correctly," Dermot added.

"Ah-right. Maybe it was now," Donal said with a smile. "So, I became more desperate as Friday approached."

"You couldn't just break up with her on the grounds that you didn't see her enough?" Marielle asked.

Donal sighed. "That didn't occur to me. So, I rang her Friday afternoon to tell her I couldn't make our date because my friend was hit by a lorry and he was in a coma, like, and I was going to hospital to sit by his bedside."

"Oh no!" Marielle exclaimed as Mrs. Campbell began a laugh that would end in tears.

"Didn't she ask you who it was and when it happened?" Marielle asked, laughing more at Mrs. Campbell's reaction than the story.

"She did at that."

"And he hadn't concocted a good cover story a'tall," Dermot said, smiling happily at Sean's mom.

"No, I hadn't. It hadn't occurred to me she'd ask. It was a bit insensitive of her now, if you ask me. So, I said it was a bloke we attended school with at St. Clement's, forgetting entirely that her uncle teaches there."

Marielle gasped. "How long before she found out?"

"That Monday. Her uncle approached me at school and accused me of dating someone else. So, I admitted it had nothing a'tall to do with another girl. His niece was merely too fat for me. Well, your man explained that her asthma had gotten worse for a time so they put her on a steroid that made her retain water—"

"Prednisone," Marielle said with wider eyes.

Donal nodded. "I believe that's right. How did you know that?"

"I have asthma," she said, ignoring Dermot as he turned towards her.

"Ah, well, he said she'd lose the weight soon enough when her breathing improved, and it did. And she did."

Marielle sat back before looking at the roof of the car to laugh.

"Has she talked to you since?" Mrs. Campbell asked, wiping her eyes.

"No. She blanks me every time I see her."

"Which is unfortunate since she's one of the better looking girls in Galway," Sean added.

"Sean's turn!" Dermot declared.

Sean looked at his friend sternly. "Not in front of me mam."

"Your mam promises not to be surprised," Mrs. Campbell replied.

Sean sighed and gave Dermot a dirty look before speaking. "Well, now, I have a similar story to Donal's. In fact, I believe my story inspired Donal to promulgate such a hateful lie, I'm proud to say. I was dating someone who seemed nice and aloof at first—"

"The way you like 'em," Dermot noted, leaning forward to make eye contact with Sean.

"I'll not deny that," he replied. "Well, next of all, your woman introduces me as her boyfriend and that was grand, I suppose, but it made me uncomfortable all the same. Before long, she said people remarked on what a lovely couple we made and what lovely children we might have. At one stage, she began considering baby names, and I've only ever kissed her, like. So, I'm thinkin' the girl's stark raving mad, but I'm too frightened to cast her aside."

"She might boil your rabbit," Marielle remarked.

"I hadn't thought of that, but I wouldn't put it past her, now. So, I'm wracking me brain for a way out and death is the only solution that occurs to me."

"Sean!" his mother scolded.

"I didn't mean to really die, Ma. I merely thought I'd convince *her* I was dying."

Marielle closed her eyes as a huge smile overtook her face.

"So, I told her there was something important I needed to tell her and I took her down to the sea for effect. I looked her straight in the eye and told her I had a brain tumour and we needed to break up so she could go on with her life without me."

"No!" Marielle proclaimed.

Sean nodded with a delicate mixture of shame and pride.

"Did she believe you?" Marielle asked.

"Not a'tall. She asked what the doctors advised in terms of treatment and I confessed I hadn't seen a doctor, but I recognised the signs of a tumour all the same from watching *St. Elsewhere*. She asked if I was messing, but I took offense, like, and she walked away. She told her friends I was unsound and refused to see me anymore."

"Well done," Marielle said, regarding Sean with respect. "Can I borrow that one if I need it?"

He glanced at her before saying, "Indeed."

"Okay, Dermot's next," Marielle announced as the car slowed beside a lake and a small peninsula.

"Ah, but we're arriving, so. Too bad, that," Dermot replied.

"I believe we're willing to wait on your story," Mrs. Campbell offered.

"Ah-right," Dermot said with resignation. "But I'm certain you'll not be impressed, Mrs. Campbell."

She turned toward Dermot, wearing a kind expression. "I'm quite certain I'll maintain my regard for you."

Dermot drew a deep breath before addressing Marielle. "Do you remember I told you about a girl I met at a match in Dublin last year?"

She nodded as she said she did.

"I told you she went to university and she seemed interested in me until I told her my age and she walked away, laughing."

Marielle nodded again.

"But in truth, I didn't tell her my age a'tall and she didn't walk away. In fact, we wrote to one another and spoke on the phone and she travelled to Galway once or twice to see me. It was only lunch or dinner and a film, and she always returned to Dublin the same night. So, that was grand until we won the All Ireland match and my picture was in the paper, and she discovered I was only in 5th year. Well, you can imagine the abuse in the letter she sent with the newspaper clipping an' all!"

"It was nice of her to send the clipping," Marielle noted.

"Yes, well, I won't tell you what she did to my photograph."

Marielle chuckled. "How old was she? A freshman?"

"Not a'tall," Dermot replied, unprepared to divulge this information.

"You didn't seem overly shy about her age on the pitch," Donal remarked before smiling at Mrs. Campbell's shocked expression.

"She was in her second year at university," Dermot said, quickly glancing at Mrs. Campbell before turning red.

"That's terrible!" Marielle said, unable to suppress a smile.

"Some might even say illegal," Sean added.

Mrs. Campbell turned to Dermot. "Tell me you won't make that mistake again, love."

"I promise I won't. I've learnt," he replied, looking back at her in earnest.

"Well, fair play to you for convincing the university girl you were out of secondary school, anyway," she said, finally breaking into a chuckle as she opened the car door.

***

"Do you have a fishing license?" Marielle asked Dermot after they carted the supplies to the peninsula and bid Mrs. Campbell farewell.

"Ah, shite! I hadn't thought of that," he replied.

"Do they enforce that sort of thing?" she asked.

"I'm not sure." He looked towards Donal and Sean as they baited their hooks. "Do you lads have your fishing licences?" he asked.

"Of course," Sean said. "You'd have to be a flamin' eejit to forget something like that whilst fishing."

"Ah, feck!" Dermot exclaimed. "Only two of us will be able to fish at a time."

"Well, what in God's name will you do to occupy yourself?" Sean asked sarcastically before smiling at Marielle.

"Shall we walk?" Dermot asked Marielle with a twinkle in his eye.

"Sure. I could use a good stretch of the legs," she replied.

"Do they say that in America?" he asked as he reached for her hand.

She shook her head. "No. I picked it up watching *The Quiet Man*."

"Well, let's stretch our legs, then," he said, looking at the narrow, gravel road which seemed to end at a small hill farther ahead. "You know, that was filmed near us, in Connemara or Mayo, I believe."

Marielle nodded. "A bunch of places north of here, actually. One of them was Tully Strand, Connemara."

"You amaze me," Dermot said with wonder in his eyes.

Marielle narrowed her eyebrows. "Because I know how to pause a VCR during the credits?"

"Not a'tall. Because you're so curious, and funny. I have to say, I love your mad stories, especially the ones about your boyfriends."

She released the tension in her eyebrows as she raised them briefly. "Well, it's easy to be funny when you're not in love."

"But you're funny with me," he brooded as he turned her in front of him.

She smiled as she looked up at him. "I am, but I'd never make fun *of* you. Ever. My female friends think you walk on water."

He returned the smile. "And what do your male friends think?"

"They think you're just trying to get me into bed and then you'll break my heart. They also think your incredible accent and Irish wit give you an unfair advantage."

His smile broadened. "And do they?"

Marielle gasped. "That's not how you're supposed to respond to that. You're supposed to deny you're trying to get me into bed."

"Well, see now, I'd have to be mad not to want you in my bed. You wouldn't believe me a'tall if I claimed it."

She smiled. "You're right, actually… that I wouldn't believe you."

Dermot used Marielle's hands to pull her closer. "So, do my wit and accent give me a leg up on the American competition?"

"Of course. I'd try to sound deep and talk about how sweet and amazing you are, but it's hard to get past your good looks and your accent. It's all just a deadly combination. Going back to the left side of the Atlantic should be pure hell."

Pain flashed across Dermot's face. "See, I'm torn now because I want you to be happy when we're apart."

She grinned mischievously at him. "So, is that why you looked so upset when I told you about the cabin on prom night? Because you wanted me to be happy?" she teased.

He looked at the gravel his foot accidentally kicked towards her, apologising. "I didn't think you noticed that," he admitted.

She nodded slowly. "I did. I also noticed that you must have talked-up Ashley and your regard for her to Sean quite recently."

Dermot's mouth opened well before he spoke. "How on earth did you know that?!" he asked.

"It was the surprise on Sean's face when you said you'd break up with her if she made trouble."

Dermot continued to regard her with awe. "Inferior test scores aside, it would be a mistake to underestimate the Americans."

"I believe those were Hitler's last words," she replied, laughing with Dermot until his smile turned into longing, and his mouth approached hers. Marielle's knees gave out slightly as Dermot's tongue teased her own, but she quickly recovered.

"Do I really make you swoon?" he asked with a proud grin. "I've only ever heard of such things in books and films."

Marielle's cheeks turned red as her eyes began to water.

"Am I making you cry as well?" he asked with sudden concern.

"No. My eyes always water when I blush. I'd be grateful if you didn't tell anyone about this. I have a reputation for being cold and heartless to uphold."

"I promise not to tell anyone in America," he said happily.

She stared at him through the top of her eyes. "Which means you'll tell Sean."

He squeezed her slightly. "If you don't mind. He's my best mate after all and I guarantee he'll want to know every last detail about your visit."

"Did he tell you this or do you just know it?"

"He told me in the house earlier when we were getting sorted."

Dermot chuckled at the memory. "He nearly tackled me in the dining room after you left."

"Why?" Marielle asked, still blushing.

Dermot shook his head twice. "Come now! You know yourself. I don't mind giving you a compliment, but let's not pretend you're unaware of your effect on the lads, now."

Marielle looked away for a moment. Never in her life had she been called-out by a boy who observed as much about human nature. She made a mental note to give Dermot more credit in the future, then spoke. "I might have assumed it, but is it so terrible that I'd want confirmation?"

"Yes, well, it's safe to say that if I cast you aside, not only would it shock the ENTIRE population of Galway, but you'd have a fair few options within mere minutes."

She nodded. "That's good to know. I may have to make use of that."

"I guarantee you, you won't," he replied decisively. "So, I make you weak in the knees and yet you won't allow me to make love to you," he remarked, though it was clearly a question.

Marielle closed her eyes.

"I'm sorry," Dermot said, but he reserved real remorse until Marielle turned away.

"I swear I'd have no ability to deny you anything if I hadn't made that pact, but I'm pretty sure God gets pissed when you break your promises, even if I was the type of person to go back on my word, which I'm not."

"Well, now," Dermot said, lacing both of his hands into hers as a smile appeared upon his face. "I believe I have a way around this."

"Really?" Marielle asked with too much hope to feign idle curiosity.

He inched closer. "I do. See, you made the pact with God after the trip was cancelled the first time."

Marielle nodded, afraid opening her mouth might tempt her to question him further on that topic.

He stepped closer again. "Then, you bought the second ticket, correct?"

"That's the order of things," she agreed.

He rested their joined hands upon Marielle's shoulders. "So, one might rightly assume the pact was associated with the second set of tickets."

"Okay," she said, squinting her eyes slightly.

"But, as I recall, you didn't use the ticket to Shannon a'tall. So, as I see it, God abandoned you in Heathrow, and therefore, didn't live up to His end of the bargain, forcing you to find your own way to Ireland via Cork."

Marielle pushed their hands against Dermot's chest. "That only works if you assume the pact was specifically associated with the tickets and not with my arrival in Ireland."

He pushed their hands towards Marielle. "True, but don't you find it a bit unusual that trained staff on a transatlantic flight wouldn't know baggage procedures at a major international airport?"

She pushed back. "Are you saying God went back on his deal and sabotaged my connection?"

Dermot moved their hands to their sides. "Well, now, you're a smart girl. I have a hard time believing you wouldn't make your connection if something or someone didn't get in the way of it."

Marielle smiled brightly. "You're beginning to make a good deal of sense."

He studied her face intently before asking, "Does this mean you'll reconsider, like?"

"I think it means I'm beginning to," she replied.

Dermot smiled before the sound of an approaching car caused him to pull Marielle through bushes lining the road.

Marielle pulled a leaf from her hair. "Even if I said yes, and I haven't yet, we can't do it here. The condoms are back at your house."

Dermot laughed. "I know. I didn't want a car to find us. God knows who it could be."

"Like your mom or Ashley," Marielle joked, placing her arms around his neck.

He rested his hands on her waist. "That would be frightful. So, you brought condoms after all, then?" he asked happily.

"I brought six, but I can't imagine we'd use all of them."

Dermot's eyes shifted to the sky as he raised his eyebrows and smiled.

Marielle chuckled quietly. "You're far too handsome," she murmured.

He began stroking her sides lightly. "And you're far too beautiful," he replied as his eyes penetrated hers. "Tell me Sean's story didn't scare you off."

"Why?" she asked with genuine confusion.

Dermot continued to study her. "Sean's girlfriend mentioning children."

"Oh, because you brought up a daughter this morning?" Marielle

asked.

Dermot nodded slowly.

"Not at all," she replied. "If any other boy on the planet brought it up, it would—scare me that is—but you're a special case."

"You can't imagine how lucky that makes me feel," he said, moving his hands to her back.

"Wait," she said suddenly. "You haven't had sex with someone else yet have you? Not even the college girl?"

Dermot shook his head vigorously. "I swear to you, I haven't."

"Okay," she said, relaxing.

Dermot noticed the plant beside them. He picked off a blackberry to offer to Marielle before picking one for himself.

"This is my favorite berry," she said, smiling.

"Mine as well," he replied before grabbing another for Marielle, feeding her as he cleared his throat. "Now that we've established that I'm *likely* meant to be your first, may I touch you, like?" he asked, opening his eyes wider for a fraction of a second.

She looked down to pick a berry for Dermot. "Where exactly were you thinking of touching me?" she asked, feigning indifference.

Dermot opened his mouth to accept the berry before kissing her finger tip, causing her eyes to close involuntarily. "Well, presently I can't keep my eyes off your breasts, but I'd like the option to explore lower."

"How can you see my breasts through this jersey?" Marielle asked, looking down.

"I could see them against your seat belt yesterday and today. At the moment, I'm using my imagination." He raised his eyebrows as he shamelessly looked down at her shirt.

"What exactly were you thinking of doing to my breasts?" she asked as if the answer held only scientific interest for her.

He moved uncomfortably before clearing his throat again. "Well, I'd settle for touching them through your clothes, but I'd much prefer to touch them directly. I believe I could die happily if I saw them as well as kissed them," he said, losing his breath at the end of his sentence.

"That's interesting," Marielle replied, looking at her fingers which were now stained. "I'll take that under advisement."

"Marielle!" Dermot pleaded, tugging on her lower back. "You're torturing me."

She smiled broadly. "I'm sorry. You look so cute when you're

504

pouting." She glanced away as she deliberated. "I believe I might be willing to accommodate your request."

"Which request?" he asked excitedly.

"All of them."

His eyes lit up. "Wait, now. All of them regarding your breasts or all of them regarding everything, like?"

She grinned at his enthusiasm. "Everything regarding my breasts. I need to consider the other matter further before I cross God."

Dermot nodded. "When exactly—regarding your breasts, I mean?"

She looked up at him with a reddening face. "That depends. How many breasts have you touched before?"

Dermot sighed as his eyes closed to the sky.

"Alright," she said. "Your reaction told me at least one. If I were a betting person, I'd say three."

"That's right!" he exclaimed.

"Three through the shirt or three directly?"

"Three through a jumper. Irish girls won't allow a bloke to touch them directly or go any further than that a'tall."

Marielle eyebrows immediately narrowed. "Are you saying American girls are sluts?"

"Absolutely not!" Dermot said with feeling. "I can't stop feeling grateful that you're not Irish."

Marielle laughed. "You're smooth. Okay. So, let's say I accommodate your touching through clothing request now. What do I get in return?" she asked with mischievous eyes.

Dermot brightened. "Make your request, then. Anything."

She smiled at the blackberry bush. "Hmm. You're not exactly negotiating from a position of power."

"Does any lad?" he asked.

She offered him a berry before she shook her head. "I suppose not. Okay, so I'm a real fan of your kissing, but you must have kissed dozens of girls. Has anyone kissed your neck?"

"Only one girl and that was only briefly. I think she got lost, actually. She hadn't a clue what she was doing."

"What about your chest?" she asked before placing a berry into her mouth.

"No one," he said, studying her closely.

"Hmm. I may start with your neck then, but I get to kiss you where I like, whereas you only get to touch me to start. It's only fair since women have more places to protect."

"Agreed!" Dermot said quickly as a grin overtook his face. "So, how might we start, then?"

"I have no idea. Although, according to my Catechism teacher who's a born again virgin (don't ask me what that means), all carnal evil begins with a French kiss."

"We should take her at her word, then," he said before losing his smile.

Marielle shivered slightly as Dermot approached her lips. His tongue teased hers before adeptly and softly probing her mouth. She moaned as he supported the back of her head, moving his fingers gently against her hair.

Dermot smiled an inch from Marielle's lips a moment before she opened her eyes. "Did I pass the first gate?" he asked softly.

"I believe you did," she replied before drawing a deep breath.

Dermot's eyes opened wider for a moment.

"But I go first!" she declared.

He nodded as the gold in his eyes flickered.

"And you'll have to sit on the ground so I can reach you properly," she added.

Dermot felt the ground before he sat.

Marielle knelt in front of him, then pushed him over backward as they laughed. She resisted the magnetic pull of his lips to find the crook of his neck, lightly introducing her tongue when his body told her she had found the right spot. She moved slowly to his ear, causing Dermot to tremble before lightly working her way back down his neck again.

"That's brilliant," he said with appreciative eyes before they suddenly widened. "Now, it's my turn."

Marielle bit the right side of her bottom lip as they both sat up. "Wait!" she said as Dermot's left hand approached her jersey. "Your hands are stained now and I believe a giant handprint on my white shirt won't fool anyone, especially your mother. You'd better just touch me directly instead."

"Really?" he asked with a man's voice and a child's enthusiasm.

She smiled through red cheeks as she covertly unfastened the front clasp of her bra.

Dermot's eyes locked onto Marielle's while his hand reached under her shirt, pushing aside her bra to gently cup her breast.

Marielle's eyes closed as she took a deep breath.

"You fit perfectly into my hand," he said softly into her ear.

She turned to kiss his neck again.

"Oh, Marielle," he said breathlessly as his hand gently massaged her.

A rush of heat entered Marielle's pelvis unlike anything she had ever felt before.

"I'll die if I don't make love to you," he murmured.

"Me too," she replied, then pulled back from Dermot as though her own words startled her. "We should stop. We should go back."

Dermot approached her lips, switching hands and breasts to better lay her down with his stronger arm.

She looked up at his dark hair and skin against the blue sky as he pulled up her shirt, baring her chest to the warm Irish air. She closed her eyes as he looked down at her.

"You're gorgeous, Marielle," he said softly. "Tell me no one has ever seen or kissed you before."

"No one has," she replied, beginning to tremble.

"Please, Marielle," he begged, looking at her face before turning to regard the breast his hand touched.

She nodded, unable to speak.

Dermot kissed one breast while teasing the other with his fingers, causing her legs to move involuntarily.

"There's no way you haven't done this before," she said, thinking out loud.

Dermot looked up at her eyes in earnest. "I swear to you, Marielle. I haven't. You're my first. Swear to me again I'm yours."

"I do. I swear it," she replied.

Dermot leaned back down with more enthusiasm.

Air refused to fill Marielle's lungs completely as heat continued to course through her body.

Dermot's hand slowly abandoned her breast on its journey south.

"You have to stop. Really, Dermot," she said, arresting his hand's progress.

He disengaged his lips from her breast, releasing a quick breath from his nose before looking back at her face with concern. "Have I taken liberties with you?"

"No, love. We're just making each other crazy. It's not fair to start this when there's no way to finish it," she reasoned, pushing down her shirt.

"I don't mind going crazy with you," Dermot countered, lightly biting his bottom lip.

"What if Mrs. Campbell comes back and we're missing? It wouldn't look good at all. I think we should get back," she said decisively as she sat up to re-clasp her bra.

Dermot closed his eyes.

"Are you angry with me?" she asked, touching his arm.

"I'm not a'tall, but I'm *desperate* to be near you."

She smiled lovingly at him. "We still have five more days. There's time."

"Alright, but I won't have you leaving before you're mine," he replied in his soft brogue, causing Marielle to lay back down and object to the heavens while silently pleading with her lower body to stop pulsing.

"Are you alright, love?" he asked, employing a coy smile before offering his hand.

"No," she replied, standing up.

***

"Well, there you are," Sean said as Dermot and Marielle approached. "Your face is looking a bit red there, Marielle. Were you running?" He exchanged a smile with Donal before apologising to Dermot.

Marielle cleared her throat. "No, I wasn't running. I was kissing Dermot's neck, and he was kissing my breasts," she replied, enjoying the stunned expressions of all present.

"You're mad!" Dermot declared.

"Shall we pretend they won't find out anyway?" Marielle asked lightly. "I'm just saving them the inconvenience of getting you alone later."

Sean's face turned red as he surrendered to laughter while Donal had a hard time moving past shock.

"Fair play to you, Marielle," Sean finally said. "I look forward to more candid conversations with you in future."

Donal cleared his throat. "So, in your absence, we've caught three tragically small fish."

"Will you not throw them back?" Dermot asked.

Donal shrugged his shoulders. "I think they're dead anyway. They survived the hook an' all, but the knife lopping off their heads was the real problem."

"You didn't!" Marielle said.

"Not a'tall," Donal replied, smiling. "They're in the cooler there."

Dermot consoled the fish as he transferred them back to the lake, smiling at Marielle as each swam away.

"Maybe it's your bait," Marielle suggested to Sean. "Or you might want to weigh down your line. What are you fishing for?"

Dermot and Donal looked at her with interest while Sean stared at the water. "We generally catch trout, pike, perch, roach, and sometimes the odd salmon," Sean replied.

"Salmon? Really?" Marielle asked.

"Indeed. They swim up from the bay."

"Well, I don't know anything about catching salmon, and I've never heard of roach before, but I believe perch and pike swim close to the bottom. You'll want to weigh down your line for them. You'll also want to weigh your line slightly if larger trout aren't biting at the surface."

"Are you sure about that, Marielle?" Donal asked, reeling in his line with nothing but half a limp worm at the end.

"I think so. I haven't been fishing for months and it's possible that your pike and our pike are completely different, but I'm willing to bet a warm Coke I'm right."

Sean reeled in his line while he and Donal discussed the depth of the water.

"So, you fish often, do you?" Dermot asked, nudging Marielle's shoulder after sitting beside her on a large rock.

"Only when I visit my grandfather. His boat has a leak so you end up bailing as much as you fish and my grandmother always packs finger food which is nice and all, but not helpful when you have worm guts on your fingers.

"When I get home, I have to buy a new reel. My grandfather attempted to fix mine this summer, but he took it apart and couldn't put it back together. He actually returned it a couple weeks ago in a thousand pieces. He looked really cute when he handed me the bag of parts and declared it a goner. The crazy thing was that reel was just fine before he touched it. Well, it stuck a little, but he was just supposed to adjust the tension."

Marielle laughed at the water. "You'll think I'm crazy, but picking night crawlers with my grandfather is the most fun you can have in

Wisconsin. He even added a red filter to his flashlight that he says sooths and confuses them. Do you have night crawlers here?" she asked, turning to Dermot.

"We do," he replied, studying her as though night crawlers were his hidden passion.

She bent down to pick a wide blade of grass. "Well, when I live here we can pick them together. I'm very good at it."

Dermot smiled. "Would you be keen to live here, then?"

Marielle looked back at him with surprise. "Would you prefer to live in the U.S.?"

"Maybe," he admitted. "Maybe we could live half the year here and half over there."

Marielle nodded. "That seems reasonable."

Dermot picked up a flat rock, resisting the urge to stand and skip it for only a moment.

"How did you do that?" Marielle asked in awe as Dermot's rock skipped three times across the water.

He turned to her with surprise. "Have you never tried?"

"I have. I just stink at it."

"Here," he said, choosing a rock for her, then standing behind her as he moved her arm in a sideways motion twice before urging her to continue on her own. She did, to no avail.

"That just plopped right in," she said with disappointment as Dermot's eyebrows furrowed sympathetically.

"Give it another go," he encouraged. "It takes a bit of practice, that's all."

She picked up another rock, but it only skipped once before it gave up the surface.

"Well, now, that's better," he remarked.

She smiled weakly before picking up another rock.

"Let me see that one, love," Dermot said, walking over to her. He rubbed the stone against her palm. "That's a good rock," he said softly. "See, you want it nice and flat, and the rounded edges should help as well." He looked down at her, still rubbing the stone as if he was thinking of something else entirely.

"We should research the physics of rock skipping," Marielle muttered, looking up at Dermot like she had never seen a boy before.

Sean and Donal gave up their fishing poles to grab their own rocks.

"Three is the record," Marielle announced, sliding the rock into her pocket as Dermot reluctantly stepped away from her.

Sean and Donal both skipped a rock twice while Marielle's next rock skipped once.

Dermot turned to smile at her, studying her as she took a deep breath and grabbed another rock. Marielle waited until Dermot bent down for a rock of his own, assuming he wasn't looking as she pulled her right arm back, then forward, flicking her wrist as she released the stone. The rock bounced twice before dropping into the lake.

"Brilliant!" Dermot exclaimed.

Marielle turned toward him with her mouth agape. "Did you see that?!" she asked, then covered her mouth for a moment. "I've never done that before in my life!"

"Yes, well, there's clearly nothing you can't do," he said, walking a step towards her before the gaze of his friends stopped him.

"No. I'm not athletic at all. It was just your incredible coaching."

"Not a'tall. Well done. Really," he said with pride.

Dermot's next rock skipped seven times, causing Sean and Donal to groan and curse before walking back to their fishing poles.

"When we return, I'll be asking your mother if she mightn't force you to quit rock skipping as well," Donal declared.

Marielle gasped as she turned toward Dermot. His eyes narrowed slightly before he looked at Sean and both laughed.

"Aren't you supposed to be practicing your Irish?" Marielle asked as they returned to their large sitting rock.

"Ah, you're a hateful girl," Dermot said, smiling after she opened her eyes wider for a moment. He turned towards the water as he began to speak.

"Is that Irish?" she asked. "It sounds French."

He turned back to her. "Yes, it's French. You won't tell Mother will you?"

She shook her head. "I won't, but I can't speak for the fish."

Sean cleared his throat behind them. "Surely you and Donal can speak enough Irish to make the fish bite," he argued, casting his line farther into the lake than he had previously done.

"Alright," Dermot said. Placing his arm around Marielle as she leaned into him, he began a long sentence of incoherent speech.

"What's *mo chara*?" Marielle asked.

"My friend," Donal replied. "Your man's after asking the fish if they wouldn't mind biting our hooks. Did you call *us* your friend or the fish, Dermot?"

"Neither," he replied. "I merely asked the fish to impress Marielle by biting whilst I spoke to them."

Donal objected, claiming his Irish wasn't that desperate.

"I like the sound of Irish," Marielle remarked. "It sounds fierce."

"Only a German could truly appreciate it," Dermot reflected before turning Marielle's chin with his right hand to kiss her, ignoring the eyes and potential ridicule of his friends.

Marielle inhaled deeply as Dermot slowly disengaged his lips. "You know, you need to be very careful about kissing me so well," she warned. "I believe you could pull all of my breath away."

"That sounded poetic," he said, smiling.

"Don't tell my Creative Writing teacher. She'll accuse me of plagiarizing it."

"I shan't," Dermot said, looking at her with a coy smile before turning towards the water as he began to recite, "Writhing in reality, humult complete; Twisting in history, surely repeat; Fire breathes hot as dew catches cold; Youth seeks lust as death catches old."

Marielle sat up to look at Dermot more closely. "You memorized that?"

He smiled back. "I did. I like your poetry a great deal and I like how you created your own word. Humult. Did you mean humiliation there?"

"I did. I was annoyed that you can say tumult for tumultuous and you can't say humult for humiliation."

He nodded with appreciation. "Like Shakespeare."

"Exactly! You're one of the few people I know who knows Shakespeare made up his own words. That's what you meant, right? You weren't equating my poem to a great work by Shakespeare?"

"I wasn't," he admitted, "but I'm not saying you don't have potential there. Do you write poetry for your other boyfriends as well?"

Marielle twitched uncomfortably. "I didn't write that poem with you in mind," she said, thinking of all the poems she discarded as unworthy of him.

"I disagree, and it's not my ego speaking here."

Marielle's eyebrows furrowed through a smile. "What makes you say that?"

"The last line is easy. Youth seeks lust—that's us. I can't imagine you feeling lustful for Gary."

Marielle scrunched up her nose at the thought.

"As death catches old—that's your job at the old folk's home. A job you worked to bring us together, and strategically avoid Gary. The fire line is poetic licence while repeating history is a certainty, but it's the first line that concerns me."

"Why's that?" Marielle asked, staring at Dermot's cheek.

His eyes looked farther away than the opposite shore. "Because I fear I made you feel like you didn't matter to me. You wrote this poem after your first trip was cancelled."

Marielle turned to the water as she let the first line repeat itself in her head. She didn't know if Dermot was right or wrong, but she couldn't let him suffer. "That wasn't you," she said abruptly. "I was thinking of someone else."

He turned to her as if he hadn't heard a word she said. "I don't want you to *ever* think I didn't want you here."

She studied the pain on Dermot's face for a moment. "Okay. I won't question that again," she said, grimacing at her last word.

Dermot thanked her as he blinked slowly.

"And the answer is no," Marielle said brightly, causing Dermot to look at her with confusion. "I don't write poetry for my other boyfriends, and you're the only boyfriend who counts. Why don't we call them something else so I can reserve that word for you?"

Dermot grinned as he pulled her closer. "Excellent idea. Regarding the other lads, you seem quite fond of the words *dumb ass*."

She released air through her nose. "I am, but you have to say it as one word if you're going to be a true Wisconsinite."

"Dumbass," he said.

"Good, but you can't pronounce the B just because it's attached to a vowel. This isn't French."

"Alright," Dermot said before repeating the word.

"Perfect!" Marielle declared happily. "Now, when you spend six months a year in Wisconsin, you'll fit right in... except that you have dark hair and skin. I guarantee they'll think you're an Italian from New York or Northern Michigan... though we only see people from New York on TV."

"Did you see many lads who looked like me when you were in New York?" Dermot asked.

"I didn't, actually, but I didn't know what you looked like. If I go back, it should be pure torture."

"I'm sorry about that," he said before becoming distracted by Donal's Irish.

Marielle looked over her shoulder as Sean joined the chanting.

"I thought you didn't know Irish," she remarked to Sean.

"I didn't say that a'tall," he replied with an air of disdain. "You assumed it 'cos you're a know-it-all American."

"Am I?" she asked as Dermot's arm twitched. "Defend your argument."

"Well, now, you assumed that your man here would share your private details with us—"

"Am I wrong?!" she asked aggressively.

"I'll not be tellin' you that. My point is, you assumed it. You also assumed you knew more about fishing than us. I expect you'll be schooling us in Irish shortly."

"I will," she replied confidently. "Your second declension nouns need some work."

Donal guffawed until something tugged at the end of his line.

"Well, there we are," Marielle said, smiling proudly as Dermot began to laugh.

Sean regarded Donal with a mixture of wonder and annoyance as he reeled in a fish at least double the size of their previous catch.

Marielle stood up, approaching Sean without making eye contact. She stood beside him for a moment, following his line of sight to the water.

Sean breathed more determinedly as he feigned interest in only his fishing line.

"Would ye say now tha' the Americans know what the feck they're talkin' about, like?" she asked with a Dublin accent.

Sean closed his eyes as his body gave in to laughter.

Marielle guffawed as Sean dropped his fishing rod, retrieving it for him before she returned to a beaming Dermot.

"You're the most competitive girl I know," he noted, placing his arm around her again.

She turned toward him with surprise. "I can't believe that's true. Your mom seems very competitive."

"Is she? I hadn't noticed," he said, not noticing the confused look on Marielle's face as well. "Why did you allow me to win at Mercy earlier?"

he asked. "Don't say I really won because I shan't believe you."

Marielle looked between his eyes and his lips. "Can I ask you a question first?"

"Of course."

"Do you suddenly feel more comfortable with me right now?"

Dermot smiled. "I do. I feel as though I've known you my entire life."

She nodded as she leaned into him again.

He turned his head to whisper into her ear. "How did you know that?"

"Your accent becomes thicker when you're nervous or excited."

Dermot sat up a bit. "Now, why'd you have to go sayin' that?" he asked.

Marielle laughed. "Sorry. Why don't we have a Mercy rematch and we can see if that puts you at ease."

"What are you doing to your woman there?" Sean asked as Marielle's right hand did battle with Dermot's left.

"Mercy!" she called.

"Not a'tall!" Dermot protested.

"I swear!" She disengaged her hand to shake it. "My left hand is stronger than your right, but your left hand is like a vice!"

"You're not having me on now?" he asked.

"I'm not."

"Alright. We'll try Splits, then," he decided, standing up before offering Marielle his hand.

"What's Splits?" she asked with concern.

"Oh, Jaysus!" Donal proclaimed. "The knife is on the ground there by the cooler, Dermot."

"Knife?" Marielle asked with alarm as Dermot smiled back at her.

Moments later, they stood near the road, facing one another three feet apart while Dermot held a fillet knife by its tip.

"So, there are two ways to play this game," he began. "The first is that we spread our legs as far apart as possible, then the other person throws the knife into the ground between them, and you have to move your leg to the spot where the knife lands. If you bring your opponent's legs together, you win. The safer way is to do the opposite. You begin with your legs together, then you move them apart to the location where the knife lands until your opponent is doing the splits and can go no farther."

"Isn't this a little dangerous?" Marielle asked with abundant caution.

"We played it when we were kids, and my father played it when he was a kid, and so on. It's perfectly safe as long as you don't stab the other person's foot—though if you do, you lose immediately."

"Is that supposed to be comforting?" she asked, terrified by the idea of stabbing Dermot.

He puckered his lips slightly as he shook his head. "I've played loads of times and I've never been struck."

"But I've never thrown a knife before!" she protested.

"Well, give it a go," he said, handing her the knife before covering his private area with both hands as he spread out his legs.

"So, I'm supposed to throw this between your legs now?" she asked in dismay.

He nodded once. "After you spread your legs as well."

Marielle squinted at Dermot. "Is this a trick?"

He laughed. "It might very well be. Spread your legs as far as you can," he said with mischief.

Marielle sighed before moving her legs apart as far as they would comfortably go.

"Come now!" Dermot protested. "Surely you can go farther than that."

"I might," she admitted, "but it seems a little undignified to try."

"You're among friends," he comforted.

Marielle flashed him disbelieving eyes. "Then, why do none of my friends look at me the way you do?"

Dermot smiled more broadly as he pleaded.

Marielle closed her eyes as she walked her feet out farther.

"Is that all, then?" he asked.

Her eyes opened. "It's farther than you when you account for my height!"

"I was hoping for more."

"Are we still talking about Splits?"

His eyes nearly sparkled as he said, "No."

Marielle looked toward the road as her cheeks turned red.

"I've never seen a girl blush as often as you," he thought out loud.

Marielle looked back at him aggressively. "I've never blushed this much in my life."

"I don't know if I should feel honoured, or badly for putting you through it."

"You should feel badly! Now, can I throw the knife at you?!" she

516

asked impatiently.

"Wait!" Dermot lifted his hand. "I'm not sure I like your tone."

She blinked hard. "I promise not to stab you, if I can help it."

His eyebrows furrowed. "I'm not certain I like your assurances either."

"Well, *you're* the one who thinks this is no big deal! I've already admitted I don't know what I'm doing," she said, her voice cracking.

"Alright, let's practice first," he said calmly.

Marielle sighed as she turned away, dropping the knife onto the ground.

"What's wrong, love?" he asked as tears welled up in Marielle's eyes. He turned her towards the road as he placed his arm around her.

"I'm not built for this, Dermot," she said desperately. "I can barely breathe around you."

He turned to stand in front of her. "That's a *good* thing. Why are you so frightened of me?"

She moaned, closing her eyes and shedding the water which had accumulated.

He smiled kindly. "I'm frightened as well. I didn't say it before, but I swear to you it's true. Have you any idea how I felt when you missed your flight? I turned away from my father to hide it, but he's a smart man. He knows you have me completely wrecked! My mum knows it as well which is why she's so blasted rude."

Marielle looked up swiftly. "I didn't say she was rude."

"No, you've been wonderful about it all. I told her myself, and I dare say my father did as well."

"Should I stay at a B&B?" she asked weakly, wiping her cheeks. "I don't want to cause trouble."

"If you go to a B&B, I'll go after you and then there'd be real trouble!" Dermot warned.

Marielle nodded. "I just need to catch my breath," she said. She turned her head, freezing in place when she noticed Sean staring directly at her.

"Do you have your asthma medicine about?" Dermot asked with concern.

She shook her head. "I don't. I never take it with me."

Dermot looked at her with questioning eyes.

"I don't need to be reminded of my weakness. I'll get it under control.

I just need to concentrate," she explained, attempting to take deeper breaths.

"Does it help to walk, love?" he asked as his concern grew.

"Sometimes. Just give me a second," she said, turning in a circle. "I think I'm just hyperventilating a little." After a moment she said, "I'm fine now."

Dermot grabbed both of Marielle's arms firmly. "Promise me you'll carry your medicine with you at all times from now on! What if you became sick here? We're miles away from help. If you mean to be my wife someday, you need to mind yourself! I'll not negotiate with you on this!"

Marielle smiled despite herself. "I promise, but you showing so much concern doesn't help matters any."

He chuckled as he pulled her close. "I'm in love with you," he said softly.

She pressed her cheek against his chest. "I'm in love with you too, Dermot. Please make it stop."

Chapter Thirty-Two

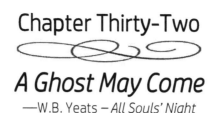

A Ghost May Come
—W.B. Yeats – *All Souls' Night*

"We owe Marielle five quid," Mr. MacManus announced at the dining room table, watching the smile on Marielle's face grow.

"Why's that?" Dermot asked with concern.

"You had a visitor today whilst you were fishing," his mother explained before placing a small piece of chicken into her mouth.

"Ashley?" Dermot asked, nowhere near touching his food.

"Indeed," his father replied.

"Did she say what she wanted?"

His father smiled. "Well, now, I'd say that's quite obvious."

"Was she angry?" Marielle asked eagerly, suspending her fork and knife over her plate as she looked between Dermot's parents.

"I've seen her *more* pleased," Mr. MacManus replied, chuckling.

"But Marielle doesn't win for that!" Dermot objected. "She bet that I would *speak* to Ashley before the end of the week. I haven't spoken to her a'tall."

"Are you certain the bet wasn't that Ashley would *attempt* to speak with you before the week was over?" his father asked.

"Definitely not!" Dermot replied. "Marielle, what was the bet concerning?"

She lifted her hand. "I don't think it's wise to get between a father and a son."

Dermot shook his head in frustration. His father smiled at Marielle knowingly while his wife smiled despite herself.

"No matter what the bet, however, I'd say you'll lose soon," Marielle added, finally cutting her chicken.

"That's probably true, Marielle, but it's a shame Dermot didn't make a similar bet with you," Mr. MacManus added.

Marielle's head rose as her eyebrows furrowed.

"We received a phone call from America today," Mr. MacManus explained.

Marielle's mouth began to open as Dermot looked from her to his father. "Gary?" he asked.

"Indeed. He was a bit concerned to hear of Marielle's plight in London and wanted to confirm for himself she had safely arrived."

"How would he have our number?" Dermot asked Marielle with something approaching annoyance.

Marielle closed her eyes briefly. "It had to be Jeanette. She loves him. He reminds her of her fiancé which is just another reason to hate him as far as I'm concerned. I wrote your number next to our phone at home before I left."

Marielle looked at Mr. MacManus with regret before she apologized.

"Not a'tall," he replied. "He seemed a very nice young fellow. He thanked us for looking after you and said he shan't disturb you again, but he was gratified to know you were safe and wanted me to relate to you that he phoned."

Marielle shook her head in disgust.

"What is it?" Dermot asked, eager to move past jealousy.

"He's pathetic. He's terrified I'll forget about him for the five minutes he's not talking, writing or visiting me, and he's such a show off. Right now, he's regaling everyone at football practice with the story of his call and my missed flight, like it's *his* story. He's only disappointed I made it here at all since a girlfriend dying in a fiery plane crash makes for a much better story."

"Good God!" proclaimed Mrs. MacManus as the men laughed.

Marielle turned toward the woman to determine if her judgment was directed toward herself or Gary.

"Aren't you being a bit hard on the lad, Marielle?" Mr. MacManus asked as if fully prepared to judge either way.

"Well, I absolutely trust your judgment if you say you think him nice, but he loves attention and he has a history of doing crazy things to get it. For example, he'll suddenly stomp on the brakes while driving 55 miles per hour on a county road. He calls it a brake check. One time, he pretended to have a heart attack while driving me home from the movies. He actually held his chest while counting up to seven, then he turned to me and said, 'Thank God! If my heart murmur had lasted three seconds longer, I'd've died.' My grandmother and little sister have started calling him *Heart Murmur Gary*."

"That's terrible!" Dermot said, laughing with his father. "I'd hate it if my girlfriend spoke about me the way you do about Gary."

"Yes, well, we shouldn't date, then," Marielle said with feeling. "I have zero tolerance for idiocy or childish cries for attention."

"Which is where Led Zeppelin comes in," Mr. MacManus noted.

"Exactly!" Marielle replied happily as Mrs. MacManus looked confused.

"We'll tell you later, Mum," Dermot promised before his mother pushed away the idea with her hand.

"Anyway, enough about me," Marielle said, turning to Dermot. "I'm dying to meet your girlfriend. I double-dog-dare you to call her over while I'm here. I'll even drop the bet."

"Not a'tall," Dermot said, dismissing the idea out of hand. "There would be ructions."

"Probably," Marielle admitted, stabbing a piece of chicken. "What on earth are ructions?"

Dermot chuckled. "Fighting."

"Ah, well, I won't pick a fight. I swear. I might tell her my opinion if she's disrespectful toward you, but I'd be well mannered otherwise."

"Even though you have zero tolerance for childish antics?" he asked with scepticism.

"Are you saying she's childish?" Marielle asked, raising her eyebrows as Mr. MacManus laughed.

"I'm not... exactly," Dermot replied.

"Then, call her! Or give me her number and *I'll* call her."

"You wouldn't dare!" he said, leaning towards Marielle.

She leaned forward as well. "Double-dog-dare me, then."

"Well, this is fascinating, but I'd much prefer to know how Mrs. Campbell is getting on," Mrs. MacManus said with an air of superiority.

Dermot looked up as amusement vanished. "She seems well enough, doesn't she Marielle?"

Marielle nodded. "She does. I didn't even remember she was sick until the trip home—I mean, back." She looked down at her plate as she began to blush.

"Is her chemotherapy finished?" Dermot's mother asked.

He cleared his throat. "For now. She goes back again in six months."

"Any chance of Sean's brother returning?"

"Not a'tall. He's too much like his father by half."

Mrs. MacManus turned towards Marielle. "Sean's brother emigrated to Canada over five years ago, and I truly pity the family. Can you imagine a son abandoning his mother like that?"

Marielle shared a grin with Dermot as her eyebrows narrowed. Dermot nearly spit out his water.

"What happened to the father?" Marielle asked in an effort to change the subject.

"He went off to work the oil rigs in the North Atlantic," Mr. MacManus replied. "He sent money and letters and visited the odd time, but all communication eventually stopped. Mrs. Campbell and the boys left Dublin to move into her family home. They began the B&B to make ends meet."

"Is the father alright?" Marielle asked.

Mr. MacManus nodded once. "Quite alright. He began another family in Scotland."

"But I thought divorce was illegal in Ireland," Marielle said as a question, looking around the table for the answer.

"Oh, i'tis, but it doesn't stop people from running off with other people and starting second families," Dermot said with distaste, turning towards his mother to accept her silent rebuke.

"Do many people still leave Ireland?" Marielle asked before she could stop herself.

"Far too many," Mrs. MacManus said, seizing on the topic. "My sister-in-law moved to New York when she was 18. When was the last time you saw your sister, Eamon?"

"Nineteen-seventy-five," Mr. MacManus replied mechanically.

"Dermot doesn't even remember his aunt, do you Dermot?"

Dermot shook his head as he grabbed a jar of pickled beets from the centre of the table.

Mrs. MacManus looked back at Marielle in earnest. "She encourages us to visit, but she won't even put us up, like. She said her neighbourhood is far too dangerous, and she wouldn't take responsibility for our safety. I ask you now, what kind of life is that?"

"I agree," Marielle said, covering her mouth until she swallowed. "During our visit to New York, one of the girls in our choir group was slashed with a knife. She was swinging her purse and a man tried to cut the strap, but missed and slashed her leg instead."

"That's dreadful!" Mrs. MacManus said with a degree of excitement.

"Yeah, but she was pretty stupid to swing her purse around like that,"

Marielle remarked, "and she and another girl had wandered into a bad neighborhood."

"Was a chaperone not minding her?" Dermot asked.

Marielle shook her head. "We didn't have chaperones. Well, we had our choir director and his wife and a couple other teachers around for our formal events, but the rest of the time they let us run around the city on our own."

"You're joking!" Mrs. MacManus said with judgement.

Marielle glanced at Dermot before she smiled. "I'm not, actually. It's funny because a Wisconsin statute requires our whereabouts be accounted for at all times. So, my choir teacher asked our principal if knowing we were on Manhattan Island was specific enough and he said it was. I really love our principal."

"Well, that's all well and good until someone gets lost or injured," Mrs. MacManus said, then turned to her son as he stared at Marielle.

Marielle nodded. "True, but aside from that cut, nothing has ever happened, and they've gone every three years for decades."

"Well, a slashing is quite serious enough!" Mrs. MacManus declared.

Marielle exchanged a look of amusement with Dermot before saying, "'Twas only a flesh wound," using a British accent to better quote Monty Python.

Dermot laughed with Marielle until both began to cry.

"Are you quite done now?" Mrs. MacManus asked, regarding the teenagers with disapproval.

Both apologized in their own way, but they convulsed at intervals before gaining control long term.

"Have you been to the U.S.?" Marielle asked Mrs. MacManus as she picked up her water glass.

"Not a'tall," she replied without making eye contact. "Wild horses couldn't drag me there."

Marielle's expression turned sober.

Mrs. MacManus finally turned towards her. "Sure, I have the history of the civilised world at my doorstep. Why would I waste my time in a place where there's no history or culture and people haven't the decency to sit down when they eat?"

Dermot noticed Marielle's confusion. "Do you sit down when you eat in Wisconsin?" he asked.

"Yes," Marielle replied. "You might be thinking of New York."

"Maybe," Mrs. MacManus conceded. "But I still won't be going. You have no art or culture a'tall."

Marielle's shocked face turned toward Dermot's before both began to laugh again. Dermot stopped first, allowing Marielle to follow and eventually speak.

"I see what you mean in terms of history. We only have a couple hundred years of that if you ignore the natives, but in terms of culture, I go to my father's parents' house and they speak German and live in a house with German decorations. I go to my other grandmother's house and she speaks Italian and serves Italian food. I guess I always thought living on a block where each house had a different heritage was an expression of culture."

Mrs. MacManus looked down to her napkin as she straightened it. "Well, we spend entire summers in Europe with no additional expense besides the ferry. There's no reason to incur the expense of an airline ticket to visit America."

"How do you travel to Europe so cheaply?" Marielle asked with genuine interest.

"We trade houses," Mr. MacManus interjected as he turned away from the study of his wife.

"How does that work exactly?" Marielle asked him.

"They have a catalogue of homes for people amenable to trading in each country," his wife replied.

"The posh ones include pictures of their houses as well," Dermot noted.

"It's not that much of an additional expense, Dermot," his mother chided before turning to Marielle. "You find a location and a house you like. You settle on a time, and then you trade."

Marielle's eyes lit up. "That sounds lovely."

"'Tis if they don't have a grandfather clock banging away at all hours of the day and night," Dermot said, causing his parents to laugh.

Mrs. MacManus stared lovingly at her son before she shared a happy glance with her husband. "I thought Dermot would go mad at the sound of the clock in France. We allowed it to wind down which it did after about a week. In any event, trading houses is only useful if you have at least a month of holidays."

"It's nice you have that much time together," Marielle said wistfully. "My parents are lucky to get a week of vacation in the summer and another for Christmas."

Mr. MacManus cleared his throat. "Yes, well, it helps when you have the summers off."

"What subject do you teach at the University?" Marielle asked him.

"I'm a dean now, but I taught Gaelic for many years," he replied, causing Marielle to turn quickly toward Mrs. MacManus.

"What?" Mr. MacManus asked his gasping wife.

"I spent the entire day teaching her to say *Irish* and you go and ruin it all!" she complained.

Dermot winked at Marielle as she smiled.

"And you teach French?" Marielle asked Mrs. MacManus in an effort to take the heat off Mr. MacManus.

She nodded. "I do."

"Mum can teach German as well," Dermot said proudly.

"That's incredible!" Marielle replied. "I have to practice my German with my grandmother and my other pen pal when I'm not in school. It would be great to declare a German week at home."

"I don't think anyone in this house would agree with you," Mrs. MacManus said, looking down at her plate.

Marielle turned toward Dermot as he shook his head. "I can't tolerate the sound of it," he explained.

"Well, French, then. If I knew French better I'd ask if we could try that now."

"Are all Americans as curious as you, Marielle?" Mr. MacManus asked, seemingly impressed.

"I don't know. Some definitely are. Though my grandmother said they had to stop speaking German at home when her older brother married an Irish girl. I never understood why she couldn't just learn German instead."

"So, you have another pen pal, do you?" Dermot asked as he set down his water glass.

"I do," Marielle replied, ignoring the urge to explain that letters to that pen pal had ended before letters to Dermot began.

Mrs. MacManus studied her son.

"I write to her in German and she responds in English. I correct her letters and she corrects mine," Marielle explained, feeling the slightest pang of guilt for using the present tense of her verbs.

"Well done," Mrs. MacManus said with sincerity.

"*I* correct your letters," Dermot argued.

"Yeah, with completely irrelevant points like adding a U to color, harbor and honor. That won't help me in school at all. In fact, it can only hurt me. I accidentally spelled theater with an R-E at the end instead of an E-R and my 8th grade English teacher made me spell it the American way 100 times."

"If your 8th grade is the same as our second year, that wouldn't be my fault," Dermot countered. "We weren't writing one another in second year."

"I know. It was a separate point."

"So, you only know German, yet you knew I was speaking French at the lake?" Dermot asked, then looked at Marielle's shaking head before he closed his eyes at his mistake.

"You mean I noticed when you *started* speaking French, then switched *immediately* to Irish?" Marielle asked.

"Yes," he said with gratitude which appeared to convince no one.

"I think I mentioned we have a very nice French exchange student who I try to speak with," Marielle began. "She's from Clermont-Ferrand, actually. She showed me a picture of her house and you can see the Puy de Dôme from her backyard so it's a coincidence you climbed it this summer. I'll tell her that when I get home. Anyway, she teaches me a new French phrase every time I see her. The last one was, '*Quelqu'un me regarde bizarrement.*' "

Dermot laughed while his parents smiled. "And do people often look at you strangely?" he asked, easily translating her sentence.

"When I'm speaking French they do… but now that I think of it, she taught me that on the city bus, so we needed it for obvious reasons. Anyway, she can't stand my pronunciation. Every time I speak she says, 'Oh, Marielle. You speak French like a Russian!'"

"You do, actually," Dermot's mother remarked.

"I speak German like a Russian too. I'm not sure if that's a Wisconsin accent issue. My friend's brother was an exchange student in Austria and he was told the same thing, but for me it's more likely attributed to the semester of Russian I took sophomore year. Unfortunately, I was pretty good at it."

"Why's that unfortunate?" Mrs. MacManus asked somewhat aggressively.

"Well, I don't want anyone thinking I'm a commie pinko," she said, not noticing Dermot's warning expression until it was too late.

"I wouldn't think there would be anything a'tall wrong with people thinking you're a communist," Mrs. MacManus declared.

"Really?" Marielle asked, thinking of Senator McCarthy and every person she had ever met, all of whom would say otherwise.

"I actually think the communists have it right," Mrs. MacManus continued, lifting her wine glass.

Marielle looked around the table to determine if she was the victim of a practical joke. When no one smiled, she looked behind Dermot to see if a SWAT team might jump through the window to take his mother into custody. "Do you mean the Soviets?" she asked.

"The Soviets, the Cubans, the Chinese, the Vietnamese. I think it's a much fairer social order," Mrs. MacManus said with no hint of sarcasm or embarrassment, and no indication she heard the air that escaped Marielle's lungs.

The Judge would hate her, Marielle thought, but instead she said, "But there's no freedom, and it doesn't work. No one's going to work hard for the same pay as someone who does nothing. Communism assumes people are selfless, but unfortunately they're not."

"Well, I'm a bit more optimistic about human nature than you are," Mrs. MacManus said with an air of superiority.

Marielle sat still, gob-smacked until the telephone rang.

"I've got it," Dermot said, standing up too quickly to avoid hitting the edge of the table.

Mr. MacManus waited for his son to leave the dining room before he leaned towards Marielle to ask, "Who do you think i'tis?"

"Hmm," she said, concentrating hard as though tapping into the collective unconscious. "I'd say it's Donal."

"I say it's Ashley."

"Not a'tall. It's Sean," Mrs. MacManus said with confidence.

Dermot walked into the dining room moments later, startled by the number of eyes upon him.

"Who was that, Dermot?" his father asked.

"It was Sean," he replied, causing his mother to beam for the very first time. "He asked if we're keen to go dancing tonight."

"Sure, you won't, Dermot," his mother said. "Wasn't someone shot there only last month?"

"Not a'tall. He was only stabbed."

Marielle and Mrs. MacManus exchanged an amused expression. "Well, surely that's bad enough!" his mother declared.

"Would you like to go dancing, Marielle?" Dermot asked.

She glanced at his mother, then replied, "I don't mind either way."

"Why don't you go to the cinema instead?" Mr. MacManus suggested.

Dermot sighed before exiting the dining room again.

"They're playing *Batman* and *The Three Fugitives*," he said upon his return. "Have you seen either of those, Marielle?"

"I've seen both, actually, but I'm happy to go. Have you seen both?"

He shook his head. "Only *Batman*."

"Well, why don't we see *The Three Fugitives*, then?"

"Are you certain?" he asked with questioning eyes.

She nodded. "Positive. I liked the movie a lot."

***

Gryphon raced to Dermot as he and Marielle exited the front door. Dermot bent down to look into the dog's eyes and rub his silky brown ears. Marielle knelt beside Dermot, rubbing an area above Gryphon's tail until he decided a belly rub was in order.

"What kind of dog is he?" Marielle asked, looking down at the brown and cream patchwork colouring.

"He's a Brittany Spaniel," Dermot replied.

"He's a very sweet boy," she said, stroking his belly. "You know, we can just skip the movie and pet him instead."

Dermot smiled at his dog. "You're quickly becoming Gryphon's favourite girl."

Marielle turned to him. "It's amazing that he runs around the city on his own and you don't need to worry about him."

"Yes, well, he's very smart. He always looks both ways before entering the road, don't you boy? And he only crosses at the Zebra Crossings."

"Would that be your version of a crosswalk?" Marielle asked, smiling.

"It would, but I was only joking. He crosses where he likes."

Dermot began to stand as he suggested they get going.

Marielle sighed while continuing to scratch Gryphon's belly. "Alright, but you have to tell him. I don't want him blaming me."

Dermot crouched down again, speaking to his dog in Irish.

Gryphon stood up, looking nose to nose with Dermot.

"What did you tell him?" Marielle asked concernedly.

"I told him you were forcing me to run off to America with you. He's not a bit impressed."

Marielle gasped. "Oh, don't say that! Tell him the truth."

Dermot laughed. "I'm only teasing. I wouldn't say a word against you, especially to Gryphon," he said, standing to offer his hand to Marielle.

She reached down one more time to pet the dog as Dermot pulled her upward.

"He's following us," Marielle whispered when they reached the sidewalk.

Dermot groaned softly. "I hate this part," he said before walking back to the dog. He pointed his finger at Gryphon while demanding in English that the dog sit and stay.

Marielle's eyebrows furrowed sympathetically as she saw the sadness in both the boy and his dog. "We don't have to go. Really, Dermot. We can sit in the yard with Gryphon and look up at the sky instead."

"Not a'tall. My parents would think us mad," he said, forcibly turning her away from his dog.

"Don't look back," he warned after walking several feel, but Marielle disobeyed, finding Gryphon still looking after them.

"But he's still sitting there," she said, her eyes watering.

Dermot stopped, then lost all of his breath when he spied Gryphon silently begging to follow. "He'll be alright, love. I honestly could never leave the house if I stopped every time he looked at me that way."

Dermot pulled Marielle's hand farther down the street.

"I didn't realize the theater was so close to your house," Marielle remarked when they arrived at the Claddagh Palace cinema only a block south of the intersection with Lower Salthill Road.

"Didn't you walk past it this morning?" Dermot asked.

"I did. I meant I didn't realize it was so close until this morning."

"So, you understand now why we don't need a car," he said, stopping at the outdoor ticket window.

"I do. It's making a great deal more sense. I feel terribly that I haven't been able to change my money yet," she said, watching Dermot hand a twenty pound note to the cashier.

"Not a'tall. My father said, 'Tell me what you need, Dermot. Anything a'tall. Even if it's a hundred quid.' "

"That was very kind of him," Marielle replied, watching the cashier hand two tickets and the change to Dermot.

"Well, he thinks the world of you," Dermot said, moving to hold the door for Marielle.

The old fashioned crimson foyer gave immediately to open doors leading to a concession area with three lines crowding the small space.

"Would you like popcorn or a drink?" Dermot asked.

"No, thank you," she replied, not wanting to waste more of the MacManus' money or stand in line and potentially meet Ashley.

Marielle moved toward the theatre doors to the left of the concession counter until Dermot pulled her hand towards the stairs against the wall.

"You have a balcony?" she asked with excitement. "I've never been in a theater with a balcony before."

Dermot smiled at Marielle's childlike enthusiasm as he led her up the stairs. When they reached the top, he suggested Marielle choose their seats, then quickly abandoned her choice for a double-wide chair in the front row.

Marielle regarded the double seat as though it was the best and most scandalous thing she had ever seen.

Dermot sat down first, propping his feet against the balcony half-wall. He hugged Marielle with his right arm as she leaned into him, then kissed her ear with more breath than lips. After a moment, he rubbed her shoulder, his hand pulsing with feeling.

Marielle turned to kiss him, but was frustrated by the extreme angle. She turned back toward the screen, placing her left arm across his lap and lightly rubbing the area of his jeans which pulsed to the same rhythm as his hand.

The audience laughed more heartily during the movie than Marielle remembered the Appleton crowd doing. The idea that the Irish needed a laugh more than Americans occurred to her as she continued to stroke the area of Dermot's jeans which refused to remain still. Near the middle of the movie, Dermot moved his right arm under Marielle's to touch her breast as two teenagers giggled behind them.

"Do you see that little girl?" he asked, indicating the young actress in a brunette bob, long pleated skirt, and bobby socks. "I believe our little girl will look like her."

Marielle turned her body toward Dermot, ignoring the angle and the giggling. She kissed him as she rubbed his jeans more vigorously until the crowd roared again in laughter.

The teenagers sighed as they looked back at the movie.

"I have to say, I love this film!" Dermot declared, causing Marielle to laugh out of step with the crowd.

Marielle marveled at the ability of Dermot's jeans to remain animated during the entire movie, having watched enough soap operas to know men often experienced issues with animation.

"Where should we go?" she asked as they left the theatre, desperate to be alone with Dermot and oblivious to the crowd exiting around them.

"Shall we walk to the sea?" he suggested.

They ignored the cold wind that rushed up Lower Salthill Road, leaning into it until they heard the crashing of the water on the outline of rocks before them.

Marielle shivered as she looked up at the stars while Dermot rubbed her arms from behind. "What's the name of that constellation?" she asked, pointing directly above them.

"I was afraid you'd ask. I'm not brilliant at astronomy, I'm afraid. I believe that's Ursa Minor."

"Aha." Marielle pointed to the right of it. "So, that must be Lee Major."

"Ah, you're right!" he said with enthusiasm. "Did you know there are six million stars in that constellation?"

Marielle doubled over in laughter until Dermot pulled her upright to kiss her. She willed away the cold during the kiss, but jumped as Dermot's cold hand reached beneath her jersey.

"Tell me I'm still permitted to do that," he said anxiously.

"Oh, you are. I just need to get used to the temperature of your hand," she replied as her teeth began to chatter.

"Bloody!" Dermot said. "We should turn back before we freeze."

"I think I see now why Irish girls don't let you reach under their sweaters."

"You believe it's the cold weather?" Dermot asked genially.

"I do. No girl could say no to your soft hands otherwise."

***

Dermot removed the rocks holding open each side of the iron gates before latching them closed behind them. Outside the front door, he looked at Marielle with a pained face. "Oh, God," he said, "I know I will die if I don't have you."

"I feel exactly the same," she replied, studying his eyes as they

531

widened. "I've considered your argument, and I believe your case has merit. I want you to be my first, Dermot, and I would love it if you were my last."

"I'd be honoured," he replied with all of his breath. "Let's get you indoors. You're trembling."

The house remained quiet and dark as they entered the foyer. Dermot locked the front door before halting Marielle's progress at the bottom of the stairs. He leaned down to kiss her while pulling up the front of her shirt. With ease, he unclasped her bra, then lightly stroked her right breast with his fingertips.

Marielle lifted Dermot's shirt, causing him to shiver as her cold hands touched his skin. "I'm sorry," she said, retracting her hand.

"Not a'tall. Move your hand back," he demanded softly.

Marielle made a fist as she breathed into it, causing Dermot to laugh.

"Really. It's quite alright," he whispered happily.

Marielle replaced her hand, feeling Dermot's body throb against his jeans as she reached down to unbutton them.

"Oh, Marielle," he said, exhaling with force as she reached inside his pants, touching his penis for the first time.

He reached down to unbutton her jean shorts as Marielle groaned.

"What, love?" he asked.

She looked down with shame. "It's not exactly that time of the month for me, but I took precautions in case it was." She looked back at him, expecting reproach or disgust, but he smiled instead, grabbing her hand to lead her upstairs. When they reached the top, he whispered, "Take care of that, then meet me in my bedroom."

Marielle turned to Dermot with alarm, but he moved past her quickly.

She changed, then walked to the bathroom. She studied her face as she washed her hands and brushed her teeth, not remembering ever having looked so red before. She turned off the bathroom light before walking to the room which held the toilet. Avoiding eye contact with Dermot, she turned on the light, then closed the door from the outside.

Dermot regarded her from his bed with questioning eyes.

"It's my cover story," she whispered.

"Ah," he said with sudden appreciation. He reached for her hand which she held back until she scanned the hallway one last time.

"We'll hear anyone if they get up. The house creaks like mad," he reassured her.

"I'll remind you of that when she catches us," Marielle replied, only half joking.

"Not a'tall," he said dismissively, pulling her closer to the side of his bed. "Lie down," he demanded.

"Does anyone say no to you?" she asked, in awe of his power over her.

"No one else matters but you, and I'm hoping the answer is no."

"Wow. Good answer," she murmured, beginning to tremble as she lay down on her back.

Dermot propped himself up on his right elbow to loosen the ties of Marielle's bathrobe.

"You're crazy. You know that?" she asked, turning toward him.

"I do, but you make me that way."

"Jesus, you have the best lines in the universe! You know, boys in Wisconsin are still stuck on 'Do you have any Swedish in you?' and if you tell them you don't they ask, 'Would you like some?'"

Dermot turned to laugh quietly at the ceiling. "That's dreadful! Do you have Irish in you?" he asked, looking down at her again.

"Yes, I do," she replied, smiling.

"Ah, see, you're no fun. Wait. I didn't mean that," he said before she had time to object.

Marielle laughed until Dermot placed his hand delicately upon her cheek, tilting her head towards him to better kiss her. Marielle surrendered to the kiss and to Dermot's hand as he unbuttoned the four buttons of her nightgown, smiling when he reached for buttons which weren't there.

He leaned down to kiss the limited area the buttons exposed, then abruptly stopped. "What's this?" he asked, holding the chain of her necklace.

"My Christmas present from my Irish pen pal. I've worn it every day since it arrived. Didn't you see it while we were, ahem, fishing?"

"No. I didn't somehow."

"It's my talisman against other boys."

"I appreciate that, but it's in *my* way just now," Dermot complained.

"Well, I wish I could take it off, but I promised my future husband I wouldn't."

"Let me move it off to the side here," he said, then continued to kiss the top of her breasts.

Marielle shivered as heat entered her lower body. "My God! You're making me crazy."

"Am I now?" he asked.

Marielle jumped slightly as she heard a noise in the hallway. "What was that?" she asked.

Dermot looked up at his door cautiously, then quickly relaxed. "It's only the spirits," he said matter-of-factly.

"Pardon?" she asked as though his answer didn't settle anything at all.

"We have spirits in the house," he repeated, leaning down to kiss her again.

"Oh," she replied, giving up on an explanation.

Marielle ran her fingers through Dermot's hair as he began to tremble with her.

"Are you cold?" she asked.

"No," he replied without further explanation as his hand looked for the bottom of her nightgown.

A loud creak from the hallway caused Marielle to jump to her feet.

"It's nothing, love," he said with feeling, reaching for her.

"I really need to go," she replied, backing away as she tied her bathrobe.

Dermot groaned. "How can you have so much self-control?"

"I'm the patron saint of self-control," she whispered.

"*Please* don't talk about religion," he pleaded.

"Is it a turn-off?"

"Not yet."

Marielle guffawed in her most undignified way, then placed her hand over her mouth and looked anxiously toward the door. "Goodnight," she said, backing up farther. She opened the door to the next room, flushing the toilet before turning off the light.

"Goodnight, love," Dermot said, rolling onto his back.

Marielle heard him sigh deeply as she rounded the corner. A few cautious steps later, she closed her bedroom door, then leaned against it as she realized the error of her plan. Had Dermot's parents heard Marielle flush the toilet, they would have expected her to wash her hands in the bathroom afterward. She considered returning to the bathroom until approaching footsteps interrupted her thoughts.

She listened closely as floorboards creaked outside the door, holding her breath until the footsteps retreated.

Marielle trembled as she lay down slowly, fearing what might have happened had she remained in Dermot's bed five minutes longer, and thankful to whatever spirit told her leave his room.

Chapter Thirty-Three

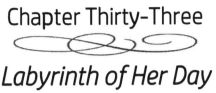

Labyrinth of Her Day

—W.B. Yeats – *Against Unworthy Praise*

Marielle squinted toward the digital clock seconds after her eyes opened. *It's half-nine*, she said to herself, chuckling. She was beginning to tell time like an Irish person.

She looked through her suitcase for something acceptable to wear, deciding on the peach sweater and khakis made famous by her senior pictures. Bathrobe on and slacks in hand, she ran downstairs.

Peeking inside the dining room, she found Dermot and his mother sitting at the table, already dressed for the day. Dermot wore jeans and a maroon-coloured rugby shirt whose sleeves he pushed a third of the way up his forearms, accentuating his lean muscles.

"Good morning," Mrs. MacManus said, approaching the door, thereby blocking Marielle's view of Dermot.

"I'm sorry I slept so late," Marielle replied. "I should've set my Indian Alarm Clock."

"What's that?" Mrs. MacManus asked at the same time Marielle wished she hadn't said it.

"Sorry. It's a crass way of saying I should have drunk water before going to bed."

"My word!" Mrs. MacManus chided as a smiling Dermot suddenly appeared behind her. "Well, that's a lovely bathrobe," she said, feeling Marielle's cuff, "but you might have easily borrowed one of ours."

"Thank you, but it was a birthday present from my mom so I kind of *had* to bring it," she replied, disengaging her eyes from Dermot's with difficulty. "Would you mind if I showered and used your iron as well?"

"Not a'tall," Mrs. MacManus replied, leading Marielle to the door at the bottom of the stairs which had never been opened in her presence.

Marielle looked around the large mint-coloured room whose beauty was hard to disguise behind disorganized bookcases and boxes stacked throughout. The ironing board and iron stood within a few feet of the door and Marielle attempted to follow the electrical cord with her eyes, but lost it behind a wall of boxes a few feet away.

Marielle thanked Mrs. MacManus, then allowed her eyes to examine the room more closely after the door closed. A desk sat trapped inside an alcove window with a view of the back yard, unencumbered by curtains. Wide crown moulding graced each wall, including the alcove. Walnut floor planks appeared nearly new, and somewhat nautical, where visible.

Marielle wondered what series of events might cause a graceful, light-filled room to be demoted to a storage space. She could imagine the upstairs table resting comfortably in the center of this room with people sitting and moving around it easily, and a doorway opening to the kitchen.

She looked down at her khakis as steam from the iron turned them a darker shade of tan, then looked up again, wondering where the hutch would go if the wall between the kitchen and the current dining room was knocked down.

The double-buzzing of the telephone distracted her from her thoughts as did Dermot's soft brogue when he answered it. Marielle turned off the iron as Dermot implored the caller to calm down, then folded her khakis over her arm before opening the door.

Dermot's right hand rested atop his head while he held the phone with his left. He stared out the window to the driveway, seemingly oblivious to his father standing with crossed arms in the doorway of the sitting room.

Marielle exchanged a smile with Mr. MacManus before making her way upstairs, nearly reaching her bedroom door before Dermot spoke again.

"I really can't cope with your abuse, Ashley! We're not married, like. I can be friends with whomever I choose!"

Marielle retrieved her sweater and underwear before quietly making her way to the bathroom. She closed and locked the door, then cursed as she remembered her towel still hung on the hook behind her bedroom door.

"I think that's a splendid idea," Dermot said sarcastically as Marielle quietly retrieved her towel. "Why *don't* you go out with Alan?!"

She returned to the bathroom and nearly closed the door as Dermot yelled, "Piss off!"

Marielle tried not to laugh as she undressed, or as she closed the two panes of frosted glass which met at the corner of the standing shower. She pushed a button and turned a knob on a wall-mounted white box which together heated the water before it slowly trickled from the shower head.

After washing her body and hair, Marielle looked up at the door with a start, wondering if she had locked it when she returned to the bathroom the second time. She turned off the water, then pushed aside the glass, taking special pains not to dislodge the aluminium union strip which fell the first night.

She looked helplessly at the towel resting on the side of the tub which now seemed farther than five feet away. There was no alternative but to risk the walk.

She looked nervously toward the door as she stepped outside the shower, taking only two steps before the door opened. "Wait!" she said, covering what regions her arms and hands could manage before Dermot's head peeked inside.

"I wanted to confirm you kept the door open for me," he whispered.

"I didn't. I forgot to lock it," she replied nervously.

"Did you now?" he asked in disbelief as he scrutinised her body. "Would you remove your arms, please?"

Her eyes opened wider as she said "no" with as much force as whispering allowed. "Leave before we get caught!" she demanded.

"I won't move an inch unless you uncover your breasts," he replied decisively.

She closed her eyes for a moment. "But you've already seen them," she reasoned.

"True, but not in this light. Claude Monet viewed the subjects of his art in every possible light."

Marielle shook her head as she laughed. "You're ridiculous, you know."

Dermot expanded his eyes for a fraction of a second in response.

"If I show you, do you promise to leave?"

"I promise," he replied as a grin became a smile.

Marielle moved her arm away from her breasts.

"Jesus, you're beautiful," he said breathlessly.

"Now go!" she demanded.

Marielle dressed quickly, leaving the bathroom completely clothed minutes later.

"Ahem," Dermot said as he exited his bedroom wearing a victorious grin. "Did you need to use a hair-dryer? Our French friends left this for us," he said, lifting a rust-coloured blow dryer from the hall table.

"Please. Are you reading *Silas Marner*?" she asked, noticing the book which rested at the head of the table.

"I am, yeah. It was our summer reading assignment."

"Really? We have none of those at Appleton East."

"I think I might fancy attending Appleton East," Dermot remarked. "I'm nowhere near the end of it."

"Well, you don't have much time. We could read together this afternoon. Just lend me your dust jacket and I'll read *Ulysses* at the same time."

Dermot leaned against the table wearing a mischievous grin. "I might actually borrow that book from you before you go."

"Do you *really* need to think about sex *more* often?" she asked.

Dermot chuckled. "Probably not. Did I tell you I'm nearly finished with *Johnny Got His Gun?*"

Marielle studied his face to determine his veracity. "Really? How did you have time for that?"

"Well, I can't sleep a'tall well with you so near." He raised his eyebrows with meaning. "And I feel closer to you reading something you've read as well."

"That's sweet, but I don't understand why you can't sleep. I thought boys took certain matters in hand, so to speak."

Dermot's head tilted back as he laughed.

"We do, and it usually helps, but not with you," he replied, turning towards her as he lost his smile.

"Stop!" she demanded. "I really can't tolerate another lovely comment. I'll need to provoke you so you'll tell *me* to piss off." She smiled mischievously as Dermot groaned.

"Did you hear that?" he asked. "I was hoping you were already in the shower."

"I would have been, but I forgot my towel in the bedroom. I'll move quickly past the fact that I won since this is no time for gloating." She cleared her throat and smiled. "So, did you break up?"

He turned his gaze towards his bedroom, nodding with a degree of regret. "I believe so. I think she was poised to cast me aside well before I told her to piss off."

"You hung up on her or she hung up on you?" Marielle asked.

"We might have done at the same time."

"Hmm, that's hardly definitive. Anyway, as a gesture of goodwill, I'll break up with Gary if he calls here again."

"Where's his number?" Dermot asked, looking around the table playfully.

Marielle smiled. "What did your parents say?"

"Well, my mother scolded me on account of my rudeness, but my father told her it was perfectly warranted on account of Ashley's."

"I love your father! He reminds me of my grandfather—not that he's old or anything," Marielle added nervously.

"I knew what you meant," Dermot said, looking at her the way he always did before he kissed her.

***

"So, how would you like your five quid, Marielle?" Mr. MacManus asked from his chair at the end of the dining room table.

"I think we should pay her in pennies," Dermot suggested as he rounded the table to sit down.

Marielle looked at him pensively for a moment, trying to remember if he should have used the word *pence*. "There's no need to pay me at all," she finally said, sitting down. "Hearing Dermot curse over the phone was payment enough." Her nose twitched at Dermot in response to him doing the same.

Mr. MacManus shook his head. "We must pay our debts."

"Well, I believe I owe you a dozen times more than that for gas, and the movies last night, but if you're not amenable to that, we can consider a double or nothing arrangement."

"That sounds interesting," Mr. MacManus remarked, nodding to prompt her to continue.

"If Ashley calls or comes by again, I win ten quid, but if she doesn't, or if Gary calls again, we're even."

"What if Gary rings and you tell *him* to piss off?" Dermot asked to the amusement of his father.

Marielle's eyebrows narrowed in concentration. "Well, it would be hard to work that into an American sentence, and he might not take me seriously, but if I do, I think it should be worth five quid to me."

"That seems fair, wouldn't you say, Dermot?" his father asked. "If only to hear Marielle work such a rude comment into a transatlantic telephone call."

"It does indeed," Dermot replied, smiling as his gaze pierced Marielle's.

Movement in the kitchen caught Marielle's attention. "Excuse me," she said, standing.

"Do you need help?" she asked Mrs. MacManus when she found her near the sink.

"Not a'tall," Mrs. MacManus said as she washed lettuce.

"I could do that for you. I'm not much of a cook, but I can certainly clean food," she offered, reflexively rubbing the pendant of her necklace.

"You haven't eaten breakfast yet," Mrs. MacManus objected, then sighed when she turned to Marielle. "You're wearing that necklace," she muttered.

"Yes. I always do. I'm not hungry, but I can help you wash dishes. That's my job at the nursing home."

"Why don't you empty the dishwasher, then? I'll direct you as to where everything goes."

Marielle spied the impressed look Mr. MacManus gave Dermot as she opened the dishwasher.

"May I help you as well, Mum?" Dermot asked, running more than walking into the kitchen.

"Since when do you help?" his mother asked with wide eyes, causing her son to blush. "You might help Marielle put the dishes into the press," she suggested.

Dermot and Marielle quickly collided near the dishwasher.

"We're experiencing diminishing returns," Marielle noted, then added, "Economics," when Dermot appeared confused. "How 'bout if I hand you the dishes and you put them away?" she said, handing him a stack of plates.

"Should I put four plates into the oven, Mum?"

"Why would you put plates into the oven?" Marielle asked.

"It's to keep the food warm longer," Mrs. MacManus explained. "My husband wouldn't be a'tall impressed if I served dinner on a cold plate."

Marielle furrowed her eyebrows at the idea that Mr. MacManus had a say in anything at all, much less the temperature of plates.

"I hope you weren't reminded of work," Dermot said as all three returned to the dining room, carrying tea.

"No, this is much more fun than work, though I do miss Lars," Marielle said, handing Mr. MacManus his tea before sitting down with her own.

"I hope you're not speaking of an elderly person there, Marielle," Mrs. MacManus said severely.

Marielle's cheeks became warm. "I was, actually."

Dermot smiled towards his mother as if he was about to enjoy what came next.

"If some young girl called me by my first name, I wouldn't be pleased a'tall!" Mrs. MacManus declared, looking away at the thought of it.

"Well, sometimes we call them *dear* or *sweetie*," Marielle said.

"Ah! That's worse!" Mrs. MacManus exclaimed as Dermot and his father laughed over their teacups.

Marielle waited for the laughter to subside before she spoke. "Well, we have a lot of Alzheimer's patients and many of them, especially the women, don't remember their last names. In fact, one woman only answers to her maiden name."

"Well, maybe, then," Mrs. MacManus relented, sharing a smile with her husband.

Dermot nodded at Marielle appreciatively. "My friend Thomas called Dad by his first name once."

"Yes, and I called him something far worse," Mr. MacManus added.

"Does Lars have Alzheimer's?" Dermot asked.

"Dermot! I'll not have *you* calling the elderly by their first names!" his mother scolded.

"But I don't know his last name," he protested weakly.

"Knutson," Marielle replied with a smile. "He's just beginning to show signs of dementia. He sometimes asks me to write a very similar letter two days in a row to his nephew."

"I thought you worked in the kitchen," Mr. MacManus said as a question.

"She does. This is during her time off," Dermot explained, smiling proudly at Marielle.

"Well, you're very good, Marielle," Mr. MacManus said with feeling.

"Thank you," she replied, looking down at her mug.

"And she doesn't like compliments a'tall," Dermot added as he studied her.

"I suppose I could accept it this one time," she replied before clearing her throat. "I wouldn't be too impressed with me, though. I don't do that for everyone. Lars—sorry—Mr. Knutson is a special case."

"He holds her hand every day," Dermot said to his parents, then apologised to Marielle when she narrowed her eyes at him.

"I remind him of his wife," she explained. "She was Danish."

542

Mr. MacManus regarded Marielle's hair and eyes. "I could see that," he said with a smile.

"Sure, Hitler would have spared you," Mrs. MacManus said with disdain, causing Marielle to flinch.

"So, did you tell Mr. Knutson you were leaving for Ireland?" Dermot asked quickly.

"I did, but sadly it's his birthday this week—tomorrow, actually. He was so upset about me leaving that the staff lied and told him my trip was moved to the week *after* his birthday. So, we had to pretend it was his birthday last week. We had a party and everything before I left."

"How horrible!" Dermot said with amusement.

"I thought so too at first, but then I couldn't figure out a good reason why. I mean, it makes him happy, so what's the harm? A worse story is the people I babysit for telling their children Christmas was on the 26th when they passed-out drunk Christmas Eve and didn't put out the presents from Santa in time."

Mrs. MacManus waited for the men to stop laughing before she declared the story terrible.

"I know," agreed Marielle. "I feel badly laughing about it."

Dermot wiped his eyes, then turned to his father with a more serious face. "What do you think of me bringing Marielle to Dún Aengus tomorrow?"

"That's fine if the seas are calm," his father replied. "You'd be better advised taking the train to Dublin to show her Trinity and the Book of Kells. The weather is meant to break by midweek."

Dermot nodded.

"Did Dermot tell you he was almost swept out to sea on the Aran Islands as a small boy?" Mrs. MacManus asked, studying Marielle as though she were a science experiment.

"What happened?" Marielle muttered, the color in her cheeks disappearing as if the incident occurred recently.

"There are holes in cliffs where the sea shoots straight up. I believe they'd be classed as puffing holes," she said, glancing at her son as he nodded. "He lost his footing when the sea shot up, and he began sliding towards the opening. Well, I *barely* grabbed his hand in time," Mrs. MacManus said, smiling like she told an amusing story rather than a tragic one.

Dermot's eyebrows furrowed at the look of pain in Marielle's eyes.

She cleared her throat as she looked away for a moment. "No matter what we do tomorrow, I'm paying," she said.

"Not a'tall," Mrs. MacManus said as the table turned cold.

Marielle looked around. Discussing money was obviously considered gauche. "Will you come with us?" she asked Mr. MacManus hopefully.

"We're working," his wife replied. "I'm surprised my husband took time on Friday to pick you up a'tall. He works morning, noon, and night. Sure, he leaves before any of us wakes and only returns home shortly before dinner," she said, staring down her husband over her teacup, then setting it down when she realised it was empty.

"Can I get you more tea?" Marielle offered.

Mrs. MacManus regarded her with surprise before handing over her cup.

Everyone flinched as someone knocked on the front door.

Dermot stood quickly, flashing a worried look at Marielle and touching her shoulder as he walked towards the foyer.

Marielle heard Dermot say hello when she reached the kitchen. She poured the remainder of the hot water into Mrs. MacManus' cup and added a tea bag before Mrs. MacManus exclaimed, "James!"

Marielle peeked into the dining room to see Gráinne's father standing inside the doorway.

"How's everyone keepin'?" he asked happily, nodding at Marielle as she waved from the kitchen.

Marielle studied Dermot's father's less than pleased expression as she returned to the dining room, setting down Mrs. MacManus' tea in front of her before standing against the wall on the window side of the table.

"Are you excited for the final?" Mrs. MacManus asked James.

"I am, indeed. Most people are a bit balmy at this stage, aren't they?"

She shook her head. "Oh, I can't be bothered with it."

"Were you not converted whilst watching your son crush his opponents, like?" James asked, looking with respect at Dermot who stood beside him near Marielle's vacated seat.

"I only tolerated it for Dermot's sake, but I can't claim to be a fan, no. Now, my husband on the other hand nearly had a stroke at the Junior Final."

Mr. MacManus finally smiled just in time for James to peek his head around the door.

"I'll say you were wrecked on many an occasion, eh, Eamon?" James remarked.

Mr. MacManus nodded, but didn't reply.

"So, are you missing it yet?" James asked Dermot.

"Not a'tall," Mrs. MacManus answered for her son. "Sure, whilst in France, we left him alone at the house with a full bottle of wine. When we returned, there was only a drop or two remaining. Here Dermot was splayed out on the couch. He had a head on him shortly thereafter, I can tell you. His training would have made no allowances for that sort of behaviour."

Dermot looked across the table at Marielle, his smile disappearing as color again abandoned her face. His father noticed her reaction as well.

"That's quite unusual for Dermot, now, you must admit," Mr. MacManus said to his wife before glancing at Marielle again.

Mrs. MacManus followed her husband's line of sight, then smiled. "I imagine he's only a year or so away from pub crawls and the like anyway," she added.

Dermot regarded his mother critically before looking at Marielle with remorse.

"Well, I wondered anyway if you were interested in a swim tonight with Gráinne and her friend Dawn?" James asked Dermot, seemingly oblivious to the undercurrent around him.

"That would be lovely, I'm sure," his mother replied.

"We'll be at Thoor Ballylee," Dermot objected.

"Not all day, Dermot," his mother said with annoyance.

"We'll be attending Mass as well," he added.

"Ah, save yourself a half-hour and go to Salthill," James advised. "They breeze through Mass there."

"I thought the Mass at St. Mary's was quicker," Mrs. MacManus remarked.

James shook his head. "Not a'tall. Salthill has a new priest. Sure, he can't be bothered with a long Homily."

Marielle looked from Dermot's mother to Gráinne's father. Never in her life had she expected adults to celebrate teenage drinking seconds before conspiring to attend a short Mass.

"Okay, so. I'll tell Gráinne you're up for it. She'll be glad to see Marielle again," James said before offering his goodbyes.

"May I speak to you in the other room, Mother?" Dermot asked from the dining room door, seconds after showing their guest to the front door.

Mrs. MacManus turned an alarmed expression towards her husband as she stood. He grinned in return.

After the dining room door closed, Marielle asked Mr. MacManus if he wanted more tea.

"No, thank you," he replied. "So, what do you think of our Mr. Maguire?" he asked as Marielle resumed her seat.

"Gráinne's father?" Marielle inquired.

Mr. MacManus nodded.

"Oh, I think he's well-liked by Gráinne, Mrs. MacManus, and most assuredly his mother," Marielle replied, but quickly apologized before Mr. MacManus erupted into laughter.

"Why don't we watch the news, Marielle," Mr. MacManus suggested as his son and wife returned to the dining room.

Marielle accepted with gratitude, then followed him into the sitting room, leaving Dermot's longing expression and Mrs. MacManus' retribution behind.

"So, this particular news is in Irish," Mr. MacManus said from a hard, wooden chair he pulled alongside the large, burgundy, leather couch.

Marielle nodded, noticing the spare news set resembled that from Rhinelander, Wisconsin.

Throughout the broadcast, Mr. MacManus interrupted a serious looking lady with flat, dark hair to translate her words into English.

"The rest is about the weather, which is always meant to change, and the Senior Hurling Final, of course."

Marielle smiled brightly at Mr. MacManus, catching him off guard when he looked back at her. "Thank you," she said. "That was wonderful. So, I got up early last year to watch the Final and I've read a little bit about the sport since you explained it to me over the phone last summer. Mrs. Campbell also clued me in on a few things. She said the Full Forward is a key position, making most of the goals and that's what Dermot played. She said they generally put tall players there."

"That's right," Mr. MacManus replied. "All positions are important of course, but I would argue Full Forward is the most tactical. The strategy Sean's mother mentioned is fairly recent, though the game is thousands of years old. Did you notice the elements of field hockey and American baseball when you watched last year's match?"

Marielle nodded. "I did. I noticed the players can throw the ball to each other and catch it with their hands or throw it up in the air and bat it away with their sticks. I also saw them hit the ball with their stick when it was on the ground."

"That's right. The stick is called a Hurley and it's made of ash wood. That's why people call hurling *The Clash of the Ash*."

"Ooh, that sounds medieval," Marielle said with excitement. "Did you play?"

"I did, in fact. I was fairly good, but on my best day I couldn't hold a candle to my son. Watching him in the spring was fantastic fun."

Mr. MacManus sat back in his chair with a deep sigh.

Marielle conveyed to him a sympathetic nod, knowing without asking that Dermot's retirement would be hard on his father.

"Sean and Dermot think there's no way Antrim can beat Tipperary today," Marielle remarked.

"I think they saw the size of Antrim's goal tender before making that decision," Mr. MacManus replied with a chuckle.

Marielle narrowed her eyebrows.

"He looks quite overweight. I'm not sure how he manages it. I dare say the boys are right, though. Tipperary will not be beaten."

"Well, I'm sorry we can't watch it with you," Marielle said with remorse. "I promise I'm respectful of the *no talking during a game* policy. I would just need to take notes so I'd remember my questions afterward."

Mr. MacManus smiled, then opened his mouth to speak as Dermot called Marielle's name from the foyer. Marielle sighed in reply, causing Mr. MacManus to study her more carefully.

"Well, thank you for introducing me to the Irish news," she said before reluctantly departing.

"Are you alright there?" Dermot asked, noting Marielle's disappointment as she joined him at the bottom of the stairs.

"I'm fine. We were just talking about hurling and I was enjoying it."

Dermot chuckled as though her comment was meant to be a joke. "Are you able to go swimming tonight?" he asked with concern.

"I'll have to see if I brought my swimsuit, but I'll be fine," she lied.

"But you *do* swim?"

"Badly, but yes."

"Well, I promise to look after you. I won't allow you to drown," he said, still studying her eyes for the answer to a question he wouldn't ask.

"That's very kind of you," she replied, looking away.

"I'm sorry about the wine bit. I swear to you I don't make a habit of it.

547

It was a particularly good wine, and I was bored, like."

Marielle noticed a shadow move on the floor near the dining room doorway.

"You don't need to explain anything to me," she said curtly, causing Dermot to look at her with confused eyes as she walked toward the dining room and the retreating shadow.

"So, my son tells me you don't swim," Mrs. MacManus said with her back to Marielle, having reached the kitchen.

Marielle thought for a moment before she spoke, sure that Mrs. MacManus was in the room when this fact was mentioned the day before. "I don't swim well, but I do swim," she replied, stopping on the dining room side of the kitchen doorway.

"I was thinking about our conversation yesterday," Mrs. MacManus said, opening a heavy wooden drawer to the right of the refrigerator.

"About Adam Clayton?" Marielle asked as Dermot approached.

"No," Mrs. MacManus replied impatiently. "About backpacking across Europe. I have brochures for youth hostels—"

"You mean the business about Adam Clayton and the drug charges?" Dermot asked Marielle.

Marielle turned toward Dermot with playfully wide eyes as his mother sighed.

"It wasn't drugs, Dermot! It was alcohol related."

He turned towards his mother. "That's not what the papers said."

An enormous grin overtook Marielle's face.

"Well, paper never rejects ink!" his mother exclaimed as if the matter were settled. "Have you phoned Sean today?" she asked, still searching the drawer.

Dermot stared at Marielle's face before shifting his eyes slightly downward in an attempt at making her blush. "No, why?" he asked his mother.

"He rang again last night. He was under the impression you meant to go dancing with him. Did you not ring to tell him you were going to the cinema instead?"

Dermot cringed. "I didn't, actually."

"Well, he had you and Marielle paged at the club and he didn't sound pleased a'tall."

"I'm thinking he'll get over it," Dermot decided without removing his eyes from Marielle's sweater.

"Well, that's a fine attitude!" Mrs. MacManus said, pushing hard on the stubborn drawer.

Dermot groaned. "He was upset about his pet fish the other day. I spent at least 20 minutes comforting him, which is ridiculous, like."

"What happened to his fish?" his mother asked, turning to hand Marielle the youth hostel brochures.

"Thank you," Marielle said before walking to the table.

"He named it *Fish* so of course it killed itself. Well, that's what I told him," Dermot said more to Marielle than his mother as he walked towards his dining room chair.

Marielle chuckled as she opened a brochure. "That doesn't sound very comforting."

"I wanted him to have a laugh. He did, and he was grand afterwards. It's an outrageous name anyway, though no different than naming your daughter *Colleen*, I suppose." Dermot looked at his mother, then back at Marielle. "It means *girl* in Irish."

"Ah," Marielle said to the brochure. "I suppose it's the same as naming your son *Guy*."

Dermot looked severely at Marielle, but relaxed when she looked up, her face betraying only amusement.

It took a moment for Marielle to process the expression which had already left Dermot's face. It seemed ironic to her that the casual use of Guy's name would elicit the reaction Guy always encouraged in others, and Marielle regarded as weakness—until now.

The presence of Dermot's mother frustrated Marielle's need to reassure him as his eyes escaped to the front window.

Mrs. MacManus examined her son's failed attempt to conceal emotion. The scene to which Marielle arrived late obviously played for her in real time. Her expression told Marielle she had never seen her son like this before, and in an instant, the rest was clear. Dermot's feelings for and connection with Marielle were a betrayal of his mother, at the same time they called into question the years she had left with her son.

Marielle regarded Dermot as his mother returned to the kitchen. "Maybe he named his fish after the character on *Barney Miller*," she suggested.

Dermot turned towards her.

"Do you get *Barney Miller* reruns here?" she asked.

"We did, actually. I hadn't thought on that before, but Sean liked that show a great deal."

"Well, it was probably just death by old age then, unless he didn't explain his reasoning to the fish. By the way, don't you find it a little odd that he'd go fishing only days after getting upset over a dead fish?" Marielle asked before an idea suddenly presented itself to her.

"What?" Dermot asked with abundant curiosity.

"It's not about the fish at all! Sean is worried about his mother. He's equating the death of his pet fish with the fear that his mother's cancer might have a bad result."

"Bloody!" Dermot declared. "How am I meant to react if his real worry is about his mother dying?"

"Exactly the way you did," Marielle replied. "You joke about fish suicide."

***

"Someone may sit in the *front* seat," Mrs. MacManus said with exasperation as both Marielle and Dermot opened the rear car doors.

"Oh, sorry," Marielle replied. "I forgot Mr. MacManus wasn't coming along."

"Are you joking? He won't be parted from the telly today," Mrs. MacManus scoffed, then smiled as she spied Dermot offering Gryphon an aggressive ear scratching.

"Is Gryphon coming along?" Marielle asked hopefully.

"Could he, Mum?" Dermot asked pleadingly.

She expelled breath through her nose. "Fine. Put him in the boot," she said before sitting in the driver's seat.

Marielle walked to the trunk as the hatchback opened and Gryphon happily jumped inside. "Will he be okay in there?" she whispered.

"Absolutely. He rides in the boot on a regular basis," Dermot replied, stroking the small of her back as they moved to the left side of the car.

"You take shotgun," Marielle offered, opening the rear passenger's-side door.

"Not a'tall. I'm grand in the back seat."

"Really?" she asked with narrowing eyes.

Dermot nodded, opening his eyes wider for a moment.

Marielle laughed, then quickly took her seat, expecting Mrs. MacManus to object to the time spent deliberating.

Mrs. MacManus looked from the back seat to the front with surprise, but said nothing as Marielle fastened her safety belt. After several seconds

550

of thought, Mrs. MacManus shifted into neutral, allowing the car to roll down the driveway and into the street before turning the key in the ignition.

"Is that to save gas?" Marielle asked.

"'Tis. There's no need to turn over the engine if gravity will do the work for you."

Marielle nodded. "Has it ever *not* started once you reached the street?"

"Not a'tall. We buy *Japanese* cars in Ireland," Mrs. MacManus said, and Marielle understood as a slight against American manufacturing.

"Mr. Ferguson has a Ford van," Dermot announced, leaning forward without the restriction of a seat belt. He reached around the window side of Marielle's headrest to stroke the back of her neck. "He has an automatic transmission and the steering wheel on the wrong side an' all. He must have a terrible time driving it, though I don't believe he's ever been in an accident."

"That's a big old smelly thing," Mrs. MacManus complained.

Marielle looked out the window, watching the pedestrians walk the tight rope between high stone walls and cars parked at least a third of the way onto the sidewalk. Insofar as she could analyze anything with tingling sensations running up and down her spine, she noticed very few kids their age could afford name brand sneakers or jeans the way Dermot did.

Soon after leaving Galway city limits, Dermot proclaimed, "Tinkers!" as a large red keyhole-shaped wagon came into view farther ahead.

"Dermot! Don't teach Marielle such rude language! We call them Travellers now."

Marielle turned toward Dermot as he rolled his eyes.

"Do you have your camera with you, Marielle?" Mrs. MacManus asked as they passed the wagon.

Marielle closed her eyes involuntarily. "I don't," she replied.

Mrs. MacManus sighed. "Look under your seat there. My husband might have left our camera in the car."

Marielle found the camera with ease and confirmed there were six pictures remaining on the expensive-looking camera.

"The Tinkers don't fancy having their photo taken," Dermot cautioned.

"Just like those tribes in *National Geographic*," Marielle remarked. "They think you're stealing their soul."

"That seems inconvenient," Dermot replied. "To lose your soul in a photo, I mean."

"True, I can think of much better ways to lose it," Marielle said, then cringed.

"Mum, tell Marielle about all the Tinkers in the public schools."

Mrs. MacManus shot her son a displeased look through the rear view mirror before she spoke. "A friend of mine teaches in a public primary school and she's driven mad by the children of Travellers starting the year, then disappearing, or appearing in the middle of a school year. It's an immense challenge for her to bring them up to the level of the class and it's extremely disruptive to the other students."

Marielle nodded. "I wonder how they pay taxes with no fixed address."

Dermot scoffed. "I shouldn't say they pay taxes a'tall."

"Maybe not payroll tax, Dermot, but everyone pays sales tax," his mother argued.

"Are payroll taxes very high here?" Marielle asked, causing Dermot to sigh at the tirade he apparently knew was coming.

Mrs. MacManus drew a deep breath. "I can't be bothered to look at my pay deductions anymore. Sure, you'd be driven mad to see the amount of money the government takes! It's nearly half!"

Marielle smiled, thinking how strange it was for a communist to complain about taxes.

"Have you ever heard of E.O. Wilson, Marielle?" Dermot asked, resting his chin upon Marielle's seat.

"No, I haven't," she replied, trying to say the last word with an intellectual flare to make up for her ignorance.

"Well, he says that species are not as cold and heartless as Darwin suggests. That, in fact, they will sacrifice themselves for the greater good of their kin or species."

"Do you believe that?" Marielle asked.

"I don't know. Mum definitely does," he said, smiling towards his mother as she nodded her head. "What do you think?" he asked as though he expected an intelligent response.

Marielle thought hard as she ignored Dermot's roaming fingers, as well as the vivid green fields outlined by stone walls which were home to painted sheep. "I think it depends on the species," she replied, "but I think there's an evolutionary advantage to self-sacrifice among humans. For example, I've noticed at the nursing home that patients who help other patients—who read, who write, or keep other people company—tend to live longer. Now, it's possible that patients who aren't healthy enough to do those things aren't healthy enough to live a long life, BUT I've also noticed that people who come in just for rehab—who seem just as healthy as the volunteering patients, but who are too lazy or angry to do anything constructive—tend to get sick and die before the happy patients."

"Maybe they're depressed and they give up," Dermot theorized.

"Maybe," Marielle agreed. "Or maybe we're hard-wired to self-destruct once we're no longer useful to society."

Dermot raised his eyebrows. "So, we should investigate if anyone lived a long life who wasn't contributing to the greater good."

"Yes. Well, or who *thought* they weren't contributing to the greater good. After all, if someone's mind turns on itself, it only matters how the person assessed his usefulness, not society's view of him... unless they're the same."

"That's brilliant," Dermot said, rubbing the base of her neck.

Mrs. MacManus squinted at the road in front of her as Marielle cleared her throat. "I notice the sheep have different colors spray-painted on their sides. Do you know why?"

"I believe it signifies they've received their vaccinations," Mrs. MacManus replied.

"Does it not show which farm they belong to?" Dermot asked his mother.

"Don't contradict me, Dermot!" she demanded, causing him to sit up straighter before sliding back in his seat. "Bloody!" Mrs. MacManus said, looking down at the dashboard. "Did your father not say we required petrol?"

Dermot regarded his mother with unhappy eyes. "He didn't, no."

"Well, we'll have a fine time finding a station open during the match!"

"It hasn't started yet," Dermot murmured.

Marielle turned around in her seat to make eye contact with Dermot, temporarily turning his annoyed expression into a smile. "Didn't you say the match will be on the radio?"

"It will, but Mum wouldn't be keen to hear it."

Marielle kept her eyes from rolling as she turned back toward the front.

"I don't care either way," Mrs. MacManus said, moving her palm from the steering wheel to regard the fuel level again. She looked in the rear view mirror. "If we run out of petrol, you'll need to hitch-hike to the nearest station."

"Is that safe?" Marielle asked with alarm.

"Perfectly," Mrs. MacManus replied, clearly taking issue with Marielle's tone.

Marielle scanned the horizon. "Do you have service stations at rest stops or waysides in Ireland?"

"What do you mean by waysides?" Mrs. MacManus asked impatiently.

"An area where you pull off the road for service or rest."

"A lay-by," Dermot said with amusement.

Mrs. MacManus nodded. "A wayside for us is something quite different. It refers to a fall from grace. For example, we might say, 'The girl became pregnant, dropped out of school, and fell by the wayside.' "

Marielle cringed. It was clear Mrs. MacManus had something very specific on her mind.

"Here's a station, Mum," Dermot said in time for his mother to stop.

Dermot jumped from the car to ask the proprietor if the station was open. The man reluctantly left his perfectly good television set inside the small cement block building to say it was.

Marielle breathed a sigh of relief, then laughed when she noticed the sign in the station's window which read "In God We Trust. All Others Pay Cash."

"That's ridiculous!" Mrs. MacManus declared after reading the sign herself.

"How much would you like, Mum?" Dermot asked through the driver's-side window.

"Twenty quid for now," she replied, parting unhappily with her bill before rolling up her window. "I filled the car on Thursday and it's already empty," she said to Marielle accusingly.

"I'm sorry about that. It's my fault. I can give you the money tomorrow when I change my traveler's checks."

"Not a'tall," Mrs. MacManus said, looking away.

Marielle attempted to catch a glimpse of Dermot through the car mirrors. Although he stood only a few feet away, the distance seemed too far.

"It's odd," Mrs. MacManus said, waiting for Marielle to turn toward her before continuing. "Dermot and his sister argue over the front seat during every car journey, yet he willingly gave it to you."

Marielle smiled weakly. "Well, he's obviously a gentleman. You've done a wonderful job in raising him."

Mrs. MacManus narrowed her left eye before smiling unhappily as though Marielle spoke in a cunning rather than a sincere manner.

Dermot jumped back into the car a few minutes later. "Alright, let's turn on the radio," he said excitedly as he reached between the front seats. "I heard the announcers talking over the man's telly."

"It's a capacity crowd here at Croke Park," the announcer began as Dermot accidentally squeezed Marielle's shoulder in full view of his mother. Marielle and Mrs. MacManus looked toward one other at the same time with similar shocked expressions.

Within minutes, the announcers yelled "Nicki English!" before declaring Tipperary had scored a point. At intervals, Marielle thought the announcers changed to Irish, but Dermot assured her it was still English. Sixteen minutes into the game, Antrim answered Tipperary.

"Did they just say the goal keeper was hit in the head?" Marielle asked.

Dermot nodded happily.

"It's five wides for Antrim!" the announcer yelled before reciting a barrage of names such as Cleary, Donnelly, Kennedy, MacDonald—or maybe MacDalton—and Armstrong.

Dermot turned from the radio to Marielle. "Tipperary beat Galway awhile back, but they haven't won the final in 18 years. There are actually two brothers on their team."

A deafening noise was heard over the radio as they pulled into the Thoor Ballylee car park. "Nicki English has immense skill," Dermot declared, then sighed as the radio stopped with the car engine.

"Can we discuss Yeats now?" Mrs. MacManus asked in her usual way before opening her car door.

Marielle apologized softly to Dermot as they closed their respective doors.

"Not a'tall," he said, smiling back and rubbing her backside as though it was a consolation prize.

Gryphon alighted from the trunk no worse for wear, then ran off in the direction of a stone bridge.

"So, Dermot tells me you're a student of Irish culture," Mrs.

MacManus said, seemingly prepared to judge for herself.

Marielle glanced at Dermot before adopting a serious expression. "Well, I've grabbed a book and read it every time Dermot has mentioned a historical event or an author. I'm not sure I've made a lot of progress though."

"I don't know anything about Yeats," Dermot confessed, resulting in a non-verbal scolding by his mother.

"I thought you did," Marielle said with a quizzical face.

"Why don't you educate my son on Yeats then, Marielle," Mrs. MacManus suggested.

Marielle took a deep breath. "Well, he was Protestant. Born in Dublin, and eventually attended high school there, but in between he lived in London. His family had money, or maybe it was just his grandparents who did because his father didn't make a lot of money as a portrait painter. William began the Abbey Theatre and wrote plays in Dublin, but he preferred to spend his time in Sligo and Galway. His greatest poetry was written here," she said, looking at the short, square, medieval tower with appreciation.

She took another deep breath. "When he was young, he slept outside as much as possible—in the woods and in caves, and he was interested in stories of fairies and banshees. Apparently, his brother died after a servant heard the cry of a banshee."

"His interest in folk tales was purely an intellectual one," Mrs. MacManus interjected. "He didn't actually *believe* those stories."

Marielle furrowed her eyebrows briefly before continuing. "He died on vacation in France—a heart attack, I believe—but they couldn't bring his body back right away because World War II was about to break out." She stopped walking. "Today is the 50th anniversary of the start of World War II so he must have died 50 years ago this year. That's quite a coincidence," she said, feeling a shiver run up her spine without the aid of Dermot's fingers.

"Was he buried here?" Dermot asked.

Mrs. MacManus answered quickly. "No. His wife, Lady Gregory—"

"I'm sorry, isn't her name George?" Marielle asked, trying to sound less sure than she was for politeness sake.

Mrs. MacManus exhaled sharply. "You're showing me up, Marielle!"

Marielle turned a smile toward Mrs. MacManus, expecting the same in return, but found none. "Sorry," she said anxiously. "I was confused myself at first, so I checked out two books at the library. Lady Gregory was a widow friend who lived near here. She helped Yeats with his research on folklore, but there was nothing else between them. He didn't find her attractive at all, but I believe there's some speculation that he had an affair with an Olivia—"

"No, she was his muse," Mrs. MacManus interrupted.

Marielle narrowed her eyebrows again as she looked at the gravel road before her. *So, Irish rock stars didn't do drugs and Irish poets didn't have affairs. Next, she'll say Irish rain doesn't make you wet,* thought Marielle.

"Do you actually have a favourite Yeats *poem?*" Mrs. MacManus asked as though Marielle's story about the man rather than the poetry left her wanting.

"Well, um, I can't remember the name of it offhand," she replied after dismissing *Leda and the Swan* whose title she never forgot. "It's a little spooky, actually. It's about a child being coaxed into the water by a fairy. It keeps telling the child that life is too sad and lonely and it would be better to come into the water and drown, and in the end, the child does."

"That's *The Stolen Child,*" Mrs. MacManus said with an unhappy smile, and a slight shaking of her head as if she found the name all too fitting.

"Do you have a favorite Yeats poem?" Marielle asked Dermot as she leaned forward to make eye contact with him.

"Oh, I don't know," he sighed. "I do like the short ones best." He smiled brightly as Marielle laughed.

Mrs. MacManus reproached her son as Gryphon ran alongside, distracting him from his mother's scorn.

"Do you have a favorite poem?" Marielle asked Mrs. MacManus.

"I do," she replied, but showed no sign of divulging the name, making Marielle wonder if it was in fact *Leda and the Swan.*

"Don't allow Gryphon inside," Mrs. MacManus warned Dermot as he held the door open to a small white cottage attached to the tower.

"Tipperary scores again!" the radio behind the counter announced.

"It's a scandal to play the match inside the museum!" Mrs. MacManus said loudly enough for people behind the gift shop counter to hear, along with three men who pretended to peruse gifts nearby.

Marielle smiled at Dermot. "It looks like you and Sean were right," she said proudly before walking toward the books. A few minutes later, Dermot called her to a table stacked with flags, tablecloths, runners, and banners where he read a story entitled "Letter to an Irish Mother." Marielle laughed at the first three paragraphs before Dermot's mother appeared to her right and Dermot retreated to her left.

"That's foul and outrageous!" Mrs. MacManus declared.

Marielle drew a restorative breath as she set down the banner.

"No. Keep reading it. It becomes more offensive further along."

Marielle nodded, but didn't look down at the banner again. She had reached her limit for negative comments within a 15 minute period, and as the child of an alcoholic, she assumed her tolerance was higher than most.

She walked to a table of books near the door as Dermot lingered by the counter with other men.

"A free out for Tipperary," she heard one man repeat as she picked up a collection of poems. She searched the index for *The Lost Child* as Dermot appeared beside her right shoulder, startling her.

"Sorry," he said, smiling.

She shook her head to dismiss his concern. "How goes the clash of the ash?" she asked, smiling as Dermot brightened.

"How did you know that?" he asked.

"Your father told me."

"So, you *were* speaking about hurling, then."

Her face adopted a dead serious expression. "I would never lie about hurling," she replied.

Dermot laughed before relating that Tipperary held a nine point lead.

"We'll be going into the movie now," Mrs. MacManus said from across the table.

Dermot rubbed the small of Marielle's back as they entered a dark room with several long, backless benches in front of a large, white screen.

"Would you like a photograph together?" Mrs. MacManus asked Marielle.

"Sure. Thank you," she responded happily, handing over the camera.

Dermot's mother stood in front of the screen, looking through the camera's view finder for a moment, a shocked expression overcoming her face. She moved the camera away from her eye to confirm what the camera displayed.

Marielle followed Mrs. MacManus' line of sight to Dermot who nearly glowed as he leaned happily into her.

Mrs. MacManus eventually summoned the strength to take the photograph, but turned away as she handed the camera back to Marielle and sat down.

Marielle looked up suddenly as the tiny speakers began delivering surprisingly crisp sound.

Dermot pointed at the speaker near the upper-left side of the screen. "Can you believe that sound is caused by an electromagnet attached to a cone which is attracted to and repelled by a fixed magnet?"

Marielle turned to whisper directly into his ear. "That is the sexiest thing any boy has ever said to me during a documentary."

"You're joking," he whispered back.

Marielle pulsed her eyelids open once as she shook her head, then gasped as a wet nose lifted her right hand.

"Gryphon!" Dermot declared. He leaned forward to exchange a grin with his mother, then ordered his dog to sit, petting Gryphon with his left hand while stroking Marielle's pinkie with his right.

A half-hour later they exited the theatre to urgent noise behind the gift shop counter. Two men turned to each other to say "McCarry" before Marielle asked Dermot what that meant.

"I believe Antrim finally scored a goal," he said, then approached the counter.

Marielle turned her amused grin toward Dermot's mother, determined to make her smile or keep the grin despite Mrs. MacManus' hardened opposition.

Mrs. MacManus finally smiled at her son as he ran back.

"It's over anyway," he said. "Antrim is down by 18 points. They're committing penalties now."

"How much time is left?" Marielle asked as a book across the shop caught Mrs. MacManus' attention.

"Two minutes," Dermot replied, staring into her eyes.

"But that's only six goals. From what I hear, you could score that in your sleep," she teased.

Dermot laughed through his nose. "True, but sadly for Antrim, I'm not on their team."

Marielle nodded. "I wonder if they know you're the difference between winning and losing the McCarthy Cup."

Dermot's mouth opened with surprise. "You amaze me every day!" he exclaimed.

Marielle smiled as her face turned pink. "Hopefully you can say the same when we're married."

"I believe I will," he muttered as if thinking aloud.

***

"Do you study Irish writers in school, Marielle?" Mrs. MacManus asked the gravel road on their way back to the car.

"No, ma'am, we mostly focus on American poets and authors such as Robert Frost, Mark Twain, Longfellow, Hemingway, Thoreau, uhh, Steinbeck," she looked toward the top of her brain to see if that was indeed the name of *The Grapes of Wrath* author.

"Not James Joyce, Oscar Wilde, or Jonathan Swift?" Mrs. MacManus asked with reproach.

"No, though I intend to read them on my own."

"But you wouldn't be *required* to read them?" she asked again.

"No, but other schools might."

Mrs. MacManus regarded Marielle with exasperation. "But how can your teachers provide you with an adequate education if they neglect those authors? Have you not *even* read Bram Stoker?"

"Mom!" Dermot interjected. "She said she doesn't study our authors."

Mrs. MacManus turned sharply towards her son before looking back at the stone bridge they had already crossed.

"Maybe we'll discuss them in college," Marielle mused, losing interest in her own sentence toward the end.

Dermot offered her a silent apology, then turned towards his mother, watching her as she watched Gryphon relieve himself on the side of the stone cottage. "Bloody!" Dermot exclaimed before calling his dog.

Gryphon ran towards the bridge at a near gallop, then diverted from the path to throw himself into the river.

"Oh, Gryphon!" Dermot protested while Marielle threw her head back to laugh. Mrs. MacManus turned to walk in the direction of the car, wearing an expression of one who is amused by nothing.

"Ah, you think it's funny until he shakes himself in front of you," Dermot warned. "Gryphon. Come here, boy!" he called, snapping his fingers in front of Marielle.

Her mouth opened in shock as she backed up quickly, ready to turn and run as Gryphon neared, but Dermot grabbed her arm to stop her. "Dermot!" she protested, not sure if she was annoyed or amused, but having no time to consider the matter further as Gryphon shook his body violently, unleashing several waves of river water onto her khakis and sweater. Marielle looked down at her clothes, then up at Dermot who couldn't stop laughing even after his mother turned around with annoyance.

"Your son is horrible," Marielle complained weakly.

"I'm quite certain you don't believe that," Mrs. MacManus replied, causing Dermot to raise his eyebrows victoriously, and Marielle to curse under her breath.

***

"Well done Tipperary," Dermot said, collapsing into the back seat. "The *craic* there should be mighty tonight!"

"Would you ever want to go to Croke Park for the Final?" Marielle asked, turning around in her seat.

"I played in Croke Park, actually."

Her eyes widened. "Really?"

"Really," Dermot said happily as his mother backed from the parking space.

"I wonder how difficult it is to get tickets to the Senior Final," Marielle mused.

"I'd say it's nearly impossible," Dermot replied.

"So, you wouldn't want to try?" she asked with surprise, holding onto the seat back as the car lurched forward.

He chuckled at her excitement. "I would, actually. Have you ever seen a major sporting event in person?"

"I have," she said, turning toward the windshield to ward off car sickness. "I went to a Packers' game last season. It was well below zero and, not surprisingly, a season ticket holder wanted to watch the game from home instead. We bought the tickets from him for only $20 each."

Dermot leaned forward. "Did you not freeze, like?"

"We did. We were wearing three layers of ski clothes, sitting on a sleeping bag, with a sleeping bag over our laps and we were still cold. In fact, Joy got us hot cocoa at halftime and I could distinctly feel the warmth going down my neck and into my stomach. It was the weirdest feeling ever."

Dermot's eyebrows furrowed. "I thought you barely tolerated Joy."

Marielle glanced over her shoulder. "Oh, I do, but she makes me feel like a brain surgeon so I keep her around."

"In what way?" he asked with anticipation.

"Well, she screws up basic analogies and historical events like it's her job. For example, she thinks a major event in American history was The

561

Last Custard Stand."

"Do you mean Custer's Last Stand?" Dermot asked.

Marielle nodded. "Yeah, but she thinks it was the last place anyone could buy custard in the late 1800s."

Dermot rested his chin on her seat. "How does she explain the angry natives?"

"Well, I guess they loved their desserts."

Dermot chuckled. "Right, well, who wouldn't kill for custard?"

"Exactly," Marielle replied, exchanging a smile with him before looking back at the road.

"I'll need other examples as well," he said tenderly, covertly stroking her neck again.

Marielle turned back. "Alright, but you can't go around sharing these stories like they represent the average American."

"I won't. I promise."

"Okay. She thinks a revered group of women in ancient Rome were called 'Vested Virgins.' I guess she assumes they wore vests over their flowing robes. Also, when someone completely changes their attitude, you say they've done a 180, right?"

Dermot nodded.

"Well, she says they did a 360. She thinks spinning around and facing the same direction is the most anyone could change."

"How irritating!" Dermot said with abundant breath.

"Yeah, and the worst part is you can't reason with her. For example, you can't show her a diagram of the human muscular system to prove there is no such thing as a 12 pack of abdominal muscles—"

"Rather than a six pack?" he asked.

"Right. My friend Joel actually held the book in front of her face and she refused to look at it."

Dermot shook his head. "Isn't she a bit too much work?"

"Often, but sometimes she's really funny like when she accused me of driving erotically instead of erratically, and there are a few crass American phrases she can't get right, but I should probably keep those to myself."

"Please do," Mrs. MacManus interjected with feeling.

Marielle and Dermot looked at his mother before turning toward their respective windows.

"Are we going to Mass now?" Dermot asked after several kilometres separated them from Yeats.

"We are. We should make it in time for Salthill."

***

Dermot's mother seemed distracted as she parallel parked in front of a bookmaking shop on a wide stretch of Lower Salthill Road. Without speaking, she walked along the footpath well ahead of Marielle and Dermot in the direction of the sea.

"This is my *least* favourite church," Dermot complained.

Marielle looked down at her watch. "Well, at least they have Mass late into the afternoon. Our church has nothing after 11:30 in the morning."

"Yes, well, that would make Mass easier to miss," he said optimistically.

"You'd be surprised. Will Gryphon be alright?" she asked, glancing back at the car.

"Sure. It's cool enough for him anyway. So, what are the crass American phrases Joy gets wrong?" he asked with an expectant grin.

"Hmm, well, when people are living together in a sexual relationship, we sometimes say they're *shacking up* together. Well, Joy says she's shacking up with someone even if she's just sleeping over at their house. One Monday, she returned to school declaring she had shacked up with her grandparents over the weekend."

"That's awkward," Dermot said as he moved to the street side of Marielle.

"For her *and* her grandparents."

"Any others?" Dermot asked eagerly.

"Absolutely. Last spring I spent far too much time telling her that the *nether regions* and the *Netherlands* were completely different places, and *slipping someone the banana* is completely different from *slipping ON a banana*—" Marielle turned as Dermot stopped walking to close his eyes and cover his face with his hands. "Oh, and she frequently leaves out the L in *public* whenever she writes it. I'm starting to wonder if she does that on purpose."

Dermot looked up a moment before guffawing.

"So, public school and transportation take on a whole new meaning," she added as Dermot began walking again.

"I imagine public toilets do as well," he said, wiping his eyes with the thumb and index finger of his left hand.

"Right, well you'd never want to sit on one of those."

563

"Eww!" Dermot exclaimed as Marielle laughed. "So, this is one of *your* friends?"

"Yes, well, I use that word *friend* in the loosest possible sense."

Dermot nodded. "Yes, I've heard all about how loose Joy is."

Marielle stopped walking to hold her stomach as laughter overcame her. "My stomach actually hurts from laughing!" she objected.

"Well, my cheeks are practically numb from smiling!" he argued.

Marielle breathed through puckered lips as she walked forward. Seconds later, she bumped into Dermot's arm which he reflexively raised to keep her out of the roadway a moment before a car raced past.

"My God, Dermot! I didn't see that," she admitted, biting her lip to prevent a nervous smile.

He turned towards her with reproach. "You promised you would look both ways before crossing the road!"

Marielle studied Dermot to determine if he was more worried than angry, receiving her answer when he looked down at her lip and relaxed his jaw.

"It must be hard for you," she thought out loud as they waited for the right to cross the road.

Dermot chuckled through the word "what."

"To *want* to be angry with me, but not be able to manage it."

"I AM angry with you," he said, still chuckling.

Marielle studied his face a little longer. "Has anyone ever told you how intimidating you are when you're angry?"

"Yes," he said with a smile.

"That's surprising," she said before looking across the street at the large, cream-coloured, stuccoed church set back from the street at least a third of a block. "I saw this the other day. It doesn't look so bad," she said, assessing three distinct sections—the center having a peaked roof while the flanking roofs were flat.

"It's dreadful," Dermot replied, holding Marielle's elbow until the green man told them it was safe to cross.

Bells tolled from the square tower above the flat roof on the left side of the church as they walked to the open double doors where Dermot's mother waited.

Marielle followed Dermot down the main aisle to the front. Ignoring his example, she genuflected outside the pew, nearly causing a collision with his mother who clearly expected to walk into the pew without one.

While kneeling alone to say her pre-Mass prayers, Marielle heard whispering between Dermot and his mother, who had no intention of kneeling or praying before the Mass required them to do so.

Mass began precisely on time and hosted fewer stragglers than Marielle expected—possibly owing to the minimal time necessary to complete it. She was caught off guard by the Olympic pace of the Our Father, falling miserably behind until she accessed the auctioneering area of her brain. Despite the speed at the Communion rail, no hosts were lost to the effort, and as Mr. Maguire promised, Mass ended 25 minutes after it began.

"I think more people in the U.S. would attend Mass if it was this quick," Marielle remarked as they walked outside.

"Sure, there's no point in risking the guilt of *not* attending," Dermot agreed as several college-aged girls accosted his mother several yards in front of them.

"Oh, Jaysus!" Dermot exclaimed, grabbing Marielle's arm to lead her to the left. He turned his back to the crowd, rolling his eyes at one girl who couldn't stop remarking on how brilliant she found a UCG professor. "They're Fiona's friends," he explained. "Actually, to be clear, they're not friendly a'tall."

"So, how is Fee gettin' on?" a tall redhead asked Mrs. MacManus.

"She's grand," Mrs. MacManus replied.

"Is she really?" the student asked with disbelief. "It seems Ryan misses her anyway and I do feel badly that she won't graduate with us on time."

"The cheeky bitch!" Dermot said, turning towards the girl as though he meant to either start or finish a fight.

Marielle touched Dermot's arm in an effort to calm him. "What's going on with Fiona?" she asked gently.

He closed his eyes briefly as he shook his head. "She had a difficult time at UCG last year. There was a terrible row between her and my mother when her scores arrived in the spring. Mum was at a total loss for what to do. In the end, Fee told Mum to fuck off, and found a job in France."

Marielle waited a moment for the shock of someone cursing at Mrs. MacManus to wear off. "Do you like Ryan?" she asked.

Dermot nodded. "I do. We all do."

"Even your mother?" Marielle asked with surprise.

Dermot smiled. "Yeah. He's the type of bloke to sit down and have tea with the family."

"I have tea with your family," Marielle argued.

"You do, but you're a bit more controversial," he said, taking a step closer to her while wearing a rebellious grin.

Marielle's smile turned into a sigh. "If that girl declares one more thing brilliant, I might be forced to yell 'Oh, my God!' repeatedly the way Joy does."

"She's clearly a pseudo-intellectual," Dermot remarked. "Now, what PS type would you class her as?"

Marielle beamed. "I continue to be amazed at your memory for random thoughts in my letters."

Dermot locked eyes with her. "Yes, well, your letters have been read and reread on multiple occasions. They keep me company when I'm lonely for you."

"It's a good thing I've written so many of them, then."

"And that they're so immensely long," he added.

She glanced away to break his spell over her. "Do you prefer writing or calling?"

Dermot inhaled slowly through his nose as his eyes narrowed. "It's hard to decide. I prefer you in person, actually."

"That wasn't one of the choices," she said like a disappointed high school teacher.

"Then, I prefer your letters—only because I can go back to them to remind myself what you've said. Also, I can hear your voice speaking to me as I read them now." He looked down at her in earnest. "Do you know how much it aches to wait for a letter from you?"

"No, but I know how much it aches to wait for a letter from you. It feels the way the song *With or Without You* sounds."

Dermot nodded as his eyes became glassy. "I'm sorry again about the wine incident."

"Oh! I'm sorry about being stand-offish with you earlier when you apologized. Your mom was listening near the doorway and I wanted to cut you off before you said something wonderful."

"Oh, thank God!" he said, his chest relaxing noticeably.

Marielle looked up at Dermot with wonder in her eyes. "I don't think my opinion has ever mattered to anyone the way it matters to you."

"And no one's opinion matters more than yours," he replied, forcing

Marielle's eyes closed before they opened with tears present.

"Oh, love," he said empathetically, dropping the hand that nearly touched her face.

Marielle swallowed hard before she spoke. "You shouldn't worry what I think because I respect and love no one above you. If you get the impression I think otherwise, you need to say something because I promise you it's just a misunderstanding."

Dermot nodded, then bit the inside edge of his bottom lip.

"That's one of the sexiest things you do," she murmured.

"One moment," Dermot said, looking away with a mischievous grin, then back again as he nonchalantly bit his lip.

***

"Well, we'd better be off," Mrs. MacManus said after they had expended an equal amount of time outside of church as within.

The redhead looked at Marielle and Dermot for the first time as the teenagers took their cue to follow Mrs. MacManus.

"Did I really park that badly?" Mrs. MacManus asked, her car sticking out at an angle and at least a foot farther from the kerb than any other car on the street.

Marielle smiled sympathetically. It was clear that Mrs. MacManus had more on her mind than parking her car in Salthill.

Chapter Thirty-Four

The Unappeasable Host
—W.B. Yeats – *The Unappeasable Host*

"How did you find Mr. Yeats?" Mr. MacManus asked Marielle, sinking his fork into a piece of apple tart.

"Very well. They're keeping his house up nicely which was a concern of his."

"Was it now?" he asked with amusement.

She nodded sharply. "He wrote a poem or a letter about it in his old age," Marielle said, cutting into her own tart. "Oh! And I realized while we were there that he must have died 50 years ago now since his body was stuck in France for the war. Was there much about the anniversary of his death on the news?"

Mr. MacManus nodded slowly. "I might remember a mention of it this past winter, actually. There are non-stop programs on the war tonight, as you can well imagine."

"We should watch some," Dermot suggested, smiling at Marielle.

"You'll be swimming tonight with Gráinne," Mrs. MacManus interjected.

Dermot turned to his mother with irritation.

"I don't know why you are taking issue with this, Dermot! You enjoy spending time with her well enough when Marielle isn't here."

Marielle grinned from her tart to Dermot, turning his shocked expression into an amused one.

Mr. MacManus cleared his throat. "Well, there should be plenty of programming when you return."

"Will you have more tart, Dermot?" his mother asked with a more solicitous tone.

"No, Mum, I'm full," he said, pushing away his empty plate.

"I cannot get accustomed to his appetite now. When he was hurling, he nearly ate us out of house and home," Mrs. MacManus said to Marielle before looking back at Dermot. "Wait, are you certain you're full?"

Dermot chuckled. "I am, Mum."

Mrs. MacManus turned to Marielle again. "In Ireland, you never say yes the first time someone offers. When we were in France, the neighbour asked Dermot if he fancied a piece of cake and he said "no." She pulled it away and you should have seen the look on his face!" She smiled as she regarded her son lovingly.

Dermot returned his mother's affection as if they hadn't fought at all that day.

Marielle smiled at Mr. MacManus for a moment. Though she appreciated the affection Dermot and his mother shared, it would make the next wave of conflict all the more jarring.

***

Marielle and Mrs. MacManus still sat at the table when Gráinne arrived with a curly blonde-haired girl several inches taller than herself.

"Did you miss me, Dermot?" Gráinne asked him in the foyer.

"I wasn't aiming for you," Dermot replied coolly.

Marielle suppressed mirth as Mrs. MacManus narrowed her eyes.

"Hello, girls," she said in startlingly pleasant tones.

"Hello, Dr. MacManus," Gráinne replied as she and the blonde girl passed behind Marielle's chair. "Do you remember my friend Dawn?"

"I do indeed. How lovely to see you again," Mrs. MacManus replied, holding her hand out to shake Dawn's.

Dermot called for Marielle from the doorway, moving his head towards the foyer when she turned around.

"Are you certain you're able for this?" he asked, holding both of her hands at the foot of the stairs.

"Well, you've promised not to let me drown, and I trust you," she said, smiling as she looked up at him.

Dermot drew a deep breath. "Alright, my mother put her swimsuit on your bed."

"Why?" Marielle asked, trying to mask horror at the thought.

"Because you hadn't brought your own."

"Did you tell her that?"

"No, I thought you had."

"No," Marielle said, grinning as she shook her head. "I guess we have definitive proof now that she overheard our conversation earlier. Anyway, I lied when I said I didn't know if I brought my swimsuit. I was just trying to get out of going."

Dermot chuckled. "Right, well, you can decide which one to wear, then."

Marielle assumed this was a joke, smiling as she took her leave and ran up the dark stairs.

Dermot opened the door to the dining room.

"You should have seen the look on Dermot's face yesterday when—" Gráinne's voice carried upstairs as Marielle felt for the light switch in her room.

Marielle changed into her black one-piece bathing suit, in lieu of the larger black, pink, and purple flower-printed suit with gathered sides.

"Did you find the bathing suit I left for you?" Mrs. MacManus asked as Marielle emerged from her bedroom.

"I did, but I brought my own after all. Thank you for the offer though."

"Well, mine should be warmer in the sea. You should wear it instead."

"I appreciate that, but I already have mine on and I'm used to the cold."

Mrs. MacManus' eyes narrowed.

"Let me get your suit for you," Marielle added quickly, turning toward the bedroom.

***

"Do you have a windcheater, Marielle?" Dermot asked in the foyer as everyone regarded her green cardigan sweater.

"I don't. Why? Is it cold out?" she asked.

"It's lashing rain at present," Gráinne said with judgement as she and Dawn turned towards the door.

"You can take my coat," Mrs. MacManus offered, handing Marielle a dark blue windbreaker almost identical to Dermot's.

"Dermot, are you coming?" Gráinne urged from the open door.

Marielle thanked Mrs. MacManus as she accepted the jacket.

"Dermot," Gráinne repeated.

"I'm waiting on Marielle," he replied impatiently before looking at his mother with defiance.

Marielle's shaking hand fumbled with the zipper for several seconds before it caught. She looked up to see the concern on Dermot's face, then looked out the window, spying the girls standing halfway down the driveway.

"Where's Ashley?" Gráinne asked as they walked along the footpath together.

"How would I know that?" Dermot replied aggressively before covertly grabbing Marielle's hand.

Gráinne turned a confused face towards him. "I thought you were dating."

He avoided eye contact as he said, "Not anymore."

Gryphon ran past the teenagers, then stopped to sniff something along the kerb, causing them to pass him in turn.

"What did you do yesterday after our lesson?" Dawn asked Dermot with abundant curiosity.

"We fished and went to cinema," he replied.

"Did you see *Batman*?" she asked with enthusiasm.

"No, *The Three Fugitives*."

"Ah, Dawn and I saw *Batman* last weekend and I have to say it was a typical Hollywood film."

Dermot turned narrow eyes at Gráinne. "Aren't most films typically from Hollywood?" he asked.

"Yes, but it's not terribly imaginative and Kim Basinger is a bit *common* if you ask me."

"What makes her so common?" Dermot asked.

"I heard she gave Jack Nicholson oral sex based solely on a bet. Is that sort of thing typical in America, Marielle?" Gráinne asked, leaning forward to address her for the first time.

"I heard most American girls will do that," Dawn remarked to Gráinne before Marielle could reply.

"What are you saying?" Dermot asked aggressively.

"They're saying all American girls are sluts," Marielle clarified.

"Is it *true*?" Gráinne asked eagerly.

Marielle nodded. "It is. I've held hands with dozens of boys, including Dermot. I don't even want to discuss all the boys I've kissed on the lips. It's got to be, hmm, nearly seven. Well, if you don't call that a slut, I don't know what you call it."

Dermot squeezed Marielle's hand as he smiled proudly at her.

"Did you see *The Wizard of Oz* was on tonight?" Dawn asked. "My brother couldn't take his eyes off the telly as I was leaving."

"Oh, I love that movie!" Marielle proclaimed. "I watch it every time it's on TV."

Gráinne and Dawn exchanged a glance before they giggled.

"Do you not like it?" Marielle asked.

"Sure," Gráinne said with disdain. "Maybe when we were still in our nappies."

Dermot laughed with the girls, causing Marielle to pull her hand away from him.

"Are you wearing Nikes, Marielle?" Gráinne asked, pronouncing the brand with a hard vowel sound. "Those look a bit different than the ones we've seen."

"I am. They're new, and you're pronouncing it wrong. They're Nike-eez, not the I form of nukes."

"Sure, they're not," Gráinne countered.

"And which of us is more likely to know?" Marielle asked impatiently. "They're an American company and I'm American."

"Are you in school now?" Dermot immediately asked Gráinne.

"We are. We started Monday."

"You should see their ugly green uniforms, Marielle," Dermot said as he seized her hand again.

"I like green," Marielle replied.

"But their uniforms are the worst possible shade. It's like the green of the school on Fr. Griffin Road."

"That's very unkind, Dermot," Gráinne said as if genuinely wounded.

Dermot shrugged his shoulders.

The wind gusted as Lower Salthill Road joined the Seapoint Promenade, causing Marielle's hood to fly backward. Dermot squeezed her hand harder as she began to shiver.

Gráinne yelled as Gryphon ran between her legs.

"What does he have in his mouth?" Dermot asked as the rain began to sting.

"I don't know," Gráinne replied, grabbing Dermot's left arm to better engage him. "Do you remember when Gryphon ran up and down the Prom with a dead rat in his mouth?" She laughed. "We screamed and ran away, but he thought it a game and chased us."

Dermot nodded, then cursed as rain turned to sleet.

Gráinne released Dermot to open a golf umbrella. She placed it directly in front of Dawn, Dermot, and herself as the sleet moved sideways. "I'm sorry, it's only big enough to cover us three," she said to Marielle.

Marielle feigned a smile in reply while silently debating which was worse: spending time with these girls; the sideways sleet; or the fact that the journey would end with jumping into the sea. It was a "horse a piece," Grandma Richter would say. Or maybe it was a "horse of peace." Either way, Marielle didn't know what it meant.

"Why don't you and I change places?" Dermot suggested as he grabbed Marielle's arm to move her toward Gráinne.

Marielle pulled her arm away. "I'm fine. Really. Don't forget, I'm from Wisconsin."

"Where's Wisconsin?" Gráinne asked.

"It's between Chicago and Canada," Marielle replied.

"Ah," Gráinne said. "So, it gets cold there? Like on the Kelvin scale?" she mocked.

Marielle nodded as her eyes narrowed. "Yes, we maintain a temperature very near Absolute Zero," she replied with ample sarcasm.

"Oh, I know this from the Inter," Dawn replied excitedly. "That's—"

"Negative 273 degrees Celsius," Marielle interjected.

Dermot turned to her, wearing a huge grin.

"Negative 273.15," Gráinne clarified.

Marielle rolled her eyes.

"So, you know a fair bit about science I see," Dermot said to Marielle.

"Yes, and I know a bit of Irish as well," she replied loud enough for the girls to hear.

"What do you know?" Gráinne asked.

"NO!" Dermot replied as a mischievous grin overtook Marielle's face.

"I'm not allowed to say it," she said, reluctantly passing on the opportunity to say "kiss my ass" in Irish. "Where are we going exactly?" she asked instead.

"It's the pier where we took our class yesterday," Dermot replied.

"Does the pier have a name?" Marielle asked, noticeably less irritated than a moment ago.

"Yes. Blackrock."

Marielle exhaled disappointment.

"What's wrong?" Dermot asked.

"Well, I always thought it would be funny to name a pier *Shakes*."

"Shakes Pier?" Dermot asked, then chuckled.

"Yeah, I think it's an opportunity lost. Just like Pope Sixtus the Sixth," she added as though her meaning was clear.

"Pardon?" Dermot asked as Gráinne began her own conversation with

Dawn.

"In the 1500s, Pope Sixtus the Fifth died. So, the title *Pope Sixtus the Sixth* has been dangling out there for 400 years with no takers. If I were named Pope, I'd grab it before anyone else could. It's the same with Shakes Pier. How long has Shakespeare been dead and I've heard of no piers named Shakes?"

"You're right," Dermot replied with an air of seriousness. "It does seem an opportunity lost."

"So, it seems a bit cold tonight," Marielle remarked as her teeth began chattering. "Will we still be swimming?"

Dermot nodded. "Well, we've swum in worse. The water is cold no matter the air temperature, so that's comforting in a way."

Marielle drew a deep breath, finding nothing about swimming in a cold, dark sea comforting.

***

"Should I wear my t-shirt?" Marielle asked as they disrobed under an L-shaped structure of covered benches.

"No," Gráinne replied. "It seems counter-intuitive, but you want to wear the least amount of clothing possible when you go into the water."

Marielle thought herself crazy as she removed her jacket and sweater. No matter how cold it was in Wisconsin, no one outside the Polar Bear Club would jump into water while it was sleeting. She dropped her jeans, then immediately tied her towel before turning toward the multi-level pier.

"You'll want to leave your towel by your trousers or it's likely to blow away," Dermot said with mischievous eyes.

Marielle turned a disbelieving face toward him.

"He's right," Gráinne agreed as they reached the pier.

Marielle cursed to herself, then returned to the bench with Dermot in pursuit, waiting eagerly for Marielle to shed her towel.

"Stop!" she said playfully.

"I've seen you completely naked," he whispered. "I don't know why you're attempting to hide from me now."

"Yes, well, you didn't see me from behind," she explained, beginning to blush.

"I'm quite certain you're lovely from all angles," he assured her a moment before Gráinne jumped into the water.

"You *are* dangerous," Marielle noted, shaking her head as Dermot raised his eyebrows.

"Are you afraid of the cold, Dermot?" Gráinne yelled as Dermot and Marielle approached the pier.

Without reply, Dermot ran past Marielle to dive into the water, quickly surfacing near Gráinne.

"Is it cold?" Dawn asked, wearing the same frightened expression Marielle buried.

"I'tis," Dermot replied calmly.

"How deep is it?" Marielle asked, looking down at the black water.

"Oh, about three meters," Gráinne answered.

"Ah," Marielle said, looking up to the top of her brain for the translation.

"Nine feet," Dermot clarified.

"Jump in!" Gráinne demanded. "Don't worry. Both Dermot and I are lifeguards."

"Jump at the same time as Dawn," Dermot suggested.

Dawn held out her hand which Marielle took before they counted down from three, and jumped together.

"My God! The salt!" Marielle exclaimed as she surfaced.

Dermot laughed. "You're not complaining about the cold?"

"No, well, I haven't gotten to that part yet. The salt is overwhelming!"

His chin rose slightly as he said, "Ah-right. You've never swum in the ocean before, have you?"

"I've never actually *seen* the ocean before flying here," she admitted.

"Let's swim out, you'll feel better," Gráinne recommended, turning to swim away without waiting for an objection.

Marielle's eyes opened wider at Dermot. He chuckled, then tilted his head as a directive before swimming towards Gráinne.

Marielle took a deep breath as her body began shaking uncontrollably and her muscles tightened and cramped. For a moment, she thought she wouldn't survive treading water, much less swimming the several yards the others had already covered.

"Marielle!" Dermot called, his head only a dark outline above the water before her.

She drew another deep breath before kicking her legs and moving her arms in a loose form of swimming.

"Are you alright?" Gráinne asked as a cursory question when Marielle reached them.

"I'm well, thank you," she replied in a calmer person's voice.

The Irish teenagers joked and exchanged stories as they treaded water in a circle, but Marielle had difficulty paying attention. Something had brushed her leg and she needed all her brain power to maintain composure. It was probably someone else's foot or leg, she reasoned, but she had no way of knowing what lurked beneath.

"Are there sharks here?" she asked Dermot when conversation lapsed.

"Some," Dermot replied, "but they're generally harmless."

"What about Porbeagles?" Gráinne argued.

"Well, besides that one," Dermot replied, opening his eyes wider for a moment.

"What's that?" Dawn asked nervously as if something touched her underwater.

"It's only me, you ninny!" Gráinne said a second before she lunged at Dawn, pushing her head beneath the water.

Marielle backed away as Dawn surfaced, flailing her hands and gasping for air.

Dermot looked across the chaos to Marielle's wide eyes as Gráinne turned towards her. He lunged at Gráinne, arresting her arm above Marielle's head. "Don't. Touch. Her!" he yelled.

"Oh, please!" she protested, pulling her arm free to swim towards Dawn.

"Are you alright?" Dermot asked Marielle when her eyes failed to return to their normal size.

"I am. I'm sorry," she said mechanically, her teeth chattering as Dawn and Gráinne swam to shore.

"There's no reason a'tall for you to be sorry," he comforted, turning towards the pier when he heard Sean's voice.

"We'd better hurry back," Marielle said with a mischievous grin. "She's got a serious crush on you."

"I know. It's dreadful," he replied, waiting for Marielle to begin swimming before he did.

"Your mom will be disappointed when you two kids don't end up together," she reflected.

"Did she tell you that?" Dermot asked, swimming farther in one stroke than she did in two.

Marielle shook her head with a shiver. "No. Did she tell you?"

He grinned. "She might have mentioned it once or twice."

"Well, your kids would be good swimmers."

"Could you not cope with the cold, Ladies?" Sean asked Dawn and Gráinne as they made a hasty retreat to the benches. They yelled something back to him, but he was already smiling at Dermot and Marielle as they neared the pier's stairs. "Well, there you are—the elusive Marielle," Sean said happily. "Have you not cast aside our young Dermot yet?"

"Not yet," she replied. "Sadly, he hasn't given me cause."

"Well, it should be a blow to the other lads, now, I have to say."

"Hello, you feckin' eejit!" Dermot said as he reached the top of the ladder.

"What the fuck is wrong with those two?" Sean asked, nodding in the direction of Gráinne and Dawn.

"I'll tell you later," Dermot promised.

"So, what do you think of our bay there, Marielle?" Sean asked as they neared the benches.

"I think it's rather crisp and salty," she replied.

"It sounds nearly edible," Sean remarked to Dermot with amusement. "Have you never swum in the ocean, Marielle?"

"No, she's only swum in fresh water," Dermot explained as Marielle picked up speed to reach her towel.

"Ah-right," Sean reflected.

"I'm sorry about the misunderstanding about the club last night," Marielle said to Sean, wrapping herself in her towel.

"Not a bother," he replied amiably.

"So, how did you find us?" Dermot asked, eagerly grabbing his own towel from the bench.

"Your parents. By the way, they looked rather serious when I stopped by earlier."

"Both of them?" Dermot asked concernedly.

Marielle turned when she didn't hear Sean's response, but it had been non-verbal and it clearly weighed on Dermot.

Marielle stepped into her jeans.

"Would you not take off your swimsuit first?" Sean asked.

"How can I do that?" she asked, then appeared shocked when she noticed Gráinne and Dawn disrobing beneath their towels. "Well, it's too late anyway," she said. "My pants are already wet."

Dermot's head shot up while the girls exchanged a look of horror.

"What?" Marielle asked, well-acquainted with the look people gave

577

when she said the wrong thing.

"Oh!" Dermot said, addressing the others. "She means trousers."

"What else would I mean?" Marielle asked.

"Well, here *pants* are knickers," Sean explained.

"Like 1920s bloomers?"

Sean laughed. "No. Undergarments."

Marielle's eyes widened, not only because she had inadvertently referenced her underwear in public, but because she remembered telling Dermot that Americans didn't wear knickers. "This place is a verbal mine field," she muttered.

"You'll be soaked, Marielle," Dermot said with his soft voice.

"I'm sure I'll be fine," she replied, although her jeans and sweater were already cold and wet.

"Sure, it's madness to swim in this weather," Sean remarked as he and Marielle waited for the others to dress.

Marielle whispered into Sean's ear. "I'm glad you said that. I was beginning to fear the Irish were stronger than Americans."

"Well, that goes without saying," he replied seconds before teenagers shot a flare from the end of the pier, causing Marielle to jump.

"Are you alright there?" Sean asked, placing his arm around her, but removing it when Dermot shot him a warning glare.

"Sorry," Marielle said, shivering. "I'm grand, as you say."

"You should visit my farm this week," Gráinne suggested, looking back at Dermot as they began walking in the direction of home.

"You don't have a farm," Dermot replied dismissively.

Gráinne drew a sudden breath. "We do indeed!"

"What do you raise on this farm of yours?" Sean asked sceptically.

"It's a sheep farm. We have several lambs at the moment."

"That sounds lovely," Marielle said happily.

"She's having you on," Dermot interjected. "She doesn't live on a farm a'tall."

"Yes, I do, Dermot!" Gráinne replied angrily, grabbing Dawn's arm as she turned away.

"So, Marielle, would you say you like America or Ireland better?" Sean asked, walking his bike beside her.

Marielle looked up from the sidewalk, unsure if she should answer with European reserve, or American exuberance, deciding on the former with Gráinne and Dawn still within earshot. "Well, it's hard to say," she replied as Dermot studied her. "I've only been here three days and I've lived in America my whole life."

Sean's face registered disappointment before he addressed Dermot. "Will you be going out tonight?"

"Not a notion," he said, grabbing Marielle's hand. "We mean to leave for Dublin early in the morning."

"Will you not go to the Aran Islands, then?" Sean asked.

"Later in the week when the rain eases."

Marielle looked up with surprise. "When did it stop sleeting?" she asked.

Dermot chuckled. "Shortly after you jumped into the sea. I'd say you were preoccupied by sheer terror."

She glanced at his smiling face. "I meant to hide that."

"Sure, you can see what you're thinkin' better than any girl I've ever met!" Sean declared.

Marielle turned to study him. "Really? I was hoping I was mysterious like Jackie Onassis."

"Not a'tall," Sean replied. "Wouldn't you say, Dermot?"

Dermot shook his head. "You should've seen her face when my mum declared herself a communist."

Marielle cringed as Sean laughed. "I've never heard *anyone* say that in my entire life," she explained. "It's considered such a huge insult back home to call someone a communist. To hear someone admit it proudly completely blew my mind. Is your mom a communist too?"

"Not a'tall," Sean replied. "She can't be bothered with politics. Sure, one politician is as corrupt as the next."

Marielle smiled as her culture shock eased. "Did Dermot tell you he told Ashley to piss off on the phone this morning?"

Sean made eye contact with Dermot before smiling and shaking his head.

"It was rather rude," Marielle continued. "I took issue on her behalf."

"This one has loads of cheek!" Dermot retaliated. "Her boyfriend rang whilst we were fishing yesterday and she had nothing but malice for him when my father related the conversation."

"True, but Gary deserved it!"

"And Ashley didn't?"

"I have no idea. I only heard you say she should *go out with Alan, then* seconds before you dropped the *piss off* bomb."

Sean chuckled. "Did she say she's going out with Alan?"

"She said she's *been* going out with Alan."

Marielle's mouth opened as she looked at Dermot in shock.

"The cheeky bitch!" Sean declared.

"I agree with Sean," Marielle said. "There's no excuse for cheating."

"Oh, really, missus? And what would you call what you and your man were up to on your walk yesterday?" Sean asked.

Marielle began to blush. "That's different. We're part of an exploratory committee in furtherance of Irish/American relations."

"As far as I'm aware, those committees aren't meant to explore one another," Sean retorted.

"Maybe, but there would be fewer wars if they did," she replied, causing both boys to laugh, and the girls to turn around.

***

"Will you come in for tea, then?" Dermot asked Sean after Gráinne and Dawn walked through the front door of his house.

Sean looked from Dermot's questioning face to Marielle's nodding head and expanding eyes. "Sure, but I won't be held responsible for speaking my mind."

"To whom?" Marielle asked happily.

"Gráinne," Dermot clarified.

"Ah, the next Mrs. MacManus," Marielle remarked, exchanging a smile with Sean.

"Would you jump on her, then, Dermot?" Sean asked as he winked at Marielle.

"Not to get over a wall!" Dermot replied, causing Marielle to stop walking until laughter passed.

As they entered the foyer, Dermot looked at the closed sitting room door and the TV light beneath it. He turned to Sean. "Marielle and I will check on my father, and then meet you in the dining room. Can you behave until then?"

"That's anyone's guess, mate," Sean replied before turning towards the dining room.

Dermot knocked softly on the sitting room door, but made no movement to open it. Moments later, Mr. MacManus opened the door only a few inches, blocking any view of the room with his body. "How was swimming?" he asked.

"Grand," Dermot replied. "Everyone returned for tea. Would you like a cup?"

"No, thank you. I'm watching my program here," Mr. MacManus said as though he had no plans to leave the room or allow anyone to enter.

"Ah-right," Dermot said tentatively.

"We'll see you shortly," Mr. MacManus continued before closing the door, causing Dermot to look at Marielle with concern and Marielle to wonder who "we" was.

***

"So, Katie blanked me in the square yesterday," Dawn declared when everyone sat at the table with their tea.

"Did you not lend her ten quid last week?" Gráinne asked, her voice dripping with scandal.

Dawn nodded. "She's positively irritating! I believe she's ignoring me in hopes I'll forget, like."

"I never lend money unless I'm prepared to never see it again," Sean said matter-of-factly. "It removes all stress from the process."

Gráinne rolled her eyes before she addressed Dawn. "You should call her out on it."

"How long has she been blanking you?" Dermot asked.

"Three days, excluding the weekend," replied Dawn.

Dermot cleared his throat. "Tell me this: on an average day, how much would you pay Katie to ignore you?"

"Five quid," Dawn answered with conviction.

"Then the beauty of it is that after two days you broke even, and now you're well ahead. Consider it an investment on a Katie-free life. It's probably the best ten quid you'll ever spend."

"Dermot's right," Sean remarked. "Anyway, I have larger problems than that."

"Do tell," Marielle said before remembering his mother's illness.

Sean smiled. "Nearly every teacher I have this year either hates me outright or barely tolerates me."

"For reasons other than the obvious?" Gráinne asked.

Sean pretended to laugh. "I have the same teacher this year for religion, and as you may recall, he can't abide my frequent toilet breaks. Last year, he declared them a disruption to his class and wouldn't allow me to go a'tall."

"Why don't you go between classes?" Marielle asked.

"That's what *he* said and I told him it takes far too long to use the toilet

581

in the manner I generally require either before or after his class."

"Is there something about his class that makes you want to use the toilet?" Dermot asked with amusement.

"I haven't a clue. Maybe it's discussing religion, now that I think on it. I haven't attended Mass in nearly four years, and I must admit they've been immensely satisfying years."

"You should go to Salthill," Marielle suggested. "Sure, the priest can't be bothered with a long Homily."

Gráinne's eyes expanded. "That's what my father says!"

"What a coincidence," Marielle replied before drinking her tea.

Sean inhaled deeply. "Ever since my Granddad died, me mam has been seeing a fortune teller who says she gets messages from the Virgin Mary."

"They must be pretty boring messages," Dermot remarked.

"*Ja,* like 'eat your broccoli,' " Marielle said in ghostly tones.

"And 'isn't that skirt too short?' " Dermot added in the same ghostly voice.

"She doesn't sound like Count Chocula!" Sean protested.

"How do you know?" Marielle asked.

"Because even an angel wouldn't procreate with someone who sounded like that."

"I agree," Dermot said. "He would've gone to the cousin in the next room and pretended he didn't understand God's directive."

"That makes sense 'cause wasn't Elizabeth pregnant first?" Marielle asked. "That must've been the first time God sent an angel and—"

"Don't say the mission was aborted," Sean teased, causing Marielle and Dermot to laugh.

"An angel can't lie to God! He's all-knowing," Gráinne said haughtily.

Dermot shook his head. "If that were true, he'd've known it was a bad idea to ask a self-respecting angel to impregnate a woman with a speech impediment."

"Right, isn't that what drunk men are for?" Sean asked, causing Marielle to close her eyes and surrender to laughter.

"Enough!" Gráinne yelled.

Marielle's face changed from pleasant to angry in under three seconds. She considered responding to Gráinne, but turned to Sean instead, allowing her anger to dissipate. "You should consider wearing adult diapers like the residents in our nursing home do."

"And go to the toilet right there in class?" Sean asked.

"*Ja,*" Marielle replied.

"That's disgusting!" declared Dawn.

"Won't that smell?" Sean asked with interest.

Marielle nodded. "A little, but that's your teacher's problem."

Sean's eyes lit up. "It would be satisfying to look at his big, bloated, red face and take a piss now, I have to say. It would be better if he knew I was doing it though."

"I imagine the change in your begging routine and the smile on your face would be enough to give it away," Marielle noted. "I hate to state the obvious, but number two would be especially disrespectful."

"I don't mean to alienate the entire class, now," Sean said, looking at the front window as he considered the idea.

"Can you imagine bearing down in the middle of his lecture?" Dermot asked, surprising everyone at the table.

"That would be tremendous, actually. What do they call these nappies of yours?" Sean asked Marielle.

"Depends," she replied.

"On what?" Sean asked.

"No, that's the name of it."

"Oh, okay. I'll go to the grocery tomorrow to look for them."

"Are you not embarrassed to buy *anything*?" asked Gráinne.

"Not a'tall. Do you need more haemorrhoid cream?" Sean inquired.

Gráinne looked to Dermot for relief, but found his eyes closed as he shook his head.

"How have you alienated your other teachers?" Marielle asked, prepared to take another sip of her tea.

"My Maths teacher is cross because I told her it looked as though she's been working hard."

"Did she have loads of paper in her hands?" Dawn asked.

Sean shook his head. "No, her hair was messed about, and she had dark circles under her eyes."

Dermot set down his tea as he chuckled. "You know, teachers like it when you say, 'It looks as though you've had loads of kids,' as well."

"Or, 'Did you have a birthday recently, because you're looking older?'" Marielle added.

"What do I know? I don't even have a girlfriend, like," Sean argued.

"And that's not likely to change unless you stop talking like that,"

Dermot warned.

Gráinne leaned towards Dermot suddenly. "Did you hear what happened to Helen's boyfriend?"

Sean exchanged a sideways glance with Marielle, then both drank their tea to conceal grins.

"The one from Oranmore?" Dermot asked as he held his own teacup near his lips.

"Yeah. He died hours after summer exams."

Dermot pulled his cup from his lips. "How?" he asked.

Gráinne smiled in response to Dermot's attention. "A disconnected aorta, I believe. He walked into his house and dropped dead inside the threshold. He didn't even make it to hospital, like."

"Oh geez," said Marielle, furrowing her eyebrows before glancing at Sean as a grin formed. "Did he pass his tests?" she asked Gráinne.

Sean's laughter drowned out the gasps of the girls, but it was Dermot's shocked expression that held Marielle's attention.

"Sorry," she said, smiling at her tea before looking back at Sean as both chuckled.

"It was a terrible funeral," Gráinne continued. "Helen was a complete wreck."

Marielle bit her lip, turning away from Sean when it was clear he intended to make her laugh again.

"I imagine the family was wrecked as well," Dermot said with sympathy.

Gráinne nodded.

"My sister's boyfriend nearly died last year," Dawn announced. "He had a heart palpitation and he was meant to take medicine for it, but he stopped suddenly—"

"Why'd he stop?" Dermot asked.

"I don't know. I believe he felt better and thought the pills unnecessary. Anyway, he collapsed and nearly died," Dawn continued.

"He didn't die though," Sean said dismissively as he leaned back in his chair.

Dawn's face registered offense. "No, but he needed surgery an' all."

Marielle glanced at Sean again. "Did that particular surgery fix stupid?" she asked before Sean's guffaw pulled her with him.

"Really!" Dawn protested while sharing a shocked expression with Gráinne.

"What time is it?" Gráinne asked.

"Five minutes past time to leave, I imagine," Sean replied, wiping tears from his eyes.

Dermot gave Sean and Marielle a disapproving look as he stood to walk the girls outside.

"Ooh, I think we're in trouble," Marielle said.

"He'll forgive you soon enough, I'm thinkin'," Sean replied with a self-satisfied grin.

Marielle nodded. "True. I'll just flash him later and he'll forget all about how rude I was. Too bad you can't do the same."

"He never stays cross for long. Sure, by tomorrow he won't remember why he's irritated a'tall."

"Would you like more tea?" Marielle asked as Sean placed his empty cup on the table.

"Would you mind terribly? I should ring me ma so she doesn't worry on me."

"Of course," Marielle replied, walking to the kitchen as Sean moved to the foyer.

The outside door to the kitchen opened as Marielle poured water from the electric tea kettle into Sean's cup.

"Well, they're off," Dermot said as Marielle smiled over her shoulder.

"Are you angry with us?" she asked, staring at Sean's tea.

"I've been *more* pleased with you," he replied.

She turned around. "Well, I'm sorry. I know it reflects badly on you when a guest of yours makes trouble and for that I am genuinely apologetic."

"But you're not sorry you offended them," Dermot said, leaning against the sink with a twinkle in his eye.

She shook her head. "I'm not, actually. But I'm sorry I'm not sorry," she said with a mischievous grin.

"Do *any* of your boyfriends stay cross with you?" he asked, pulling Marielle toward him after spreading his legs apart to even their height.

She looked down at the part of his t-shirt exposed by two open buttons. "Some do, actually. It's hard to imagine, I know, but I'm glad you're over it."

"What if I'm *not* over it?" he asked, locking eyes with her.

Marielle turned toward his shoulder. "Then I'd have to kiss you to see if you'd relent."

"And if I didn't?" he asked, attempting to engage her eyes again.

She glanced at him nervously. "I'd need to up the ante."

"Well, I must say, you make fighting enormous fun," he replied with diminished breath as he reached down to hold her hips.

"I like wrestling as well," she said, raising her eyebrows briefly.

"Winner takes all?" he asked.

She glanced at him again. "With you?"

Dermot nodded.

Marielle looked slightly to the left for the answer. "Oh, yeah," she replied softly.

"Jesus!" Dermot exclaimed as his body responded to her.

Marielle smiled as she looked down at his jeans.

"That's your fault," he declared.

"Well, I assumed it wasn't Sean's!" she replied.

A look of disgust overcame Dermot's face. "Why did you say that?!"

"I'm testing to see how durable it is," she replied, still looking down.

Dermot laughed until he kissed her, then jumped as his father called his name from the dining room doorway. Dermot stood up as Marielle turned her back to add milk to Sean's cup. "We're in here, Dad," he replied.

"What are you up to?" Mr. MacManus asked happily.

"Well, our guests have departed, and Marielle is currently making a cup of cold tea," Dermot replied, noting the lack of steam rising from the cup.

"Is it cold?" she asked.

"Dermot, make Marielle a proper cup of tea," Mr. MacManus ordered with more vehemence than was necessary.

"I shall," Dermot replied, crossing his arms as he studied his father.

"How was your program?" Marielle asked, abandoning Sean's cup.

"Grand. It's still playing, but I'm off to bed."

"Oh, you have to work in the morning," Marielle said with disappointment.

"Yes, not all of us can mitch-off school to travel the world," Mr. MacManus replied genially.

"Yeah, it's hard to be me," Marielle said, smiling brightly.

"Your classmates must be quite envious," Dermot remarked as he finally looked away from his father.

She nodded. "They are. I can't repeat the rude names my friend Joel called me."

"I wish you would," Sean said from behind Dermot's father.

Marielle leaned to her right to make eye contact with Sean. "I'm afraid your tea is cold now."

"No worries," Sean replied. "Me mam needs me home now anyway."

Marielle's smile disappeared. "Will we see you tomorrow?"

"Perhaps. What time will you return from Dublin?" he asked Dermot.

"We'll return before dinner anyway. I'll give you a buzz."

"Ah-right," Sean said before offering his hand to Dermot's father. "Dr. MacManus, a pleasure as always."

Marielle extended her hand as Sean approached her, but he pulled her in for a hug instead. Mr. MacManus raised his eyebrows at a distracted Dermot.

"It was grand to see you again, Marielle," Sean said.

"You too," she replied, stepping back, but still holding his hand. "Maybe we can do our best to offend Dermot tomorrow as well."

"I'll count on it," he replied happily, nodding to his friend before leaving.

"He's a good lad," Mr. MacManus reflected before exhaling audibly. "But I fear he and his mother are a bit strapped at the moment." He looked at the counter. "Will you not fetch Marielle a proper cup of tea, Dermot?!" he asked impatiently, causing Dermot's eyes to narrow slightly.

"I promise I will," Dermot said with calm authority as if he was the parent rather than the child.

"Alright, then. Sleep well, all," Mr. MacManus said before departing.

"Is everything alright?" Marielle asked as Dermot studied his father's wake.

"Sorry," he said, looking at Marielle. "Let me get you some tea."

"May I confess something to you?" she asked, looking up at him with regret.

"Anything," he replied, looking from one of her blue eyes to the other.

She grimaced slightly before she said, "I hate tea."

Dermot looked down at the cup. "I actually find it dreadful myself," he confessed before both laughed.

"Wait. Is that allowed?" Marielle asked cautiously.

"What do you mean?"

"I mean, you being under the thumb of Great Britain for so long. We started a whole war over the stuff. I hear they don't tax tea in Boston because they're still mad about it."

"Come here," Dermot said, pulling Marielle with him as he moved back to the sink. "You'll pay for your rude comment."

"Ooh, you hug almost as well as Sean does," she said as he wrapped his arms around her.

"Can you believe the cheek of him?!" Dermot declared.

"Nonsense! I love Sean... in a completely platonic way. He reminds me of my brother Stephen, only less angry."

"Really?" Dermot asked with genuine surprise. "Stephen must be quite angry, then."

"Yeah, anger isn't something my family has in short supply."

"It would appear you're full of mischief as well."

Marielle chuckled. "Well, that's true. Holidays are generally a game of verbal chicken to see who can offend everyone else first."

"Who is most likely to be offended?" Dermot asked, rubbing Marielle's waist.

"My mother first, then Anna—both Italians."

"You'd expect that," Dermot remarked.

Marielle nodded. "Then it's a tossup between John, my dad, and me."

"What about Stephen?" Dermot asked.

"Stephen and Jeanette make it an Olympic sport. You can't beat them, but mostly because they're a tag team."

"That seems a bit unfair," Dermot noted before kissing Marielle's forehead.

"*Ja*, but they can't help it. They're Irish twins."

Dermot moved a piece of Marielle's hair from her cheek. "Nine months apart?" he asked.

"Just about," she replied.

"And Jeanette resembles you?"

"Well, in that respect, people think she and *I* are twins."

"Lucky her," Dermot replied, pushing Marielle's hair from her right shoulder.

"Now, she'd say lucky me."

"That's what I was thinking. That *I* was lucky, I mean," Dermot clarified.

"I knew what you meant," Marielle replied softly, placing her arms around his neck as she waited for the kiss she knew was coming.

Floorboards creaked near the dining room door, but no one called

Dermot's name.

"Do you know where my cup is?" Marielle asked as she rushed toward the dining room, pretending to look startled when she saw Dermot's mother.

"Is everyone off, then?" Mrs. MacManus asked while pushing her hands deep into her bathrobe pockets.

"They are," Dermot replied, rinsing Sean's cup in the sink.

"Why don't you make us some tea and we can have a chat about your evening," his mother suggested.

Marielle sat in her usual dining room chair as she described the sleet and the cold water.

"You should've seen her face when she came up for air, winjin' about the salt!" Dermot said, smiling lovingly at Marielle.

"I've never tasted so much salt in my life! I was sure my arteries would harden instantly." Marielle laughed, but Mrs. MacManus wasn't listening.

"Why don't you go dry your hair, Marielle?" Mrs. MacManus directed more than asked. "You look absolutely miserable!"

Marielle paused for a moment, startled by Mrs. MacManus' vehemence. She confirmed Dermot appeared startled as well as she took her leave.

Marielle closed the bathroom door tightly before switching the dryer to its lowest setting, only turning it on for a few minutes to avoid disturbing Mr. MacManus' sleep. After changing into her nightgown and bathrobe, she returned downstairs to a foyer whose only light was that which spilled from the crack in the dining room door.

Marielle knocked on the door, causing it to open wider, then froze as she looked at Dermot's pained, red eyes. He still sat in his chair between the table and the window, but he looked more trapped now than before she left.

Marielle turned to Mrs. MacManus as both she and her son looked down at the table. "I'll just be heading off to bed," she said reflexively, wanting to remove herself from the gravity of the room even if her presence had been welcome. "Will we be getting up early for Dublin, then?" Marielle asked Dermot.

"Don't worry about it," Mrs. MacManus replied impatiently.

Marielle swallowed hard. "Alright. Well, thank you for everything today."

"Not a'tall," Mrs. MacManus said to the table.

Marielle backed away from the doorway and began shaking on her way up the stairs, feeling considerably colder than she did on the way down. She closed the bedroom door, but it popped open slightly as she crawled into bed.

After only a few minutes of trembling, she considered retrieving her bathrobe as an additional cover, but she remembered that blankets didn't create heat, they reflected it. The sea had penetrated her bones and there was no way to feel warmer when her bathrobe and comforter could only reflect cold.

Marielle's teeth chattered as she remembered her bedroom two houses ago. The walls held no insulation, allowing her to etch designs into the ice which accumulated on the window beside her bed. She could still feel the cold under her finger nail and see the fog she made with her breath, but she had never felt this cold before.

She heard movement downstairs before two people walked up, minutes apart. The first paused outside her door. The second did the same before closing it.

Marielle shuddered as her thoughts gave way to speculation, then immediately gave up. There was no way to know what Mrs. MacManus felt at any given moment. Although her mind's current flowed in one direction, the shifting wind of her mood made Marielle seasick. She only knew for certain that tonight was the night Mrs. MacManus revealed something big to her son, and that something broke his heart.

Marielle lay in bed, looking up at the dark ceiling, unable to catch her breath. She thought about the car and truck lights dancing across their ceiling in Kleiner and the helicopter lights above the bed that awaited her in Appleton. But this bed in Galway wasn't so high, and this room wasn't so cold which belied the fact that she was freezing. Lights didn't dance in this room, but she could hear the sound of traffic until shivering gave way to fatigue and she drifted off to sleep.

Hours later, a motorcycle engine revved loudly as if poised to jump through the window. Marielle opened her eyes suddenly, staring in the direction of the window until she remembered she was on the second floor, facing the rear of the house and, therefore, unlikely to be the victim of a motorcycle attack. She took a deep breath before turning her head toward the hall as the floorboards creaked.

No, Dermot, she thought, assuming the footsteps were his before the sound retreated. Moments later, the sound returned, then retreated again. Someone paced the hall or guarded it and she felt certain without looking that she knew the identity of the sentry.

Marielle closed her eyes with force. Whatever had occurred that night, she knew her days with Dermot were numbered.

Chapter Thirty-Five

The Parting Guest
—W.B. Yeats – *Youth and Age*

Marielle awoke to a room bright with sunshine and starkly at odds with the dark cloud above her head. She stared at the wallpaper as she wondered when she had stopped shivering. Her eyes followed the fern pattern to the corner, but she couldn't find a break or a seam. Whoever hung this paper had an unusually good eye for detail.

She closed her eyes as she remembered the pain in Dermot's. She considered what might have occurred between the time she left the dining room the night before and the time she returned, causing her to shiver again—this time from fear rather than cold. After several minutes, she decided she couldn't remain in bed any longer doing nothing but waiting and wondering. She would go for a run and by the time she returned, it would be time for bad news.

She pushed back her covers as she sat up, then cursed as she fell back onto her pillow. She couldn't leave the house without locking the door behind her and she didn't have a key. There was nothing to do but await her fate, stare at wallpaper, and contemplate the mind of the hanger.

Marielle dozed off before a door opened, then closed below. Hurried feet ascended the stairs past Marielle's door, around the banister, and down the hall. A moment later, the same person made her way downstairs again, closing the front door with purpose. Marielle thought she heard a car door, but that could have been her imagination. A faint knocking at her bedroom door might have been her imagination as well, but she answered it anyway.

Dermot opened the door wearing his smoke blue t-shirt, his arms appeared more muscular than she remembered and his legs looked tan against his dark blue boxer shorts. Even after a long and difficult night, he still looked perfect.

Marielle sat up on her elbow. "Is your mom gone?" she asked.

"She is." Dermot motioned in the direction of the door. "She left just now, in fact."

Marielle studied Dermot's face. "Are you alright?" she asked softly.

Dermot regarded the wallpaper as if the proper response could be found there.

"What's going on?" she asked in her kindest voice. "You looked terrible last night."

"I have some bad news," he said, looking at her as pain returned to his eyes.

Marielle steeled herself before repeating her question.

Dermot rubbed his arms. "It's awfully cold. Do you mind if I get into bed with you?"

"But, what if your mom comes back?" Marielle replied in a tone meant to show less shock than she felt.

"She won't. She has a lecture in a few minutes."

Marielle lowered her head slightly. "Are you sure?"

"Yes. It's quite alright."

Dermot waited until Marielle acquiesced, then took a running start, jumping over her onto the wall-side of the bed. He crawled under the thick comforter, smiling as he snuggled beside her.

Marielle marveled at his child-like enthusiasm, then flinched as his cold feet touched hers.

"Sorry," he said quickly.

"No, I prefer you near me," she replied happily, her feet pursuing his.

"I did this when my sister was home," Dermot mused. "We would lie in bed and talk for ages."

Marielle's eyes widened. Although she regarded Dermot's relationship with Fiona as enviable, she thought it unusual that he would feel comfortable lying in bed with her, and even more unusual that he would admit it so freely.

Dermot noticed Marielle's surprise and shrank from it.

She quickly said, "I shared a bed with my little sister when we lived in Kleiner. It was actually hard to get used to sleeping alone when we moved." Her teeth began to chatter. "Sorry, I've been cold since we got into the water last night. I don't know what's the matter with me."

"Here, I'll warm you up," Dermot offered, rubbing his hand against her arm.

"Ooh, that's much better," Marielle joked, smiling until her happiness wasn't returned. "What's your news?" she asked.

Dermot drew a sharp breath. "I'm not permitted to see you off on

Thursday. Mum prefers I rest and get everything sorted for school on Friday. So, I won't be able to give you a proper goodbye."

"Oh, that's alright," Marielle said with relief. "You couldn't give me a proper goodbye with your father standing there anyway." She stroked his hair as she examined his face.

"I suppose so," he said, looking deep into her gray-blue eyes before shutting his.

"There's something else," Marielle said more than asked.

He groaned as he opened his eyes again. "Mum told me I must stop writing to you and speaking with you after you leave. I have until Christmas to cut with you altogether."

Marielle didn't gasp so much as stop breathing. "Why?" she whispered as her hand dropped.

"She thinks you're too mature for me and it's too serious between us."

Marielle attempted to clear her throat. "Wow. She really *does* hate me," she muttered.

Dermot squeezed her arm. "I said that very same thing, but she said that wasn't it a'tall."

"Well, what exactly *is* it?" Marielle asked aggressively, causing Dermot to smart. "Sorry. I tried so hard not to say anything or look annoyed when she called America a cesspool and communism a religion. I really did!"

"I know. You were wonderful," he said, regarding her tenderly. "I told her I thought she was treating you very unfairly. She said she had her reasons, but she wouldn't explain further."

Marielle jumped as she turned toward the door. "Is someone in the hall?" she asked.

Dermot shook his head. "It's nothing. It's merely an old house."

She looked back at him, unconvinced.

"Really," he said with more confidence.

Marielle willed her mind to return to their dilemma. "Couldn't you tell her I mean nothing to you, that we're not serious at all?"

Dermot released a wry laugh. "After last night, I shan't be believed."

"Why not?"

"Because she was surprised by my reaction. She said she had no idea I would take it so badly and it confirmed in her mind that she made the right decision."

Marielle closed her eyes for a thoughtful moment. "Couldn't your dad

594

intervene?"

Dermot shook his head. "He wouldn't."

"Really? In my house, my mom can say anything she likes, but it's what my dad says that matters."

"No," he said gently. "It's not like that here. Mum makes the rules."

At that moment, Marielle was surprised by how much she missed patriarchy.

"We can still marry," Dermot consoled. "It merely requires we plan ahead and employ a bit of perspective."

Marielle regarded him severely. "Don't you think we're a little young for perspective?!" she asked before diffusing her words with a smile.

Dermot pulled her towards him as he turned onto his back. "Last night, I determined how we might marry in six years rather than eight."

"Really?" she asked, her cheek resting on his chest as she stroked his t-shirt. "How's that?"

"If I swot mercilessly as an undergraduate, I might get a position with the university whilst I work on my doctorate. It might allow us to live on our own."

Marielle lifted her head abruptly to make eye contact with Dermot. "They have married student housing at U.W. Madison. We could go there for grad school. It would allow us to get married in four or five years."

"That would be brilliant!" Dermot replied. "I wonder if I might be admitted."

A mischievous grin overtook Marielle's face. "Well, I hear you have a superior educational system in Ireland. So, I'm sure they'll be able to sense your enormous intellectual power just by reading your transcript."

Dermot smiled at the ceiling. "God, I'd hate to argue with you if you were educated."

Marielle continued to stroke his t-shirt. "Don't worry. I'll study covertly like women in Iran do."

"Do they?" he asked the top of her head.

"I have no idea," she said, joining her right hand with his left. "Do you want me to change my name?"

Dermot narrowed his eyes as he considered the matter. "Well, that's up to you. You could hyphenate it to Richter-MacManus."

"Ooh, that rolls off the tongue nicely," she said sarcastically.

"Or we could combine our names to—"

"MacRichter," they said in unison, then laughed as though the world wasn't ending in four days.

Marielle pushed herself up on her left elbow as she smiled down at Dermot, and a moment before both jumped at a creaking sound near the top of the stairs.

"I'll check," Dermot said, throwing back the covers before he leapt over Marielle and ran from the room.

Marielle heard Dermot run the length of the second floor, then down to the first. A moment later, he walked through the bedroom door. "It's nothing, but I locked the front door to be safe."

"Don't your parents have keys?" she asked as he resumed his position.

"Not to this particular lock," Dermot said with confidence. "No one does."

Marielle regarded him admiringly as she declared him brilliant.

"Thank you," he replied, encouraging her head to return to his chest.

Marielle listened to Dermot's heart as she reflected on six to eight years of waiting. It felt very nearly like a death sentence, she decided, more so since heaven was on the other side. She closed her eyes as tears silently fell.

"Are you alright, love?" Dermot asked, looking down.

She refused to look at him as she said, "Sorry. I'll stop in a minute."

He turned onto his side to better see her face, kissing one tear, then another.

Marielle took a deep breath as Dermot's lips approached hers, then shuddered as a rush of warm energy cascaded across her stomach. Dermot's body responded in kind as they inched toward one another. Marielle lifted the back of Dermot's shirt as his left hand attempted her nightgown buttons, then gave up. He pulled her knee over his before moving his hand along the back of her leg, pausing where he expected to find underwear that weren't there. His fingers traced the inside of her thigh, then explored in between. She winced as he pressed his fingers inside of her.

"Am I hurting you?" he asked.

Marielle shook her head while shivering unexpectedly. He kissed her harder as he continued to move inside of her and she continued to shake. Marielle pulled back the elastic of Dermot's boxer shorts to move her hand inside.

"I want you," Dermot proclaimed.

"You have me," she replied, gently kissing his ear as she stroked him.

"You have no idea how long I've dreamt of this moment," he said, as though thinking aloud.

She stopped kissing his ear to whisper, "I think I do."

Dermot sighed before exasperation turned into amusement. "Must you be so competitive?! Even in bed?"

"Is this a competition-free zone?" she asked innocently, looking around, then began to stroke him again.

Dermot laughed. "I have no idea. I've completely forgotten English just now."

Marielle smiled as their lips touched again.

"Where are the condoms, love?" he whispered.

"They're in my purse. I'll get them," she said, beginning to turn from him when a loud creak from the hallway caused her to jump off the bed with a curse.

Dermot looked at the door with alarm, then lay back down with a sigh. "Damn it!" he yelled before asking the ceiling "Why?!" repeatedly.

"It's an old house," Marielle explained, smiling down at him.

"I hate this fucking house!" Dermot exclaimed, resting the back of his hand on his forehead.

Marielle turned toward the clock. "It's ten-thirty. What time is your mother's lecture over?"

"Any time between eleven and half-past."

"Right," Marielle paused. "Is she going to wonder why both of us are still in our pajamas when she gets home?"

"I was just thinking on that," he said, turning a tortured face towards her.

Marielle kissed Dermot's forehead. "I'll jump into the shower. You get dressed and pretend like nothing's happened when your mom walks in."

He nodded. "Right, I'll avoid telling her that the spirits of this house are ruining our sex life."

"Good plan. I'm not sure she'd be sympathetic."

Marielle passed Mr. MacManus' bedroom door when she heard Dermot's desperate moan. She considered returning to him, but quickly disregarded the idea. If she went back now, she couldn't guarantee self-restraint on her part, and having sex with Dermot while his mother pounded on the front door was bad form, she thought, then laughed.

Marielle glanced at the mirror above the sink before returning to it.

She touched her flushed skin with wonder as she heard Grandma Richter's voice say, "You've got it bad, kid."

A slow trickle of shower water failed to encourage washing as Marielle studied the embedded sticker in the centre of the soap, deciding she had never seen or smelled anything quite like it. A pounding or thumping noise caused her to turn her head toward the door. Seconds later, she heard two voices speaking with purpose. She listened for only a moment before moving her head under the water again.

***

"Good morning!" Mrs. MacManus said in disarmingly high spirits as she rapidly crossed the dining room toward Marielle.

"Good morning," she replied, attempting to match the woman's tone while watching Dermot scowl at the back of his mother's head.

"Dermot will need to make you lunch," she announced, brushing past Marielle into the foyer. "You'll want to look in on Ronan as well. He's back from his holidays and he'll be keen to show you his colour before it washes off. I'm off, then," she said, closing the front door heavily.

Marielle turned from the door to Dermot, waiting to speak until he finally smiled at her. "Do you know what a whirling dervish is?" she asked.

He shook his head. "I don't, no."

"I don't either, but I think your mother might be one."

Dermot expelled an angry breath.

"What's wrong?" she asked, fatigued by the question.

"Auch!" Dermot exclaimed, turning toward the window behind his chair. "I forgot to unlock the door."

"You mean the lock no one has a key to?" she asked, tempering her concern.

Dermot nodded before shaking his head in frustration.

Marielle pulled back the corners of her mouth. "What did she say?"

"She gave out to me of course, and demanded an explanation."

Marielle stared at Dermot, waiting for one as well.

He drew a deep breath, but there wasn't enough air in the room to release the tension in his brow. "I said I didn't want her running through the door, yelling at you."

Marielle steadied herself against the dining room chair.

"She said I should know she would never do that."

"It's not your fault," Marielle said reflexively. "I should've reminded

598

you to unlock the door. I thought about it on the way to the bathroom, but I guess I'm used to you and I having the same thoughts all the time."

Dermot studied her for a moment. "I seriously doubt you have the same thoughts as I do all the time," he said, a grin returning colour to his cheeks.

"I wouldn't be so sure," she replied, smiling before she looked away.

"You're so cute when you do that!" he proclaimed, closing the distance between them.

She looked up at him. "Do what?"

"You get nervous and look away from me."

"No, I was just thinking of something else," she said, blushing.

"Bollocks," he replied, wrapping his arms around her.

She cleared her throat. "I'm offended you would say that."

"More bollocks."

She stepped back to better regard him. "Stop reading me, please."

"Surely, I'm not the only lad who can read you," he said, clearly confident that he was.

"You are, actually, and it's more than a little irritating."

"I think you'll recover," he said, pushing her hair off her shoulders before tension returned to his brow.

Marielle smiled. "I imagine Dublin's off the table."

"'Tis. Are you disappointed?"

She shook her head. "No, but we'll need to decide what to do today or we won't withstand the inquisition tonight. Should we invite Ronan over to watch a movie?"

"No, Mum wouldn't like that a'tall."

Marielle stared up at him, allowing her eyes to ask the obvious question.

"Too intimate and not active enough," Dermot explained.

"But we're unlikely to have sex with Ronan in the room."

Dermot chuckled. "Still, she wouldn't like it."

"You could take me to the library and we could investigate whether Columbus actually prayed at St. Nicholas Church before going to the New World," Marielle suggested.

Dermot shook his head. "He didn't. That's a ridiculous notion. Next option," he said, grabbing Marielle's hand to lead her from the dining room. "Wait," he said, turning to walk backward through the foyer while holding both of her hands. "Tell me why you locked the bathroom door."

599

"I was afraid you'd get curious," she replied. "It sounds like you did."

Dermot looked away as he smiled.

"See, you do the same thing!" Marielle proclaimed.

His eyebrows rose briefly. "I have no idea what you mean."

"Bollocks," she replied as they entered the sitting room.

Dermot laughed at Marielle's word usage, calling her an Irishwoman.

"I thought you were grateful I was American," Marielle remarked as they neared the couch.

"I am. You're making me nervous just now," he said before lying down and extending his hand to her.

Marielle lay on her back with her head on Dermot's right shoulder. Dermot laced his right hand into the back of hers, then crossed his ankles on the armrest at the end of the couch. "I think your mother wouldn't appreciate us putting our sneakers on her furniture," Marielle said, looking at their Nikes nearly side by side.

"I hardly think my mother's greatest concern with finding us together would be our shoes on the couch," he retorted.

"Touché," Marielle replied.

"Though my Nikes are considerably whiter than yours," he added.

"*Bullscheiße!*" Marielle exclaimed. "Mine just have dust on the leather, whereas yours are less white on the fabric. Since it's easier to clean leather than fabric, mine are cleaner overall."

Dermot pulled Marielle closer with his arm. "Are all Americans this competitive?" he asked.

"Yes. About every. Single. Thing."

He smiled at the ceiling. "It must be exhausting."

"You have no idea," she said, then took a determined breath without continuing.

"What?" he asked.

"Did an American serviceman break your mother's heart when she was young? She seems to have an irrational hatred for us."

Dermot considered the matter with some amusement. "Not that I'm aware of, but I see your point. I believe she views Americans as environmentally irresponsible and violent."

"I'll own up to the violent part," Marielle replied, "but I'd just like to say that we recycle aluminum cans at my house and you don't. So, if it comes up again, I'd like you to state my case."

Dermot said he would.

"She may never come around to liking me," Marielle continued pensively, "but it's clear she loves you a great deal which is nice."

"Yeah," Dermot said, sighing at the ceiling. "I try to appreciate that, but it's its own burden."

Marielle smiled with mischief as she said, "Can you imagine what she'd be like if you were an only child?"

"Oh, Jaysus!" Dermot said with a chuckle. "Or if she were a widow?"

"That would be much worse. Thank your lucky stars your dad is still alive... for lots of reasons."

Dermot flinched at an unpleasant memory. Before Marielle could ask, he said, "Do you know she kicked my father out of their bedroom when I was born?"

"No! Really?" Marielle asked, turning to see Dermot's face.

"She wanted a son and when I arrived there was no reason to sleep with my father anymore."

"So, they haven't—"

"Stop!" he protested. "I know what you're meaning to ask and I honestly can't think on it."

Marielle turned her sympathetic face toward the ceiling. "Your poor father. Well, I promise not to kick you out of our bedroom no matter how many sons we have." She paused. "I'm surprised your father doesn't hate you."

Dermot flinched again, but Marielle didn't notice as she began to chuckle. "I was just thinking about Sean telling his girlfriend he had a brain tumor based upon watching *St. Elsewhere*. Did he really only do that because she mentioned children?"

"He did, yeah, but she honestly should've known better. No one in their right mind would bring up marriage and children to Sean."

"I wonder what names she suggested," Marielle mused. "Maybe his real problem was the names."

"Those would be some pretty terrible names now, I have to say."

"Give me an example," Marielle said happily.

"Gary, for starters."

Marielle guffawed. "You're right. That's a horrible name. Ashley is as well."

"Too bad, that. I was hoping to name our little girl Ashley. I'm only joking," he said quickly when Marielle gasped. "I'd like to name our daughter Eva, actually."

"Wow, that's my middle name!" Marielle remarked.

"Is it?" Dermot asked with excitement.

"No," she said as she lay on her back again.

He nudged her with his arm. "What's your middle name, then?"

Her eyes remained fixed on the ceiling. "I don't talk about my middle name."

"Why?" he asked, attempting to make eye contact.

"I just don't," she said, shifting her eyes toward him for a moment.

He nudged her again. "Were you named after someone you hate?"

"No," she replied.

"Were you named after anyone a'tall?"

She shook her head.

"Why won't you tell me?!" he asked with exasperation.

Marielle smiled impishly. "Because it will make you crazy if I don't."

"I won't make love to you if you won't tell me," he threatened, staring at her cheek.

She shifted her eyes as she shook her head. "You don't mean that."

"Tell me, Marielle!" he demanded as he propped himself up on his right elbow.

"Alright." She laughed. "It's Ruth."

"Liar! It starts with an E," he declared.

"How on earth do you know that?" she asked, rolling her head toward him.

"Because your initials are M-E-R, like the sea."

"I share too much information with you," she reflected.

"Now, tell your future husband your real middle name. I demand it!" he said, turning her onto her side to face him.

"I'm not sure you can do that," she replied. "It appears husbands over here have far less power than they do in the U.S."

Dermot turned away to laugh. "I intend to change that," he said.

She raised her eyebrows with an air of surprise. "Right now?" she asked.

"Yes. Tell me," he said, an inch from her lips as he held her wrist firmly.

She glanced at her wrist as she said calmly, "That doesn't hurt. You can't take me in a fight."

Dermot's smile broadened. "I think I can."

"You'll be disappointed."

His eyebrows narrowed. "Are you saying that because you want me to pin you, like?"

She shook her head slightly. "No. You won't pin me."

"Are you mad?! I weigh at least three stone more than you."

"True... I think, but I'm compact and scrappy."

"You're enraging as well! Alright, I refuse to fight you," he said, loosening his grip.

"Because you can't win," she said matter-of-factly.

"Stop!" he demanded.

She narrowed her eyes in thought. "Because I'm right or because you're wrong?"

"How's that an option?"

"It's really not."

"You're beginning to make me daft, Marielle."

She smiled victoriously. "I'd say you're well past daft."

"Is there *any* way to resolve this argument and discover your middle name without wrestling you?" he asked.

Marielle consulted the corner of her eye. "No," she replied.

"Fine," he said, tightening his grip a moment before Marielle rolled her wrist from his grasp.

"That was quite good," he said with surprise as he looked down.

Marielle leveled her eyes at him. "I know," she said.

Dermot joined his hands to both of hers. "Will you give it another go, then?"

"Of course. The first battle ended too quickly," she said with disappointment.

Dermot narrowed his eyes playfully before declaring a start to the second round.

Marielle's left hand began to overtake Dermot's right as he pinned her right hand against her chest. Both looked at the other with a pained expression, waiting for the other to surrender.

"Do you give up?" he asked.

"No," she replied through a tense jaw.

He used his left hand to turn Marielle onto her back without regard for the lack of couch beneath her. She gasped as she fell, and just before the floor knocked the wind from her.

"Jaysus!" Dermot yelled as he jumped off the couch to kneel beside her.

Marielle held her stomach as spasms of silent laughter began, due in part to the expression on Dermot's face.

"Oh, thank God you're alright," he said.

She closed her eyes as tears filled them.

"You *are* alright?" he asked.

She nodded her head against the floor as speech was impossible.

"You're mad!" he remarked, finally smiling.

Marielle wiped tears from her red face. "Well, you're a brute!" she declared as she sat up.

"Wait now!" Dermot objected.

Marielle lifted her hand. "I'm only joking."

"Oh, alright, then," he replied, resting his back against the couch. "I believe you owe me your middle name now."

Marielle nodded. "It's Edwina."

"Not a'tall!" Dermot said with dismay.

"No, it's not," she admitted, then yelled, "Fine!" when she faced Dermot's disapproval. "It's Elyse," she finally admitted.

"What's wrong with that?" Dermot asked.

Marielle shook her head. "Nothing at all. I like it, actually."

His expression became severe. "Then why did you say you didn't?"

"I never did. You just assumed it because I said I wouldn't talk about my middle name."

"No, I'm quite certain you said—"

"Wrong!" she interrupted, blowing an errant piece of hair from her face. "I made a point *not* to say that. You're easily misled."

Dermot looked up as though replaying the conversation in his mind. "Are you—"

"I'm sure," she insisted.

"Alright, then. What do you think about the name Eva for our daughter?"

"Okay," Marielle said amiably, scooting beside Dermot.

"Do you like it?" he asked with impatience.

"I do."

He stared at her profile. "You don't, do you?"

Marielle turned to him with an air of annoyance. "I just said I did."

"But you have the look of someone who's lying."

A grin appeared upon Marielle's face. "I have the look of someone who's honored to be discussing children with you."

"Ooh, that's quite smooth," he said, moving closer to her.

Marielle flashed her eyebrows. "Will she be a hurler, then?"

Dermot shook his head. "Only boys hurl. Girls play camogie. It's the female version of hurling."

Marielle looked at the wooden chair across the room. "Was your father alright with you quitting?"

"I don't think he was part of the conversation, actually."

Marielle nodded. "I have to say, it's good we're waiting six to eight years to get married. It'll take me at least that long to get used to a family where the woman calls the shots. I need to be rewired or at least reprogrammed."

"Can you wait for six years?" he asked softly, taking her hand.

Marielle shook her head. "No. I think I may die first."

He looked at her with concern that her smile overtook.

"I mean it only feels like I'll die first," she clarified. "I *have* had two recurring nightmares about dying, but waiting wasn't among them."

"You really die, like?" Dermot asked tenderly. Watching Marielle nod before he said, "I heard you can only have dreams where you *almost* die, but if you actually die in them, you're already dead."

"Well, if that's the rule, I'm either the exception, or I'm in heaven right now." Marielle smiled as Dermot anticipated what she would say next. "Which makes sense since I'm with you."

"Two smooth comments in one conversation! I believe you *are* becoming an Irishwoman."

Marielle continued to smile as she turned away. "I absorb culture like a sponge."

"So, what are these dreams of yours?" Dermot asked before he kissed her hand.

"Well, in one of them, it's graduation night and I'm alone in my parents' old LTD (that's a car) and a song named *Mary's Prayer* comes on the radio. I reach down to turn it up, but I run off the road and hit a tree and the last thing I see is the clock on the dashboard announcing the time I died."

Dermot stared at her quietly before he said, "That's dreadful."

"But not as bad as the second one. In that one, I'm in the middle of a lake in my old town and a skeletal hand from a submerged train latches onto my leg and pulls me under."

"I thought that wasn't a passenger train," Dermot murmured.

"It wasn't. There's no logic to it. Anyway, to answer your question, if I don't drive a car we don't own anymore, and I don't swim in a lake we don't live near, I should be able to wait six, or eight, or a hundred years as long as you're at the end of it," she said, watching him play with her hand.

"I promise I will be," he whispered, turning toward her with serious eyes.

"What's that picture over there?" Marielle asked, spying a photograph on the television.

"No," Dermot objected weakly as Marielle abandoned him.

"Is that you?" she asked, staring at a much smaller version of Dermot in a dark suit standing beside his beaming mother in front of the church near the Docks.

He followed her, then indicated it was.

She lifted the photograph. "Is this your First Holy Communion?"

"No, Confirmation," he said, kissing the back of Marielle's head as he rested his hands upon her shoulders.

"Really? We don't get confirmed until this year. How old are you here?"

"Twelve," Dermot replied.

"That's only four years ago," she noted, continuing to study the photograph.

"Nearly five," he clarified.

"Well, no wonder your mother is so protective of you," Marielle reflected. "She still sees you as this cute, innocent little boy."

"And how do your parents see you?" Dermot asked.

"They don't," she replied reflexively, returning the photograph to the TV. "I'm only joking," she said quickly. "They think I'm a big bucket of awesome."

Dermot smiled as Marielle scanned the area in vain for pictures of his sister.

"Do you know my mother went pub to pub raising money for our hurling club to go to Wales? And she hates pubs, like."

"That's incredible," Marielle said, turning around.

"It was, though many of the parents contributed. Ronan's father took loads of photographs during the Final in Dublin as well as the match in Wales, and gave each of us an album. Would you like to see it? It's up in my room." He raised his eyebrows briefly.

Marielle suppressed amusement. "Why don't you bring it down here instead?"

He cocked his head to the side. "Don't you trust me to be a gentleman?"

"No," she replied, then laughed when he appeared wounded. "I'm sorry. I'm only joking. I believe you're a gentleman."

"And how else do you see me?" he asked, grabbing both of her hands.

"Wow," she remarked. "That's a brazen request for a compliment. I usually insult people when they're this obvious."

Dermot's gaze penetrated her before he said, "Maybe, but you won't insult me."

"I have a long track record of insulting you."

"True, but you won't now," he said with confidence.

Marielle shook her head. "You're right, and your perceptiveness is upsetting. The problem is, I can't answer your question without sounding like one of those sappy holiday TV shows I hate."

"Say it to me then and no one else need know," he urged.

"You won't tell anyone?" she asked, looking down at their hands. "Not even Sean?" She looked up at Dermot again even though she knew his eyes would lock onto hers when she did.

"Well, maybe Sean, now," he admitted. "But no one else, and I guarantee he won't tease you for it."

Marielle squinted as she considered her words carefully. "Well, I think you're really asking two questions: how do I see you and what do you mean to me? It's easier to answer the first one by saying how smart, and handsome, and fun you are."

"Answer the second one," he said gently, rubbing the top of her hands with his thumbs.

"Give me just a second," she said, swallowing with difficulty before she began. "You feel like peace and love to me. I feel like I've always known you, almost like you're a part of me I hadn't met before. You hear about women who refuse to remarry after their husbands die or who die minutes after their husbands do even though they were never sick at all. (That actually happened to the parents of a nun in our parish.) I've always wondered how anyone could feel that strongly for another person, and now I know. I don't *think* I would die if anything happened to you. I *know* I would." Marielle shook her head in disgust. "And that sounds like a made-for-TV movie," she said as she pulled her hands free to walk to the piano beside the couch where she began to play *Pomp and Circumstance*.

607

Dermot walked up behind her, resting his chin on her shoulder while hugging her tightly. "Stop playing and come to my bedroom."

"Do you really think that's a good idea?" she asked as she turned around.

He held out his hand as a smile overtook his face. "I think it's a brilliant idea."

Dermot pulled Marielle upstairs quickly, then pushed his bedroom door closed nearly the entire way.

Marielle looked at the door, wondering why he needed to close it if they were the only people home, but she decided not to ask. It was Dermot's home and Dermot's call.

"Sit here," he said, indicating the end of the bed as he bent down to open a small box on the bookcase in front of her. He turned around as he handed her two Irish coins from the late 1920s. "I want you to have these," he said. "They belonged to my grandfather. The one I never met."

Marielle shook her head as she examined the coins. "No. I can't."

"I want you to keep them," he repeated, sitting beside her.

She turned to him. "I can't take something that belonged to your family."

"You will be family soon enough and you can bring them back to me. Until then, I want you to look at them and think of me."

Tears formed in Marielle eyes. She looked away to take a deep breath. "How am I going to live without your letters and phone calls?"

"You won't. I can still write," he said, rubbing her back.

"But I can't write back."

"You can. You just can't post them."

Marielle wiped her eyes as she laughed. "Can you imagine the number of letters you'll receive in six years?"

Dermot smiled. "I was thinking the same. A lorry will pull into the drive and dump enormous quantities of paper onto our doorstep."

Marielle nodded at Dermot as their eyes locked.

He groaned suddenly. "God! I want to run away with you, Marielle, but I need the bitch! I can't pay for UCG on my own."

"I know," she muttered.

Dermot brushed his hand against her cheek as his composure returned. "It will be fine. I promise you."

She cleared her throat. "So, where's this album of yours?" she asked, placing the coins into her pocket.

Dermot regarded Marielle appreciatively before turning to the bookcase again. He retrieved a two-inch-wide binder, setting it on his lap as he happily explained each photograph. The last was a close-up of Dermot's beaming face, hurling stick raised victoriously into the air.

"Do you think I can have a copy of this?" Marielle asked.

Dermot nodded at the picture before smiling at her. "Certainly. The chemist should be able to make a copy anyway."

"Good, because I believe it's a conspiracy that you never sent me a clear picture of your face. Did you worry I'd only love you because you're hot?"

Dermot laughed. "Not a'tall. Mum never gave me duplicates of any close-up photos. She saved those for relation."

Dermot closed the album with enthusiasm, not noticing the skepticism on Marielle's face. He returned the binder to the bookshelf, then scooted back onto his bed until his head rested upon his pillow. "Come here," he said to Marielle.

Marielle looked between the door and Dermot nervously.

"If you mean to be my wife, you must come when I call you," he said with a serious expression which quickly transitioned into a smile. "Sorry. That was very bold."

Marielle smiled in return. "It was, but I'll come to you anyway," she said, crawling up the bed. She placed her head upon Dermot's chest when he moved his arm to make space. After a moment she said, "I can hear your heart."

"Is it—"

"PLEASE don't ask if it's saying my name!" Marielle interrupted.

Dermot laughed at the ceiling. "You *are* psychic."

"No, I just know how smooth you are," she remarked, beginning to stroke his t-shirt.

Dermot kissed the top of Marielle's head. "When I was training, my heart rate was 47 beats per minute."

"Is that good?" she asked.

"'Tis. The average Olympian has a similar heart rate."

"Yes, but you're not average. If you were an Olympian, I'd say your heart rate would only be 20 beats per minute."

Dermot laced his left hand into her right. "I think I'd be classed as nearly dead with a heart rate like that."

"Well, 35 then," Marielle offered, puckering her lips in thought as she noticed the walls in Dermot's room were painted the same color as those in the mint room. "You know, you're lucky that you had a desire to do something and your parents took an interest. I told my parents in 1980 that I had to start training if I was expected to be ready for the '88 Olympics."

Dermot smiled. "And what did they say to that?"

"Nothing. They just looked at me like I had three heads."

"Well, the head you have is lovely. You'd only be lovelier with three."

Marielle laughed as Dermot pushed aside the sheer curtain.

"What is it?" she asked.

"Only the neighbour hanging clothes on the line."

Marielle regarded the woman on the other side of the hedge. "She looks very unhappy."

"Her husband died last year of a heart attack," Dermot explained before dropping the curtain abruptly.

"Did she see us?" Marielle asked with concern.

"I don't think so. I wonder if Gryphon is climbing up," he said, pushing aside the curtain again.

"How can he climb up here?" Marielle asked, raising her head so Dermot could move unhindered.

"The roof slopes beneath this window. He jumps onto the bin, and then the shed. Then he climbs right up. It's how I sneak him into my room without my mother knowing."

"Wow," she said with respect. "You're both very clever."

"That's hardly news to me," he said seriously before laughing at his boldness.

"So, it wasn't him?" Marielle asked when Dermot encouraged her to resume her position on his chest.

"No," he said with concentration on his brow.

"*Du bist sehr klug,*" she said, merely because the phrase repeated in her brain.

"That doesn't sound very nice," Dermot remarked.

"German never does. It means you're clever, but you're also funny," she said, scooting up to kiss the corner of his mouth. "And gorgeous." She kissed him again, then considered whether she was the kind of girl who used the word *sexy.* "But my favorite thing about you is—"

He hushed in anticipation.

"How gentle you are."

Dermot's body language said Marielle's compliment disappointed him which was too bad since she wasn't sure she meant it. She thought to take it back, but she didn't want to appear indecisive, thereby calling into question the sincerity of her previous comments. She decided to kiss Dermot again and tell him she loved him. So she did, and nothing had ever felt more sincere.

Their hands joined as they turned onto their sides, facing one other. They kissed lightly with their eyes open, closing them as the kissing became more passionate. Dermot released Marielle's hand to move under her form-fitting cardigan sweater. He unclasped the front of her bra with only one hand before cupping her breast.

"I love you," he said with feeling.

"I love you," she replied, unbuttoning his jeans.

Dermot's eyes closed suddenly as breath escaped him. "You make me daft," he murmured.

"I want you to make love to me now," Marielle said, pushing down the waistband of Dermot's jeans.

He stopped to look into her eyes with fear in his own. "Are you certain?" he asked.

"Yes," she replied with resolve.

His eyebrows furrowed.

"Is something wrong?" she asked concernedly.

Dermot cleared his throat, glancing away nervously. "After events this morning, I thought it might be safer to wait until Tuesday night."

"What's happening Tuesday?" she asked.

"My parents have tickets to the theatre. A comedy. I told my mother you wouldn't understand Irish humour. I thought we'd make love whilst my parents were at the play."

Marielle's eyes closed suddenly. "Okay," she said with difficulty.

"Is that not better?" he asked.

She nodded with her eyes still closed, opening them when Dermot didn't speak. "Sorry. You're right... even though nothing seems better than right now."

He took a determined breath. "Alright. We need to fetch the condoms, then."

"Maybe if we're quick, we won't need them," she suggested, kissing his neck.

"Pardon?" Dermot asked with surprise.

"Maybe if we do it quickly, we don't need condoms."

"Oh," he said, glancing at the door.

Marielle turned toward the door as well, then noticed her passport picture hanging on the bed side of the chimney. Above the picture were the two postcards she sent from Great America and below hung five postcards she sent from New York.

Marielle touched her picture. "You *did* save it," she said as her eyes lit up.

"I told you I did."

She nodded slowly, unable to speak.

"Shall we make love now?" Dermot asked with sudden intensity.

Both of them stood up to remove their shoes, jeans, and underwear.

"Are you frightened?" Marielle asked as she freed her jeans from her ankles.

"Terrified," Dermot replied, then smiled. "Will you be on top?" he asked hopefully.

She shook her head. "I've never done this before."

"Neither have I," he argued.

"True, but you're the boy. It's your job to be on top."

Dermot waited for Marielle to lie back on his bed. He positioned himself on top of her with his legs outside of hers before both realized the opposite arrangement was the only one that would work. Marielle laughed as she moved her knees outside of Dermot's, then looked deep into his eyes as she felt him press against her. She pulsed her eyelids to diffuse the look of intensity on Dermot's face, but he didn't smile as she expected. Instead, his eyes became large as a creaking floor caught Marielle's attention. He cursed as he jumped to the end of the bed and a second before his mother's voice called his name from just beyond the doorway.

Marielle jumped to the side of the bed. She looked quickly to the corner for a hiding place, and the floor for her jeans, but there was no time for either as footsteps neared.

The hinges creaked halfway through the door's swing, but the house was otherwise silent as the teenagers lowered their heads and Mrs. MacManus looked into the room. Marielle looked up in time to see shock pull all available air from the space. She grimaced as Mrs. MacManus ran toward her to slap her across the face. The force of the slap turned Marielle's head, but she only felt the shame.

"The cheek of you!" Mrs. MacManus yelled. "I knew you were like this from the moment I laid eyes on you!"

Marielle blinked slowly. "I've never done this before," she muttered.

"Do you think I believe you?! You dirty bitch! Irish girls aren't like this! We never wanted you here! We put you off in the spring but you can't take a hint!"

"Mom!" Dermot said in an agonised voice before he closed his eyes. "It was me."

"What?" she asked, turning abruptly toward her son.

He looked up at her. "It was me. It was my idea. I'm the one to blame."

"No," Marielle said at the same time as Dermot's mother.

"I have spoilt you!" Mrs. MacManus yelled, her voice cracking.

"I know, Mum. I'm sorry." He lowered his head again.

"Did you have intercourse?" she asked her son.

"No," Marielle said softly when Dermot didn't reply.

"DID YOU HAVE INTERCOURSE?!" she yelled.

"NO!" Marielle yelled.

"Don't you raise your voice to me, you dirty bitch!" Mrs. MacManus said, raising her hand to strike Marielle again.

Dermot stood quickly, intercepting his mother's hand. "Don't touch her!" he said as a warning in the same tone he used with Gráinne the night before.

His mother looked up at him with a child's bewilderment. "Why?" she asked.

"Because I'm going to marry her," he replied.

Marielle closed her eyes as she silently cursed.

Air was pulled from the room anew as Dermot dropped his mother's hand and she backed into the hallway, looking very much like a woman who had seen a ghost. "You're only 16 and 17 years old! This is illegal! I'm calling the *Gardai*," she said, continuing to back up.

"No, Mother!" Dermot demanded, ready to run after her before remembering his lack of trousers. He cursed as he grabbed his jeans, jumping into them as he left the room.

A moment later, Mrs. MacManus yelled into the phone. "Come here! I need you! I need you!"

Marielle hastily grabbed her jeans, causing the Irish coins to fall from her pocket and roll under the bookcase and bed. She picked up the only Nike she could easily find before running to her room. She slid her things from the dresser into her suitcase with her forearm, exactly as she had seen in the movies. She tied her navy blue, canvas sneakers before grabbing her bathrobe from the hook on the back of the door. She looked for her gray duffel bag, but it was gone. Her purse was gone as well.

She looked toward the wardrobe as a middle-aged woman wearing a sweater and corduroy skirt walked through the door. The woman didn't say a word as she stood over Marielle, arms crossed.

Marielle zipped her suitcase before looking again at the wardrobe, wondering how she could pack the new emerald green dress she bought for her cousin's wedding.

The door hit the wall with force as Mrs. MacManus ran into the room. "I want you out of my house this instant and I never want to lay eyes on you again!" She raised her hand to strike Marielle, but the helmet-haired woman shook her head, immediately causing Mrs. MacManus' hand to retreat.

"I need my duffel bag," Marielle muttered.

"It's on the street where you belong! So is your purse. I'm calling your parents. They should know what a whore their daughter is," Mrs. MacManus said, then ran from the room with her sentry in pursuit.

A moment later, Marielle stood up as Dermot ran through the door with eyes more pained than the night before.

"I'm so sorry, Marielle," he said with a trembling voice as he touched her arm.

She grabbed both of his forearms as she looked into his eyes, willing him to be strong. "It's not your fault. It's mine."

The sentry spoke a sentence bearing Dermot's name from the floor below.

"I need to go," Marielle said, unsure of what to say next.

Dermot pulled her to him as incomplete words exited his mouth in halting patterns.

"Dermot!" his mother yelled, "get out of that bitch's room!"

He turned toward the door as he yelled, "Mother!" Then he ran from the room for the last time.

***

Mrs. MacManus stared with narrow eyes, clenched fists, and a red face as Marielle descended the stairs, suitcase in hand.

"Give me your calling card!" she demanded as Marielle reached the landing. "I'm calling your parents."

Marielle drew a deep breath. "No," she replied with quiet

determination.

"What?!" Mrs. MacManus yelled, running to the bottom of the stairs.

"I won't give you my calling card. If you wish to speak with my parents, you'll do so on your own dime," she said, then descended the last step, staring down several inches at Dermot's mother with the look of someone determined not to be struck again.

Mrs. MacManus stepped backward with concern, allowing Marielle to cross to the door unhindered.

"You will reimburse us for our petrol!" she yelled as Marielle exited the front door.

Marielle hesitated for a moment at the sight of a driveway filled with people middle-aged and older. Whispering and murmuring halted as they noticed the young American. She reached down to pick up her purse from the sidewalk, then walked a few feet farther to retrieve her duffel bag. She skirted the crowd until she approached the gate. "Excuse me," she said several times as spectators reluctantly made way until she reached the footpath.

She struggled under the load of her heavy suitcase for several yards before a car stopped and a young woman suggested she get inside. Marielle considered disobeying, but not seriously. It was possible the driver was an axe murderer, but she didn't care. Nothing could be worse than the yelling of Mrs. MacManus and the scrutiny of her neighbours.

"Where are you off to?" an attractive, dark-haired woman asked.

"The youth hostel. Thank you," Marielle replied.

"Not a bother," the woman said before resuming her conversation with a man of a similar age who sat in the passenger's seat.

Marielle stared at the stone walls, then down at her shaking hands. She wasn't crying and she had no ability to change this anytime soon.

The car turned right before the bridge and alongside the Docks before it slowed. "This is grand, thanks," the man said, kissing the driver before exiting the car.

The car made a three point turn, passing the church in Dermot's picture and the Claddagh sign before turning briefly in the direction they had traveled.

"If you don't mind, I'll leave you at the end of the road here," the woman said. "The youth hostel is down there a short distance." The woman pointed to a building a few hundred feet along, across the street from a pub named Monroe's.

"This is perfect. Thank you," Marielle said before exiting the car.

***

Marielle lay on one of five bunk beds delineating a room with unusually large windows. She stared at the bed above hers, wondering why she thought she might cross God and get away with it. She had no one to blame but herself, and now Dermot was imprisoned in a house with nosy neighbours on the outside and an angry mother on the inside. There was nothing Marielle could do to save Dermot or make anything better. She placed her forearm against her head as she willed herself to cry.

Two women spoke with Australian accents as they walked from the hallway into the room, but Marielle didn't acknowledge their presence.

"Are you alright there?" one asked in a kindly voice.

Marielle turned to see a short, dark-skinned woman standing beside a taller, sandy-blonde one.

"I'm fine, thanks," she replied with red eyes that held no tears.

"You don't look fine," the blonde woman remarked.

Marielle sighed. "I'm not. I just got kicked out of my pen pal's house."

"Oh?" the blonde asked.

Marielle sat up on her elbow. "His mother caught us… kissing."

"It sounds like you could use a drink," the dark one said. "We're heading out for tea soon, are you interested?"

Marielle shook her head. "No, thank you. I need to think for awhile."

"Alright, then. We'll be at Monroe's if you change your mind."

"Thanks," Marielle replied, lying back down as they departed.

She wondered when the call to her parents would occur, if it hadn't already. She thought of the rudeness of Mrs. MacManus and the terrible words she would use. The story would be completely devoid of any explanation, least of all that Dermot and Marielle were in love and had every intention to marry.

She concentrated hard in an attempt to sense whether her parents already knew, but she felt numb and disconnected from everyone and everything around her. For all she knew, tables were overturning in Appleton at this very moment. Vows to shun would come next, just before everything she owned was thrown onto Oneida Street. It seemed strange somehow that one might lie in peace when wars were declared in one's name at that very same moment.

Marielle chastised herself for worrying about her parents' reaction

616

when Dermot sat in the middle of an active war zone with *Gardai* arriving at any moment. He would explain to the police that intercourse had been a near miss and, therefore, they had broken no laws at all, but the interview would demean and embarrass him further. Marielle wondered with malice why they didn't just bring a priest or torture equipment or a lie detector test to interrogate him, given the severity of the crime.

Surely, Dermot's father would return home soon and inject sanity into the situation. He might even allow his son to leave the house to find Marielle, if only to gain a full explanation for the teenagers' misdeeds. Even if Mr. MacManus didn't allow his son to leave, Dermot would probably sneak out the way Gryphon snuck into his bedroom window. Marielle was sure of this.

She sat up. If Dermot left the house without his father's consent, he would have very little time to find her before his parents discovered him missing. Marielle needed to go to the place where he would look for her first.

She stood up, then began to pace. After several minutes of incoherent thought, a feeling of hunger descended upon her. It was a foreign feeling since she hadn't felt it in over three days.

She knelt beside her bed to retrieve a book of traveler's checks from her suitcase. A few minutes later, she walked down the sidewalk in the direction the hostel proprietor suggested as the nearest currency exchange.

Marielle calculated the conversion rate of $100 into Irish Pounds and even after the fee for converting checks to cash, and the fee for converting dollars to pounds, she still found the amount given her suspiciously small. *Maybe 68 pounds stretched further than dollars*, she thought.

Marielle looked both ways to cross the street as a strawberry blond bicyclist on the opposite side of the road caught her attention.

"Sean!" she yelled, but questioned his identity until he made a U-turn, crossing to her side of the road.

"Hiya. Where's Dermot?" he asked, looking around.

"At home."

"I thought you meant to go to Dublin today?"

"We didn't after all."

He nodded while wearing a confused expression.

"Are you busy right now?" Marielle asked.

"I am at present, but I should free up later in the day." He looked up as a thought occurred to him. "No... Wait, now."

617

"Do you have school tomorrow?"

He shook his head. "No, I'm off like Dermot. What's this about?"

"Dermot's mother found us kissing. She's kicked me out of the house. I'm staying at the youth hostel now."

"Well, she likely lost her temper. She'll get over it soon enough."

"No. Trust me, she won't. Can you meet me tomorrow at McDonald's at 10 a.m.? I'll explain everything then."

"Ah-right. I'll see you in the morning," Sean said as he departed, now pedalling in the direction of Dermot's house.

Marielle walked into a music store, looking for a tape to buy Dermot for his birthday. She would place a letter inside the tape case and ask Sean to deliver both in the morning.

The store offered *Rattle and Hum*, but she was sure Dermot already owned a copy. The song *Anything for You* played in her brain, or maybe it just played over the music store's sound system. In any event, Dermot would hate it, but the lyrics might remind him that she would remain devoted to him always. She picked up the tape to examine the orange sticker before cursing silently. It cost 12 pounds while they were 12 dollars at home. Maybe her Irish money wouldn't stretch so far after all.

Marielle exited the store feeling there was little time to waste. She needed to visit the post office to rent a mailbox where she could send her letters to Dermot. Then, she could provide the key or combination to Sean as well.

"Excuse me," Marielle said as she ran into a short, stout, bald man just outside the music store's doorway.

"Not a'tall, young lady. You're in a mighty hurry."

Marielle prepared to speak before the man whistled to a Chihuahua with one hand, and leaned on his cane with the other.

"Is that your dog?" Marielle asked, noting the lack of collar or leash on the animal who explored the sidewalk farther ahead.

"Yes, but she likes to wander from time to time."

Marielle nodded. "Do you know in which direction I can find the post office?"

"Certainly. I'll walk you there myself," the man said, whistling again for his dog.

"No," Marielle said quickly, looking down at the man's stiff leg. "I couldn't ask you to do that, but if you—"

"Not a'tall, a'tall. Come along, now, young lady," he insisted.

They walked in the direction of Eyre Square, then stopped outside a nondescript building. "Here you are. Is there anywhere else you mean to go today?"

"No, well, I'll just walk to the sea after this," she said, having decided it was the most logical place for Dermot to search for her.

"I'll wait for you here, then," he said before whistling to his dog again.

"I hate to keep you from your day," she objected.

"I had nothing a'tall planned except to get some fresh air which I'm doing in spades."

Marielle smiled. "Thank you. I'll try to hurry."

By the time Marielle reached the front of the line, she was sure the man and his dog had already departed.

"Next!" an unhappy young woman called from the counter.

"Hi," Marielle said tentatively, wondering how many times Dermot had dealt with the same woman while posting his letters to the United States. "Do you have post office boxes for rent?"

"Yes. Fifty-three pounds per year."

"Fifty-three," Marielle repeated.

"Yes. Fifty-three pounds per year," the woman said as if the question bored her to tears.

Marielle calculated the money in her pocket since buying the cassette tape, quickly realizing she didn't have enough. "Thank you," she replied before turning away.

"Next!" the woman yelled.

"Are you all sorted, then?" the man asked Marielle as she emerged from the building.

She nodded. "I am. I'm sorry you waited so long."

"Not a bother. Sure, everyone knows what the post is this time of day."

"What time is it?" Marielle asked, having no idea where she left her watch.

"It's half-one, I'd say," he replied.

Marielle blinked heavily. Only two hours ago, she was still with Dermot.

"Would you like to walk down to the sea now?" the gentleman asked.

"Please," she replied quietly.

The man spoke to Marielle about his deceased wife and the children who emigrated to New Zealand.

619

"Do you see your children often?" Marielle asked.

"Not a'tall. My youngest daughter is a bit of a daddy's girl now, I must say. She does plead with me on a regular basis to move to Wellington, but my doctors are here and Galway is my home. I'd feel a stranger anywhere else. I'm sure you know what I mean."

Marielle didn't reply.

"Do you not?" he asked.

She glanced at him. "Feel like a stranger?"

He nodded, then whistled for his dog again.

"Yes, but unfortunately that's how I feel when I'm home."

The man looked at the footpath before speaking. "Pardon me for saying so, miss, but I believe that means you're not at home a'tall."

Marielle looked up as the man said hello to a woman who scowled in return.

"Is that a friend of yours?" Marielle asked with a smile.

"Yes. A lovely woman. So you're home from America, then?" the man asked.

Marielle squinted. "Sorry? I don't understand."

"Are you originally from Ireland?"

"No, I'm just American," she replied.

"What brings you to Ireland, then?"

"I'm here to visit a friend. I think he might be waiting for me in Salthill."

"Right now?"

"I'm not sure," she said, wishing Dermot's location was something she could feel.

"Why don't you run ahead, then? If your friend doesn't turn up, meet me here in an hour and we'll have tea together."

Marielle smiled at the man with gratitude before running down the road. She passed shops and pedestrians without notice until she reached the spot where the Promenade met Lower Salthill Road. Although the traffic light was green, she stopped in order to consider a bench across the road. Dermot would likely pass that bench on his way to just about anywhere in Salthill so it made sense to wait for him there, but the coast farther along to her right drew her instead. No matter the strength of her reasoning, she couldn't resist Blackrock Pier, having last seen it with Dermot the night before.

Children ran upon the pebbled beach, as well as the boulders which peeked through cement slabs near the pier. Parents walked past Marielle, holding the hands of happy children wrapped in beach towels. A boy in stars and stripes swim trunks canon-balled off the lower pier near a little girl, eliciting admonishment from his mother. It was the same spot where Marielle had jumped into the water with Dawn 18 hours before.

She sat down upon semi-circular amphitheatre steps which faced the sea. Shading her eyes from the sun, she imagined Dermot standing in line with his lifeguarding class to her right. It was only two days ago, she told herself, but didn't quite believe it. Too much had happened for those two days to feel like less than a lifetime ago.

She turned her head suddenly as a boy with dark hair and a navy blue windbreaker walked through her peripheral vision. She studied the boy's wake for several seconds before determining it wasn't Dermot. Farther down the Promenade, another dark-haired boy of Dermot's height wore a navy blue windbreaker. Marielle jumped up to run after him, waiting to say his name until she stood directly behind him. The boy turned the second time she said the wrong name, causing her to apologize before she turned back to the pier. Moments later, she spotted another dark-haired boy walking farther along the footpath in the opposite direction.

Marielle chased shadows for what seemed like hours, forgetting her agreement to meet the kind, elderly man for tea. She sat down with a sigh on the bench near Lower Salthill Road. Breaking her appointment was only one of the sins she committed this day.

She stared at the water until the sun sank into the bay. The worst day of her life was officially over, but across the Atlantic, daylight still held ample time for retribution.

Young couples and groups of teenagers passed Marielle until artificial light cascaded down the Promenade. For a time, it seemed only Marielle kept the bay company, and she wondered how long she could stay on this bench before someone discovered she had nowhere else to go and made her leave.

Along the coast, people walked into houses filled with light. Chimney smoke rose from rooftops as the sweet smell of peat filled the air. People waited for loved ones to return home, but no one waited for Marielle. She could return to the youth hostel after midnight or disappear entirely and no one would know for several days. She was on her own, but far from free. She felt empty and diminished.

She gathered the last of her strength to stand and walk up Lower

Salthill Road toward Taylor's Hill. From across the street, she stared at the house named Seaview and the gates which remained open, but were now closed to her. The house glowed from nearly every window, including Mrs. MacManus' room. Twenty-four hours ago, she sat within that light, but now she stood in the darkness.

Marielle shivered as the temperature suddenly required a jacket, but was otherwise immobile as pain washed over her. Life moved with more ease while pining for Dermot across the Atlantic, imagining his face and his house. Standing under his sky, across the street from his house with no way to reach him conjured feelings she couldn't bear. She walked away with difficulty, feeling not all of her soul left with her.

Meandering dark streets returned her to the youth hostel. She jiggled the handle of the locked door before placing her head against it. Again, she willed herself to cry, but failed. After calming herself enough to reason, she read a sign instructing residents to use the after-hours code. She vaguely remembered the proprietor saying something about a code when she checked in, but she couldn't quite remember it now. She reached into the pocket which held Dermot's grandfather's coins that morning, finding a piece of paper with four numbers instead.

She opened the door to a quiet, darkened foyer. Unable to locate a light switch, she held both sides of the wall as she climbed the stairs. Several steps after turning right, she bumped into the doorknob of her dormitory.

Lumps on each bed were easily visible by the street light which poured through the windows. Marielle kicked off her shoes before lying on her bed and pulling the comforter over herself. She would brush her teeth and wash her face extra well in the morning, she decided before drifting off to sleep.

Chapter Thirty-Six

Even Lovers Drown
—W.B. Yeats – *The Mermaid*

Marielle swam alone in the middle of Kleiner Lake as a canary yellow Jeep honked its horn twice from shore. She looked down as something brushed her leg, hoping to find only a weed, but a skeletal hand grabbed her ankle, swiftly pulling her under the lager-colored water. She twisted out of its grasp, then reached the surface before it grabbed her again. Yellow water swirled above her head, turning brown, then black.

Marielle sat up with a start, scaring the blonde Australian standing at the sink near the end of Marielle's bunk.

"Are you alright there?" the woman asked.

"Fine, yeah, sorry," Marielle said, lying back down.

"Late night?" the woman's friend asked, looking at Marielle's clothes.

Marielle nodded. "It was too dark to change when I got back and—"

The blonde glanced at her friend before asking, "Do your parents know where you are?"

"They know I'm in Galway," Marielle answered.

"But they don't know you've left your friend's house?"

Marielle shook her head. "No, though Dermot's mother probably called to tell them."

"They must be worried sick about you!" the dark woman declared.

Marielle smiled unhappily. "I wouldn't say that's their primary emotion."

"Sure i'tis. You need to ring them. What do you have planned for today?"

Marielle drew a deep breath, attempting to separate fact from hope. "I'm meeting a friend and then nothing after that."

"Well, you're coming out to Monroe's with us tonight," the blonde said with determination. "They have live music an' all. We met some nice blokes from West Germany last night. One of them is quite a spunk."

The dark one chuckled as she glanced at her friend. "He tried to crack onto Stephanie the majority of the night."

623

"Sure, but in London, all of the pommies wanted Jackie," Stephanie retorted.

Marielle's eyebrows furrowed, feeling she was learning yet another new version of English. "Well, I need to leave early tomorrow morning," she said.

"We won't rage on much past midnight, will we now, Jackie?" Stephanie said.

Marielle nodded with her best attempt at a grin. "Do you know what time it is?" she asked.

"It's only half-seven. They don't use curtains to ensure everyone's up at the crack of dawn," Jackie explained with displeasure.

Marielle pushed back her covers, then knelt on the floor to retrieve her suitcase from beneath the bed. She opened the blank, turquoise notebook meant to journal her trip, then commenced writing a letter to Dermot. Halfway through the letter, she decided to put it in code so Sean couldn't read it. A short time later, she began again in backward code. If the letter fell into Mrs. MacManus' hands, Dermot could plausibly state he couldn't decrypt it, but if left alone, he would certainly discover that one equaled Z, rather than A.

Once complete, Marielle decoded the letter again to make sure it made sense before folding it into the space between the new tape cassette and jacket cover.

Dear Dermot,

I'm at a loss for what to say to you. I have too many things going through my mind and I'm afraid saying nothing might be the result or that I'll think of what I really mean to say after Sean walks away with this letter. Let me start by saying how sorry I am for what I've done to you and your family. I wish I could take it back or make it up to you more than I have ever wished for anything in my life. I don't expect you to forgive me, but if you could wait for me for six or eight years, I promise to make this up to you somehow.

I know you'll hate this tape, but it's important that you know I would do anything for you. If you needed to get away, I would find a way for us to be together. I would work two or three jobs and move to any state or country you like. Home is where you are, and every minute away from you is torture.

Please don't worry on my account for how things ended here. I don't fault your mother or take issue with what she said. I know this is my fault and I am shamed by it.

Please tell me how you are from time to time.

I will miss and love you always!
Marielle

A woman bent down to speak to Marielle in a rapid succession of French, using the same word for shower that she had learned in German. Marielle stood to follow the woman to the bathroom, then pulled and twisted the nozzle to find the right water temperature.

"*C'est bon?*" Marielle asked.

"*Oui,*" the woman replied.

Marielle returned to her suitcase to retrieve a new pair of jeans, a clean t-shirt, and a gray cardigan sweater, then returned to the bathroom. A hot shower failed to lighten her mood and the mirror above the tooth brushing sink only highlighted a complexion which now matched her sweater. She wondered if everyone who crossed God lived the rest of their lives in black and white before deciding they probably did. At least pictures would remain in color, she thought with gratitude, then cursed. She hadn't taken any pictures of Dermot with her own camera. Not one. If her memory of his face faded, she would have nothing of Dermot for her own. She held the sink as she closed her eyes, but tears failed to form. She didn't know why she couldn't cry except everything about her was very nearly broken.

***

Marielle walked to Eyre Square to check the bus schedule to Shannon Airport, then bought a newspaper before making her way to McDonald's. She drank her orange juice sparingly, pretending to read her paper as she sat in the same yellow semi-circular booth she shared with Dermot three days before.

At precisely 10 a.m., a woman resembling Mrs. MacManus walked past the window of the restaurant before turning to open the door. Marielle's paper shook as Dermot's mother walked directly toward her, maintaining eye contact the entire distance. As surprised as Marielle was to see her, she was equally surprised by the expression on her face. Rather than a woman seeking revenge, she resembled a teenager determined to confront her tormentor. At that moment, Marielle realized the past two days had nearly broken Mrs. MacManus as well.

Marielle thought to apologize as the woman placed a paper bag in the chair opposite her, but decided such an apology would seem hollow. Mrs. MacManus turned around without a word, and departed as quickly as she arrived.

It took many minutes for Marielle to appreciate that Sean wouldn't arrive, and that it was he who had given her up to Mrs. MacManus. It took only a few seconds longer to realize that if Sean had given her up, so had Dermot.

She looked around the restaurant to see if bystander shunning would begin anew, then rose with cassette in hand before anyone could start. She picked up the paper bag on her way to the door, leaving her newspaper and juice behind.

***

Marielle sat on her bed in the youth hostel, staring down at the contents of the bag which now rested on the floor—a watch, one Nike, a candy-striped nightgown, two airline tickets, and a passport. She shook her head. She had only missed her Nike. In any event, none of it mattered anymore. She shoved the bag under her bed before rising to walk to the sea.

No one said hello to her on the footpath, and nuns and priests scowled at her when she offered a weak greeting. Everyone knew her sin and there was no hope of absolution. There would be no option to go to the convent and no Dermot at the end of college. Chances were that Mrs. MacManus had already called her parents and Marielle had no home in Appleton any longer. For all intents and purposes, she had no way to go forward and no way to go back.

What began as an innocent exchange of letters, triggered a course of events which would end today in Salthill.

Marielle had always thought it romantic to have a grave marker bearing the words "Lost at Sea," but romance had faded now that this was a distinct possibility. She considered her headstone with a strange detachment. Instead of dates delineating her life, one could easily write "Letters" for her birth, and "Salthill" for her death. People would repeat the words and wonder what they meant. "Letters to Salthill," they would say, assuming the engraver was confused, disgruntled, or underpaid. Marielle groaned quietly. Grave markers and strangers mattered little when all she wanted was a release from pain, rejection, and frustration.

626

A half-hour later, she sat on the bench which she occupied the night before, waiting for teenagers to leave the jetty. The bench still faced Galway Bay, but it now rested in Purgatory. She told herself she wasn't being dramatic. God had abandoned her. For the first time in her life, she sat without feeling Him near her, and for the first time in her life she was completely and utterly alone.

Grief still overwhelmed Marielle to a level which frustrated expression, but she would not end her life for grief's sake alone, she decided. Logic would still prevail. She began making a mental list for and against death, and for the first time in her life, she felt no compunction to write it down.

She thought of her initials and her lifelong fear of water, wondering if both foreshadowed the way she would die as words by Yeats repeated in her mind:

Come away, O human child!
To the waters and the wild
With a faery, hand in hand,
For the world's more full of weeping than you can understand.

Mrs. MacManus had thought the poem so fitting, and Dermot had indeed been stolen, but not by Marielle. Now, she was left to ponder what a world without Dermot might look like and if an American boy—or any boy—could take his place. She thought about Gary and the difference in his mother's reaction at finding the teenagers together. Life with Gary would be easier on the whole, or in part, because he lived in Freedom. Marielle chuckled unhappily. Gary lived in Freedom, but she wanted the boy imprisoned in Galway.

She scanned the beach, certain she was being watched. Children jumped from rock to rock while their parents walked along the Promenade nearby. Teenagers stood at the end of the jetty, laughing. Cars passed behind her bench, and the world went on without her as all hope was lost and she sat drowning under a tidal wave of shame.

Her parents would kick her out of the house as soon as she arrived home and her grandparents' opinion of her would be forever tarnished. Even if her family didn't cast her aside, the retribution would be swift and absolute. There would be no letters, no phone calls, no job, and nothing that might distract Marielle from the hell of living in her house.

She squinted toward the sun as she considered the alternate point of view. She might be washed away and never found. There would be an investigation, an international incident even, and everyone in the world would know what she and Dermot had nearly done. Worse yet, if never found, her parents would always wonder what had become of her. They would hold out false hope that she was alive, and they would never forgive themselves for letting her go. Strike that. Mom would never forgive Dad for letting her go and he would never forgive himself, though he would likely take it out on the entire family after dark.

Her disappearance would also begin a new round of scandal and suspicion around Dermot and his family, and Marielle's experience in the driveway showed her that shame on a large scale in Galway would be too much for anyone to bear.

Again, she felt eyes upon her and she heard someone call Dermot's name from the group of teenagers which now moved behind her. She twitched, but didn't look. Sitting alone was torture enough without looking for someone who wasn't there. A car started nearby, then quickly drove away.

Marielle decided to consider her grandparents before sending the matter to the jury. Given her grandmother's heart problems and her grandfather's propensity for vengeance, someone would surely die as a result of Marielle's suicide. She rested her face in her hands. There were no real choices, only responsibilities, and there was no need for a jury. The only way to protect her family and Dermot's was to walk away from the sea rather than sink beneath it.

She attempted to summon tears again before giving up. Anger would be a much easier emotion to express from now on, she decided. If she was cursed to live, things would be different when she returned to Wisconsin. She would never allow anyone to diminish her or injure her again, and she vowed that Mrs. MacManus' was the last hand that would ever slap her. Anyone attempting to strike her subsequently would face as much wrath as Marielle could mete-out, and she felt sure this was substantial.

If she had something to say to her father, she would just say it. She wouldn't look at the time, count empty beer cans, wait for a commercial, or attempt to gauge his overall mood. She would no longer lie or hide or shrink from scrutiny, and if the room was dark, she was going to turn on a fucking light!

Marielle shook her head. There was no reason to pick a fight, but she knew with equal certainty that the only way to meet a conflict or fight a war was hand to hand, and head to head.

After minutes which felt like hours, she decided to walk to the pay phones near Eyre Square to call her parents. There were closer phones, but she required a long walk even as she decided she couldn't put off the present any longer.

She walked along the bay until the intersection with the Docks made her turn north. She turned away as she passed Dermot's church and closed her eyes as she passed the Claddagh sign, remembering the conversation the latter inspired about rings and marriage. That was three days ago, and 24 hours ago she was still with Dermot. She consulted her watch. Exactly 24 hours ago, everything changed.

She turned toward the boats as she stopped walking. Fittingly, *Honora* was gone. She wondered if will power and concentration might bring it back or even turn back time. Instead of coaxing Dermot to get undressed, she would suggest they read their books at the hall table, or walk downtown, or meet up with Sean, or Ronan, or demand they visit the library. Dermot could help her swim better in the cold sea. There were a dozen things they could do which wouldn't ruin their present as well as their future.

Marielle picked up a rock from the footpath as she wondered how he could betray her—and she couldn't decide if *he* was Sean or Dermot. How could Sean tell Mrs. MacManus where to find Marielle without showing up ahead of time to warn her or afterward to apologize? And how could Dermot allow Marielle to meet his mother alone? As she looked over the railing at the dark water, she knew the answer. It was the same reason American boys used when coaxing girls into having sex, then called them sluts afterward. Joel was right. Irish boys were no different than Americans!

She threw the rock into the water as she realized she had finally been duped by a boy smarter than herself.

She glanced at the sign again, and paused as it brought to mind Dermot's declaration to his mother. Would an American boy announce to his mother that he wanted to marry a girl he regarded as a slut? Marielle wasn't sure. In the absence of certainty, it was only fair to assume Dermot was sincere, even as she wondered what kept him from leaving his house.

She turned away from the Docks. There was no way to know anything anymore.

***

Marielle heard the single ringing of their phone in Appleton and the operator ask her father if he would accept the charges.

"Marielle?" he asked with a parent's concern.

"Dad," Marielle barely said before dissolving into tears.

"What's wrong?" he asked frantically.

She looked outside the booth at the jagged metal fountain, grateful to Mrs. MacManus and God that he didn't know. "I just miss you guys," she said.

"Are you okay?" he asked with worry that bordered on agitation.

She cleared her throat as her mother's voice asked her father what was wrong. Instead of answering, Jack instructed Maria to take the phone.

"Marielle, what's wrong?" her mother asked with more authority.

"I'm not staying with the MacManuses anymore. There was a fight. I'm in a youth hostel now."

"What happened?" her mother asked breathlessly.

"I'll tell you when I get home if she doesn't call you before then. It was very, very bad."

"Are you alright?"

Marielle paused to consider the question her mom posed rather than the one she expected: namely, what terrible thing had Marielle done to shame the family? "I'm fine," she finally said. "I need to take the bus to Shannon tomorrow since the bus on Thursday won't arrive in time for my flight."

"Where will you stay?"

"I'll sleep in the airport."

"Oh, Marielle!" her mother protested. "Just a moment. Your sister wants to talk to you."

"What's going on?" Jeanette asked with as much interest as concern.

"Mrs. MacManus walked in on Dermot and I when we were about to have sex. She kicked me out of the house."

"You're joking!" Jeanette exclaimed before she began to laugh.

Marielle smiled for the first time. "I'm not."

"You?"

"Yes, me. I guess I'm an idiot after all. Promise you won't tell Mom and Dad. I'll tell them when I get home."

"Sure you will," Jeanette said through a smile.

"Can you do me a huge favor and put $60 into my checking account?

630

I'll try to get a hotel room in Shannon tomorrow night if I have enough money."

"Okay. I'll do that in a little bit."

"Thanks," Marielle said with relief. "Are Mom and Dad okay?"

"No. They thought you'd call before today and when you didn't, they thought something was wrong."

Marielle studied the fountain as her eyebrows furrowed. "Why's that? I didn't tell them I'd call."

"How should I know? You know how parents are."

"Oh, one more thing. I forgot the dress I bought for Ellen's wedding at Dermot's house. Will you bring something to Milwaukee for me to wear?"

Jeanette said she would and Marielle thanked her in a voice meant to double for *I love you.*

"No problem, dumbass," Jeanette replied, in a way that doubled for *I love you, too.*

Marielle returned the receiver to its cradle, then breathed deeply for the first time in 24 hours. As screwed up as her family was, they still loved her, and they were likely able to weather this storm better than most.

She walked from the booth to the edge of the fountain, looking up at the pieces of rust-coloured metal. She didn't know if the centerpiece had a name, but she decided the artist disliked birds enough to create an air hazard.

She turned toward the plaque Dermot showed her on Saturday before taking her to McDonald's. It commemorated JFK's visit to the square shortly before his assassination. At least one American would be revered in Galway regardless of his sexual exploits, she reflected. She stared at the profile of Kennedy's head wondering if this was gender hypocrisy or a newly-discovered life formula. Ethnic identity, plus fame, plus martyrdom equaled eternal adulation. She wondered if scandal would subtract from this equation, or if fame, martyrdom, or ethnic identity nullified it. All she knew was that she was shamed for attempting to sleep with a boy she loved while Kennedy was revered despite sleeping with dozens of women he didn't. She didn't feel sorry for herself, per se, she just found the fact noteworthy.

"Hiya!" a woman's voice called from the footpath.

Marielle turned to find the Australian women waving at her, their smiles widening as Marielle jogged toward them.

"Did you ring your parents?" the tall, blonde Stephanie asked.

631

Marielle smiled. "Just now."

"What did they say?" Jackie inquired.

"That they were worried about me. Nothing else."

"See, we told you they wouldn't be angry with you for kissing a boy."

Marielle squinted. "Well, that's not the whole story," she admitted.

Stephanie and Jackie turned toward each other and laughed. "We know well enough what happened. Not even an Irish mother would throw you out for kissing her son."

Marielle considered the comment before she said, "I'm not sure about that."

"Well, did you meet your friend anyway?" Jackie asked.

"No. He didn't come. Dermot's mother showed up instead."

Both women inhaled sharply. "What did she do to you?" Jackie asked.

"Nothing. She just dropped a bag full of my stuff on the chair across from me and walked out. It was worse than you can imagine though since I was going to give Sean Dermot's birthday gift and a letter, but now I can't." Marielle glanced away, shaking her head.

Stephanie placed her arm around Marielle, turning her toward the youth hostel as they began to walk. "I believe you need a drink," she decided.

***

Jackie returned to the table with three pints of Guinness.

"I'm not sure I can drink something that big," Marielle protested weakly.

"Give it a go, anyway," Jackie encouraged.

"So, I believe Jackie and I may have a solution for your problem," Stephanie declared.

"Do we?" Jackie asked with surprise.

"We do," Stephanie said before turning to Marielle. "Is his mother home during the day?"

Marielle nodded. "Yesterday and today anyway."

"Have you attempted to ring?"

Marielle smiled with half the mischief she generally employed. "Yesterday, when I thought she might have gone back to work and later to ask her how I should give her her money back."

"What money?" Jackie asked.

Marielle raised her pint glass as if she meant to drink from it. "The money they wasted on gas picking me up from the airport."

"She asked for that?"

Marielle took a sip and held back a grimace before she said, "She did."

"Well, she wasn't too bothered at finding you and her son together to forget about money," Jackie said with judging eyes.

Marielle shook her head. "No, or to forget about our ages. In the middle of yelling at us, she said quite accurately that we were only 16 and 17 years old."

"Which one are you?" Stephanie asked.

"Seventeen, but Dermot's only a month away from 17 too. It just seemed odd to me that she would yell something so accurate when she seemed out of her mind otherwise, and it would be easier to yell one age or the other."

"That *is* odd," Stephanie decided. "How did she catch you?"

Marielle looked a thousand miles away before she looked back. "That's a mystery. The house creaks like crazy and she had just gone back to work from lunch. She somehow got into the house without us hearing the latch and walked up the stairs and down the hall without us hearing the floor creak. Well, Dermot heard one creak, but there wasn't time by then."

"So, she expected to find you together," Jackie reasoned.

"I think so. It was weird because we were supposed to go to Dublin yesterday, and she basically canceled our plans, leaving us alone at the house all day."

The Australians narrowed their eyes at one another before Stephanie asked, "Is Dermot well experienced with girls?"

"Not really," Marielle replied. "We were meant to be each other's first."

"So, you've never had sex before?!" Jackie asked.

Marielle shook her head. "No, and we didn't manage it this time. We're both still technically virgins."

Jackie covered her mouth to stop laughter while Stephanie bit her bottom lip to do the same. Watching the reactions of both women caused Marielle to laugh, allowing the Australians to follow suit.

"I don't see you trying again for a good long time," Jackie finally said.

"If ever," Marielle replied, picking up her Guinness.

"Do you think this boy is worth forever?" Stephanie asked with scepticism.

Marielle squinted slightly. "I thought so, but now I don't know. The only thing that makes me think yes is that he made his mother stop hitting me—"

"She struck you?!" Stephanie asked.

Marielle chuckled as she confirmed she did.

Stephanie shared indignation with Jackie before she asked, "Did you not consider phoning the police?"

"No. She called them herself. Apparently, it's illegal to have sex when you're under 18, or maybe if you're not married. I forget which."

"This is madness!" Stephanie declared. "So, you can hit people, but you can't love them?"

Marielle shook her head. "Apparently not."

"Is it like this in America?" Jackie asked.

"Yes," Marielle replied decisively. "So, I should have known better."

"Okay, so, he stopped her from hitting you," Stephanie said, urging Marielle to continue.

"Right, and he told his mother he wanted to marry me."

Stephanie drew a deep breath before something outside the pub's window demanded her attention. "Jackie, are those the two girls from Bath we're meant to have tea with?"

"They are," Jackie said, jumping up to run to the pub door.

Marielle stood as introductions were made, then offered to help Jackie retrieve two more beers.

When all sat down again, Stephanie said, "Would you mind if we ask our friends here how we might help you with your Dermot?"

Marielle immediately turned red. "Not at all," she replied.

Stephanie and Jackie related the details of Marielle's story as well as her disappointment that day.

"And she said that to you, did she—that Irish girls weren't like that?" the plump brown-haired girl named Mary asked with unmasked annoyance.

Marielle smiled as she nodded her head.

"I do get fed up with Irish mothers thinking their daughters are so pure!" she exclaimed.

Marielle smarted, feeling she had just betrayed Ireland. "Well, it sounds like they are," she explained. "At least that's what Dermot said."

"Trust me, they're not," the thinner brown-haired girl named Claire replied. "They visit London and Bath on a regular basis and they do sing a very different tune when their mothers aren't in tow."

"So, how might we deliver Marielle's letter to Dermot?" Stephanie

asked.

"Is he permitted outside the house?" asked Mary.

"No," Stephanie replied as a lightbulb went off in Marielle's eyes. "What is it?" she asked.

"He wouldn't be allowed off the property, but he might be allowed out of the house to close the front gates at night," Marielle replied.

"So, you could wait for him to close the gates and hand him his present then," Mary suggested.

"No, it's too risky," Jackie said. "His mother will surely monitor his progress to and from the gates."

"Marielle could place the letter in the gates," Claire offered.

"Or next to one of the rocks that holds open the gates," Marielle said with excitement. "He has to bend down to move the rock anyway. He could pick up the tape at the same time without anyone noticing."

"Brilliant!" Stephanie proclaimed. "See, well there you have your solution."

Marielle nodded. "Right, but I need to find some way of telling Dermot to look for the tape."

The women's eyes narrowed in a nearly identical way, causing Marielle to chuckle.

Jackie turned toward the pool table at the centre of the pub. "I've got it," she said. "We pay one of the lads playing pool to ring Dermot, pretending to be one of his chums. When Dermot gets on the line, the chap will hand the phone to you."

"That could work," Marielle said happily.

"Right, now go chat up those boys," Mary encouraged.

Marielle approached the pool table, then waited for a break in play.

"Hiya," one boy said as he raised his pint from the side of the table.

"Hi," Marielle replied. "I'm wondering if one of you would mind doing a favor for me. I need someone to call my friend's house pretending to be someone else."

"Aengus is the man for you," the shortest boy said as he pushed forward the tallest.

The women smiled as Marielle walked outside with the boy.

"Alright, your name is Séamus and you live in Dublin. You're asking for Dermot and when he gets on the phone, I'll take it."

"Right, so," the boy said as he walked into the telephone booth across the road. He looked well at ease as the phone double-buzzed and he asked to speak with Dermot. "This is Séamus," he said, sounding more like Sean than he did a moment ago. "I am at the moment, yeah." Seconds later, he handed Marielle the receiver and she handed him a five pound note as she whispered thanks.

"Dermot?" she asked.

"Hello?" he replied with a faraway voice.

"Dermot, this is Marielle," she said happily, but she could only hear his breath as he began to weep. "Please don't," she said quietly as her eyes closed and sorrow found her again.

"I'm so sorry," he said through a voice burdened with tears.

"It's not your fault. It's mine. Please don't worry about me. I'm fine. I really am."

"This is not what I wanted for your holiday," he said.

Marielle's eyebrows narrowed.

"Please don't be angry with Sean. She made him tell her. She knew as soon as he arrived—"

"I'm not angry. Dermot, you need to listen to me," she insisted. "After dark, I'm going to place a tape behind the left hand rock that holds open the gate. Inside, there will be a letter. Do you understand?"

"I'm desperately sorry for the things she said to you. I've been tormented—"

"Dermot, please! I don't care what your mother said to me. I just need you to listen to me now—"

"I don't see how this can work. It won't work."

"What won't work?" she asked, her blood pressure rising.

"Us," he replied before submitting to tears again.

Marielle rested her head against the booth. "We have time to talk about this later, but I need you to go to your gate after dark and pick up this tape."

"What tape?" he asked with confusion.

Marielle sighed. "After dark, I will place a tape behind the rock that holds open the left side gate. The left side as you walk down the driveway, that is. There will be a letter inside."

"Alright," he replied.

"I love you," she said.

"I love you," he whispered.

Marielle walked back into the pub triumphantly.

"Did it work?" one of the women asked.

"It did," she nodded.

"Well done, you," Mary remarked as Jackie added, "Good onya."

"Thank you. I'd like to buy the next round," Marielle declared.

***

Marielle felt slightly tipsy as she tightened the laces of her Nikes and picked up the tape from her bed. She checked for the second time that the letter was safely tucked inside before smiling at the Australian and British women.

"We're waiting on you, so don't delay," Stephanie said with the authority of an older sister.

Marielle nodded. "I won't. I promise. But I'm not sure how long the phone will take."

"Do your best to be quick about it," Mary urged.

Marielle smiled at the four women, then ran toward the exit. She continued running without a break until the road intersected with Lower Salthill. Moments later, she stood across the street from the house named Seaview one last time as she studied shadows of gables and windows fronting unlit rooms. Dermot would come and go from his house multiple times per day for at least the next six years, and she hoped that as he passed this spot he might feel that part of her soul which she willingly left behind.

She waited for traffic to clear before crossing Taylor's Hill Road, then walked into the driveway to approach the designated rock. As she dropped the tape, Gryphon jumped up, barking loudly as he gave chase. Marielle ran as far as Fr. Burke Park before looking back. Gryphon was gone.

Melancholia overtook Marielle as she crossed the River Corrib. She wondered how the dog could have forgotten her so quickly, hoping this wasn't a sign of his owner's affection.

Dermot's words from earlier replayed in her mind. He didn't see how their relationship could work, but that wasn't his job. It was *her* job to find solutions to impossible circumstances, and she knew she would, or she would die trying.

***

A woman looked down from the window of the youth hostel as Marielle stood in the phone booth, waiting for the telephone to ring in Appleton.

"Marielle?" Jeanette asked as the operator departed the line.

"Hi there. Did you put money into my account, by chance?"

637

"I did."

"Thank God, and thank you!" Marielle exclaimed.

"No problem. Look, Dad's here," Jeanette said soberly. "He wants to talk to you."

Marielle's watch arm twitched, but she refused to look at it.

Jack cleared his throat before he said, "Hey, kiddo."

"Hello, sir," she replied as she watched patrons open the door of Monroe's Pub.

"Look, your sister told us what happened over there."

This time, Marielle's whole body twitched as her lungs released the last of their oxygen. "I'm sorry," she said, placing her forehead against the side of the booth.

Jack cleared his throat again. "You know, we love you."

She closed her eyes. "I love you too, Dad."

Jack paused as if contemplating his next words carefully. "I sure do miss you, kid. There's no one here to cover me up at night."

Marielle looked up at the light from the youth hostel window as it became more blurry.

Jack continued, "Come home soon, kid."

Marielle's voice cracked as she said, "I will, Dad. I promise."

**

Years later, Marielle looked back on her father's words as the turning point when she finally understood the man behind the shadow. Her father regarded her differently as well, and that generally included a healthy dose of love and respect.

Although Dermot forgot his promises, or perhaps he never meant them, Marielle couldn't help feeling grateful for his influence in helping her understand the one man who, despite his many flaws, would always love her.

The End